KNOTTED

LAXMI HARIHARAN

D1737727

PART I

TAKEN

1

Zeus

"Boo!" I bare my teeth.

The soldier cringes, and sweat beads his forehead.

"Really, Z?" My second-in-command narrows his gaze.

I raise my shoulders then let them drop. "Okay, a bit over the top." But, cut me some slack, okay? I like to play with my prey.

Besides, I have a flair for the dramatic, one of the few redeeming features I inherited from my bastard of a father. Except, oh, wait, I was the bastard in that relationship, given he'd never acknowledged me...not until I had my fingers around Golan's neck and recognition had dawned in his eyes. Too late, Pater. Thirty years too late.

The soldier's skin is stretched so tight over his cheekbones that I expect it to crack any moment. The reek of piss stinks up the warehouse. The fool, clearly a beta by the way his shoulders are hunched, has wet himself.

I yawn aloud. The sound of my jaws cracking seems to snap the man into action, for he staggers forward, followed by his partner. They haul a rolled-up carpet between them.

Strings of thread trail from the edges to sweep over the wooden floor. The patchwork on the outside of the carpet is peeling. The fabric seems so innocuous, so unassuming, it's precisely that which sends all of my instincts on alert.

A sliver of awareness ripples over my skin. Thud, thud, thud, my heartbeat accelerates. The fine hair on my neck rises.

What the bloody hell? I can't take my gaze off that damn rug. "Unfurl it."

The edge of impatience in my tone must have signaled the impending flare of temper, for Ethan, my second moves forward—not that the soldiers will dare try anything. The stripes on their vests mark them out as emissaries of the Leader of Scotland, and Kayden doesn't have the balls to put them up to breaking into my stronghold. I drum my fingers over my chest. Nah! It's exactly the kind of move, I'd expect that twat to try to pull off.

Adrenaline laces my blood. I curl my fingers into fists.

That piece of shit wants me out of the way so he can take over my position. Well, he and most of those gathered here. Don't everyone rush all at once. I snicker.

The Scot nearest to me pales.

He expects me to kill him. The body count I've left behind in the past year ensures that most fear me. But I might spare these men; for now, and only because it keeps them guessing about when they are going to die. Can't have them getting too comfortable now, eh?

I lean forward on the balls of my feet.

The sudden movement draws a gasp from the beta. He bends and places his side of the rolled-up cloth on the floor. The other man follows.

I take a step forward. Honestly, I don't show any other outward sign of threat. I don't even peel back my lips, or speak…well, okay, I glare at the soldier on the right.

With an audible gulp, he turns and scampers down the big hall toward the still open doors. His partner blinks then scoots after him. My gaze is already on the piece of fabric left behind.

"I don't think it's wise to open it, General," Ethan warns.

Since climate change unleashed tsunamis and wrecked Earth's sublayers thirty years ago, trace metals all but vanished. Electronics can no longer be powered up, and technology collapsed, leaving no means of communicating. The only way to check what's inside that rug is the old-fashioned way. To open it.

"Consider yourself heard." I crack my neck from side to side. "You've done your duty, Second, so can we get this charade over with?"

Sure, his concern is genuine, and yet it doesn't sit easily with me.

Not since he betrayed the ex-General, aka my dear departed father, by aiding me in killing the old man.

"Allow me, sir." Solomon, my third, grabs the open seam of the curled-up mat. He heaves, but it doesn't budge.

Ethan moves to the other side, and together they tug at it. The cloth unfurls… and flattens out into a pool of turquoise and green.

The illumination from the solitary skylight far above floods over it and the entire rug shimmers.

My pulse races. The breath catches in my throat. My heart hammers and I am sure it's going to jump out of my ribcage.

The next second, a figure springs up from the carpet and launches itself at me. Head bent, dressed all in black. There's a blur of movement, and a blade whines through the space.

I slide aside.

The breeze displaced by the stranger shimmers over my neck. A flash of pain cuts through me as the blade nicks my skin.

I thrust out my leg, and the intruder goes sprawling to the floor, only to turn in a move which should have been near impossible.

It calls attention to the lithe lines of the body that is wrapped in that jumpsuit. The figure launches itself back at me, and I bend my knees and throw the intruder over my shoulder.

There's a thump, then the sword skitters across the wooden floor.

I swivel around and close the distance to where the infiltrator leaps up from the center of the carpet.

The colors fade, the room shrinks around me. My vision narrows in on the face, to where the dark cloth has unraveled from around the head of the newcomer. Eyes of shattered green blaze at me.

The hair on my nape rises.

It's her, the woman from my dreams.

A strand of dark-red hair slinks free.

The scent of rain on cool dawn air bleeds through the space, interlaced with that sugary essence of slickness.

Blood rushes to my groin.

Every instinct inside me goes on alert. "Omega," I rasp.

2

Lucy

I lift my chin, then farther up, then all the way up, to meet his gaze. To call the General massive is an understatement. He is a monster. A man-mountain, the biggest, most powerful alpha I have ever seen.

His blue eyes blaze at me.

A ripple of fear mixed with something else—lust? Anticipation? —tightens my stomach.

His face is all hard planes and dark angles. Long black hair flows to his shoulders. His lower lip is full, obscenely so. It should soften his looks; instead, it only heightens the sense of danger that clings to him like a rich coat.

It's the exact opposite of the faded vest that embraces his torso.

His clothes strike a jarring note in the middle of the most prosperous pocket of this city, which is where we are, but it suits this alpha. Declares exactly what he is: an asshole who doesn't give a damn about anyone else.

Who takes pleasure in surprising his friends and outwitting his enemies—no, he doesn't have friends...doesn't need friends...or lovers or... How would he be as a lover? A dominant? A male who'd take without mercy? That feminine, omega core of me quivers in anticipation.

A pulse flares to life between my thighs.

An age-old instinct deep inside awakes...and insists this alpha will pleasure me. He'll bite me, lick me, suck me...and a piercing wave of desire twists my stomach.

Heat flushes my skin, and yet I feel cold, so cold.

I try to take a step forward, but my feet feel weighed down.

The alpha thrusts out his chest, and the force of his dominance crashes over me.

My breath catches.

I can't move. Can't think. Can't do anything but stare at his face, drink in his features. Open my heart and absorb every last particle of impact that his sheer charisma has on me.

I want to trace that long, hooked nose of his. To close the distance between us and bite his square, pronounced jaw. Lick it, nibble on it, then pull his head down between my thighs until his hard whiskers rub across my sensitive core.

Heat floods my skin.

My nipples tighten.

I don't need to look down at my breasts to know they're thrusting out, their sharp edges a palpable outline against the material.

He must know the effect he has on me, for the strong cords of his throat ripple. His sculpted chest seems to widen as he straightens and plants his arms on his trim hips. His powerful shoulders block out the sight of the room. His entire presence sucks up the air in the space. The strength of his personality is a visceral force that crashes into me and threatens to overpower me. I want to reach for the throbbing space between my legs and relieve the pressure that is building in my womb. What is happening to me?

"Do you know what I do to those who challenge me?" He growls.

The rich sound grates over my sensitized nerve endings and shudders straight to my center.

My thighs quiver, my stomach trembles, and I thrust my pelvis forward in blatant invitation. What the hell? It seems my body has already arrived at a decision and the rest of me is struggling to catch up.

I grit my teeth. "I am sure you are going to tell me." Every instinct in me tells me to cower...to give in to him. But I cannot. Will not. The part of me that is honed to fight back, insists I resist.

I jut out my chin.

My heart pounds in my rib cage, and a pulse flares to life between my thighs.

He growls again, and the sound tugs at my nerves. The vibrations roll over me and surround me. Cocooning me in the center.

It's like nothing I have ever heard before.

Moisture pools in my core. The scent of slick bleeds into the air. I gasp. No, not now. I can't be heading straight into a heat cycle, not when I am here on a mission. Is it the adrenaline of the attack that has brought on this sudden wave of need?

His lips, those sensuous lips, tighten.

A vein throbs at his temple, and his cheeks flush as he looks down at me from his superior height.

I should feel emboldened that I am having an effect on him, the most powerful alpha in all the land, but instead a writhing need to challenge him tears at me. To ask him. To give in to his every demand. And that confuses me.

"You are an omega but not a submissive?" He frowns.

The hackles of my neck rise. I had not expected this alpha to figure that out.

Genetic mutation brought on by climate change has divided the human race into three subspecies: alphas, betas, and omegas, and I happen to belong to the weakest of them. But the warring sides of my personality have made me an anomaly in this world where alphas take, and omegas are raised with the expectation of being bred.

"It's why you should let me go. I am not suitable for reproduction." My stomach trembles, my palms begin to sweat. I am trying to rationalize with a savage.

Accelerated cellular transformation over the past few generations has equipped the alphas with the ability to knot the omegas and increase the chance of impregnation.

As for omegas, the onset of heat cycles at puberty compel most to seek out an alpha to rut them through it. Nature's way of balancing out the dwindling population count, helped by the fact that heat suppressants are banned. Even black market supplies of the precious chemicals have run out.

I'd managed to hide myself away during the worst of these phases, had never felt compelled to lay with any alpha, not until this monster.

I need him, yet I want to fight him.

I must show him he can't just take. Not without paying a price first. Not without begging, pleading, making me scream.

Anticipation stretches my belly.

An age old instinct inside me jolts to life. My core clenches. My knees quake, and I push my boot-clad feet into the dirt for purchase.

He angles his head and peels back his lips. "On the contrary, it renders the entire process so much more interesting."

There is so much cruelty in his look...so much lust...so much everything.

My skin tightens.

Every single emotion that I have fought against my entire life, denied myself, all of it drips from his gaze.

I can't tear my gaze away.

I clench my fingers, my muscles strain, and I try, once more, to move. It only sends another pulse of pain through me. Being in this particular alpha's presence is weighing me down, making me feel like I am already in his control.

How is that possible?

The General takes a step forward, and his scent slams into me. Earthy, woodsy, and liberally laced with pheromones.

I am sure he can see every single emotion, every nuance of the feelings that tremble over me right now.

My belly clenches. My womb spasms. Slick pools between my legs and slides down my inner thighs.

His nostrils flare. He leans back on his heels. One side of his lips rises in a smirk.

The alpha knows exactly what he wants. His eyes gleam. His features flush.

Fear twists my insides. My limbs tingle.

It's as if I am watching everything unfold in front of me from a distance.

Setting my jaw, I square my shoulders, only for another burst of pain to radiate out from my center.

I arch my back, thrust my breasts out at the keening need that grips me.

I wrap my arms around my waist and cannot stop the groan that ripples up my throat. Even to my own ears it feels more like an invitation, a call to the alpha to do what he was born to do to an omega. To mate me, knot me, and make that pain inside me go away.

To fill that emptiness that is once again writhing, gnawing, and tearing at me, growing inside me with every passing millisecond until it feels like I am one big mass of yearning that will not stop. Not until he slams into me, and no, no, no! This can't be happening.

I'd starved myself of food for days to weaken my libido; I'd also calculated the time of the month to make sure I am between heat cycles. I hadn't counted on the proximity to this particular alpha sending me straight into one.

My head spins with the overload of endorphins that my overwrought nervous system is dumping into my blood. All brought on by his presence. Him. He's the reason why my body is responding with such primal need. The omega in me recognizes him. Only him.

My pulse thuds in my head; my vision blurs.

Pain cramps my womb, and I double over.

The shortage of omegas has led to alphas exploiting them, taking them at will. As he no doubt intends to overpower me now.

I will not let him do that. I straighten in time to see the General stalk toward me. His masculine presence tugs at my nerves, pushes down on my skin, sinks into my blood. My head spins.

Heat sweeps over my skin and heads to my lower belly. My core weeps.

All of my life I have tried to deny that I am an omega: the receiver, the nurturer whose insides are ravenous for an alpha's touch, who has been deprived of the sensory stimulation that only comes from an alpha's rut. Now, his scent, that concentrated testosterone, sinks into my blood, forcing a reaction.

The General growls.

It's a long, drawn-out purr that seems to emerge from the very depths of his masculine body.

The hair on my neck stands on end.

Liquid need radiates out from my womb, bleeds through my skin, and flares up in the air around me.

My womb cramps, and a fresh burst of slick gushes down between my legs to wet my pants. I don't dare look down, don't dare acknowledge the liquid pooling under me.

I should be mortified, ashamed at my public display of what I am…an omega meant to be mated and bred, who cannot physically hold back her reaction, not in the presence of this prime male specimen, and yet the survivor in me says I need to fight. Fight! My shoulders shudder, and I straighten my spine.

The General slams his fist to his chest. "Leave us," he roars.

The aggression comes off him in waves, surrounding me, cocooning me. Is he trying to shield me from the sight of his own men?

Footsteps sound, then fade away. Of course they'd rush to obey him. No one will dare stand up to him, and I'd walked into this predator's lair and challenged him. Sweat beads my palms.

The doorway to the warehouse slams shut. The echo resounds through my head. The blood thumps at my temples. A pulse flares to life between my legs.

"You scared?" His voice bleeds through the space.

"What do you think?" I grit my teeth.

"I think I am going to enjoy breaking you." He peels back his lips, and my knees tremble. The fine hair on my nape stands up.

The scent of my fear is so strong I am sure he can smell it, and that's not good. The first sign of weakness and this dominant alpha hole will pounce. My belly twists. A flare of heat tugs low below. No, that should not excite me. The thought of him delivering on his earlier promise should not make my thighs clench in anticipation.

I need to get away from that lethal, coiled, powerful male, before he senses how his nearness is affecting me.

I stagger away from him only for my feet to tangle in the carpet, and I cry out. I go sprawling on my back and stay there.

"Get up," he snarls.

I blink then slap my palms onto the carpet for leverage and stagger back to standing. Thrusting my chin forward, I meet his gaze. Those startling blue eyes burn into me. Concentric circles of aquamarine, teal and a wild blue, that draw me in. Trapping me in the sphere of his influence.

"Kayden sent you to kill me."

My chin quivers, and I ball my fists at my sides.

His jaw firms. "I should kill you for daring to burst into my stronghold and trying to assassinate me—"

"But you won't." Yeah, that would be too merciful of him.

He's a monster, and I don't expect any pity from him. But every alpha has an ego. And this predator more than anyone else I have met. Perhaps I need to appeal to that?

He tilts his head. "Feisty, aren't you?" His voice is soft, almost casual.

My stomach churns. Whatever he has in mind for me, it's not good. The thoughts skitter through my head, and I force my brain cells to knit the words together in a coherent sequence.

"You bet." I set my jaw.

His gaze narrows.

My stomach twists, and not only with arousal. My heart hammers, and a bead of sweat trickles down my spine.

"You are a big powerful alpha. Me, I am but a helpless omega." I flutter my eyelashes.

So, I am overdoing this, he's going to see right through my act. "Why don't we make this more exciting for you?" I force out the words through a throat gone dry.

He angles his head.

Guess what? He bought it. A flicker of hope sparks in my chest.

Then his lips widen in a smile, and it's so feral, I know, he's not going to let me go. Not that easily. There's a heavy feeling in the pit of my stomach. My heart thuds, and I almost lose my will to resist—almost.

"I agree." He thrusts out his chest.

"Huh?"

Why am I having this conversation with him? I am only delaying the inevitable, that's all, but I have to try, have to.

"Run." His nostrils flare, "I'll even give you a head start. You have until I count to ten."

"What do you mean?" I gulp down a breath.

"You are losing precious seconds."

No, it can't be. This is not exactly what I'd had in mind when I had suggested making things more exciting. Not.

"Nine."

The alpha is toying with me? He's going to hunt me? My palms sweat. It can mean only one thing. He wants to increase the anticipation of whatever is to come.

The violence, the ultimate conclusion to this game is only one, and it's not going to be in my favor.

I close my fists so tightly my nails slice into my skin. The scent of copper leaks into the air.

"On the other hand, perhaps you'd rather we conclude this farce right now?" His eyes gleam.

The bastard no doubt thinks I don't have a chance of outrunning him. I square my shoulders and thrust out my chest. I will not submit, not so easily.

His gaze sweeps over my breasts, down to my core, and he stares at the space between my legs. There's no mistaking the anticipation that laces his features.

I want to scratch that look of satisfaction off his face, to deny that my insides tremble in response. More moisture gathers between my legs. What is wrong with me? I am here to kill him. Not to mate him. Not. To. Mate. Him.

My pulse races.

I turn on my heels so fast I almost stumble, then find my balance. A scream boils up, and I bite down on my lips to hold it back.

"That the best you can do?" His voice mocks me.

My legs feel weak, yet I force myself to move, to put one foot in front of the other. Keep going. Don't stop.

Reaching the exit of the warehouse, I throw myself against the doors.

3

Zeus

The double doors swing open, and she races through, leaving behind the sugary scent of her slick. The spicy scent of her fear leaks into the air, laced with that spoor of the rain on cool dawn air that is so uniquely her.

My cock throbs, straining against my pants. Adrenaline pumps through my blood. I walk after her, my pace leisurely, yet everything inside pushes me to hurry. Hurry. Go after her, claim her, take her.

I've never felt such a powerful need as this to have an omega. Never felt this overwhelming urge to shield her from the gaze of other alphas, to hide her from sight until I have had my way with her. I speed up my steps and walk out into the wilderness surrounding the warehouse.

Ethan and Sol stand on either side of the doors, their gaze trained on the figure weaving through the trees.

One of the other alphas breaks formation to run after her.

"Stop."

He halts and, his shoulders bunch. The fucker angles his body to face me over his shoulder, and his torso leans forward. Every muscle in the man's body is coiled. "You don't intend to keep her all to yourself now, do you, half-breed?"

"That's General half-breed to you." I stalk over to him.

The man turns his gaze to follow the omega who is now almost out of sight. "You'll give her up to the omega harem, and then I am going to rut her and mark her and —"

Reaching him, I wrap my fingers around his neck and squeeze. The alpha is bulked up to the point of being almost obese with muscle. But I am taller than him, and while I am leaner, I know I am more powerful, and that's not ego, just a fact.

The man gasps, "Surely you are not going to kill me over an omega."

"Wrong comment." I increase the pressure of my grip, hear that sweet snap as his spine breaks. I remove my hold on him, then tap his forehead. His body tumbles over.

I walk over the body of the fallen alpha. "No one hunts her but me."

Ethan stiffens behind me, but he doesn't protest. "Of course, General."

Not that his agreement fools me.

My second has questions, but he'll table it for later. Much later if I have my way with the omega. "Make sure there's food and water in my suite."

"As you wish." Ethan's voice has an edge to it this time. He knows what I have in mind and is not happy about it. Big fucking deal.

He's this close to insubordination, and I need to tell him off. My second is not indispensable, and it's time he realized it. But right now, I have more pressing things to take care of.

"One." I complete the countdown.

Adrenaline pumps through my blood. The thrill of the chase kicks in, and I take off after her.

Heart hammering, pulse-pounding, my feet slam into the dirt, and mud flies up behind me. Reaching the end of the path, I follow the still fresh scent of her sugary essence and that unmistakable trace of fresh rain that sinks straight to my blood. My cock throbs. Warmth floods my chest. My fingers tingle with the need to touch her. I follow the trail to the pool of water in the center of the forest surrounding the stronghold.

She swam across it, in a bid to dissipate her scent and throw me off. Clever omega.

She can fight and she knows how to evade a hunter—this is not an ordinary submissive on my hands. She's unlike any woman I have ever met, someone who challenges me, faces up to me.

My groin tightens.

I quicken my pace and run around the perimeter of the pool. Her scent fades on the other side. Where could she have gone? I scan the area. Trees line the edge of the open lawns that lead down to the parapet walls. The water of the Thames River glimmer beyond that.

I run towards it, calculating how far she could have gone. It wouldn't be like her to do the obvious and hide in the forest on the far side of the stronghold. This way is more exposed, more dangerous. It's exactly the route she'd take.

I run across the grass, straight through the last line of trees.

There's a rustle from the branches above, and that sweet scent of her pours over me. My instincts scream at me to swerve; every part of me stiffens to alertness. But if I were to move aside, she'd hit the ground. The thought of that soft body being hurt, being marked by anything else except my fingers sends a primal burst of anger through me.

She slams into me from above.

The force of it topples me on my back. And then she is on me, her legs squeezing my waist, her fingers around my throat.

"Round one is mine, alpha-hole." She pants then rams her forehead down on mine.

Sparks of red and white flare behind my eyes, pain shoots through my head, but already I am moving. "Not yet, omega-*hole*." I bare my teeth, grab her waist—she's so small that both my palms meet on either side—and then I twist my body so she's lying under me, her strong thighs still gripping my waist, her ankles locked around my back. I bend over her.

Her cheeks flush; her chest heaves.

I push my arousal against her core. It's a blatant sign of who is more dominant, not that there is any doubt about that, okay? Still, it doesn't hurt to show her who's in charge here, does it?

Her gaze widens, her lips part, and fuck! I want to lean down and slide my tongue into that ripe mouth even as I ram my cock balls deep into her pussy.

She must sense my intention, for that sweet, sugary scent of her slickness leaks into her air.

"Does the thought of being taken by me turn you on, Omega?" I lower my voice to just short of a purr, holding back the rich sound that I already know will arouse her further.

Her eyelashes flutter. She swallows, and her hips wriggle under me, brushing against my iron-hard shaft.

Heat bursts through my veins, radiating through my blood, until it feels like every part of me is on fire, with need. For her.

She thrusts out her breasts, and her nipples are outlined through the material of her tight black T-shirt, so sharp, so enticing.

"Oh, Alpha, please take me, rut me."

She flicks out her tongue to lick her lips, and I feel it all the way down to the tip of my shaft.

"Said not this omega." She bares her teeth.

With a move I don't see coming—and I have faced down some of the best hand-to-hand fighters in this land and won—she twists her body, then makes to slide out from under me. I let her go until she is sure she is almost free. Almost. I wait until her features relax, then snake out my arms. I grab her wrists, and twist them up above her head, shackling her there.

A growl rips out of me and her gaze widens. The green of her iris lightens. The scent of her arousal deepens. A pulse tics to life at my temples. My cock throbs in tandem.

I hold her down with my more powerful body, and this time there is no finesse. Only brute force. An alpha laying claim to his omega. "Oh, you will be begging for a lot more before I am done." I take her mouth.

I had meant to punish her for what she'd done. Not the physical hurt when she'd rammed her head against mine. It's my ego that is more bruised—the one that cannot accept that this sprite of an omega could have flounced into my stronghold and then attempted to kill me. It's that which makes me ram my tongue between her lips and swirl it over her teeth, and then I suck in her essence.

Honey and melting ice and sweet, tangy berries, the taste goes straight to my head. I growl low in my throat. The sound rips out of me. Possessive, harsh, it rolls over her. Her entire body seems to stiffen, then relaxes.

Her thighs quiver.

I smell the dampness of her slick, wetting her pants and sinking into the seams of my crotch. My dick throbs, needing to be inside of her.

I transfer her wrists to one hand and sweep the other palm down the side of her arm, to her breast, squeezing that ripe nipple.

I feel the shudder flow down her side as her pelvis thrusts up to cradle my hardness.

Another growl wells up from me, rippling over where her breasts are crushed against the planes of my chest. The sugary scent of her arousal is all around me. I slide my hand down her hips to squeeze the lush curves of her butt. Mine. All mine.

Her body arches under me, her spine curves, the cradle of her hips calls to me. All her muscles shudder, and it's so fucking hot. A primal need grips me. My shoulders go solid.

I slide the heel of my hand between us to rub against her core, her still-fabric-covered center, needing to feel that slickness, wanting to lick it up, pushing, shoving, cupping her core, dry humping her with my hand. Wanting to see her come.

A low moan bleeds up her throat. Her teeth dig into my lower lip, and shock waves ricochet down my spine.

"Fuck, Omega." I tear my mouth from hers.

"Not yet." She twists her body, wrenches her wrists from my grip, and slides out from under me. This time she breaks free.

4

Lucy

The alpha of alphas had all but fucked me right here in the open, and I had let him.

Not that it should come as a surprise, him trying to take me right here in the open without finesse. It's exactly what I'd expect of a brute like him.

But my response to him, the way I had opened my mouth, my legs…my heart… no, not that, not yet, but if I let him, he could get under my skin, and what am I thinking about?

He's treating me like I am a caged animal. To him I am another omega he can drag off to his lair and rut and—my belly tightens—I want him to do it.

I want him to reach down and place his lips where his hand had been between my legs. I need to feel his tongue thrust inside me, feel that thick shaft whose length had throbbed against my waist, fill me, take me, knot me. "Fuck." I scream more to hear the sound of my own voice, so I can try to shake off this sexual haze that has gripped me. This need that twists my insides, that makes me want to turn away and retrace my steps and throw myself at him.

"No. Fucking. Way." I will not let him capture me.

I push my feet into the ground, focus my eyes on my goal. The wall, get to the wall.

My belly clenches; my skin heats.

The thud of his footsteps draws closer, as he chases after me. The scent of burned pinewood pours over me. His scent. So evocative, so potent. It's laced with the tangy spoor of his arousal. It sinks into my blood, and my core clenches.

Goosebumps flare over my skin. "Keep going," I swear to myself, then blink the sweat from my eyes. I hit the wall and clutch at it. My hands slip on the surface, and I almost scream out in frustration.

"Stop, Omega." His voice is low, resonant, and it slides over my skin, incessant, incandescent.

It calls to me.

"No." I shove my hand over the top of the wall, and this time find purchase. I haul my body over it, almost go over the side, then at the last second straighten myself to stand poised on the narrow length.

"Don't do this." His voice is soft, so tempting. So enticing. I hear the promises hidden in the tone and don't dare turn. If I do, I'll be lost.

I grip the surface with my boots, stand there balanced on the wall, trying not to stare at the churning mass of water far below. The wind blows over me, and I sway with it, trying to keep my balance.

The breeze cuts off, and I know he's there behind me. His big body is shielding me from the elements. And it shouldn't feel like he's trying to protect me. But it does, and that doesn't make sense.

"Turn around, Omega."

I shake my head, glance at the other side of the river. Can I swim across? That's assuming I survive the fall. I glance down at the water and mistake!—my knees quake. I lose my balance, doubling over all the way from my waist. My heart pounds, my leg muscles scream in protest, then I straighten again.

There's silence behind me. I don't see him, don't hear him. His scent fades away, and I miss it already. I miss his presence. How bizarre is that?

How can you miss something you've never had?

I've never had anyone watch out for me, not until now. But he isn't my protector. He's an alpha who'd take me and rut me, and my heart stutters. The horrible thing is that I want him to.

I don't want to die without knowing what it is like to have an alpha's cock—not any alpha, *this* alpha. *His* shaft. I need it inside me, and what does that make me? Another omega who is driven by her needs. Yeah, that's all I am. But maybe, if I take the plunge and dive into the water…I can redeem myself. Perhaps this is the way to prove to myself that I am not just a pussy driven to find fulfillment in the arms of an alpha. A man I hadn't met until less than half an hour ago.

A low purr bleeds through the air. It loops around me, surrounds me, sinks into my blood. Warms me, enfolds me, caresses me.

How is it possible for one single consonant to carry so many complex notes, so much need?

I feel myself sway, feel my muscles relax, even as the still thinking part of my mind screams at me to fight. Fight. I half-turn, shuffling my feet, on the wall. Pieces of gravel slide off and over the side.

"Look at me." His voice is soft and insistent, and yet there is a trace of steel running through it. "Now."

The dominance in his tone cuts through the thoughts swirling around in my head, and slams into my chest. It pushes down on my shoulders, tugs at my nerves, forcing me to obey.

I lift my gaze to his.

Find myself drawn into those deep-blue eyes. So calm, so serene, so false, and yet so true. So intense. Deeper than the water behind me. Brighter than the skies above.

Standing on the wall, I am about level with that gaze.

Another low purr rumbles up his chest, his throat, pours out of his mouth, and I sway toward it. Toward that massive chest that can take my weight. A dense cloud of heat spools off his body and slams into me. I gasp.

My insides churn, my toes curl, everything in me insists I close the space between us, that I throw myself at him, rip off his clothes, feel his naked skin, lick the sweat that drips down his throat and ask him to take me. Right now.

This is insane.

There is a buzzing in my ears. I shake my head to clear it, then stagger back, taking a step away from him, and into space. I fling out my hand, and then there's only the whine of the breeze.

5

Zeus

Her gaze widens, and then her body begins to fall. My heart slams against my rib cage. I leap across the distance that covers us and, leaning over, grab at her hand. I close my fingers around her wrist.

The weight of her body pulls me over the side. I hook my foot under the space at the bottom of the wall for leverage. She is not very heavy, yet my arm feels like it's being pulled out of my socket. Sweat beads my forehead. Her body sways in the breeze. Her features tighten, and the color slides from her face. Still, she doesn't scream, doesn't panic. That surprises me and turns me on. She's fucking strong, doesn't scare easily, and I can't wait to break her.

It's even more important that I save her.

I strengthen my stance and then take a step back. Flexing my biceps, I heave her up. All the while, I hold her gaze. Those green eyes of hers stare at me; in their depths is a grim determination.

She actually thought she could have survived the fall and escaped, and perhaps she might have, but if I have my way, it will be a while before she sees any open space. Not until I have shown her who is her master. Not until I have taken her body and soul. Not until I own her thoughts, know her feelings, can second-guess her every move. Not until every part of her is mine. Only *mine.*

I don't realize I have spoken the word aloud until her gaze widens. I can see the exact moment it sinks in about who is her rescuer. Her green pupils dilate. With fear? Arousal? Then, she kicks out her legs and pulls me over, almost all the way over the side.

Once again, I press my feet into the ground to find purchase. Then, hanging over the side of the parapet, I fling out my other arm to grab her shoulder.

"Let me go." She snarls at me, holding my gaze.

"Never." I bare my teeth, widen my stance, and yank her up.

The leverage pulls her up and over the side, and the weight of her body crashes into me. This time I am prepared. I heave her over my shoulder and then, swiveling around, I race up the lawns. I need to get her to where she is safe, where she can't harm herself like that again.

She squirms in my hold and I sense her draw in a breath. All her muscles tense. Oh! No, she is not going to escape, not this time.

I tighten my hold and squeeze her thighs into my chest. Reaching the staircase, I race up the steps two at a time.

She begins to struggle harder, wriggling in my grasp. Each twitch of her hips only bleeds more of that omega scent of her arousal into the air. My cock hardens so much that it makes me stumble and almost fall, and fuck, I've had enough. Something inside me snaps. I slap her butt, once, twice, a third time. I intend to hurt. Intend to quieten her, need to feel that curved flesh give under my palm, feel that firmness resist. My fingers curl with the need to feel her naked skin slide against mine.

She stills.

I fling open the double doors to my suite and stride in. The sound of the bolt crashing home echoes around the space.

"No, no. No." She punches a fist against my side.

Damn but she doesn't give in, does she? A part of me relishes the fact that she still resists me. It's going to make her submission so much sweeter.

She sinks her teeth into my back, and the sharp edges graze the skin through my vest. I feel it all the way to the tip of my cock.

Hell, I've been hard from the second I set eyes on her. She'd charged me, armed with nothing but that puny knife and had drawn blood. She'd taken me by surprise.

When was the last time anyone had managed to do that? Not since I had dueled with Ethan, and we'd been teenagers then. *And Kayden had sent her.* Had he anticipated that this omega would get through my defenses much easier than any alpha would?

A prickle of awareness tugs at my subconscious, and I push it aside. Not even Kayden could have expected this omega getting as far as she has.

It should piss me off really that she thinks she can go toe to toe with me, and yet it's alluring. And exciting. She is wild, this one. She will not give in easily. Her audacity is an aphrodisiac that calls to me. And there is no way I am letting her out of this room, not for a long time.

She knows it, too.

And perhaps it is that which makes her struggle afresh.

She snarls and tries to knee me in the groin. I swerve, and her leg scrapes my waist, her inner thigh brushing my hardness. The scent of her arousal is heavy in the air. Honeyed, yet with a hint of something deeper... I have no doubt she will taste sweeter.

Desire tightens my groin.

She slams her fist into my back. The vibration shudders through me. I don't stop the growl that escapes my throat and am rewarded with her body trembling against mine.

It's cute that she thinks I will actually heed her cries, that I might consider setting her free. Not when she'd walked right into the den of the big bad alpha. I angle my head and sink my teeth in the curve of her butt.

She screams out. "You bit me?"

"*You* bit me first," I growl. "I only returned the favor."

She thrashes her legs, her body bucks, and she pounds her fists on my back.

"Behave." I drag my arm down to below her hips and hold her there.

"You haul me away, capture me and bring me here, and you expect me to stay quiet?" Her voice is muffled, but I still hear her.

Her knees dig into my waist.

"I gave you a chance to escape, you failed. You are mine." I snap my teeth.

She trembles.

A primitive surge of satisfaction tightens my groin. She's afraid. Good. "It seems it's finally sinking in you are in my control." I sneer.

She brings down her joined fists on my back. The blow only sends another pulse of heat tearing through my veins.

"Have you lost touch with reality so much that you don't know right from wrong anymore?"

There's a touch of anguish in her voice and helplessness, and it tugs something inside me. Some long-forgotten, humane part of me that only one other woman has ever touched. What am I doing? I'd seen her and lost control. Had smelled that essence of ripe omega mixed with a dash of something forbidden, something so tangible that I had wanted to throw her down on the floor and rut her right there in the open.

It had blinded my senses to everything else. Except her. I am the hunter. She is my spoils. So why am I so hesitant? I cross the floor toward my bed.

She must realize that I am approaching my destination for she begins to struggle again. Arms and leg thrashing, she writhes in my grasp.

Another flare of her arousal hits me, and on cue, my cock thickens. What the fuck? I tighten my grip on her, "Keep that up and I won't be responsible for what happens to you. I've been a gentleman so far."

"You are kidding, right?" She yells, "If this is how you treat your guests—"

"That's where you are mistaken." I reach the bed. "You aren't a guest. And I am not your host."

I am a callous bastard who does not hesitate to plunder first and ask questions later, as she's going to discover soon enough.

She knees me in the stomach, and the breath whooshes out of me. Another shudder of arousal tightens my belly.

"Let me go," she pleads.

"You bet." I throw her down on the mattress.

She bounces once, then springs up on her feet. Of course, she does. She's already demonstrated that she knows how to fight, and she'd almost held her own…almost, even against someone as powerful as me. And that's not ego, just a fact.

It's imperative that I make her a conquest. My dick throbs. The beat echoes the pulse thudding at my temples.

Swiveling around, I stomp to the table by the window and stab my finger at the tray of food there. "Eat." I jerk my chin at the omega.

Her features grow pale. Her gaze drops to the tray, and she purses her lips. "I don't want to eat, you fool."

Her choice of insult is almost anticlimactic.

I snicker, and the skin at the corners of her eyes tightens.

Still holding her gaze, I kick off my boots. "In that case, let's fuck."

6

Lucy

Bastard! He knows that pronouncement while not exactly a surprise is only going to alarm me, and that is his intention: to frighten me so that I'll submit to him like a nice docile omega. Well, he's got that so wrong. I am not going down, not without a fight. The alpha-hole can go screw himself if he thinks I am going to make this easy on him.

He shrugs out of his vest, then places it over the chair near the bed.

The arrogance of the brute! He turns his back on me. I bare my lips, then lean low to charge him.

He tears off his tunic to reveal his naked back.

My breath catches, and my thigh muscles freeze.

Without his clothes, this alpha is overpowering.

I swallow, and my heart hammers.

Nothing has prepared me for those shoulders that seem hewn out of stone. His biceps flex, and I don't need to touch them to know they'll be hard and ungiving, like the rest of that body he is so casually baring to my gaze. Colored ink marks one side of his back and continues up and over his shoulder.

This is when I throw myself at him and catch him unawares. When he is the most vulnerable. I force my brain to connect my thoughts with action and place one trembling foot in front of the other.

He bends and pulls off his pants.

The scent of him, that earthy, woodsy, packed-with-need aroma intensifies. It's laced with something deeper, the tang of his precum, all of which sinks into my blood and heads straight to my core.

My throat closes; my mouth goes dry. Moisture seeps out from between my thighs.

The muscles of his back ripple, the intricate tattoos on his skin undulate like the patterns on a rattlesnake.

The man is deadlier. He'll hypnotize me, seduce me, take me, and I'll not be able to protest. A shiver runs down my spine.

He drapes his fatigues over the seat, and all thought dribbles out of my head. His corded flanks are a thing of beauty that sweep down to meet the backs of those muscled thighs.

I must have made some noise, for he turns and gives me a full-frontal view of that sheer unleashed dominance of his physical self.

His chest is sculpted. There are tattoos colored across those angles and planes. His honeyed skin sweeps over a torso that has weathered many fights. A tattoo slashes diagonally across the expanse, and I want to touch it. Trail my fingers over those pecs, down to where his concave stomach dips to meet his shaft. His fully aroused massive dick that stands up almost vertical with need.

Heat sweeps through my body, chased by chills. Goosebumps flare on my fore-arms. Every pore of my skin seems to open as if to absorb each nuance of his touch, the feel of him. My body is preparing for the invasion by this alpha that is bound to come. My stomach lurches. I want to look away but I can't.

I want to move but my body feels too heavy.

A ripple of need pierces my core.

I want to taste him. Want to lap up the seed that drips from him and rub it all over myself.

I can almost feel that slithery moisture trickling over me. The sensations twist my insides. My thighs clench and a low, keening need rocks my belly.

His gaze narrows and those blue eyes seem to lighten into colorless mirrors that amplify my own desires before throwing them back at me.

My skin chafes with the need to go to him, to throw myself at him and rub my skin over his.

He holds his arms loosely at his sides, then widens his stance. I can see every last nook and hollow of that beautiful, delectable, hateful body.

The cords of his strong throat flex, the planes of his chest rippling as if there is an unseen force unfurling inside him.

The brute is preening for me, making sure I know exactly who is going to possess me. A powerful dominant alpha male who will take without mercy.

I should back away, scream, try to plot on how to get out of there. But that omega core of me insists I am exactly where I should be. The need to draw into myself, and make myself smaller is overwhelming. I will not do that. To do that will only give him an advantage. I jut out my chin and stay where I am.

His jaw firms. Then, he angles his head and studies me. His gaze is brooding, calculating, stained with lust and a strange cruelty.

My throat closes. My fingers tingle and the hair on my nape hardens. Why doesn't he do something? Say something? Anything to break the silence that fills the room and presses down on my shoulders. Sweat beads my palms.

The chiseled planes of his chest tense, tightening his skin that is the color of honey. I want to run my lips over the demarcation of those powerful pecs, to lick and suck my way down to those thighs shaped from sheer muscle and tendons and covered with a smattering of light hair. The chafing of his rougher skin on mine would set off delightful trails of friction over my belly, leaving tracks of redness where they'd scrape the insides of my thighs.

Sparks of heat jolt through my chest.

The tension in the room ratchets up, and my nerves feel like they are being strained to the breaking point. Every part of me feels like it is on fire, yearning for his touch, yet he stays unmoving. He could be a sculpture or an obscene dedication to everything that is lethal.

My eyelids feel too heavy, and I lower my gaze back to where that massive shaft throbs. In the last few seconds, his shaft has grown bigger, harder.

My breath stutters. He's too large, too massive. Every part of him screams that he is bent on dominating me, that he will not stop until he gets what he wants, and not even then. Not until every single inch of my skin bears his imprint.

Something very much like anticipation grips me. The still rational part of my brain screams out a warning.

I need to get out of here.

Out of these clothes which feel too tight on me. Out of these barriers which I have imposed on myself. Tear through the walls and expose that giving, needing omega inside me.

The yearning is so primal that my womb cramps and slick gushes down my inner thighs. I wrap my arms around my waist and groan.

The sound seems to turn him on even more, and his already engorged shaft thickens further.

He takes a step forward, and I have no doubt that he is going to close the distance between us. He is going to lick up the sweat from between my breasts, then thrust his tongue inside my pussy and absorb my essence, and the awful thing, the beautiful thing is that I can't wait. I need him to take the choice out of my hands and put me out of this misery.

The image cuts through the haze that the heat cycle has brought on. I straighten my shoulders and tear my gaze from the part of him that promises me the ultimate freedom.

He stalks toward me to stand at the foot of the bed.

This close, the dominance of his presence weighs down on my chest, presses down on my shoulders. The fine hairs on the nape of my neck rise. A plume of heat spools off his chest and slams into me, a moan whines out of me.

His gaze widens, those cruel lips curl in a smirk.

My sex quivers in response. Every pore on my skin pops open tuned into him, waiting for him… waiting.

He leans forward on the balls of his feet. His scent crashes over me, sinks into my blood and tugs at my nerve endings. My skin puckers.

Closer, I need him to come closer, why has he stopped? No, what am I thinking? What's happening to me? My throat closes. "Don't you dare," I gulp.

7

Zeus

"Don't challenge me." I keep my voice casual when every part of me aches to cover her body with mine.

Waves of fear roll from her. Yet she holds up her fists in front of her. The skin stretches white over her knuckles.

Standing on the bed that is on a raised platform, she is still not at eye level with me.

I frown. "You are tiny."

Her chest rises and falls; her thick hair curls over her face and around her neck. Red highlights gleam in it. How will it feel to have those locks wrapped around my palm as I yank back her head and close my mouth around those delectable lips?

"My looks are deceptive." She raises her head and meets my gaze.

"I said tiny...not fragile," I smirk. "Your will is strong enough that you walked into my turf and took me on, not to mention facing down a crowd of alphas. Clearly, you are also stupid."

"Stupid?" She blinks as if she can't quite believe that I said that to her face.

Hey, I did compliment her first, didn't I? Backhanded as it was, I was still appreciative of her fearlessness...or should I call it recklessness?

"Not as much as you are." She thrusts out her chin.

"Oh?" I angle my head. "Pray, tell me what you mean by that?" My voice is casual...and while my men would have given me a clear berth on hearing the threat in my voice, it seems to have the opposite effect on her.

"I'll go one better," Her shoulders tighten. The muscles of her arms bunch, and I know she is preparing to attack me.

I brace myself for the inevitable when she snaps her shoulders back, and her breasts strain against her jumpsuit. Those nipples outlined through the material tease me, call to me, begging me to cup them, massage them, curve my tongue around the hard nubs and pull on them.

All other thought goes out of my head.

Everything except that I am an alpha and this luscious omega, ripe for the plucking, going into her heat cycle, is here, in my room, in my bed. On my turf.

Fuck everything else.

My thighs go rock-hard.

Her gaze slides back down to my dick. Her little pink tongue slides out to lick her lips, and I feel the ripples of need all the way to my groin.

I have to have her now.

I growl my intention, drawing that harsh purr out, all the way from the depths of my being, up through my ribcage, pouring it out, unfurling the notes over her, lassoing her with it and pulling her closer, closer.

She groans and stutters mid-step. Her gaze widens; the black pupils in those forest-green eyes bleed out. "That's not helping."

"On the contrary. I'm making sure you are wet enough to ease my penetration."

I breathe out a low purr. And am rewarded when the sugary scent of her arousal grows deeper.

Her cheeks flush. "Thanks for painting—or should I say panting—that for me in graphic detail."

I can't stop the surprised chuckle that cracks out of me. "Not only gorgeous, and a fighter, but also smart." The compliments roll off my tongue so easily. I hear my own words and start.

Just a one-off, that's all it is.

I never waste time on words, definitely not before I fuck. Not ever. And certainly not to sing the praises of the omega who's already in my grasp. I have no need to tell her what I think of her. Really not.

Her cheeks flush. "You going to say now that your approving talk will also ease your infiltration of my body?" She huffs out a breath.

"No, actually... I am deciding how to put that sharp tongue of yours to better use." I gaze at her mouth, knowing that will only turn her on further. Somehow, my plan of taking her has turned into a full-blown seduction. It feels so right, and yet it's not what I want. Is it? I need her to fear me, lay with me, fuck me back perhaps, just as I intend to worship her body, too.

Molten heat courses through my blood.

She must sense my thoughts, for her lips tremble. Her chest heaves. She curls her fingers into fists at her sides, and I know it's because she's stopping herself from touching me.

"You want me, admit it." I run my hands over my chest.

"No." Her gaze follows my actions as I slide my palm down to my thick cock and palm it at the base. Squeezing it down the length until a drop of precum oozes out.

She licks her lips. Oh, yeah, she wants me, wants my dick inside her all right. "Why are you fighting the inevitable?"

"Because... I have sworn to only lay with my mate."

Her features freeze as if she can't believe she's blurted that out. I angle my head. Interesting. A strange warmth pools in my chest. I don't want to examine it. Don't care what it is. Nope. No way.

"So you haven't been with any other alpha?"

She squares her shoulders. "Your ability to deduce the obvious is overwhelming." She tries to sneer, but her voice trembles, spoiling the effect.

I don't need her confirmation to reaffirm what I've already sensed. She's held back from anyone else having her, and that knowledge shakes me to the core.

I want to shove her on her back, bury myself inside her, sheath my cock in the depths of that sweet omega essence right before I turn her over, then bend her and slam into her from behind, taking her in every conceivable position.

She must read the intention on my face, for she shakes her head. "No."

I peel back my lips. "Yes."

This is when she retreats, perhaps falls on her knees and submits to me—better still, lies back, opens her thighs, and stays that way. I growl low, anticipating that sweet taste of her coating my tongue, that complex, seductive omega scent rolling through my blood as I raise and lower her on my cock. I can literally feel her skin give under my fingers when she snarls and bows her head and comes at me.

For a second it is I who blinks and freezes. I stare as she charges at me.

Little hellion.

I almost admire her for her fighting instinct, for that need to not give up, to fight back until the last breath, that intuition that had kept me going all through my growing years. That had brought me here to this fine suite in the palace in the richest district of the city.

I sense a kindred spirit in her. Which is why I am going to have to break her. I almost feel remorseful at that. Almost. But I have no choice. I have my plans all laid out. I haven't come all this way to let an omega derail me.

So what if she smells like sunshine and heat and that faint sugary taste of musk that hints at her arousal?

So what if she has the most beautiful, most desirable, most luscious body that I have ever encountered?

So what if given half a chance she will claw her way under my skin, rip out my heart, and trample all over it, even as she claims ownership of my soul…and I must put an end to this. To whatever spell she is casting over me. Her omega essence is clearly ensnaring me, making me lose my composure, and that I will not allow. No way.

When she rushes at me, I take the brunt of her hit. I don't feel it. No, that's a lie. The feel of her breasts sliding against my chest, the scrape of her knuckles as she smashes her fist into my side, all of it turns me on.

I don't move. And it's not the fear of hurting her that keeps me immobile. It's just that I relish the splatter of her punches on my chest until the fight finally goes out of her.

She falls to her knees, head hanging forward, shoulders slumped.

She's breathing heavily, her lips parted, her spine curved down. It's a gesture of total submission, one I appreciate.

My cock twitches and I delight in every second of the tension building in my groin. The inevitable coupling is going to be so much sweeter. So satisfying, that bite of pure satisfaction that comes with having broken an omega completely and utterly.

Reaching down, I swipe her hair away from her face, then clamp my fingers around her neck.

Her body tenses, then she springs up and snaps her head forward.

8

Lucy

I rear up and smash my head into his chin. Shock waves ricochet down my neck, down my spine. Sparks of red flash behind my eyes.

It feels like I've run into a brick wall. The impact slices through my body.

I cry out and fall back on the bed. Tears run down my cheeks. I'd known I wasn't going to be able to escape, knew it from the moment I'd agreed to this half-assed plan to assassinate the General, that this could go either way. But until that moment I'd not realized I'd held out a last sliver of hope that I'd be able to break out of the grasp of this alpha.

He'd given me a chance to escape, and I had failed.

Then he'd allowed me to go at him, and the one solid hit that I'd got in at him had laid me low. The physical pain from the impact rips through me. A dull pressure pushes against the back of my eyeballs. More than the fact that I am utterly and completely at his mercy, it is the humiliation that I can't hold my own against him that frustrates me. I've honed my fighting skills against some of the most skilled warriors, and all of it is to no avail.

It's strange that more than the possible rape of my body that this alpha no doubt intends, it is the rape of my pride that hurts me more.

The throbbing in my head increases in crescendo. My guts twist, and the band around my chest tightens.

Sweat drips down my back, down my forehead, creeping into the space between my eyelids, and they sting.

I squeeze my eyes shut and lie there waiting for whatever punishment he has in store for me. Knowing only to expect the worst. Every last nightmare version of what I have heard from other omegas of how alphas will take from you, tear into you to slake their thirst...all of those scenarios crowd in on my head. My shoulders hunch. Tears slide down my cheeks and dammit, but I can't stop them.

I am aware of him swooping down on me.

The world tilts as he slides his body under me, stretching out and cradling me close to his chest. There's a strange gentleness, an almost awkward reverence to how he holds me. He doesn't soothe, doesn't say anything. His arms are around me, bands of steel that tie me to him. To keep me prisoner, to stop me from escaping, no doubt. I should feel threatened...yet I am not.

There's only a relief that I can stop pretending. Is that what I have been doing so far? Pretending? The thought brings on a fresh wave of tears, and a sob racks my body, then another. Before I know it, I am holding on to the same arms that imprison me, hanging on to him for support as I bawl my eyes out.

My insides twist.

I curl up my legs and bring them close. I am wound around this man's chest like a baby clinging to her mother.

My sobs intensify. What the hell is wrong with me? This is not the time to have a full-blown breakdown. Not in the arms of my captor. Yet surrounded by the heat of this alpha's body I feel secure in a way I've never felt before, not even with my own family. I don't have many memories of my mother who died too young. My father was a warrior, the Czar of Moscow. Though I was an omega, he'd recognized the fighter in me. He'd made sure to train me. I'd been fortunate that as a member of the royal family I'd had the choice of when to mate with an alpha. I'd managed to delay it, too, until now.

The tears keep coming.

My throat is so dry I am sure I shouldn't be able to cry anymore, and yet I can't seem to stop. It's as if all the years of pent-up hatred, fear, recklessness, all of it wound inside comes bubbling up. I am falling apart, and it's in the arms of the most powerful alpha in the land. The one who will no doubt take my virginity against my will.

But even that thought doesn't stop my weeping. Nothing matters anymore. Nothing except the feel of his arms around me.

The soft growls that rumble up his chest rock my body.

The rich bass of his purring crawls up the space between us, vibrates up his throat and curls around me. Sensuous, gentle. His tone is almost sub-vocal, and yet it's unmissable. It's hypnotic. I listen to it. Am entranced by it. I hiccough once. My ears pop, and the sound grows deeper. A soothing, resonant murmur that rolls over my skin and sinks into my blood.

Each new wave of purring sets off sparks of heat in its wake. Seducing. Comforting. Like he's weaving a cocoon around me. I am caught in the wonder of this new experience.

The earthy scent of him, mixed with the dark cinnamon of his arousal, sloshes over me. I breathe it in, not aware that I am doing it, not until the hard planes of his chest bite into my cheeks. I become aware of digging my nails into his skin, which is streaked from my tears.

My tears.

It's so intimate. And yet it shouldn't be like this. It shouldn't feel so right when everything else is wrong, so wrong. I shouldn't be here. With him. In his bed.

Enfolded in his arms. Soaking in his warmth. Reveling in that entrancing alpha scent of his, seeking out his touch…his caresses. Him. Only him.

How can I feel so much, in such little time? And for someone completely and utterly wrong for me? My eyelids grow heavy. I try to crack them open, but it's too much of a struggle. I push against his hold, knowing I should try to break free.

Another soothing purr rumbles over me, and the muscles of my shoulders unwind.

He slides his thigh between mine, but I am too weak to protest. The rough hair of his upper thigh brushes the tender skin between my legs. I was wrong. The feel of his skin on mine is not only pleasurable, it heightens the contrast between what only he can offer and the emptiness swirling inside me. Something like pain skitters down my spine.

I swallow and reach once more for that rumbling that is growing in volume, deepening around me. Pulling at me. Tugging at me. I want to protest, say something. But I feel too weak. Like I have been running, fighting too hard.

The purring changes tenor becomes deeper, resonant. It sparks a response from my nerves which immediately seem to catch fire. I shudder, not sure exactly what he's doing to me.

If this is what it means to submit, so be it.

He may as well take me when I am half out of my head with grief, with sadness, and an overwhelming desire to be done with whatever it is that an alpha does to an omega. Or not. I've heard of it but I've never been with a man before. Not because I am a prude, not for my lack of trying, but because for an omega, once you get an alpha to mate you to break the heat cycle, then you can't stop, not until the heat cycle has run its course. More often than not it results in an omega's pregnancy.

And I've never thought I'd want to bring a child into this world, not until I'd met the right alpha. Which isn't him.

My muscles tense.

His arms tighten as if he senses my discomfort.

I wriggle in his embrace, pushing against the sculpted planes of his chest.

His breath raises the hair on my head. Another purr builds up from his groin. I am lying on him so I can track exactly the source of that sound, follow it as it shivers up his iron-hard stomach, ripples through his rib cage, vibrates up his throat and then pours out in mellifluous chords that slide into my blood, straight to my core.

My thighs clench.

The soft flesh of my center quivers. A trickle of slick spurts down my inner thigh.

And it is that which brings me to being alert. Awareness tugs at my nerves. It pushes aside the haze of desire that has clogged my mind.

All of his gentleness, his tenderness, it is all a front. It has to be. A way to lull me into comfort, to make me trust, enough to allow my hormones to regroup, my core to relax and ready itself for my alpha. Which he is not; he never will be.

I raise my head, gaze at him through hooded eyelids, then lean down and sink my teeth into his neck.

9

Zeus

Her teeth dig into me, and the shock of it surges down my spine. There's a primitive satisfaction that she wants to own me, while a part of me cannot believe she took that liberty with me. It is my prerogative as alpha to mark her first.

Mine to own, to claim, to do with her as I want.

I've been holding back, and she has taken advantage of that; she has taken the lead in this mating game. More than the physical hurt, it's my ego that roars in protest at the liberty.

With a roar, I flip her over, pinning her to the bed.

I snag her arms together to pull them up and over her head, shackling her wrists. I want to ask her what she's trying to prove, but one look in those green eyes, and the words stutter in my mouth. I am not someone with a soft heart, I have no tenderness inside me. I take, that's what I do, yet one whiff of the fear that vibrates off her, and when I open my mouth all that emerges is a rumbling growl.

Her lips are stained by the blood she drew from me when she bit me.

It's primal, and so fucking arousing. The evidence that she already marked me, has staked her claim on me, does she realize it? It sends a fierce surge of need pounding through my veins.

My cock twitches and I grind the evidence of my arousal into her soft core—not because I want to show her how turned on I am, though that, too—but it's more a clear sign to her as to who owns her and that there is no escape from me.

"You fought well, little warrior; you can take comfort in that."

She bares her teeth, showing gums stained with my blood. "I'm not done yet." Her green eyes are so large, the pupils so dilated that it's a clear sign she is nervous, afraid, and also aroused.

"Yes, you are." Something like tenderness flushes through me. Nah. It can't be that. Me? Wanting to take care of this omega who tried to kill me? I must be losing my mind, or perhaps I have been too lenient with her. I've indulged this wildling for too long. It's time to show her the kind of pleasures only an alpha can give his omega.

I lean down and lick my blood from her lips.

Her shoulders shudder. Every muscle in her body goes on alert.

I nibble my way up her cheek to the shell of her ear, then suck on her earlobe.

She shivers. Her eyelids flutter down. A low groan spills from her lips.

"That's it, submit, give in…go with your instinct, and then it'll be easier for you."

As the words leave my mouth, her body tenses again. It seems if I speak it breaks the trance she falls into when I purr for her. And it's no hardship to do that, mind you. I'll force her if needed. I'd much prefer someone more submissive, someone more pliant, open to do my bidding…not. If that were the case, wouldn't I have taken an omega from the ones stocked in the harem, the ones my alphas lay with whenever the need to rut comes over them?

I'd done so on one occasion, but the encounter had been so unfulfilling I'd not bothered again. Then I'd caught a glimpse of that dark-red strand of her hair tumbling free of its restraint to curl over her shoulder and I'd known what was missing. Her. Her fire, her breath. Her scent. I have to have her.

My dick pulses in agreement. My shaft pushes against the softness of her core.

Her eyes fly open, and the green in them has faded to light gold. My breath stutters. She is much more breathtaking than I'd thought. It makes me want to see how the rest of her is.

What is so special about this female that she is already in my blood?

Why is this prickly omega the only one I want?

The thought pulses a trickle of discomfort down my spine. No, I have no intention of feeling anything for her. The only reason I brought her here was to punish her. To show her she can't challenge me on my own turf.

And, yeah, because the thought of any other alpha violating her is something that affects me in a way I still can't understand. It's that which makes me pull my weight off of her and stand back.

Her legs are flung apart, her breasts rising and falling, her cheeks flushed. And the remnants of the jumpsuit cling to her body like petals from a rose on damp ground.

Bending down, I grab the seam of her collar and rip the fabric to her waist. Yanking it over her legs, I pull it off her.

She is naked underneath.

Her full, lush breasts spring out, dark-pink areolae crowned with the most delicate of buds for nipples.

Desire grips me, hot and hard. I can't tear my eyes away from the perfectly formed specimen of femininity.

Her slim waist seems impossibly narrow. I trail a finger over her navel to where her waist slopes to meet the dark-red hair that points to her clit.

Goosebumps pop on her skin. Her muscles tense.

I look up to find those green eyes dilated yet burning with a fire that entrances me. She flexes her jaw. A muscle throbs above her cheekbone. She is gritting her teeth, to stop herself from making any noise, knowing that will only encourage me. And suddenly I want to hear her voice more than anything else.

I trail my finger down to the edge of her clit and hover there. Her thighs clench. Moisture trickles between her legs and pools below. The scent of her deepens and goes straight to my head.

My cock hardens and aches with the need to feel her warmth clench around me. I raise my gaze, up her trembling stomach, over her swollen breasts to her face.

Those green eyes, the gold in them sparkles and burns. Yet her lips are pursed in defiance. She is aroused. She wants me. Yet she is still able to resist me. A fierce surge of pride grips me. It makes me want her more but also slows me down. I want to seduce her until she has no choice but to give in to me. And give in she will. I've never lost a fight and don't intend to start now. Certainly not to a weaker omega.

"Does the thought of my hands on your flesh, discovering all your secrets one by one, stripping you of your layers and baring you to my gaze...does that turn you on?"

She raises her chin but doesn't answer.

She doesn't need to.

Her chest rises and falls, and her belly trembles. That sugary-sweet musk of her arousal laps at my senses.

My mouth waters.

And yet I pause and wait...for what? I can't understand my own hesitation. She is mine to take, to ruin, to do with as I want.

I am the most powerful alpha in the land, the newly ascended leader of this city.

So what stops me from having my way with this wisp of an omega who dared try to assassinate me?

Precisely nothing.

I drop to my knees and lower my mouth to that trembling flesh between her legs.

10

Lucy

I see the play of emotions on his face…and, really, it should not be possible to differentiate the lust that leaks from his every pore with the flicker of something very much like confusion that I am sure I glimpsed there for a second. No, surely, I am mistaken.

This is Zeus, the fiercest alpha in the city, the man who killed his own father to become the General. The very hungry male who licks his tongue from the bottom of my pussy all the way to my clit at the top.

No, no, no.

I must have said it aloud, for a low purr flows over me. This sound is tenacious, insistent, like the vocal equivalent of a battering ram, seducing me, asking to be let in. And that confuses me. I am at his mercy. He is the alpha, I am the omega, in his suite, on his bed, and his tongue is writhing inside me, and yet a part of him tries to soothe me.

I almost wish he didn't.

I wish that he'd take me and be done with it.

If it is my heat cycle that is making him want to claim me if that is all this is about, then I want him to be done with it, so I can get down to business and perhaps ask him for a way to help the rest of my omega clan. If… His fingers join his tongue in my core, stretching me, hooking inside and finding a vulnerable, delicate patch of skin that is so responsive, so delicate, so everything that I know he's found that secret place inside of me that I hadn't known existed.

I thrash my head from side to side, and my back arches off the bed, and my hands, they are buried in his hair. I should drag them away. Instead, all I can do is rake my fingernails over his scalp until they snag on his heavy locks that are…

smoother than they look, silky. Like how my skin must feel in comparison to the second calloused digit he's pushed inside me.

"No, please." I moan, trying to push him—at least I think I am trying to shove him away; the fact is, I am holding his face close to my pussy and thrusting my pelvis into his face, offering up all of myself to him.

He can take me now and I wouldn't stop him.

Another deep purr from him crawls over my skin, settles in my belly.

More slick oozes from between my legs and a wave of dismay grips me. Around him, I can't control my own response. It's alarming and also makes me want to give in.

He draws in a deep breath as if he is inhaling my very essence, taking a part of me inside him. It shouldn't be so arousing, shouldn't turn me on, but it does.

Primal lust tightens my skin. I pant, only to scream when he circles his tongue over my clit, then drags it to the entrance of my channel where he licks up my moisture. Leaning up and balancing his weight on his forearms, he dribbles the liquid into my mouth. And I slurp it up from his lips and swallow it down.

I taste myself, sweet and musky, and him...spicy with a honeyed edge that is a shock. It's far from unpleasant. There's a strange intimacy in this, in tasting our joined-up essences, and it's the closest, the nearest I have ever been to anyone else. My soul seems to intertwine with his in that instant. I shake my head, trying to deny these strange feelings of heat and lust and sheer passion that are tearing me apart. It can't be like this. It can't feel so right, not when he is all wrong for me.

As if sensing my confusion, and how close I am to either submitting completely or retaliating with a fresh burst of anger, he raises his head and stares into my eyes, that startling blue gaze of his holding mine. It keeps me still for a second. I find myself slipping, sliding into those molten, colorless depths. Pulled into a strange vortex that I hadn't expected to encounter.

A jolt of awareness tugs at my nerves. Every cell in my body seems to be sensitized and yearning for his touch. The hair on my forearms harden.

I've fought enemies on the journey from my home country to get this far...but faced with the biggest monster of them all, I am speechless. A low moan swells up from the pit of my belly. I open my mouth, and all that emerges is "Please..." I gasp.

There is a flash of satisfaction in his eyes, then he leans down. The hard flesh of his shaft grazes the melting folds of my pussy. My insides twist, my belly churns... but it's not with fear. A shudder of anticipation tightens my skin. Heat enfolds me, and sweat pops on my brow.

I swallow and try to speak, but all that comes out is a mewl.

"I know." His voice is soft, so gentle, deceptively so.

My muscles relax and I spread my thighs wider. Then I raise my pelvis, a millimeter more. My core skims his swollen shaft.

He groans and rubs the head of his cock over the entrance to my throbbing channel.

A searing need sweeps over me, followed by a jolt of fear. An awareness of what I am, of what he is going to do filters into my mind. He's going to take me, and this is wrong.

This is not how I wanted it to happen for my first time.

Not with an alpha I didn't choose.

With the one who my body aches for. With the one who can match my needs.

Who makes me feel this depth of yearning I'd not thought possible. I want him to break my heat cycle, I need him to fuck me, knot me, fill me with his cum, breed me. What am I thinking?

He brushes his shaft over my melting core.

His movement is almost tentative, and that is my undoing. A groan spills from my mouth. His lips fasten over mine, absorbing the sound. His hands shackle my wrists above my head, and between my legs, that vicious part of him throbs. And his mouth, oh, that hot, needy mouth of his sucks from me, drinks of my essence. It's as if he's trying to rip out the very depth of my soul and fuse it with his. I squeeze my eyelids shut and am no longer sure what I am fighting. Him? Me? This keening need that churns my gut, leaving me hungry and shaking and needy for more, so much more.

I shake my head, trying to dislodge his sensuous tongue with which he's licking the inside of my mouth.

His body shudders. He pulls back, his shoulders trembling as he props his body over mine, holding his weight up with his biceps.

And it is that unexpected gesture, the fact that he restrained himself instead of ramming into me and taking me, that has the desire roaring through my veins. Heat sears my cheeks.

I crack my eyelids open in time to see the sweat run down his temples and plop on my cheek.

His lips slow their assault, his tongue licks the inner seam of my lips…and that softer, gentler touch is so seductive, so full of promise that I tremble. In that second, he reveals a tenderness that connects with me. That omega instinct of mine rushes to the fore and tells me to grab him, hold him, take what he is offering… Do it. Even as he holds back and waits and watches me out of those searing, almost colorless eyes that mirror back my own desires.

His features are strained, his lips swollen, and yet he stays where he is.

Why is he holding back?

What is he waiting for?

Only he can give me the relief I crave. Only he can make me forget everything I have endured to come this far.

I bare my teeth and in one swift move wrap my legs around his waist and angle my hips so he slides in, a fraction more. His shaft brushes against the barrier inside me.

I shudder.

Desire pools in the pit of my stomach. Goosebumps flare over my arms. Another millimeter more…that's all that stands between this yawning emptiness and…that feeling of something I crave that I still don't understand.

His eyes flash blue with shades of a deep, dark violet in them that hints at secrets, at nightmares.

A growl rips from him.

I shiver. Then, still holding my gaze, he pulls out, all the way out of me.

11

Zeus

I stay poised at the entrance to her moist, trembling core.

Her body heaves and bucks and strains to get closer. Her skin grazes over mine and my blood pulses with need.

That ache inside me for more, for so much more, to own her, to break her, hammers at my temples. I sniff the blood in the air, and it reminds me that it was she who had bitten me first...and yet I can't just take her.

Surprise! Apparently hidden inside is a kernel of someone decent, someone I thought I'd lost a long time ago, someone I still don't recognize. It's probably an aberration. And I am sure the restraint on my side is only because she is a virgin. No one, not even an omega who'd dared to break into my stronghold, deserves to be taken against her will for her first time.

And I *am* her first.

I grow impossibly hard at the thought. Yet I also want to watch her closely, study her reactions as she responds to my touch.

I plan to be her only. I don't question the complete, utter truth in it that I feel all the way to my core.

It was she who came to me. She, an omega on the verge of her heat cycle, knowing full well that being in the company of so many alphas was only going to drive her over the edge. She knew it...yet she had burst into my ascension ceremony. It was she who'd made the first move to claim me.

As I am going to claim her.

Slickness floods her channel, and despite myself, I slide in farther.

She groans.

So do I.

I lower my head and hover above her, balancing my elbows on either side of her body.

Her eyes are squeezed shut, and sweat beads on her upper lip.

"Look at me."

My voice comes out rough, and it feels like I have drawn it out over cut glass that lines my throat. I pinch her chin. "Open your eyes."

She must see me. Know who the alpha is who is taking her, staking his claim on her. She has to acknowledge me.

Her eyelids flutter open. Her black pupils have grown to expand, covering almost the entirety of her green irises.

More of her slick flows over my cock as I angle my hips and pause there, my stance planking over her with my weight balanced on my forearms and my feet.

A slight move and I can slide into her, ram into her all the way and give her the relief she craves. But not yet.

She moans again, fine lines appearing between her eyes. Her lips part, and her arm comes up to grip my biceps. "Please," she gnaws on her lower lip.

"Please what?"

She shakes her head and purses her mouth. Her cheeks are fiery with color. Her cheekbones stand out under her skin. Her shoulders heave, and her breasts thrust out, the nipples so hard I swear I can cut my skin on their sharpness. Desire coils and tightens my groin. I throb inside her. Every part of me wants to plow into her, to show her who she belongs to, to take her again and again. My biceps tremble with the strain of holding my weight back. "Tell me, Omega?" My jaw firms.

I move my hips and my cock scrapes the sides of her walls. A shiver of heat sparks down my spine. Her throat moves as she swallows. Her chin wobbles and her eyelids flutter down.

"Look at me," I command.

Her eyelids snap open. I hold her gaze.

"What do you want?"

Silence.

Tears lighten her eyes and tremble at the corners. I should feel remorse but I don't. All I feel is satisfaction that I moved her to this. Moved her to feel the kind of emotions I can't.

"Say it." I lower my voice, soften it so it sounds like I am cajoling her.

Why is it important that she tell me that?

Why can't I simply take her, show her that I am truly the monster everyone thinks I am? And yet somewhere deep inside, that last civilized part of me, the part that has seen my alpha father take my omega mother against her wishes, that part that had known it was wrong even then, resists.

Even as every cell inside me pushes me to move, to take her, knot her, stake my claim on her.

"It's now or never, Omega." I lean away from her and she reaches for me. Eyes half-dazed with desire, nostrils flaring, sweat shining on her skin.

She juts out her chin, "Fuck me, now."

Before she has completed the sentence, I thrust into her slick, wet channel and break through the barrier.

Her body bucks under me, and she flings her head back and screams.

The keening sound shimmers over my skin, tugs at my nerve endings.

The need in her voice is laced with a touch of desperation. Lust and fear roll off her in equal measure.

I want to ram into her again and again, but I stay where I am and let her adjust to my size.

My breath rasps out of me, and my heart hammers like I have been running for miles. I grit my teeth and stay unmoving, even as her moist pussy embraces my shaft.

She's so fucking tight and hot and wet.

Her body writhes and shudders; her nails dig into my biceps, rake over my back. Pain shudders down my spine and twines with the sheer pleasure of being inside her

I pull out again, all the way out.

I angle her hips up for better access and plow into her slickness with such force that her body moves up the bed and the frame slams against the wall.

Her body bucks, her hips wriggle under me, and her chest rises off the mattress.

A shudder rips through her.

A fresh spurt of moisture swirls out to greet my shaft.

I slam in all the way to the hilt. My knot engorges and following instinct, I hook my shaft behind her pelvic bone. Mine. Only mine. A fierce need coils in my chest and I thrust forward locking in as deep as I can.

Her pussy clamps around me, seducing me, giving me the pleasure of submission I so crave. Her spirit may deny it, but her body wants me, fucking needs me. Giving in, I let the hot streams of cum flood through her womb.

My hips clench, my groin tightens, and I know I am not done. I will not be done, not until I truly claim her.

Heat tugs at my nerve endings, the thought arousing me further. It shouldn't be possible, and yet I grow more hard. My balls feel too heavy and seem to drag me down.

Feeling my desire seems to affect her.

Her eyelids flutter open. Her pupils are dilated. The black of her pupils has completely taken over her irises, except for the pale, emerald-green ring around them. She swallows, looking at me completely dazed.

Fresh slick flows from inside her, tugging me, asking me to keep going.

I lower my mouth to her throat and sink my teeth into that soft skin at the curve of where her neck meets her shoulder.

12

Lucy

He bites the skin of my shoulder, and a flame of white heat arrows out to hurl through my veins, toward my chest. I scream out in pain even as a ball of heat throbs against my rib cage. I moan and thrash, but he doesn't let go.

The worst thing is that the pain clashes with my arousal and the mixture of the pain-pleasure only turns me on more. How is that possible?

I shouldn't be feeling the white-hot sting of arousal that guts me, that draws at a climax low in my belly.

His bulbous knot is locked inside me, and more hot streams of cum sear my womb.

I arch my legs up and hook them around him, digging my heels into his back. My spine curves off the bed; my chest thrusts out.

He grips my breast and squeezes a nipple. Another spurt of pain jolts down my spine.

Intense pleasure rolls over me, and the climax roars forward, then stops waiting for his touch, his hated…needed touch to make me come completely. "Please…" There's that word again. Why am I asking my tormentor for something my mind insists I don't want?

For something, my body insists that only he can give me? Only he can break this tearing need inside me. At this moment I loathe myself. That I was born an omega when all my life, all I've ever wanted was to be able to take, to fight for myself, for my clan…my family. The thought cleaves through the haze of need that has blinded me. Any moment now I'll tip over into the burning heart of the heat cycle and then I will no longer remember anything, not me, not him, not the goal I set out to achieve.

I need to do this while he's still inside me. While his knot pulses and my pussy clamps onto him and milks him. I need to do this if I want to see my fellow omegas go free.

With a last burst of clarity, I yank my hand still shackled in his grasp.

His grip loosens, and I slide my arm out.

I fling it to the side and reach blindly for something, anything I can use as a weapon... There, my fingers brush the lampshade on the side table.

I grab at it, but my sweaty fingers slide off it. I almost cry with frustration.

His muscles go solid, and his forehead crinkles. The desire in those glowering eyes is joined with a tinge of something else. Caution? And I almost regret doing this, almost. For a second, all I can think is damn them all, damn the world that always demands more than I am ready to give, my clan who always turn to me for protection... For with this man, the roles have reversed.

I can come into my omega self, I can allow myself to give up the part of me that caused so much strife and be what I am deep inside: a softer, more delicate, caring nurturer.

As if in agreement, my core pulses more moisture.

The heated walls of my womb clasp him hard, drawing out a fresh load of cum. The blue in his eyes recedes, and those eyes burn with a strange violet-tinged flame. It's fascinating. And I want him to always look at me that way. Then he raises his head, and blood gushes from the wound in my throat. The beast marked me... The horror of it sinks in. He claimed me...why would he do that? He could have rutted me and broken my heat cycle, but he went further.

His lips twist in a smirk.

My blood drips down his lips, down his chin to merge with the scarlet of his that bubbles from the wound where I had bitten him first. The ball of heat in my chest pulses.

I was wrong...we marked each other.

We claimed each other.

I am bonded to a stranger.

To someone, I don't know.

To only the biggest monster of all the land.

The one I came to kill, the one whose death will save my clan.

I raise the lamp and bring it down on his head.

13

Zeus

I sense her move, then the lamp smashes into the side of my head. Pain slices through my temples, and sparks of red flare behind my eyes. My hold on her loosens. But my knot inside her only strengthens. A fresh burst of desire slides into my blood, flowing all the way to the tip of my cock, engorging it further. Guess I should have told her that I have this propensity for violence… The harsher she is with me, the more it turns me on. I'll leave that information out for now. Just to see how far she'll go. How far can I hold out before my mind shuts down and the lust takes over? And what will that do to both of us?

I lower my head and purr, a long, low, angry purr that rips out from inside and folds over her.

Her gaze widens. The scent of her arousal intensifies. Her arm trembles and her grip on the lamp loosens.

I smash my head into the lamp and send it flying from her hands. It falls on the bed, then rolls to the floor and crashes. The sound doesn't penetrate the haze of the heat cycle that has her in its grasp.

Yanking her hand above her head, I wrap my fingers around both her delicate wrists. With my free hand, I reach down between us, scoop up some of our joined juices, my cum, her slick, a mixture that is pure aphrodisiac, and wipe her lips with it before shoving my finger inside her mouth.

Her lips curve around it, and she sucks on it. The feel of her lips on my skin dumps a wave of adrenaline into my blood; mixed with it is this primal need to finish what I started.

I move inside her, this time only with intent to punish. She mewls then cries out as I slam inside her all the way and let myself come again, coating her insides with hot, ropy streams of cum. Marking her inside and out.

"Mine," I growl.

Her eyelids fly open. Dark, fevered eyes stare back at me. The black of her pupils have completely taken over the green—the sign of an omega having completely submitted to her heat cycle. She bares her teeth.

I expect her to attack me again, or at the very least scream at me to get off of her, when, "More," she snarls and digs her heels into my back.

I freeze. Did I hear that correctly?

Her eyes narrow, then she raises her hips so I slide deeper inside—the swollen head of my cock brushes against her cervix.

She cries out, color draining from her cheeks. Her eyes plead with me. Her lips seduce me, and I can't stop myself. I take her lips and close my mouth over hers, fucking her with my tongue as much as my erect shaft penetrates her the way neither has ever pierced anyone else before.

The climax builds up from my groin, tightening, stretching, becoming big enough to overpower every part of me, plowing through me.

Her body shudders, and her teeth bite down on my lips as she falls apart.

I stay as I am, still half erect inside her.

She cracks her eyelids open and peers up at me.

I want to ask her why she tried to kill me—well, I know the answer why: she hates me. There's not much she can do about it, though. I claimed her as mine; she is my mate.

Her hips move of their own accord, her breath catches, and her lips turn downward. She rakes her nails down my biceps before clasping her fingers around my forearm.

I lean in and blow over her flushed face.

It's hot inside this room. Not only is it the height of summer, but I've nailed tight all the windows. I don't want the exterior of this city intruding and polluting the atmosphere inside.

Sweat drips down my chest. A drop plops on her breast, then another. Her gaze veers to my chest, to where my shaft is still locked inside her.

The sight arouses me again.

I move against her, and she croaks, a harsh sound. Her eyes fly open, and her gaze locks with mine. The dark of her irises deepens.

I am hurting her but also arousing her. And that pleases me immeasurably. The glow of satisfaction flushes my skin, and I don't question it. It doesn't matter to me that she gets as much pleasure from our coupling as I do. It doesn't.

I lean in and lick the bleeding wound on her shoulder.

She shudders, and a moan of pleasure is drawn from her.

I growl, a low, soothing purr, and her shoulders relax. Her thighs clench around my waist; the scent of slick deepens the air.

I want to hear her voice calling my name as she comes once again, as she rides my cock and her core shatters around me.

Still knotted inside her, I flip her over and above me.

14

Lucy

He flips me over so I am straddling him.

His knot is still heavy inside me, weighing me down, blocking all the cum that has streamed out of him.

The thought only makes me hotter. Desire ripples down my spine.

A low purr rumbles from his throat, stretching in the space between us. My stomach cramps, and I groan.

Inside me he grows bigger, and his knot flexes. Every part of me aches, and yet there is still this hunger. An emptiness that seems to grow bigger by the second, filling me, making me feel like I am searching, yearning for something more.

So much more. Of him. Of me. Of what he can do to me. Of what I want him to do to me. The force of my thoughts sends heat shooting through my blood. I bend down and hook my fingers in his hair, raking my nails down his scalp.

His shoulders flex. Red streaks his cheekbones. He growls again, but this time it has a tone of challenge laced through it.

His nostrils flare.

His gaze narrows.

He grips my waist and raises me, all the way up, until his shaft slips out and I stay poised right there with his knot blocking the entrance to my wet channel.

The feel of that roughened, ribbed skin against my soft inner walls sends a pulse of heat scrambling over my skin.

My toes curl; my thighs flex as I grip his waist. The feeling is so erotic, so much everything that starbursts of color flash behind my closed eyelids. I sway a little, and his grip firms on me.

"Look at me," he growls.

The command in his voice cuts through the intense feelings that have me in thrall.

I crack my eyelids open and meet his gaze—and hold on to that liquid blue in his eyes that seems to mirror back every last fragment of lust that I am feeling now.

It's as if he can read me, see through my soul, and I know I am being fanciful. Because he is an alpha who wants to show me that he is more superior, more dominant, yet my instinct says there is more, so much more to this man.

Right?

Wrong.

Was that why he'd dragged me here to his room and proceeded to bury his cock in me? His very large, very beautiful cock which he lowers me on again so the knot locks into place, holding me to him.

There's a low keening cry, and I realize it's me. I sound so aroused. So needy. Hungry for more. My chest pushes forward, my breasts thrusting out. I know my nipples are swollen, and my hair flows around me as I hold on to his forearms for balance.

The alpha is so damn massive, and the way he raises and lowers me again and again… And I am small, of course, in comparison. Still, the fact that he handles my body like I weigh nothing is both erotic and at the same time it makes me realize how much more powerful, how dominant he is.

A shudder of fear tugs at my nerves.

The still barely thinking part of my hindbrain, the one I've relied on to flag danger in all the time I'd been on the run from my homeland, sends a pulse of warning that creeps into my blood. It shoves away the sheer need that grips my body, that has pushed away all rational thought so far.

His hardness throbs inside me. Need radiates out from my core all the way to my toes.

And it feels so damn good.

I moan. Then shake my head, trying to clear it.

As if realizing that I am fighting the high of mating, and not wanting me to regain my composure, as if his very goal is to enfold me in the waves of pleasure which seize me, which roll down my spine, and make me hunch my back to try to keep in every last drop of moisture that is oozing out of me, he slides an arm up my back and grips the nape of my neck.

His touch sends a wave of intense desire surging through me. Sweat trickles down my throat, and my hair sticks to my forehead.

"Stop torturing me." I moan out the words, hear the pleading in them and refuse to let myself blush.

I am too far gone down this maze of pleasure in which he has me trapped.

My body is not my own anymore…it's an instrument of desire that he can tweak and play and tune to his heart's content.

He tugs me close so I am balanced above him, my breasts swinging right in front of his face.

"So fucking beautiful." His gaze rakes over my features—my lips, down to my chest. "I am going to give you so much pleasure you are going to forget everything: where you came from, what brought you here, your past, your present, everything except my name."

There's an authority in his voice that insists I agree with him. That I submit to the strength of his personality and give him what he wants. And it is precisely that which makes me straighten my spine. "You can't force me to do anything I don't want."

His gaze narrows, then his lips peel back in a smirk…which is not really a sign of amusement. Nope. It's a look so cruel, so full of the need to torment, so full of satisfaction that I blink. Not what I expected.

I'd thought he'd rage at me, perhaps turn me on my back and fuck me again. Instead, he gentles his hold on my neck and drags his palm over my skin, up into my hair.

His fingernails rake my scalp in a parody of what I'd done to him earlier. Goosebumps flare on my skin. The fine hairs on my forearms harden.

The difference between the intent I read on his features and the way he tailors his touch to seduce me, is so contradictory, that my head spins. My belly tightens, and to my horror, a fresh burst of slick gushes out to bathe his already swollen cock.

"You know exactly the right thing to do." His voice is soft.

His features compose into a look I cannot quite comprehend. His gaze is intense, brooding even, as if he's only now noticed me properly, realized I am not a submissive omega…and that's not what he wanted in the first place.

The realization sinks in.

This monster needs a challenge. He thrives on reaching for the unattainable. I've given him the perfect reason to redouble his efforts to mate me. To break me. He will not stop, not until he owns me completely, body and soul…not until he's ingrained his essence in every cell of my body.

The thought sends a wave of panic skittering over my skin.

At the same time his sheer confidence in how he thrusts his hips up so his massive shaft penetrates me, spears me, until it feels like I am being broken in half, is so completely arousing.

It feels like his very essence is reaching out to me, trying to overwhelm me, subsume me, and that's when the panic sets in.

I bite down on my lower lip.

Pain cleaves through the desire in my head. I bite the inside of my cheek, "Let me go."

One side of his lips curls and he takes his hands off of me, holding his arms up in front of me. In this moment I hate him more than anyone else I have ever hated before in my life.

He's doing this to prove a point. To show me that I am here of my own volition. That I don't have a choice but to be here impaled on his shaft. I push down on his chest, and the feel of those hard planes under my palms is so erotic, I don't realize I am sliding my palms in circles, cupping his skin, not until his gaze drops down to my hands, then back to my face.

"What have you decided, Omega?"

His voice is soft, confident.

His gaze holds mine steady.

Those irises of his are almost colorless. Gone is the passion that lurked in them earlier. Now they are considering, watching, stalking me. Waiting for me to move. He knows what I am going to decide, and I am helpless, caught in this trap he's woven around me.

Inside me, his shaft pulses. I gasp. My pussy clenches around the hard flesh. I squeeze my eyes shut to better absorb each ripple of desire that floods over my skin.

He's letting me go; he's giving me the perfect opportunity to tear myself off of him and stagger out. I push down with my knees into the mattress to do just that. But my body has other plans.

A tremor of heat flushes my skin; sweat breaks out on my brow and beads my upper lip. A spasm unfurls in my center and throbs out, asking, begging, needing this alpha to break my heat cycle.

I've only heard from the other omegas how agonizing it can be to see this through on your own. For during this very delicate time, your body is ready to receive, ready for the seed of an alpha to take root. Ready to be fucked and knotted, for that clawing, aching hollow inside to be filled with the engorged flesh. That shuddering, rasping friction that only comes with the thick, swollen alpha's member inside you, slamming through you, piercing you...as he is. Now.

"I hate you." The words sigh out of me, even as I slide up until my soft core catches on his bulbous knot, drawing a keening cry of delight from me. "Hate." I pant and lower myself around the knot. "You." The breath whistles out of me. The pleasure is so intense, I cannot stop myself from gripping his hair with renewed ferocity, holding on to him, pulling at the tufts, knowing I must be hurting him...and he deserves it. He deserves every last fraction of the pain that I am causing him, for not even that will make up for the anguish he's putting me through right now.

"You think you hate me." He slides one hand up my side to cup my breast, then positions the swollen flesh over his mouth. "But by the time I am done with you, you will no longer think so. No longer will you have the capacity to deny me...or yourself. For I intend to give you so much pleasure...so much pain, that it will wipe out everything that came before."

He closes his mouth around my swollen nipple and bites down. Not with so much force to hurt...and yet the surge of vibrations that rips through me, heads straight for my core, lighting up all my pleasure centers. All my nerve endings seem to fire at once. The sensations arrow down to collect right there around my already engorged clit. It's too much. Too soon. Yet not enough. I pant and strain against him. Needing, wanting, what? What do I want?

He lowers his head, and his gaze locks on me. He waits, every part of his body tense, his muscles shuddering, watching me, stalking me, holding out for something more from me. I swallow and wait. Wait. My chest heaves and sweat beads my forehead.

He slides his palm between our bodies and grinds the heel against my clit. Red and white sparks flash behind my eyes and I cry out. My hips jerk, slick gushes from my channel, and my inner muscles clamp down on his throbbing dick.

His eyes flare and his shaft thickens even more inside of me, the knot widening until it seems to fill me completely. With a harsh growl he lunges forward, going impossibly deep inside of me. My body bucks; every muscle in my pussy quivers. The climax rips up from my toes and then sweeps up my thighs, arches my spine, bouncing over my skin, vibrating up my throat, and I scream as I come.

He peels back his lips, and with a last thrust, locks into place behind my pelvic bone. His muscles ripple and with a triumphant roar he shoots hot jets of cum into my womb.

My eardrums pop, and then there is complete silence.

A velvety white, so soothing that I know it cannot possibly be real, flows over me, cocooning me, and I let it drag me down.

15

Her body goes limp, and she falls over.

I guide her down to lay on me. Her shoulders twitch, and then her muscles relax as sleep takes over.

Sprawled across my chest, her head fits under my chin. Her breathing is deep, like one who has been spent.

It satisfies me to know that my omega is content, for now.

There are things I want to do to her which I've never wanted to do to anyone else, and that in itself is a shock.

Since she'd walked into my space and I had taken a whiff of her scent, I'd known she was mine.

Call it primitive, but it is the wont of the alpha to dominate, and any omega chosen by me had better be grateful I am going to see her through her heat cycle.

I tighten my arms around her, and she moans. It's such an inherently feminine sound, so completely contradictory to everything I am, that I harden again.

She burrows in deeper, and warmth floods my chest.

I unhook one arm from around her. Reaching up I brush my fingers over her mark at the side of my throat.

No one has done that before.

Not even the more uncontrollable alpha females who I have on occasion taken to bed. And only for the satisfaction of bending them to my will before allowing them to find release. As for the omegas? Most had been too tame, too ready to spread their legs so I could rut them to release.

This wildling is unlike any female I've met. She'd gone straight for the jugular, literally speaking. And it doesn't bother me as much as it should. And it should really. It should worry me very much that this little slip of a not-very-submissive omega swept in and seduced me with her cunt, her heat, her scent. She could distract me from the plans I'd worked on for so long. A skitter of apprehension tugs my nerves.

I am so close to taking over the Scots and becoming far more powerful than Golan ever was. Nothing and no one can sway me from my goal. She's a pleasant distraction, no more. My very own plaything, who will do as I bid her. I'll seduce her, make her so hungry for my touch, for every shred of my affection, that she'll beg me for satisfaction.

I will shield her from the world, and in return, she'll provide me with many moments of pleasure. She's a means to forget where I came from, a relief from the responsibilities that lie in store for me, for even the alpha at the top of the food chain, aka me, needs an omega to satisfy him.

While she marked me first, it is the alpha's claim that matters. I forged the mating bond with her and took her as my mate. And she'd better be grateful for that.

I rub my cheek against her hair. "Wake up, sweetheart, your true mate is here."

16

Lucy

His voice whispers in my ear. Seductive, beautiful, it shivers over my nerve endings. The heat of his body cocoons me. I feel safe and secure. And that can't be right. A flicker, a hum of contentment rolls out of me. I rub my cheek against the hard, unforgiving planes of his chest. He curves his body around me, and it feels so right.

Is this what it feels like to be home? But I don't have a home. Not since my country was invaded, and my father made a deal with the Vikings — virgin omegas for the life of his people.

I'd managed to escape with as many of the omega women as I could save.

We'd stowed away on a ship to Scotland, and the leader of the Scots had agreed to protect us. On one condition. I had to comply with his plan of sneaking into the General's stronghold and killing him.

I had failed in my mission.

Now I was going to meet the fate of almost every omega captured by an alpha. I was going to be mated and I am sure, eventually, bred. Only omegas can give birth. In these times of declining population, it should have been a blessing to be born one. Why, then, has it always felt like a curse?

He yanks my hair back, and heat prickles over my scalp. It doesn't hurt not exactly…more of that pleasure-pain I am coming to associate with him.

I moan and force my eyes open, knowing already what I am going to see. That I am trapped, under the watchful gaze of my mate.

My monster.

Chills rack my body, immediately chased by heat. It rises from my belly, bubbling up to the cord that is curled against my breast bone. The heavy coil that binds me to him.

A hum of betrayal tightens my chest.

He is the strongest alpha in the land, yet he's also the General, the ruler of this country.

Will he listen to me if I explain why I broke into his stronghold?

As if sensing my emotions and realizing that my rational self is asserting itself despite the heat cycle in which I am still trapped, he flips me over. I am on my back, and his big hulking figure is bent over me. He's all around me, and I should feel what? Threatened? Afraid? But I am not. And that scares me further.

It also arouses me.

All other thought spills from my head. I cannot think about the world outside, about the other omegas who wait for news from me.

"Do it," I narrow my eyes.

His arousal throbs.

His lips curl in a smirk, then he pulls out of me. The knot has lessened and he slips out with very little pain. Had he waited until now so he didn't hurt me? If so, why didn't he let go of me earlier? Why has he held me on his chest, his fingers running over the back of my hair, my spine? Goosebumps flare on my skin. Had he taken care of me? No, I don't want that. I want him to be exactly what the role demands of him. An alpha. Who takes and rapes and pillages?

He didn't rape me, though, did he?

He'd waited and seduced until I'd asked him to fuck me.

My face heats at the memory.

I hadn't wanted him, and yet my body had given in and been a willing participant in how he'd taken me.

My shoulders tense at the thought, and a whimper of protest coils up my throat. I don't stop it; I couldn't if I wanted to. Without him inside me, that emptiness crawls in on itself. It aches. I ache.

Every part of my skin feels like it is being stretched.

Heat flushes my skin. Sweat drenches my back. My lips are dry, so dry. And yet between my legs a fresh dose of slick trickles down.

His nostrils flare, and a low purr grumbles up his massive chest. It only sinks into my skin, rolls over that damned throbbing in my chest, and twines with it.

It hurts me and yet it also feels right.

It doesn't make any sense.

Nothing makes sense. Except the animal on top of me, who'd rutted me not a few minutes ago. Of whom I want more.

I raise my chin and lick my lips. My hips arch of their own accord so my melting core brushes against his already hardening cock.

His gaze narrows; silver sparks flare in those blue eyes. His lips pull back in a snarl. And I am almost relieved. This I know, this creature born of need, of hunger, trying to fulfill the most basic of desires, hunger, sex, thirst…these urges I can manage. I don't want to think beyond that, not now.

He slides down my body, and as if knowing exactly what I had thought, what I had wanted, he grabs my thighs and shoves them apart. Sliding his big palm under my hips, he holds me up and fits his lips to my core.

My eyes roll back, and my mouth opens in a silent scream, only his hand glides up, and he shoves his thumb between my lips. I don't question it. I bite down around his digit, to anchor myself.

His tongue is inside my pussy, licking me, sucking me. A growl rumbles up from him and draws forth a fresh stream of slick. He licks it up, swallows it, then comes back for more.

He fastens his teeth around the bud of my clit, and stars explode behind my closed eyelids.

He still doesn't let me go.

My fingers are wrapped in his hair, trying to pull him away, trying to hold him close.

My thighs are wound around his head, and I am half off the mattress, and all I can think is: fuck, more. I want more.

Then he drags his other thumb down my butt and toward the puckered hole between my ass cheeks. I freeze. My eyes fly open. But he's a step ahead of me. His finger slips into my wet, streaming channel, scoops up my slick, and spreads it around my back hole.

He traces the puckered ring of the hole, and a shiver runs up my spine.

He thrusts his tongue into my pussy, then with the heel of his hand he rubs my clit.

His finger slips into the hole.

The combination of his tongue inside me, his thumb in my mouth, and the finger in my back hole is too much.

The climax crashes over me. I scream and bite down on his thumb; my back arches up and off the bed. Before I can collapse, he flips me, yanks up my hips, and enters my wet channel from behind.

17

Zeus

I'd meant to take her, put her in her place, show her that she is an omega who has to submit to me. I'd meant to be harsh, not caring for her needs. And I wasn't. I was only satisfying myself. If, during that time, I also gave her pleasure, well, what is the harm in that?

As it is, I can't get enough of her body, her soft skin, her warm, tight pussy that clasps around me.

The still rational part of my brain twinges, and I push it away.

I shove aside all thought, everything except for the desire that tightens my groin. The blood that rushes to my shaft, thickening its head so it flares up and knots into place. I am going to make sure that none of my fluid slips out. Make sure every part of my hardness is sheathed inside her. Under me, she thrashes her head from side to side. Her back arches off the bed and slams into me. Her arms push down on the mattress, shoving the curve of her spine into my chest.

I am bent over her, covering her with my much bigger self, protecting her... I clamp down on that emotion. Nothing, I am allowed to feel nothing for her, remember?

Nothing except this greedy need to take...to give, to bring her to climax again and again, to make her take every last bit of my cum as I gush into her, jetting the very essence of what I am right inside her, hitting her womb.

I cry out, and then for a second time, I bite down on her shoulder, right over where I'd marked her the first time. This time it's a true mating, one in the heat of passion, one without any ulterior motive, one meant to solidify my claim on her. She throws her head back and screams, and the sound bounces around the room and slams over me, and it feels right. I taste her blood and draw back, licking the puncture marks, trying to soothe her, to deaden some of the pain. I shouldn't be doing it, but I can't help myself anymore.

Everything in my past has already vanished. All I am is an alpha, and she is my omega.

My mate.

That's all that matters.

I lower her, even as I turn her on her side and keep her wrapped in my arms. I purr, letting the vibrations of my chest resonate against her back. She moans in her throat, rubs her cheek where it is pillowed on my biceps. I let her draw comfort from me.

I want to deny it.

I should deny it.

But I can't. And I am too content, too replete to not give in to the need to comfort her either.

I wrap my other arm around her waist and draw her close. I'm flaccid now, the knot having diminished in size so that I can pull out of her, but I don't. I stay right there. After all, she is mine, isn't she?

Over the next two days I manage to persuade her to eat at regular intervals. It's not altruistic of me to do so, nor is it that I am worried about her in any way. Nope, it's purely selfish, honest. I want to keep her energy up, so she can be an active participant in our mating. I need her to be conscious, to feel every ridge of my engorged dick when I bury myself balls deep in her; as I bring her to climax and knot her over and over again. And the feral thing that she is, she takes from me, matches me move for move, until finally sated and stripped of all defense, she curls up at my side and falls into exhausted slumber.

I throw my thigh over her hip to hold her captive, then close my eyes.

A loud banging echoes through the room. I grab my omega and pull her close, wanting to shield her from whoever is behind the door.

"Who the fuck is there?" I crack my eyelids open.

Her body shudders in my arms. Her gaze is bewildered, her lips swollen, the claiming mark at the base of her neck still bleeding. Every part of her has been marked, ravaged, taken. She is caked in my cum, and it's so glorious. I don't stop myself from throwing back my head and shouting my exultation. That pure animal feeling of satisfaction that comes from having rutted so thoroughly.

When I look down, I expect to see her cowering against the pillows, perhaps curled up and crying. Instead, she's watching me with an intent gaze as if she's trying to understand what I am feeling right now.

It feels so right...that I know it's wrong.

There's another loud knocking on the door.

"I don't mean to coitus interruptus," Ethan's voice filters through, "but you'd never forgive me if I didn't remind you about the meeting of the Council that you called for to discuss the situation with the Scots?"

Right. Meeting. About the Scots. I should have pushed it back, but I hadn't been in my right mind when I'd barged in here with the omega. I'd expected to have stayed for a few hours... normally that's all it's taken for me to have broken an omega's heat cycle in the past.

"You've been in there for a straight seventy-two hours, General," Ethan helpfully informs me again.

The fucker is probably gloating at how the mighty Zeus lost all track of time buried in his omega's sweet pussy.

Not any omega. I'd been wrapped up in my mate for three days. Which is understandable, even for a bastard like me. It takes months to consolidate a mating bond. I could be forgiven a few days. Not. Nothing comes between me and my plans to take over the Scots.

I square my shoulders. A better man would explain to her why it is important that I have to leave, and that I won't take too long. That I'll be back before she has a chance to fret and miss me.

She pushes at me, and I loosen my arms from around her. She moves away and her breasts sway. The rounded flesh is reddened from my ministrations. Her dark-pink nipples swell under my gaze. A shudder of heat tightens my gut. Perhaps I should stay with her, bring her down from the high of the mating before I leave. Yeah, a considerate alpha would do that. Which I am not.

"How long do your heat cycles last?"

She swallows then, some more of the haze from her eyes clearing, and it makes me want to cover her body with mine and fuck her all over again, until that dazed, dilated look is permanently etched in her eyes. The sheer primal need of it thickens my shaft which is still inside her.

As if sensing my need, a fresh stream of slick shivers down her thigh.

"Answer me." I'd wanted to be curt, but the words had come out almost soft.

"Three." She shakes her head as if to clear it. "Perhaps four days."

So she's almost at the end of her heat cycle. A surge of something suspiciously like relief lightens my chest. Nope, that can't be right.

Why should it matter to me that she should be able to cope fine when I leave her? Why does a part of me want her to miss me? And the fact that when I return, she'll still be here waiting for me? I need to hurry and get the meeting over with.

I really should leave right now.

She shifts in my arms. Her hair flows over her shoulder, and I can't stop myself winding it around my palm.

She bites her lip.

I bury my nose in her neck and draw in that sweet, sugary scent of hers, laced with that deeper, spicier tang of me.

The bond in my chest writhes. I stiffen. The mating bond. I rub the skin over my heart, trying to settle the restless ball of heat lurking under my ribcage.

I'd known what I was doing when I'd marked her.

Had decided as soon as I'd set eyes on her that I was going to claim her, so why does this reminder of what she is confuse me?

Why do I want to hold her close and explain why I must leave her, just for a little while?

I pull out of her and my dick slides out with a wet plop. Liquid gushes out of her pussy and sloshes down her inner thigh. My cum. Her juices. The interlaced scent of our joined arousal reeks into the air.

A pulse springs to life at my temples, in my balls, even at the back of my eyelids. Fuck me. What is this omega doing to me?

She gasps and my skin tightens, a jolt of unease crawls down my spine. How am I already so tuned into her? Fuck this. I need to walk away from her, show her she has no influence over me.

I swing my legs over the side.

Rising to my feet, I stalk away from the bed to where I'd disposed of my clothes and slide them on.

Dense clouds of tension roll off her, and I feel her uncertainty tug at me through the bond. She doesn't say anything. Had I been expecting her to call out to me?

To stop me?

Perhaps ask me to take her again? She doesn't, and something like disappointment weighs me down. I pull my boots on, then walk out of there.

18

Lucy

I am not sure how long I snoozed for, but the sound of the door opening sweeps through my subconscious mind. I stir and wake up, wondering where I am. The ceiling above is unfamiliar, the bed below me too smooth, too soft. I shudder and take in a breath of air and find it is scented with his fragrance. The beast has left, but his musk is everywhere, on me, in the room.

I turn and crack my eyelids open. My eyelashes are caked. I wipe away whatever is clogging them, knowing it is a mixture of sweat and his cum and our fluids, the fluids he'd dribbled into my mouth that I had swallowed down like it was the last drop of moisture I'd find in the world. The memory of how I'd given myself to him and asked him to take me, all of it crowds in on me.

My body shudders in remembrance of his touch. Slick gathers between my legs. There's movement in the room, and I know I must sit up, but I can't. I groan, and my voice comes out all wrong. I can barely swallow.

I need water.

My tongue is so dry it feels swollen and fills my mouth, along with his taste. The salty taste of his skin, the sweet musk of his essence, the sugary, tangy mixture of both fluids…all of it pops goosebumps on my skin. I push myself up against the pillows only to find that every part of me aches. Through half-closed eyes, I see a woman place fresh food and water on the table.

She doesn't look at me, keeps her eyes averted. "The General has commanded that you eat and drink before he returns."

"Who are you?" I try to say the words out loud, but of course, nothing emerges.

Before I can repeat myself, she turns and leaves. The door shuts behind her with a soft snick. Whispered words filter through, then the bolts drop into place. I am alone once more. And truth be told, I am relieved. I wouldn't want anyone else to witness how far I have fallen. That I am here wallowing in the outcome of my mating still in the last throes of my heat cycle, floating in and out. I'd let the General break my cycle and stake his claim on me.

I hadn't resisted enough.

Yet a part of me insists there is nothing I could have done. I am an omega, and this was bound to happen. He'd taken me so many times I'd lost count. Soon he is going to be back and no doubt he is going to fuck me many times more. A shudder of heat flushes my skin, and my guts twist with apprehension.

I have to resist him.

I must push back. It'll only make things more difficult for me. But that's fine. I've come this far; I've infiltrated the General's stronghold. Now all I have to do is wait for the opportune moment and try to kill him again. Once that is done, I can return to Kayden, and he will free my clan. My stomach twists. With grief…with hunger.

The scent of food teases my nostrils.

But I shouldn't eat. I shouldn't.

I am here being fed, so I can get energy back, no doubt for another mating, while the other omegas must be eagerly waiting for news of my mission.

I need to complete my mission and rescue them.

Straightening my spine, I swing my legs over the side of the bed and stand. My knees almost buckle. My thigh muscles scream in protest. My left shoulder throbs. A fresh surge of blood drips down my throat. I hold my palm to the wound where he marked me, the wound I don't want to acknowledge, but the throbbing in my chest responds to the ache.

It's as if the cord that binds me to that monster recognizes its master.

My body may crave him, may want him, may even acknowledge his dominance, but not my soul. Not my mind. Not my emotions. I know I can hold out on him. When I am not in heat, when I am more myself…when.

The scent of food grows stronger. Sometime in the last few minutes I've crossed the floor to the table in my confused state and now I stand in front of the table bearing the tray. I should eat it. I shouldn't. I can't. I must. To keep up my strength. To keep myself together. Just until I find a way to kill the monster.

I had been wrong to approach Kayden and agree to his plan. I'd foolishly thought I had a chance. Truth is, I hadn't been thinking straight. I'd gone with what my instinct said was right. And look where that landed me.

Imprisoned in the den of the monster, in the middle of a heat cycle which twists my guts. Sweat breaks out on my skin and my womb clenches in need. My teeth chatter, my toes dig into the floor. I am hot and cold all at once. Not good, this is not good. I am going into the home stretch of the heat cycle. The last day is always the worst.

Why isn't that alpha-hole here when I need him, when I want him to take me and rut me and shove away the pain that taints my insides?

Moaning, I wrap my arm around my middle and reach for the plate, only for it to crash to the floor.

I cry out in anger, in fear, in shame, then drop to my knees, curling up on my side in front of it.

19

Zeus

I stride down the corridor without cleaning myself up. Perhaps I should have showered, but the fact is that I want her scent on me.

I want to show her claiming mark and I am still unsure why. It isn't that common for omegas to mark their alphas. Rarer still for alphas to flaunt them. But I want to do so.

A sign to them she is mine and off limits to anyone else. She is my mate, the one I chose…the one who chose me.

Or maybe it's just this primal need inside me to make sure they can smell her on me, feel my satisfaction and know that she waits for me back in my suite.

Not that any of them would dare to touch her, and if anyone dares look at her, I'll burn out their eyes, I'll gut them… I'll —

A touch on my shoulder snaps me out of my thoughts.

"She's in your head." I look around to find Ethan standing at my shoulder. His features are calm, his gaze wary.

When I had killed my father and taken his place, Ethan had been the first to pledge his loyalty to me. It still didn't change the fact that he came from the ruling classes. The same as the alphas who had misused their power and hastened my mother's death.

"Second." I stalk to the head of the table.

Ethan drops into the chair on my right.

I glower at the assembled men. "When do we attack Scotland?"

My gaze sweeps the room.

There's silence, then Solomon leans forward. "It's not a good idea, General."

I train my gaze on Sol. "Is that right?" My voice is low and measured.

Solomon pales under his tan.

I'd hand picked him to become my Head of Troops. Not that it matters. As long as he follows my lead, I'll be tolerant of him.

"Answer me." My voice rings through the room.

Sol's gaze flicks to Ethan.

"The timing is not yet right to take on the Scots." He swallows, then squares his shoulders. "We need to arm the soldiers and train the new recruits. Also need to source more weapons. It's premature to attack."

"All of you agree?" I look around the table.

"We are not yet prepared," Liam growls.

"Care to elaborate?" I thrust out my chest. It's a subtle act of dominance, warning off the other man, telling him that I am stronger, more powerful than him, and not just physically.

"I am the first to want to wipe out the Scots for their slaughtering my family, but I know the importance of not rushing in." The tank of an alpha pounds his fist on the table for emphasis. "When we finally attack, I want to do so with all our might. Kill them in one go."

Well, at least he speaks his mind.

"Anyone else?"

"Since we are all in such a chummy mood," Ryker drawls from the other side of the table, "perhaps you need to spend time consummating your bond with your omega, get it all out of your system so you are not distracted when we fight the Scots."

Anger bubbles up, the emotions ripe and thick and coiling through my blood. I taste the need for violence on my tongue, so rich, so strong. "Is that what you'd do if you were in my place?"

Ryker's shoulders stiffen. He's one hell of a marksman, the best on my team. Doesn't mean I have to spare him. No one is indispensable, and he knows it. He swallows, then nods.

"You're right." I let my lips twist in the semblance of a smirk.

A breath rushes out of Ryker; his shoulders visibly relax.

"That's the last time I tolerate anyone talking about my omega. No-one is to even glance at her, got it?"

Silence.

I glower around the table, making sure to look each alpha in the eye.

Ryker gets to his feet. "That's our cue then." He glides out of the room.

Sol and the other alphas follow.

Well, all except Ethan who stays seated. He brings his fingers together in front of him. A nerve tics at his temple. He sets his jaw. Adamant fucker. He will not leave without having his say, and the frustrating thing is that I am going to let him do just that, too. Fuck! Leaning forward, I brush the dust off his shoulder. "What?"

He doesn't get the threat inherent in my gesture, or if he does, he chooses to ignore it. Fucker has some balls.

"You count on me to tell the truth." He holds my gaze.

He's right, and fuck if that doesn't infuriate me. Anger heats my blood. "I keep you because you had no other place to go."

"And isn't that a fact." Ethan lowers his palms and drums his fingers on the table. "I was born here; these are my people, and I plan to do my best by them."

"Your misplaced sense of loyalty will bite you in the ass," I glower.

"Your trying to hide what you always feel whether it is to your men or to your omega will—"

Only when I feel the rough cloth of Ethan's collar under my fingers do I realize I've closed the space and hauled the slimmer man up to his toes. "I warned you not to talk about her," I snarl.

"And if I obeyed you every single time you issued a command, I'd be mistaken for a beta." Ethan's lips twist.

Annoyingly, he is right again.

Sure, I have an ego, but I also know I don't want to surround myself with men who agree to everything I say. That's what Golan did, and look what happened to him. A harsh chuckle rolls out of me. "Speak then." I let go of him.

He crashes into the table, then rights himself. "You should have sent the omega to the harem." He pauses as if choosing his words with care.

Ethan thinks things through down to the last detail before he takes action. Me? I lead with my gut.

"Go on." The mating cord nestled under my breastbone throbs. A shudder of awareness rolls down my spine, twining with something else, a faint sense of unease. I rub the skin of my chest above my heart.

"It's the deal you made with us." Ethan sets his jaw. "No alpha is allowed to touch omegas without their permission. How do you expect your men to live by your code when you can't follow it yourself?"

The blood thuds at my temples, my left eyebrow throbs. "I wanted her; I took her." I lean forward and shove my face close to his. "No one comes near her, until I decide what to do with her."

His lips tighten. His entire demeanor is one of censure. And I thought when I'd killed off Golan, I'd gotten rid of the ghost of parental disapproval. Fuck this. I don't owe an explanation to anyone.

"I don't march to anyone else's tune or follow anyone else's timetable, only my own." I grind my jaw so hard that pain slashes down my throat. "We will attack Scotland and bring Kayden to his knees."

"We need more time—"

I raise my hand, cutting him off. "We will wait a few more days… Until I have made sure my omega is settled. Then we attack." I turn to leave.

"We chose you for our leader, Zeus. The underbelly of this city needs to be swept clean of the criminals and the corruption fostered under your father's rule. You are the only man who can show us the way."

I pause halfway to the door. A cold feeling rolls in my gut.

He is wrong, so wrong. I'm just the bastard from the wrong side of the tracks who is always on the outside looking in. I believe in only one thing: fighting for myself, for my survival. That is it. Nothing else matters. Not this city. Not the people. Not my Council. Nothing.

I glare at him over my shoulder. "Don't patronize me." My voice is deceptively light. Blood thuds at my temples. "Do. You. Understand?"

Ethan's jaw hardens, then he lowers his gaze. "General."

I should feel some satisfaction that the other man has submitted, has acknowledged my superiority.

Yet it only leaves a feeling of distaste in my mouth.

The mating bond shudders and pushes up against my chest. Dense waves of fear bleed from the cord. My gut churns.

The omega…she is restless and afraid. She needs me. I stride to the exit and shove the doors open.

20

Lucy

The pain shudders over my skin. My shoulders jerk, and my chest thrusts up and off the floor.

My stomach twists, and I taste the acidic tang of bile. I want to scream, but all that emerges is a whimper.

I moan and curl in on myself.

There is this hunger gnawing at me. It churns at my guts, growing bigger by the second, as if it's going to tear open my skin and rip out of me at any time. I am hungry, so hungry. And it's not for food. I want him…need him…to fill me. To shove aside this hollowness that's drawing me in, threatening to overwhelm me.

I want him throbbing inside me. The thought is so intense I almost imagine he is here, his massive body bent over me, his hard thighs pushing my legs apart, then him slamming into me, burying his brutal length in me, holding me down, folding his body around me, protecting, taking me, cherishing me. The thought sends heat shooting through my veins. Sweat beads my brow.

My chest heaves.

My breasts ache.

Every part of me screams and begs for his touch.

I want to call out to him. I need to call out to him. The urge is so overwhelming that I feel every last coherent thought trickle out of me, leaving only the pure essence of the omega I am behind.

To be a receiver, to take, the breeder.

Isn't that what my mother told me? And I had resisted it every step of the way. At least my father, for the short time he'd been around, had encouraged me to fight the urge.

He'd been the rare male alpha who'd actually not conformed to the stereotype. Who'd seemed to understand what it means to live a life where you are constantly living from one heat cycle to the other. Fighting it each time. Terrified of that hunger that sweeps in with the onset of each mating loop. Worried that this cycle is the one where you give in and seek out an alpha to break the cycle and put an end to the suffering. It was one-sided. So unjust. Nature had decreed that with the plummeting population count, omegas in the heat cycle would attract every single alpha in the square mile around them. Send enough into the rut that they would seek you out and try to take you.

Most of my omega friends had rejoiced with the onset of their cycles. Dreaming of the alpha who they would choose as their mate. Not me. I wanted to hold on to my independence for as long as I could. No alpha-hole male is going to break me. No, I am my own person and intend to be this way for as long as I can. I had opted to take fertilization blockers—fringe benefits of being royalty? I had the means to purchase the drugs from the black market—and subdue my hormones. I'd pushed my heat cycles further and further apart, and been able to spar with alphas without attracting their attention.

I thought it was working…until I had sensed him and my true nature had come roaring out.

Another white-hot cycle of pain rips through me and catches in my throat. I don't have the energy to scream to try to relieve some of that burning pressure.

My womb cramps, and the fluid begs to be secreted.

All it needs is an alpha's purr, his scent to draw it out and satisfy this hunger that demands his touch. Where the hell is he when I need him? I bang the side of my head against the floor in the hope of relieving some of the pain, or at least to hurt some other part of me so as to distract me from the core source of pain. Inside me.

Deep inside me.

In the very center of my being.

The sound of footsteps grows closer. Am I imagining it? A faint rumble of voices, then the air from the corridor flows over my flushed forehead, then the door slams shut.

I scent him first.

That spice of burned pinewood seeps through the air. My mouth waters. Or maybe it's just that I am thirsty?

The pace of the footsteps increases, then I feel him kneel down next to me.

I expect him to berate me, to perhaps hit me for messing up his space or maybe slide me on my back and take me…which is what I want, damn it!

Tears prick the backs of my closed eyelids, and I let them trickle down my cheeks.

I couldn't stop it if I wanted to.

I want him to fuck me, to take me mercilessly and put an end to the dense, cloying pain that thuds through my guts, that fills my head, pounds at my temples. I just want it gone.

I open my mouth to ask him to do just that, while a part of me cringes at the shame of it. This is my sworn enemy—he'd taken me against my will, and now I want him to do it again. And again.

I try to move my limbs but only manage a slight jerk of my hands.

He seems to understand, though, for his arms come around me and scoop me up.

Every muscle in my body tenses.

I am sure he is going to fuck me when I am at my weakest.

When I need him the most. When I don't really want him, but my body is not going to cooperate with my will.

I want…to get the hell out of here.

I want...to turn back time to when I'd met Kayden, and tell him I do not agree to his plan.

I want…the feel of the alpha's arms around me, cradling me closer, his lips sliding over my fevered forehead as he walks into the bathroom holding me.

The sound of running water fills the space. It splashes over my face and I gasp. It's cold. Too cold. Goosebumps pop on my skin. My shoulders quiver. I gulp, and the breath catches in my throat. I open my mouth, and water slides in. I gurgle and shove at the wall of muscle at my back.

"Shh."

Has he actually placed his chin on my head? Is he actually being this gentle with me? I feel the purr vibrate up his chest as he holds me flush against him. Instantly, my muscles unwind.

My shoulders shudder.

It feels like every part of me is reacting to him, tuning in to him. Drawing in every last cadence of that purr that rolls over me, sinks into my blood, uncoiling that tension that grips my flesh.

My shoulders slump, my knees go weak, and I would have fallen, except his arm is around my waist, propping me up.

The water is no longer cold.

It seems to hit my fevered skin and to absorb some of the heat before it flows away. The throbbing in my forehead dulls.

All through it, he keeps purring— a low, deep, comforting sound that coils around me, soothing away more of my aches, trembling down my spine, down the backs of my thighs.

I am floating; my limbs feel so heavy. My eyelids feel like they are weighed down. I should protest and tell him he can't manipulate my body like this. He has no right.

My muscles tense again.

My hands twitch as I try to raise them. I fold my other arm above my chest, place my mouth next to his ear, and allow another husky purr to wind around me.

He pulls me back against that solid wall of his chest. My head rolls back, and I let sleep pull me down.

When I awake next the room is dark.

I feel the soft sheets under my cheek; something silken covers me. My insides twist, but this time it is something else…a different kind of hunger. My limbs feel too weak, but I force myself to open my eyes.

A shape moves in the dark next to me.

I scream and spring up.

21

Zeus

She screams, and the noise rips through my guts. It shouldn't affect me. She is just someone I had decided to take for my own and keep on a whim...except that's not true, not anymore. Fact is, from the moment I had seen her, scented her, laid eyes on her, there was a powerful pull toward her. One I can't yet understand.

Except I need her with me, need to bury myself in her softness and slake my hunger.

To satisfy her while I am at it, too. Why is it so important that I soothe her? I don't want to go to her and yet I cannot help myself. I am not aware that I am on my feet and moving to her, not until I am sitting next to her on the bed. Not until she's flung herself at me, tearing at me with her nails. She growls, and there are tears dripping down her cheeks as she flings herself at me again and again. Pain comes off her in waves. And terror, the sheer terror of the unknown. Mixed with it is the whiff of hunger. A need so powerful that a growl rumbles up my chest. It's torn out of me, flowing through the air. My very insides seem to be begging me to stop her, take her close, protect her. I curl my fingers into fists at my sides, digging my nails into my flesh. Pain shudders up my arms, but I push it aside. All my attention is taken up by the tiny thing who is trying to climb me, who is crawling up my chest, to wrap her arms and legs around me.

"Please." She clings to me.

Her voice breaks.

I need to bring her closer, take her to me, draw her essence inside me...and yet I resist. I am not sure why. Is it because the way she suffers satisfies some deep-rooted hunger inside? The need to rut, to kill, which has been with me from the very start, from the time I saw my father hurt my mother, over and over again as he tried to take her, make her bend to his will? And my mother had resisted every step of the way. Until the bastard had broken her physically, and yet her spirit hadn't given in. She'd resisted.

Like she is. My little omega who bares her teeth at me.

"Why are you not taking me, fucking me as a red-blooded alpha should?"

"Is that what you want?"

My voice comes out harsh, and I don't recognize it. It sounds like a man at the edge of despair, an alpha at the edge of his control. And I have been holding on to the shreds of that ever-weakening control of mine. I hadn't been aware of that, not until now.

Not until she snarls, "I demand that you fuck me and take my pain away. That you break me and find that part inside of me that wants to be revealed to the world. I ask that you then feed me, for I am hungry. Hungry. Do you understand, Alpha?"

The crudeness of her words sends a keening cry of desire rippling down my spine. My cock hardens. My groin throbs. "You are not in your senses; you don't know what you are asking—"

She grabs the back of my hair and yanks me close with such force that my head snaps forward.

"How do you know what I want? How can you possibly know the depth of hunger that twists my insides, that bubbles up from my very womb, that yearns for your touch, your heat to fill me, that needs your seed to soothe it, to fulfill it? To take root. How can you know the depth of want that drives me to open my eyes, my mouth, my soul and ask for you to take me? Even as the part of me that is rational and independent that was taught to fend for myself and survive without an alpha cringes and wails at the depths to which I have fallen?"

She pants to a stop, chest heaving, red lips glistening. The scent of her need fills the space, crashing over me.

I lean in until our noses bump, until I can see the pores on her cheek, the flush that stains her skin, the freckles that dot the creamy expanse of her breasts. "Once I start there is no going back." I want to smirk, to pretend it's a joke, to show her that I am the dangerous one in this relationship—and I am, of course I am.

For I am bigger, more physically powerful, much stronger than her.

And yet, as she raises herself on her knees so her eyes are level with mine, so the heat of her core flows over my chest, I know she packs a powerful punch, too. Perhaps we are more equally matched than we realize. Perhaps that is why the force in me that needs to take, relishes the challenge. For that's what she is. A challenge. Prey. One I can toy with, play with, without fear. For she will not break, not that easily.

And I will keep trying over and over again, so she gives a little every time.

And when she finally goes over the edge, I'll be there to taste my spoils.

Her complete submission, it will be so beautiful.

So erotic.

A thing of pleasure that will be well worth the effort. And break she will.

I intend to take every single part of her until she is pleading with me to stop.

Until she is begging for more.

Until her very spirit cries out for me.

Until I own her. Absolutely.

The thought of it is such a turn-on that desire hardens my groin. My cock strains against my pants, its need twisting my insides. While every part of me readies to take her, to bend her to my will.

"Promises, promises, Alpha. Are you going to just sit there talking or are you going to live up to your words?"

Anger brushes my nerves. My skin tightens with the overwhelming need to take, to possess, to consume. "Don't provoke me, Omega."

I shove her away, not gently. "Not unless you can take the consequences of your actions." I am past any pretense. She wants to see what I am. She wants to feel the monster inside. The one who is insatiable, who will not stop, not until one of us breaks, and it will not be me.

22

Lucy

He pushes me away, and I am not sure why. Does he not want me anymore? No, that can't be true.

I sense the need in him, the want to tear into me, to break me. And I am not unhappy about it or threatened.

All I feel is a relief that finally he's revealed his true self to me. Just as I have to him. I watch him walk to the door, open it, and speak in a low voice to the soldier stationed outside. Footsteps approach up the corridor. A tray exchanges hands. He steps back, holding it. The door snicks shut behind him. It's a soft sound and yet it shivers over my sensitized skin. The scent of food wafts over to me, but that only twists my stomach.

He places the tray on the table, then turns and folds his arms over his chest. He doesn't say anything, just waits for me to comply with his unspoken command. Every line of his body indicates he'll patiently wait until I give in.

I want to say no, want to deny him, but all that comes out is a snarl. It's as if whatever I am becoming is cutting through the civilized veneer in me, marking me what I am. An omega with the desire to breed.

"You know what happens when you disobey me."

"So you'll fuck me?" I smirk. "Guess what, big man? That's what I want anyway."

"If you continue like this, I won't give you what you want."

What the—? My breath catches, and I feel the color leave my cheeks. "You wouldn't dare."

He bares his teeth, then grabs his crotch. "I can scent your arousal, the moisture that your body is producing as we speak."

His every word sends a fresh need rippling over my skin.

He growls, and the purr slashes through the hunger that has me in thrall. "Just my very nearness makes you want my cock thrusting inside you."

My spine arches back and my breasts grow heavy.

Every part of me wants to go to him, to throw myself at him and beg him to take me.

"And you will have it, but only when you do as you are told."

Rage thrums my nerve endings. That I needed him to fuck me and break my heat cycle is bad enough. That he taunts me about my dependency on him and holds back, is far worse. I feel like I am losing the very last of whatever pride I was holding on to. Pride? Hah! I have nothing left, nothing but this fiery will to fight back. To take what I need instead of always being put in a position where I am being manipulated and used.

Something inside me snaps.

I've had enough.

Enough.

I can't do this anymore. I can't always be the responsible one. The one who should provide for my clan. The one who found a safe passage to this country. The one who negotiated with the leader of Scotland. The one who took the initiative to walk into this alpha's palace determined to see his demise. Not knowing it was my own that was in sight. If this is all that's left of me, then so be it. If I am reduced to this sniveling, wanting mass of emotions that cannot survive on my own anymore, then so be it.

I am tired of hiding what I am.

An omega who chooses to take.

A woman who will let herself feel.

A lover who will revel in her alpha's skin sliding over hers.

Who will be broken and filled again because she derives pleasure from it.

I am tired of asking. It's time I take what I need.

Everything around me fades. The room recedes. Everything except him. His scent, his face, those blue eyes that tear into my soul. It's all I can see. My gaze focuses in on him. Springing up on the bed, I run to the edge then jump across the space and throw myself at him.

His body sways. The breath slams out of him. He takes a step back but doesn't fall. He grabs my waist and holds me in place. I snap my legs around him, loop my arms over his shoulders, and fix my lips on his.

His mouth opens in surprise, and I slide my tongue in.

I drink of him, suck of his essence, I take from him and keep taking. I don't stop. At some point he responds. He yanks me close enough for my skin to rasp over his vest that he still hasn't removed. I smell blood in the air. Mine? His? I don't know.

A growl rumbles up his chest, flowing up our joined bodies. My thighs spasm and I dig my heels into the hard planes of his back.

He slants his head and sucks on my tongue.

The taste of him sinks into my mouth, flowing through my blood, and goes straight to my head.

Everything inside me comes alive.

My toes curl, and I dig my heels into his back. I am likely hurting myself, hurting him, too...and that doesn't matter. If anything, it only feeds that hunger inside me that is pushing to get out. That writhes and groans and wants more, so much.

I realize then I can't stop.

Not until I have him.

Not until I have it all. Not until I am in him, as he is in me. And it's not fair that this monster, this alpha who has the future of my clan in his hands is the one who can arouse these feelings of complete submission in me. But I am not submitting, am I?

All I am doing is tearing open my heart, my soul, my body, and offering it to him. And him? He takes.

Without tearing his mouth from mine, he walks to the bed. The world tilts; I feel the bed at my back. He pulls his mouth from mine and rises to his feet, putting distance between us.

My pulse quickens. Eyes half blind with desire, my senses alive with need, I move to rise with him. "No, please, don't…" Don't what? Don't go? Don't leave me? I want to say it out loud.

But that tiny, rational part of me that is still functioning holds me back. I have all but submitted my body to him, not my soul. Not my will. I cannot give him that. I will not put myself through the ultimate betrayal and give up everything. Not yet.

Tears prick the backs of my eyes, my chest feels like it is going to burst, and there is a growing pressure in my head. My brain cells seem to be melting, and surely, he can see it? Can't he tell how difficult this is for me? Can't he see how much I need this, need him? How much I want him to just take me, to give me the oblivion I so crave?

And maybe he does, because he cups my cheek. "Shh! I am not going anywhere. I just need to take off my clothes so I can feel you completely."

I swallow, registering the change in him. When did that happen? When did he go from being the aggressor to the comforter? I blink, and a teardrop runs down my cheek. His gaze follows it. Then he leans down and licks it up.

"You taste so sweet, so haunting." He brushes his lips over mine and straightens.

Every part of me wants to follow him, to fling myself back at him. But I wait. Wait.

I don't move. I can't take my gaze off him as he unhooks his vest.

Walking to the chair, he drapes it over the backrest.

The thick muscles of his triceps bulge. The scent of him deepens. Pungent, tangy, and so evocative. My mouth waters. The muscles low in my belly tighten. I clench my thighs but cannot stop the fresh burst of moisture that flows out. A low whine is drawn out of me.

I hear the keening need in it, and that turns me on further. "Hurry." My breath comes out in puffs. My chest rises and falls.

I want to lie back and shut my eyes, then fall into that black, yearning mass of need that is me. And yet a part of me cannot take my gaze away from the complete picture of maleness that is unfolding in front of me.

He slides the pants down and steps out of them.

Every part of me snaps to attention. My palms and feet tingle. I've seen him naked before, and yet the sheer poetry of those angles and planes of his body hits me anew. Heat flushes my skin. Every pore in my body is focused on him.

His wide back narrows to tight flanks that contract as he turns to face me.

I've sensed his strength, and yet the force of his dominance takes me by surprise.

He's so very male, every inch of him. My fingers twitch to grip his muscles and feel the unleashed power that hums under his skin.

His thighs are already taut with need, and between them his arousal which is large and veined. Saliva pools in my mouth. The size of him, the smell of his arousal, how he'd filled me earlier and pumped into me. The warmth of his cum filling my channel, his tongue thrusting into my mouth...the images flicker across my mind, speeding up. My breath comes in quick gasps. Sweat beads my palm. I know I am staring and I can't stop. Not even when he circles his shaft and runs his hand up the length. The slit glistens with beads of precum.

I lick my lips, wanting to taste him again.

I open my mouth to tell him, but all that emerges is a moan.

It seems to galvanize him into action, for he strides to the bed, leans above me, and rubs the liquid over my lips. "Tell me you want me."

I stare but can't stop myself from flicking out my tongue and slurping up the moisture.

His gaze grows lighter, and those irises of his turn almost colorless. "Say it. I'll give you what you need. All I need is to hear you say it now."

"No," I growl.

He holds my gaze.

And that connection is so hot, so unnerving that my hips seem to jerk forward of their own accord. I raise my pelvis, and scissor my legs around his waist so my core meets his cock. The swollen head of his shaft nudges the entrance of my wet channel, then he plunges inside.

23

Zeus

I plunge inside her.

Hot. Moist. Sensations spiral out from my groin. Warmth fills my chest. All my nerve endings seem to fire at once and I grit my teeth. The feeling is so different, so intimate. My muscles bunch, my throat closes, and…this can't be right.

It can't feel so good to be inside her, to have her pussy clamp around me and milk me. The need to pound into her is so strong, and yet, overriding it is this need to protect. All emotions I have never experienced before, least of all for this omega whom I hadn't known until a few days ago.

My thigh muscles lock, and my biceps tremble as my arms support my body weight.

She digs her heels into my back. "What are you waiting for?" She bares her teeth.

And, really, she is only a tiny thing, less than half my size. And I am leaning over her, my muscles far stronger. It would take only one flick of my wrist to overpower her. The sheer audacity of her approach has me in thrall. I slide my fingers around her neck and grip it tightly.

If I wanted to, I could kill her right now.

Her gaze widens. The black pupils expand, not with fear…but arousal. A fresh pool of slick spurts out of her and coils around my cock. I grow bigger and fill her up inside, until my hardening flesh brushes against the walls of her womb. She groans. So do I.

She flings back her head, her neck arches, and she bites down on her lips. And that sends me over the edge. I pull out of her and stay poised at the entrance to her wet channel.

I know I am going to hurt her and yet I can't stop myself. Her gaze widens. She mewls, scrunching up her face, and her cheeks flush…with anger? With desire. She peels back her lips and digs her fingernails into the back of my shoulder.

"Don't you stop now, Alpha. Or else—"

"Or else?" I growl and more moisture gushes from her.

Her eyes roll back, and she moans. "Or else, I'll never spread my legs for you again, not willingly."

I almost laugh aloud. Oh, the irony! She is throwing my words back at me.

Her chest heaves, and her breasts rise and fall, the nipples hard enough to scratch a furrow down my skin.

Does she really believe that she has a choice in how she'll submit to me? That she could hint at that should bother me, but it doesn't. Not as much as the sheer possessiveness that grips me. I lean in close and pinch her chin, forcing her head down. She cracks her eyes open, the green a ring around the darkness of her pupils almost filling her entire eyes.

"Whenever I want, however I want, I'll fuck you, and you'll take it all."

She pauses; her breath hitches.

I lower my voice. "And you'll ask for more."

Her eyes dilate until the green completely vanishes. The color fades from her cheeks. The honeyed scent of her arousal deepens, laced with the acrid scent of fear. And I want to soothe her and tell her I'll never hurt her.

Even as a part of me is pleased that she is still afraid of me. She should be, for she has no idea how close I am to binding her to me and never letting her go.

It would serve her right if I did.

I should.

Bind her. Knot her to me. So she can never belong to anyone else. "No one but me," I snarl. My voice slices through the haze in my head. "Do you understand?"

She nods.

"Tell me." Why is it so important that I hear her acknowledge my dominance? I am not sure. Except that possessive part of me, the one that demands her complete subjugation, wants her to say it aloud. Craves it with a fierceness I can't fathom. But I can't fight it either—I don't want to fight it.

"Yes" she snaps, tears glittering in her eyes.

"Yes, what?"

"Yes, Alpha." She hisses through lips bitten from my ministrations.

A part of me registers the anger and the frustration that emanates from her. But I ignore it all.

"My name. Say my name."

She grits her teeth and sets her chin. Her eyes glow with that light of stubbornness that both frustrates and also excites me.

"Say it." I harden my jaw, knowing I am dangerously gone in my passion, in my anger; knowing that I am on the verge of hurting her in the middle of my lust, and yet I know there is no turning back. Not now.

She clenches the walls of her pussy around my dick.

A fierce surge of desire tugs my groin. Lust flows down my spine, filling my balls until I am hurting. Until I know I can't hold back.

I growl loudly and her stomach muscles cramp. Her body responds to my every nuance. I know I am taking advantage of the fact that I have pinned her in place.

That I can control her body as easily as I can control my own. Too bad I can't tame her mind or her spirit. Yet a part of me rejoices at the challenge. Knowing there can be no other mate for me.

Mate?

Yes, she is, and no, it doesn't mean anything.

It's the most convenient way of keeping her with me.

My lips twist in derision at myself. At the sorry man I have become. One reduced to trying to subdue the one thing that has come into my life and has sparked the urge to fight again, for myself, for her. For everything I hold dear. I feel more alive than I ever have before.

As alive as the day I killed my father and took revenge for my mother's death.

"Say. It." I growl once more and deepen my purr.

This time I feel the slick gather at the base of her core. Feel the hunger that rips through her so her back arches and her breasts thrust up. Her nipples tighten. Her hips tremble. The scent of her arousal flows over me. Crashes over me, tightening my need. Stretching it until I am sure I am going to snap. I can't hold back. I can't. And yet… "Please." The word dribbles out; my voice breaks.

"Zeus," she whispers on a breath.

The sound of my name from her lips sends a pulse of desire tearing down my spine. The blood thunders at my temples, my shoulders bunch, and every muscle in my body tenses in preparation. I will invade her, take her, fucking own her. I must. Liquid lust rams through my blood demanding that she scream when I do so. Knowing she will throw her head back, kick her heels into my back, dig her nails into my neck, and tear grooves down my skin when I rut her, and all of it sends me over the edge.

I plunge into her, sinking all the way inside her melting channel. I tilt my hips, and grind myself in to the hilt. The blood rushes to my groin. The bulbous knot at the base of my shaft swells. I thrust forward that last millimeter and hook behind her pelvic bone, locking her to me. Her body bucks and her pussy clamps onto my turgid flesh, drawing me in even closer. Tight. Hot. Succulent. Mine. The feel of it, the complete rightness of it floods me, filling every last cell in my body and overflowing. My balls draw up, my thigh muscles spasm and I want to come inside her, mark her, claim her and yet something makes me wait. Wait. Leaning down, I take her lips, thrust my tongue inside her sweet mouth, and rake my fingers through her hair.

Her little body goes stiff, and then I feel her climax shudder up from her toes, sweeping over her thighs, pinning her waist to the bed, her chest vibrating, then her throat ripples, and she screams, and I absorb it all. Only then do I let the hot streams of cum gush forth as I empty myself inside her.

24

Lucy

When I come to it is to the thud of his heart under my cheek. I slide my fingers over warm skin. Turn my face and bury my nose in the light smattering of hair on his chest.

The scent of his sweat and musk of his arousal turns me on, and it also strangely soothes me. I feel protected and cherished, and the still thinking part of my mind warns me I am falling into a place from which there is no return. I try to move only to find there is a heavy weight around my waist. It's his arm, which is massive enough to hold me down.

It feels so right that I know it's wrong.

Not like this.

All my life I've spent fighting that core inside me, the part that was intrinsically omega that needed to be tamed, subdued, knotted, and bred. And in one stroke he... this alpha, the most monstrous of all in the city, has done just that. And I had encouraged him. The faint recollection of giving him what he wanted, of calling him by his name tumbles over me.

My cheeks flush.

That is more intimate than anything else we've done.

And it shouldn't be.

I'd called him by his name, that's all. We all have one. Then why does it feel like I have broken a pact with myself? That I have gone back on the promise made to my clan, that I have betrayed myself by doing that?

I wriggle against the massive chest of the alpha, and he doesn't let go. Big surprise.

He folds his other arm around me and purrs. The sound is low, and soft, and flows over my skin. Its soothing in a way it shouldn't be. He rubs my back as if trying to pacify me. He rests his chin on my head, and I have this insane need to bury myself in his chest, to surround myself with his warmth and his heat, to draw that shroud of protectiveness over me and let it consume me. I squeeze my eyes shut, not sure why I feel the need to cry. It's only my life that will never be the same. A sob catches in my throat. My shoulders shudder as I try to bite my lips, try to consume every last depressing emotion that wells up. What is happening to me?

The giant purrs once more, and the sound instantly sinks into my blood.

The tension drips out of me, and my shoulders sag. No, no. I don't want that to happen.

I don't want him to be able to manipulate me such that even my grief is something that is not my own.

I want to rage at him and tell him that.

Instead, I let the tears flow down my cheeks. The warmth pools on his chest, and he must feel it, for he firms his hold on me.

"You are upset at how you responded to me." His breath raises the hair on my head. "Don't be."

He runs his palm from the nape of my neck down to my hips and back up again. The moment is soothing, and soft…tender. "You are the most passionate woman I have ever met."

He praises me.

And it's all wrong. He's not meant to soothe me or take care of me. He's meant to overwhelm and threaten and force himself on me. Truth is, he didn't do anything I didn't want. Even now, caught up in the throes of the end of my heat cycle, with my mind half hazy with the need for him, with my body already signaling that I need the alpha to fuck me again, the rational part of my brain insists that I can't put all the blame on him.

Perhaps I had been stupid to walk into his lair and let myself be caught by him, and yes, he had taken me, but everything that had happened after that, I had wanted it.

I can't blame myself for getting caught, for as soon as I had seen him, had sniffed his luscious alpha scent, I'd known it was him. Only I had been denying it to myself so far.

The thought quiets me…my muscles relax, my toes uncurl. I let my body sag against him.

Zeus seems satisfied by the response, but he doesn't stop his purring. His large palm continues to soothe me. He drags his fingers through my hair, scraping his fingernails across my scalp. Ripples of pleasure undulate down my spine. A moan dribbles out of me.

I sense the change in him at that. Feel the hardness that nudges against my hip.

He rakes his fingers over my nape, over my spine, cupping the curve of my hips before sliding his hand into the space between my legs. I can't stop the groan that wells up. My thigh muscles clench, locking his fingers in place.

Moisture pools inside my core and trickles down my thigh. I know this time it's not his purring or his cajoling that has drawn out the slickness from me. It's me enjoying his body, his nearness, his presence. It's the way he's tried to claim me, tried to draw the uncertainty from me.

And I feel grateful. There. I've acknowledged it to myself. I am grateful that he found me in the middle of my heat cycle, that I had gone into my heat cycle right there in his presence, that he had taken me and helped me through it, that it is him who broke me and knotted me. My clan... The thought of them waiting crashes through my head, and I push it away. I need to get to them, and I will get to them. But I need to use this to my advantage. Clearly, he wants me, he finds me attractive, he claimed me, and the only thing I can do is use this to help my clan. Barter my submission for them. Pretend an acquiescence I don't really feel, to draw him into his comfort zone, until he lets his guard down, and then... My muscles tense.

A growl rumbles up from him. His hands grip my waist and, lifting me up, he slides me down the thick girth of his shaft.

Just like that, he fills me, the hard, engorged flesh dragging against my softer inner walls, sending a pulse of desire up my spine. Little bursts of flame explode behind my eyes. I moan at the feeling of being completely full, and the sound of his growl twines with mine.

He raises and lowers me on his shaft, and again. Desire thrums my nerves, liquid heat pools in my core, and I clench my inner walls around him. I can't stop, not even if I wanted to. I am rewarded with another snarl from the alpha.

"Look at me."

I open my eyes and am caught in the swirling depths of his silver gaze. Flickers of gold spark in their depths. It captures me, holds me in thrall. When he slides his hand up to grip my nape and brings my face forward, I don't resist.

Not even when he holds me there, poised over him, staring down into his face, my position that of mock dominance, but I am not fooled. He controls me, his anger holds me in check, the feeling of unleashed power that hums under his skin binds me to him, and the low hum of the mating cord under my rib cage tells me I am his as much as he is mine.

He lowers me down his shaft until my hips slide over his. I grip the sides of his waist with my knees and squeeze my inner walls. The burst of gold in his eyes glows brighter, and it feels...so good that I can give him pleasure. I squeeze again. A groan rumbles up his massive chest, color burning high on his cheeks.

Just like that, the sexual tension ratchets up. His nostrils flare, his eyes narrow and his gaze falls to my breasts. He flips me over so I am under him and without pulling out of me,he leans down and bites my nipple. Flares of need sizzle over my skin, leaving little sparks of fire in their wake. My eyelids flutter down.

"No."

The command in his voice whips through my mind, and my eyelids snap open. My gaze is caught in his.

"Mine," he growls.

I swallow. Something stretched tight inside me dissolves.

He hooks his hands under my knees, yanking my legs up and over his shoulders, so I am spread wide. I thrust my hips up, and the angle means he slides in deep. Deeper than he's ever been before. It feels like he is piercing me in half. He seems to touch the very secret core in me where no one has, where no one else will ever be, no one but him. Why does it feel like he's ripped off every single mask I've worn to the world and made me his?

Something seems to change in him, too, for he lowers his head and slants his lips over mine. He thrusts his tongue into my mouth, and his cock expands inside.

The knot snaps into place.

Like it was meant to happen. I know then that everything that has happened in my life has brought me up to this point: to submit to him, to give him pleasure, even as I take from him.

My soft core tightens around him, milking him, and the climax slithers out from my center, flooding me, embracing me as the thick juice of his cum bathes my channel. His big body shudders; the muscles of his back clench.

He kisses the edge of my mouth, the gesture almost tender, then he rests his forehead on mine. A bead of sweat drizzles down his temple. I flick my tongue out to lick it up.

"Yours."

I only realize that I've said the word aloud when he stills over me. Then he scoops me up and turns me over to rest on his chest. He runs his palm over my hair. Once again, his touch feels almost tender. But that's not possible. Surely, I am mistaken. The most brutal alpha in this part of the world is not capable of a soft touch. He is not.

Is he?

"Sleep now and recover your strength." His voice sinks into my blood.

There is a subtle command to the words that insists I obey him. I want to resist him, and yet, this once…just once, will it not be okay to shut my eyes and give in to this feeling of warmth and comfort and safety which cocoons me? Can I not give in to that part of me that wants to be owned?

When I wake up, I am alone.

25

Zeus

I walk into the war room for the daily recon to find the place is empty, except for Ethan. He rises to his feet as I walk in. I slow my steps.

It's not in the man to be that formal. Oh, he respects me all right, only he's not given to such outward gestures, not when we are on our own.

I pull out a chair, drop into it, and tip it all the way back. "Kayden is preparing to attack?"

Ethan goes still; his gaze narrows.

"Don't be so surprised, Second." I set the chair on its front legs with a thump. "The fucker is bound to spring that on us when we least expect it—"

"Namely right after initiating the peace talks?" Ethan frowns. "Why am I not surprised that you'd have already anticipated it?"

"Admit it, you are impressed." I push back the chair, then prop my legs on the table.

Ethan watches me with a frown. "That's an antique table."

Boo fucking hoo. I scratch my chin. Nevertheless, I swing my legs off the table and set my feet on the floor with a snap. "You're delaying the inevitable, Second."

"Oh, what the fuck." Ethan shifts his weight from one foot to the other. "Fine, I am impressed."

I drum my fingers on the table. "Why do I feel a 'but' coming on?"

"You are so able to anticipate Kayden's moves. Sometimes I think the two of you have some kind of a past that I don't know anything about."

My shoulders freeze. "How did you guess?"

"What the fuck?" Ethan's features harden. He marches to the table and pounds his fist on the surface. "Why didn't you tell me anything about this until now? Do you know how important this piece of information is to the future of this city, for the future of coming generations? For—"

"Relax, brother," I drawl. "I was yanking your chain."

"Oh, for fuck's sake!" Color rushes to his cheeks

"Calm down, asshole. At this rate, you'll have a coronary and die in this room instead of going out with a bang in a fight."

"Is that what you want, to meet a bloody end?" He leans down and grabs my collar. "Is this why you can't wait to leap into a fight with Kayden, so the two of you can slaughter each other?"

"You want a fight, Second? You only have to ask." I hold his gaze. And it feels weird that I am calm while Ethan, the sensible one, is all worked up. "If I didn't know better, I'd think you were worried about losing me."

"Oh, bloody fuck." He lets go of me and steps back.

"Can't remember when you used that four-letter word so many times in one conversation last." I grin.

"What-fucking-ever." He rakes his fingers through his hair, but his eyebrows draw down.

"Now you are borrowing my dialogue." I click my tongue. "Really, E, it's time you think of something more original."

"Time you think of how we put an end to this Kayden-shaped problem. It's bad enough that you took the omega to bed—"

"What's your point?" I crack my neck from side to side. My shoulders flex. Ethan's right, much as I hate to admit it. Kayden had sent the omega to kill me...and I had mated her.

What a fucking mess. "The bastard is as much in my head as I am in his," I growl, more disturbed than I want to let on.

Our two countries have been at war for so long that I'd known it would come to this—a bloody battle which I intend to win. Not for my Council or the citizens of this fair city. I don't owe any of them anything. Nope, it's my pride that insists I defeat Kayden, quash any resistance. That and being able to use his resources to restructure this city. Wipe it clean of the dirt and muck, the corruption that grabs at its roots. I am so close now, to getting what I want, I can taste it. The fine hairs on my neck harden. I drum my fingers over my chest. It can't be that simple.

Kayden couldn't have been so careless that news of his plans would so conveniently reach me, giving me time to plan a defense.

I rise to my feet, only to pace along the length of the room.

Ethan watches, his gaze hard. "Aren't you going to gloat we should have listened to you and attacked a few days ago when you first mentioned that offense was the best form of defense?"

I pause and swivel around on my heels. "It's not in me to strike a man when he is down...not." I peel my lips back at him, let the glint of satisfaction show in my eyes.

"It's clear we need to get our troops together, to prepare for a fight." He turns to leave.

"No."

He pauses mid-step, then shoots me a glance. "*Excuse me?*"

So fucking polite. I much prefer the Ethan who says what is on his mind. But then he's the gentleman, trained in the etiquette that makes him the kind of alpha that omegas yearn for.

Me? I am the marauder, the one who takes. Who protects, too—not that I'd ever admit to that—just without the finer points of behavior that Ethan can lay claim to.

"You heard me." I rub the back of my neck. "How many people know of this?"

"Just you and me, and the spy who brought the news."

"Keep it that way." I set my jaw.

"What are you playing at, Zeus?" He frowns.

"You knew what you were getting when you chose me. You know I don't trust anyone with my plans."

"A strength."

I nod.

"Except when it isn't. When you hold your cards too close to your chest, when you don't allow anyone else to see what you are, then what you become is a dictator."

"Right on first count." I chuckle, the sound harsh. "I have never tried to hide what I am. I am not the idealized version of the leader you think I am.

"You are not a monster, Zeus." He leans forward on his feet, his gaze measured, his chin rock-hard.

"I didn't take you for an ass-licker either." I grin.

"You are too smart," he continues as if I hadn't spoken, "too intelligent to waste your position, the title you carry, your bloodline...you wouldn't use it without reason. You have a plan all right. It's just not the one you are sharing with me and the Council. And unlike them—"

"You're not gullible." A smile tugs my lips, the first genuine one of the day since I fondled the omega and touched her face and reluctantly left her sleeping in the bed stained from the evidence of our rutting.

I shouldn't let thoughts of her interrupt this important session. This is the reason I've fought so far, the reason I'd overthrown the old order, brought in people of my own, cultivated the city. And yet when the goal is so close, when I can all but taste the revenge, the fruit of my years of struggling, all I can think about is her.

"You are losing your focus." He grimaces. "*She* is making you lose your concentration." And the smile on his face is one of satisfaction. As if he's been waiting so long to see me fall. He'll relish every last second of seeing me drown in the feelings that are engulfing me.

"I hear every word you say, friend." I emphasize the last word, making it a mockery of what it is meant to be. "Do not for a second think I have lost sight of what I want."

"Except what you wanted forty-eight hours ago...is it the same as what you want now?"

"Of course it is. I—" The words cease. Something very much like an epiphany sweeps over me. He's right. It's not sufficient to kill Kayden. Not adequate to raze this city to the ground. Not enough to organize for those who are loyal to me to be part of the new world I hope to build. No, there is something more. Her. I need her with me. Want her close by so I can bury myself in her sweet cunt when the need takes me. So I can feel her soft skin, twine the silky hair around my fingers, see her grow fat with my child, and kiss her and love her and mate her and... Sweat beads my brow. My vest sticks to my back. The heat in the room is suddenly too much to bear.

I stalk to the window and fling it open, leaning outside. I'd never done this before, looking for fresh air in a city where there is none. Where the smoke from the charcoal fires that people burn at night to keep warm settles over the space, coating everyone in fine grime.

Where a deep breath in the open will clog the pores on your skin. Yet I find myself leaning out and gasping lungfuls of the pollution. Laced below the pea-soup fog I smell the moisture from the Thames. The sluggish brown sludge of the river flows in the distance. Over the years the water has reduced to a trickle of what it was. The ruins of the bridge that had been destroyed by the bombs mock me from a distance.

There's a touch on my shoulder, and I know it's Ethan.

"A mating bond goes both ways, or didn't you realize that."

He's right, and yet a part of me doesn't want to accept it. The mating bond was not spontaneous. It was something I had decided on the moment I'd set eyes on her. I'd known that I was going to claim her. And yet I shake his hand off.

"You gloating now?" I turn on him.

"You know I don't do that." He puts up his palms.

"Yeah, you leave the finer points of being an asshole to me."

"Like I said, you are a better man than you give yourself credit for." He grips my shoulder, his gaze serious.

I almost tell him what I have in mind for the city then. Almost. "You're wrong." I step back. "You don't have to worry that this will derail our plan to fight the Scots."

"I never doubted that anything would take your mind off the goal at the end." His voice is sincere. He sounds exactly like the Ethan I know.

"Power. Ultimate power, that's all I crave." I say it aloud and I know it's to remind myself of what I have at stake.

A way to help focus my mind which insists on reaching out through the mating bond to her.

As if sensing my interest, the mating bond twangs. Grief and loneliness sweep through. It twists my heart. A band of ice tightens around my chest. A feeling of such utter dejectedness crawls into my gut, and I know without a doubt it is her. That the omega is awake and needs comforting and tending. Likely she is coming down after the high of the heat cycle. As the reality of what has been done sinks into her, she will rebel and try to escape. And I cannot, will not let that happen. "I need to go to her."

My gaze snaps on Ethan. My voice sounds hollow and desperate, and I don't try to mask it.

"It's normal for the first months of a newly paired bond for each to be so attuned to the other that you have difficulty telling your emotions apart from hers."

His voice is solicitous, and it should soothe me that he is trying to calm me. Instead, a burst of anger twists my insides. "And how would you know that?" I snap.

His gaze widens, but there is no other change in expression. "So I have heard. Consider it advice from one friend to another. The crux of my experience should help an alpha who is about to enter a very tumultuous stage of a relationship, one that will affect your mind and hence the plans that the entire Council has worked on so meticulously over months."

I look at his features, trying to detect any trace of the fact that he was making fun of me, or that he was speaking in jest, but all I see is seriousness, a trace of concern perhaps. I drop my hands and step back. "Advice accepted."

I swerve around him and head for the door.

"I let go of the omega who could have been my mate and I will forever regret it."

I pause at the exit, then turn to him. "She's—"

"Alive. I met her on my last trip to Russia, was attracted to her instantly, wanted to claim her..." His voice trails off.

"But you didn't." I angle my head, watching him closely.

His lips firm. A pulse ticks above his jaw. "I waited too long. I didn't act on my instinct. When I went back in search of her she was gone. The Vikings invaded Russia and all hell broke loose. They caught me and almost killed me. Only let me go when they realized I was your second." His lips twist. "Even those barbarians did not want to cause a diplomatic incident with you."

"My reputation precedes me." I should feel a fierce surge of pride that news of how I had taken power in London had traveled that far. I should feel gratified that the fiercest warriors in the land hesitate to challenge me. Instead, all I can think of is the softness of her curves under my fingers. Smell the scent of her arousal as I bury my nose in her core, the taste of her essence as I lick her moist folds. And all of it insists that there is more to life than absolute power.

How can I think that? I roll my shoulders and try to school my thoughts into some semblance of familiarity. Soon I'll be taking pity on my own people, pardoning their faults, rebuilding the infrastructure for them, and what the fuck? Obviously, the proximity to the omega is softening me up.

"So you see, I understand a little of what you are going through... Hell, I am envious that you found an omega who calls to you the way she does." He drags his fingers through his hair. "And ignore what I said earlier. Ultimately if she is the woman for you, then nothing else matters, certainly not the fact that Kayden sent her to kill you."

"And the surprises keep coming." So not what I'd expected to hear from Ethan. That must have cost him, given how much he hates the Scots. This fight with Kayden is personal for him. For me...it's a means to show the world I am better than my father.

"We'll find her." I stalk back to him. "I'll help you find her." I grip his shoulder.

His gaze widens. Guess he hadn't expected me to say that. Hell, I hadn't expected myself to say that. The omega's influence is more consuming than I realized.

The mating bond stutters, and a cold feeling coils in my gut. My shoulders stiffen, and I half turn toward the exit.

Ethan's eyebrows furrow. "Go." He jerks his chin to the door.

I don't question the urgency that sweeps through my blood. She needs me. Swiveling around, I rush for the exit.

26

Lucy

I look at myself in the mirror and wince. My hair is caked with cum, and there is fluid drying on my body. My lips are swollen, the skin around my lips is chafed, my nipples look unusually larger, and my breasts…?

I cup them and grimace.

They feel sore, like they have been squeezed and pummeled.

Well, to be fair, he had been gentle with my breasts. Overall, he'd been gentle with my body. For a big man like him, his fingers are unusually light in their touch. He'd rubbed his cum into every part of me that he could access, then poured some of our joined-up liquids into my mouth, and I had…loved it.

I admit it.

I had relished every touch, feel, taste of him.

I had reveled in his scent. I had fucked him right back.

I grasp the edge of the wash basin and lean forward, my hair falling over my face, bringing with it the scent of sex. That darker, deeper, muskier essence of his laced with the lighter one that I recognize as the spoor of my own arousal.

It feels like he's right here with me in the room again. His scent, his touch, his caresses surround me. My lower belly cramps, and liquid seeps out from between my legs.

I squeeze my eyes shut and will back the sickness that twists my gut. The mating bond twangs and coils inside, trying to reassure me that this is as it should be, that he is my mate, he had taken me, used me. Claimed me. It is only right that my body responds to him.

No, no, no. I swing out and smash my fist into the mirror. Cracks spider over the surface and pain slices through the sexual haze that has gripped me. Scarlet drips down my fingers and splashes on the floor dripping over the shards of broken glass. I swear bring the side of my palm to my mouth and suck on it. I have made a mess of this place. Is he going to punish me for this? Probably. Most likely he'll fuck me again, and my body will enjoy it and ask for more.

My shoulders hunch, and the adrenaline fades. I am bleeding, and I know I need to stop the flow of blood, and yet my legs feel too heavy to move.

Every part of my body aches.

Not surprising, though, for it's been what, five, six days since he brought me here and locked me in his space? Since he ravished me and forced the mating bond on me?

I only have myself to blame. I made the first move. I bit him, I staked my need for the bond. It was the heat cycle, of course, and I can keep telling myself that.

That my hormones are at play and I am not really aware of what is happening. It doesn't change the reality of everything that has taken place.

Tears burn at the backs of my eyes and fall on my hand, burning the broken skin that still bleeds. I need to get ahold of myself. The bond twinges again, and a feeling of warmth pours down it, bleeding into my muscles. It's as if he knows of my discomfort and is trying to soothe me. Lies, all lies. I don't trust him. All of it: his taking care of me, making sure I am fed, trying to get me to say his name, seducing me by sharing a little bit of the broken man I sense inside the monster on the outside. All of it is an act.

I feel his presence creeping under my skin, twinning with my blood. He's becoming a part of me.

Just as he'd rubbed his fluids into every crevice on my body, making sure to strengthen the bonding process. Making me a part of him, too. The thought sends a shudder of fear down my spine. I am losing myself in the omega I am at heart. That core of me who is bonded to an alpha, who wants to be taken and cared for. Who needs an alpha to rut her through a cycle. I am all of that and more. So much more. I need to stop resisting him. Need to let him in, let him take, allow myself to dissolve into him...then find myself again.

I stare at the woman whose face is reflected in the cracked mirror. Something inside me tells me I am right. The sooner I put this plan in action, the faster I can find a grip on my destiny, find a way to help my clan. All without telling him. If I tell him the real reason I am here, he'll only find a way to get to my clan, many of whom are omegas like me. He'd make them join his harem, and I am not that stupid.

No, I need to play him at his own game.

He wants an omega? A meek woman? A breeder? I'll become that. I'll throw him off my track, then find a way to get what I want. I must bide my time until I find a weakness and then I am going to kill him...break the bond he forced on me.

The mating cord writhes at the thought, sending a shudder of pain so sharp that I double over. My body cannot stand the thought of him dying. Every second I am here with him, in his room, every time he fucks me, cares for me, makes me think of him, the bond only deepens. I need to kill him before the bond becomes so strong that his dying would kill me, too. I have no intention of dying, not like this.

Turning, I walk to the shower closet, wrench the door open, and step in. The water is blissfully hot, and I let it pour over me, let it clean away the residue of the various times he took me.

My skin is so sensitive that the water sliding over it sends a shiver of need coursing through me.

The wound at the base of my neck where he bit me throbs. I had avoided looking at the broken skin in the mirror. Trying to deny what he'd done to me. I needn't have bothered.

The wound softens under the water and pulses with need. It seems to be calling for its maker to touch it, caress it, and soothe away the pain. The cord in my chest pulses, and a dense plume of heat flushes my skin. I imagine I hear his purring, feel his massive chest at my back, his arm a steel band around my waist, sliding up until his big palm cups my breast, tweaking my nipple.

His other palm slides down to part my lower lips. He drags his fingers through the folds, slipping into my wet, needy channel. Heat coils low, tightening my belly, and I lean forward to rest my forehead against the wall.

His presence only follows me. His big body shields me from the shower. His lips touch the claiming marks—he licks it, his saliva sealing the wound. The pain recedes and is replaced by pure primal greed. For him. To take me all over again. It shouldn't be possible to want him again. Not after the number of times, he's taken me already.

Not after I'd allowed myself to be used over and over again. And not after my heat cycle has simmered to an end, and yet here I am, in the shower imagining he is here with me and…

"You can't shut me out." His breath shudders over the shell of my ear.

The hair on my nape rises. It was him all along. He'd been here with me, and I'd known it and yet I'd tried to ignore it. Hoping if I pretended enough, he wouldn't actually be here…if I tried enough, I'd forget everything that had happened to me.

I sense his presence pull at me through the bond, feel his need seep through my blood, my soul, and I know then, as much as I pretend, things will never be the same. That I can't hide from him, or from myself. He places his palm over my hand, then spreads my fingers flush against the shower wall before doing the same with the other.

Trailing his hands over my arms, he traces the lines toward my back, down my spine to the curve of my hips.

I sense him sink to his knees, then he licks the swell of my butt to where the cheeks part in the middle.

Desire thuds at my nerves. I feel the blood rush to my face and huh, why am I blushing now? He's already done so much to my body, he knows every inch of my skin, and yet as he parts my butt cheeks and slips his tongue into the puckered hole there, I find my muscles clenching. I press my fingers into the stone wall. His arm wraps around my front, and he skims his fingers through my core, his touch gentle, almost comforting. He thrusts a thumb into my soaking channel, and I moan, my lower belly stuttering then unfurling. He moves his other arm up to cup my breast, caress it, tweak it.

The first stirrings of a climax tremble up from my soles.

I shudder, and my knees quake. He seems to sense it, too, for he grips my hips and turns me around.

Before I can crack my eyes open, he spreads my thighs apart, then flips one of my legs over his shoulder.

Then he plunges his tongue into my wet core, sucking, nibbling, biting on my clit.

The climax surges up my spine and sweeps over my nape to break into little flickers of light behind my closed eyelids.

My other knee gives out from under me, and I slide down against the shower wall, only for him to rise, and prop me up. He wraps my legs around his waist, angles his hips and plunges into me, again and again.

I can't stop myself from holding on to his broad shoulders, from burying my teeth into his shoulder, from groaning, moaning his name, and letting the slickness flow out to welcome him as his knot locks into place.

His groan echoes over the sound of the shower and he pours his very essence into me.

We stay that way, joined up until the water runs cold.

Then he flicks off the shower and, with him still inside me, steps out of the stall. He grabs a towel and covers me with it, running it over my back, my hair.

I cling to him, refusing to open my eyes, letting the tiredness tug me under, allowing him to care for me again. Knowing I must protest. Knowing I will take every last drop of concern he shows me, and hating myself anyway.

This time when sleep claims me, I embrace it just as I embrace the monster to whose chest I cling as I burrow into it.

When I wake, I am alone in bed.

I watch him as he works out in a corner of the room, naked from the waist up. Seeing the light that filters through the window to frame him, lighting the honey brown of his skin, tracing the scars that mark his back, the tattoos on his arms that move with each ripple of his muscle, I realize he is not only powerful but there is a certain poetry to how he moves. A fluidity. He goes through what is clearly a morning routine...a mix of tai chi and calisthenics and yoga, which seem easy to follow but I know must take complete concentration.

Sweat glistening on his shoulders, he finally stretches out. There's a knock at the door, and the alpha I'd noticed when I'd broken into the Ascension ceremony walks in.

Zeus crosses the room and takes the tray of food from him. He shoves his considerable bulk in front of the other alpha, shutting out the room and me from sight.

They speak low enough that I cannot decipher the words. The man nods, then leaves without a glance in my direction.

When Zeus turns, his gaze locks with mine.

I expect him to command me to eat... To drink... To fuck... To sleep?

I brace myself for his touch, for him to show me again that he is more powerful, my alpha. Instead, he swaggers to the table by the window and slides the tray onto it. He slugs down half a bottle of water, then places it back on the table. He grabs up the vest that's flung over the chair and shrugs it on, then drops into the chair. Reaching for the pot of coffee, he pours himself a cup.

A tangy, bitter aroma fills the space. My nostrils twitch, and my mouth waters.

He takes a sip of the steaming liquid and his eyes close in appreciation. My stomach growls. The bastard's not going to offer it to me. I need to go there and get it for myself. I swing my feet over, looking around for clothes. There are none, except for a shirt that belongs to him. Standing, I reach for it, pull it on. It dwarfs me, and the fabric smells like him. It feels like I am wrapped up in layers of his essence. I open my mouth to protest then pause. I need him to think that I am accepting my situation. Crossing over, I slide into the chair opposite him.

"Good morning." I pour myself a cup of coffee. So fucking civil. I sound so fake even to my own ears, he's going to see right through me.

He nods at me over his cup.

Well, what do you know? He's buying my act?

His lips curve up, and the skin around his eye's crinkles. He's been expecting me to fall in with his plans all along.

I curl my fingers around the cup and very much want to fling it at him. Instead, I lower it and place it carefully on the table.

Reaching for a buttery croissant, I drop one on his plate, then slide another onto mine and break it.

"I don't trust this supplication from you." He leans back in his chair. "What is it you really want, Lucia Erasmus, Czarina of Russia. Why are you really here?"

27

Lucy

I pause with the croissant halfway to my lips, and stare at him.

Spit drools from my open mouth.

For once, all of the graces instilled in me since childhood, since I was brought up as the treasured omega in the household of the Czar of Russia, desert me. But then it has been a long time since anyone has called me by my full name. The name which I'd hoped I'd left behind when I escaped from Russia.

I'd run away from the arrangement my father had in mind for me...straight into a bond with an alpha who is much more fearsome.

Why is it that everywhere I turn there is always a man who wants to hold me down, collar me, bond to me, make me feel like I am secondary, only an omega?

'You're not an average omega...' My mother's voice echoes in my ears. *'You are a pure-born omega who carries in your blood the genes of the Russian royal family. The genes that guarantee your offspring will not only be strong but be resistant to most diseases, blessed with the ability to foresee, a kind of intuition that many would kill for.'*

And yet I hadn't foreseen my own future, that I would walk straight into this trap, have an alpha cage me, bond to me.

Or was that why I had brokered the deal with Kayden, knowing I couldn't possibly trust the Scottish alpha? Knowing it would be a trap, that he was bound to claim me? No, even before. From the time I first heard my father mention Zeus' name, talk about his prowess and how he'd taken over as General, I'd known an affinity for him right from then.

I had refused to accept it. Not until I'd walked into that grand hall and seen him and scented him and then...then there had been no turning back. I'd known then I was his.

"You…" The piece of croissant slips from my fingers and falls to the plate. "How long have you known?" I pick up the piece and pop it back into my mouth. I can't taste it, yet I force myself to bite into it, chew it, then swallow.

Zeus tilts his head and surveys me with that steady gaze.

"Your second, he told you…" I don't need to look at him to sense him nod his confirmation.

I reach for the coffee cup and drain it. And, damn it, I should be raging, or be afraid or throw a tantrum, or something. Yet all I feel is a strange calm.

I'd known it would come to this, had known inside, that from the time I'd walked into his stronghold, this confrontation was coming. Or perhaps it I'd lost every shred of feeling, of my identity, when I had gone into heat, had crawled into that bed with him and asked him to take me.

When my body had led the way forward and the rest of me had no choice but to follow.

When everything I'd learned about myself, my self-respect, my pride…all of it had been swept aside in that carnal need to mate. Because ultimately that's what I am deep inside, a female whose omega instinct will always be in the lead.

"Don't you have anything else to say for it?" His voice is low, his gaze steady. He hasn't eaten anything on his plate so far either.

And I don't know why that simple detail sticks in my head. Either he's more upset than he's letting on… Or, nope, can't be that. He had a need, he sensed me, he wanted me, he took me. There's nothing more to it than that. He can't possibly be upset about the fact that my identity was a surprise to him.

"You don't seem surprised?" I want to be as casual as him and reach for the rest of the croissant, but my stomach suddenly feels heavy, my guts lurching. I lean back and rub my forearms.

"Should I be?" He places his elbows on the table.

"Shouldn't you?" I raise my eyes and meet his gaze.

His cheekbones stand out in relief. Some of the color has faded from his face. It only makes his features look more austere, more brooding. He seems strong and powerful and formidable. Waves of tension roll off him. I sense a pulse of heat and something else… A spark of anger rolls down the mating bond; it tugs at my nerve endings. I wriggle around in my chair, trying to find a more comfortable position. I shouldn't feel so guilty, I shouldn't. I am not the one at fault. I am only trying to do right by my clan, aren't I? Then why does his very presence make me feel like I tried to pull a fast one on him? That I lied to him?

"I did not…" Only when I hear the words aloud do I realize I have spoken.

He angles his head. His eyes darken into flints of ice. So cold. So terrifying.

He can be far more formidable than he's alluded to.

He'd taken me against my will and yet he'd also cared for me. He'd made sure to rut me through the cycle, had never hit me or abused me. Why am I making excuses for this monster? It still doesn't negate the fact that he'd killed some of his own men, taken me from the court to his room, and he's kept me here since.

"You were saying?" His fingers drum next to his plate. Fingers with clean-cut nails, long, lean fingers that have been inside me, that have known exactly which part of me to press against, which part to arouse and bring to climax.

My belly cramps, and I clench my thighs tighter. No, no… I can't be turned on by just thinking of everything he's done to me. And yet there is no mistaking the moisture that dampens between my thighs, that makes the shirttails stick to my underside.

He stiffens; his big shoulders bunch. His nostrils flare. The beast knows that I am turned on.

"It seems even though you are past your heat cycle your body still wants me."

"I don't."

His lips curve up in a smirk. "The sweet musk of your arousal says otherwise."

Hearing the words only turns me on further. A moan ripples up my throat, and I bite down on my lower lip to stifle it. "You shouldn't say such things aloud," I mumble, and heat flushes my cheeks.

His gaze widens. He watches me from under hooded eyelashes.

A spurt of heat tugs at my lower belly and I look away. I can't meet his eyes, not without giving away how much I am feeling right now. And it's lust, only lust.

The cord trembles against my rib cage, unfurling, sending a pulse of such need shooting down to my core. "Ah hell!" I huff out a breath.

There's a low chuckle from him.

Bet if I look up I'll see a smirk tugging at his lips. The one that draws attention to his mouth, that makes me want to rake my fingers through his hair and drag his face down to nestle between my legs. I squeeze my thighs together. "It can't go on like this."

"Like what?"

"Like every time we have a conversation or if we are in the same space, there is this need to…to…"

"Fuck?" His voice is rough.

Sweat beads my palms. My toes curl. I squeeze my eyes shut, and try to block the sight of him from my head. That only heightens my other senses. My skin tightens. The hair on my forearms rise.

I sense his big body shift. Feel the heat roll off him and know he's crouched down in front of me. His legs brush mine and I try to slide back in my seat, but he only shifts his bulk in synchrony with me.

"Oh, what the hell are you playing at?" My eyelids fly open. Mistake. He's so close now, too close. He's within touching distance. The skin around his eyes tightens. A pulse tics at his temples. That complex woodsy scent of his bleeds into the air. Images of his hands on me, his lips on my mouth, of how hard he felt inside me. How good. How right. All of it crashes over me.

The force of his personality is a living breathing thing in the room. It pushes down on my chest, squeezing my rib cage. My shoulders hunch. "Don't." My voice breaks. That familiar ball of emotion is heavy in my throat. "Not like this." I ball my fingers into fists. My lips tremble.

His gaze falls to my mouth. His breath grows rougher.

He leans in close and the heat from his body slams into me. Dense clouds of warmth swirl over me, and sweat breaks out on my brow. Then, as I think that he's going to pull me up—or worse…or better still, drag me to the floor, push aside my shirt, and take me right there—he moves.

28

Zeus

I am so close to her that I can see the little creases around her eyes. I can see the pores on her skin, the freckles on her nose, the creamy expanse of her throat; I want to lean in and touch to remind myself she is as soft as I remember her to be. Then her throat moves as she swallows. Nervousness and fear come off her in waves.

And that stops me.

When I had dragged her here and fucked her... It wasn't completely against her will, for she had all but begged me to take her, but she was also in the high of her heat cycle then, had not been in her right mind, and her body had needed me. But now?

Her gaze is clear even as those green eyes burn with desire. Her body trembles. The sugary scent of her arousal fills the air. She presses her bare toes into the floor. Every part of her is eager for me, and yet she holds back.

"Don't be afraid."

She starts at my voice, her gaze flying to my face.

Her pupils have dilated again. She is more aroused than she realizes. A yearning flows to me down the mating bond.

It tugs at me, pleads with me to take her, yet I sense a resistance. A reluctance to give herself to me. I could overpower her and take her...but... No. I rise to my feet so fast that she gasps and pulls back into the chair. And she's not meek—at the height of her heat cycle she fought me, she wanted me, but didn't want to give in to me. It was only when the hormones had overridden every other part of her rational mind had she asked me to take her.

I feel a grudging respect for that, though I shouldn't.

I know then that I can't stop at seducing her into giving me what I want, and that only turns me on even more.

The hardness of my arousal strains against my pants. Yeah, like her, my body, too, has a mind of its own. Given a choice, I'd drag her to my bed, and then proceed to mate with her over and over again until I'd marked her completely. I'd own her such that she'll never again refuse me, that she'll never again be scared of me.

Why is it so important that she comes to me of her own accord? That she wants me as much as I want her? That she accepts the mating bond?

"How long can you resist?" I take a step back.

She stares. Color rushes to her cheeks. She swallows. "You will be surprised. Remember, I was a virgin all these years. I managed to see through many heat cycles on my own, without asking the first alpha to cross my path to take me."

"And yet you did." I smirk, my lips pulling up at the sides. I sound like I am gloating, and I am. It is the truth, after all. "You did ask me to take you. The alpha who rescued you from a room full of marauders."

"And yet, you weren't careful with me either." Her hand flies to the shredded, still-healing marks on the side of her neck.

I angle my head and survey my handiwork. Satisfaction curves my lips up in a smile. "No. I mated you."

"Why?" She shoves back her hair so the strands float around her shoulders. "You could have rutted me through the heat cycle, could have taken all you wanted from me and then let me go."

"But you see that wasn't my plan."

"You didn't know who I was then, did you?" Her body stills, and she stares at me

"I didn't," I agree and lean back on my heels. When did this entire conversation change tack? Why is it that she always refuses to follow my lead?

With my men, I tell them what to do, and they bow and scrape to please me. They follow my command.

Except Ethan who has a mind of his own. Which is why I respect him…which is why my admiration for her ticks up a notch. "You are no ordinary omega, Lucia."

"Lucy." She folds her arms over her chest and thrusts out her chin in a gesture I am beginning to recognize.

"You know why I brought you here, Lucy. I intend to keep you here for as long as it takes."

"As long as what…?" Her lips tremble.

I want to go to her and soothe her, and yet a part of me says if I do that I'll be lost. That I'll give her the power if I do so, and then what? Would that be so bad?

I pace.

When I'd mated her, my only thought was that she was mine, that she belonged to me.

What I hadn't counted on was for the mating bond to go both ways. That I belong to her as much as she does to me.

And I want to tell her that, but something in me refuses.

I can't.

I am here in this palace for one reason only. To destroy the legacy of the man who had shown my mother no mercy.

Her gaze bores into me.

The tension grows in the room, filling the space, mixed with that edge of sexual need that always seems to be there between us. That will never go away no matter how many times I mate her.

"Answer me," she says, her voice low but firm.

"I intend to keep you here for as long as it takes for you to acknowledge who I am."

"Who are you?"

"Your mate."

29

Lucy

I hear his voice as if from a distance. See his face set in an expression of determination. His jaw firms. A nerve ticks at his temple.

His chest planes ripple under his dark skin, and all I can think of is going to him, dragging my fingernails over his chest and marking him. Then, throwing myself at him and asking him to take me over and over again until I reach that space where all that remains is that bare essence of my soul — a naked need, a burning desire to be part of something.

To be joined to him in a way that I have never been to anyone else and never will be again. And that thought is a shock.

But is it, is it really? When I'd known from the time I'd set foot in this palace that there would be only one logical conclusion. That I was going to be taken and knotted, and not by any alpha, but by the most powerful of all of them. And inside I'd been ready. More than ready. Maybe it was that genetic superiority in me that came from being part of the royal family of Russia that expected to only be united with a bloodline that was different from the norm.

Which was what my father had intended for me, with the alliance he had forged with the leader of the Vikings. I had turned my back on that and run away…straight to a fate that was apparently not very different.

"Why me? Why choose me as your mate?" A shudder of nervousness runs down my spine. The hair on my neck prickles and stands up. It shouldn't be important to hear his answer. It shouldn't matter what his reasons were to bond with me. And yet it is. Something primal inside me insists that I force him to admit what I'd already sensed. "Tell me." I hold his glowing blue gaze.

A myriad of expressions flit across his face. For a second, I sense that vulnerability that I thought I'd touched, that I'd felt when he was deep inside me, when he'd insisted that I say his name.

It is then that I realize that behind that charade he projects to the world he is as lonely as me...and I am sure he is going to finally tell me something that is real, that matters.

Something that will give me a reason to push aside everything else that binds me to the outside world and gives me the space to finally be myself, to accept the bond that tugs and pulls at my gut and is worming its way into my soul.

He straightens his spine.

His shoulders stiffen.

His features form into a mask of indifference. Once more he is the General, the leader of the insurgents, the alpha who killed his own father and took over.

"Because I need a mate by my side, to win the respect of my followers. To show the old guard that I am serious in my claim to being their leader. To cement my position of power."

"So it is to further your own needs?"

"Obviously." He angles his head.

His gaze narrows and he searches my face. Does he expect me to react with surprise? Or perhaps he wants to see some other emotion; one that will set right everything that has happened.

"No." I gulp. Is all of this a ploy for progeny? My palms fly to my belly, and I want to tear them away and tuck them at my sides; but I don't.

"Yes." His voice is soft but firm. "I want to control, command, dominate and use you."

My nerve endings stretch. My core trembles, and I fight the need to cover myself. To throw myself at him and ask him to follow through on his words.

Then, "I want to touch you, hold you, kiss you, and protect you." He frowns as if his words puzzle him. "To keep you safe so that someday you may carry my child." His gaze drops to my stomach and stays there.

His voice cuts through the thoughts skittering in my head. A child. Someone of my own. Someone born of my own flesh and blood. It pulls at that nurturer I've hidden deep inside of myself, that I've tried to drown out all of these years under the voice of rebelliousness, under the need to be independent.

And I am still all of that.

Only, I am also an omega. A fierce provider, someone who was born to procreate. And the thought doesn't fill me with horror. Not even the fact that it is this monster...this alpha who could have already impregnated me, and that he'd done it without sharing his intentions with me. That he'd done it in a cold, calculated manner. All of it...he'd planned all of it. I sink against the back of the chair. "You'd been looking for an omega for this reason."

"Not any omega, but one of superior breeding to ensure my future generations can weather everything that the future is going to bring. Imagine my surprise when you sweep right into my clutches? One sniff of your scent and I knew your genes were exemplary. Learning that you came from the royal family of Russia only sweetened the deal further. And, of course, then there is your cunt." His gaze slides down to the apex of my thighs.

I resist the urge to squeeze my legs shut. Try to pretend that hearing him talk about that part of me is not making my flesh weep with need. That his gaze sweeping over me does not encourage moisture to trickle from my core.

"Your sweet pussy that made it abundantly clear that it ached for me." He raises his gaze to my face.

Those molten eyes deepen until they seem to be almost clear pools of spring water.

A mirror in which I can see myself reflected.

One that I want to shatter, but which I know is going to tear me apart instead. My stomach twists.

"I don't want you." I force myself to keep my features straight, to keep all emotions from showing on my face. To clamp down on the lust that pushes at me and thumps at my temples. "I don't want you…" I shake my head. "I don't."

"So you keep saying."

His jaw firms, and I am sure he is going to close the distance between us and take me and throw me on the bed and bury himself in me. And I want him, too… with every fiber of my being. I tense my body, grip my forearms so my nails dig into my skin. My toes scrunch into the floor, and I wait…and…he swivels on his heels and stalks to the door.

I watch, not sure what's happening.

A part of me already aches that he is leaving. While my core throbs with unfulfilled lust and my lower belly pulses with readiness, my mind says this is the right thing, that he did not force himself on me. That he did not seduce me to give in to him. There's a ball of emotion in my chest that's growing larger by the second. The breath shudders out of me.

He pauses with his fingers on the door handle.

Every part of me tenses up again.

He turns and fixes that glorious blue gaze on me. "When you face up to the fact that this is not one-sided, that you want me, that you need me to break you, that you revel in it, that more than that, you are but this…an omega who wants every depraved thing that only me, only your alpha, can give you. That only I, Zeus, can fulfill you. When you finally accept that and ask me to rut you…only then will I mate you again." He shoves open the door, which slams shut behind him.

30

Zeus

I'd walked out of there and that was not what I had intended. I'd wanted to try to be civil, to stay with her, make sure she was okay after the last few days. And that thought itself is so unnatural. What does it matter how she feels? She is my hostage. The daughter of an enemy who'd walked into my palace with the express need to hurt me. Why did she agree to do that?

I'd never bothered to ask her of her intentions.

I didn't need to.

The look on her face when I had called her out on her own identity was proof enough. Besides, I am judge, jury, and executioner. I don't need to explain my decisions to anyone, and certainly not to an omega.

And yet that part of me that seems to come alive when I'm around her, insists that I give her the benefit of the doubt.

Why is it that the sight of her green eyes, wide and with tears shimmering in them, haunts me? That scent of hers, that familiar, honeyed, sugary essence clings to my every pore, tugging at my nerves, while the mating cord in my chest thrums with discomfort.

A feeling of sadness seeps through the bond. She is hurt and lonely, my omega.

Well, she deserves it. Doesn't she? She'd known what she was getting into when she'd flounced into my lair. Surely, she hadn't thought I'd go easy on her. She couldn't have possibly known that I'd spare her...and yet something inside me insists I should have treated her with care.

That I should have asked her first, given her a chance to defend herself. Right... Next, I'll be asking her permission before I mate her. I have already done that...in a sense. I'd told her I was going to wait until she came to me. That until she really wants me, I won't take her again. Fuck this! I am losing my mind and all over a timid omega, over a pair of green eyes that haunt my soul, over a sweet cunt that grasps my shaft and milks it as if it has been designed for me. Whose womb throbs in readiness, and I know that she is the one who is meant to birth my offspring. Did I just think that? Am I am waxing poetic about her…? Do I still have my balls? No fucking way am I letting a female get the better of me.

Striding out of the palace into the courtyard, I stop at where my troops are practicing.

"So our mighty leader arrives," the hulking alpha lurking in the corner of the courtyard drawls. "I take it you found the omega satisfactory? Given we haven't seen you here for a few days. Most unlike you, mighty Zeus, the Bastard of the East End."

I swerve toward him.

Jerome sniggers, then the fool saunters out into the center of the court to stop in front of me. "Yet by the glowering darkness on your face it seems perhaps she is not to your satisfaction? Care to pass her over perhaps? Maybe what she needs is a real male to satisfy her."

Blood thunders in my temples, and red sparks flash in front of my eyes. My fingers twitch, and the next second, I find myself hauling Jerome up in the air, his legs suspended off the ground. A fight is exactly what I need, and this…this sniveling excuse for a man will do quite nicely for getting his head pounded into the wall.

I stalk toward the wall, carrying him along with me, then slam his head against the hard surface, again and again.

Blood sprays out, and bits of his flesh fall to the ground.

There is the sickening sound of his skull cracking, but I don't stop. All I can think of is no one dares talk about her like that in front of me. No one dare look at her again. "She is mine," I roar. "Mine." I slam the man's head into the wall with such force that it flattens all the way down to his neck. His body grows limp, and I throw the irritating burden to the side. Turning, I pound my chest. "Anyone else?"

The soldiers have formed a wide circle around me. On their faces I see fear, desperation, also resignation. What's missing is respect. What I've craved from the beginning.

The need to redeem myself in front of the people who've made me their leader.

I've wanted this, craved this power since I was five and had caught a glimpse of my father sparring with his troops right here in this courtyard. And yet every time I'd tried to live up to his expectations, tried to live up to my own dreams, I have failed. The only thing left for me is to destroy this town and show them once and for all who is the most powerful alpha.

No one meets my gaze, except Solomon who stands there, eyes narrowed, a look of understanding on his face. I glance away.

Ethan steps forward. "Want to take on someone your own size, Alpha?"

"You have a death wish, Second?" I crack my neck from side to side. Truth is, that's exactly what I need. A chance to pit my skills against someone who can hold his own, who will challenge me, push me, take my mind off the annoying, beautiful, alluring woman whose thoughts send a pulse of desire shooting to my groin. Yet who I've sworn not to touch, not until she asks for me to take her.

Ethan's lips pull up in the semblance of a smile. He has his armor on already. He holds up his sword and takes position.

My gaze falls to it. "Barehanded. No weapons."

The color slides from his face. A nerve ticks at his temple.

He is unsure of how he'll fare against me without his favorite weapon. Good. When I was running wild on the streets of the East End, I had no access to fine weapons. All I had were my wits and my bare fists. Fighting freehand is what I still excel at. No one has defeated me, ever. Many have tried and been hurt.

The same thoughts must have run through Ethan's mind, for he nods and hands his sword to Solomon.

He shrugs off his armor and lets it fall to the ground.

I take off my vest and fling it aside.

We walk to the center of the courtyard and face each other.

The heat of the morning sun pours over us. People begin to stream onto the balconies above us.

I bend my knees, raise my fists, and am about to charge forward, when a soldier runs into the courtyard.

"The omega. She's gone."

31

Lucy

The shirt I wear, *his* shirt, whips around my thighs. Reaching the other end of the building, I hear the shouts as soldiers pursue me.

I still can't believe he'd left the suite without locking it behind him, that there had been no guard on duty. Zeus was crude and an alpha-hole, but he wasn't sloppy. Had he done this deliberately?

Yet, this is too good an opportunity, and I have to take it, even if it means being caught and punished. I have nothing to lose.

The sound of footsteps racing in pursuit thunders, and blood thuds at my temples; my pulse beats so fast that I feel dizzy, yet I keep going.

I run through the gardens, to where the scent of the river floats to me. A cry breaks out behind me, and I pick up my pace.

My feet skid on the stones, and pain rips up my legs. I bite my lip to hold back my groans. Stumbling over the uneven ground I reach the parapet wall and peer over the side. The water of the Thames churns below.

My heart pounds. A chuckle rips out. I thought I was so clever to escape. Thought I would be brave enough to jump and leave the alpha behind.

The mating bond in my chest throbs and a shudder of desire races down my spine. My throat closes. No. No. This is not happening. I cannot be bonded so closely to him that he can anticipate my fears, my uncertainty, even predict what I am going to do next. Once more I glance over the parapet at the river.

My head swims, and a moan emerges from my mouth.

I grab the platform of the parapet. Can I do it? Can I take this final step? Or am I forever fated to be here, bonded to a man I know nothing about? Who knows my identity? Who probably suspects that I had an ulterior motive to have come this far?

He'd found out my real identity but he still doesn't know the real reason I am here. This is my chance. This.

My heart stutters. The mating bond pushes against my chest. He's coming, he is. I don't need to look over my shoulder to sense his presence.

"Lucia."

His voice shivers over my skin. The mating bond stretches and pulls at me to turn around. I squeeze my eyes shut.

"Don't…don't come closer or…" Pain floods down the mating bond.

The fear that comes down the connection almost blinds me. It also confuses me. He can't be afraid for me. He doesn't care for me. But he'd walked away from me that morning and given me a choice. In this instant I know I've made a mistake. I've found the one person who finally recognizes what I am inside. Not any omega. Not a meek female. Not only a submissive. Someone who is his equal. Someone he won't treat as another breeder, but one who he'll want to please. He'd grabbed me from that room full of alphas, but he'd actually saved me from them. He'd taken me for himself, yet each time he'd also made sure to pleasure me. And his touch…his feel… his caresses. Desire tugs my groin, and slick gathers and drips from my core.

"I am not going anywhere, Lucia."

Another pulse of heat trickles down the bond. There's a yearning there. A need to fulfill, to take care of me that I had refused to accept. And now? It's too late, it is. I turn to him.

"But I am." I smile at him. Tears prick my eyes.

"Wait." He flings out his hand and closes the distance between us.

I push back against the wall. The breath catches in my throat. My hands slide on the parapet, and then I am falling, falling. I think I scream, but I am not sure. The wind gushes past me so fiercely, so strong that my eardrums seem to rupture. Then there is only silence and pain that rips through me as I hit the surface of the water and sink under.

32

Zeus

"No!" My heart slams against my rib cage, and I race toward the parapet. I throw my leg over the wall, but arms seize me and yank me back. "Let me go," I roar at the intruder.

I scan the river, searching for her. There is only the churning, swirling mass of water that is the treacherous surface of the Thames.

I can't see her.

There's no sign of her.

Another pulse of worry twists my guts. My stomach lurches, and my breath comes out in pants. My vision narrows. The hair on my skin pops. I grab the arms that restrain me and rip them off of me, then leap for the wall and jump over the side.

Keeping my arms close to my body, I hit the water and go through. Opening my eyes underwater, I look for her. Nothing. I don't see anything. There is a ball of fire in my chest, squeezing my heart. I fall inside myself and reach for the mating bond and find it quiet.

So quiet.

Fear shudders down my spine. Surfacing up for another gulp of air, I then dive below, my gaze scanning the space. And again. My arms are so tired, legs so heavy I find the current overpowering me. Know I must swim to the riverbank, else I'll likely drown, too.

Closing my eyes, I reach for the bond and stretch my consciousness out through it, searching, sensing, and all I find is white.

A silent whiteness so blank it could be a canvas that will never be painted on.

My guts twist, my stomach churns, but I can't give up. How can I when the one thing that brought the color into my life is gone? Darkness closes in on me, the water tugs me down, and I try to push back, knowing I can't give in to the tiredness, cannot let myself fall.

Everything I've faced to come this far seems to hit me. Images of my father, my mother...my followers, the need to destroy the city...all of it is chased away, and all there is, is her.

The sugary scent of her slick, the softness of her skin, the brilliant green of her eyes when she is aroused, the fear that rippled through her, the first time I'd seen her, her fighting me...submitting to me... The mating cord twinges, once, so faint I should have missed it except I've been waiting, waiting for that.

My eyelids fly open, and I aim for the faint light that filters through the waves, sinking through the green depths, the color so like her eyes. I am going to see again. I will see her safe, I will find her, rescue her, bring her back, and when I do, I am never letting her go. Never again. I push back strongly and rise to the surface. When I break through, my lungs expand, and I draw in huge gulps of air.

"Zeus."

I look to the other side to see Ethan waiting for me.

It was him who'd tried to hold me back from jumping; no one else would have dared. Only he has the guts to face me, and I want to rage at him for trying to hold me back. Yet, when he wades out to grab my arm and hauls me to the shore, I don't shake him off.

I am too tired, too overwrought, too anguished to think of anything else but her.

Reaching land, I keep walking, Ethan at my heels.

He touches my shoulder. "We'll find her, Z."

I stiffen, then jerk my chin.

Notice I don't admonish him for reassuring me. Me? The alpha who's never needed reassurances, who'd never have accepted comfort from another, hell, who'd never have revealed his vulnerabilities to himself let alone the world—that alpha; he's the man I used to be. I set my jaw and stalk forward. I am changing and there's not a damned thing I can do about it. It's her fault. The damned omega is softening me up. I'd almost flung myself into the river without caring for my life. I've never put myself on the line for anyone else, for no one except my mother. "Alert the troops, send out search parties, alert the guards along the river."

"Now you insult me."

I turn and narrow my eyes at him. "Fucking Second," I snarl without heat. "Always one step ahead of me."

He meets my gaze. "Of course, you'll want to be part of the search party and head out yourself?"

I angle my head, not bothering to reply.

When I reach the bridge leading away from the palace, Solomon is already there with my armor.

I shrug into my suit. "Put out a reward."

"Already done—"

"A million quid."

There's silence. I shoot him a sideways glance, "Stop trying to second-guess me...*Second*." I peel my lips back at Ethan.

His lips firm. "Of course, your omega is worth that and more."

"Another million if she is found unwounded. I want her unhurt, if so much as a hair on her head is touched I'll set waste to this city, you understand?"

His features are frozen, all the expression wiped off his face.

He's going to protest that we are stretching our already lean financial resources to find a woman, I wait for him to say it, just so I can pick a fight with him, put him in his place. One excuse that's all I am gonna need to lay into this motherfucker. My fists clench.

Ethan's gaze narrows, then he angles his head, "Of course, General."

Bloody fucking hell! It seems I don't need to explain to him exactly how much she's come to mean to me.

Reaching the bridge, I slide into the armored car which Sol has brought around for me.

"She could be dead..." Ethan gets in the front next to me.

Sol takes the back seat.

I snarl, "She isn't." I start the armored vehicle and roar up the bridge.

"How do you know?" Ethan scratches his chin. "Ah, the mating bond."

"You can sense her?" Solomon leans forward.

I shoot him a glance in the rearview mirror and he pales, then folds his arms over his chest.

Ethan turns to me, "You know what this means, right?" His voice is quiet.

"I am sure you are going to tell me," I grit my teeth.

I shouldn't allow this degree of familiarity from him, but whatever.

We are going to search for her, and yet the fact that we are under so much pressure has brought down any walls there may have been between us.

There's silence in the car.

When it has continued long enough, I curl my lips. "Say it fucking already."

"It means"—he pauses for effect and turns to Sol—"he is aware of her through the bond. He can track her through the connection. It also means if one of them dies—"

I set my jaw. "The other dies, too."

33

Lucy

I wake up with a gasp, sitting up so fast that the world spins around me. I am not sure where I am. The bed is rough under me, not as rough as some of the places I've slept, but different to the silks of the bed that I'd become accustomed to over the last few days...or is it weeks?

In Zeus' stronghold, I'd lost track of time, and suddenly I can't wait to see the outside world. One look...one glance to see where I am, enough to get my bearings. I swing my legs over, and when my feet touch the floor a pain shoots up my legs. My guts churn, and bending over, I try to retch, managing only to dry heave.

Footsteps thud toward me, and before I can straighten, hands grasp my shoulders, holding me as I cough.

The acidic taste of bile is in my nose, crowding in on my throat, and I rest my forehead against my knees.

I feel lifeless, like everything in me has been brushed out, like every part of me has been broken and then put back together again, only whatever has been formed now is something different, a body with which I am not quite familiar. I feel... discombobulated. Where did that word come from? My English tutor who had taught me in Russia, was from London, but her accent had been different to his.

"Zeus." I breathe out his name, and the sound of my voice echoes hollowly in my ears.

The person holding me urges me to sit up. Soft hands pull back the hair from my face. A pair of warm brown eyes peer into mine. "You need to lie back, you are hurt, and your feet are not in great shape," the woman says.

I glance down and wince. My feet are dirty, toenails dark around the corners. I don't need to look at the underside to know they are scratched and bruised.

There's blood smeared on the floor.

The scent of copper is suddenly too intense for me. My stomach twists; my chest heaves. "I am going to be sick again."

The woman nods and springs up, dragging me up with her. She pulls me along to the bathroom. Every step I take hurts, but I'd rather bear the pain than be sick all over the floor.

The bathroom tiles are cool under my feet, and then I am doubled over the ceramic bowl in the corner.

I hold on to the rim and puke until it feels as if I've coughed up every single thing I've eaten in the last week. By the time I collapse back onto the floor, sweat beads my forehead. My chest heaves, and I can't feel my legs or my hands for that matter.

A cold towel is pressed to my forehead, and I moan my appreciation. She holds it there with one hand, then offers me a glass of water. I try to take it from her, but my hands are shaking so much the water splashes all over the long shirt I have on. The mating bond coiled against my rib cage throbs, sending a pulse of pain shooting down my spine. I rub the skin over my chest. My gaze darts to the woman.

"You're bonded to an alpha." It's a statement, not a question.

I frown. "How can you tell?"

She jerks her chin toward the wound on the side of my neck. Only then do I become aware that it's bleeding again. My entire side screams with pain, and there are splotches of blood over the cloth covering my chest. "A shower. I need a shower."

"You are too weak—"

"Please." I let the glass slide from my fingers so it falls to the floor and rolls away. Reaching out, I grasp her arm.

She tosses her dark-brown hair over her shoulder. Her jaw hardens, and those warm eyes glow with understanding. "Let's get you up."

She rises and helps me to my feet.

She's taller than me. Muscles weave across her arms. She's wearing dark pants and a shirt. There's a whiff of dominance around her that marks her out as alpha...almost.

Except she isn't. The delicate features of her face, her soft touch as she staggers with me to the shower, the fact that she took me in... The concern that rolls off her says she must be omega.

"How?" I force the word through a throat that feels that it's been sliced with knives.

"How do I manage to survive as an omega in a city full of alphas gone rogue?" One side of her lips twists. "We have much to catch up on...but first." She helps me into the shower, turns on the warm water.

Then assists me in taking off my shirt and props me up. She proceeds to bathe the mating wound which has softened and oozes pus and blood under the hot water. By the time she helps me back into the bedroom and helps me pull on a T-shirt and drawstring pajama bottoms, I am shivering and hot at the same time.

My chest hurts. The mating cord whines and throbs, and there is a pounding at the back of my eyes that feels like it's going to rip through my brain.

I don't protest as she half carries me to her bed and shoves me under the covers.

The bed smells of that strange alpha-omega confluence. How the hell had she managed that? Most omegas yearn, to be born a beta, or better still an alpha or at least find a way to hide their smell. While this woman hasn't completely succeeded, her scent is confusing enough to buy precious seconds by throwing an alpha off track. Enough to give you time to escape in a struggle. A few seconds, that was all it took for him to capture me; to make me his.

She tugs the blankets all the way up to my chin. "Sleep, recover, and we'll talk more about what brought you here and how we can help each other."

Something at the edge of my consciousness prickles at that. "Help each other? How can we?" I mumble.

She runs a cloth that smells of something fragrant, something that slides into my blood, calming the mating bond. Darkness tugs at the edges of my vision and I slide under.

When I wake again, there is a man in the room. "Zeus?" I crack open my eyelids.

The shape moves. The light shines over his face, a lean face so handsome it's unmistakable.

Indigo eyes glow at me. So familiar, yet different. His lips pull back in a smile that is so pleasant it coerces you to trust him. I am not fooled.

He's the predator here in this room, but I am done with being prey.

I try to rise, and the room spins around me. My heart thuds against my rib cage. This can't be happening. I didn't just escape one alpha only to be cornered by another.

The same woman who'd taken care of me earlier moves to stand next to him. "You promised you wouldn't shake her composure, brother."

"Brother?" I groan out the word, then swallow down the dryness in my throat and ask the question I should have asked earlier. "Who…who are you?"

Silly, trusting me.

I'd never stopped believing in the kindness of strangers. I'd simply accepted her help, and now here I am facing the biggest enemy of all. Kayden. Alpha of the Scots.

He rises to his feet. He's almost as tall as Zeus.

I'll always measure any man I meet against the prowess of my own alpha.

My alpha? Where did that thought come from? Why do I still think of him as mine?

I try to sit up, but my arms can't take my weight. The woman who hasn't yet told me her name sits on the bed and supports me. I pull away from her, but my movements are weak.

"I'm sorry I had to drug you, but it was the only way to make sure that you'd stay."

"And I thought I could trust you."

"It was for your own good, I promise, Lucy."

"Who are you? How do you know my name?"

"Reena Kane. I am Kayden's sister."

"You called him here?" I cough. My pulse thuds in my temples. How do I evade Kayden? Assuming I did manage to escape, where would I go?

By now Zeus has alerted his troops and is no doubt searching for me. He may already be on his way to the city. My mating cord twinges and unfurls, insisting that Zeus won't do me any harm.

Why would my very consciousness already be one with him?

Why does my instinct tell me to trust him…more than the man sitting opposite me?

The man who'd promised to help me, who'd sheltered my family?

"Where are the other omegas?" I focus my gaze on him, ignoring the way his figure weaves in and out of the picture in front of me.

"They are safe and waiting for you."

"Safe?" I chuckle and cough again.

Reena rubs my back, and once more I try to sidle away from her. She lets me move out of her grasp, and I fall back against the pillows. My shoulders shake with the effort, and sweat beads my brow.

"Well, by the looks of what happened, they are safer where they are at any rate." Kayden takes a step forward.

The alpha scent of his presence grates on my nerves. This is not the man I want. This presence is foreign, intrusive. It is hurtful to me, to what I could one day carry inside of me.

My throat closes.

Zeus had wanted to impregnate me. Could that have happened already? The mating cord thrums with emotions, and tears well up in my eyes. There's passion and joy and a need to survive that ebbs and flows inside me. I've never felt like this before. Helpless and yet also hopeful.

Knowing he will come to me.

If I let him find me, I won't be able to resist him. I'd let him take me again and again, and I'd enjoy every second of it even as I hate myself. It's inevitable that I fall pregnant if I am not already.

I cannot let an alpha who took advantage of my heat cycle to bond with me, also plant his seed in me.

I will not let any child of mine grow up in the shadow of the man who is so confused he doesn't even know himself.

I must not let him near me again.

The mating cord pulses against my rib cage, insisting that I am wrong. But I shove it aside.

"Kayden." I push back on the bed and this time sit up without any help. "Why are you here?"

"Isn't that obvious? You want the safety of the omegas. I want this city."

"Isn't there any other way but to kill Zeus?" The moment the words are out, I know it's a mistake.

Kayden's features form into a mask. He's so good at hiding his emotions; his face is inscrutable. Unlike Zeus, who as much as he tries to keep his feelings under control, I can always sense them lying there under the surface. Waiting for me, calling to me, aching…for me. The mating cord whines and shivers. A shudder runs down my body.

"You are bonded to him." Kayden angles his head. "You care for him."

My breath catches in my chest. I want to deny it, but from the silence in the room, the way that Kayden stares at me, the way Reena moves away from me, her nostrils flaring as she sniffs me, the realization that Kayden is right dawns on her face, and I know it's too late.

"So it is him? He is the alpha you are bonded to." Reena wrings her fingers together, and in this moment it's clear she is much more omega than alpha.

"Are you going to give me up to him?" I glance from Reena to Kayden.

His lips peel back in a smile. "Give you up? Hell no." He stalks to the seat and slides back into it, legs parted, chest planes wide, hands gripping the arms of the chair and dwarfing it. "You are bait, sweetheart. The alpha is hunting his mate, and when he gets to you, guess who will be waiting for him?"

34

Zeus

I wake up with my heart pounding. Sweat drips down my back so my vest is stuck to it. There is a feeling of impending darkness, of something so heavy in my chest that it seems to get larger by the minute.

I swing my legs over the side of the bed and stay there, panting. My heart stutters, and I rub my chest.

The beats are erratic. There is a sense of impending gloom. Of something coming at me, something more sinister than anything I've faced before. I hang my head forward, grip my knees, and will myself to breathe. One breath, two breaths, slowly, in and out. Focus, I must focus. The mating cord in my chest strains and a groan rips out of me.

My scalp prickles and I wipe my damp palms on the sheet covering the bed. I know it's her emotions I am feeling. She's afraid.

When I'd taken her, I had only meant to bind her to me. My only thought had been to ensure that I had someone who belonged to me. Not to the city, not to my men…not to the sense of duty that despite everything I do, I carry with me.

Perhaps I am my father's son more than I'd known. Perhaps hidden somewhere inside is this need to do right by the city, and I don't understand where it is coming from.

This sudden attack of conscience that's forcing me awake in the middle of the night.

This need to keep my omega safe.

My Lucia…it is because of her that I am being tainted. Her thoughts, her emotions, her idealistic need to do good by all, it's dripping into me. Creeping in my subconscious. The mating cord binds her to me, but it also ties me to her. It's influencing me in ways I cannot begin to understand.

Fear shudders down my spine, and helplessness…and mixed with it is this urgency. Is she trying to get to me, to warn me away?

My shoulders bunch.

I raise my head, firm my thighs, and push myself up on my feet. I walk out of the door of the bedroom in the warehouse that I've kept in the city. Another relic of my father's days. He'd kept this house incognito in order to be able to go about the city without being recognized.

One of the traditions that I decided to continue.

I stagger into the living room to find Ethan walking in from the other room.

Solomon, who's been keeping watch in a chair by the window, rises to his feet. "What are the two of you doing up? It's only four a.m." He yawns and scratches his chin.

"I need to go to her." I strive to keep my voice low, but it comes out harsh. I shake my head. I have to find a way to control myself. Whatever is happening to me, there's an easy explanation for it. It's normal, isn't it, when an omega is bonded to an alpha, to be aware of her emotions, to perhaps also want to take care of her?

I squeeze the bridge of my nose. Where are these thoughts coming from?

"You okay?" Ethan's voice cuts through the thoughts swirling around in my head.

"Why wouldn't I be?" I snarl out, angrier with myself for feeling this vulnerable.

It's as if the mating cord is burrowing inside my soul and ripping out all the layers I've built over the years. It's laying my emotions bare, making me feel naked and exposed, and I don't like it. Not one bit.

Walking to the table next to the surveillance equipment that Sol had been monitoring, I pick up the bottle of water and drink from it.

It does nothing to soothe the sick feeling twisting my stomach.

Pouring the rest of the water over my head, I then drop the bottle back on the table. "What's the latest? Have any of the soldiers seen anything?"

The mating cord throbs and a wave of terror engulfs me. My skin seems to burn, and there's a ball of emotion in my chest so huge that I cannot breathe.

I stumble to the window, and grabbing the sill, I shove open the pane and lean out.

It's a security risk to do that. Anyone could recognize me…which is not the issue. My own citizens aren't exactly filled with love for me. Not like I've done much to deserve their respect either. And fuck…there I go, playing the violin again.

I've never, in all these years, thought of their needs even once, about what I can do for them.

My father had done his version of the right thing. He'd flung my mother back to the East End of the city, the gutters where she'd come from.

He could have kept her, taken care of her and his son, but he hadn't cared. Not for her, not for any of the omegas. He'd only cared about his precious city…well, for the parts that are filled with the upper classes, the rich and wealthy who live in the districts closest to the palace. He'd made sure they had everything they needed. He'd turned his back on the poor. And me?

I'd gone a step further.

I'd wanted to punish the ruling classes but I'd ended up doing my worst by both the rich and the poor. It didn't matter what your class, or your status or indeed where you lived. I was an asshole to everyone alike. Everyone except her. With her, I cannot keep up this charade; it has always been nothing but a front.

Just, I've never wanted to own up to it. I cannot let her do this to me.

Being near her, in her, having her essence mixing with mine is changing me from the inside out. It's making me...more empathetic, wanting to do good for my people, but this stinking city has given me nothing but fear and pain and a start in life that I'll never be able to live down. I cannot allow myself to develop a conscience, not now.

I cannot let myself care for my people.

Cannot let the man I really am come to the surface. The one who feels duty-bound to do right by his city.

The one who wants to use his power to change the flawed system that my father had so callously imposed.

I've come too far.

Planned too long.

Lost too much.

Too much to let one omega sweep in and upset all my plans, to change me, mold me into a version who is half me...the real me who is a responsible, conscientious leader who wants to protect his people.

The kind who, no doubt, the fucking history books will love to sing about...no, that isn't me.

I am a monster, an illegitimate bastard who took great pleasure in using his power for one thing. The downfall of the bloodline that had given birth to him and given him nothing else. Nothing. This city is going to Hell. And I am going to be responsible for it. That's how I want the future to remember me.

And I intend to live up to my reputation.

Starting with her.

I am going to find her and teach her a lesson, the kind that will ensure she never dares face up to me, never dares run away from me again. The little princess of royal blood is going to be broken completely by the most nefarious bastard in all the land. Me!

The mating cord in my chest thrums and pushes against my chest, warning me I am wrong. Telling me not to do this. Pleading with me to reconsider. Nah. No way can a simple bond do that. So what if it links me to her?

So what if I am using the connection to find her. It is only a means to chain her to me. To bond her to me for now. Forever. So no one else can have her. No one except me. That's all it means.

That. Is. It.

I turn to Ethan. "It's time to move."

35

Lucy

I walk to the window and look out over the grimy city.

The buildings are all low, a relic of the past when government laws decreed that no construction would be tall enough to block the view of the parliament building from anywhere.

The same structure that the monster now uses as his base.

The same monster who had taken me, rutted me and broke my heat cycle. A trickle of slick dampens my core. I squeeze my thighs together.

He is still a monster.

He may have not fucked me against my will, still, he had taken advantage in the midst of a heat cycle when I had been desperate for any alpha's touch.

No, not any alpha…but him.

I push the thought away.

He hadn't given me a choice. He hadn't restrained himself. But then…I hadn't wanted him to either. So why are my thoughts still on him?

Why does every part of me want to go to him, to feel his touch on me, his wide palm gripping my hips as he brings me closer and lowers me down on his shaft, and again… A moan is torn out of me. There has to be a way out. I can rip the bond from my chest, break this connection so he won't be drawn to me as I am to him.

So I won't imagine that he is already somewhere in this city, getting closer, closer, closer to me.

Wanting me, missing me, yearning for me as much as I am for him.

The mating cord thrums and gnaws at me, tugs at my nerves and stretches, pushes into my chest.

My spine curves and my eyelids fly open.

My breath is coming out in gasps, and my heart is racing. Fast, so fast. My chest thrusts out, and I feel like I am being pushed forward to the tips of my feet, yanked out of my body. My very soul is fluttering inside, slamming against my skin as if my very essence wants to pour itself through the cord to him. Him. No! I curl my fingers into a fist and slam it on the wall. Pain flutters over my skin, but the wall doesn't crack.

Of course not.

Physically I am still an omega.

Still weak.

I may be fast on my feet, quick with my thoughts, know how to use my intelligence and my beauty to seduce, but I'll never be as powerful as an alpha. Did I really think I could break out of here? Out of the prison that another alpha had imposed on me?

It isn't fair that omegas have to always depend on someone else; wherever you turn, there is always someone bigger, more powerful, one step ahead of you. Someone strong enough to do the things you want to do. To reach the heights you want. Who takes what you need. I always feel like I am lacking, as if I am secondary, and the world would rather I give in, roll over, and submit...except when I am with him.

Oh, make no mistake, he wants me to submit to him...and I want him to make me. A shudder of fear laced with desire tightens my stomach. Can he sense that I am I thinking of him? Am I drawing more attention to myself? Calling him to me? I stand there yearning for him, hating myself for it, yet unable to stop the shudder of pleasure that runs down to my core. My stomach cramps in anticipation, yearning for that deep, rich fullness that only an alpha, *only he* can fill.

That feeling of utter completion that I'd felt only once when he'd covered my body with his and slammed into me again and again; that feeling of oneness as he'd bitten me and the pain had swept through me, pushing away all other thoughts except that it was me...and him...and I was his. Irrevocably, completely, fully his.

He is the monster; I am his victim. And yet he owns me, and not against my will. And that is the sad truth. Only with Zeus do I feel like I am something, that I am at the center of his world.

The city may hate him or love him. Either way, they want a piece of him.

Yet with him...I am his world.

He may deny it, may not acknowledge it, perhaps abhor the idea, but the fact that he wanted me, needed me...enough to have mated me.

The mating bond tugs and whines in my chest, yanking me forward with such force that my spine curves again.

My chest thrusts out, and my spine curves. A force that I cannot see urges me to keep going. I fling open the windowpane, shove my leg over the sill, and begin to slide forward to the muddy ground three floors below. All the time my gaze is still on the palace in the distance, across the river.

The site of my mating.

By knotting me, had he bound me not only to his body but also to his soul, to that very place where he had taken my virginity? And what will I do when I find him again? Ask him to take me back? To forgive me, and then what? I sit here, legs dangling, thoughts buzzing in my head, my vision narrowing, focusing. My thighs firm, my shoulders bunch, and I lean forward when arms grab me around my waist and yank me back. No, no, no. I fight against the restraints, rake my nails over the barriers that hold me back. I push, wriggle, bring down my head and bite, and kick out.

"Let me go, please." I hyperventilate.

"No." Reena's voice whips through my ears.

The strength in her grasp digs into my waist, and the ground recedes.

Another strong pull and I fall back into the room, to the floor. I hit my side and the breath whooshes out of me. All thoughts spill from my mind. Pain shudders through me, and I focus on that. The mating cord writhes in my chest and I hate the damned thing. Loathe it.

How can something unseen control me like that?

I am not a coward. I've never thought of taking my life no matter how rough things were in the past. And I hadn't meant to put myself in danger, not like that, and yet when I'd seen his palace, all that had mattered was that I get out of there and go to him and find him…and he wasn't even there.

The cord pushes me to get to my feet. The hair on the back of my neck rises. Every instinct tells me to get out of here and find him. I don't question how, but I know where I must go. It's the only way out.

If I want to salvage anything of myself, if I want to retain my own identity, then I need to put enough of a distance between us. I must slam down a barrier that separates me from him before his essence bleeds through me and mingles with my thoughts and I don't know who he is and who I am; before we become the kind of bonded pair that not even death can part, I know what I have to do.

I stop struggling and let my body go lax. My shoulders hunch, and I let my muscles loosen.

Reena exhales a breath. She pulls her arms from around me and moves away, pushing herself to sit. "What were you thinking?"

Her voice is disturbed and angry, and yet I also hear genuine concern. She is Kayden's sister, a man I now know I can't trust, and yet Reena is like him but also not.

She's the one who asked him not to hurt me, who tried to hold him back. And Kayden, it seems, respected her wishes and left right after that meeting. I haven't seen him since. Is that good? Or bad? Where is he? What is he scheming about now? I am not quite sure, to be honest.

I am relieved that he isn't around. It seems wrong to be in the presence of any other male, any other alpha except the one who is my own.

Except he isn't…my own.

He belongs to no one—not to me, not to this city.

The mating cord shudders and cringes inside my chest. I rub the skin over it. It shouldn't hurt so much to think of him.

To feel him flow through my blood as if his essence is already inside and mingling with mine. It should scare me to realize that I am sensing his thoughts, that I am seeing him more clearly than anyone else has. A deep loneliness bleeds down the bond, and uncertainty, and fear…so much fear. About his past, his future, about losing me. I shouldn't feel it. I don't want to feel it. It's not right. I shouldn't feel this close to a man, a monster who took me when I was at my most vulnerable, the one who bonded me before I had a say in the matter. He used my heat cycle, my need to be physically rutted through the cycle against me…a man who used my vulnerability to claim me?

Can I trust him?

Can I allow myself to see the sliver of genuine goodness I sensed somewhere deep inside him?

More than that… It is a strength, a passion, a fierce will to follow his heart, to do what is right. Except what he feels is right is not always right for the world. And I am the only one who can see it, feel it, sense it deeper than he ever has. What am I going to do about it?

Should I allow myself to draw him out, let Kayden capture him? Do I have a choice? If I don't, Kayden will kill my clan. Yet, if I lead Kayden to Zeus, if I allow Zeus to walk into the trap, Kayden will kill him, and as one half of a mated pair, my days will be numbered. Either way, only one thing is certain—I am going to die.

A calm descends over me.

That is right. A peace, an end to this existence which has become so twisted and convoluted, so entwined with the life of another who I have no desire to call my own. To whom I am becoming more attached with every passing moment.

If I kill myself first…? It is only a matter of time before Zeus dies, too.

Kayden will get what he wants. And my clan will be safe.

The more I think about it, the more I know this is the only way out. The mating cord curls on itself and anguish pours from it. Fear pounds through it, slamming into the presence at the other end, and I know Zeus can sense I have decided on a course of action.

He doesn't know what it is, but he knows already that he does not like it.

I sense his will flood down the bond. Sense him pulse reassurance, heat, a lick of fire…enough desire for my nerve endings to flare, to cramp my womb, my core moistening with need. He's not holding back, Zeus. He's trying everything possible to change my mind…from what, he can't know, but it's as if he's thrusting the very force of his will, his dominance on me to stop me from what I am doing.

Sweat breaks out on my forehead.

At the same time, moisture laces my core.

My heart pounds so fast I am sure it is going to burst out of my rib cage at any moment.

A breath wheezes out of me; my lungs seem to be unable to take in any more oxygen. Every part of my will resists Zeus' influence, even as my body insists I go to him. That I am half of him. I am nothing without him.

"No," I scream and slam my fist on the floor. The skin over my knuckles breaks, and the smell of copper is in the air. I let the pain center me.

"What is it?" Reena's voice sounds over me. She grips my arms and tries to hold me down.

"Help me," I gasp out.

The world whirls around me.

My vision wavers. If I don't see Zeus soon, feel him, scent him, lick him, and draw of him, I am going to be reduced to a blubbering mass of need that nothing and no one can fulfill. This is not what I want. Not to be bonded to someone who feels so close that they are a part of me…even as my mind, my very will, that primal, rational thinking part of me still resists. The fight is going to kill me anyway…if I let it. I didn't choose how to come into this world, but I am going to choose how to end my life…in a way that benefits those I love the most. My family.

Reena's face fills my vision. Her chin trembles, and her grip on my arms firms. "Tell me what you need."

36

Zeus

I race out and onto the streets I'd traversed as a child. The safe house is in the East End of the city. I am sure this is where my father met my mother. Neither of them mentioned it to me, but the thud of my heart, the heavy feeling in my chest, and that sinking hole in my gut confirm to me this is where the two of them had run into each other. This is where my father took her for the first time. For all I know he fucked her in the very house, in the bed where I had lain at night. My gut churns, and leaning over, I puke. I've never done this before, been so affected by the thought of my parents, been so tuned in to the plight of my mother.

I cared for my mother, protected her from hoodlums in the neighborhood when I came of age…but had always consciously blocked out all thought of how it could have been for them to be together. How it was for her to have run into him, to be attracted to him, to submit to him knowing all along he was never going to recognize her. A whore from the wrong side of town, who survived the wildness of the streets. She had enough courage to face up to the alpha who wouldn't let go of her, not until he'd had his fill of her…and yet she hadn't been able to protect her heart from him.

She'd fallen for my father, the General, had been taken in by his fine clothes, his power, his charisma, and had submitted to him. Golan never gave her the recognition she deserved. He'd never taken her for a mate, not officially.

I realize now that my mother must have begun to affect him, too. He must not have realized how much the mating bond goes both ways. He'd thought with her death he'd be rid of her influence. He hadn't bargained on how much her death would shorten his lifespan, too. He'd gotten progressively sicker, weaker after her death, and when it came to killing him, I'd eschewed the weapons and used the ways of the street.

The mighty Golan, killed by old-fashioned strangulation. Oh! The irony. I chuckle.

This scent of blood is heavy in the air, and the reek of poverty is all around me. The stench of desperation and helplessness that permeated my childhood clings to my skin, twists my insides. And I have had enough. I need to get out of here.

Pulse pounding in my temples, I swing into the armored car and set off. Sol and Ethan are following me separately. Ethan had insisted on that, and I know he is right. I owe my second a lot, not only for thinking on his feet but also for agreeing to me embarking on this harebrained mission on my own.

He'd known there was no way out.

He'd sensed how much the bond was affecting me.

He'd gleaned how much she meant to me.

And he hadn't said anything, not made a fuss, not protested. Had stepped up to the role I need of him. To agree, yet watch out for me.

Yeah, he is one smart motherfucker, and I am never going to let him know that. I am never going to share with him how much his actions and that of Sol's in following us, no questions asked, have made me feel like the lowest heel ever. I had only questioned, resisted, pushed them at every turn. Yet they are loyal to me.

Loyalty. An alien concept, that I still refuse to accept. Unlike her. The only thing I believe in is her.

I am going to get to her and claim her all over again, but it isn't for the reasons Ethan thinks. It isn't because I can't live without her. Not because every cell in my body throbs for her, not because the mating bond yanks me forward, showing me the way, unerring in its direction as it leads me through the twisting alleys, onto the broken expressways of a once proud city, and away from London... Where is she? A few miles of driving, and I smell the sea. She is headed to Dover? Why? Is she planning to leave this city? Take a ship somewhere?

My heart stutters.

My guts twist.

I press my foot on the accelerator, and the vehicle leaps ahead, almost colliding with a slow-moving caravan. I swerve around it and keep going, knowing it is going to take Ethan and Sol longer to catch up in whatever mode of transport they have decided on. Nothing is as fast as my custom-made truck, my one insistence...almost a compulsion, this need for speed and control. And dominance. Everything that had come together in one perfect pattern when I had claimed her. I hadn't thought then. I had ridden that rush, that feeling when I was inside her when her soft core had clamped its moist heat around me, tugged me in... It had been like coming home.

"Fuck." I slam the wheel with my fist and step on the accelerator. The tires squeal, and the hated countryside streams by, still green despite the fact that the rains have been failing over the years and the weather has gotten more erratic. Too hot one day, snow the other, an unpredictability that has reduced lifespans and altered genes, all in one generation. Enough for humans to be divided into alphas, betas, and the rarer omegas.

Enough for me to realize that I was meant to be the strongest alpha of them all, from the time I had taken on the beasts who had tried to rape my mother and killed them. Then sealed my future when I had taken over as General of the city.

Enough to be sure that I have to get to this omega before she does something she will regret. I will make her regret it. And I am looking forward to it.

I plan to wrap those glistening strands of her hair around my fist, yank back her head to reveal the expanse of her neck, then sink my teeth into the claiming mark to reaffirm my ownership.

The mating bond screeches with need, and fear pours down it. The heaviness in my chest is so big, so cold, I know she is in danger. I need to get to her.

My chest thrusts forward, and my breath comes in pants. The force inside me grows larger, pushing out, shoving against my rib cage. It propels me forward. To keep going and get to her before it's too late.

I veer off the road, onto the muddy path leading uphill, then that, too, fades. I keep going, through the mud and faded grass, onto the flat plateau that soars up to a cliff.

The wheels churn, and the truck's tires strain for purchase. I brake to a stop and jump out of the vehicle, not caring that the truck begins to roll back. I can't retrace my steps. I don't care about what I've left behind. My heart stutters, stops, then ratchets up in speed. The mating cord urges me on, farther, faster, keep going. Now.

I reach the first peak and then I see her.

Poised ahead, at the top of the second peak of the cliff right ahead. Around her the white chalky surface gleams a dull creamy silver. So like her skin…no, her skin is softer, richer, smoother.

Waves of fear pour down the mating bond, so intense, so strong, that they threaten to overwhelm my senses. My breath comes in heaving pants.

Sweat pours down into my eyes. Still I push forward. When I am not ten feet from her, she turns.

Her long hair gleams with hidden golden highlights, red in the fading sunshine. Suddenly I can't wait to discover everything about her. Her secrets. Her lies. Her truths. Her fears and innermost desires. I want it all.

She angles her head at me. "You shouldn't have come."

"I couldn't stay away." I slow my steps.

"You should leave."

"Not without you." I come to a halt not five feet from her.

"Go." She raises her chin.

I chuckle, and there's nothing happy about the sound. It's twisted, yearning, full of fear and anger. At her. At me. At this damn city that brought me to this place. Facing the woman who is becoming more important to me by the second, who I'd taken without mercy, who I haven't yet broken, who I know I am going to own, and not only because she is my mate…well, maybe that, too, but really, it's because I want to.

Because no one can stop me.

She throws her head back and laughs.

No one except her.

My heart stutters.

I know what she is going to do, even before she takes a step back.

Even before she has swiveled to face the open sea.

"No!" I leap toward her, close the distance between us, and grab her hand.

My fingers touch her skin and slide off.

Then she is falling, falling.

I keep going and dive off over the edge of the cliff.

To find out what happens next get **CLAIMED BY THE ALPHA, KNOTTED OMEGA 2, HERE**

Read an excerpt...

Lucy

When I come to, it's to the sense of heat enfolding me. I burrow into the warmth, the hard planes of the chest that shift under my cheek. The scent of fresh rainwater on parched earth fills my nose.

That alluring, growing need curls in my belly and my core trembles. Every instinct tells me I am safe.

Safe?

I try to move and find there is a heavy arm around my waist, its weight both brutal and soft.

The friction of his skin over mine sends a tremor of heat down my spine.

Slick pools between my legs. My stomach cramps, and the mating bond in my chest pulses with life. Heat. Life. Energy. My scalp stings, my fingers and toes tingle.

Every part of me prickles like it's coming back to life. Like I have been asleep for a long time. Like I'd never jumped off the cliff and straight into that blue-green water, hitting the waves, going through and—my eyelids snap open.

I am surrounded by his smooth, honey-brown skin, which is broken by the scars on his throat, the wounds I had marked him with. They bleed into the tattoos on his chest.

I reach out and trace my fingers over those swirls and curves, those colors that are as stark as the monster I'd thought him to be, as poignant as the lost boy I had glimpsed in his eyes in the seconds before I'd jumped off the cliff and into the sea below.

Why had I done that?

Willfully sent myself to a possible death, while deep inside I'd known it wasn't going to happen that way? That I'd just started living. I'd just met him, and I wasn't going to let go of him or the future I'd glimpsed.

Had I been testing myself? To see if I was as brave, as fearless as I'd thought myself to be? To test him to see if he'd come after me? And he had.

The thoughts tumble around in my head. There is a fluttering in my stomach, and I push against his chest.

A growl rumbles from him. "You're awake?"

"Where am I—?" My voice cracks; my tongue sticks to the roof of my mouth.

When was the last time I drank water?

Well, if you don't count the gallons I swallowed as I sank under the waves, eh? A chuckle wheezes out of me.

I feel lightheaded, enough to be able to laugh at this strange scene which might well be from a dream. Except it isn't. The man-mountain moving under me, his flesh surrounding me, the pulse of need flooding down the bond...all of it tells me I am alive. "Why did you save me?"

He doesn't reply at once.

Is he considering his words before speaking? Strange. The Zeus who'd taken me like it was his due had never given thought to the feelings of another.

He cups my cheek, and his touch is so gentle, so sweet. "You didn't leave me a choice, little squirrel."

My throat closes. That term of endearment...does it mean that he cares for me? Nah. Not possible. So why does it feel like I betrayed him when I ran from him? He took me without giving me a choice, I was right to leave him.

"It won't work, you know." His voice reverberates under my cheek, so growly and yet so soothing.

I want to close my eyes, burrow into him, merge with him, and go right back to sleep.

"What?" I swallow, somehow knowing what he is alluding to, but that isn't possible. He cannot read my thoughts, can he?

"You keep trying to leave, not realizing that I will follow you."

His words send a wave of need coiling through my womb.

What the hell is wrong with me?

"I will always find you, and claim you." His jaw tics, and a nerve throbs at his temple. "You are mine to own. To claim. To possess."

The passion shimmers in the air between us.

The hair on my neck prickles. The flood of raw emotions, of fear and lust and his utter need to take, flows down the bond. My chest hurts. The back of my eyeballs begins to throb.

It's not like he doesn't know every inch of my body, or how my flesh responds to him, not like he hasn't shown me how much he wants to dominate me. He wants to break me.

His gaze narrows; the skin stretches over his cheeks.

My chest grows heavy. There is a ball of emotion inside clawing, waiting to get out. The force of it is bigger than the mating bond, more profound than the physical urge to want him to rut me, more primal than the need to procreate that is inherent in my omega state.

It is real, alive and writhing inside of me, and that scares me.

This need to tell him that I am his.

To respond to that call of his mate, to tell him I am here for him, that he can take me, slake his thirst in me, bury himself inside me, and knot me all over again. And I want it all. So much.

The depth of my emotions washes over me and floods into the bond, sweeping through it.

Under me, his heartbeat increases in speed. Heat pours from his chest, and his muscles go rock-hard. Can he sense what I don't dare tell him? That I hadn't meant for it to be this way?

Why is it that he just has to look at me, touch me, hold me, and I will dissolve, shatter into a million pieces, each of which reflects his name? Screams this monster's status. Alpha. My alpha. Mine.

The mating bond curls inside me, tugging at me, yanking at me, pleading, urging, begging me to accept.

"No." I yank myself from his hold with such speed that I must have taken him by surprise.

His grip loosens, and I wriggle out from under his grasp. Hitting the hard floor, I push myself to a standing position. The world swings around me. His big body moves. His muscles tense, and he springs up to his feet, arms outstretched to catch me.

My legs tremble, and I punch my toes into the floor for support. "Stay away…" I gasp.

I don't need to ask him to know that he saved my life.

I lurch to the door and shove it open, stepping onto the fine white sand. There is a beach in front of me, sloping down, ringed with coconut palms, and beyond that the sea, waves, and the blinding sun shining off of it for as far as I can see. It should be idyllic but it is not.

It should gladden me that I am away from the smoggy, dirty streets of London, but it doesn't.

I am here alone with him. My skin puckers.

I stumble forward and onto the beach. My feet sink into the sand. I look down and draw my gaze up the curve of my ankles, to my legs, over my bare thighs, to my stomach. My breasts are bared to the sun.

I am naked.

Heat flushes my cheeks. All this time, in his arms, I didn't have any clothes on.

Something sounds behind me, and I swing around and flush. Blood rushes to my cheeks, and I know my neck must have turned an interesting shade of scarlet. For the man is naked, too.

He has not a stitch of clothing on.

Not his pants or those massive boots I've seen him in. Nope. There's a vast expanse of honey-brown skin, marked with those tattoos I'd been admiring down to the sculpted planes of his stomach, and below that his shaft, which is already semi-erect.

"Wh…why did you bring me here? Why did you rescue me?" Why am I bothering to ask him this question?

He confirms my fears. "One guess?"

"Uh, because you needed time away, and this is your island retreat?" I swallow.

"Wrong answer." His stance is patient. He's waiting, waiting.

"And because I am your…" I squeeze my eyes shut.

"Say it." His voice is soft.

"Your…" I force myself to open my eyes. "Omega."

"And?" He takes a step forward.

I hold my place. I will not be scared. I am not going to step back. Not going to show him how afraid I am. That my heart is pounding, my throat is dry, while sweat breaks out on my forehead. "And I need water. I am parched."

He turns and walks inside the house, then reappears at the door with a bottle of water.

A bottle?

So someone has stocked this place. I lean back and take a better look at it. The structure is rudimentary but seems secure. It must be for Zeus to bring me here. Why is it that I trust this alpha so implicitly with my safety? Was it because he'd jumped into the ocean after me and saved me?

I want to ask him why he did it but I am not sure I want to know his answer. Not least because I don't want to question the warmth that pools in my chest at the thought of him risking his life for me. My captor had become my savior and how do I feel about that, eh? Why am I not panicking? My toes curl and my fingers and toes tingle. With fear? Anticipation? Both?

I close the distance between us and snatch up the bottle, "This place belongs to you?" I gulp down the water then hand the bottle back to him.

Without wiping the top, he tilts it to his lips and chugs down from it, too.

It feels very intimate. My lips tremble. I want his mouth on me again. Longing sears my belly, and I push back the need to press my thighs together. But I must have given something away, for his gaze drops right back to my core.

He bends to place the bottle at the side, on the ground, then straightens. "It's just you and me, and no one is going to come here, not until your lesson is complete."

"Lesson?"

"Yes, little omega. The one you need to learn." He looks at me. Hooded eyelids. The silver in his irises is as liquid as the sea behind me. As tempting as the water, I had dived into when I had jumped off the cliff. There's a pleasure-pain of calling in them. They scare me and seduce me at the same time.

"Which one is that?" I dig my toes into the sand.

"You want me to spell it out for you, little squirrel?" His lips thin. His nostrils flare.

That threat in his tone sets my nerves jangling.

I know what he means. And it should terrify me. Should warn me to stay away from him.

Still, that spirit of disobedience that has brought me this far, that has gotten me into trouble so many times, urges me not to cooperate with him. Not when I am so clearly in his control. "I have no idea what you mean."

He closes the distance between us so quickly that I gasp.

He grabs my nape and pulls me close. His fingers are long enough to curl around my neck all the way so his fingers meet in the front.

My pulse rate ratchets up.

He lowers his face and his nose bumps mine. His eyes narrow, and his jaw goes solid. The scent of dominance leaps off him, so thick and fast that it plows into my chest. Sweat breaks out on my forehead.

He rubs his thumb over the front of my neck. "Perhaps I should show you what happens to omegas who run away from their mates."

My breath hitches; anticipation tugs at my belly, and moisture beads my core. Why does the brutality in his voice turn me on so much? Why do I want every depraved thing that he can do to me? It should feel wrong and it doesn't.

I can't stop myself from pressing my thighs together to hold in the moisture that threatens to leak out from my core. I need to put an end to the hold he has on me. I must.

"You are not my mate." The skin over my heart ripples. The bond pulls at me, scolding me for not accepting what I already know.

"You are right."

"I am?" I stare.

"I let you out of my sight. I left you before the ending of your heat cycle, when you needed me, instead of consolidating the bond." He pauses, surveying me, watching me, stalking me like the prey I am.

And I am tired, so tired of being on the defensive with him.

Mates aren't supposed to trap you or drive you out of your mind with need until you yearn for their touch, then deprive you.

Mates who are alphas are supposed to hold you, rut you through your heat cycle, then cherish you and bring you down from the high, none of which he has done.

A pulse ticks at his jaw. "I am going to set that right." He steps forward and cups my face.

"No." I shake my head. "I don't want that…I don't."

Swooping down, he places his forehead on mine and purrs, a low, glorious resonance that is drawn up from the depths of his core. The notes ripple up his massive chest with such strength that the vibrations thrum over my breasts.

My nipples pebble and the flesh between my thighs weeps.

The sound of his purr strums my sensitized nerve endings. My core clenches and moisture gushes from between my legs to form a puddle under me.

A sob rolls up my throat. My chin wobbles and I raise my hands to his chest, wanting to push him away.

All I end up doing is spreading my palms, sensing the vibrations that throb up his ribcage. It's strangely soothing. An affirmation that he is alive. That I am still alive. I push back from him. "Why do you insist on doing that?"

He bends and scoops me up in his arms then walks back toward the house. "You like it when I purr." His forehead furrows. "It brings out the need inside you. Speaks to the omega essence of you."

"Exactly!" I peer up from between my eyelashes. Those piercing blue eyes of his deepen in color. Mistake. Why am I trying to reason with him when all he has to do is look at me and I want to fling myself at him and ask him to take me all over again? "That's why I don't want you to do it." I shove my hair over my shoulders. "It's diffi-cult to think, let alone speak when you do that, and then it leads to the inevitable."

He steps over the threshold. My gaze flies past him to the narrow bed at the far end of the room.

There is barely enough space for one person. An image of me curled up against his broad back, my face pressed into those sculpted planes washes over me. It's both arousing and reassuring, and the mix of emotions confuses me.

I shouldn't be so needy for him.

And it's not just my body.

My will is melting along with the rest of me, getting used to his presence in my head, in my heart, in every part of me which has begun to recognize his flavor and thirst for it.

His essence flowing down the mating bond is bending me to his will. I drop my head.

I have been fighting this attraction to him for so long. My shoulders slump. I lower my chin toward my chest, and my hair spills over my face.

"So what would you rather do?" His voice reverberates up his chest.

My insides quiver. Why is it that as I am trying to be logical, my body is hyper-aware of him? I huff out a breath. "I just want us to have a conversation without any distraction."

He crosses the floor toward the bed. "Okay."

"Huh?" I blink, staring up at that impenetrable visage. Whatever it was I expected, it wasn't for the devil to agree to my request. "So you'll be willing to answer a few questions first?"

"One." He sets his jaw.

"Three." Guess there is some use of having grown up in a royal household and eavesdropping on discussions my father had with his Council. All those negotiations, all that give and take I've witnessed is ingrained in my blood.

"Two." He straightens his shoulders, and I sense he's back to being the General again. He also doesn't seem very surprised that I'd tried to talk him up.

"Okay," I agree before he changes his mind.

"Hmm." There's a low exhale of breath from him, then he lays me on the bed. Pulling up a chair, he flips it around and goes to straddle it.

"Wait." I spring up on my knees.

"Now what?" he growls, his massive shoulders flexing as he folds his arms over his chest.

"You may be used to being naked, but I am not." I jerk my chin at his body, not daring to lower my eyes to that chest. If I do, I'll be lost. If I look down to where his shaft is growing harder by the second, I have no doubt I'll close the distance, grab it, lick it, and then lower myself onto it…and…not yet. I squeeze my eyes shut. "Let's put on some clothes. Please, just until we have this conversation."

He turns and stalks away.

I blink.

Not what I'd expected, okay? I mean, this here is an overbearing alpha-hole, the monster who runs this city as if it is his personal dictatorship and…maybe I misjudged him.

I push the thought away. Nah. Being this close to him, sensing his warmth, the tug of the mating bond, all of it is skewing my judgment. Next, I'll be thinking of playing happy families with him, of him and me and our children in his stronghold. I shake my head to clear it.

Clearly, I am losing it, and the worst part is, none of it seems wrong.

It feels natural, more organic than anything I've ever felt before. How can it be a mistake, when all my instincts scream that it's right?

"Give an omega an inch, and of course she's going to take over your whole damned life." He strides to the closet I'd glimpsed in the corner.

It's so unexpected. The General of the city, the alpha of alphas, muttering under his breath like he is a henpecked man. I giggle.

He shrugs into a pair of loose linen pants. He stalks back to me and flings a tunic at me. It's big enough to cover me all the way to my knees and smells of the sea.

I slide it on then plop down on the bed. "You've used this place before?"

He angles his head. "Even a bastard like me needs a retreat, somewhere to get away and clear my head."

"You mean regroup on the assholeness inside so you can go back and be more of a bastard?" Oh, hell, there I go again, inciting him. Why can't I just stay quiet? Why can't I conform to the stereotypes of omegas? Gentle. Docile. Right. So not what I am.

He frowns. A nerve ticks above his jaw.

My pulse thuds at my temples, but I hold his gaze. So, the guy's a monster. No argument there. Still, he's been less of a jerk than I'd thought. He rutted me, gave me what I needed, saved me…from the stupid-ass attempt at trying to drown myself, and now he's actually trying to have a conversation with me?

Everything I've always expected from someone normal. Someone who isn't a monster inside. Which he isn't. And I have never wanted someone average, normal…have I? That would bore me.

And here I go making excuses for his behavior again. I rub my palm over my face.

Walking back to the chair, he straddles it. Then smirks in that way I am beginning to think of as The Zeus Special. "Yeah, that's exactly right. And I'm done being patient. You get one more question, Omega. You'd better make it count."

Turn the page to keep reading…

PART II

CLAIMED

37

Lucy

When I come to, it's to the sense of heat enfolding me. I burrow into the warmth, the hard planes of the chest that shift under my cheek. The scent of fresh rainwater on parched earth fills my nose.

That alluring, growing need curls in my belly and my core trembles. Every instinct tells me I am safe.

Safe?

I try to move and find there is a heavy arm around my waist, its weight both brutal and soft.

The friction of his skin over mine sends a tremor of heat down my spine.

Slick pools between my legs. My stomach cramps, and the mating bond in my chest pulses with life. Heat. Life. Energy. My scalp stings, my fingers and toes tingle.

Every part of me prickles like it's coming back to life. Like I have been asleep for a long time. Like I'd never jumped off the cliff and straight into that blue-green water, hitting the waves, going through and — my eyelids snap open.

I am surrounded by his smooth, honey-brown skin, which is broken by the scars on his throat, the wounds I had marked him with. They bleed into the tattoos on his chest.

I reach out and trace my fingers over those swirls and curves, those colors that are as stark as the monster I'd thought him to be, as poignant as the lost boy I had glimpsed in his eyes in the seconds before I'd jumped off the cliff and into the sea below.

Why had I done that?

Willfully sent myself to a possible death, while deep inside I'd known it wasn't going to happen that way? That I'd just started living. I'd just met him, and I wasn't going to let go of him or the future I'd glimpsed.

Had I been testing myself? To see if I was as brave, as fearless as I'd thought myself to be? To test him to see if he'd come after me? And he had.

The thoughts tumble around in my head. There is a fluttering in my stomach, and I push against his chest.

A growl rumbles from him. "You're awake?"

"Where am I—?" My voice cracks; my tongue sticks to the roof of my mouth.

When was the last time I drank water?

Well, if you don't count the gallons I swallowed as I sank under the waves, eh? A chuckle wheezes out of me.

I feel lightheaded, enough to be able to laugh at this strange scene which might well be from a dream. Except it isn't. The man-mountain moving under me, his flesh surrounding me, the pulse of need flooding down the bond...all of it tells me I am alive. "Why did you save me?"

He doesn't reply at once.

Is he considering his words before speaking? Strange. The Zeus who'd taken me like it was his due had never given thought to the feelings of another.

He cups my cheek, and his touch is so gentle, so sweet. "You didn't leave me a choice, little squirrel."

My throat closes. That term of endearment...does it mean that he cares for me? Nah. Not possible. So why does it feel like I betrayed him when I ran from him? He took me without giving me a choice, I was right to leave him.

"It won't work, you know." His voice reverberates under my cheek, so growly and yet so soothing.

I want to close my eyes, burrow into him, merge with him, and go right back to sleep.

"What?" I swallow, somehow knowing what he is alluding to, but that isn't possible. He cannot read my thoughts, can he?

"You keep trying to leave, not realizing that I will follow you."

His words send a wave of need coiling through my womb.

What the hell is wrong with me?

"I will always find you, and claim you." His jaw tics, and a nerve throbs at his temple. "You are mine to own. To claim. To possess."

The passion shimmers in the air between us.

The hair on my neck prickles. The flood of raw emotions, of fear and lust and his utter need to take, flows down the bond. My chest hurts. The back of my eyeballs begins to throb.

It's not like he doesn't know every inch of my body, or how my flesh responds to him, not like he hasn't shown me how much he wants to dominate me. He wants to break me.

His gaze narrows; the skin stretches over his cheeks.

My chest grows heavy. There is a ball of emotion inside clawing, waiting to get out. The force of it is bigger than the mating bond, more profound than the physical urge to want him to rut me, more primal than the need to procreate that is inherent in my omega state.

It is real, alive and writhing inside of me, and that scares me.

This need to tell him that I am his.

To respond to that call of his mate, to tell him I am here for him, that he can take me, slake his thirst in me, bury himself inside me, and knot me all over again. And I want it all. So much.

The depth of my emotions washes over me and floods into the bond, sweeping through it.

Under me, his heartbeat increases in speed. Heat pours from his chest, and his muscles go rock-hard. Can he sense what I don't dare tell him? That I hadn't meant for it to be this way?

Why is it that he just has to look at me, touch me, hold me, and I will dissolve, shatter into a million pieces, each of which reflects his name? Screams this monster's status. Alpha. My alpha. Mine.

The mating bond curls inside me, tugging at me, yanking at me, pleading, urging, begging me to accept.

"No." I yank myself from his hold with such speed that I must have taken him by surprise.

His grip loosens, and I wriggle out from under his grasp. Hitting the hard floor, I push myself to a standing position. The world swings around me. His big body moves. His muscles tense, and he springs up to his feet, arms outstretched to catch me.

My legs tremble, and I punch my toes into the floor for support. "Stay away…" I gasp.

I don't need to ask him to know that he saved my life.

I lurch to the door and shove it open, stepping onto the fine white sand. There is a beach in front of me, sloping down, ringed with coconut palms, and beyond that the sea, waves, and the blinding sun shining off of it for as far as I can see. It should be idyllic but it is not.

It should gladden me that I am away from the smoggy, dirty streets of London, but it doesn't.

I am here alone with him. My skin puckers.

I stumble forward and onto the beach. My feet sink into the sand. I look down and draw my gaze up the curve of my ankles, to my legs, over my bare thighs, to my stomach. My breasts are bared to the sun.

I am naked.

Heat flushes my cheeks. All this time, in his arms, I didn't have any clothes on.

Something sounds behind me, and I swing around and flush. Blood rushes to my cheeks, and I know my neck must have turned an interesting shade of scarlet. For the man is naked, too.

He has not a stitch of clothing on.

Not his pants or those massive boots I've seen him in. Nope. There's a vast expanse of honey-brown skin, marked with those tattoos I'd been admiring down to the sculpted planes of his stomach, and below that his shaft, which is already semi-erect.

"Wh…why did you bring me here? Why did you rescue me?" Why am I bothering to ask him this question?

He confirms my fears. "One guess?"

"Uh, because you needed time away, and this is your island retreat?" I swallow.

"Wrong answer." His stance is patient. He's waiting, waiting.

"And because I am your…" I squeeze my eyes shut.

"Say it." His voice is soft.

"Your…" I force myself to open my eyes. "Omega."

"And?" He takes a step forward.

I hold my place. I will not be scared. I am not going to step back. Not going to show him how afraid I am. That my heart is pounding, my throat is dry, while sweat breaks out on my forehead. "And I need water. I am parched."

He turns and walks inside the house, then reappears at the door with a bottle of water.

A bottle?

So someone has stocked this place. I lean back and take a better look at it. The structure is rudimentary but seems secure. It must be for Zeus to bring me here. Why is it that I trust this alpha so implicitly with my safety? Was it because he'd jumped into the ocean after me and saved me?

I want to ask him why he did it but I am not sure I want to know his answer. Not least because I don't want to question the warmth that pools in my chest at the thought of him risking his life for me. My captor had become my savior and how do I feel about that, eh? Why am I not panicking? My toes curl and my fingers and toes tingle. With fear? Anticipation? Both?

I close the distance between us and snatch up the bottle, "This place belongs to you?" I gulp down the water then hand the bottle back to him.

Without wiping the top, he tilts it to his lips and chugs down from it, too.

It feels very intimate. My lips tremble. I want his mouth on me again. Longing sears my belly, and I push back the need to press my thighs together. But I must have given something away, for his gaze drops right back to my core.

He bends to place the bottle at the side, on the ground, then straightens. "It's just you and me, and no one is going to come here, not until your lesson is complete."

"Lesson?"

"Yes, little omega. The one you need to learn." He looks at me. Hooded eyelids. The silver in his irises is as liquid as the sea behind me. As tempting as the water, I had dived into when I had jumped off the cliff. There's a pleasure-pain of calling in them. They scare me and seduce me at the same time.

"Which one is that?" I dig my toes into the sand.

"You want me to spell it out for you, little squirrel?" His lips thin. His nostrils flare.

That threat in his tone sets my nerves jangling.

I know what he means. And it should terrify me. Should warn me to stay away from him.

Still, that spirit of disobedience that has brought me this far, that has gotten me into trouble so many times, urges me not to cooperate with him. Not when I am so clearly in his control. "I have no idea what you mean."

He closes the distance between us so quickly that I gasp.

He grabs my nape and pulls me close. His fingers are long enough to curl around my neck all the way so his fingers meet in the front.

My pulse rate ratchets up.

He lowers his face and his nose bumps mine. His eyes narrow, and his jaw goes solid. The scent of dominance leaps off him, so thick and fast that it plows into my chest. Sweat breaks out on my forehead.

He rubs his thumb over the front of my neck. "Perhaps I should show you what happens to omegas who run away from their mates."

My breath hitches; anticipation tugs at my belly, and moisture beads my core. Why does the brutality in his voice turn me on so much? Why do I want every depraved thing that he can do to me? It should feel wrong and it doesn't.

I can't stop myself from pressing my thighs together to hold in the moisture that threatens to leak out from my core. I need to put an end to the hold he has on me. I must.

"You are not my mate." The skin over my heart ripples. The bond pulls at me, scolding me for not accepting what I already know.

"You are right."

"I am?" I stare.

"I let you out of my sight. I left you before the ending of your heat cycle, when you needed me, instead of consolidating the bond." He pauses, surveying me, watching me, stalking me like the prey I am.

And I am tired, so tired of being on the defensive with him.

Mates aren't supposed to trap you or drive you out of your mind with need until you yearn for their touch, then deprive you.

Mates who are alphas are supposed to hold you, rut you through your heat cycle, then cherish you and bring you down from the high, none of which he has done.

A pulse ticks at his jaw. "I am going to set that right." He steps forward and cups my face.

"No." I shake my head. "I don't want that…I don't."

Swooping down, he places his forehead on mine and purrs, a low, glorious resonance that is drawn up from the depths of his core. The notes ripple up his massive chest with such strength that the vibrations thrum over my breasts.

My nipples pebble and the flesh between my thighs weeps.

The sound of his purr strums my sensitized nerve endings. My core clenches and moisture gushes from between my legs to form a puddle under me.

A sob rolls up my throat. My chin wobbles and I raise my hands to his chest, wanting to push him away.

All I end up doing is spreading my palms, sensing the vibrations that throb up his ribcage. It's strangely soothing. An affirmation that he is alive. That I am still alive. I push back from him. "Why do you insist on doing that?"

He bends and scoops me up in his arms then walks back toward the house. "You like it when I purr." His forehead furrows. "It brings out the need inside you. Speaks to the omega essence of you."

"Exactly!" I peer up from between my eyelashes. Those piercing blue eyes of his deepen in color. *Mistake.* Why am I trying to reason with him when all he has to do is look at me and I want to fling myself at him and ask him to take me all over again? "That's why I don't want you to do it." I shove my hair over my shoulders. "It's difficult to think, let alone speak when you do that, and then it leads to the inevitable."

He steps over the threshold. My gaze flies past him to the narrow bed at the far end of the room.

There is barely enough space for one person. An image of me curled up against his broad back, my face pressed into those sculpted planes washes over me. It's both arousing and reassuring, and the mix of emotions confuses me.

I shouldn't be so needy for him.

And it's not just my body.

My will is melting along with the rest of me, getting used to his presence in my head, in my heart, in every part of me which has begun to recognize his flavor and thirst for it.

His essence flowing down the mating bond is bending me to his will. I drop my head.

I have been fighting this attraction to him for so long. My shoulders slump. I lower my chin toward my chest, and my hair spills over my face.

"So what would you rather do?" His voice reverberates up his chest.

My insides quiver. Why is it that as I am trying to be logical, my body is hyper-aware of him? I huff out a breath. "I just want us to talk without any distraction."

He crosses the floor toward the bed. "Okay."

"Huh?" I blink, staring up at that impenetrable visage. Whatever it was I expected, it wasn't for the devil to agree to my request. "So you'll be willing to answer a few questions first?"

"One." He sets his jaw.

"Three." Guess there is some use of having grown up in a royal household and eavesdropping on discussions my father had with his Council. All those negotiations, all that give and take I've witnessed is ingrained in my blood.

"Two." He straightens his shoulders, and I sense he's back to being the General again. He also doesn't seem very surprised that I'd tried to talk him up.

"Okay," I agree before he changes his mind.

"Hmm." There's a low exhale of breath from him, then he lays me on the bed. Pulling up a chair, he flips it around and goes to straddle it.

"Wait." I spring up on my knees.

"Now what?" he growls, his massive shoulders flexing as he folds his arms over his chest.

"You may be used to being naked, but I am not." I jerk my chin at his body, not daring to lower my eyes to that chest. If I do, I'll be lost. If I look down to where his shaft is growing harder by the second, I have no doubt I'll close the distance, grab it, lick it, and then lower myself onto it…and…not yet. I squeeze my eyes shut. "Let's put on some clothes. Please, just until we have this conversation."

He turns and stalks away.

I blink.

Not what I'd expected, okay? I mean, this here is an overbearing alpha-hole, the monster who runs this city as if it is his personal dictatorship and…maybe I misjudged him.

I push the thought away. Nah. Being this close to him, sensing his warmth, the tug of the mating bond, all of it is skewing my judgment. Next, I'll be thinking of playing happy families with him, of him and me and our children in his stronghold. I shake my head to clear it.

Clearly, I am losing it, and the worst part is, none of it seems wrong.

It feels natural, more organic than anything I've ever felt before. How can it be a mistake, when all my instincts scream that it's right?

"Give an omega an inch, and of course she's going to take over your whole damned life." He strides to the closet I'd glimpsed in the corner.

It's so unexpected. The General of the city, the alpha of alphas, muttering under his breath like he is a henpecked man. I giggle.

He shrugs into a pair of loose linen pants. He stalks back to me and flings a tunic at me. It's big enough to cover me all the way to my knees and smells of the sea.

I slide it on then plop down on the bed. "You've used this place before?"

He angles his head. "Even a bastard like me needs a retreat, somewhere to get away and clear my head."

"You mean regroup on the assholeness inside so you can go back and be more of a bastard?" Oh, hell, there I go again, inciting him. Why can't I just stay quiet? Why can't I conform to the stereotypes of omegas? Gentle. Docile. Right. So not what I am.

He frowns. A nerve ticks above his jaw.

My pulse thuds at my temples, but I hold his gaze. So, the guy's a monster. No argument there. Still, he's been less of a jerk than I'd thought. He rutted me, gave me what I needed, saved me...from the stupid-ass attempt at trying to drown myself, and now he's actually trying to have a conversation with me?

Everything I've always expected from someone normal. Someone who isn't a monster inside. Which he isn't. And I have never wanted someone average, normal...have I? That would bore me.

And here I go making excuses for his behavior again. I rub my palm over my face.

Walking back to the chair, he straddles it. Then smirks in that way I am beginning to think of as The Zeus Special. "Yeah, that's exactly right. And I'm done being patient. You get one more question, Omega. You'd better make it count."

38

Zeus

I can't help it if the words come out more hurtful than I'd meant them to be.

I am trying, aren't I?

I brought her here, gave her time to recover, then allowed her to ask me questions. Questions? You'd think this is an interrogation, and I owed her answers.

Most of my Council don't have the courage to challenge me. Well, okay, except perhaps that dickwad Ethan, and he wouldn't do it with such audacity as this little omega. The sprite demands a response from me like it is her freaking right. And it is. My shoulders still.

It *is* her right as my mate to ask me anything…except, no way is she going to find out that I just thought that. I am noticeably softening toward her. I conceded to wearing clothes, allowed her to cover herself up, too. She distracted me—and why am I not surprised? I brought her here with the need to keep her on her back, legs spread so I can fill her up again and again.

"Why…why are you growling?"

"Am I?" I realize my thighs are rock-hard, and my spine is stiff. Bloody hell, every muscle of my body is buzzing with need. The pulse pounds at my temples, at my jaw even in my fucking balls, and I don't like it, not one bit.

All this time, I've followed my instinct…whether it was in killing the alphas who'd hurt my mother, taking out Golan—that was completely deserved. I jumped into the sea after her…not what I'd expected of myself, okay? I did all that, didn't I? I've kept her safe, made sure to protect her from herself, and here she is, staring at me. Her gaze accuses me, tells me that I am in the wrong.

I wrench my thoughts back to the present and force my shoulders to unwind. But the muscle between my legs, that part of me refuses to comply.

"Why do you think?" I snarl out the words.

She winces at my tone. Some of her color fades.

I should be glad she's still afraid of me. But honestly, that isn't my intention. And that confuses me more. For the first time, I am fighting every instinct. Which dictates right now that I shove aside this fake conversation. Push aside my chair, tear off my clothes, strip her naked, and then…hold her. Skin to skin, cheek to cheek. Bring her close to me and purr for her and soothe her. Holy fuck. I am completely losing it. Was it a mistake to bring her here? To keep her in such close proximity to me? To have just taken off from London without informing my team, purely so I could carve out this time and space for myself, for her… I've never done this before, never brought anyone else here.

I hadn't even realized this was where I was headed, not until I'd arrived here with her in my arms.

"Are we here for small talk? Are these the questions you wanted to ask of me?" I set my jaw, angrier with myself than anything else. And that surprises me. I am not used to this kind of self-questioning. Life had been easy in that sense. Fight for what I believe in. Take revenge. Eat, fuck when I felt the urge. Straightforward. Simple. Boring. Yeah, it had been too easy. I had been jaded. Been waiting for a diversion. Been waiting for her?

From the time she'd launched herself at me, my life had turned upside down. But I didn't resent it, when I should be livid that she'd completely blown me off course.

For the first time since I can remember, my mind is not occupied with the need to take revenge on the city, on all those who did wrong by me. It also helps, of course, that I've killed many of them. But it isn't just that. Every part of me insists it is important that I spend time with her, get to know her…be gentle with her, give her the chance to get to know the real me. That I am not what I seem.

Now that's a surprise. And I am tired of the thoughts that chase around in my mind.

I stand and shove the chair aside. My chest heaves. I know I am purring again. The notes leak from my throat and charge the space between us. The sound swells over her.

Her shoulders draw back, and her breathing steadies.

If I could use my voice to pull her to me and bind her to me and not talk anymore, I would. If I could lapse into that masculine part of myself that wants to claim her, consolidate the bond, and force her to accept it, I would. I take a step forward.

She doesn't shrink back.

And that…confuses me. "Why are you not afraid of me?"

I broke my own rule. I wasn't going to engage in more conversation with her than what was necessary, but for once, I don't care. "Tell me."

She holds my gaze.

Her chin wobbles. She's scared of me, but she is trying hard not to show it. Strong omega. She is beautiful, gorgeous, and magnificent. And I don't deserve her. For fuck's sake. It really had been wrong to come here. If I'd realized that instead of teaching her the lessons I intended, I was going to indulge in a bout of self-recriminations, I'd never have brought her here… No, not true. I'd still have come. I am many things, but a coward is not one of them.

"You won't hurt me, Zeus."

"You sure of that?" I bare my teeth.

She raises her chin. "You don't hate me, Zeus. You hate…yourself."

"What the fuck?" My heart stutters.

Her words sink into me. They shake me in a way nothing and no one ever has before. The way I'd taken her the first time, the sense of coming home…all of that pales in comparison to the sheer terror that grips me.

My scalp tingles with the knowledge of what she's implying. But I don't want to accept it. Cannot accept it.

I plant my feet wide apart. "You pull a fast one on me? Is that why Kayden sent you? To undermine me? To crawl into my head and fuck around with me? Why did you agree to the mission to kill me?"

There, it's out.

The question that has bothered me for so long and which I haven't asked until now. Because I've too busy trying to fuck her brains out. I'd wanted to knot her to me. And I had…and guess what? It isn't enough. Fuck. I need more than to just own her in the physical way.

I need her to trust me. To believe in me, and…there you go. I've heard of this type of connection between mated pairs. To be fair, I'd thought it was an exaggeration, stories that were propagated in a romantic vision by omegas. Well, whaddya know? There's a grain of truth to it after all.

The bond in my chest twangs, and it's not her…it's just that deeply ingrained part inside of me that insists that despite everything else, I am not beyond redemption. That this is my chance to atone for everything I have done. This is my salvation. She is my salvation. My answer. This is my chance to find something that is good and real and belongs just to me. She is my property. The thought shakes me to the core.

"I did come to kill you." She smiles, but it doesn't reach those beautiful green eyes. "But not once did you bother to ask me why."

"I am asking you now."

"Maybe it's too late. Maybe everything that's happened between us has shown me that I can't trust you. That if I tell you the real reasons for my coming, you'll use it against me."

Her shoulders draw up, and she tucks her elbows into her sides.

"And maybe if you don't tell me, it will be so much worse for you." I close the distance between us. "Or perhaps that is what you want, Omega?" I bend my knees and thrust my face close to hers. "You want to drive me over the edge until I take you again and again? Until I fuck you, and knot you, and ensure no thoughts rattle around in that pretty head of yours?"

Her breath hitches. The pulse thuds at the base of her neck.

The golden sparks in those green eyes flare. I want to reach out and lick up those lips, to drop to my knees and raise that damn tunic and bury my face in her pussy. Bring her to climax and forget about everything. And that would be so easy. To follow my instinct and be what I am, an alpha who takes, and fuck everything else.

Fuck these doubts I am having about myself.

I reach for her.

39

Lucy

He drops to his knees in front of me and yanks my thighs apart. His touch is rough, and I am sure his fingers have marked me. The heat from his body infiltrates through the thin tunic and suffuses my skin.

Goosebumps rise on my forearms.

The scent of my arousal seeps into the air. Sugary, spicy, and that arouses me further.

I don't need to tell him how much I want him; I don't need to say anything. My body, it seems, does all the talking. It insists that I want him.

He flicks his gaze up and I swallow.

Violet flames flare in those blue irises. That only happens when he is angry or aroused or both. His nostrils flare, and I know he's smelled my body's response.

He pushes the thin tunic all the way up until it's bunched around my waist. I don't have any underwear, and of course, he knows that.

If he looks down, he'll see exactly how turned on I am. That my core quivers and moisture clings to my swollen sex, which is throbbing for him. He holds my gaze, and the color heightens on his cheekbones.

There's no other change in his features.

Still holding my gaze, he glides his palm up my inner thigh to come to a stop right before he touches my clit.

I shiver, and heat flushes my cheeks.

With his other hand, he massages the outside of my thigh, then slides up to grip my butt. "So fucking gorgeous." He massages the curve of my ass. "So perfect. So soft and firm and all mine. Mine to break. To do with as I want."

There is a brooding quality to his voice as if he's talking to himself. That dark edge of cruelty I've glimpsed in him laces his tone. Coating it with intent. I have no doubt that he will follow through with his words. It's why he brought me here. It's why I am powerless to stop him. Why I revel in every depraved thing he wants to do to me. Why I want it more than anything else.

A shudder sinks into my blood and whips straight to my core. My pussy trembles. My thighs quiver. A moan wells up, and I bite down on my lower lip to stop it from streaming out.

"I want to mark you all over, so every time you look at any part of yourself, you'll know it belongs to me." His voice lowers, and the meaning in his words heats my skin.

Yes. I pant. My heartbeat thunders. Sweat trickles down my throat, hugging the valley between my breasts.

The emotions that pour off him are so intense... Like he's baring his soul, and I am sure I am mistaken.

This is Zeus, the father killer. The alpha who tricked me into laying with him. Except, the skin is stretched across his features, and his voice is rusty.

My instincts insist that he's never said this to anyone. Not man or woman. To no one but me. Only I have this effect on him.

I made him lose his control enough for him to take me from the warehouse.

It's because of what I do to him that he jumped into the sea to save me. Then, instead of returning with me to his stronghold, he brought me here. Away from everything. Away from his Council, from the other alphas. He doesn't want to share me with them.

He wants me all to himself.

The sheer possessiveness of his gaze, the raw need implicit in his touch, all of it should fill me with power knowing that I have this effect on him.

Instead, fear laces my nerves.

I can't do this.

I don't want to be the woman to tame this beast. I don't want to be at the receiving end of this alpha's affections. It will tie me down, surely, more than anything else. He will demand a response, one that will not be adequate. I can't... I don't have it in me to want him the way he needs me. "I belong to no one," I firm my lips.

"Wrong again." His fingers squeeze my hip, sending a pulse of pleasure-pain streaming straight to my core.

My thighs clench, and I ache to press them together to hold in the moisture that's pooling at the base of my channel.

I don't want him to know how much his words are affecting me. More than the raw way he'd consumed my body, the sound of his voice, the intensity with which he is searching my features, looking into my eyes, demanding I give him that part of myself I have sworn I'll never share with anyone else, definitely not this alpha...all of it prompts me to scoot back from him.

He lets me.

That should have warned me, but right now, all I can do is pull up my legs. I fold them against my chest, yanking my tunic down to cover myself, then I retreat until my back is to the wall.

"If you think that's going to stop me, you are mistaken." He leans back on his heels.

"Wha…what do you want from me?" My voice comes out in a squeak.

"Haven't I already told you?"

I clear my throat. "No."

"You've sensed it, Omega. You know what I need."

"I don't know what you're talking about." Why can't he just keep it simple? Take my body, own it, plunder it, use it as he needs. "Why are you complicating everything?" I throw up my hands and swear.

He laughs then.

A full-blown, from-the-belly laugh. His features light up. His eyes gleam. The sheer charisma of his presence calls to me. Heat curls low in my belly. My throat goes dry. I curl my fingers into fists, and my nails dig the palms of my hands. I don't trust him. Not one bit.

He rises to his feet, and glares down at me from that great height. "Only you, Omega, would say something so completely audacious and so completely true."

"You are not listening." I huff out a breath. "I can't give you what you need."

"You can and you will, this, I promise you."

That hard tone in his voice drives me over the edge. Anger thrums at my temples.

"I cannot be the kind of omega you expect me to be." I bounce my fingers on the bed. "You have some crazy image of me as a breeder, someone who will happily submit to you whether in heat or not, get pregnant, and bear your bastards."

"Didn't hear you complain the last time you asked me to take you. Your exact words I recall were: Rut me, Alpha. Fuck me," he smirks, "Alpha."

Jerk. And why do I find his words so damn hot? My pussy quivers. Heat sears my cheeks and I glare at him.

"You wanted to have a conversation, then you complain when I oblige." He holds my gaze and I don't trust that oh-I-am-so-innocent look of his features.

He's right though. It's the first time we are talking for any length of time without the man trying to stuff his dick into me. Only I hadn't counted on his words being as much of a turn on as his moves — and fine, I admit it, a part of me misses his touch, his primal hunger, the way he consumes me every time he takes me.

Things were much easier when there was just lust between us when I could blame my body's response on the fact that he didn't give me a choice. Which he is now. I press my arms close to my sides. "I don't want to do this."

"We are not doing anything…" His gaze rakes over my huddled-up self. "Yet."

"That's what I mean." I firm my lips. "Why aren't you throwing me down on my back and shoving my legs apart and slamming yourself into me?"

"I already have."

And isn't that the truth? My shoulders hunch. I lean forward, agitation squeezing a band around my chest. "Why aren't you doing it again? Isn't that why you brought me here? Isn't that what this entire 'teach your omega her lesson' is all about?"

"It is."

"So, then?" I spring up on the mattress and close the distance between us. I peer up into his face, trying to read his features, trying to figure out what the hell he is thinking.

The alpha who had fucked me, knotted me and rutted me over and over again — that, I get. That was when he was behaving true to form. But this? Him revealing his true self—that he is an intelligent man who wants to talk with me. Who speaks in riddles, who keeps his distance from me...this Zeus scares me more. I want to approach him, claw at him, and ask him exactly what he is up to...this...this is exactly what he wants from me.

I fold my arms over my chest. "What's your game?"

His eyebrows lower. "Now you are the one speaking in riddles, little squirrel."

"I have a name," I snarl.

"I know."

"So use it." I curl my fingers so my nails dig into my forearms.

"When you decide to call *me* by my name without my prompting you, and when we can speak without you losing your temper." One side of his lips curls into a smile.

I raise my fists, wanting very much to punch him, claw at him, throw myself at him, and lick the beads of perspiration that glimmer on his chest. "I hate you."

"No, you don't. You are just getting to know me."

"So that's what this is about?" I flatten my lips. "That's why you brought me here away from everything and everyone, so we can have, what, some quality time?" My voice trembles.

He angles his head and watches me with that brooding gaze I love...and which drives me a little crazy, for it's so fucking sexy. And it shouldn't be. The alpha can be charming when he puts his mind to it. When he isn't getting all macho and over the top with his masculinity, which he is. Face it. He's the most macho, most lethal man I have ever met. Every pore of his skin drips with danger, every glance of his is laced with the need to dominate. With the promise to take. My skin tightens. My fingers tingle. He keeps me guessing what he's going to do next. My insides quiver. I want to throw myself at him and plead with him to have his way with me. Damn this alpha!

The very fact that he'd actually thought this through and brought me here implies that he intends to follow through with this plan, and I so don't want to fall in with whatever he has in mind. "You're going to keep me a prisoner here until I decide to fall for your swoon-worthy charms."

"You noticed them?"

"Noticed what?" I widen my gaze. Sure I have an inkling what he means but I'm not going to give him the satisfaction of acknowledging it.

"You know." He squares his shoulders. "My charms, my attributes, my rather larger-than-life features."

"You have a big ego." I swipe my hair from my face.

"It's not the only thing that is big." The bastard smirks. He actually smirks at me.

"I hadn't noticed." I mean that in the most sarcastic way possible, but it seems it's completely lost on him.

"You want a repeat, Squirrel? You just have to ask."

He drums his fingers over his chest, drawing my attention to that sculpted flesh. I can't stop myself from admiring those beautiful pecs. I slide my gaze over that incredible eight-pack, farther down to where the drawstring pants dip low on his concave waist. No one has the right to be that perfect, that handsome. My mouth waters.

Moisture pools in my core.

I can't blame him for my state of arousal. He hasn't done anything. Nothing except smirking that wicked, drenched-in-sex look of his.

He widens his stance just enough for my gaze to lower to that part of him I have been trying to ignore. Not that I haven't seen it before, but ah! Hell, that massive bulge that tents the fabric over his crotch arouses me even more than seeing him bare. The dampness on the front is a clear sign of the precum dripping from his shaft. My womb contracts. My throat goes dry.

He grabs my nape, and that's when I realize that I've leaned into him. Dense heat spools off his chest and slams into me. I gasp.

He yanks me up to my toes and pulls me close enough for our breaths to mingle.

"And if you did that, you'd never forgive me, or yourself." His voice, low and seductive, ripples over my skin.

I shiver. "Is that what you want from me? My forgiveness?"

40

Zeus

This is not how I had intended for this conversation to go. I'd wanted to find a way to put her at ease.

Who am I kidding?

I'd wanted to soothe her and get her to unwind. Hey, nothing altruistic about that. All a ploy to win her trust. I'd hoped a few words, a smile, a bit of tenderness, and she'd be falling into my arms. I mean, how difficult can it be, right? But the princess has completely turned the tables on me. She peers up at me with those mesmerizing green eyes.

There's a look in them I cannot understand.

She's waiting for me to tell her something.

To give her a signal. To show her I meant it when I said I wanted her forgiveness.

Am I ready for this, though?

My plan had been simple. Bring her here, away from my men, away from Kayden and anyone who'd try to use her or distract me. Then fuck her and keep her high on the endorphins from our coupling. I wanted to keep her blissed out with the pleasure of sex until her next heat cycle rolls around. At which point I'd impregnate her, and then...yeah, return with her as my mate.

The very omega who'd come to assassinate me, I'd planned to return with her and introduce her to the Council, as the woman who is going to stay with me by my side.

It had seemed easy, plausible.

I'd had long moments to think about it as she'd slept and recovered from her ordeal. I had looked at her sleeping face, relaxed, and known then I couldn't afford to lose her again.

I'd pushed her, and she'd tried to take her own life, and that...that had completely surprised me and yeah... scared me. Me the alpha of alphas, worried about an omega? Fuck me!

But there's no denying that her actions had made me vulnerable to her in a way nothing and no one else ever has. Except perhaps my mother. But the relationship there was different.

A fierce need to protect this omega grips me, and I cannot explain why. Sure, I am an alpha, and there's a part of me that is drawn to protecting those less able than I am, but with her, it's more.

I want to own her and take care of her, break her and put her back together, mark her, knot her and take her again and again until she knows no other feeling, no other emotion, nothing except me. Only me. My blood surges and I can't hold back the growl that reverberates up my throat. "Mine," I snarl.

She shakes her head. "No. Not after what you did to me. You took me from that warehouse."

"I gave you a chance to escape." A vein throbs at my temple.

"You mated me against my will."

"You asked me to." A pulse ticks to life at my jaw.

"I was in the middle of my heat cycle, of course, I was going to demand that you fuck me."

"So you expected me to turn my back on an omega who bares her cunt to me? Whose slick drizzles down her thighs to stain my bedroom floor, whose sugary arousal surrounds me and clings to me until it drives me out of my head with need?" My chest heaves, " You would have me leave *that* omega to writhe in pain?"

The color drains from her face. Her green eyes narrow. "Yes." She nods. "That's exactly what I would have expected of you."

"Liar." I lean in close enough for the heat from my body to envelop her, but I don't touch her.

She shivers and grips her fingers together in front of her. "See...this is what I mean. I thought we were finally talking, but you can't keep your dick in your pants. All you want to do is fuck."

"Of course, woman," I roar. "I am an alpha. I am driven by my needs. Of course, I want to fuck...just not anyone."

"Huh?" Her gaze widens. "Wha...what do you mean?"

I really hadn't meant for that to slip out. Hell, I hadn't meant for any of this to happen. Too fucking late. I have no choice but to tell her now. Taking a step away, I pace. Back-forth-back in front of the bed.

She doesn't say anything. But I sense her gaze following me. And the omega is quiet. Another surprise. I'd have thought she'd throw more questions at me. After all, speaking is not something she is averse to, or fighting, for that matter. A low chuckle boils out of me. The great Zeus, alpha of alphas, General of London, rendered speechless by a little squirrel of an omega. Fuck. I rake my fingers through my hair, still liberally matted from the seawater, then turn to her. Dropping my arms to my sides, I raise my head and meet her gaze.

"The omegas from the harem, I never fucked any of them."

"You didn't?" Her eyes light up, and her features shine. She looks too damn pleased.

I shift my weight from foot to foot. "Not that I am a virgin," I smirk.

"Not that I'd have mistaken you for one." One side of her lips quirks in a smile, but her tone is soft.

There. Something in her gaze—a kind of wary attention, bordering on seriousness, not a look I've seen before. But then how long have I known her? Less than a week, and here I am telling her my life story...yeah, a complete goner, that's what I am. And strangely, it doesn't matter. Not as important as it feels to finally come clean and tell her about my past.

"I gave the omegas my word that they could choose the alphas with whom they mate."

Her eyes gleam. "You've made sure you keep them supplied with the pharmaceuticals needed to control their cycles?"

"It's not a big deal." I scratch my jaw. A tingling sweeps the back of my neck. Her approval means nothing to me. Nothing.

"Heat suppressants are unavailable." She purses her lips. "Their production was stopped years ago."

I stare at her.

"Right." She blows out a breath. "You are the alpha of alphas. It's easy for you to get them produced again."

"Damn right." I shift my weight from foot to foot. "I have them made to help the omegas in the harem."

"You took care of them, you were considerate enough to help them get through their difficult heat cycles without always needing to resort to an alpha to rut them." She takes a step forward. Her green eyes shine.

I move back, "Don't mistake me for something I am not."

"Oh, and what is that?" Her chin trembles.

What the fuck? Is she laughing at me? No way, she didn't just do that. Pinpricks of alarm flare over my skin, "I am not someone who does good."

"You had me fooled." She peers up at me from under hooded eyelids.

Blood rushes to my cheeks, what the fuck is she doing to me? "Don't push it Omega."

She bites her lip, then bobs her weight on the heels of her feet.

"Well whatever is on your mind, say it." Now I am giving her a chance to speak? Do I still have my balls or did I leave those behind when I pulled her out of the river?

Her features brighten and fuck if a wave of heat doesn't pool in my chest.

She presses a finger to her chin, "Just, you know, your reputation being what it is...then the way you acted with me, rutting me, breaking my cycle...and you did admit to protecting the other omegas." Her gaze sweeps over my features. "It's confusing."

"I am not going to apologize for taking you the way I did." I thrust out my chest. My scalp tingles, and my skin feels too tight. And why the fuck do I feel so defensive about what I've done?

"You'll never do it again with any other omega either." She slaps a palm over her mouth.

Every muscle in my body tenses, "Is that right?" I lower my hands to my hips.

"Forget I said that."

"Nope. Na-a-h. No way." A smile tugs at my lips. I know I'm smirking, but hey, I'm allowed. Maybe, just maybe having shared what I feel—and that had not been easy—has been worth it. Perhaps. But I'm not ever doing this again.

"You are overbearing," she huffs.

"You bet." I drum my fingers on my chest.

"Only you would take that as a compliment," she grinds her teeth.

"Only you would stand there, without your underwear, on my bed, and parry words with me, when I'd rather be exchanging something else entirely."

She makes a noise suspiciously like a snarl and bares her teeth. "Is that all you think about? Sex?" She punches her fist into my shoulder.

The jolt ripples all the way down to the tip of my cock.

I cover her palm with my much bigger one, then drag it down and hold it flush over my heart.

"This is where I need to come clean about something else. Or better still, show you." I gaze down at where my cock tents my pants.

She follows my gaze and her chest heaves. When she raises her face, twin spots of color burn on her cheeks, and her pupils have dilated again.

Holy fuck. "You may have already guessed, but in the spirit of this new relationship we seem to have now, I need you to know that every time you hit me, you turn me on."

41

Lucy

I hear his words, and an illicit thrill grips me, and I don't understand it.

"No answer, little squirrel? For once, that smart mouth of yours is speechless?"

"Ah…" My skin tingles with need, and there's a scratch at the back of my throat. *Don't say it, don't say it, don't—* "It turns me on when you're rough with me, too." I drop my head forward. "Did I just say that aloud?"

He tilts his head. "Perhaps for the first time, you're being honest with yourself?"

"Or maybe it's the impact your nearness has on me?" I set my jaw.

Those blue eyes blaze.

I clench my fingers into fists. I've gone and done it again, given him more ammunition with which to get back at me.

"So you admit I affect you?" He moves closer, close enough that I have to tilt my head up, all the way up again to meet his gaze.

"Not that it's such a secret." I jut out my chin. "And I am not going to say anything else to you. It will boost your already inflated ego if I do."

His lips widen. "You're right. I think we have been talking too much."

"I think we have barely touched the tip of a myriad of things I want to ask you." I hold my stance.

"You had your chance to ask questions earlier, remember?"

"You distracted me."

"Not as much as you are distracting me right now." He stares at my mouth, then slides his gaze down my breasts to the space between my thighs.

A tremor of heat runs down my spine and my knees quake. Moisture gathers between my legs, and I clamp down on the need to squeeze my thighs together. No, no, I am not going to acknowledge how turned on I am just by being near him. Not just as we are beginning to finally communicate…sort of.

"I'll make another deal with you."

"Ah…" I open my mouth to refuse his offer.

He holds up his hand. "Hear me through, then think carefully before you refuse. There is no easy way out of here." He swirls his finger.

I look around the space, the clean, spacious but bare room, the fireplace in the corner, the single bed, the closet pushed up against the corner next to a table and chair, and through the window, I can see the sea not far away.

It strikes me again how isolated we are and that I have no way out of here. I don't know where we are, though I guess we are not far from Dover but I am not going to ask him. It would be a sign of weakness, and I don't want him to use that against me. I don't have a choice but to do as he tells me. The very fact that he is still talking to me instead of taking what he wants, well…perhaps it means that he's making an effort? That he wants to find some semblance of a relationship here?

"Fine." I gesture to him, making sure to keep all emotions from my face. I guess all those years of discipline drilled into me by my nannies is finally coming into good use.

He steps back and jerks his chin to the table. "After you?"

"Huh?" I blink. So polite. His demeanor is such an about-turn from the alpha-hole I am coming to know. What is he up to? My pulse thuds and my mouth goes dry.

"Better take a seat, before I change my mind."

I scoot past him. Walking to the table by the window, I plop into a chair.

He drops into the other one, and our knees bump below the table. I instantly pull back, but he doesn't say anything.

Another surprise.

Somehow, the more accommodating he is, the more I don't trust him. Resisting the urge to draw up my leg—because, ah! No underwear—I cross one leg over the other. "I'm listening."

He leans forward and places his elbows on the table. "I think we should come to some kind of agreement."

"Hmm?" The alpha who is used to just taking what is his wants to extend a deal? I wring my fingers together in my lap. "Whatever you're offering, I am not buying."

His lips turn up in a smirk. "You haven't heard what I have to say."

"You don't have anything I want." I square my shoulders.

"Oh, we both know there is a lot I can offer that you need. What's more, you'd beg for it, if you followed the true nature of what you are."

"If this is a lecture of how a good little omega should behave—"

He holds up a hand. "That's not it."

"No?"

"If I wanted a compliant omega, I'd have found one in the harem or in the wider circles of my team."

"No doubt," I mutter.

A guts churn. My chest feels tight, and that is stupid.

Why should it matter to me who he has slept with?

The thought of his hands on anyone else, those lips kissing anyone else, bringing anyone else to climax, knotting any other omega, makes my stomach burn. I shove the hair out of my eye. Damn it, I don't want to be jealous of all those females he has bedded.

I can't afford to be envious.

Not when my family is still under Kayden's control.

The very Kayden who is no doubt hunting for me right now.

I am running out of time, and I don't know what to do about it. I need to get back, but just me on my own is not going to be much help to them.

I need Zeus with me.

I need to take him back to Kayden, then hand Zeus over to Kayden, and get out of there.

Or I need to kill myself…no, I am not going to try that again. What I'd done the last time…it had been irresponsible, too instinctive.

I had not been thinking straight then, but somehow seeing death so up close has clarified so much. I want to live. I want my clan to stay alive. The one person who does not belong here is him. So what if I am mated to him?

The mating bond hasn't been completely consummated. It takes weeks, months sometimes, for a newly mated couple to settle and for the bond to take root. I have a little more time to wrench the bond out, to take him back and release my family. But first, I need him to trust me again.

"What's the deal?" I choose my words carefully, intent on keeping the nature of what this is. A transaction. That's all it is.

"I suggest we use this time wisely. Let me show you the heights of pleasure I can take you to. Give me a chance to be the alpha I am." He leans forward and places his elbows on the table, joining his fingers in front of him. "Allow yourself to be an omega."

A thrill of anticipation clutches at me. I can't be turned on by the very thought of him possessing me, can I?

I am not sure what I feel for this man.

I didn't know he existed until a few weeks ago. But every part of me insists I need him, and not in a way I am going to appreciate. "What does that mean?"

"Let me show you how it can be between us."

"You want me to give in to your demands?"

"No. I want you to fight, hurt me if you want. Resist. I promise I won't do anything you don't agree to. I promise I will not reciprocate or hit you back. You don't have to submit to anything." A nerve ticks to life at his temple. "Give in to your complete defiance. For once, you don't need to hide. Neither do I. Let yourself go. Just once allow yourself to be free."

42

Zeus

"No restraints, no masks to wear, no one knows what we do here." Am I saying this for her benefit, or is it more to remind myself?

I am not sure.

Fact is, I've never before actually negotiated the terms of how I am going to take an omega.

I am still not sure why I am doing this now.

I am the most powerful alpha in the city. I am used to getting what I want when I want it. Still, something tells me I need more than brute strength to tame her. I need to give her a reason to put aside whatever is holding her back. Because the surrender of her body is not enough. I need her soul. Her will, her trust—there's that word again. It never stopped me from taking what I wanted before, so why is it so different with her?

She hesitates. Her eyebrows draw down, and she sweeps her gaze over my features.

I want to tell her she can trust me...not. Truth is, I don't know if I can stick to the rules I am laying out. I go by my instinct, and right now, all I know is that I'll try every which way to compel her to submit. On my terms, of course.

I am not above promising her anything she wants to hear.

Does that mean I'm a bastard? Yeah. But I have never given anyone else cause to think otherwise. Why start now?

I am acting in the way nature intended, the way it is most natural for me. I always take what I want.

I am not in the habit of holding back my needs.

Just sometimes the means to the end can be different. Doesn't matter. The goal is still the same—to coerce her to accept our connection. And she won't take the bond, not unless our mating becomes something she wants as much as I do.

She springs up from her seat and paces.

The long tunic flies around her knees, showing off glimpses of that pale thigh. The skin covered in soft freckles, that I want to trail my fingers over on my way to that sweet triangle in the center of her thighs. The moisture and everything there belongs to me. Only to me. She knows it; I know it. But she needs to give it to me willingly.

She pauses mid-step and turns to me. Her shoulders pull back, and she runs her fingers through her hair. "I so want to believe you. I do."

"But…?" I want to go to her and reassure her that of course, I mean it. That I saved her, brought her here, for her to heal as much as me. But I can't quite form the words, so I stay where I am. "You can say it, Omega. Tell me what is on your mind."

"Why don't you call me by my name?"

My shoulders bunch and my jaw goes solid.

"Tell me, Alpha."

"For the same reason, you don't call me by mine." I flatten my lips.

"I did already." She carves her fingers through her hair, holding it back and then releasing the strands.

Her cheeks go rosy. "When it matters most. When I can't lie. I called to you then. And—"

"I gave you what you wanted, didn't I?" I want to remind her how it was between us, that when we boiled it down to our basic needs when I took her, none of this mattered. Not the fact that I am the General of London, or that she was once the czarina of Russia.

All that mattered was that I was born to take, she was made to give, and when we got together, it was different from anything I had ever experienced. I want to say all that, but I don't. "I am still waiting for your answer."

"I know what you are doing." She splays her hands out wide to stretch her fingers, then relaxes them.

"Oh?"

"Once again, you are pretending to give me options." Her lips curl. "You are making me think that I have a say in all this. That if I don't submit, you'll let me walk away, when we both know that's not true."

It isn't.

Of course not.

I don't intend to let her set foot off this island, not until she is completely bonded to me; not even death will let her escape me…she can't fool me again. Not like the last time. "You're right."

Her forehead furrows, and her cheeks pale. "So you admit that all this is a farce." She waves her arms around her.

Her chest heaves.

"All of this saving me, bringing me here, telling me that I should let go of all my inhibitions, it's just a way of, what? Taunting me? Showing me that I am in your power? That I can either accept and come willingly, or you'll take me anyway?"

Yeah, that's exactly what it is. I stiffen and drum the table with my fingers, knowing I need to choose my words carefully. Ha? Me? The one who never holds back, not even in the thick of a war discussion, is trying to figure out how to seduce her.

The realization sweeps over me.

That's what I have to do. Play with her, toy with her, seduce her into coming to me.

Where force had not worked, maybe being more strategic will. I am not one to mince words or hold back. But just this once, maybe just a little more restraint is called for? I need to change tack, enough to disarm her. I must pull back and confuse her…and then when she least expects it, to strike. Yeah, that will work.

"What are you thinking?" She takes a step forward, then twists her fingers together. "Whatever it is, I don't appreciate it."

"Oh, so now you can read my mind?" I smirk. If I put on that alpha-hole face of mine, it will get her all riled up, right?

"Hell forbid." She props her arms on her hips. "I don't want to know what depraved, filthy things you are thinking of."

"Speaking of filthy…" I allow my gaze to sweep down to her breasts and am rewarded when her nipples pucker. "I rest my case."

"So you can turn me on with a look. You can purr, and I am all but ready and moist to spread my thighs for you." She juts out her chin. "I thought you wanted me to be willing and come to you of my own accord?"

"That would help." I bring my fingers together and hold her gaze, seeing the different expressions scurry across her face. She has no idea how easy she is to read. How her every thought, feeling, emotion, is reflected in the way her features mirror her internal conflict.

But I don't say anything, merely school my features into a mask of indifference. Sometimes you have to wait. Bide your time. I don't have patience, but I am not foolish.

"But?" She tilts her head, throwing my own words back at me.

I can't stop the laugh that barks out of me.

This feisty woman will never hesitate to go toe to toe with me. I know now that I don't have a choice. I'll never meet anyone who will match me so well. Action for action. Word for word. In bed, in a fight. At every level, she is mine. She truly belongs to me. I want to bare my lips and snarl and tell her that she can never escape me, never. That I intend to take what I want by force if she doesn't accept the terms I am laying out.

I grind my jaw so hard it hurts.

That's not going to help. That would get her back up, and she'd flounce out of here…to where? She has no way of leaving the island. All options outlined to her lead back to one thing. Me.

I rise to my feet.

The color pales from her cheeks. I know by now she will not cower or shrink back or try to escape.

My omega with the spirit of an alpha holds her ground, "I am not scared of you."

"You should be."

"I don't trust you." She squares her shoulders.

"So what's new?" I drum my fingers on my chest.

"But I do trust that sliver of something I sense inside of you."

All of my senses go on alert, "Whaddya mean?"

"Inside you is hidden a real man, an alpha who wants to protect what is his, cherish what you believe in, go after what you know is right."

Her words sink into my skin and warm my chest. My heart begins to hammer. The fuck? She almost had me convinced there. Clever omega, trying to make me out to be something I am not. Me, wanting what's right? Not-fucking-true. No way. "You are mistaken." I close the distance between us and stare down at her from my superior height.

She still doesn't shrink back. Huh? Woman has no thought of self-preservation.

She squares her shoulders and juts out her chin. "You protest too much." Her tone holds a challenge. And fuck if that doesn't turn me on.

A growl rumbles up my chest.

The scent of her, that sweet arousal bleeds into the air, and my mouth waters. She wants me as much as I need her.

But the power struggle between us is about so much more than dominance or submission. It's a battle of wills, taking this fight to an entirely new level, and I don't intend to lose. Never. I set my jaw.

"The deal is off."

She blinks; her chin trembles.

"I have a better idea." My chest rises and falls, brushing the tips of her nipples.

She shudders. "Wha…what?"

"Let's cut to the chase." I peel back my lips, knowing that base instinct inside me is taking over. Knowing I am done talking. Hey, I tried to reason, tried to give her a way out, didn't I? But I am not a saint or a diplomat. I am a marauder. I am similar to the berserkers who'd taken over her country and set her on the run…to me.

Her breath comes in pants. She licks her lips and straightens her spine. A pulse flicks to life at the base of her throat.

My mouth goes dry. I want to throw her down and tear into her. I need to rut her, now. I clench my jaw, curl my fingers into fists at my sides. "Run, little squirrel. I'll give you a second chance to escape. If I catch you, you are mine. Mine to do with as I want. Mine to take as I need. Mine to ravish until you are so fulfilled you'll never think of leaving. Mine to fill, to plunge right into, until there is no me, no you, until we wear the same skin. Until my spirit merges with yours."

Her shoulders tremble, and the sugary sweetness of her slick rents the air. Her pupils dilate. Her lips part. Fuck me…but she is turned on, and my cock throbs… and I keep my promises. Not. But she still doesn't realize that. Poor trusting thing. Is she in for a surprise?

I bend down to peer into her eyes. "Go."

43

Lucy

His voice snaps through the sexual haze that fills my head. Big surprise? I just have to be in his presence, to smell that burned pine scent of his, to sense the heat of his body bleeding through the space, and my core throbs for him. Violet sparks flare in his eyes, and I cannot look away.

His gaze bores into me as if he's reached into the very depths of my soul. As if he's read every filthy, degraded image that fills my mind, sensed every horrible need inside, every lust-filled thought I've had about him, about what I want him to do to me. The heat cycle was the perfect excuse to let go of all inhibitions and ask him to hurt me, to take the pain away from inside of me.

But this, here, when I am in my senses and stone-cold sober…this is when I hate myself. Hate that independent spirit inside me which refuses to submit willingly. He wants me to initiate the first move this time. And I will not. Cannot do that.

"Last chance, Omega."

The heat from his body envelops me, and the force of his dominance is overpowering. My heart stutters.

It's as if he's projecting his will at me and forcing me to take a step back, and another. He leans forward and snarls at me.

My mind goes blank.

Every thought inside me dribbles out, and my core clenches with need. My pulse rate ratchets up, my vision tunnels and everything else fades from around me. Everything except this fierce need to escape.

Swiveling on my heel, I race out of here. Out of the doors, onto the beach, my bare feet digging into the sand, and the warmth of the particles slither between my toes.

I run up the beach. Veering to the side, I race toward the tree line. *Keep going, don't stop.* My breath catches in my throat.

Sweat slides down my forehead, and I blink it away.

My leg muscles burn, and a laugh tears out of me.

I feel alive, so damn alive. I am running away from the monster, the man who bonded me, whom I refuse to accept as my mate. I should be rejoicing that I have a chance to get away from him. But deep inside, I know this is all a game. I want him to catch me, to find me, to take all choice away from me, to fuck me and knot me again and never let me go, and…no.

The thought sends a pulse of adrenaline racing through my blood. No, I will find a way off this island, I will hide from him. I have to. The thought overpowers me. The sound of my breathing, the thud of my footsteps fills my ears. I close my mind to everything else. *Don't stop, not now.*

There is a catch in my side, and pain floods my chest. I come to a clearing and pant. Ahead a pier juts out to sea, and tethered to the edge of it is a boat. Is that how we got here? I don't know, don't care. It's a real chance to get away from here. Bet he didn't think of that, eh? Another peal of laughter spills out of me and is chased by a need to cry. I recognize the signs for what they are—hysteria. I run toward the boat. My footsteps pound on the wooden walkway. It's too loud. He's going to hear it; he'll be here any second. *Don't look back, keep going.* The breath screams through my lungs. Skidding to a stop in front of the boat, I try to unwrap the rope from around the pole it's tied to. My hands are sweating so badly that my fingers can't find purchase. I sense him a second before his heavy footsteps thump on the wood. He steps onto the pier and the entire structure rocks.

"Fuck, fuck, fuck." My heartbeat thunders in my chest. Sweat stings my eyes, and I blink it away.

His footsteps draw closer. Steady. Ominous. He doesn't slow down, just keeps coming.

The rope tears at my skin, taking off the tip of a nail. I wince and the scent of blood seeps into the air. I sense him start. He's halfway down the pier. *Damn it, come on.* I can't lose. Not now. The blood pounds in my ears. Tears prick the back of my eyes. I yank at the rope and it comes undone. Yes! I throw it aside then push the boat away from the pier.

"What are you doing, Omega?"

A low purr accompanies his words, bleeding through the air, pouring over my back, sinking into my skin. And my heart, my stupid heart skips a beat. The bond in my chest throbs. A pulse of heat sweeps over me. My belly tightens. *No, no.* I push away all emotions, clamp down on every need inside of me that insists I turn and go to him. No, this is my chance. This. This is what I trained for all that time, to fight for myself. To show that I am not just an omega who submits and opens her thighs at an alpha's command.

Taking a step back, then another, I race to the edge of the pier and jump; my spine curves, my legs pedal in the air as I clear the water and hit the edge of the boat.

The impact reverberates through me, then the side of the boat bites into my chest. White sparks sear my brain and I scream in pain. My muscles spasm, my legs crumple from under me. The water sloshes over me. My eyes burn, and my hair clings to my throat.

I grab the side of the boat and clamber over. Lurching onto the deck, I swing up to my feet.

My shoulder throbs and my chest aches, and it's not from the physical pain of having crashed into the boat. The bond twists and turns and yanks me to my feet. There's a force inside, gnawing at me, begging to be unleashed; something that's me and yet so different. One that insists I cannot leave, not now. Not when he's there, waiting for me. Not when he is the one for me. He's not. He isn't.

I slam my butt onto the wooden bench, grab the oars, and begin to row. My muscles protest, and my arm shakes. The oars dip into the water, swelling up and over one wave, then down.

"You can't leave me, Omega." His voice follows me, seeping between the holes in the wind. Has nature itself conspired to hold me back and ensure that I hear him?

"I have to go," I say it aloud, not sure if he can hear me. Dip the oars in the waves, try to push forward. A gust of wind pushes me back, toward him, toward the shore.

Why is this happening?

I grit my teeth, set my jaw, then bend forward and row.

The sweat pours down my spine; the backs of my thighs flush with sweat. I slide down the bench and almost tumble off.

"Come back, Omega. You know you want to."

"No," I scream. At him? At myself? At my pathetic attempts to get away from him, when everything inside me insists I turn around and go back to him? I am conforming to what I am, another omega who wants to be mated and bred. So what if I was once a princess, someone of high blood, who had the freedom of choice? I did choose. I chose him.

The oars slip from my hands and hit the side of the boat with a clatter.

"Come back, little squirrel. You know I want you."

I look over my shoulder, into the distance, to where the white peaks of waves in the middle of the sea are visible. The wind picks up, hurling back the boat, shoving it in the direction I'd come.

"I need you, Omega"

My shoulders hunch. The fight goes out of me. I slap my palms over my ears, not wanting to hear that cajoling voice. Not wanting to sense the plea, the absolute need to possess me that leaps from his tone.

No one else can want me with this intensity. No one can take me as he does. No one else can…love me with the sheer unadulterated pleasure he can. Not in the conventional sense, not in the sense of soul mates. He cannot be my mate.

He's someone who bonded me, whose essence is in me so much that I am lost, and I want to leave him. My pulse skitters. My limbs twitch. The mating bond yanks at my chest and my spine bends.

An unseen force tugs at me, and my entire body tilts in his direction.

The edge of the boat crashes into the pier.

The sound screeches through the air, and the hair on the back of my neck rises, echoing the screaming that is locked inside of me.

He grabs the boat and hauls it close to the pier, then rescues the rope and knots it over the post, like he intends to knot me again. And he will. And I won't resist this time. What does that make me?

"Mine." He hauls me up and into his arms. His mouth closes over mine. I don't react.

He sinks his teeth into my lower lip and heat sears my lower belly. A moan dribbles out of me. He swallows the sound, then shoves his tongue into my mouth, filling me, consuming me. Liquid lust curls down my spine and my thighs spasm.

He sucks on my tongue and the salty taste of blood explodes on my palate, laced with that deeper, more complex taste of his. That burned pinewood scent of his floods my senses. I squeeze my eyes shut.

He tears his lips from mine, then licks the moisture that trickles down my cheeks.

A low, soothing purr rumbles up, swirling around me, tugging at me. It tightens and yanks my spirit closer to his. I still don't move. Don't touch him. Don't say anything.

A gust of wind blows over me, and I shiver.

He pulls me closer to his chest as his heart thuds under my ears.

I sense him walking, his footsteps pounding over the pier. I burrow in deeper, wanting to hide away, to deny what I have become. To not recognize how dependent I have become on him.

Walking to the beach, he keeps going. When he steps into the bungalow, the wind drops.

The world tilts, and I sense the mattress at my back. Of course, he's placed me down there.

He tugs the tunic up and over my head. I stay still. Force my muscles to relax. Force myself not to open my eyes. The purring creeps up a notch. My nipples pucker. My heart races, not in fear but in anticipation. My thigh muscles clench, and my belly quivers. That insidious slick inside me creeps toward the entrance of my channel.

"You are angry with yourself. I understand that."

Sure. He knows exactly what I feel, now, does he? I want to snap at him. But what's the point? I can't fight him. Can't fight myself anymore. Why am I still resisting him? I may as well give in. Doesn't mean I have to enjoy it. Though I will. I can let him take my body. I won't fight him. But I won't be a party to it either.

"Open your eyes."

The force of his dominance weighs down on my chest. The fine hairs on my nape rise. My shoulders jerk and everything in me wants to obey him, but I will not. If I give in, all will be lost. I'll never find myself again, the strength of his personality will overwhelm me and swallow me whole... and then... there will be no more Lucy. There will only be Zeus and his omega, and I am not ready for that.

I squeeze my eyes closed and just lay there. Elbows tucked into my sides.

He pulls my legs apart, and his breath sears the soft flesh of my core. Goosebumps rise on my skin. I can't stop that. My toes curl, and I dig my heels into the bed, holding back.

He licks my slit, then thrusts his tongue inside my channel.

Desire pounds at my temples. My breath screams in and out.

He rubs the heel of his hand over the swollen bud, and the moisture inside me flows out to greet his intrusion. I can't control my body, not where he is concerned.

Grabbing the underside of my thighs, he yanks my legs up and over his shoulders, deepening the angle.

He plunges two fingers into my squelching channel, then adds a third and my entire body spasms.

Heat shoots up my spine and a scream coils in my throat. I bite down on my lower lip and swallow it back.

His fingertips twist inside me finding that hidden core of me with perfect accuracy. My pulse rate shoots up and my skin tightens until I am sure it's going to crack. I can't stop the moan that spills out of me.

My inner walls convulse, and a rush of desire floods my core.

His hand slides up to curve around my breasts to pinch a nipple. A tremor runs down to meet that sweet pain in my core. Swelling with it, overflowing my center. The beginning of a climax cracks out from my womb.

He bites my clit and I scream. The pain streaks over my skin and white sparks shriek through my head. My mouth goes dry and my heart hammers as if it's going to break out of my rib cage.

He lets go of my pulsing sex, slides out his fingers, and drops my hips back on the bed.

The change is so sudden that my eyes fly open, to be captured by that liquid violet of his gaze.

44

Zeus

She looks at me, and I can sense the surprise in her gaze. Her green eyes deepen in color until they seem to reflect the hue of the water that surrounds this island.

When I had seen her fall through the cold waters of the sea, I'd known fear, the kind I'd never experienced before. Not when I had lost my mother, not when I had been about to kill my father. Not when I'd known I'd be faced with being alone…a fear that had been wiped out when she entered my life. It's been replaced by this complete confirmation that she is mine, and I am not letting her go.

It's that which pushes me to slide up her body and lean my weight on my elbows as I plank over her.

She stares up at me, her breasts heaving. Tears slide down her cheek, and I cannot stop myself from bending down and licking them up. She shudders and opens her mouth, and I brush my lips over hers.

"Don't speak."

She swallows but stays where she is.

"I want you, Omega. I'd give up my life for you."

"But you won't let me go."

My lips twist into a smile. The defiant woman will not listen to me. That's why she is unique. She'd never hesitate to speak her mind, to put me in my place.

"You are mine, little squirrel. Mine to be with, to protect. To cherish."

"To break." Her voice is low.

"To mate with." I rub the swollen head of my shaft over the opening of her pussy.

She moans, and her pelvis thrusts forward, brushing my turgid cock.

A low growl tears out of me.

Her shoulders hunch; her hips twitch. "I can't fight you anymore." Her eyes dilate and turn that golden green I am beginning to recognize.

"So don't." I flutter little kisses over her forehead, down to her cheek. It's not in me to be gentle, to be so amorous. But this feisty creature imprisoned under me brings out that innate need to protect and also to ravage. How is it possible that two completely contradictory emotions can live side by side and mesh...the way I want to lose myself in her?

"I can't let myself submit to you." She hiccoughs.

"You don't need to." I lick a trail over her lips, down to where the pulse flutters at the base of her neck.

"Then how?" She draws in a breath.

"You just need to be yourself."

"What am I anymore?" Her voice lowers to a whisper. "A failed assassin? A princess from a once glorious land?" She swallows. "Or an omega you stole away in front of your men, all of whom knew you were going to rut me?"

The anguish in her words twists my heart.

I flip her over, then slide her up and over me so she is balanced on my chest. That dark-red curtain of her hair pours over my face. I want to wrap the strands around my palm and tug it back, to bury my teeth once more in the curve of her shoulder and claim her all over again.

"You are my mate. I will take you back and introduce you to the Council as such. Give you a formal place by my side. None of them will dare look you in the eye."

"I'll know what they are thinking." Her gaze slides away.

I cup her cheek so she has no choice but to meet my gaze. "Does it matter so much to you what others think? Isn't it enough that you seduced me, that it is your cunt that owns me, that it is your pussy that I want to bury myself in? That it is you I mated, you." The words fall thick and fast, and I hear myself in surprise.

Do I have so much passion, so many emotions inside me?

The mating bond throbs and knocks into my chest. The intensity of the emotions pour down the connection, and I let them bleed out. I let her sense it, let my emotions brush over the barrier of her mind so there is no doubt I mean what I say.

Her eyes widen, and the color pales from her face, leaving the smattering of freckles over her nose highlighted in response.

"I want more."

"Take it." I grab her hand and slide it down my chest to where my shaft throbs between us. "This is for you. Nobody can bring me to arousal as fast as you."

Her fingers curl around my hardness.

I cannot stop the purr that winds up my chest.

She squeezes the turgid muscle, and my cock jumps in her hand.

"Oh." The surprise has her mouth falling open.

Desire hurtles down my spine, and all I can think is I fucking want those lips locked around my dick. "Take me in." I hear the words torn out of me and bloody hell, is that my voice that sounds so hoarse, that has a pleading edge to it?

I've never begged a female to suck me off. Never. The omegas I'd fucked had been more than willing to submit to me and do whatever I wanted them to do.

But there is a sweet intensity to asking the only female I ever want in my bed again to make love to me.

Love? The fuck? Where did that thought come from? A concept as outdated as the unblemished world before the tsunamis and earthquakes ripped us apart. Before climate change threw the seasons upside down, and nature sped up genetic mutation among humans, making us what we are today: animals in touch with our base instincts. Closer to what our ancestors had been long ago. And here I am pleading with her to take me in her mouth. Bloody-fucking-hell. Last I checked I still had my balls, and yet I can't stop myself. I need her, want her, must have her now.

"Please." The word dribbles out of me. It feels strange as I roll my tongue around it. It feels right as I hear it stretch out in the space between us.

Her chin trembles and her little pink tongue slides out to lick at her lips. And fuck, I can't wait anymore. My groin tightens.

A purr rumbles up my chest.

I swirl the sound over her, enveloping her in the resonance. The next second, slick gushes out from between her thighs to pool on my waist. And fuck me if that isn't the most erotic thing I have ever seen? "Do it." I growl.

Her lips turn up at the side, and golden sparks flash in her eyes. Then she slithers down my body and closes her mouth around my aching dick.

45

Lucy

The scent of him fills my nose. The taste of him, salty and deep, with the tang of his precum that sinks into my tongue. Desire flushes my skin, and my core clenches.

The mating bond tautens, aching to get closer, pushing me to open my mouth and swirl my tongue around the rigid muscle.

I take him inside until he hits the back of my throat.

He groans, and the sound cascades down my spine. I squeeze my thighs together but am too late to stop the fresh burst of liquid that slithers down from between my legs. The scent of my arousal intensifies.

His waist goes rigid; the muscles of his thighs spasm. "Your mouth is so fucking hot, so tight. You are killing me, Omega."

His voice is laced with pain. He wants more, something only I can give him. He sounds like I do when in the middle of a heat cycle and yearning for him. A fierce need thrums my chest.

I drag my mouth up, all the way to the tip, licking up the trail of precum.

"Grip me harder."

I stare at him.

Color stains his cheeks, while his breath comes in hard gasps. Sweat beads that wide plane of his chest and he looks so powerful, so magnificent, my heart stutters.

He must have sensed my scrutiny, for he cracks open his eyelids and meets my gaze. The color of his eyes intensity to twin points of indigo, almost black. I have never seen him this aroused, this wanting, and I am doing this to him.

He takes the hand I've balanced on his hip and slides it down to his shaft. The hard length throbs in my hand, the pulse echoes the beat that flares to life at my core. I want him inside me. So this is how it feels to communicate on a primal level, where no words are needed. Where all I am is an omega, and he is an alpha. My alpha. Is this what he meant earlier when he said we should take this chance to shed all our masks and be what we are?

He squeezes my fingers around the swelling knot. His jaw firms, the skin stretching over his features. All along, his gaze holds me, doesn't leave my face. The connection is disconcerting. Can he sense how in sync our spirits are?

The pulse in my chest agrees with my assessment. I swallow. Warmth floods my skin.

I knead hard, and he groans. The cords of his throat move and his shoulders flex. His hand drops away. He curls his fingers into a fist and slams it into the bed. "Fuck."

The tension spools off him, and I know it's because he's close, very close to coming. I want to see him shatter, to bring him to the edge of something I sensed before. I just want... I dip my head, still gripping the base of his shaft, and take him all the way inside my mouth until I almost gag. I can't stop the whine that tears out of me. Tension threads his muscles, and I allow my instincts to consume me. I want him to fall apart. Now. I draw my mouth back to the tip, then take him in again.

He grabs my hair, yanks it back just enough that I am forced to meet his gaze. "I am going to come, and you are going to swallow every last drop, Omega. Do you understand?"

My eyes widen, my heart hammers, and I pant. Then, with him still holding my gaze, still tugging back my hair, I sense the tremors that surge up his legs, to his groin; his knot pulses. Hot streams of cum flow into my mouth, down my throat.

I swallow, almost gagging again as the rich liquid pours out, and there's so much of it. It overflows my chin, down my throat, dripping onto his skin.

He pulls me up, balancing me on his chest. Then, squeezing the nape of my neck to hold me in place, he rubs his cum into my skin, over my breasts, shoving big handfuls down to my pussy where he rubs it into my folds.

Those blue eyes of his bore into me, and he rams two fingers into my moist channel.

I moan, and he kisses me, plunders my mouth, his tongue thrusting into me as he fucks me with his fingers, in-out-in.

The tension is too much.

The pleasure builds from my core.

Then, just as I think I can't last, that I am going to come, he pulls his fingers out and grabs my waist, holding me above him before lowering me onto his still rigid shaft.

"Fuck me," he growls.

And his words are so filthy and so right, the command in his voice is such a relief that I don't need to think for myself anymore. I can give in now. I clench my inner muscles around his pulsing shaft.

He raises and lowers me again and again, each time going a little deeper, a little more inside, hitting the walls of my cervix. A low, keening moan spills out of me. Waves of pleasure build-up from my heels.

His shaft grows bigger, more rigid, his knot expanding and slotting into place. The pressure of it seizes me, drawing out waves of heat so intense that I fling my head back and cry out. My climax shatters over me. Bursts of light explode behind my closed eyes. The mating bond snaps tighter, and I gasp.

Sweat pours down my back, and I squeeze my thighs about his waist. I clamp my pussy around his dick, milking him, taking from him. Taking what's mine. Only mine. The world shrinks to that intense source of pleasure between my thighs, and nothing else matters. The climax surges through me again. Intense pleasure sweeps over me, crashing over my shoulders, then as suddenly it fades away.

My muscles quiver and a trembling seizes me.

My breasts flatten against the planes of his chest. Only then do I realize that he's lowered me to lie on his torso.

His arms come around me, his fingers trailing through my hair, soothing, comforting. And it shouldn't feel so good, but it does. His lips brush my forehead, and I let myself slide into sleep.

When I wake up, he's still inside of me.

I raise my head and rest my chin on his chest.

I find him watching my face. Is he trying to decipher me? I reach out to trace the furrow between his eyebrows.

His arm snakes out, and he shackles his fingers around my wrist.

"Now we speak."

46

Zeus

No fucking way did I actually tell her that we should speak. While my dick is still knotted inside her? My cum streaks the valley between her breasts, and my sweat laces her cheeks.

My scent clings to her skin, and those green eyes are half dazed from the aftermath of the climax that still shudders through her. Next, I'll be asking her to move into my suite. Oh, wait, I already did that.

I am turning into someone I don't know, and you know what? It feels okay. It doesn't seem wrong. It feels pretty good, actually. Fuck if that doesn't freak me out further.

I let go of her hand, then grip her hips and try to pull her off of me, but she wraps her legs around my waist, straddling me. "Oh, no, you don't pull away, not after that statement."

"I don't know what you mean," I glower.

She raises her finger and trails it over the outline of my nose. "That's the first thing I noticed about you. Your hooked nose."

"You mean my patrician nose." I glare down said nose at her.

"Hmm." She bites down on her lower lip. "Ego much?"

I grunt, then grab her ass and adjust her position. My shaft thickens. The ridges pulse against her inner walls and a frisson of lust crawls up my spine.

I groan.

So does she.

For a second, I stare at her, taking in her flushed appearance, her still dilated pupils, her red hair caked with sweat and my drying cum.

"You are glorious." The words are out before I can stop them. I've never complimented any omega as much I have her.

A flush steals over her cheeks.

Interesting.

After everything I've done to her body—I've invaded her, knotted her, fucked her—and still she blushes.

"Are you for real?" A sense of foreboding tugs at my mind and I push it away.

"What do you mean?" She firms her jaw.

"Why did you agree to kill me?" Something prickles my subconscious.

"Now you ask." She stirs, then wriggles in my grasp. Her body begins to slide, and I squeeze her waist and hold her in place.

"Answer me." I lean up, close enough for our noses to almost bump. For our breaths to mingle. For me to see that dimple that furrows her cheek as she grimaces.

"Why did you sneak into the warehouse with that pathetic excuse of a weapon? You stood little chance of hurting me, let alone killing me, and you still did it?"

"Your timing sucks, you know that?" She wriggles in my grasp.

I slide my hands up her back and yank her closer. Her breasts graze my chest, and my cock pulses inside her.

She moans, and the color of her eyes deepens to an emerald green. "Fascinating, your eyes. Do you know that when you are aroused, they dilate enough for the black to bleed out, and when you are about to climax, gold sparks flare in them?" And I am waxing poetic. For fuck's sake.

She stills, and the blush deepens down her throat, creeping toward her breasts. Her nipples pebble, their diamond-hard edges drag over my skin. Blood rushes to my groin and I want to fuck her all over again. No, not yet.

I clamp my lips together and wait.

Her gaze skitters away. "Kayden is holding my clan hostage. I agreed to his plan because I didn't have a choice. I knew when I walked in there, there was a good chance I would be either killed or worse—"

"Knotted to me?" I move my hips enough for my knot to slide and bloom inside her once more.

Her eyes dart to my face. Her breath quickens, and her cheeks flush. "When you do that...I..." She swallows. "I—" She bites her lips.

I grip her chin so she has no choice but to meet my gaze. "Tell me. What does it do to you when I knot you?" I lick her lips.

Her breath hitches. "It's overwhelming and so filling." Her chest rises and falls, matching the tempo of my breathing. "It compels me to want you even more."

Our pulses are in synchrony, and it's the hottest, most intimate thing I've ever felt.

"Why didn't you tell me all this before?" As soon as the words are out, I curse myself. Wrong question.

She frowns. "You didn't give me a choice, alpha mine. You were too busy satisfying your hunger."

"I couldn't stop myself from jumping to your command. After all, you did ask me to fuck you." I smirk, knowing it isn't completely right, and yet, hey, I am not above bending my facts to fit the situation. Know what I mean?

"So you'll do anything I ask you to?"

"Hmm." I narrow my eyes. "Not sure I like the direction of this conversation."

"I need to get out of here and save my people."

"Your problems are mine now. You don't need to worry about your clan. I'll rally my troops, and we are going to attack Kayden. It's about time. And we'll free your people."

"What if it's too late?"

"It won't be." I set my jaw.

"How do you know that?"

I pause, wondering how much to tell her. "Just know that it will be okay."

"You are watching Kayden? You knew he put me up to this and that he was holding my people hostage?" Her features crumple as the full understanding of the situation dawns on her. "You were aware that he intended to surprise you with his sham of a gift?"

"I am the General." I jut out my chin. "I know everything that happens in my country, in my enemies' domains, and definitely what goes on in Kayden's space." It seems arrogant, but what the fuck? I can't hide who I am. Dominant. Alpha-hole. Yep. That's me. She knows it already, so why is she so surprised?

"I didn't anticipate he'd smuggle an assassin into my stronghold. Except the killer turned out to be the biggest surprise of all. She turned out to be mine." I tighten my grip around her.

She pants a little. "You are squeezing me."

"Good."

"I can't breathe." She gulps.

"I'll share my breath with you."

"My muscles ache." She wriggles her hips, and of course, my dick twitches.

"I'll stretch them out for you."

"You have an answer to everything?" She pouts.

"Finally, you are getting to know what I am?" I smirk, knowing I have won this round. Knowing I have her where I want her. In my arms, almost submitting to me. Almost.

"Did you mean it when you said you'll help me save my clan?"

"I don't repeat myself." I stare at her.

She leans down and kisses me. For the first time, it is she who licks my lips.

I part them, and she fastens her mouth around my tongue, then sucks on it.

The tug ricochets all the way to the tip of my cock.

Without pulling out of her, I flip her over so she's under me. Raising her hips, I pull back, then plunge into her.

She screams, and the sound turns me on further.

The warmth of her inner walls clamping around my dick is more than I can bear. A deep purr rumbles up my chest, and her pussy clenches around my shaft.

My groin tightens. My balls grow heavy.

Slick flows out of her, and the scent of her is everywhere around me.

"All mine," I glide my hand up the outside of her thigh, wrapping her leg around me. I angle her hips enough to slide in deeper.

Her head thrashes to the side, and her eyes roll back. Those mewling noises whine out of her. My dick pulses. My groin hardens. I pinch her chin and lower her head.

She cracks open her eyelids, the black of her pupils having bled out enough for me to know she is losing herself in me as I am in her. "Who do you belong to, Omega?"

Her shoulders go tight.

"Tell me."

"I—" She shakes her head.

She's trying to clear her mind, to get a lock on where she is, but I can't let that happen. I want her to tell me now, while she is in the throes of a sexual high, as I am going to knot her. I need her to tell me the one thing I want to hear. If that means I am an asshole, so be it.

I thrust into her, just enough for my cock to graze the slippery walls of her channel.

She moans.

And again.

This time, her breasts tremble, and color sweeps over her shoulders up to her face.

"Tell me." I pull out, all the way, and stay poised at the entrance of her channel.

"Please, I need you inside me."

"And you'll get what you want. Tell me who you belong to." I rub the swollen head of my cock up and down her slit.

"You." She shudders. "I belong to you."

I pound into her before she's completed the statement. She opens her mouth to scream, and I am already there, absorbing the sounds that are torn out of her. Every breath, every cry, her every moan of ecstasy belongs to me.

Sliding into her, deep inside, deeper than I have penetrated before, my knot clicks into place. I tear my mouth from hers. "Come for me, Omega."

A low scream rends out of her, then her body trembles as the tremors weave up her legs, her thighs, over her quivering waist. Her breasts tremble. She throws her head back and breaks under me, just as her wet, moist core clamps on my dick and milks me.

My balls draw up, and then cum shoots out of me again.

I collapse over her, making sure to keep my weight off her tiny body, but my arms are too weary to support myself.

I find myself falling on her and try to move away.

Her arms come around me, holding me in place. I sink down on her. Hearing the sound of my own heartbeat, the harsh in and out of my breath, the echo of her pulse at her temples, her breasts flattened against my chest—I've never felt so close to another. My heart hammers. The hair on the back of my neck rises.

Something is wrong.

The sound of an explosion rips through the air.

47

Lucy

The ground around me seems to shake. I've never had a climax like this. Bits of plaster rain down on us from the ceiling. Huh? So it's not just my orgasm that's rocking the space, but the explosion I heard is real?

His knot loosens, and he starts to pull out of me.

"No." Panic twists my guts. "Don't go."

A sudden tension grips my body. Terror squeezes my guts.

My pulse rate ratchets up, and I am sure it's the pounding of my heart in cadence with his that I am hearing.

I dig my heels into the back of his thighs and lock my arms around his neck. I clamp my inner muscles around his cock and he groans.

It's not lost on me that I am going through the very actions I'd accused him of doing to me a while ago. "Don't leave me." I clutch at his shoulders, hauling myself closer to him, thrusting my breasts into his hard chest.

"Shh." He leans his forehead against mine.

The delicacy of his gesture, the sheer gentleness of his embrace, sinks into me. My throat closes.

The mating bond thrums between us, and an inkling of fear bleeds through it. "What's happening?"

"I really don't want to leave you, Lucy, but I fear we have company."

The hair on my forearms rises. He called me by my name for the first time. My pulse rate ratchets up. I know then there is danger surrounding us, that he means to protect us, and I don't…can't let him go.

If he leaves now, I'll never see him again. Things will change, and I don't want that.

Just as I'd begun to get a sense of how it could be between us, everything is being torn away from me. This isn't fair. It isn't. "Don't go." The words bubble up out of me. Tears prick the backs of my eyes.

His body stiffens, and his shoulders go tense. He's already pulling out of me. His shaft slides out with a wet sound and another shiver of apprehension tightens my skin.

I reach down and clasp my fingers around his semi-erect dick, then tilt up my pelvis to take him back inside me. "No, don't go. They'll kill you, Alpha."

"I'd like to see them try." His forehead creases and a slow smirk curls his lips. "Nothing and no one gets to me or what's mine."

I swallow.

He leans back on his knees between my legs. The light from the open door pours over his shoulders, haloing that thick, dark hair that flows around his neck. The sculpted planes of his chest ripple, and the muscles of his forearm flex as he holds out his hand to me.

Sheer dominance pours off of him. The confidence and the primal strength implicit in every angle of his body is a turn-on.

I drink in the sight of him greedily, committing every single detail to memory. That burned pine scent of his mixed with that lighter sugary smell of my arousal, that tang of his cum that bleeds through the air, the deep blue of his eyes with the indigo fires that flare in them and call to me. Those strong cords of his neck that I want to kiss and lick my way down to where the massive shaft of his stands still semi-erect.

"Take my hand." The tattoos on the side of his biceps flex as he holds out his arm.

I place my palm in his, and he pulls me up so I am balanced on his thighs.

"Listen to me, Lucia. You are going to get dressed, and then you are going to stay here and not come out, no matter what happens."

"No, Alpha, don't go." Fear compresses my chest, and a ball of emotion grows bigger in my throat. "They are going to hurt you."

He bares his teeth, "Nothing can harm me, not when I know I have you waiting for me."

I swallow at the intensity in his voice.

This is when I tell him it's a trap, that everything that's going to happen is my fault, but still, I can't speak. I can't breathe.

The fear for him is a living thing in my chest, clawing at me to get out.

The bond twinges and shudders. And then a slow cloud of heat comes down the connection. It's filled with strength and possessiveness and something else. Love, so much love, the intense kind of want that promises me that he'll never let anything happen to me. And I love him for it. This monster who'd claimed me and rutted me, I'd trusted him from the moment I'd set eyes on him. The mix of sensations calms me more than anything else. In this instant, I know that come what may, he'll find a way to resolve this situation. *I* will find a way to resolve it.

"You will wait for me, Omega." He raises his head.

It's not a request, of course not. A command. A statement of intent, one that clearly says I belong to him.

He leans down and sinks his teeth in at the junction of where my shoulder meets my neck. Pain twists my insides, and I scream. He tears his teeth from my skin, then kisses me, dribbling blood into my mouth.

I suck on his tongue, then lick the blood off his lips.

The pain pulses and arrows down to meet the ball of heat in my chest.

"I will," I breathe out.

He wraps his big hand around the nape of my neck and yanks me close so my breasts are flattened against the hard planes of his chest. His shaft throbs against my still dripping core. "You are my property. Mine."

My heart feels like it's going to shatter. My scalp tingles and my hands and feet grow numb. Everything I have always wanted, that I had dreamed of is in front of me and I am going to lose it.

"Do. You. Understand?"

His voice lashes through the thoughts rolling in my head. The dominance of his stance demands only one fitting response. I jerk my chin, "Yes."

He cants his head and I swallow. "Yes, Alpha."

"Good girl." He kisses me again, then lifts me up by my waist and places me on the floor. "Get dressed."

I stare, not wanting to let go of him. He turns me around and points me toward the closet. "Wear your pants, don't forget the shoes."

I stay where I am.

"Go." He swats my butt.

I stumble then run to the closet, pulling out the clothes, putting them on with trembling fingers.

"Shoes. What shoes can I wear?" I am talking to myself, and that's okay. It's one way to focus, to stay present. Spying a pair of sneakers that seem to be my size, I slide them on.

By the time I turn, he's dragged on his drawstring pants and is walking through the door. It slams shut behind him. I race to it and peer out through the window. My breath stutters.

"No."

48

Zeus

Fuck, fuck, fuck. How did I let them get that close?

I stalk out of the bungalow. The sand in front of the building is hollowed out. The shrubs have been torn up by the roots and a fir tree burns to my right. As I walk forward another tree shudders, there is a creaking sound, then it crashes to the ground. The vibrations rip toward me. A cloud of sand billows up and spatters over me.

I clench my hands.

I should have known it was risky to bring her here, and without any of my team on guard.

But I had been selfish when I'd rescued her. I'd known there was no way I was willing to lose her again.

Which meant I needed time and space away from what I was…the alpha who ruled the city. I'd wanted time to explore the depths to which I had fallen in mating her the way I had. I'd wanted to make it up to her.

I'd brought her here, hoping to shut out the world. I should have known I couldn't stay hidden for long.

You don't get to commit the kind of crimes I have, piss off the number of people I have, without realizing you can run but never hide.

They'll track you down, hunt you down, bury you alive, and hurt those who matter to you.

Fear whips down my spine. My insides twist. I am not going to let anyone harm her. Not now, not ever. They'll have to kill me to get to her.

The cloud of dirt clears. I come to a halt not five feet away from my nemesis, the man who covets my power, "Kayden."

...eus."

The Leader of the Scots glares at me. Bet he wants to rip through me. He'd challenged me at my Ascension ceremony, and I had defeated him in front of my men. I had made him lose face and now he wants revenge. Anger radiates off of him in waves. His eyes spark with hatred.

Had I made a mistake in sparing my half-brother's life? The band around my chest tightens. My throat closes and I wipe all the expression from my face.

"Nice day for a walk?" I keep my voice casual.

Everything inside me wants to shove him away, push him off the island, and lead him away from my omega. But I don't say anything, don't let on how afraid I really am. A cold bead of sweat slides down my spine.

"I always did admire you for not losing your shit in a crisis." Kayden cracks his neck from side to side, and the gesture is familiar. It's something I am prone to do when I am angry or upset or when I want to dominate. Of course, asshole, he is your half-brother, there are bound to be similarities. And where had that thought come from eh? Fuck this conversation, what are we doing shooting the breeze anyway?

I cup my palm behind my ear, "Is that praise? Not something I'd ever thought I'd hear from you…half-brother."

His shoulders bunch, "Don't remind me." He sets his jaw.

"Unfortunately, there's no denying the resemblance between us." I drop my hand and lean forward on the balls of my feet. "Our father dealt us the ultimate blow, for his genes were too strong. Enough to paint your features and mine with the same brush strokes. There's no getting away from the fact that we have blood ties. Except"—I drum my fingers on my chest—"Don't expect me to honor it, hmm? Our fight to the death will be so much more entertaining for that, don't you think?"

"I am not here to talk about what we have in common." He raises his gun and aims it at me.

I draw myself up to my full height.

I will not show how afraid I am and it's not about losing my life. It's her. I cannot let anything happen to my omega, to the one thing that belongs to me, only to me. Not to this stinking city, not to my men, not to anyone else. She is mine and I will protect her at any cost. "Why do you hate me?" Yeah, that's me resorting to the oldest trick in warfare: trying to distract my enemy. It's a testament to just how out of ideas I am. Just keep the man talking while you work out what to do next.

He stares at me and his lip curls, "Is that all you have to ask? Are those going to be your last words?"

Fucker grins at me like I am losing my mind, and perhaps I have. I am going out of my head with worry. For her. Fuck me, what is this omega doing to me? My scalp prickles, the back of my throat hurts. The mating bond jolts and I raise my palm to rub the skin over my heart where it aches. What the hell? Did I just give away another clue to just how torn inside I am? I tuck my elbow at my side. "Answer me."

"Golan paid me a visit when I was five." He widens his stance. "Bastard revealed that he was my real father. Like that was a surprise, eh? My adoptive father never hid my origins from me so I knew that already. No, what took me unawares was Golan declaring how much he loathed me. How unworthy I was, unlike my older half-brother, Zeus who would one day inherit everything from him."

I stiffen. "Motherfucker played you." I clench my fingers at my side. "He played both of us," I mutter.

"He did it well." He chuckles, the sound a harsh whine in the space.

"He made it clear that you were his heir, while I was just the product of a rape, an illegitimate son who'd never scale the heights of his older sibling. I'd never hated anyone more than him...and you from that day. I swore I'd not stop until I took down both of you. Too bad, you beat me to him." He waves his gun at me.

A bead of sweat trickles down my back.

"Now I am going to defeat you and take over your city."

"So that's what this is about?" I purse my lips, "Sibling rivalry?" Soldiers have killed for less, so what he says doesn't surprise me, but that humane part inside of me that I have discovered since meeting my little squirrel rears its head insisting that I try to find a way out that would spare his life. Again. Me, showing mercy? Fuck me, I am going soft in my head.

"It's about power. You, of all people, must know the importance of absolute dominance." Kayden leans forward on the balls of his feet. "The kind that makes alphas tremble in your presence, that has omegas baring their pussies for you to ravage."

"It has its benefits," I keep my voice casual. The mating cord twinges in my chest and I shift my weight from foot to foot.

His gaze sweeps over my frame and comes back to rest on my face. His forehead creases, "Don't try to downplay the sole reason for your existence. You were right, we are similar, both driven by power, by the need to stamp out any trace of our blood-father and leave behind a legacy that re-writes history completely."

His words are too close to what I was, how I used to think, to everything that used to drive me until... one pint-sized omega swept into my life and turned it upside down. The blood rushes to my head and my stomach rolls. What the fuck is wrong with me?

Why can't I be as single-minded, as focused as I used to be? I used to want just one thing: the destruction of everything that motherfucker Golan stood for. And I am as driven, as needy, as one track as I have ever been. I do still crave one thing and one thing only. Her. Only her. Her lips. Her scent. Her cunt. "The fuck?" The roar rips out of me, and fuck me, but I can't rein in my emotions anymore.

Kayden's features light up in a look of utter delight, "Who'd have thought the mighty Zeus, the Beast from the East who killed his own father to gain the leadership of the most powerful city in this region, would meet his end deceived by an omega."

Deceived? A chill floods my chest. I clench my jaws so hard that that pain bleeds down my neck.

"Explain yourself." I drop my hands to my sides, straighten my fingers, and keep my feet firm on the sandy ground.

I need to stay calm, stay focused. Kayden is canny and trained at ways of pulling a fast one over his opponents.

Hell, he's proving to be as ruthless as me when it comes to navigating the corridors of power. But the one thing I have which he doesn't? Instinct. It's never failed me before...and it insists now that...he is right. She betrayed me.

Every muscle in my body goes solid, and she must sense the complete and utter feeling of loss that engulfs me, for the ball of heat nestled under my ribcage rears up. The omega's trying to reach me, trying to weaken me, and no way am I going to let her infiltrate my heart again.

I slam down a barrier on the mating cord. The emotions that pour from her end and into my veins cut off.

Kayden's lips twist. His gaze narrows on my features.

I shouldn't give away more of just how much this revelation has shattered me, but my brain, my heart, my soul, all of them seem to have a different plan. "You knew…" I try to complete the sentence, but the words stick in my throat.

Me, the alpha-hole of alpha-holes, struck dumb because the first time I trusted someone, she played me. Anger squeezes my chest and the blood pounds at my temples.

"Did I know you would claim the omega I sent you? No." He taps his foot on the ground. "But I'd calculated the odds. I knew she was exactly the kind of woman to appeal to you. Strong, feisty, and with that core of helplessness to her which would call to the gallant in you. I gambled."

"And you won." I pull my spine upright. There is a rolling in my gut and my chest aches. Blood-fucking-hell. Apparently, I have a heart. Who knew? And hey, I have feelings for her, too. Wonderful, let the realizations keep rolling forward, no matter that it seems like someone punched a fist through my ribcage and tore out that piece of flesh that used to beat there.

"She led you to me." My voice comes out hollow and the back of my throat hurts. It fucking hurts. Every part of me already knows what the look on his face confirms.

"Correction. She made you vulnerable, brought you away from your stronghold to this unguarded location, kept you wrapped up in the high of mating so you didn't even register our approach."

Anger squeezes my chest and I can't breathe. And it's not the fact that I let my guard down, though that too, but the fact that he dares talk about our mating as if it was just another callous coming together of bodies and it is not. It isn't. The mating chord slams into my rib cage and a groan tears out of me. Fucking get your head back in the game. He is going to kill you…worse he is going to hurt her and you are mooning over what could have been, how he is insulting her…and I am so screwed.

"How did you find us?" I force the words out. I don't want to know. If he tells me, that last sliver of hope that I am holding onto will shatter and then…then I will be gutted, absolutely, I know it and yet I can't stop myself from deepening that wound in my chest. Masochist that I am.

"I had her followed, had my soldiers posted across the city and at sea to track any move from either of you. You didn't think she could escape unless I had allowed her to, did you?" Kayden's eyebrows knit. His gaze sweeps over my features.

He's going to see the truth in my eyes and damned if I am going to glance away. I am not a coward, never turned away from a fight. I have my faults, but turning tail and hiding was never one of them. Not even when it's clear that I am losing… for the first time.

"Bloody hell." Kayden's gaze widens, then he throws back his head and laughs. That full, unabashed chortle from the depths of his belly which changes his countenance and which makes him look more familiar. Which highlights the similarity between us again.

"You have feelings for her." He props his hands on his hips.

No, it's worse. Much worse. I had fallen head over fucking heels with the omega. I'd claimed the one woman who could go toe to toe with me, and she'd deceived me, she was going to wipe me out, and you know what? None of that matters. I am going to die...but damned if I am going to let Kayden or anyone else get to her.

"You won't harm her." I thrust out my chest and put every bit of dominance I know into my voice.

He stiffens, his eyebrows drawn down. "Once the alpha, always the alpha, eh? Tell me, if you were in my position, if you had the gun trained on me, if I was the one thing standing between you and the woman I'd claimed, what would you do?"

"I'd kill you both," I say that without hesitation, because that's what I would have done, and because right now, lying won't serve me. "But you're not me. You have a conscience, Kayden. It's why you are not the leader of the most powerful city in the region. I am." I widen my stance. "I am going to crush you and there's nothing you can do about it."

His features go white as the color fades away, then he chuckles. "Fucking Zeus. Your balls are bigger than your brains."

"And your balls never did match up to the ambitions you had." I want to wind him up, to push him over the edge, so he loses control of himself and slips up. Or at least I hope so.

His lips thin, his skin is stretched over his cheeks, and a pulse beats at his temples as he walks toward me with his gun raised, then darts past me, picks up speed, and keeps going.

"No, no, no." Adrenaline spikes my blood. I break into a run, but it's too late.

49

Lucy

Kayden jams the barrel of the gun against my temple, and I freeze. I shouldn't have come out of the bungalow. I should have stayed inside as he'd asked, but I couldn't help it. When Kayden raised the gun at Zeus, I knew I couldn't stand by and do nothing.

Now Zeus looks at Kayden, his nostrils flared, those blue eyes burning with an unearthly light, every muscle in his body coiled with tension. I sense the anger surging from him in waves, and I know he is about to do something very stupid that will get him killed, and that I cannot tolerate. I've come this far, led Kayden to him, all without the view of finally handing him over to his sure death. But now, faced with the evidence of what I have done, with Kayden ready to kill him, I know I'll do anything to stop it. I'd give myself up to save Zeus.

"Don't do this." I turn to Kayden.

He steps back, gun still trained on me and beckons me to step toward Zeus.

Zeus starts to move forward, but Kayden growls. "You were right, I am going to kill both of you."

"You don't have the balls to do that, so why don't you hand over the gun to me?" Zeus slides his bulk between me and Kayden. He props his arms on his hips so his body covers me from sight.

Kayden shoots, and a surge of heat rips through my shoulder. A scream tumbles from my throat.

In front of me, Zeus' big body sways.

He takes another step forward and, closing the gap between them, grabs Kayden's gun. Another shot rings out.

I hear the bullet punch into his chest, scent the heavy, coppery burst in the air.

Then Zeus collapses to the ground. My alpha, who is invincible, his big body crumples.

Kayden steps over him and seizes my arm.

I snarl and slam my fist into his side. His arm shakes, and the gun falls to the ground. I grab for it, and he jumps on me, his body crashing into me.

My shoulder is whacked into the sand. Pain rips up my arm. The gunshot wound from earlier rips open, and red and silver sparks behind my eyes. My head whirls. He hits my hand, and I groan, then loosen my fingers.

He snatches up the gun and pulls me up with him. "Move," he snarls in my ear.

Tears prick my eyes, and I turn, trying to get a glimpse of Zeus. He's on the ground with blood pooling under his big body. The ball of emotions coiled against my rib cage screeches and pain floods down the bond. I tug at the hand holding me. His grip loosens, and I pull away to run toward Zeus.

Before I can reach him, Kayden is on me.

He seizes me around the waist and hauls me up over his shoulder. "He's dead, and you are mine."

"No." He's not dead. He can't die. "Zeus, Alpha," I sob.

The pain in my chest is huge and growing, taking over every part of me. My palms and feet grow numb. The mating bond twitches, then its resonance begins to ebb. Fear threads my spine, and at that moment, something inside me snaps. I cannot leave Zeus.

I will not allow him to die.

He has to live.

For me.

For what the future holds for us.

I bite down on Kayden's arm. He roars in pain, and his grasp falters. I twist my body and fall to the ground, rolling to break the fall, and then run to Zeus. I turn his body over.

His eyelids flutter open. His chest is splattered with blood and with sand. The mating bond stabs into my chest.

He tries to speak, and blood spurts out.

"Don't you fucking die on me Alpha," I snarl. "You hear me?"

Tears flow from my eyes and fall on his cheek.

He swallows. "I'll find you where you are. This much, I promise you."

Reaching down, I slide my arms around his shoulders, pull him, hold him close, feel the breath from his lungs sear my throat…then, nothing. His body goes limp.

I hear screaming and realize it's me. Fear curdles my gut, my heart feels like it is shattering, then I am being hauled away from him.

His limp body rolls to the ground.

"No." I shake my head.

Kayden begins to drag me away.

There's a pounding in my ears, and my vision narrows. I throw myself at Kayden, scratching his face, his chest, going at him with my teeth and nails and kicking him, howling at him.

"Let her go," a voice snaps through the violence that fills my mind.

The sound of a gun being unlocked snaps through the space. Kayden turns, still holding me.

"The alpha is dead. Long live the alpha." Kayden jerks his chin at the new arrival.

"Ethan," I croak.

He doesn't look at me. "Let her go if you value the life of your sister." He tugs the woman he's holding forward.

"Reena." Kayden stiffens, but his hold on me doesn't waver.

She stares at him, her eyes troubled. Her features are set in a look of resignation. She knows this is going to end badly for all of us.

And why is Ethan asking Kayden to release me? Am I not the enemy here? My mind whirls.

Before I can say anything, there's a flurry of movement, footsteps, and a bunch of men wearing the Scottish colors surround us.

"You didn't think I'd come on my own, did you? I am not as foolish as my half brother." He nods over his shoulder at the fallen Zeus.

"Half brother?" I breathe out.

Ethan's eyebrows furrow. "Let her go. Tell your soldiers to step back, else I'll kill your sister."

"You keep her." Kayden peels back his lips in a grin. "I'll take Zeus's omega."

50

Zeus

The sound of her screams rips through the haze that envelops me. I rush toward her, but my feet sink into the sand and drag me down. There are hands grabbing at her, pulling her away. She turns to me and extends her hand. I reach for her and grab at thin air.

"No." I spring up to find I am back in my suite in London.

The pulse thunders at my temples and my breath comes in pants. The mating bond screeches at me, slams against my ribcage, and yanks me up. My spine bends, my chest snaps forward, and I gasp.

Adrenaline spikes my blood.

Waves of stress and helplessness and so much hurt bleed down the bond and slams into me. Sweat beads my forehead.

"Fuck." I try to growl, but my throat is so raw as if I have been screaming for her. And for a second, I can't understand why I am doing this. I've never felt so gutted. My insides churn, my chest hurts. Every molecule in my body yearns for her. My very life is ebbing out of me, for without her, I am nothing…nothing.

The realization sinks in, and the tension drains from me. I bow my head.

There! I've admitted to myself that I cannot live without her. I am as good as dead if I don't have her.

I am going to do everything to protect her.

She is mine, and no one is going to hurt her.

Least of all that asshole, my very own half brother. And the fact that he is family means he is more dangerous. I snicker, the sound echoing through the space. To think people rely on those closest to them. My nearest blood has always been the bloodiest to me.

I am going to break that cycle. I am going to see this through to the end and save the one thing that has made me feel alive, made me connect with the truth of what I am inside. Not just an alpha, but also a protector.

I fling off the cover and swing my legs over the side of the bed. The effort sends pain shooting through my chest. I rub the space over my heart to find I am bandaged up all around my torso. My shoulder screams, my thigh muscles spasm, but I push on. I need to get to her.

I rise to my feet, and the blood drains from my head. The world tilts around me, and my leg muscles quake with the effort of trying to hold up my weight.

"Easy there." Ethan strides in from the door and steadies me.

"I am fine," I growl at him.

He lowers me back to the bed and grips my shoulders. My limbs twitch. The mating bond tugs at me, and I bend over with a groan. "Fuck," I try to breathe, but my lungs hurt. The band around my chest tightens and waves of agony crash over me. I drop my chin toward my chest and dry heave. The mating bond thrums, and adrenaline laces my blood. "I have to get to her."

Another wave of pain floods my chest, and I almost blackout this time. What the fuck? I am not some bloody weakling, I am the General of this city, and I am going to rescue my mate.

I grab the frame of the bed and push my feet into the wooden floor for purchase. Sweat pours down my chest in rivulets with the effort.

My muscles tense, and everything in me feels like it's fine-tuned to do one thing. "I have to find her." I hear myself, hear the helplessness in my voice, the anger, and that twisted desire all mixed with pure, unadulterated fear, and I cannot understand it.

How can I feel so much? Like she is the other half of me. She, an omega I'd met just a few days ago, has distilled her presence into me, and her essence now occupies that very core of me.

I rub the skin over my chest again, over the bandages, over where the bullet had gone clear through me. Right at the point where the mating cord is embedded into me.

The void personifies what is left of me.

Emptiness, a raw, searing wound that grows deeper by the minute, throbs with need, churns with that ache to be with her. The wound seems to ebb and contract, then fills with a surge of fear so strong that my throat closes. My knees crumple, and I sway.

"You are in no state to leave." Ethan folds his arms over his chest.

"Nothing and no one stands between me and her."

I hear my own words, and fuck if I don't sound obsessed. For I am. With her. My fingers tremble; sweat beads my forehead. I need to get to her; instead, I huddle here, helpless. Adrenaline spikes my blood.

I stagger to my feet. My leg muscles seize and I sway but manage to stay upright. Thank fuck.

The breath whooshes out of me. My lungs fucking hurt. My limbs twitch. My shoulders bunch. Every part of me screams in agony, but it's nothing compared to the void in my chest which threatens to grow bigger, until it fills every part of me, until I am one big mass of pain, every molecule of which still wants to go to her and rescue her.

"If you leave in this condition, you won't clear this stronghold, let alone infiltrate Kayden's fort where he's keeping her."

I turn on him so fast he has no time to react. But, of course, Ethan doesn't blink. He holds my gaze.

"You know where he's holding her?"

"At the Isle of Wight, in a tower that is virtually impenetrable."

"It's a trap." Another surge of pain blasts through me. It radiates out from the point where the mating bond is coiled in my chest, where it's now a long, dark hole, a furrow that rips out my guts, leaving only emptiness behind. For that's still what we are to each other, nothing. "She brought Kayden to me." The realization punches me with the force of a storm.

Ethan doesn't reply. He doesn't need to; the furrow between his eyebrows say everything.

"I am sure there's an explanation to everything—"

"Stop." I take a step back and hold up my hand. My voice is soft. Yet anger bubbles up from deep inside. This feels right, this acidic tang of hate that sweeps through my gut, that churns my insides, that eats away at my cells and bathes me in numbness. Welcome, hate, old friend. This I embrace with gratitude. I know how to deal with rage. I know what I need to do. I square my shoulders and straighten my spine.

"Don't go, this will not end well if you do." Ethan's voice is low and hard.

"Don't try to read my thoughts." I grit my teeth.

"You forget I've studied your behavior and your thinking patterns."

I blink. "That's bizarre, even for you, Second."

"It's the logical approach." He rubs the back of his neck. "One way to predict your moves, which, to be honest, are not always rational."

"What-fucking-ever," I growl at him. "What are you getting at? Spit it out, and in simple English. In a form that even I, the Bastard of the East End, will understand."

Ethan chuckles, and the sound is not kind. "Do I detect a streak of self-pity in the mighty Zeus?"

"Don't provoke me." We are so different, this man and I, and we are synced by something I cannot define.

He'd turned on the man he'd taken an oath to protect…then he'd helped me save her, and I've grown to rely on him.

Like I'd come to trust her, love her…and look at what had happened. She'd led Kayden straight to me. She'd almost killed me, and…I cannot live without her.

The mating bond aches and swells and burns in my chest, and… "Enough." My voice rings through the space.

Am I telling that to her? To Ethan? To myself? I am not sure. I drop into myself, draw on my instincts, and snap down a barrier on the bond.

A last pulse, a gasp, and then it stills.

Silence sweeps through my mind. The darkness crowds in, laced with hate. The need to hurt. Familiar emotions. This I can deal with. This is me. Empty, lifeless, a man who cannot be redeemed.

I swivel around and stagger to the bath at the far end of the room.

At the door, I grasp the frame and turn to look at him over my shoulder. "Tell the doctors to pump me up with enough painkillers. They need to get me functional, long enough to get to her."

"You sure that's wise? Why not wait a few days, until you have recovered enough—"

I stare at him, clamping down on my jaw so hard it hurts.

The color fades a little from his face.

He drops his head forward in a gesture of submission, but I am not fooled. Ethan doesn't bend to anyone; this is temporary. But it will do. Until I get to her, until I show her who is the real alpha in this relationship. She betrayed me once, and I will not let her fool me again. This time, I will bring her back and cage her and keep her. She will be my guilty pleasure, a possession to be taken and touched and then put back.

I'll ensure she understands the price of betraying me. No one, no one hurts me and gets away with it. Least of all an omega who has nothing to her name, a princess without a kingdom, a waif who wanted to save her own clan. A woman who smells of honey and sunshine and…I slam my fist into the wall next to the bathroom door. The surface cracks, and the plaster floats down on me.

My knuckles ache, and I smell blood in the air.

Pain floods my brain, and it helps me focus. Focus. Just one thing to do. Find her. And show her who is her true master.

51

Lucy

I am numb, so numb, I am sure I've drawn into myself, become an empty shell, and floated away, high up in the sky.

Away from where it hurts, away from the pain that floods my chest. The mating cord has been silent since Zeus fell. Emptiness swells in my ribcage. He can't be dead. Not my alpha. Not my vital, larger-than-life, dominant mate. He has to be alive. Has to… I grab at my chest. My fingers dig into the bandage that is wrapped over the crook of my shoulder.

The bullet that went through him grazed the side of my throat. It hurt me, but it almost killed him. "Zeus." I spring up in the bed and look around, my pulse pounding at my temples, but the room is draped in shadows. I clutch at the space above my left breast, trying to prevent the escape of any lingering vibrations.

I need to contain the last beats of the mating cord, lock in the thud-thud that beats in tandem with my heart.

My soul.

My everything.

He's everything to me.

And I betrayed him.

A trembling grips me. A pulse of heat drips down the mating bond. He's trying to block me out, and yet despite everything, he's helpless in the face of the intensity of our connection. He cannot stop a part of him from reaching out to me.

The scent of him floods my senses, that burned pine and cinnamon of his essence. I draw it in and pull it over myself, positioning it between me and the world.

The fine hair on my neck rises, and I know I am not alone. But I am not ready to face whoever is watching me.

For these last few seconds, I want to be alone with the essence of the person who can fulfill me, my alpha, my mate. My all… The mating cord thrums. It's pleased with my thinking, then a hint of belligerence bleeds through. And hate, mixed with confusion and love, so much love. But I am mistaken—he's an unfeeling monster. It's not possible for him to love, is it?

Not possible for him to give himself over completely to who I am. Especially now that I've betrayed him.

The mating cord pulses in agreement, then cuts out.

It just shuts down.

A chasm gapes in the space where it had once been. "No." I grip my side.

My heart hammers and a chill rattles my chest. The cord can't just dissolve.

Mating bonds between an alpha and omega cannot be broken.

I am alive, so he must be too.

The only explanation is that he's placed a barrier on the bond so I can't reach him…which means that he knows I betrayed him. I need to get to him and put things right. But how? I straighten my legs. I'll do what it takes to remedy the wrong I did him.

"You're conscious?" Kayden swaggers forward to stand a good five feet from me.

The arrogance of those flared nostrils, the haughtiness with which he surveys me—that curved nose, that build—he's so similar to his half brother. The same half brother who no doubt hates me now. The pressure increases at the back of my eyes and I bite down on the inside of my cheek to hold back my tears.

"What do you want, Kayden?" I infuse my voice with disdain.

His gaze rakes my features, "Not what you think."

"How do you know what I am thinking?" I try to chuckle, and the sound comes out on a gasp. Pain throbs through the wound at the side of my throat, but I can take it. It's a sign I am alive and here…unlike the emptiness that permeates my chest, filling it with nothingness.

"You're an omega in an alpha's domain. Of course, you'd think I want to rut you, but I don't take what belongs to another." His gaze falls on the claiming marks on my throat. The marks are still visible around the space where he'd shot me and where the bandage had been wrapped.

The way he looks at the wound, realization sinks in.

"You shot me over the claiming marks on purpose?" I grip my fingers together to stop myself from attacking him again. That's not going to help me, not right now.

"You could say it was a healthy coincidence."

Oh, the conceit of this man. "You half brothers talk the same. Did you two have the same teacher?"

His features tighten. "I am nothing like him. I am alive, and he's—"

My skin prickles. "He's not dead." I gasp out the words, rushing them out before he can say anything else.

Kayden angles his head, and his gaze narrows. "So, you do have feelings for him." He purses his lips and a smile tugs at the corners. "Apparently my plan worked, all too well."

"I…I don't understand." I wring my fingers. "Why did you bring me here?" I swallow.

"I have something bigger in mind for you. If it was Zeus's death I'd wanted, I'd have killed him already. No, this is more—much bigger. I need him to acknowledge his bond for you. I need to lure him here where I can barter him to the Vikings."

"You wouldn't." I stare at him in horror.

The Vikings are merciless, the worst of the alphas.

They are berserkers with no emotion, nothing to distract from the sheer blood craziness that takes them, and they go on killing rampages when that happens. They want power, land, and omegas.

Fear grips me. I force the words out, despite the lump in my throat. "You are going to trade me to them?" I hate that he can hear the tremor in my voice.

"Not you. They want my half brother. And I'd have taken him if his second hadn't intruded." He inhales, then releases his breath with a whoosh. "No, this is better. You are bait, and one a wounded alpha will covet, now that you are bonded to him."

I firm my resolve and meet his gaze. "Barter me instead."

"They want more." He rubs the back of his neck. "You are taken. They seek virgin omegas to mate with and breed—"

"You are going to barter my clan? You promised to protect them."

For a moment, he looks uncertain. "I am sorry, truly." He sets his jaw. "If I don't do as the Vikings say they will destroy my city and kill my people." He clenches his fingers into fists.

My palms sweat. "You'd give up your own half brother?"

"I'd do anything to save my clan, you of all people must understand that." His shoulders sag, then he squares them.

I swallow and look away. He's right. Hadn't I betrayed my own mate to save my kin? There is a sinking feeling in my stomach. My insides roil.

"It's not something I take lightly." He shifts his weight from foot to foot. "I came to this conclusion after much deliberation. If there was any other way, I'd take it."

"I will not let you hurt those I love." Rage pounds at my temples. Adrenaline spikes my blood. I stumble to my feet and throw myself at him.

He steps aside, and I lurch forward, toward the floor.

He catches me and shoves me back on the bed. It's not a gentle push, but he could have used more force.. I sit up.

He props pillows behind my back, then moves away, putting space between us.

It's clear to him that I am bonded.

That I belong to another.

Of course, he can scent another alpha on me, but it's not that. "You don't want to hurt me."

"Smart omega." His gaze sweeps over my features. "I don't want to taint you in any way that might distract Zeus from his purpose—of reclaiming you, taking you away."

The horror of what he's saying sinks in. But there's also a fierce sense of rightness, of inevitability. That come what may, he'll always return to me, as I will find my way to him. And this time, I will not let him down. I need to find a way to help him. I must. I draw myself up to my full height and meet Kayden's gaze.

"You lie."

He stiffens. His chest rises and falls, and he folds his arms over his chest. The dominance pours off of him, and those features so similar to Zeus's harden.

But he isn't Zeus.

He doesn't have my alpha's eyes. Or his chin. Or that breadth of his chest that urges me to fling myself at him and ask him to cover my body with his.

"Explain, Omega." His voice is a whiplash.

My heart hammers, but I hold his gaze. "You're not a monster, and neither is Zeus. You think you want to hurt him. You think you are going to give him up to the Vikings. But you are not."

He growls, and the sound eddies over my skin and settles in my belly. The unmistakable masculine power of an alpha tugs at my nerves and my chest hurts.

His nostrils flare, and his gaze narrows. He takes a step forward. "You don't know what you are talking about."

My pulse races. My guts twist. I want so much to cower, to fling my arms over my head and hide; instead, I grip the bedclothes and clench my teeth "I do."

"Only an omega would believe in the goodness that lurks under the skin of a beast, and that's not —"

"True. It's true." It has to be. Doesn't he understand I have to believe it to survive? I need to hold on to that kernel of possibility I sense here, what my intuition tells me is possible. I have to give it a chance.

My words seem to cut through the haze in his head, for he takes another step forward, and another, until he's standing above me. He's not as tall as Zeus, but Kayden is tall enough, mean enough, and bigger than many alphas I have met. Icy tendrils of fear have me questioning myself.

He growls and tosses his head.

"You don't scare me." I clench my fists at my sides.

He blinks, then chuckles.

I stare.

"I can see why Zeus is so taken with you. I guess I made the right choice by sending you to him, after all. Who knew I'd figured out his taste before he could, eh?" He straightens, and turning, stalks to the door.

"Wait," I call after him.

He pauses, then shoots me a look over his shoulder. "No more questions. I have told you everything I can. Rest, recover. It won't be long before Zeus arrives, and you don't want to keep him waiting, Omega."

52

Zeus

I move back, far enough from the wall to be able to take the measure of it. Then running up to it, I scale it, my fingers and toes catching the dents, tiny grooves in the wall of the castle, before getting to the top. I vault over it and drop to the ground almost twenty feet down.

Hitting the muddy earth, I roll to break my fall, then spring back on my feet, and begin to run.

I tuck my arms into my sides, lengthen my strides, and my breathing grows deeper. All the lessons I learned while racing through the alleys of the East End, evading those who hunted me, come to the fore.

My body adjusts to the pace and I race through the forest that surrounds Kayden's safe house in the Isle of Wight.

Crazy, the height of stupidity, Ethan had called it. I have come here on my own, not fully recovered from the bullet the bastard pumped into me. And here I am, being led by my dick as I attempt to single-handedly break through one of the most guarded outposts in the entire continent. Well, boo-fucking-hoo. There hasn't been a single stronghold I couldn't infiltrate so far... and I plan to do just that. I am going to spear that omega's cunt once I get to her.

Footsteps crunch through the fallen leaves near me, and I drop to a crouch. I shuffle behind the trunk of an ancient oak tree.

Soldiers walk by, clad in armor, carrying large swords and armed with organic fitted guns. Interesting. Guns are normally confined to top rank alphas, bullets being relatively difficult to come by. Which means someone is funding Kayden, probably the same people who put him up to trying to trap me.

All my instincts go on alert. The hair on my nape rises. I hadn't considered until now that Kayden might be working with someone else.

Fear twists my guts. More than ever, I need to find her and get her out of there. Now.

I draw in a deep breath, scenting the woodsy air. The smell of eucalyptus and rotting vegetation hangs heavy. Laced with it is that honeyed smell of my omega. I growl in my throat.

A sense of sheer possession overwhelms me. And anger, so much rage. She knew I'd knot her, had anticipated I would mate her, and she had played me every step of the way. Challenging me, provoking me, making me want her until it wasn't enough to crave her body. I needed her essence in me, and I had broken everything I'd stood for.

I'd forgotten about completing the revenge on Golan by destroying all trace of my inheritance, wiping out the ruling classes, defeating my half brother…I had forgotten the need for revenge that had kept me going so far.

When I am with her, all I can think, scent, feel is that skin, those lips, the scrape of her teeth on my dick as she swallows me whole. My cock throbs in response, and I don't clamp down my desire. Not my temper either. Instead, I dive into it and yank it up over myself. I use it as a shield, for I am not carrying any weapons.

Remaining in the shadows, I run through the trees. The wind has died down, and the leaves are still.

When I reach the tower in the center of the island, I don't slow. I break away from the trees and race to the entrance.

The first guard sees me. His gaze widens, but before he can reach his weapon, I kick out, catching him in the throat. He crumples to the ground.

I swing around and slam my fist up and into the chin of the second guard.

That one goes flying back, hits the side of the tower, and then his body sags to the ground. The thump from the crash echoes through the space.

Racing forward, I slip in through the entrance. I lunge up the winding staircase and keep going, up the winding steps. When I round the next corner, that aromatic rose-and-honey scent of my omega bursts over me.

I follow it, keep running all the way up, through the door at the top floor. When I push on it, it swings open. Well, no surprise there. It's a trap, but they've underestimated the fury of the beast who's taken the bait. I step through the double doors. Moonlight flows in through the windows that cover the walls of the turret. And there in the center, laid out on a bed, I see her.

Her rich, dark-red hair ripples over the white sheets. Her arms are folded over her stomach. The white of her face glistens in the moonlight. She looks untouched, almost virginal, which she isn't. I'd taken her, and mated her, and then she'd betrayed me. A growl rumbles up from my throat.

She stirs, and I forget to breathe.

Turning over on her side, she flings out an arm. Her tunic parts to expose a creamy thigh. The neckline is deep enough to cling to the tops of her breasts.

Her nipples peek through the almost translucent fabric.

Has she been laid out there precisely to lure me in? Every instinct inside me screams to get out of here. The hair on my forearms rises, and a pulse thuds to life at my temples, at my jaw, even in my fucking balls.

My body insists there's only one way out.

To go to her, take her, knot her now, and claim her all over again.

My vision closes until all I can see is her.

Only when I find myself standing next to her do I realize that I have crossed the floor.

Above us, lightning splits the sky, illuminating the entire place in relief. It brings out the hollows under her cheekbones, the purple rings beneath her eyes. She murmurs and moves restlessly, then turns on her back again.

The white wraparound tunic parts all the way down to show the shadowed valley between her thighs. The scent of her slickness bleeds into the air.

My shoulders bunch.

Her hips twitch, and she rubs her thighs together.

My mouth goes dry.

Her chest heaves, and a mewl spills from her lips.

She knows I am here. Her subconscious senses my presence, and her body is putting on a show. Only for me.

I try to take a step forward and find I can't. My feet seem to be stuck to the floor.

She flings an arm up over her head, and one nipple pops up over the neckline.

My balls tighten, and a groan catches in my throat. I can't take my gaze off her.

She moans, and her lips form my name. "Zeus," she whispers under her breath.

My heart stutters. Even in sleep she calls to me.

Lightning bursts in the distance; thunder rolls. Her eyes are shut, but her eyeballs move behind her closed eyelids. She's dreaming of me. She wants me.

She moves her head, and I see the bandage on the side of the throat over the claiming mark.

The bastard shot her.

The bullet had gone through me and nicked her, right over where I had claimed her. I clench my teeth so hard that my jaw snaps. Blind fury grips me. The fucker hurt her. He put her in danger. He used her to get to me, and he is going to keep doing it again and again. I have to get her out of here. But I need to touch her first.

I lean over her, and she parts her thighs. Her hand slips down her waist to the triangle between her legs.

She weaves her fingers through her glistening folds, then thrusts two of the digits into her cunt, and fucks herself.

The scent of her, that sugary sweetness of her is all around me. Sweat drips down my spine. I wait, frozen, undecided. Knowing I need to get her out of here. Knowing I can't yet…not without making sure I have claimed her once more, so that my scent is on her, and I've marked her as mine. That primal part of me prowls to the fore.

"Alpha…" The breath trembles out of her, and she wriggles her hips.

Fuck this, I must have her. Now.

Something inside me snaps. Everything that is human and decent, which is not much to begin with—but whatever it is that this omega had sensed—that halfway empathetic part of me gives way.

The monster in me roars forth, the one that had not hesitated to kill to protect my mother, that had throttled my father. Heat sweeps over me, and my mind empties. Placing one knee on the bed I swing my other over her hips, then lean forward.

There's a clap of thunder, and her eyes fly open.

53

Lucy

I see his big body hulked over me.

His massive shoulders are silhouetted against the glass roof, and the lightning that tears through the sky is reflected in the silver of his blue eyes.

His hair cascades behind him.

His chest muscles ripple under the black that he is wearing. The material clings to him, tracing every groove, every hard plane of his chest. It sweeps down to dip in at his concave waist.

The hard rod of his arousal strains at the front of his pants. Precum dampens the material over his crotch.

My mouth waters. My throat closes.

That deep, burned pinewood scent of his pours over me and bleeds into my veins. His purr draws at my nerves and my sex puckers with need. The tang of his arousal teases me. My stomach flutters.

I snake out my hand and grip his rigid cock through his pants.

His groin goes solid; his thigh muscles twitch.

With the fingers of my other hand, I continue to fuck myself.

His dick throbs in my palm. I am not dreaming. He is here. Real and alive and oh, so vital. My breath hitches.

"No screaming then, Omega?" He bares his teeth.

I squeeze his shaft, and his chest heaves.

Oh, he likes that. I bite my lower lip.

A pulse ticks at his jaw. He pries my hand off his crotch and shackles my wrist over my head. Then he yanks the fingers of my other hand out of my pussy. He raises them to his lips and sucks on them.

The sensation of his tongue on my skin sends goosebumps flaring down my arm. I shiver; my core trembles. Every part of my skin seems to come alive with anticipation. My nerve endings stretch until I am sure I am going to scream with the tension building between us.

His nostrils flare, and those blue eyes blaze with lust and with some other emotions I can't quite name.

I raise my gaze to meet his and open my mouth. He releases my wrist, then swoops down to wrap his fingers around my throat.

"You don't get to speak. You lost that privilege when you betrayed me. I trusted you once, but never again."

His breath is hot on my cheek, like a lover's kiss, except it isn't. He's the Devil, here to ruin me, and heaven help me if I don't want him to.

I try to speak once more, but his hold on my neck tightens. His eyes narrow. The skin around his eyes stretches.

Hatred and loathing roll off him and overwhelm me.

I stare at him and drink in his features: that patrician nose, that strong jaw, that beautiful neck. All of it pleases me and scares me. I'm so afraid of what he's going to do next. I need whatever he has planned for my body. Every touch, every nibble, every flicker of heat, of pain, I want it all.

He shoves one massive thigh between mine, then the other.

A dense cloud of heat spools off him. It crashes into my chest and pins me down.

He forces his bulk between my legs, spreading them wide apart. The rough material of his pants chafes over my inner thighs.

My pulse rate ratchets up, and my belly quivers. More slick streams from my channel.

His nostrils flare. "Does the threat of violence turn you on, little squirrel?"

Yes. No. His blue eyes hold me in thrall. Emotions bubble up and stick in my chest.

He peels back his lips. "By the time I am done with you, you'll never want to see me again. You'll loathe the day you set foot in my stronghold."

No, no, no. He got this all wrong. I want him, but not with hate. I want more. I want all of him. His heart. His soul. His very essence. I try to tell him that, but he increases the pressure on my throat, and I can't get the words out.

His gaze narrows.

He releases my other arm, then lowers his zipper. His cock springs free. Massive. Throbbing. Erect.

My heart hammers. Not like this. Don't. I must have made some noise despite the iron hold around my throat. Or maybe it's the panic in my eyes, or the pleading I pour down the bond at him. I am not even sure if he will receive my intent, but he must sense something, for he slows down.

Just enough to press his chest to mine so every part of his torso covers my much smaller body. Then he purrs. The sound sweeps out of him and pours over me, into me, heating me, enveloping me in that sheer 'Zeus' essence.

Warmth surges up from my heels, swelling over my body. Every part of my skin seems to ignite.

My core throbs, and slick gushes forth. My head rocks back against the pillows, and I can't stop the whine that dribbles out of me.

"So needy, so wanting. So fucking responsive." His eyes darken, going that deep indigo, which I know means he is going to… He plunges his hardness into me.

A scream peels up my chest only to be caged in my throat.

He spears me, slamming home in a way that's meant to hurt. He is my dominant, my master, and all I can do is thrash in his embrace.

Still, he made sure I was moist enough and wanting enough that there is no pain.

He pulls all the way out, then rams into me again. His balls slap against my flesh. White pleasure sweeps through me, and he does it again; the waves build with each thrust. I dig my fingernails into his forearm for purchase.

The need to punish leaps off him. This is different from how he'd mated me in his stronghold. Even then I'd sensed a restraint to him. This is different. This is an alpha rutting an omega, aiming to punish, to make me hate him as much as I hate myself now. He's right. By the time he's done, there will be nothing left of me to give him. No love, no need, nothing but the tatters of my pride and my shame at wanting this alpha so much.

I stretch out my hand, yearning for something more. Needing to connect with him on another level.

He weaves his fingers with mine, then draws my hand to the side and pins it there. He lunges into my wet pulsing channel and his dick penetrates all the way in. My entire body shudders from the impact. Every single ridge of his turgid flesh leaves its imprint on the weeping walls of my pussy. Intense heat screams out from my core. My hips strain to get closer to him. My spine arches; my shoulder blades dig into the mattress.

He holds my gaze and thrusts one more time. His throbbing dick slides in impossibly deep sinking into that very secret core of me. He hooks me behind my pelvic bone even as the root of his shaft expands and his knot slots into place locking me to him.

A nerve beats at his temple. Sweat drips down his throat and plops onto my chest. "Come for me." His growl sweeps over my skin and on its heels my climax surges up jolting over my legs. My thighs spasm; my stomach tightens. My entire body stiffens then shatters as waves of red and white crash over me.

His chest planes go solid, and the tendons of his throat flex. He swoops down and bites my shoulder on the unmarked side.

I fling my head back and open my mouth to scream. He slides the hand that was around my neck, to my lips to smother the sound. I bite down on his palm and taste copper.

He doesn't flinch.

He raises his head, and blood streaks his chin. My blood. He takes his hand off my mouth. "Welcome home, Omega. Your nightmare has begun."

A pressure builds behind my eyeballs, and my head spins. "I don't believe you. You are not a callous man."

"I took you without your submission." His voice is harsh.

"We took each other." I lick my lips, tasting him.

His eyes blaze; a pulse ticks at his jaw.

My heart stutters, and everything inside me shrivels. Still I don't lower my gaze. I need to hold my own. I cannot give in, not yet, not until I've figured out how to set things right.

"Semantics." He grabs the base of his shaft, squeezing it until the last streams of cum shoot inside me, enough for his knot to loosen. He slides out with a wet plop, and his seed streams down my thighs.

I want him to take it and mark me, to rub it all over me and tell me I am his. I wait…wait for him to do just that.

Maybe he senses my emotions, for his eyes widen, and he leans in close enough for his lips to almost touch mine. Almost. He bares his teeth. "Fooled you."

He pushes back and springs off the bed, then zips up his pants.

All the heat seems to be sucked out from my body. I shiver, then wrap my arms around myself. I want to scream at him. I have to tell him he's got everything wrong, but the words stick in my throat. I try to sit up, but my hands refuse to support me.

He grabs my waist, then hauls me up and off the mattress. His movements are abrupt, yet his touch is gentle.

He places me on my feet. I stumble, and he rights me, then steps back.

The remnants of our coupling ooze down my leg.

He reaches for me again, and I want to flinch. I want to but I don't. I hold his gaze as he rips the tunic off me and flings it at me.

"Clean yourself up."

54

Zeus

The hurt in her face guts me, and I cannot understand my reaction. She doesn't mean anything to me. She doesn't.

She's the omega who had swept into my stronghold, and I had taken her as any alpha would.

She fought me, and I mated her.

She betrayed me, and I…let her down, too.

I went against that trust she'd placed in me, and I rammed into her, as is my wont.

That's all an omega is good for, to breed, to be knotted and filled with spawn to level up the declining population.

The thought of her heavy with my child sends a primal wave of lust surging through me. Close on its heels is a compelling need to protect her. To keep her safe. I'll never give her my heart, or the complete possession of my body, but I'll keep her safe.

I'll keep her in my sight always. She will never escape again.

I cross the floor to the closet in the corner of the room and pull it open. Taking hold of another of those tunics similar to the one she'd been dressed in, I stride back to her then hand it over.

Without giving her a chance to speak, I stalk to the door and shove it open. I don't need to turn to know she's on my heels.

The heat of her body flows over me, and once again I am struck by how tiny she is.

My little squirrel must be caged and protected at all costs.

I race down the steps, and she is at my heels. Her bare feet slap against the tiles.

Her soles will hurt when we run through the stones and the muddy ground outside, and the rain will soak her skin. I refuse to let it stop me. Why is it that the thought of her hurt twists my guts? She's nothing to me. Nothing.

Reaching the ground floor, I wrench open the door.

The rain chooses that moment to pour down. The water flows in gusts, drenching me.

It's good, though. It will give us more cover.

I march out.

She follows me, and I hear her feet skid on the slippery ground. My heart lurches. She rights herself, and the breath I'd not been aware of holding rushes out.

I will not turn to help her along. I will keep going, keep my head bent, gaze at the tree line on the other side. I glance over my shoulder to find she is lagging behind. Her clothes are damp from the rain, and the mud flies up in her wake to splatter on her dress. Her feet will be bruised and cut at this rate.

I reach the tree line then hunch over and jerk my chin at her. "Up."

"What?" She frowns.

"Didn't you hear me?" I grit my teeth. "You are slowing me down, woman. Get up on my back so I can give you a ride."

She crosses her arms over her chest. "I can leave here on my own two feet, thank you very much."

"Fuck." My stomach lurches. At this rate, we are going to be discovered by the guards, and there's no way I am going to let them get their hands on her. I need to get her to safety. "Don't push me, Omega. I am already furious with you."

"Like that's any different than before." She tosses her head.

"Yeah, it is." Blood thuds at my temples. "I trusted you. I knew you'd come to kill me, yet I mated you. Not anymore."

"Wha…what do you mean? You can't sever the mating bond." She rubs the part of her chest over her heart, a mirror to the place in my chest where the cord burns. White noise fills my rib cage, swells my blood and pounds at my pulse points. All of my nerve endings twitch, warning me, tugging at me, telling me not to do it. Don't cause her pain. Don't. "Oh, I will keep the bond, for I intend to make your life a living hell."

Her features go pale.

This is when she'll flee from me, maybe back to Kayden, or perhaps she'll try to run, knowing she's changed one kind of imprisonment for the other.

Instead, she stomps around me and thumps me in the chest. "If you think that scares me away, think again. Nothing can change what I have been through already. Where every single part of me has been infiltrated by you, taken by you, and still I am here with you."

"That's what I don't understand." I shake my head, the rainwater bouncing off me, off her, filling the silence.

"Neither do I." Her mouth turns down at the side. Her green eyes shine…with tears?

My chest tightens, and my guts lurch. The fuck? Why am I reacting to her misery? I wanted to upset her, cause her to be angry and afraid. Instead, all of those emotions are backfiring on me.

A shout sounds in the distance.

I stiffen. "We've gotta leave."

"No." She folds her arms behind her back.

"Really?" I set my jaw.

I was insane to have come to her rescue. I was wrong to think my attachment to her is temporary. I am giving her a chance to speak, to have a say in how the future unfolds for her, and fuck me if that isn't acting out of character.

Obviously, I am losing my edge, my ability to think in coherent terms. Since I mated her, I have forgotten my goal, my past, what I am. All I know is her, and I am not going to let her order me around or defy me again.

No way.

I haul her and throw her up over my shoulder. She struggles—of course she does.

I slap her butt.

She goes still then wriggles with renewed force, kicking out and catching me in the side.

"Keep quiet. Do you want to attract Kayden's attention? I can promise you his treatment of you is going to be far worse than mine."

"Let me down, or I'll yell and attract the attention of the guards," she hisses at me.

"You won't." I chuckle.

Why would she want to stay back with Kayden, the man who kept her family captive, who put her up to the mission of infiltrating me? Nah, she knows she is better off with me. She knows it.

She throws her head back and screams.

55

Lucy

I didn't mean to do that, scream and draw attention to us, but this alpha, his sheer arrogance riles me up again.

Everything I'd decided earlier, to put right the way I'd betrayed him, to behave like a normal omega, all of that goes right out the window.

His big body freezes under me, and his muscles coil. Dense clouds of anger roll off him. I swallow. He's going to punish me for this.

Probably spank my butt again, or drop me, leave me, and get the hell out of here. He does none of that. He chuckles. A deep, sexy sound that seems to swell from his very core. It's as potent as his purrs. No, even more.

This is Zeus giving in to that sense of humor I knew he had hidden inside him. I'd sensed it, felt it, just never thought he'd show it. Not now. Not when we are facing his nemesis. His half brother who reacted so like him. For a second, my heart aches at the rift between these two. Both alphas, so similar, yet so different. One of whom is mine, and the other…he doesn't mean to hurt Zeus. He doesn't. Just as Zeus wants an excuse to settle their differences.

I cannot explain this flash of insight that sweeps over me except to say that perhaps my instinct and ability to foresee, which my mother had always maintained I had, chose this moment to reveal itself.

He lowers me to the ground, making sure to slide me down every single inch of his body.

I feel those hard planes of his chest, the taut muscles of his stomach, the rigid length of his shaft, all of it sets my insides humming with lust. Then I am standing, and he bends enough to peer into my eyes.

"You've been a bad omega."

His voice is stern. His eyes gleam.

Yeah, the alpha's eyes actually shine with a light that promises I haven't heard the last of this.

His lips turn up in a smirk. "I promise I am going to punish you for that, but for now, we need to get out of here, okay?"

Those indigo eyes of his draw me in, circles of blue and violet and turquoise, and the entire range of blues in between flare. All dwarfed by those long lashes that should make him look absurdly feminine. But all it does is emphasize his sheer masculine presence.

My heart lurches with a strange warmth.

Why am I so drawn to him, even as we are trying to escape a man who is out to get him, and me, and my family?

I stiffen. "My clan."

"We'll get them out, provided you cooperate."

I swallow and bite my lower lip.

He frowns, and his gaze searches mine. "Will. You. Cooperate with me?" His nostrils flare.

The intensity of his gaze sears me.

A growl spools from his throat, and despite myself, my thighs clench, and moisture creeps down my core. I nod. "Y…yeah."

"I didn't hear you, Omega." He draws himself up to his full height.

I jut out my chin. "I'm ready to leave with you."

He holds out his hand.

I slip my palm into his much bigger one, and he takes off, yanking me along. He sets a blistering pace. My muscles burn as I try to keep up. My heart pounds, my throat is dry, but everything inside me glories at the fact that he's holding my hand.

We are doing this together, and every pore in my skin opens and revels in being near this alpha.

The sheer vitality and energy that crackles from him is a testament to what he truly is. A full-grown, in-his-prime alpha, who is lethal, dangerous, and all mine. Mine. I almost stumble at the realization. His grip tightens on my hand, and I straighten. Then we are moving, fast, through the trees.

I hear the footsteps crashing through the undergrowth behind us the same time he does.

He increases his speed and pulls me along.

My lungs scream. I try to draw in oxygen, and my feet slap on the stones with every step I take. The skin on my soles bursts open, and I wince but don't stop.

My thighs burn, my stomach spasms, but I force my legs to move. I will keep pace with him. I must. It's the only way to earn his respect. Show him that I can match his speed.

We run until we hit the beach. He doesn't stop, keeps going, wading into the waves. The seawater burns the cuts on my feet, and a scream boils up before I can stop it.

He doesn't slow down, though I sense the tension in his body ratchet up. The stress coils in his muscles.

Half turning, in a move that takes my breath away, he snatches me up and swings me over his shoulders then jumps over the first wave and the next. A third wave crashes over us, and he loses his grip on me. I crash into the water.

The blue-green waves close over me, filling my mouth, my ears, burning my eyes. Then I am pulled under, only to be hauled up by a firm grip under my armpits.

My head clears the water, and I take in big gulps of breath. My lungs scream; my throat hurts. I squeeze the arms holding me. "Alpha."

"That's right, Omega."

"Zeus." I crack my eyelids open.

"Wrong guess."

56

Zeus

Kayden holds her up in front of him, his hands gripping her shoulders. How dare he touch her? The water streams over her hair, down her neck, plastering her dress to her chest, and all I can think is that she looks like a goddess. And he has his hands all over my property.

Anger tightens my chest.

I take a step forward, and a wave crashes in between us. I lose sight of both of them.

My heart slams against my ribcage. My throat goes dry. Where are they? A second, then another, and he resurfaces, and he's still holding her close to him.

Primal rage heats my blood, thundering in my veins. "Let her go."

"The mighty Zeus felled by an omega."

"Don't talk about her."

I keep my gaze off her eyes. Off those burning green eyes that mirror the turmoil of the sea around us.

Lightning crashes above us, and the wind picks up speed, sending another spill of water flowing over me.

I keep my feet pressed into the shallow seabed, feel the sand flake and fall away from behind my heels. A heavy weight pushes down on my cheat. My ribcage constricts and I can't breathe. The mating cord slams against the barrier I have placed on it, and my throat closes.

He takes a step back, dragging her along.

Needles of ice pierce my flesh. "What do you want, Kayden?"

"A question you've never bothered to ask before, bro."

Half bro. But whatever, I don't correct him.

When I had killed Golan, Kayden had challenged me for the title of the General. I had defeated him in front of the entire Council of my alphas. Then instead of killing Kayden, I had let him go. The only person he hates more than me is my father. Well, we have that in common.

I raise my arm and fling aside the gun I'd been holding on to, and the one on my back. Both are waterproof, and they can still be used, but I don't let on about that.

"What's this? The new, improved version of Zeus who wants to take the time for a tête-à-tête? Fancy." He bares his teeth.

The expression on his face is defiant and angry.

I see the similarities between us, everything that had been facing me for so long, and I had blindly missed it.

He's as much a victim of circumstances as I am.

As much a man misled by emotion, by fate, by the accident of birth.

He has his hands on the one thing that matters more to me than anything else, and I cannot let him hurt her. Not even if I have to die for her... The thought sweeps through me, and my insides churn, then still.

A strange sense of peace descends over me. There, in the middle of the stormy sea, as the omega I'd chosen for my mate is held hostage by my half brother, as his team of alphas stomp up the beach and line the water's edge, as I hear them raise their rifles and cock them... The sound reaches me over the wailing of the wind, and I push it aside.

"Let her go." I widen my stance.

"What will you give in exchange?"

"Me." I raise my chin.

"Not enough."

"What else do you want?" I prop my hands on my hips.

"Your title, your seat of power." One side of his lips draws up. "That you'll bow to me, accept me as leader of the joined states of England and Scotland."

"Never," I growl.

His hands curl around her neck, and his forearms ripples as he squeezes.

She gasps, and her head flies back and slams against his chest

The pulse pounds at my temple; the blood roars in my ears.

"Let her go." I take a step forward.

Only for him to bring his other arm around her neck, and I know what that means. One twist and he could snap her spinal cord.

Red haze fills my sight. Everything in me bursts into a hot, melting mass of flames then blanks out.

A cold fist squeezes my heart.

I draw the numbness over me like armor. "Don't you want to hear what I have to say?"

"I'm all ears, big brother. Tell me."

"We fight, you and me" — I thump my chest — "one on one."

"If I win?"

"You get my power, my Council, and my omega, all of it." I firm my jaw.

"If you win?" He drums his fingers on his chest.

"I keep the omega."

"Only the omega?" He frowns. "You don't want anything else?"

"Just her."

He tilts his head. "You expect me to believe that you'd walk away from everything you fought so hard for, and all for her?"

"I won it all overnight. I'll lose it again…or not." I raise my shoulders, then let them fall. "Easy come, easy go, little half brother."

His gaze widens. Realization dawns on his face.

My palms grow cold. Bloody fucking hell. Did I just blurt that out? The terms I suggested sound too good to be true. He's never going to believe that by winning I'd give up everything. Whatever happened to the alpha who had plotted and planned and muscled his way to claim the role of General of London? He's fucked that's what he is. My stomach rolls. I've given myself away.

I've revealed what I value more than power, more than wealth.

He'd guessed that I had feelings for her, but I've given away exactly how much she means to me. I've conceded the most important bargaining point to him, that I would give up not just my life but my life's purpose for her.

My breath catches. I wipe all the emotions from my face.

Wouldn't do to give away that I've realized my mistake as well. I hold his gaze and wait.

In his arms, her features are frozen. She's wondering if I have gone crazy. And maybe I have. Or maybe for the first time I am following what I want. Fighting for the one thing that makes me feel alive—her.

"Well?" I kick back on my heels, and my stance is casual. Inside, my stomach hurts, and my blood roars. Everything in me wants to step forward and snatch my omega from Kayden.

He releases her so suddenly that she stumbles.

She breaks through the water and goes under with a cry, but I don't move. Don't want to show how much it hurts me not to go to her right now and pull her up. But she's strong, my omega. She can fight this. She has to survive for me. Please. She surfaces the next instant and lurches, half swimming, half standing, the water coming to her neck. Her face is pale, but she's fine. Still alive and breathing. Her anxious gaze holds mine.

Kayden smiles.

It lights up his entire face, turns those features far more beautiful than mine into the face of a fallen angel. "Challenge accepted."

57

Lucy

I stare not understanding exactly what's happening between the two of them. I feel helpless, caught in a game, and I have no clue what the rules are. Who are these players?

It's as if everything I have lived so far is a lie.

The only truth is the harsh sting of the wound at my shoulder where he bit me again. The saltwater pours over it, and it burns.

I shudder and try to hold my own against the next wave that crashes over me. I sway and almost fall again. Neither of them notices.

Zeus turns and plunges through the water. The lash of the waves doesn't slow him down.

His hair is drenched, and his fatigues cling to him. He holds his arms at his sides, looking every inch the true warrior he is.

Kayden follows him.

Whatever is transpiring between the two of them right now is not about me. It's an old conflict, something that had taken place before I had stumbled into Kayden's stronghold. Before I'd agreed to his half-baked plan of—no, he'd planned it all down to the very end.

He'd counted on Zeus wanting me for himself, on using me as a bargaining chip to get to him.

He's using me to hurt Zeus.

I don't understand why they are setting everything else aside to fight here, the two of them. Is it just macho alphas and their ego that demands they fight it out?

Or maybe I don't want to accept what's staring me in the face. Kayden's trying to distract Zeus. But that can't be right. It was Zeus who'd proposed this one-on-one fight, right?

Another wave slaps into me from behind, pushing me closer to the shore. I wade through the water, then, reaching the beach, drag my weary body, clad in the long white tunic, forward.

Footsteps thud on the sand, and Kayden's team runs up to form a wide circle around the two of them, including me in it.

The alpha closest to me lifts his head and sniffs in my direction. Another next to him stiffens.

Of course they can scent me. The remnants of the mating with Zeus still clings to me, despite the dunking I took in the seawater. The first alpha male who'd seen me snarls and takes a step forward.

Zeus growls and puts himself between me and the man. "Call your men off, Kayden. Ask them to step back, give a wide enough berth for my omega."

"Not *your* omega…yet." Kayden shifts his weight from foot to foot as he surveys Zeus.

Zeus folds his arms in front of him. "If you want to fight me, then do as I tell you."

Kayden angles his head.

Zeus leans forward on the balls of his feet. "You will not get this opportunity again. Everything you've always wanted in your grasp, here." He draws himself up to his considerable height.

Kayden's lips draw up in a lazy smile. "Don't go getting your pants in a bunch, brother." He raises his arm. "Step away."

The alphas hesitate.

All their eyes are on me. The wind flattens the tunic against my curves. It also brings with it that deeper, danker scent of alpha arousal. The need to rut me, to hurt me. All of it emanates from them.

Goosebumps snap on my skin.

I want to moan in terror and hide myself behind Zeus's broad back. But that would show that I am weak and defenseless. And I am not that.

Omega I may be, but I am also a skilled warrior, and I will not let these alphas put me down. I bite down on my lower lip and the pain cleaves a path through the fear in my head.

"Now!" Kayden's voice cracks through the place with the effect of a whiplash.

Just now, the dominance that flows from him has the hair on my neck bristling. I sense the surprise that tenses Zeus's muscles.

He doesn't move, though.

The second alpha who'd noticed me backs away, followed by another. Then all of them step back.

"Keep going. Fifty paces, and you don't come close, you don't cross the line, not until I say so." Kayden's voice is hard.

The first alpha hesitates. "Do you plan on sharing the omega if you win her?" His gaze sweeps over me.

Lust coils in his eyes, and he smacks his tongue.

I don't need to look down his body to know he is aroused. My insides curdle with disgust.

Kayden closes the distance and slaps the alpha in the face. "Back the fuck off."

His voice is cold enough to send a quiver of apprehension down my spine. This man is not as harmless as he's portrayed himself. He's strong and powerful. Almost as lethal as my alpha.

My insides curdle.

An iciness clutches at my chest.

This is wrong; it's not what it seems.

The fight is not going to be as one-sided as I'd thought it would be. I step forward and grab Zeus's arm. "Don't do this."

He freezes. His gaze drops to where my fingers clutch his biceps, then to my face. "You don't get to tell me what to do."

"Yeah, I am just an omega you claimed and now hold captive, but you mated me, remember?"

His gaze flies to the flesh wound from when he'd bitten down on my neck. "My prerogative." He tosses his head.

"I didn't grow up in one of the most politically charged courts in the world without knowing when there is something foul afoot."

Zeus's lips twist. "Now, if that is all…" He shrugs off my arm and steps forward to where Kayden has turned back from telling off his second.

His gaze flicks between the two of us.

"Wait." I know Zeus won't listen to me, but I have to try or I'll always regret it. I'll wonder what would have happened if I'd stopped him, or at least warned him. I curl my fingers around his biceps below the sleeve of his wet shirt. The touch of his skin sends tendrils of heat racing down my spine. I am here fighting, but just being close to this man sends a quiver of desire down my spine. I want to lean in and lick his skin.

He pulls forward, and I dig my nails into his flesh. "Listen to me."

Turning on me, he leans in close enough for his breath to shudder over my dripping hair.

I swear the water turns to steam. That's how angry he feels to me right now.

Ripples of heat and disgust and raw hate pour off him. His blue eyes blaze with a kind of hurt mixed with white-hot rage. I want to throw myself at his mercy and beg him for forgiveness to take me back. And that's crazy. I haven't done anything wrong, have I?

"Don't. Ever. Tell me what to do. Again."

He bites out each word, as if they are carved out of ice. And yet seeing him in full temper is also the most arousing thing I have ever seen. I shiver.

He steps back from me, and my arms slide off him.

"You have my attention." He looks down that hooked nose.

"I have good instincts." I keep my voice low, keep my gaze on his face.

"So do I."

"No, I mean the kind of instinct that allows me to sense under-the-surface emotions, to know when things are awry. And something is very wrong here. Things are going to go against you, and I had to warn you."

"Finished?" He drops his arms at his sides.

"Y…yeah."

Without letting me finish, he turns and stalks forward. Stripping off his shirt, he flings it to the ground.

I lean forward and pick up the shirt, then sink my nose into the fabric. That deep, burned pinewood scent of his fills my senses. I am surrounded by his presence. I draw in another lungful of his essence, then shrug on the shirt.

Ahead, Kayden's stripped to his pants, too.

The two alphas circle each other.

58

Zeus

I circle the man who is my half brother and who I don't know at all.

I see my likeness in his features, in the way he peels his lips back, flares his nostrils, and bends his knees to keep his stance wide.

He is slimmer than I am, but every part of him is corded muscle.

He's a few years younger than me…I think.

I'd never really thought to ask him his age or how he'd felt about having Golan as a father. Well, no surprises there. He hated Golan, the man who'd kidnapped the omega mated to the Leader of Scotland and impregnated her. She'd died after giving birth, and the Leader of Scotland had adopted Kayden.

How did it feel to grow up knowing your mother was kidnapped and raped? Almost as bad as seeing your mother raped in front of you…by your own father.

I shake my head to clear it. Why are these thoughts shoveling through me now? Maybe it's some kind of effect of the mating bond that insists on unearthing the man I was supposed to have been? A leader protective of his people. A man who nurtures his city for future generations.

Everything I am not.

I lean forward and stalk my opponent, shutting out all thoughts. The sound of the sea drops away, as does the sound of his men who shuffle around watching us. The scent of apprehension is heavy in the air.

But her scent is stronger, slicker, closer than any of theirs. I draw in that sweet omega scent of hers and let it flow through me to clear my mind. If I do it unconsciously, that's fine, right? I have to pretend I didn't use her presence to ground me. To draw on the piercing ache in my chest to center myself. I focus my attention on the man who leans in and charges. I wait, wait until the last second, then slide aside.

Kayden charges past, then rolls to break his fall. Turning around before he can find his balance, I throw myself at him.

We go rolling toward the waves' edges. When we come to a stop my palms are wrapped around his neck.

I squeeze and try to cut off his air.

Will I add half brother killer to my list of sins?

Won't be the last.

My fingers tremble...and slip, and then he punches me in the side, once, twice. The vibrations ricochet through me. I don't let go, just use the weight of my body to hold him down. He rears up and pounds his head into my chin.

My spine curves back.

My jaws snap together, I taste blood in my mouth, and scarlet sparks flash behind my eyes. I must have loosened my grip, for he twists his body enough to throw me off, and then he's on me, his knees digging into my sides.

He punches my face to the left, right, left again. The impact ricochets down my neck and tears down my spine. The breath leaches out of me, and darkness bleeds into my conscious mind. The alpha of alphas fallen after such a short fight? No way. Adrenaline spikes my blood and my vision tunnels. With a roar, I bring up my fist and smash it up and into his chin. His head snaps back and I buck and fling him aside.

Kayden's body arcs through the air, and he lands almost gracefully on his back. Rolling again to break the fall, he lurches to a stop.

I push myself up, but my arms tremble, refusing to hold up my weight. I collapse onto the ground.

I sense liquid running down my temples, pooling under me. Scent the coppery smell of blood. Mine? His? I don't know.

My side pulses with pain. My head swirls. I can't give in. Not now. Not ever. So we're evenly matched. So what? I can win this fight. I must.

I rear up to my feet, staggering as my thighs spasm. Shaking my head to clear it, to straighten the scene that's weaving in front of me, I force myself to take a step forward, and another, and then I'm standing over him.

Kayden's arms and legs are flung out. His breath comes in pants. One eye is shut, and his other eye feels almost too bright in comparison. His chest is covered in splashes of blood, a big gash in his side.

I hold out my hand.

He stills. His jaw works. Bet the fucker's trying to figure out what the hell is happening.

That makes two of us.

I like to take my opponents by surprise. And right now I am not sure what he is. Friend? Foe? Family? All of the above, and nothing. My lone blood-tie in this world. If I don't count her, and she isn't blood...she's more, much more...and fuck this line of thinking. "You going to lay there all day dickwad?" I glare at him.

His jaw ticks. Then he grabs my hand, and I pull him to his feet. Letting go I take a step back, and square my stance.

He frowns at me and thrusts his chest forward.

There's no fear on his face. A strong sense of leashed power clings to him. It's packed with aggression and hate. Everything that he needs to hold his own in a fight. And why am I rooting for him? My own half brother, who I've hated for so long? Things are seriously fucked up in my head.

I straighten, and we stare at each other.

"This is not right."

"That's correct," he snarls. "You're still standing."

"Leave while you still can, Kayden."

"And live my life as second to you? No fucking way." He charges.

This time, I am ready.

I face him head-on as he rushes me. I swerve and punch him in the head, to the gut, back to the head, the side, then a last punch to the side of the head, and he goes down.

Adrenaline pumps through me, and I leap up and bring my fist down on his chest.

The sound of ribs breaking is loud, and blood spurts out of his mouth.

I rise and raise my joined fists and pause. I can't do this. Cannot kill him. I drop my hands to my sides and step back.

"Get up." I growl the words through a throat full of some emotion, something I can't quite give a name to.

He tries to get up and fails.

I hold out my hand, and he grips it. I haul him up. His knees seem to give way, and I prop him up.

"Leave. You have your life. Go."

He raises his chin. "I'd rather die… Fight me to the death, asshole. Only one of us leaves here today."

"Or perhaps you may be so lucky that neither of you gets out of here alive."

I swivel around at the sound of a third voice.

59

Lucy

The voice rings out, and I swivel around to look at whoever spoke. The hair on the back of my neck rises. It can't be. When I left Russia, I thought I'd left that nightmare behind.

I recall images of the berserkers riding into town, pillaging everything in sight as they'd charged through Red Square. I'd run into them as I had tried to escape the city with my omega clan. Their leader had spotted us and made straight for me.

He's looking at me now over the heads of Kayden's alphas, who are surrounded by the new arrivals. They are all tall, at least a head above Kayden's men, almost as tall as Zeus.

My throat closes. My stomach lurches. I move toward where Zeus and Kayden are still locked in a fight. My alpha's shoulders flex, and his muscles go solid. He releases Kayden and turns to glare at the new arrival. "Who are you?" He thrusts out his chest.

Zeus has automatically resumed command over Kayden, and over Kayden's men a foregone conclusion that he's won the challenge and he's not brooking arguments about it.

A flush of pride burns my chest. Following on its heels is coldness. A shiver of apprehension ripples down my spine.

The new arrivals restrain Kayden's men.

Their leader preens outside the circle, his gaze on Zeus. I can't let my alpha get close to him. If he does, the berserker will kill Zeus, just as he had beheaded my mother when she'd tried to protect me.

These men are beyond merciless. They destroy and pillage, capture omegas and breed them, while occupying new lands. And I had thought Zeus was a monster. I'd forgotten what I had escaped to get here.

Zeus props his arms on his hips. His forehead is furrowed, but his stance is as powerful as ever. His bloodstained torso heaves as he stalks toward the leader of the new arrivals. Waves of tension roll off of him. He takes a step forward, then another, until he's crossed over to me. He's putting himself between me and the new arrival.

The berserker's gaze flicks to me then back to Zeus. "Well, isn't this interesting," he drawls, his accent thick and reminiscent of the lands from which he comes.

When the tsunamis had torn through many cities of the world, they'd submerged most of Scandinavia. The melting ice caps had done the rest.

The survivors had had to be brutal to survive, and cunning, and have the strongest of genes. It's why the berserkers are so powerful, almost unconquerable. Everybody has a weakness, except with these men, they don't care much about anything, except omegas.

We are the universal currency of barter and exchange. My stomach heaves, and my mind empties of thought.

I cannot let him hurt Zeus. I take a step forward. The new arrival swaggers through the circle of men. He comes to a halt in front of Zeus. His flesh smells of the sea and vegetation, and the violence radiating from him is staggering. I gasp and huddle closer to Zeus, melting into his back. It makes me seem weak, and that's okay. I stand no chance against this animal. I don't want him to see me, don't want him to breathe the same air I do.

"I came for the omega. Hand her over, and escape with your life."

Zeus growls, a roll of aggression that tears up from him and flows into the space. There is complete silence, broken by the splash of the waves on the shore.

"You have fight in you, Alpha, I'll give you that." The stranger angles his head. "It's almost a pity to destroy you...almost."

"You didn't answer the question." Zeus' voice is low, menacing, with a ring of steel. Heat streaks down my spine.

It seems the more aggressive he gets, the more it arouses me. The more we are at the edge of danger, the more I feel alive. My sense of right and wrong is getting warped, and there's nothing I can do about it, nothing. Except squeeze my eyes shut and gather my courage.

I dig my heels into the ground and pray I can do what needs to be done. I need to find a way to save Zeus and myself. I will not let this Viking warrior hurt us.

"I don't plan on having a conversation with you." The stranger draws his sword.

The thought of him burying that in Zeus's neck, in the skin I had marked when I'd claimed him, sends sheer terror racing through me. My stomach rolls, my chest feels heavy. I try to take a breath and find I can't. My head spins and darkness bleeds into the edges of my vision. Not the best time to have a panic attack. My thighs spasm. No, no, I can't faint, not now.

Zeus must sense my terror, for he leans back on his heels, just a little, just enough to close the minuscule distance between us. The planes of his back brush against my forehead.

The touch is so minute, almost not there, but with it, he conveys everything his words never can.

That he does care for me, somewhere deep inside, where a part of him that is good and true and wants to do the right thing prevails.

That essence of him I'd sensed and believed in, right from the time I'd first heard his name mentioned.

"I am Harald, the leader of the berserkers." The Viking's voice rings through the space.

"And I am the alpha whose men now surround yours." Zeus's voice is casual in a way that has every hair on my forearms rising.

I peek around his broad back and gasp.

60

Zeus

I look up, past where Harald stands, past the circle of Kayden's alphas, who are surrounded by Harald's berserkers, to where Ethan has come up with my own soldiers.

Solomon breaks off and races to the right, and Mace and Liam run across to the other side to take up positions at the circumference of the circle.

I've never been so fucking glad to see my men.

I am a selfish bastard, but I am not stupid. I know when I need help; not above asking for it either. I am prone to being reckless, but damned if I want to end up like my old man with this berserker's fingers around my neck, or worse, with his sword buried in my chest and his dick in my omega. My guts twist. I throw my head back and roar. I gasp at the depth of rage that wrings through me. Something inside me snaps.

All I know is that I am tired of this go-round with Kayden, now with this berserker, with my own omega who's resisted me so far.

I don't care anymore that my life is at stake.

The survivor in me rushes to the fore. My gaze narrows, and all my instincts home in on the berserker.

I am going to kill this male who dares to challenge me for my omega and threatens to harm my family. Yeah, Kayden is family, my blood, no escaping that. And I protect what's mine, which includes my half brother who has more power than brains right now. I'll deal with him later.

First, I need to show this marauder his place and get my omega back home. Back where she belongs, with me. That's all.

I lower my head and roar again.

My cry is torn away on the breeze that rolls in from the sea.

Harald bares his teeth at me. His mohawk stands stiff across his scalp, the rest of which is bald. His face shines with sweat. With anticipation.

His gaze drops to where my omega is peeking out from behind me. I know her curiosity got the better of her. Of course she wouldn't stay hidden. The spirit of that woman…and don't I love exactly that about her.

I curve my arm around her and push her back, then angle my body to block all sight of her completely from the berserker.

Harald fixes his gaze on me. He licks his lips and takes a step forward. "I've chased that omega cunt halfway across the world, and she'd better be worth it." He angles his head. "Tell me, General, is she as sweet as she appears to be?" He thrusts his pelvis forward and grabs his crotch. "I bet there is an edge to her slick that feeds the animal inside you. Does it compel you to take her over and over again? Urge you to bury your cock balls deep in her and—"

I leap through the air and throw myself at him.

I don't care that I am unarmed and he holds a sword. That he probably said all that just to provoke me. All I know is that it's time to put an end to this confrontation.

I slam into what feels like a brick wall. The shock judders through me. My ribcage screams in protest. The muscles of my legs spasm before my feet find purchase.

The man is more powerfully built than I had anticipated.

He slides a few steps back, that's all the force of my impact had on him—and wraps his massive arms around my shoulders in a parody of a fucking hug.

I growl and kick his leg out from under him. His gaze widens in surprise, and he lets go and staggers back.

I punch my fist into his side, his shoulder, his face, then whack it straight into his groin.

The breath rushes out of him, and he charges at me again.

I step aside, and he staggers past, then swivels around with such speed that I blink. I hadn't been expecting that, not from a man of his massive girth.

He brings his joined fists up and sweeps them up and toward my chin.

My neck snaps back. I am sure my head has been taken off my body, and my spine screams in pain as white and red sparks sweep through me. I feel the rush of air then the hard surface of the sand as I crash into the ground. I try to move, but every part of me feels weighed down.

Pain tears through my brain, my neck, down my back, and black bleeds into the edge of my conscious mind. The great Zeus sobbing like a baby. Fuck.

Harald's grinning face comes into view. He raises those massive sledgehammer-like arms again. "Goodbye, asshole."

There's a scream, and then someone slams into him from behind. Pale arms squeeze around his neck, and shapely legs dig into his waist.

"Lucia." I hear someone call out her name and realize it's me.

Terror screams through my insides, twists my guts, and my breath catches in my chest.

I try to rise again and manage to sit up. The world swings around me.

Harald laughs and arches his back. He shakes himself, and she goes flying through the air, hitting the sand and rolling until she comes to a stop. She doesn't move.

A roar rips out of me. Red fills my head, clearing out everything else. Pushing away the sickness that bubbles up my throat, I stagger to my feet and charge him, throwing everything I have into the move. I turn at the last minute to angle my body and smash my shoulder into his chest.

He topples over and hits the ground. Sand spews up from the impact, raining down on us. I leap on him and bring all the weight of my body to bear as I grip my thighs around his waist, swinging down my fists on his chest.

There's a howl from the man, and then blood spews forth from his ribs and his side, bathing me in a hot, steamy, frothing mess. My skin crawls.

I grab his shaggy head and smash it down, again and again.

He screams, and his shoulders lock. Then with a litheness I had not been expecting, he lunges his legs up and hooks his ankles over my shoulders. His weight pins me down.

The breath burns in my chest, but I refuse to let go of him.

Sweat pours down my back. I bring my thumbs down over his eyes and press them into his skull.

He screams. For a big man, the sound is full of fear and almost feminine in its panic. The strange confluence tears at my nerve endings. The pores on my skin pop. His grip around my neck loosens. He brings his arms up and pounds me in the side again.

Each slam of his fist resembles that of a hammer smashing into me.

My side howls in pain, and I refuse to loosen my grip. He rears up with his entire body and shakes me with such force that I find myself flung off. Fuck. This beast really is a monster. Anger pounds through me. Everything is forgotten; what little bit of humanity the mating cord had bled into me fizzles out. I lock away every part of me that is reminiscent of the man I could be.

Then punch my fists against my chest and roar out my challenge again.

The berserker staggers toward me, blood streaming from his eyes. One eyeball is grotesquely pressed in.

There is a flash of silver through the air, and he holds up his hand to grab the sword one of his followers has thrown him. He charges toward me.

Kayden steps between us, and the sword goes through him. It juts out from his back and scrapes the skin on my chest.

Harald stares, his gaze so wide it should be comical, but it isn't. All I can think is that Kayden is my brother, and he sacrificed himself for me. It doesn't seem right. It can't be. It doesn't make sense. It doesn't.

Harald flexes his shoulders and reaches for his sword.

Kayden kicks him hard in the chest with enough force for Harald to grunt and stumble a few steps back.

"Take your omega and go," he pants over his shoulder.

"If you think I am leaving you behind...you thought wrong." I hear the words and know it's true.

The fucker took my omega and used her as bait to get to me, and yet...he never really hurt her.

Anger curls my nerves, but my pulse thuds in my temples and insists I cannot leave my half brother, my sibling, here at the mercy of this berserker. He is going to be taught a lesson, all right, but it's going to be me to do it. He took what was mine, and he'll be shown never to do that again. I'll use my own methods to punish him.

I step in front of Kayden and head butt the marauder.

The impact sweeps through my skull, and I am sure my teeth have all but loosened. My bones rattle, but I also hear the satisfying crunch as his ribcage gives. He screams and staggers back, blood welling up from his mouth, dripping from his nose.

I stand there panting when Kayden stumbles up next to me, his shoulder next to mine. He seizes the sword by the blade and pulls it out from where its stuck in his side. Blood gushes out, and his features whiten. But the fucker doesn't scream, not a peep. That has to hurt. My half brother is much braver than I gave him credit for. He moves the sword, its pommel facing toward me. I grab it and heave it up, then swipe it down.

Just as Harald steps back and holds up his arm in defense.

The sword cuts straight through his forearm.

He screams. His hairy arm goes swirling through the air and lands on the ground. I bring the sword up again. More berserkers run up from behind Harald and surround him.

"Coward," I growl. "Come out and fight me."

Harald's features twist. "I am not as stupid as you, Alpha General. You think with your heart, and you follow your dick."

"I didn't stay to have a bloody conversation, asshole."

"I know when to retreat. This round is yours, but the fight belongs to me. I promise you that."

There's a howl, and then Ethan closes in from the right, Sol from the left, and Mace and Liam yell as they fling themselves on Harald's men.

I look over the fighting men to where Harald staggers away to the beach. He walks to the water, three-fourths the man he was, then dives in. The fucker manages to swim, without the use of one hand. The saltwater must completely ravage his wounds and turn his entire body into a seething, burning mass. Yet the berserker gives no sign of it. He strikes out using his legs and his remaining arm. Fucking hell. The pulse thuds at my temple. He is the most dangerous enemy I have ever encountered.

More lethal than Golan, more powerful than Kayden, more cunning than any of the scumbags I'd encountered in the East End, and far more politically astute than my Council ever will be.

I am going to need every bit of power, and strength, and resources, and luck, lots of luck to get this man. Before he…regroups his forces and takes revenge.

"Zeus." Her moan bleeds into the air.

I turn to find my omega trying to sit up.

She's alive, thank fuck. My heart fills with a strange emotion, something I don't want to put a name to. I am almost getting used to the fact that she is always going to draw a very different reaction from me. Well, different than what I had expected. Something more than lust, more than the need to take…I want to…give, to share, to be with her. This is so not what I fucking expected.

I stride to her, and squatting down, lift her in my arms.

Her body trembles and she feels so fragile, so fucking delicate. The breeze blows over us, and she shivers.

I hunch over her, to protect her from the wind and shield her from the sight of the other alphas. I need to get her the hell away from here and take care of her: my omega. I peer into her face.

"Kayden." She nods to where he lies on the ground, bleeding out.

"He's alive." I scowl at her. Why is she talking about that fucker when I am right here standing in front of her, holding her in my arms?

"He saved your life."

"You put yours at risk." I clench my jaw so hard that pain slides down my neck.

She juts out her lower lip and my heart pounds. My left shoulder screams. But having her so close to me provokes the muscle between my legs to throb with a very different kind of pain. "Do that again, and I'll put you over my knees and spank you."

Color rushes to her cheeks. The scent of her arousal is heavy in the air.

She doesn't protest. Her breath hitches.

Adrenaline thrums my blood. My groin hardens.

"I won't stop, not when you beg me to, not when your pussy is soaking wet, not even when you plead with me to take you." I pause, lust oozing through my blood. "I will not hold back, Squirrel, not until neither of us can move for days." My groin hardens. "Not even then…" My voice catches in my throat. My dick strains in my pants, pleading to be let out. I am one sick fuck.

"Promise?"

61

Lucy

I am not sure what made me say that, but his words bring out that base instinct inside of me, the one that only he seems to be able to touch. It's the inherently omega part of me that responds to the alpha scent of him.

That masculinity, the need to possess that rolls off him as he holds me close to his massive chest. He leans down close enough for me to see the lines that stretch out from his eyes.

For those indigo eyes to shimmer with lust, the sparks of silver in them swirling, ebbing, and flowing.

The heat from his chest slams into me and pins me down. The fine hair on my forearms rise, and tremors race down my skin.

It seems to shake him out of the daze he's fallen into, for he straightens, then walks over to where Kayden lies on his back, blood pumping out of his chest.

Zeus lowers himself, still holding me close. I can almost convince myself that he doesn't want to let me go. He cradles me to his chest. A crooning hum bleeds from his lips and the tenderness of his touch envelops me. He holds me like I am the most precious thing in the world. But that's not true either.

I am only an omega he fucked and claimed, whose body he played like a finely tuned instrument, but that was all.

There is nothing else between us, nothing…not even the mating cord. My heart stutters, and the emptiness where the connection had once been swirls with pain. I gasp, and Zeus looks at me.

"You need to take her back." Kayden coughs.

"Why did you do it?" Zeus holds his gaze and squats before the other alpha. He cradles me closer, impossibly closer to that broad chest.

"You know why." Kayden squares his shoulders. His gaze floats to me then back to Zeus. He stays quiet.

"I need to hear it from you," Zeus growls.

There's a strange tone to his voice I cannot place. Is the alpha moved by what his half brother had done for him? Does the General actually give a fuck about his surviving blood relationship?

The tendons of his throat move. Color flushes his cheeks.

I still and watch the play of emotions on his face, fascinated and not surprised. I've always known that underneath that harsh exterior, that mask he shows to the world, is a man who feels...who knows what the right thing is to do.

"What you have with her"—Kayden jerks his chin at me—"it's not something I can hope to find. I never meant to hurt you when I took her. It was just—"

"Leverage." Zeus completes his statement.

I wriggle in his hold. "I am still here, you know."

Both pairs of eyes look at me, one filled with pain, the other streaked with incredulity and a touch of anger.

Then Zeus changes my position so I am held with my face pressed into his chest.

A low purr draws out of him and flows over me, and I want to tell him it's not fair that he's shutting me up in the most basic of ways. I open my mouth, only to inhale another potent blast of that alpha scent...a mix of pheromones, sweat, and blood, and him. Just him. My head whirls, and my heart stutters. My muscles seem to relax against my will. All thoughts go out of me, and I snuggle in closer.

The bastard is soothing me, drugging me to relax, and I... I am too tired to protest.

He keeps up that subvocal hum. The baritone is so soft that I imagine only I can hear it. The vibrations rumble up, and sink into my blood, soothing, comforting...and also arousing. Liquid lust strums at my nerve endings. Moisture pools in my core. I curl my body around him, then brush my hips against the evidence of his hardness.

His muscles jerk under me, but he gives no other sign he's noticed my casual caress.

There's a harsh chuckle, then another exhale from Kayden. "I did it to get your attention. Not that this means I forgive you for all your indiscretions." He grimaces. "I accept it wasn't right to use the omega against you, but you have to admit you'd have done the same thing if you were in my position."

Zeus straightens his shoulders. I watch the cords of his neck flex. I raise my fingers to draw my nail over those beautiful sculpted tendons that coil and react when I touch them.

A hum fills the air; this time it's me.

I am brimming with contentment, mewling tiny noises that ripple up my throat. I should be ashamed, really. After everything, all that chasing and being chased, I am back with the monster, and something inside me insists I don't want to let go this time.

Warmth flushes my skin, my heart quickens with anticipation, and that draws my attention back to the empty hollow in my chest. "The mating cord." I think I say it aloud, but he doesn't respond.

He grazes his cheek over my forehead. "Sleep now, little squirrel, before I put you back in your cage."

62

Zeus

I carry my sleeping omega up the corridor of my stronghold in London. She'd passed out in my arms and hadn't stirred once during the journey from Dover.

I am not sure what it is about her that brings out these protective tendencies in me.

She thinks she tempts me to become more human?

She doesn't know that she touches the base part of me. That primal part that wants to fuck her and hurt her, protect her, cherish her, then claim her, and give her an orgasm like she's never had before.

I want to knot her to me, so my skin can slide over her and fuse with hers. So I can pull her into me, fold her body into mine until our spirits blend. The thoughts rush through my head until I am no longer sure what I am thinking.

My muscles ache, every part of me hurts, my brain feels like it's been crushed, and yet I cannot let go of her.

Reaching my suite, I shoulder open the doors, then stalk to the bed and place her on it.

She murmurs and turns over on her side, her fingers under her cheek. Her other hand is hooked around my wrist. And that affects me most. I'd hurt her and pushed her, yet she still trusts me.

She does. I know that.

Which is why I am going to break this last connection between us.

I don't like what I become when I'm with her. That's the truth.

And it's not the fact that I want to take her with a need that is so powerful it goes beyond the physical. Nor is it the fact that every time she dares to look at someone else I am filled with the need to possess her all over again.

Normal for an alpha with his omega.

But it's the intensity with which I want her. I want to feel her flesh over mine, her thighs about my waist, her hair wrapped around my fists as I part her legs and slide into her, and her pussy milks me—all of it disturbs me. But I cannot let go of it, this need inside me that's writhing for her.

I don't realize I am on the bed and between her thighs, not until her breast curves under my palm. The nipple springs to attention through the cloth of her tunic and the shirt... *my shirt* that she's worn over it.

A fierce surge of possession squeezes my chest.

I squeeze her nipple until it pebbles enough to almost tear through the layers. Then, bending down, I take the nipple between my lips.

She moans and arches her back, thrusting her breast into my hand, then moves restlessly. She rubs her skin over mine, trying to get closer.

A growl rumbles up my chest. I hover above her, balancing my weight on my elbows but staying close enough for the vibrations of my chest to stir the air around her. I want her to feel the heat of my body, sense the musk of my arousal, the throbbing of my shaft that pushes against my pants.

Sliding off the bed, I shove off my pants, wincing with every step.

My muscles protest as I bend down and pull the tunic and the shirt up and off her, manipulating her body to give me access.

She moves again, her lips form words, a low groan is drawn out of her, and her forehead furrows. She's in pain, and I know just how to comfort her.

I crouch above her, then sniff the base of her neck before trailing my finger up the underside of her breast.

She moans again, and I growl. My tone is low, subvocal enough for her to hear me, light enough to roll over her skin. To shift the air around her and ruffle the fine hair of her forearms.

She squeezes her thighs tighter, and the scent of slickness bursts into the air. I am instantly hard. My cock leaps, blood rushing to the tip. I slide down her body, still without touching her, but her body knows I am there.

She mutters under her breath, incomprehensible words that sound almost drunk, and a flush of desire twists my guts.

She's high on my presence, my purring, on me, just me. It's how I want it to be. Just me and her and nothing else between us.

Another low growl flows out of me, and I modulate my voice so the notes loop over her waist.

Goosebumps flare on the strip of skin just above her pussy.

My gaze drops there, slides farther down to her quivering flesh. Plump, pink, and ready for me. I lower my nose to the triangle between her thighs and purr lightly. Her entire body shakes, and her hips thrust up.

Slick flows down from her core, glistening, calling to me. I lick up that sweet, honeyed essence, and it goes straight to my head. My dick throbs with so much force my groin tightens, and it's so painful that I know I need her now.

Sliding my hands between her thighs, I gently part them then gaze at the pink, succulent clit that peeks out from under its hood. My stomach rumbles, and my mouth waters. Bending down, I lick the bud just once, permitting myself to taste it.

Her entire body arches, her chest rises off the bed, and her head thrashes from side to side.

I increase the intensity of my purring, and project my voice to coil the sound waves over her skin, spooling it around her breasts, to cocoon her and soothe her.

A shallow breath quivers from her, and her breasts with those incredible nipples rise and fall. She quiets. The lines between her eyebrows lessen. Rising, the weight of my full-to-bursting balls almost dragging me down, I bite my lower lip to stifle the groan.

I stay poised over her, waiting until her breath deepens, then, gripping her hips and angling them just so, I slide into her.

She sighs and stills, and every muscle in her body tenses.

Every instinct in me tingles and warns that if I do this, I'll never be rid of her. If I take her now, I know there is no going back. I'll be taking her all over again, and then there will be no me, no her, just this intense connection which sears my soul. Every time she is out of sight, my stomach twists. I want her with a primal need that no one else can satisfy. No one but her. She is already my weakness. Can I live with that?

I stay poised right there at the entrance of her channel as moisture flows out to cover the tip of my dick.

The soft inside walls of her pussy clench around me, drawing me in gradually.

I grit my teeth so hard that pain rips through my upper jaw, joining the litany of aches and pains which riddle my torso. The sheer warmth of her, the scent of her, that essence of her that pours into my blood and draws me in farther, farther. She moans and wriggles her hips, and then I slide in, all the way into her.

63

Lucy

One moment I am aching and empty, and the next he is there inside me. Plunging into me, filling me.

I didn't realize how empty I was, not until he slams all the way home, until I am filled, and yet empty for more. My belly quivers.

My toes curl, and I dig my fingers into the soft sheets under me. I am surrounded by his heat, his scent, that sharp bite of his cum.

The pulse drums at my temples. My breasts ache. Why isn't he holding them and biting down on my nipples?

I thrust my chest up, and a warm, moist tongue swirls around my nipple. His teeth grip the throbbing flesh, and he sucks on it. The vibrations travel all the way to my core. My hot, melting core that is already filled with him. I open my mouth to scream, and my eyes fly open to meet his gaze.

That burning indigo gaze of his gleams silver with arousal.

He closes his mouth over mine and absorbs my groan. His tongue thrusts into my mouth at the same time his cock fills me to the brim. I am burning with pleasure, melting with desire, covered by him, wallowing in his scent, his sweat, his very essence that spills over me, and I know I don't want to be anywhere but right where I am.

He plunges into me again with so much force that my entire body moves up the mattress. The thump of the headboard against the wall shatters through the sexual haze filling my head.

My gaze flies around the room, and I recognize his suite. The first tendrils of uncertainty slither down my spine when he leans back and licks his lips.

Perhaps he smells my uncertainly? For his actions slow, become more coercing, seductive.

He pulls his shaft all the way out, his hand slides up the back of one thigh, and he wraps my leg around his waist so my heel is pressed into the curve of his spine, then he does the same with the other.

It's almost worse because he leans down and brushes his mouth over mine again, and a third time until I part my lips. How can I resist this sweet assault on my senses any more than when he'd taken me with all his strength?

Either way, he just has to look at me, touch me, purr for me, and I am his willing slave. Then why is he withholding the mating bond?

I start to wrap my arm around his neck when he grabs my hand and pulls it up and above my head.

He yanks up my other arm, shackling both with one hand. All along, his mouth doesn't stop that sweet, sensual seduction of my lips. Every scrape of his shaft against my sensitive channel sends shivers of lust radiating up my spine. I am one turbulent, twining mass of sensations.

Every inch of my skin hurts.

My every breath is filled with his essence. He's all I see, all I taste. I am enveloped in his touch; the dominance of his presence pins me down.

He grips my thigh and tilts my hips up another millimeter, then sinks all the way in. A groan is drawn out of me.

His gaze still holds mine.

Is he punishing me? Or himself? And for what? My brain cells refuse to function anymore, and when I think I am going to come, he pulls out, he fucking pulls all the way out and stays there, poised.

I open my mouth to protest, and he covers my mouth with his and purrs. The vibrations from his big body ripple over mine, holding me in a cocoon of sound that ebbs and flows around me, that sinks into my blood. My womb cramps, and more slick flows forth.

He moves his hips to glide his dick inside just a little, enough that it sends waves of pleasure shooting up my spine. His big palm rubs down my side, over my hips, cupping my butt and squeezing.

His other palm covers my breast and pinches my nipple hard enough for another pulse of heat to flare low in my belly. All the time, he never stops that purring, raising it in intensity to continuously flow into me. The sound weaves a cocoon of comfort over me, pinning me down.

Every part of me is aching and needy—oh, so needy.

I want to dig my heels into his back, want to bury my nails into his shoulders, want to bite down on that tongue that is teasing, swiveling inside my mouth, sucking from me, drawing this intense response from me. Want to ride the climax that shivers up from the soles of my feet, gliding up my calves, up the back of my thighs, meeting that aching, burning fullness in my center that is so close, yet so far.

I try to strain for it and find I can't move.

Can't breathe.

Can't do anything but give myself up to this intense coupling he's subjecting me to.

His big body holds me down.

His purring seduces my spirit and holds me in thrall. His touch…oh, his touch on me, in me, inside me, all of it reduces me to the very essence of what I am. An omega. His slave. His. Only his.

Something inside me dissolves—that last barrier to resistance, perhaps?

Or that last strike of independence that has me holding out for this intense assault on all my senses.

His seduction, this ultimate showing of prowess, of what he actually is. A prime dominant alpha. All of my muscles relax, my spirit breaks free, and the climax pours up from my womb. Heat radiates out from my core, sweeping over me, flushing my blood with endorphins.

Flashes of light flare behind my closed eyelids, and then I am falling, falling.

Inside me his knot snaps into place, and it's so tight, so hard, so full...so everything, that I cannot put any more words to it.

The climax picks up another notch, screaming through me. I arch my spine and thrust every part of my body, from thigh, to hip, to breast, flush against him. I hold on to him as he shoots hot jets of cum into my channel.

When I come to, it is to the low hum of purring all around me, cocooning me, carrying me away on waves of warmth and heat and security, so much security.

My alpha will always take care of me.

Protect me.

Fuck me.

Knot me when needed.

He will breed me. And I want it, want him. Heat flushes my skin, followed by chills. My muscles tense.

Bands of steel close around me. He has me coiled on his chest. A pulse in my core warns me he's still locked inside me. As I think that the knot widens, and his dick hardens, filling me up again. He draws his fingers through my hair, raking his fingernails over my scalp, and I shiver.

There's something subtly different about how he's holding me, touching me. Gone is that fierce need to possess, when he'd spoken to me and demanded I look at him and call him by name. It's almost like he's gone past that, and there's this need to play my body, urge me to respond, make me so drunk on him, so dependent that I don't want anything else. That I simply become his slave, a toy to be kept here, taken out and played with and then put back again. Something deep inside me insists I rebel. I don't want to be merely his breeder. I am so much more than that. Much more than a pussy, more than just an omega.

Everything I've fought against my entire life comes crashing over me. My brain freezes, and I shove aside that sense of warmth and security he's trying to weave over me. False, all false. Yet I want all that and much more.

I try to raise my head, and to my surprise, he lets me.

I crack my eyes open, my shoulders shaking with the effort. I feel drunk and vulnerable and open, and I want to ask him why he's doing this to me. Why he's keeping me captive in his arms, why he's making me into a parody of what I am. Those blue eyes look at me with so much clarity, there's so much intelligence shining in them...and intent and nothing else. No hurt, pain, no pleasure, no passion. All of this was meant to humiliate me and show me my place. A chill runs through me. Do I know this man? I know his body, every scar, every ink mark on his skin, but do I really know him, what he is, what he wants?

He blinks, and the blue is replaced with burning silver. Heat flows from him, and a low purring begins again.

Goosebumps flare on my skin. Every part of my body hurts and aches for him. The emptiness in my chest is matched with the blankness that gapes between my thighs, and then my core shudders, begging for release. Heat sweeps through me, from my heels all the way up to my core, and my womb clenches, begging for him. For that rough heaviness of my alpha's touch, for his cock throbbing to fill me.

I shake my head and try to speak. He leans up and once more claims ownership my mouth and takes me under.

When I wake up next, I am alone—hands still flung up, my legs parted. The flesh between my legs aches. I move, and every part of me protests. I groan, then sigh as water trickles over my mouth. I lap it up greedily. In the dimness of the room, I can make out the outline of his great height as he moves away. He walks into the adjoining bathroom.

The sound of water running reaches me, then cuts off.

He appears again and, sitting on the bed, presses a wet cloth between my legs. I can't stop the moan of pleasure that spills from me.

He drags the cloth across my thighs, wiping them.

His touch is rough, not lover-like, more like that of a master with his slave. Almost clinical. It shouldn't arouse me. It should make me feel used, but instead, a shiver of anticipation runs up my spine.

He must notice, but he doesn't say anything, just drags the cloth over my waist, around my breasts, swirling the rough cloth across my nipples, which tighten at once. My shoulders stiffen. In anticipation? In disgust, at myself? At how quickly he can arouse me? Perhaps I should push him away and tell him I can take care of myself?

His movements quicken. He's able to anticipate my needs, and I hate that.

Even without the mating cord's presence, I know he can sense my every move. He knows what turns me on, what angers me. *He knows me.* He's invaded not just my body but also peeked into my soul. It unnerves me, and yet I want it, too.

I want every single emotion that he can invoke inside me. My shoulders stiffen. No, surely, that's not right. I can't be so in thrall of him, can I?

I curl my toes and squeeze my thighs, but he still doesn't notice.

He flings aside the cloth, then drags the back of his palm up my throat, over my face, to swipe at my lips once, twice until they feel raw. Until it feels as if he's trying to wipe his very scent off me, and that confuses me. "Zeus, what—"

"Shh, little squirrel." He tosses the flannel aside.

Bending, he positions his body above mine. In the dim light, I can see the whites of his eyes, his breath low as his chest rises and falls. A low purr rumbles over me, and my eyelids flutter down. Heat seeps through me as my breath synchronizes to the ebb and flow of that hum. He licks my lips, and I shudder and reach up for more. Jutting my chin up, I open my lips.

"Greedy squirrel." His low chuckle strums at my nerves.

There's a light touch at my breast, and heat flushes my skin.

He tugs at my nipple, and I groan. I push out my breasts, not caring that I am signaling that I am in his thrall, that I am now submitting to him. I want his mouth, his fingers, his lips, his heat all over me.

I want to roll in his essence and crawl under his skin.

He trails his fingers over my waist, and a low scream rolls up my throat. "Fuck me." I heave out a breath.

"Ask me nicely."

Bending, he trails his lips and his tongue down my waist to my clit and swirls his tongue around the bud.

I explode. The low tension builds up from my core and surges through me. I strain to bring my hands down to grip his hair, to hold it there, to pull it back, to rub those whiskers against my inner thighs and feel his breath on my trembling cunt, and that's when I realize I can't.

I try to lower my right arm, but it's restrained. My wrist is tied to the headboard.

64

Zeus

I know the exact moment she realizes she is chained, for the muscles of her stomach stiffen. Her thighs clench, and the climax rips through her.

I nip at her clit and at the same time slide two fingers inside her channel, and she shatters around me.

She shatters around me, and I still don't stop. I lick her pussy, suck on her clit, then shove another finger inside of her. I hook it at the center of her.

Her body tenses; her spine rears up and off the bed. A scream rips out of her.

Oh yeah, I know exactly how to draw a response from her.

For once, it's not about me, and isn't that a shock?

I want to keep her here, pleasured and senseless, drugged with me, at my mercy. It's to keep her safe, to shield her from what I have to do over the next few weeks.

I need to fight the Vikings and not worry about her while I take on this new threat.

The scent of her is all around me, her sugary scent of slick that flows out over my tongue. I lap it up, commit it to memory for the time I have to be away.

It's right I haven't lowered the barrier on the mating bond; it would endanger her life if I did.

There is no telling if I will come back from this, and if I don't…then I have left instructions for her to be taken to the harem. She'll be well cared for.

It would be up to her if she took another alpha. My breath hitches. No, I will not let it come to that. I will be back. I will, but in the meanwhile, she needs to be here in my room, in my bed, safe, surrounded by my scent, my presence. It's the only way I can let myself leave.

Before the aftereffects of the climax have faded away I rise, and pushing aside her legs, slide into her.

I cannot hurt her this last time, cannot leave her wanting.

I want to satisfy her, and it's a strange feeling admitting it to myself.

I let myself take her, slowly, almost gently, filling her with every throbbing inch, drawing out her pleasure.

Her shoulders shudder, and her features twist as the climax builds again. She pants, and her chest heaves, up-down, in tandem with mine.

I frame her face with my big hands and place my forehead against hers. "I am sorry. It has to be this way."

She swallows, then scissors her legs around my waist, pulling me in deeper, and that fucking breaks me.

Tears roll down her cheeks, and I bend down and lick them up.

It feels like she is absolving me of all the sins I have committed so far.

I push aside the burden of guilt I have borne at killing my own father, of not being able to protect my mother. So what if I was too young to do so? I have my half brother imprisoned…but at least I didn't kill him.

She helped save my life, and I am giving my omega her due.

Keeping her here under my protection. Filling her with my dick, pumping her full of my cum, knotting her so my seed will take root, and it will. It has to this time. And all through it, she'll be safe here and cared for. Nothing will harm her. Not even me, for I will be away from her.

Her pussy clamps around my dick, and I come, shooting hot streams of cum inside her.

She shudders and slips her untied arm around my neck. She holds me as I slide my head down to her breasts.

The sound of our breathing mingles in the silence. She trails her fingers over my back, and the touch seeps through the sexual haze that dulls my mind.

Turning, without pulling out of her, I place her on my chest, then adjust the rope attached to her wrist so she is able to fold her arm with ease. I want to keep her as my prisoner but I don't want to hurt her. She came to assassinate me, betrayed me to my enemy, and instead of taking revenge, I am concerned about causing her discomfort. Fuck me.

"I know why you are doing this." Her voice is soft.

I run my fingers through her hair, down over the curve of her spine. "Doing what?"

She pulls the chain attached to her hand. "You are keeping me bound, thinking you can curb my spirit that way."

"You are wrong." I hadn't intended to deny or confirm anything, but I can't seem to stop myself from speaking.

"So explain, then, General, why do you want to keep an unarmed omega like me under lock and key?"

I gather my thoughts, wondering how to break it down for her, to tell her that she brings out a part of me that no one else can, that I'd lost her twice and I can't let her go again. That she weakens me, makes me vulnerable…more human than I've ever felt before.

"It's to show you your place." I try to keep my voice light, try to smirk.

"You are scared, Alpha." She raises her head, and those green eyes bore right into me.

My throat closes, and apprehension strums at my nerves.

"Me? You are accusing me, the most powerful alpha in the land, of being scared?" I lift her up and place her to the side on the bed, wanting suddenly to be away from the scrutiny of those eyes, needing some distance between us. I gather my thoughts again, trying to understand why I need to see her restrained.

"Yeah, that's exactly right. You are afraid of your emotions, General. Afraid that if you let on exactly what you feel for me, you'll end up as being less of an alpha." She thrusts that delicate chin out and looks at me, her nose so close our breaths mingle.

The shared intimacy is not lost on me.

I've never indulged in pillow talk. That's for weaker people, for those who actually have time to pander to their emotions…not for someone like me who is too busy fighting for power, for vengeance, who is constantly haunted by memories.

And yet, as I try to draw on that thirst for revenge that has motivated me so far, my mind comes up blank.

Perhaps it's this tentative truce with Kayden or the fact that Golan is dead while I am still alive with my omega in my arms.

Or maybe…maybe it's because this witch of an omega with her clever words, her bright eyes, and her delicate pussy which never fails to entice, has me in her grasp. And why is that so disturbing?

I clench my jaw. A ripple of worry lodges in my gut, and my knot loosens.

I pull out, and our joined fluids spill onto the bed. The scent of my cum mixed with her slick, that complex scent which I'll carry with me, which I cannot quite define, sinks into my blood. I reach down and scoop up some of the mixture and bring it to her lips.

She opens her mouth and licks it up, curls her tongue around my finger. Goosebumps flare on my skin, and a shudder runs straight down to my cock as if that particular piece of muscle is on a leash, on direct command to her.

I'd thought she was responsive to me, but nothing has prepared me for the fact that my body is as tuned in to her as it is.

With the barrier I've clamped on the mating bond, I've held back her essence from twinning with my spirit; but my physical self is completely and utterly enthralled by her. A shock runs through me.

This is not what I'd wanted.

I claimed an omega. I hadn't thought that would mean she would own me.

I knotted an omega. Didn't mean I had to be trapped by her.

Her touch, her feel, her scent that clings to my skin and to my soul. I am not ready for this. Not ready to let another into my heart… into my soul.

Perhaps physically, my body will always have this primal response to her, but I cannot, will not, let her own any other part of me.

Straightening, I get up, then climb over her and out of the bed.

65

Lucy

Emotions flicker over his face. Helplessness, a realization, a strange vulnerability, even…then a decision.

Those blue eyes of his lighten until they seem almost colorless.

A cold light shines in them, and it chills my soul.

"No." I shake my head and reach for him, but it's too late.

He's already taking a step back from the bed. He folds his arms over his massive chest, and the tattoo of wings down his biceps shudders as he flexes his muscles. His enormous bulk is powerful, lethal, and all mine. But he doesn't accept it. Not yet.

I sit up, groaning a little when my muscles protest.

The flesh between my legs is sore, and twinges of heat radiate out from my sex.

He's so damn tall and broad. The sheer dominance of his presence pins me down. Every pore in my body is aware of him, his heat, his touch, how he can ram past any barriers I dare put up between us.

I haul myself to sitting position, and my skin makes a squelching sound as it chafes over our joined fluids that coat the bedspread.

The scent of our mating is everywhere. The claiming marks on my shoulder twinge. On the other side, the bullet wound throbs. My throat is dry, my chest is heavy, and my thighs ache. I almost chuckle. I am one completely fucked omega, and I probably look it.

His gaze rakes over my breasts, down my waist, as I had hoped.

My skin puckers, my breathing grows erratic. One look from him and my body is ready for him.

He grips my shoulder and exerts enough pressure until I am once more flat on the bed. Figures, the alpha wants me on my back, legs spread open and ready to take his cock, again.

So why does the touch of his big palm seem so damn familiar? Why does he make me feel safe? I have this absurd need to cry, but I will not. Not now. Not when I need to show him that I understand him. I can take what he gives me, and more. "I am not going anywhere." I firm my lips.

His forehead furrows, and those thick eyebrows knit.

"Understatement." He jerks his chin to where the chain around my wrist is tied to the iron bedstead.

"You don't need to do that." I yank on the shackle and it doesn't give.

He smirks, those full lips curve up, and I want to lean in and bury my teeth in that lush lower lip and suck on it. And if I do that, he'll probably go all alpha on me again. He'll either fuck me or else walk away. I huff out a breath. "I mean, I am here, I intend to wait for you, while you go off and complete your warrior duties, or whatever it is you think you have to do."

"Bossy, aren't you?" His lips quirk. Then, he bends and chucks me under my chin. "But remember, in bed I am the one who takes charge."

"Like I could miss that!" I flick my hair over my shoulder.

"And still you challenge me." He draws me close and peers into my eyes, a strange litany of emotions crossing his features. "You are incorrigible."

"That's what my father said, too." I hadn't meant to reveal that.

It's the first time I've ever spoken about my past to him, not that there is anything to hide about it, but prior to this we've been a little too preoccupied with other things. Well, mainly him fucking me brainless. Once more, we are attempting to have a conversation, and—surprise—once more, we're naked. Still, it's a change from my being fixated on his body, his scent, his breath…which I have been since I first saw him.

I will myself to keep my gaze on his chest, his face, anywhere except lower down where I am sure he is still erect. The alpha has a sexual appetite which boggles me. Just thinking of the number of times he's taken me, knotted me, kissed me, all of it sends a surge of heat sweeping through my skin. I bite my lips and look away.

"Your father, the Czar of Russia?" His voice rumbles in the space between us.

My alpha is going to leave me. Nothing I say will stop him. I nod and blink away tears. I force my thoughts back to his question. "He taught me to fight."

"He taught you well."

My gaze flies to his face. My cheeks flush. "He made me take on some of the best fighters in the country."

"Well, they mustn't have been very good, considering all it took was a few well-placed hits to take you down."

He smirks that condescending smile. My fingers itch to slap his face. My body insists that I pull him closer, then run my tongue over his lips. I tug at his grip, but of course, he doesn't let me go.

"Here I had just begun to think perhaps there is something redeeming in you after all." I pinch my lips together.

"Don't make that mistake." He grips my chin and forces up my face so I have no choice but to meet his gaze. "I don't have a single ounce of sentiment in my body."

"Your big body," I blurt out as a wave of anger sweeps through me.

He thrusts his face close to mine so our noses bump. "Big, sexy, irresistible body that you can't get enough of."

My throat goes dry, "Ego much?"

"Don't forget what I am." He drops his hand and straightens, so I have to tilt my head right back to meet his gaze.

"Don't try to make me into something I am not. I am the alpha who claimed you against your will—"

"What's this? A confession."

His lips thin, his chest rises and falls. Dominance radiates from his every pore, pushing down on my chest, pressing down on my ribcage. There I go baiting the alpha again. Will I never learn?

I draw in a breath and the sudden influx of oxygen overwhelms my starved lungs. My head spins.

"I knotted you, many times during your heat cycle. I may have already impregnated you."

My hand flies to my stomach. A surge of shock…surprise…no, not that. In the back of my mind, I'd known I would fall pregnant.

It is the usual outcome of mating during a heat cycle.

Unless something untoward happens, I might already have conceived a child. *We* may have created a child. I stare at him.

"It's why, you see, you need to stay here. I can't let you escape." He turns and marches to the door.

"You bastard," I snarl, knowing I shouldn't, yet needing, wanting to do something to provoke him.

"That's General Bastard to you," he throws over his shoulder without looking behind.

My heart thuds, "I'll find a way to get rid of it," I say in desperation, while everything in me protests against it.

"No, you won't." He pauses with his hand on the door. "You'll stay here, take care of yourself, and the child." He shoots me a glance over his shoulder.

"What if I am not pregnant?" I raise my chin and meet his gaze.

"Well, then I look forward to rutting you through another heat cycle. Either way, I'll fight much more at peace knowing you are here safe and not tearing through the city." He thrusts out his chest, and his lips curl. His eyes glitter. There is not an iota of empathy in his gaze.

Any compassion I may have glimpsed earlier on his features is gone. A chill slithers down my spine. "I am your mate." I rub my upper arms. "You can't treat me this way."

He swivels around and props his hands on his hips. "I have no mate." His shoulders flex and the tendons of his throat move as he swallows. "You are my breeder, and if you are pregnant, perhaps I'll recognize you as the mother of my child, or indeed children, for there will be more. But let me be clear, you lost the right to be my mate when you led Kayden to me. You deceived me. I'll never forgive you for that."

Turning, he hurls the door open and leaves.

I stand there, and the door slams shut. It's bolted from outside, by the soldier standing guard, no doubt. Why do they bother? After all, I am chained to this bed, bonded to this alpha, and probably pregnant with his child.

If I did escape, no one would help me, not with Zeus's scent so strong on me.

I'd have to find another harem of omegas and beg them to take me in. Or become a breeder for some other alpha; perhaps an omega on hire. The thought of any other male's touch on my skin, smelling any other alpha's scent…My stomach twists. Bile rushes up my throat.

I have become exactly what I never wanted to be: bonded to a monster who doesn't want me.

Hang on there's more. Will Zeus forgive Lucy for her betrayal? Will they overcome the challenges and get together? To find out get OWNED BY THE ALPHA, Knotted Omega 3 HERE
"One hell of a primal read, this alpha is a sex god." - USA Today Bestselling Author, Lee Savino

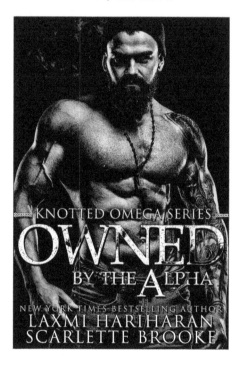

Read an excerpt...

Lucy

I sit up with a start. That scent of burned pinewood is so strong I am sure he is in the room with me. My eyes adjust to the darkness. Thanks to climate change, in this part of the world, it's hot all year around. But, early in winter the daylight breaks a little late.

The weather in my home country Russia is the exact opposite.

It's cold all year around. One perpetual winter with the snow layering over and over. I draw in a breath. Why is my mind wandering around in such random circles? Oh! Wait, maybe it's because I've been stuck in this room for a week now since he left? A bubble of laughter swells up. I bite my lip, and swallow hard. Pressure builds behind my eyeballs. I blink away the tears that threaten to overflow. Clearly, I am in shock. All thanks to Zeus.

He'd taken me in every position. On my back, on my front, me on top, me below, from the side, against the headboard of the bed...always on the bed. I curl my fingers into fists.

The bedsheets still smell of that masculine essence of his, an unmistakable complex fragrance tinged with his cum and shot through with the sweet, sugary essence of my slick.

Our scents seem to intermingle, recreating the very positions he had cajoled my body into.

I hadn't been aware of how flexible I'd been, not until the alpha had maneuvered me exactly how he wanted.

The last time he'd taken me, he'd turned me on my front, commanded me to go down on my hands and knees. When I had refused, he'd slapped my butt. I'd resisted doing as he wanted, and he'd spanked me. He hadn't stopped, not even when the flesh of my ass had quivered and ached—just not as much as my pussy which had wept with need.

Each time he'd hit me, he'd growled his approval. He'd purred his demands, and his voice had deepened with every stroke. I'd tried to pretend what he was doing wasn't turning me on, but the bastard knew my insides were wet and empty. I'd ached for him.

He'd known it and taken full advantage of it.

His spanking had grown harsher, his purring more resonant, until the sounds had mingled together.

My response had been instantaneous.

Every time he'd spanked me, my core had clenched. With the resonance of each purr, the slickness had gushed out from between my thighs. Every part of me had screamed for him to knot me and put me out of my misery.

I hadn't been able to stop the moan that had finally keened out of me. I had begged him to fuck me. Pleaded with him. I'd sunk my nails into his shoulders, thrust my pelvis up and smashed it against his dick in my agony. Still he didn't take me.

No, he'd yanked me up by my waist, until I was on my hands and knees. Then tugged my hips up, positioning me until he'd let out a grunt of satisfaction. He'd arranged me at that precise angle which would allow for the most intense penetration.

My cheeks flush. My skin burns. I can't stop the primal anticipation that tugs at my nerves.

I'd waited for him. Stayed as he'd commanded.

While a part of me had raged at my need to agree to his every whim. I hadn't wanted to do his bidding, but my body, so sensitized to his every need, had yearned for that approval. I'd hoped that if I did as he'd asked, he'd lower the barrier on the mating bond and let me see him, feel him absolutely. So I had complied.

I'd stayed butt in the air, my face pillowed on my folded arms.

He'd trailed a finger between my ass cheeks. "It strikes me, little squirrel, that there is still one virgin hole left in you."

I'd clenched my butt, my heart skittering. "You…you don't mean to…"

He'd tapped the curve of my waist. "I didn't give you permission to speak, did I?"

I'd bitten down on my lower lip and shut up. Yeah, obedient fool that I'd been.

He'd run his palm over my ass, then kissed my left butt cheek. "I told you already you were going to be punished, right?"

"Right."

He'd slapped my butt. "Just nod yes or no."

Tears had pricked my eyes. Every inch of my skin felt stretched, my nerve ends tingled, every part of me had gone rigid with defiance, while my pussy…that traitorous, needy part of me had quivered with anticipation.

"Answer me…Squirrel."

I'd nodded. Of course I had.

"Good girl." He'd dragged his whiskers over my right butt cheek then. Goosebumps had risen all over my skin. Even now, as I think about it, my ass cheeks tingle.

He'd grasped each cheek and spread them apart, then leaned down and licked my puckered hole.

Heat sweeps through my core at the memory, and I moan aloud. The sound of my voice in that empty room seems to mock me.

It mirrors the frustration that gripped me, when he'd slipped his hand around to the front. He'd dragged his fingers through my dripping folds, showing me just how much of a sham I was. How ready and open and willing I was for him to do with me as he'd wanted. He'd thrust finger into my pussy at the same time as he'd licked my back hole again, and again.

I'd tried to pull away from him, only he'd tied my arm to the bed, so my movement had been restricted.

Not that it would have mattered, for he'd squeezed my hips tightly and leaned his weight on my legs—not enough to hurt, just enough to render me immobile. He'd finger-fucked my pussy, adding two more of his digits and drawing them in and out of my channel, dragging those rough, callused fingers down the saturated walls of my cunt. All through, he'd continued to eat me out from the back.

The climax had caught me completely by surprise; it had simply crashed over me.

Liquid heat had erupted from my center, and my butt cheeks had clenched. Slick gushed out of me in thick streams, even as he'd raised his head and slipped in a finger into my back hole.

That had sent me over the edge.

Sparks of white had crashed over me—I swear I'd seen sparks of red in front of my eyes. Goosebumps had erupted on my skin, and the red and white had simply yanked me under.

When I'd come to, it was to the warmth of his chest at my back.

He'd held my limp body up, so I was kneeling and he was positioned behind me.

I'd been so far gone then, so pliant, and floating on that post climax high that I'd simply raised my arms behind and around his neck and pushed back, trying to smash as much surface area of my body to his as possible. I'd all but rubbed myself against him. I'd wanted to absorb his scent, the feeling of his skin gliding over mine, that roughness of his calluses as he'd grabbed my thighs and pried them apart... I'd wanted it all...and he'd known it.

"Ready, Squirrel?" His breath rustled in my ears, a second before he'd hauled up my hips and slammed into my dripping pussy from behind.

I'd screamed. My back had curved down. My hips had twitched and clenched and begged for more.

"You didn't think I'd take you there without preparing you first, did you?" He'd nipped the shell of my ear. "The time will come, just not yet."

The promise in his voice had curled my toes.

I'd trembled. My elbows had slipped, and I'd deepened the stretch of my body. I'd thrust up my hips, had waved them right in his face. I had begged him to take me, and he had.

He'd pushed a finger into my back hole.

I chafe my thighs together. *Don't do it. Don't.* I thrust my finger into my sopping channel. I want to come again. To ride out the climax as I had done with him earlier.

I'd felt him purr, and that had drawn forth even more slick.

That force inside me had intensified all over. It had surged up from the soles of my feet.

He'd pulled back to the edge of my channel and slammed in again and again. On the last thrust, I'd felt his knot slot into place, and he'd shot streams of cum into me, filling my womb. I'd been aware of the liquid building up, adding to the wave of climax that had crashed over me.

It had felt like the next climax had begun to build almost at once, sweeping through me. I remember throwing my head back against his chest and screaming, even as I'd held on to his shoulders and raked my nails over his skin. I'd collapsed and must have fallen asleep, for when I'd come to, he was gone.

He'd left me as he'd said he would.

My belly. I drag my finger from my channel. Raise it to my lips and suck on it.

The salty taste of the remnants of his cum fills my mouth. I roll it over my tongue and swallow it down. I taste like him. Smell like him. Behave as he'd trained me to even when he's not around.

My heart hammers, and my pulse flutters at my throat. I don't know who I am anymore. I swing my legs over the side of the bed to place my feet on floor

Every part of me feels like it's been well and truly fucked. The woman I'd been, the Lucy who'd stood up to her father, evaded the marauders and reached the shores of this country is fast drowning. I am losing myself in him. Until all that's left is the echoes of my climax. The high of the endorphins brought on by our mating lingers in my blood. My head spins.

I groan and drop my head forward. My free arm dangles between my legs. There's a liquid feeling in my limbs, as if I am melting everywhere. If I stand now, I am positive my knees will buckle. I look around and spot the tall glass of orange juice on the side table.

I snatch it up, raise it to my lips, and drain it.

The sugar seems to revive me at once. I place the cool glass against my forehead. That's when I see the note. It's folded, and there's no name on it, but clearly, it's for me.

I gnaw on my lower lip. I shouldn't read it. Don't care what he has to say to me.

My fingers tingle. Who am I kidding? I want to…need to know what's in it. I place the glass back on the table and reach for the note.

What could he have written anyway? More excuses? Lies? This alpha confuses me.

I firm my lips.

One minute he wants me, and the next he pushes me away.

The only person he hates more than me is himself, and isn't that a laugh? Surely whatever he wants to tell me can't be all that bad? I pick up the note and unfold it.

I'll be gone by the time you read this… I wanted to say thank you…

I bite the inside of my cheek.

Thank you? He actually wrote thank you? Probably just a trap. I am sure he doesn't mean it.

…for being with me for so long. I haven't always been tender with you…but, I don't think you want gentle, do you, Squirrel?

You are an omega, yet you've challenged me, baited me, you even claimed me first. It might have been your instincts as you say, or maybe I was just irresistible… (the latter, I think).

Bet he'd smirked as he'd scrawled that. Ha!

Either way, I claimed you, too. Clearly you haven't accepted the connection between us for you led Kayden straight to me and betrayed me.

My stomach flip-flops. I firm my lips.

It turned out for the best, as this way I can keep my half brother under the same roof as me.

"You had him imprisoned, asshole," I fume. Now I am talking to the man in his absence. I toss my head.

His voice comes through so strongly in the letter it's as if he's here in the room with me. My scalp prickles. Stupid dominant alpha, his presence is everywhere. Even when he's not physically with me, he is influencing me. The hair lifts on the back of my neck. I look around the room. Well, I *am* in his suite, surrounded by his scent, and faced with the evidence of our recent coupling on this bed, so clearly, I'd think of him, right?

I lower my gaze back to the letter.

The thing is, Omega, you are the one for me. The only woman who's stood up to me, gone toe to toe with me, and even managed to win a few of our encounters…which I allowed you to, of course.

"The ego of the man," My fingers press into the paper. I want to scrunch up the note and throw it aside, and yet I can't. Besides, he did write, *The only one for me…* Does he mean that? Zeus has many faults, but the alpha I have come to know does not lie. I continue reading.

Which is why I can't let you go, you understand? It's why I need to keep you chained, much as it pains me, because it's the only way to ensure you don't escape again. I need you to be safe, so I can focus on defeating the Marauders.

My heart stutters. A cold feeling grips my chest. He's gone after them. And he purposely didn't tell me. The sneaky bastard.

Yeah, if I'd told you, you'd have found a way to sneak off with us, or convinced me to take you along, and you know I can't.

You make me weak, make me care for you, make me want to protect you, all of which makes me vulnerable, and I don't like it, not one bit, Squirrel.

Doesn't change that you are my mate.

I've exercised my right to block the bond, as only an alpha can, so you cannot track me; you will not be able to read me or intuit what's happening to me, and that's for your own good. So don't try to escape and come to me if anything happens. Not that anything will.

"Overconfident alpha-hole," I rake my fingers through my hair. "You've gone and put yourself in danger. You are doing exactly what that Berserker wants. I am not going to let you die, Alpha. Not on my watch."

Turn the page to keep reading...

PART III

OWNED

66

Lucy

I sit up with a start. That scent of burned pinewood is so strong that I am sure Zeus is in the room with me. My eyes adjust to the dim light that filters in from between the cracks in the shutters. Thanks to climate change, the weather in London is hot all year round and this early in winter the daylight breaks late.

The weather in my home country of Russia is the exact opposite.

It's cold all year round. One perpetual winter, with the snow layering over and over. I draw in a breath. Why is my mind wandering around in such random circles? Oh! Wait, maybe it's because I've been stuck in this room for a week since he left me tethered to the bed stand? At least the bastard had the foresight to let out enough of the chain so I could use the bathroom unaided. I should be grateful for that, I suppose.

A bubble of laughter swells up. I bite my lip and swallow hard. Pressure builds behind my eyeballs. I blink away the tears that threaten to overflow. Clearly, I am in shock. All thanks to that alpha-hole.

A week since he left and his every touch is still imprinted on my skin.

He took me in every position. On my back, on my front, me on top, me below, from the side, me bent over on the bed…always on the bed.

I curl my fingers into fists.

The bedsheets reek of that masculine essence of his, an unmistakable complex fragrance tinged with his cum, and spiked with the sweet, sugary essence of my slick.

Our scents seem to intermingle, recreating the very positions into which he had cajoled my body.

I had never been more aware of just how much bigger and more powerful than me he was—or just how flexible I could be—not until the alpha had maneuvered my body into the exact positions that he wanted.

The last time he'd taken me, he'd turned me around and commanded me to drop down on my hands and knees. When I had refused, he'd slapped my butt. I'd resisted, and he'd spanked me again. He hadn't stopped, not even when the flesh of my ass had quivered and ached—just not as much as my pussy, which had wept with need.

Each time he'd hit me, he'd growled his approval.

He'd purred his demands, and his voice had deepened with every stroke. I'd tried to pretend what he was doing wasn't turning me on, but the bastard knew my insides were wet and empty. I'd ached for him.

He'd known it and taken full advantage of it.

His spanking had grown harsher, his purring more resonant, until the sounds had mingled together.

My response had been instantaneous.

Every time his big warm palm had connected with my flesh, my core had clenched. With the resonance of each purr, the slickness had gushed out from between my thighs. Every part of me had screamed for him to knot me and put me out of my misery.

I hadn't been able to stop the moan that had finally dribbled out of me. I had relented and dropped down on all fours and pleaded with him to fuck me. He hadn't relented.

I'd bowed my back, pushed my hips up in the air and begged him to take me. I had sobbed out the words as I'd waved my ass in the air asking him to rut me. I clench my fingers into fists at the memory.

Still he didn't take me.

No, he'd yanked me up by my waist, then scooped my hips up, positioning me until he'd let out a grunt of satisfaction. He'd arranged me at that precise angle which would allow for the most intense penetration. He'd massaged the aching flesh of my ass-cheeks. The circular motion of his rough palm seemed to rub in all that hurt and yearning that he'd created. The anticipation had begun to build inside, clawing at me; the emptiness in my womb bubbling up and eating away at me. A living breathing thing that thirsted to be filled by this alpha's cock, that yearned to be knotted and fucked in that most basic of ways.

He'd reduced me to the animal heart of me.

The one I had denied for so long.

That I had kept hidden behind the veneer of civilization, of fine clothes and wines and the best education that money could buy. The alpha-hole had stripped all of it from me. He'd shown me what I am. An omega. A writhing, keening, hollowed out shell of a woman who wanted one thing. Him.

I had thrown back my head and howled at him to mount me.

I had cursed and sworn at him, shrieked that if he didn't take me then I'd kill him and...he'd grabbed my thighs, wrenched them apart and rammed his dick into my pussy. He'd filled me to the brim with such force that I was sure he had split me in half.

The images, those sensations of how hard he'd felt as he'd plunged into me wash over me now, and my cheeks flush. My skin burns. I can't stop the primal anticipation that tugs at my nerves.

I'd clamped my inner muscles on his throbbing shaft and tried to take him in deeper and...he'd slapped my ass and told me to stay. That he hadn't given me the permission to move. That I had much to learn and he was going to take great pleasure in wearing me down—in breaking me, ruining me and putting me back together. Rebuilding me up around that pulsing, angry source of intense pleasure that was his cock.

And those harshly spoken words had sunk into my blood and resonated within my core. I'd frozen in place. I had obeyed him. While that last thinking part of me had raged at my need to agree to his every whim.

I hadn't wanted to do his bidding, but my body, so sensitized to his every demand, had yearned for that approval. My flesh so turned on by his dominance had wanted more—wanted him to fuck me harder, to take what he needed from me, to fulfill me in the only way an omega could be, and only by her mate. My soul had hungered for him on that other plane where I had sensed him in those early moments when the mating bond had snapped into place, before he'd hidden it. I'd hoped that if I did as he'd asked, he'd lower the barrier on the shared connection and let me see him, feel him absolutely. So I had complied.

I'd stayed there, butt in the air, my face pillowed on my folded arms, waiting, hoping, needing him. Waiting.

He'd paused a beat, two, then trailed a finger between my ass cheeks. "It strikes me, Little Squirrel, that there is one virgin hole left in you."

I'd clenched my butt, my heart skittering. "You...you don't mean to..."

He'd tapped the curve of my waist. "I didn't give you permission to speak, did I?"

I'd bitten down on my lower lip and shut up. Yeah, compliant fool that I'd been.

"You disobeyed me, again, now pay the price." He'd pulled out of me and I had whined...*whined)* my disappointment.

"I feel as deprived Squirrel, I don't want to hold back either, but first—" He'd run his palm over my ass, then kissed my left butt cheek, "—you'll take your punishment like the good omega you are, right?"

"Right."

He'd slapped my butt. "Just nod yes or no."

Tears had pricked my eyes. Every inch of my skin felt stretched, my nerve ends tingled, every part of me had gone rigid with defiance, while my pussy...that traitorous, needy part of me had quivered with anticipation.

"Answer me."

I'd nodded. Of course, I had.

"Good girl." He'd dragged his whiskered chin over my right butt cheek then.

Goosebumps had risen all over my skin. Even now, my ass cheeks tingle.

"If I am not inside you in the next few seconds I swear my aching balls are going to drop off, so come for me my omega, show me how much you want my cock inside of you." He'd grasped each of my ass cheeks and spread them apart, then leaned down and thrust his tongue into my puckered hole.

My core clenches at the memory, and I moan aloud. The sound of my voice in that empty room seems to mock me.

It mirrors the frustration that had gripped me when he'd slipped his hand around to the front. He'd dragged his fingers through my dripping folds, showing me just how much of a sham I was. How ready and open and willing I was for him to do with me as he'd wanted. He'd shoved two fingers into my pussy at the same time as he'd licked my back hole again, and again.

I'd tried to pull away from him, but he'd tied my arm to the bed, so my movement had been restricted.

Not that it would have mattered, for he'd squeezed my hips tightly and leaned his weight on my legs—not enough to hurt, just enough to render me immobile. He'd finger-fucked my pussy, adding two more of his digits and drawing them in and out of my channel, dragging those rough, calloused fingers down the saturated walls of my cunt. All through, he'd continued to eat me out from the back.

The climax had caught me completely by surprise; it had swept over me.

Liquid heat had erupted from my center, and my butt cheeks had clenched. Slick had gushed out of me in thick streams even as he'd raised his head and slipped a finger into my back hole.

That had sent me over the edge.

Sparks of white had crashed over me—I swear I'd seen sparks of red in front of my eyes. Goosebumps had erupted on my skin, and the red and white had yanked me under.

When I'd come to, it was to the warmth of his chest at my back.

He'd held my limp body up, so I was kneeling and he was positioned behind me.

I'd been so far gone then, so pliant, and floating on that post climax high that I'd raised my free arm behind and around his neck and pushed back, trying to smash as much surface area of my body to his as possible.

I'd wanted to absorb his scent, the sensation of his skin gliding over mine, that roughness of his calluses as he'd grabbed my thighs and prised them apart... I'd wanted it all...and he'd known it.

"Ready, Squirrel?" His breath had rustled in my ears, a second before he'd hauled up my hips and slammed into my dripping pussy from behind.

I'd screamed. My back had curved down. My hips had twitched and clenched and begged for more.

"You didn't think I'd take you there without preparing you first, did you?" He'd nipped the shell of my ear. "The time will come, just not yet."

The promise in his voice had curled my toes.

I'd trembled and opened my thighs wider. I'd deepened the stretch of my body, begging him to take me, and he had.

He'd pushed a finger into my back hole.

My thighs quiver and I chafe them together. *Don't do it. Don't.* I thrust my finger into my pulsing channel. I want to...need to come again. To ride out the climax as I had done with him earlier.

I'd felt him purr, and that had drawn forth more slick.

That force inside me had intensified all over. It had surged up from the soles of my feet.

He'd pulled back to the edge of my channel and slammed in again and again. On the last thrust, I'd felt him lock the knot into place, and he'd shot streams of cum into me, filling my womb. I'd been aware of the liquid building up, adding to the wave of climaxes that had crashed over me.

It had felt like the next climax had begun to build almost at once. It had rippled up my legs to coil in my center then surged out to fill my blood. I remember throwing my head back and screaming, as I'd held on to his arms and raked my nails over his skin. I'd collapsed and must have fallen asleep. When I'd woken, he was gone.

He'd left me as he'd said he would.

My belly quivers, my core aches. I drag my finger from my channel. Raise it to my lips and suck on it.

The salty taste of the remnants of his cum fills my mouth. I taste of him. Smell of him. Behave as he'd trained me to even when he's not around.

My heart hammers, and my pulse flutters at my throat. I don't know who I am anymore. I swing my legs over the side of the bed to place my feet on the floor

Every inch of me has been mauled by my alpha, every orifice truly fucked. He'd knotted me, and taken me over and over again. He'd absorbed my essence into himself until I am no longer sure who I am. The woman I was, the Lucy who'd stood up to her father, evaded the marauders and reached the shores of this country is fast drowning.

I am losing myself in him.

All that's left is the echo of my climax. The high of the endorphins brought on by our mating that lingers in my blood. My head spins.

I groan and drop my head forward. My free arm dangles between my legs. There's a liquid sensation in my limbs. If I stand now, I am positive my knees will buckle under me. I glance around and spot the tall glass of orange juice on the side table.

I snatch it up, raise it to my lips, and drain it.

The sugar seems to revive me at once. I drag the cool surface of the glass over my forehead. That's when I see the note. It's folded, and there's no name on it, but clearly, it's for me.

I gnaw on my lower lip. I shouldn't read it. Don't care what he has to say to me. My fingers tingle. Who am I kidding? I want to…need to know what's in it. I place the glass back on the table and reach for the note.

What could he have written anyway? More excuses? Lies? This alpha confuses me.

I firm my lips.

One minute he wants me, and the next he pushes me away.

The person he hates more than me is himself, and isn't that a laugh? Surely whatever he wants to tell me can't be all that bad? I pick up the note and unfold it.

I'll be gone by the time you read this… I wanted to say thank you…

I bite the inside of my cheek.

Thank you? Did he actually say thank you? Probably just a trap. Bet he didn't mean it.

For being with me for so long. I haven't always been tender with you…but, I don't think you want gentle, do you, Squirrel?

You've challenged me, baited me, and claimed me first. It might have been your instincts as you say, or maybe I was just irresistible…(the latter, I think).

Bet he'd smirked as he'd scrawled that. Ha!

Either way, I claimed you, too. Clearly you hadn't accepted the connection between us for you led Kayden straight to me and betrayed me.

My stomach flip-flops. I firm my lips.

It turned out for the best, as this way I can keep my half brother under the same roof as me.

"You had him imprisoned, asshole," I fume. Now I am talking to the man in his absence. I toss my head.

His voice comes through so strongly in the letter, it's as if he's here in the room with me. My scalp prickles. Stupid dominant alpha, his presence is everywhere. He's not physically with me, yet he's influencing me. The hair lifts on the back of my neck. I look around the room. Well, I *am* in his suite, surrounded by his scent, and faced with the evidence of our recent coupling on this bed, so clearly, I'd think of him, right?

I lower my gaze back to the letter.

The thing is, Omega, you are the one for me. The only woman who's ever stood up to me, gone toe to toe with me, and managed to win a few of our encounters...when I allowed you to, of course.

"The ego of the man." I press my fingers into the paper. I want to tear up the note but I don't. Besides, he did write, *The one for me...* Does he mean that? Zeus has many faults, but the alpha I have come to know does not lie. I continue reading.

Which is why I can't let you go, you understand? It's why I need to keep you chained, much as it pains me, because I must ensure that you don't escape again. I need you to be safe, so I can focus on defeating the Marauders.

My heart stutters. A chill grips my chest. He's gone after them. And he purposely didn't tell me. The sneaky bastard.

Yeah, if I'd told you, you'd have found a way to sneak off with us, or managed to convince me to take you along, and you know I can't.

You make me weak, make me care for you, elicit in me an urge to protect you, all of which makes me vulnerable, and that doesn't please me, not one bit, Squirrel.

Doesn't change that you are my mate.

I've exercised my right to block the bond, as an alpha can, so you cannot track me; you will not be able to read me or intuit what's happening to me, and that's for your own good. So don't try to escape and come to me if anything happens. Not that anything will.

"You overconfident alpha-hole." I crumple the paper. "You've gone and put yourself in so much danger. You are doing exactly what that fucker wants. I am not going to let you die, Alpha. Not on my watch." I fling away the note.

Crawling up the bed toward where he's tied me to the bed frame, I yank at the chain; it doesn't give. Try to use my other hand to untie it, but my fingers slide off. It's a silken handcuff, so it doesn't hurt my wrist. The jerk tied me knowing exactly how much I'd hate it. Just for that, I am going to find a way to escape and reach him.

The claiming marks on either side of my shoulder throb. Pain sweeps down my spine. The space in my chest where the mating bond had locked in convulses and a jolt of fear races over my skin. My stomach churns, and my womb spasms.

A hollowness fills my chest.

I try to draw in a breath, but my lungs burn. I gasp and try to rise, only to sink back. I need to go to him.

There's the sound of the door opening, and a figure walks in. She breaks into a run halfway across the floor. Reaching me, she grabs my shoulders and rights me. "What's wrong?"

I blink into the eyes of the same omega female who'd brought me food and seen to my needs over the past week. "He's in danger." I gasp.

"The General?"

I press my lips together. "I need to go to him."

She hesitates.

"Please, it's not just him, it's all his team, too." I curl my fingers into fists. "Their lives are in danger."

She goes pale. "Ethan...Ethan's with him."

"He's also at risk." I lean forward. "All of them. We need to get to them."

She takes a step back and turns to go.

"Wait...what are you doing?"

"I'm going to get Sol." She straightens her spine. "He'll know what to do." She goes to the door.

"Not here."

She shoots me a glance over her shoulder.

I wave a hand toward the messed-up bed, the evidence of my coupling with Zeus everywhere. "I don't want another alpha or anyone else to taint my space."

She angles her head, her gaze considering.

"Help me up, take me to him." I set my lips.

"It's against the General's orders."

"If you don't do that, there may not be any General or any Ethan left..." I fold my arms over my chest.

She swallows.

"You understand?"

She lets go of the door, which snicks shut. Swiveling on her heels, she hurries back to me. She grabs a key from her pocket, and reaches for my cuffs. "I'll help you to the shower."

67

Zeus

"Don't go, Alpha." Her voice echoes in my ears.

I know I am dreaming, but I don't want to break the images that fill my mind. Just this once, it's okay to burrow into the fantasy, to cover her body with mine.

That sweet scent of her arousal teases my nostrils and sinks into my skin, and I know I need more, so much more.

I trace little kisses over her cheek, down her throat, to the hollow between her breasts, licking up the bead of sweat that lingers there.

"Zeus."

Her breath sears my forehead. Her muscles tighten under my palm. I cup the firm curve of her breast and squeeze.

She shivers. Her dark-red nipples pucker up. And I can't stop myself. I curl my lips over them and bite down.

"Zeus."

Her cry sweeps over my skin, and my groin tightens. My shaft throbs.

"I need to be inside you," I whisper.

"Please." A mewl rises up her throat and curls around my shoulders.

I slide down her naked body, trailing wet kisses over the curve of her rib cage, down to where her waist dips to her belly button. I swirl my tongue over the indentation. Her muscles quiver. Her fingernails rake over my hair, and she grips the strands, pulling back my head as her pelvis pushes up toward me. Offering me her body, her soul, her everything. And I won't be content unless I have her all over again. I trail my tongue down to the triangle between her legs, where her flesh pulses, and blow on it gently. Her entire body quakes. A moan tears out of her. My groin tightens; I need her. Want her. But first, I need her to come. Just to see her fall apart around me, so she knows who controls her body. So she knows she cannot do anything without my permission. She knows who's in charge, and it's not her. No matter what, my omega is stubborn; I need her to submit to me. She must acknowledge me as her master. I flick my finger over the nub of her core. Her thighs clench. The scent of her arousal bleeds into the air and shatters over my skin. My entire body tenses. And I thought I was teasing her?

I grip her hips and raise her at just the right angle.

Then, bending close, I purr, letting the sound flow up from my core, up from my chest and out over her, modulating my tone just right so it bleeds into the air between us, surrounding us, cocooning us.

Her body shudders. Her spine arches, and her hips push up. "Take me, Alpha," she pants.

A smile curves up my lips. "Soon, my Squirrel, very soon. But first you need to learn your place."

Another growl rumbles up my chest, and I let the sound weave around her hips, lassoing the trembling flesh, bringing her closer, to the end that only I can see. Her legs twitch. She folds her knees, then widens her thighs further.

I can't stop the purr of satisfaction that drools out of me. She's beautiful, gorgeous, and mine. All mine. I will make her mine even if it means I have to rip out every cell in my body, even if it means keeping her here until I have ravaged every portion of her skin, licked every inch of her curves, sucked on every piece of her flesh—or perhaps there is another way. Seduce her, taunt her, make her beg. A shiver of anticipation tugs my nerves. I go hard just thinking of everything else I want to do to her. Just teasing her, of course. I want her to realize what she'd miss if I was not there, what she'd get only from me.

I release of her hips, and her body sinks back into the bed. Her muscles coil.

"Wha…what are you doing?"

"Shh!" I bare my teeth, knowing she can't see it. I had clamped down a barrier over the mating bond, yet she seems to glean my thoughts. Despite my trying to separate us, she is tuned in to me, and it's worrying. Damn if it isn't also intriguing. It worries me. And excites me. Enough for me to want to test it.

I reach up and tie her free arm to the headboard. "Close your eyes." I reach for a second scarf.

Her eyebrows draw down, and her mouth purses. I expect her to protest and say she doesn't want me to blindfold her, that she doesn't want to completely submit herself to my ministrations. Once again, my omega surprises me. Her shoulders tense, but she doesn't say anything. Just raises her head from the pillow so I can tie the fabric around her eyes. I don't need to reassure her, yet that part inside of me that seems to surprise me these days, ever since I met her, that is, coerces me.

I flutter my knuckles over her jawline then place my lips close to her ear. "Trust me."

She nods, a quick jerk of her head. Almost imperceptible, but I catch it.

"Good girl."

I brush my lips over hers.

Her lips cling to mine, and before I give in to the temptation of thrusting my tongue inside her mouth and drinking of that essence of her that goes to my head, I withdraw. I balance my weight on my elbows and the balls of my feet, planking over her.

My muscles strain with the weight of my entire body, but I can take it.

She must sense the heat from my body for goosebumps pop on the skin over her breasts. Her nipples pucker. A bead of sweat creeps down her temple. I lean close and am about to lick it up. Then change my mind and blow on her skin.

She shivers and sinks her teeth into her lower lip. I sense her muscles go solid under me. Ah! So she's going to hold back the satisfaction of showing what I am doing to her? She's just changed the tone of this entire game into a battle of wills. One I am not going to lose.

A harsh purr rumbles up, and I lower my chest, close enough to almost graze her nipples—almost. Her flesh tightens, the buds pucker up. She must sense the vibrations, for the muscles of her waist quiver.

I lower my mouth toward her breasts and open my mouth over the nipples and blow again. The pores of her breasts tighten, her curves swell. She swallows. Waves of anticipation roll off her, and that sweet, sugary scent of her arousal deepens. It's more arousing than touching her, the fact that just my intent of wanting to bring her to climax is turning her on so much.

I crawl down her body, making sure not to touch any part of it. Spotting another scarf, I bind it around her ankle and tug it tight to the side. Then the other so she's spread-eagled.

There's the sound of a moan from her, quickly stifled. A trickle of slick sloshes down from between her legs. My omega is aroused, and I haven't started yet.

I rise off the bed and stand at the foot of the bed frame.

My gaze sweeps over the curves of her body, a long, lean line of submission—no, not really. I bound her so I could bare her to my ministrations, but that doesn't mean she has submitted to me. If anything, her shoulders straighten, her stance wary. She is anticipating everything that's coming to her, but she's not scared and that intrigues me.

"What do you want, Omega?" My tone sounds gentle.

Not how I'd wanted this session to go, but that's how it always goes with her.

Me trying to get her to come around to my way of doing things, her resisting, and me having to unbend just a little at a time.

I'd set out to tame her, but she always manages to crawl her way inside of my heart, under my skin, right from the time I'd first laid eyes on her. No, even before, from the time I'd first dreamed about an omega with green eyes who I was going to take for my own.

I've never told her that before, but I can show her what I want to do to her. How I want to make her beg for my touch, mewl for me to penetrate her, and then, I am going to hold back. Does that me a bastard?

Probably.

It's just how I am. I prefer to tease, to draw out the need, until every single molecule of her body wants me, only me.

A harsh purr is drawn out of me. I throw my voice so that the edge of the tone lassoes over her. She tugs at her bonds, and her thighs clench. A gush of liquid pours out from between her legs, pooling below, and I can't hold back anymore. All thought of teasing her goes out of my head. I lean down between her legs, lap up the liquid, then, scooping up the moisture, smear it over my hardness.

"I know what you are doing." Her voice trembles.

"Do you?" I grip the base of my shaft, trying to hold back the need that tears at me. Just a little longer until I can have her. Just a few minutes more until I drive her to the edge. When she's about to go over, I'm going to pull her back and do it all over again. But she doesn't know that, yet.

"Let me help you, Alpha." She tilts her head.

Clever omega, she thinks she can trick me into opening her blindfold?

"I admit I am tempted." I drag my grip up my cock, all the way to the end so a drop of precum appears at the tip.

She groans.

So do I.

"Please." She licks her lips and I feel the tug all the way to the tip of my shaft.

I kneel over her, raising my torso until I am positioned right over her face. "Open your mouth."

"First take off my blindfold."

I swear. "You are not in a position to negotiate."

Her lips twist. "Neither are you."

A growl rumbles up from my throat. Low, deep, filled with every last sliver of intention of what I want to do to her. What I *will* be doing to her if she doesn't cooperate.

Color rises in her cheeks.

She curls her fingers around her restraints. "You are such a sore loser." She pouts.

"And you are going to be more than *just sore*." I rub my dick over her lips. "Everywhere." Her lips fall open, and I slam my shaft into her mouth. "Once I am done with you…"

My engorged flesh hits the back of her throat, and she gags.

"I am going to punish you for your insubordination, Little Squirrel."

She licks the head of my shaft, and another purr is drawn out of me. My balls grow heavy, and damn if I am not near coming already.

I skim my knuckles over her jawline. So gorgeous. So sensuous. And, all mine.

She closes her mouth around me, and the heat sweeps down my spine. Sweat pops over my forehead. Who is taking who here? Anger flows into my chest, and it's laced with pride…for her, for the fact that whatever I throw at her, she always takes it and comes back for more. Like she wants me…not just my body, but me, the harsh, cynical monster inside who hadn't hesitated to kill his family for power. Who is hell-bent on wrecking his legacy, until there is nothing left of the tainted blood that runs in my veins.

My nerve endings crackle with pain…with lust…with need for this omega who has me on my knees.

She just doesn't know it yet. I can't tell her, not until I come to terms with how I see her. She's not just my mate, she is more—my partner, and… no omega has ever stood next to her alpha, never fought alongside her mate, until her.

She'd put her life at stake and saved me. She'd almost gotten killed in the process, and I cannot allow her to do that again. She needs to know where she belongs. Under me, in my bed, in my space, where I can protect her and keep her safe.

My heart stutters.

I cannot let anything happen to her. If she insists on continuously challenging me, it will put her at risk.

I need to find a way to keep her here, voluntarily, and the only way to do that is to tame her spirit.

I pull out of her, until the swollen head drags over her lips. "You're going to take everything I give and ask for more, and when I am done with you—"

All of her muscles tense.

She pulls up her chin, and swipe her tongue over the edge of my cock. Liquid lust slams into my groin.

"—I'll take everything that is left, and when it's over, you won't know where you end and where I begin." I thrust my flesh inside that heated, moist mouth of hers. "You'll forget everything about yourself, everything except my name."

"Zeus."

Freezing water slaps my face, and I spring up on my feet. I swing my fists up in front of me. Water flows off of me, and my feet almost slip. I look around to find I am in the shallows of a river.

On the raised bank just a foot ahead, Ethan faces me, his chest forward, knees bent. "We tried to wake you, but clearly you were…ah…too exhausted." He chuckles. "We voted this was the best way to wake you up."

"The fuck?" I wade through the water before springing up on the bank.

Liam bursts into the clearing. His breath comes in pants. He's geared up in fatigues, a gun secured to his back, more guns packed into the belt around his waist, and a knife strapped to his thigh. "Found the Vikings."

I stride to him, shaking the water out of my hair. "How far?"

"A mile, maybe two."

I move past him to where we'd broken camp. I grab my vest and pull it on over my dripping clothes. They'll dry off in the heat of the day anyway. Already my clothes are steaming. Shoving my feet into my boots, I pick up my sword and slide it on over my back, then the organic gun which I hook onto my belt.

Ethan reaches for his vest.

"Your timing always did suck, Second." I should be far angrier at him for having interrupted what had clearly been a dream.

Though I'd clamped a barrier over the mating cord, these nightly dreams have been getting more vivid since we'd left London and headed off toward where the Vikings had last been seen. The plan is to catch them before they leave the shores of this country. Once they board the ships to Russia, they'll be invincible—in more ways than one. At the time I'd left her, I'd thought it was a good idea to keep a distance been us.

Right now, with my groin on fire, my balls straining like they weigh a ton, and that ever-present sting of the mating cord that claws at my breastbone, I am not so sure. I rub the skin over my chest and swear.

"Is it my timing or yours you are talking about?" Ethan shrugs on his vest and hooks on his guns and the bow and arrow.

"What do you mean?" I gather my hair and tie it back with a piece of leather.

"You should have stayed and completed the mating bond with your omega—"

I close the distance between us then draw my knife and press its edge to his throat, "Why do I get a sense of déjà vu, Second?"

"Just stating the obvious General." He holds up his hands in mock surrender.

"I told you never to talk about her."

"Someone has to, given you don't want to acknowledge how much she's already changing you."

I frown, "What do you mean?"

"Apparently you give a fuck about someone else other than yourself." He scratches his chin. "Not that it's a bad thing, except—"

"Except, it takes the edge off of my awareness." I set my jaw. "It's a source of distraction, one which threatens to take my attention away from what is important." I push down on the knife until the blade slices through his skin. A trickle of blood spills down his throat.

He swallows, and his eyes narrow. "Come now, Z, you know I am looking out for you."

"Yeah, the way you watched out for Golan right before you showed me to his suite and gave me your blessing to kill him?" I raise the knife, and he stiffens.

I bring it down and he doesn't move.

The knife whizzes over his shoulder. Fucker doesn't blink, he continues to hold my gaze. He has balls, I'll give him that.

I brush past him to where the blade has gone through a fox.

I slam my foot on the animal, hold down the carcass, and yank out the knife.

"I did what was in the best interests of this city." His voice follows me.

"And I am doing what's best for me." I wipe the blade on the animal, then heave the carcass at Ryker. He snatches it up.

Blood drips down from the animal.

"Tonight you're on cooking duties." I jerk my chin at him. "Assuming we haven't caught the marauders by then."

His features contort, and his lips draw down. "Aw, come on, General, you know I'd do almost anything other than cook."

"Time to learn, asshole." I toss my head. "You throw me in the water—and not that I don't appreciate the wakeup call, you get me? But every action has consequences, and don't you forget that."

He hauls the carcass over his shoulder.

"Let's get out of here before—"

A war cry rings out and a bullet whistles past a second before another slams into my shoulder. Pain burns a line down my arm.

"Get down," I yell, dropping to the muddy ground.

68

Zeus

There's another whizzing; more bullets pepper the space around us. Next to me, Ryker falls to the ground. My shoulder throbs and I wince. I shove aside the pain then grab his arm and drag him to the trees. Ethan races over and drops next to me.

"There are more than I anticipated." He pants. Sweat beads his forehead.

"Where's Liam?" I crane my head to peer across the tree line.

"He's covering us from the other side." The sound of bullets screaming back in the direction from where the gunfire came emphasizes his answer.

"We need to teach these Vikings a lesson they'll never forget." I crack my neck. "Where are the rest of our men?"

"At least two days away," Ethan replies from upfront.

"Fuck!" I growl. Blood thuds at my temples.

Another hail of bullets bursts over us, followed by a shower of arrows. One of them scrapes Ethan's arm, and he swears. "We need to get out of here."

"Cover me."

He opens his mouth to protest, and I shake my head.

"We do this my way." I spring up to my feet. The sound of gunfire follows me as Ethan trains his gun on the enemy and squeezes the trigger.

I reach Liam and squat down next to him. "You're good at hand-to-hand combat."

He frowns. "Yessir."

"You willing to follow me?"

"You bet, sir."

"Good man." I straighten and race to the tree line.

Liam is right behind me.

I take a wide detour, going all the way around the space from where the original firing had come, making a U-turn to come up behind where the group of Vikings are hidden in the trees.

"Come on." I pull my knife out.

Grabbing the Viking closest to me, I slit his throat. The man falls to the ground without a sound.

Next to me, Liam has twisted the neck of the nearest soldier with his bare hands and shoves the figure into the bushes.

I creep up on the next one and plunge the knife into his neck. Blood spurts out, and he crumples. Liam kicks out the feet of the soldier in front of him. The man crashes to the ground, and Liam punches his fist into his opponent's face.

I leap across to the last man. Snapping my arm around his shoulders, I slit his throat. His blood seeps out, and his legs convulse. I drop his still-kicking body to the ground.

The sound of bullets fades away.

I straighten in time to see Ethan cross the tree line, and head for me. He half carries, half drags an injured Ryker with him.

"It was an ambush." Ethan pants.

I hold up my hand, and he shuts up. In the distance, the sound of footsteps crashes through the undergrowth. There are more soldiers on the way.

"Let's split up." I gesture for Ethan and Ryker to stay. Shooting a sideways glance at Liam, I beckon him to come with me.

We race around the clearing.

I sprint halfway to the other side, Liam at my heels, and duck behind the trees just as Harald stalks into the clearing.

He's followed by four of his men. They are in full armor, with guns and swords strapped to their backs.

From the other side, Ethan strides in. There's a Viking standing behind him, with a sword held out in front. Its tip is pressed into Ethan's side.

Ryker staggers into the clearing, arms folded behind his neck. Two Vikings have their guns trained on him.

"Fuck." How did I let them get the better of us? I curl my fingers into fists. My muscles bunch.

I should have brought the rest of the troops with me; Ethan had been right. But there was no way I would have left the stronghold unguarded. Not with my omega there. She is what Harald covets, and as long as she is protected from Harald, well, it doesn't matter what happens to me.

I'll go to my grave trying to kill this bastard. And kill him I will, for without his death, my omega is not safe. Besides, no way does he challenge me and get away with it. I need to survive this particular encounter, that's all. I dig my booted feet into the ground.

"Zeus." Harald's voice rings out.

A flurry of birds rise from the trees in alarm.

"I have your men, Zeus." He props his arm on his hip and widens his stance. "Perhaps you have a modicum of decency in your blood, something that will compel you to fight for the lives of your men? You are not going to let them die, are you?"

I raise my gun and take aim at Harald. Liam touches my arm, "If you shoot you give away our position."

Of course he's right. I should have thought of that. It's a testament to just how fucked up I am in my head that I'd forgotten a basic defensive tactic.

Harald must have sensed something for he straightens and stares in my direction. He jerks his chin and his soldiers fire off a round toward us.

I drop to the ground, and Liam mirrors my actions.

The bullets fly over us and when the hail of firing stops, I peer up.

"I warned you, Zeus." He nods to his man, who drives his sword into Ethan's back.

"No!" I clench my fingers into fists.

Ethan falls over on his front.

The man grabs the sword and yanks it out. Blood spurts from the wound. Ethan's body twitches, then stills.

My pulse rate ratchets up. Icicles spike my blood and I clench my fingers. Fucker is going to pay for this. I didn't mean for that to happen to Ethan—so what if I didn't trust him? Fact is, that man is the reason I took over as General, why I had navigated the politics of the Council, why I am standing here today...and he...he's dead.

Harald's men killed one of my own and I am not going to let them leave without taking revenge.

I spring up and Liam blocks my way. "You step out there, General, and he'll take you captive."

"I can't watch him take out another of my own." I grit my teeth so hard that pain slashes my jaw. Somewhere along the way I'd mellowed enough to care for the lives of my team. It's the one thing that separates us from our cousins in the animal kingdom...the fact that when challenged we close ranks, and that even extends to someone as selfish as me.

Ahead, Harald raises his gun and points it at the already bound Ryker. His gaze swivels to the edge of the clearing. "Guess you really are the kind of leader who'd readily sacrifice your team for your own life."

My muscles coil, and anger whips down my spine. I shove Liam to the side.

"Your omega...if you die, she dies, too."

That brings me up short. "I've blocked the mating bond from taking root in me. If I die, she will suffer, but she'll survive." The mating cord in my chest twinges, and I resist the urge to rub my chest.

"She'll find another." Liam narrows his gaze, his eyebrows draw down.

One side of my lips curl. "That's the idea." My heart stutters, pain twists my guts, and I shove it aside.

He blinks. "You've changed, Zeus."

Thanks to her. I toss the gun over to him.

Yanking the sword off my back, I hand that over, too. "Tell her to use it to cut out the claiming mark on her neck."

I lean forward on the balls of my feet.

Liam doesn't move.

I jerk my chin. "Go."

He doesn't move. His features are solid and his eyes seem too bright.

"That's an order. You need to survive this and get out of there."

He jerks his chin, then steps back into the bushes.

I stalk forward and into the clearing.

69

Lucy

I race past the tree line. Mirela is right behind me. She pants, the sound of her breathing loud in the silence. I slow down until she catches up with me. "You need to keep it down; you are making too much noise."

"You're too fast for me." She sucks in her cheeks.

"Yeah, that's what they all say." I can't stop my lips from curving up in a satisfied smile.

The alphas of London have no idea what's going to hit them.

"I can't believe you coerced me into letting you free and also following you. If the General finds out…"

"You leave the General to me." I continue to survey the area. Did I hear a noise?

"You are too confident for an omega." She purses her lips.

"My father taught me to be a warrior. He treated me and my omega sister more akin to the alpha sons that he wanted. He trained us so we could protect ourselves." I clench my fingers into fists. "Didn't stop him from using us for leverage when it suited him." I curl my lips. "When the Vikings invaded our city, my father bartered off the virgin omegas—including me— in exchange for their leaving."

An emptiness yawns in the pit of my stomach. "I escaped with my sister and others from my clan. My mother didn't make it. The berserkers slaughtered her. She sacrificed herself so we could survive."

Mirela touches my shoulder, and I move away, not wanting her empathy.

"And your father?"

"After what he did to us?" I straighten my spine, "bartering us like we were his possessions…? I refuse to accept him as my parent anymore." My chest hurts, a pressure pounds behind my eyes. Why did my father's action hurt so much? I should have known that when it came down to it my father's alpha nature would prevail. He'd treat us like we were objects to be traded: omega pussy that could be bought and sold.

"I'm sorry." She whispers. "That's why you want to go after the Vikings? You want revenge?"

"Yes. No." I twist a strand of my hair around my fingers. "Not only." I blow out a breath. "It's complicated."

"It always is." She observes me from under hooded eyes. "It's the General, isn't it?"

"The alpha who took me when I was not quite in my senses?" I tilt my head. Did I hear something? Every muscle in my body goes on alert. I squat and pull her down next to me.

"What is it?" Her shoulders shake with fear before she rights herself.

This omega has guts. She is afraid but she hadn't hesitated to up and come with me. She'd helped me slip out from behind Sol's back. Yeah, she'd agreed to drug his food, and I'd wanted to bind and gag him, but she'd insisted I desist.

Doing so would have completely lowered his standing in front of the other alphas, and, well, we can't be having that, now can we? Macho alphas with their over-inflated egos. Get an omega to carry out his job, and she'd do it with half the fuss, better planning, and with less of the bravado.

"Can you hear anything?" She swats at her arms waving away the hovering mosquitoes.

"Shh!" I angle my head, trying to home in on the sound.

There's only the hum of crickets and a woodpecker in the distance hammering away. We didn't miss them, did we? We didn't come this far to lose the Vikings.

"How did you know where to find them?"

"Before I escaped I overheard my father talking about the trade routes of the Vikings." I glance sideways at her, "There's only one functioning port for their ships to dock in this country—"

"Southampton?"

I nod.

A moan rends the air, and I stiffen. She clutches my arm.

"I heard that," I whisper.

Rising, I follow with her close on my heels. I manage to avoid the dead trees and fallen branches, and try to keep as quiet as possible. She steps right on a fallen branch, which cracks under her weight. The sound echoes through the area.

"Damn." I swear under my breath.

She halts next to me. "Sorry," she whispers.

I strain my ears but can't hear anything. She probably alerted whoever it is that we are coming. The hair on the back of my neck stiffens. All my instincts go on alert.

"Stay silent and mind where you place your feet."

She nods, her lips draw down, her shoulders stiffen.

I swivel around to find a gun pointed at her temple. The man holding it is...

"Ethan?"

His gaze darts from her to my face. His features are dazed, his eyes are dilated, and he's holding himself straight, like he is in a lot of pain.

"Ethan, it's me, Lucy. Don't you recognize me?"

He doesn't move, but his throat muscles flex as he swallows.

"You're hurt. Let us help you."

He cocks the gun.

"Don't hurt me, Ethan." Mirela's chest heaves. "I was worried about you."

He blinks, and his gaze falls on her face. His features clear. "Mirela?" His hand wavers.

I snake out my arm and grab the gun from him and shove him aside. He topples over on his front.

Mirela gasps and drops to her knees next to him. Blood leaks from his back. His clothes are mottled with blotches of red.

"He's hurt." She swallows.

"He's dying." I rise to my feet and try to think.

"We need to save him. We have to." Her chin trembles.

I bend down and slap his face. "Ethan, wake up."

"Hey." She shoves at my arm. "What are you doing?"

"I need to know where they have taken Zeus and the rest of his men." My stomach lurches. I was wrong. I am not empty inside… Fear burns my guts.

"I thought you didn't care about the General?"

"I don't." Lies, all lies.

The hollow space in my chest seems to grow wider, deeper. A chill stutters down my spine, and I gasp.

Mirela's gaze falls to where I rub at my chest.

"You're mated to him?"

"He claimed me, only to slam down a barrier on the bond so I cannot connect to him…" His absence haunts me, and that is much worse.

Her eyes narrow, and she flinches. Her features pale, and pity fills her gaze.

"Don't." I touch Ethan's shoulder. "Did they take him to their ships? Are they planning on taking him with them?"

He coughs. Turning his head in my direction, he rests his cheek in the dirt. "They didn't say much, I didn't hear much, but it's clear they are going to take him as hostage and probably head back to London to claim the city."

"No way." I rise to my feet and slide his gun into the back of my pants. They are my alpha's and many sizes too big, but I'd torn off the bottom and managed to bunch them and hold them up with a belt. It was the best I could do, considering…I'd taken on another half-assed, not-properly-planned venture.

"Time is short." His breathing grows ragged. "You need to get to them and set him free, and he and the men will do the rest."

I almost chuckle at that, the irony. "So send the little omega on to save the big alpha, then ask her to fall back and let him have all the fun?" I jut out my chin.

"Zeus is going to have his hands full with you, isn't he?" He wheezes.

"Not just his hands." I plonk my palms on my hips. "You are obviously in no shape to fight."

"But *you* are." He narrows his gaze on me.

"You got *that* right."

"My sword…they left it in the clearing, and you'll probably find some of the other guns from those who were killed in our encounter."

I purse my lips. Should I believe him? "Don't you alphas all stick together."

"I am doing what's right to save the General. He has to live so he can lead the people."

"So can you." I toss my head.

"I am not as ambitious as he is." He frowns.

"Yeah right," I sneer.

"I enjoy the machinations of the mind too much. The parry and thrust of strategy turns me on."

Mirela tears the sleeve of her shirt. "Is that the only thing that turns you on?" She balls it up and presses it over the open wound on his back.

His entire body jerks, but he doesn't utter a cry.

"You do, too..."

"Finally!" Mirela's actions stop, she stares at him. "You must be more hurt than I thought to admit that..."

"Probably the fall I took earlier," he mutters.

"Probably." She jerks her chin at me. "Hold this, will ya?"

I place one palm on top of the other and apply pressure on the makeshift tourniquet.

She tears off another strip of cloth and binds it around his chest.

He sucks in a breath. "Woman..." His shoulders bunch. "You trying to kill me already?"

"Don't be such a baby." She ties up the bandage with a flourish. "All done."

Together we heave Ethan to his feet. He's almost as big as Zeus, and between the two of us we can barely hold up his weight. We help him deeper into the forest and lean him against a tree.

"You need to leave, Lucy. Get to him. He's not going to be happy though, that you put yourself at risk for him."

"Won't be the first time. The stubborn alpha needs to accept that I can take care of myself." I pause and step back.

He leans more of his weight on Mirela who straightens and wraps her arm around his waist. Hmm! They do fit well together, though I don't say that aloud. Nope, not that anyone could miss the chemistry sparking between these two.

"I can't leave you like this." I frown.

"I'll take care of him." She lifts her chin.

"I know you will." I peel off the gun he gave me and hand it to her.

"What about you?"

"I'll find the abandoned weapons from the other soldiers."

"Go." He gestures with his chin. "Mirela will help me back to London, and I'll alert the troops to come out and meet you."

"Umm, that may not be needed." Heat flushes my chin.

Mirela shifts her weight from foot to foot. "Yeah, we just need to stay, help is on its way."

Ethan huffs out a breath. "Sol?"

I nod but hold his gaze. "We got a head start. He must be less than a few hours away with a bunch of chosen troops."

"How dare he let you leave unaccompanied?"

I stare and his brow furrows. "Let me guess you didn't give him a choice?" He turns on Mirela.

She reddens, "I may have...uh!...drugged his food."

His jaw firms, "Who's guarding the stronghold?"

My back stiffens. "Whoever is left."

"You left us wide open to an enemy attack." Ethan swears and rubs the back of his neck. "You shouldn't have done that."

"I had no choice." I square my shoulders. "The General's and your lives are more important."

"I hope for your sake, Omega, you are right."

Yeah, me, too. I will not feel guilty for what I did. "You alphas." I toss my head, "You count your worth by power and omega pussy. It's all about saving face and damn the consequences."

Ethan draws himself up to his full height. "I am not here to debate the ethics of the situation or what it means to be an alpha."

I notice he doesn't let go of Mirela either.

"Another time." I turn to leave, then come up short.

Facing us is a contingent of Vikings.

Zeus

I stalk into the clearing, my arms held up in front of me to show I am unarmed. Every decision made in the last few weeks seems to come crashing down on me, and fuck, isn't that a surprise? I snicker.

Me, Zeus, who'd lived life without caring about what the repercussions of my actions were, who'd lived for revenge, who hadn't cared what I had to sacrifice or give up as long as victory was mine…that Zeus… The wound in my shoulder throbs from where I took the bullet. My chest hurts from what I saw.

Ethan is dead. And…I feel like shit…Fuck.

There is a ball of emotion in my chest that grows bigger with every passing moment and I cannot understand why. I feel almost as bereft as when I'd lost my mother. The fuck is that about?

I'd sworn never to let myself be as vulnerable again, yet here I am grieving for the death of a man who I'd never trusted. I had given Ethan the position of my second because it was part of our deal.

He'd supported me in overthrowing Golan and taking over as General and in return I gave Ethan power. The reality is that I'd never treated him as more than just someone to tolerate. I had never gotten over the fact that he'd betrayed the very man he'd pledged to protect.

My rational mind had always insisted that Ethan would one day turn on me, that there was a reason why he'd sided with me to help me track down my omega. There had to have been something of benefit to him in all of this. I'd doubted him and he'd given up his life for me.

It's that which makes me push on unarmed, to walk toward where Harald and his warriors wait for me.

I am not afraid.

I've faced death too many times to be scared.

A part of me realizes that I don't want to die. Not now, not after I've found my omega. I'll give anything, anything to hold her in my arms, to kiss her, ravish her, take her, protect her. I'd had my chance and I blew it. For I'd been too hung up on the fact that she made me weak. That she'd swept past my barriers and taken my focus off of what that had mattered to me so far. Revenge. For the past. For the injustice my father and this city had committed toward me. After I'd killed Golan, that emptiness in me hadn't diminished. Not until I'd scented her and taken her. And my life has not been the same since.

I'd found her. I'd also turned my back on her. And in a way...well, I deserved this. Liam was right. It's the only explanation for the emotions that swamp me. Betrayal, hurt, and what I suspect is remorse ball in my chest. I shake my head to clear it and come to a stop in front of Harald.

I left my weapons with Liam, but that had been to buy myself more time. I don't want to die. I need to avenge Ethan's death. In this moment, it doesn't matter that I hadn't trusted him—the man had helped me, had now given his life for me.

My gut churns.

Nothing like a healthy dose of revenge to get the blood flowing. To get the adrenaline pumping. To clear out all other emotions except for that hard edge of hate that pervades my mind. My vision tunnels. I narrow my gaze and stare at Harald.

"The fuck you want?" I crack my neck from side to side.

The Viking leader raises his chin. We are of the same height and almost equal in weight.

Even missing an arm he makes for a formidable opponent; and I am going to make sure he doesn't hurt her.

"You have some balls on you, General." He chuckles, "Or should I call you Zeus?"

I glare at the aging alpha, a pulse tics at my jaw.

"Not that it matters." He cants his head, "A bastard by any name smells as rotten."

I grunt. "Takes one to know one."

His shoulders bunch, and I know he's going to hit me. I duck, but his fist catches me in the side of the jaw.

White and red sparks jolt my brain. I stagger back and wipe the blood off of my lower lip. "Take me on one-on-one, and we'll see who wins." I growl.

"Oh, the fire in your belly." He shakes the matted hair back from his face. "I'd give anything for a chance to feel the extremes of emotions that fill your veins." His eyes gleam. "That lust which comes with being a prime specimen of an alpha, I want to experience it just one more time. Would you indulge me if I asked for a glimpse?"

A cloud of something dark and desperate assails me. He seems to be channeling Golan. I may have killed my father but damn if this fucker is not the same age and as depraved as my asshole old man.

"You knew Golan?"

He angles his head. "We were acquainted."

"You were one of the alphas he loaned out my mother to." As I say it, I know I am right. My heart hammers. My throat closes.

He grabs his crotch. "Your old man had impeccable taste, I'll give him that." He bunches his fingers and brings them up to his pursed lips. "The sweetest cunt she had on her."

Red clouds my vision. White noise ricochets around in my head, filling it until I can't think anymore. "You raped her." She'd mentioned to me once, when she'd gotten very drunk, about how my father had loaned her out to the leader of the Vikings.

"Now hold on." He taps a finger to his temple. "Did I rape her?" His features brighten, and he drops his arms to his sides. "I did what any red-blooded alpha would when faced with luscious pussy. I knotted her until she begged me for mercy. She screamed like a stuck pig…or is that a sow?"

Blood drums in my ears. My guts heave.

He leans forward and smacks his lips. "She enjoyed every second of it, I can assure you."

"You beat her so much that you marked her. It's because of you that she wore the scar on her face." Images of this asshole taking my omega mother, again and again, while she screamed for mercy, ricochet around in my head.

"Any self-respecting alpha would have done the same." He stabs a finger at me. "Surely you understand that."

"It's why Golan abandoned her. He couldn't stand to see his property marked." I fist my fingers at my side.

"And look at what that did." He chuckles. "She gave birth to you on the streets, and you learned to survive by your own wits."

"You took away her beauty, her youth, her confidence in herself, everything." My pulse pounds at my temples. My vision narrows.

"I gave you the means to hate, to draw on that inner fire inside of you that fuels you today. I gave you the gift of rage, son." He peels back his lips.

It's his version of being benevolent, in that very twisted way that is both familiar and cringe-inducing. "I am not your son," I snarl out, and just for a second, I am back in that bedroom reeking of sex and unwashed bodies where I had killed Golan.

"Oh, but you well might have been. Both Golan and I had screwed your omega mother around the time you were conceived." He raises his one good hand and taps my cheek with it.

He's doing it to entice me, to lure me into fighting him. I look too much like Golan for that to be true.

Anger tightens my guts. I cannot give in to it. I'd done so before, and it had led me to making mistakes. This time I need to see it through, need to understand exactly what he's up to. "What do you want?"

"Your city, your council…your omega." His gaze drops to my neck where the claiming marks peek out from under my collar.

"You'll never get to her."

As soon as the words are out, I know it's a mistake. I drew his attention to her. I snap my jaws shut and grind my teeth hard to stop myself from speaking.

It's a new feeling, this need to restrain myself, and if that isn't poetic justice, what is? Me, the alpha who's spent my entire life following my instincts, who's never held back from following my needs: for violence, for lust. For the most basic of needs. I curl my fingers so hard that the nails bite into my palms. The scent of copper reeks in the air, pain slashes up my forearm, and I focus on it. This I can deal with. This I understand. Revenge, hate, the extreme emotions that dictate you have to follow them where they lead you… I can work with that.

"You learn fast. Too bad you didn't show some of this restraint earlier when you left your omega behind." He thrusts out his chest. "You should have stayed behind to protect her, or left more of your men behind to keep her back."

A cold sensation fills my chest.

No, it cannot be.

She is back at the stronghold, tied up, and I've charged Sol, my most trusted man, to guard her, and as I am thinking it, I know I am wrong. I know she's in danger. The hollow feeling in my chest deepens. The mating cord which I'd blocked.

A bead of sweat runs down my back. "I'll never let you get to her." I charge at him.

Only for his men to grab my arms.

Another throws a rope around my shoulders, a third springs a chain around my legs. I am bound, unable to do anything but shuffle forward. "Don't you fucking dare," I growl at him.

"Or what will you do, eh?"

He raises his gaze to the side, and I follow it.

The scent of rain on dawn air fills the space. My hackles rise. *No, it can't be. Not her, please.*

Two of his men stumble into the clearing, dragging my omega between them.

70

Lucy

"Let go of me." I yank my arm away from the grip of the Viking alpha who has me imprisoned. His fingers bite into my arms, and I groan.

The sound fills the air, and every alpha in the vicinity seems to stiffen. Oh hell! This is not what I'd intended. I hadn't meant to be captured. I couldn't be caught, and not by the Vikings, the very animals I'd managed to escape from with my clan in the first place. I'd been stupid to come in search of my alpha.

I had been sure that I was as strong as any of the alphas, that I too could take on danger… Well, guess what? I'd conveniently forgotten that very basic difference that nature had imbued in us. That they could take me and possess me, claim me, and yeah, ultimately breed me.

I hadn't wanted to acknowledge that, not even when Zeus had tried to subdue my spirit. Truth is, that though Zeus had wanted to tame me, he'd never hurt me.

Everything he'd done to me…well, I had been an equal partner in it. I'd teased him and led him on, often pushing him over the edge, purely to see what he'd do to me after that.

I don't dare raise my gaze to see him now.

I'd sensed him as these Vikings had dragged me here. I'd known they were taking me to him.

My breathing grows shallow and a hollowness fills my chest. The imprint of where the mating cord had once been throbs with something like anger.

Perhaps my body knows that my alpha is close, and every cell in me seems to spring to attention.

My very flesh aches to go to him.

I don't want to show how much being in such proximity to him is affecting me.

Despite the fact that the clearing is packed with alphas, my senses are drawn to the large glowering alpha of alpha-holes standing there proudly. His vest is splattered with blood, and his eyes are wild. Every muscle in his body tenses as he tries to break away from the restraints that they have imposed on him.

"How dare you bring her into this?" He growls and my body cannot help but respond to the violence in his voice.

That fear and anxiety that pours off of him, rips through the space and clutches at me.

I want to moan, want to fling myself at him and...comfort him.

His shoulders bunch. His chest heaves.

He's very afraid for me. More than that, he's in a panic, a sheer, blind panic. I see it in the way he holds himself rigid. In the way every muscle in his shoulders strains as he flexes his arms.

"Now that's the question, isn't it?" Harald's voice mocks Zeus.

He growls again, an agonized noise that plucks at my nerves, and despite the fact that I am surrounded by danger, despite knowing that these alphas here would pick up on any kind of response to Zeus, knowing all of that, I cannot suppress the shiver that ripples down my back. My womb contracts, and slick pools in my center.

The alpha holding me tenses. His gaze flicks over my face, down my body, over my chest. My skin crawls.

The other guy licks his lips, his gaze bouncing between me and Harald.

The wind blows, a light breeze that skims my skin, taking the scent of my arousal down in the direction of where Harald's men have Zeus in shackles.

He peels back his lips and snarls.

At the same time, Harald raises his chin in my direction. "She cannot stop her excitement on seeing you, can she?"

"Don't touch her." Zeus lunges forward and flexes his shoulders. His biceps bulge.

The chains creak, then one of the bindings snaps.

He yanks an arm free and raises it at Harald who ducks.

Zeus' fist scrapes Harald's cheek before my alpha is yanked back with such speed that the chains tear at his skin and sparks fly in the air. The scent of copper grows heavy. His scent. His blood. I moan. I need to go to him and lick up the drops of blood that drip from him, run down his chest and onto the ground. My belly tightens and a chill coils in my chest.

"Don't hurt him," I croak.

My pulse thuds in my ears.

I can't understand these sensations that course through my body. Why does the sight of Zeus hurt and bleeding seem to arouse me further? I want to throw myself at him and ask him to claim me again in front of everyone. In front of these animals who've torn my life apart.

My stomach heaves. Heat flushes my skin, followed by chills. "No." This can't be happening. My body can't betray me like this. I can't be entering a heat cycle. I'd completed one when Zeus had left me, and that had been a week ago.

No, it's my very sensitized body reacting to my alpha's proximity.

Zeus had primed me; he'd drawn out the omega part of me that is pure femininity.

He conditioned my body to need him whenever he is in the vicinity. I need to touch him. Feel his skin on mine. He had slammed down a barrier on the mating cord and left without completing the bond. Now, everything in me wants him to rut me. I need him to consummate our connection, to finish what he started and consolidate his claim.

What are the chances that the alpha who I had tried to assassinate, the one who'd seduced me and rutted me, is also my true mate?

The hair on the back of my neck stiffens.

Heat fills my rib cage. My chest pushes out, and my spine curves. It's as if there's an invisible force that's pulling me to Zeus. I stagger forward, straining against the two alphas who are holding me.

"Let her go." Zeus' tone is strained.

"Only if you beg." Harald licks his lips and his gaze flicks between me and Zeus. His brows draw down.

Zeus' muscles coil; his shoulders tense.

All of my instincts go on alert. Goosebumps pop on my skin. A chill runs down my spine.

"Don't," I gasp. "Don't do it, Alpha."

I sense every part of him is attuned to me. It's evident in the way he holds himself, angles his body, how his shoulders are turned toward me, yet every part of him fights against that same force that connects us. Try as he might, there's no way that we will ever be rid of each other. Never.

His big body lowers. He drops one knee to the ground, then the other. "Leave her."

Harald strokes his chin with his one good hand. "You're forgetting something."

A pulse ticks above Zeus' jaw. He rolls his chin toward his chest and squeezes his eyes shut.

"Let her go…please."

"I'll do one better." He leans forward on the balls of his feet. "I'll let her come to you, and if the two of you put on a good enough show for me and my men, I'll perhaps, spare one of you."

71

Zeus

No way did he just say that, did he? I snarl. Anger fills my chest, and my vision tunnels in on Harald, until all I can see are those cold chips of his eyes. So lifeless. Why hadn't I notice that before? I thought I didn't have a heart, but this alpha...he is worse than Golan.

More dangerous, for he plots and plans.

The hackles on my neck rise. Had he planned this all along? Is this a trap I've walked into? But that can't be possible, can it? "You allowed her to escape with her clan. You tracked her to Kayden, let him plot to sneak her into my stronghold... You waited all this time, until we both came to you, until you had us at our most vulnerable." Blood pumps at my temple.

I want to yank at the chains that tie me and break them apart;

I am going to jump the berserker and...then what?

They'd kill me and her...worse, they'd abuse her.

Fear twists my gut, and a chill grips my chest. My hands and feet tingle. Every part of me goes on alert. I will die but will not let anything happen to her. When had that happened?

This urgency to protect her, to take her out of there, to find a way to release her, notwithstanding what happens to me. I cannot do what he asks of me, cannot. Will not.

"Untie me and fight me."

He chuckles. "I might have taken you up on that offer, but..." His gaze falls on his missing arm and...he raises his shoulders. "Well, it wouldn't be fair, now would it? Considering you have both arms and I have one, it would be a very one-sided battle."

Fucker. There's no way I'm letting him carry out his plan. No way am I going to rut her in front of him and his men.

I've never had an issue with public exhibitionism. When you grow up on the streets and live in a shantytown, everything is conducted out in the open, including the act of coupling.

It had never bothered me before, but with my omega? No way am I going to allow anyone to humiliate her.

"I'll take on five of your men, all at once."

"You are a good fighter." His gaze flows over my shoulders.

"Unarmed."

"That may be a possibility." He scratches his chin.

"And they can bear weapons."

"They'll be armed and they'll chase after your omega. It's up to you to find them and kill them before they get to her. If you fail…" He raises his shoulders and lets them fall.

"Bastard." Rage grips me, intense, the kind I've never felt before. My stomach twists in fear. Sweat drips down my spine.

"You got that wrong. I am the legal heir of my father. It's you who is the bastard."

His alphas grow restive around him.

The one holding my omega drags her close to him. "Why are you debating this with him? Kill him, give her to me. Let me take her cunt and teach her what it is to be taken by a real man. She'll keep us entertained until we reach the stronghold and take it for ours."

"Along with all the other omegas there," a second man adds.

"It's gonna be one long omega pussy-fest." The first smacks his lips.

I stiffen. Anger twists my guts, and something inside me snaps. Yanking my other arm free from the man holding it, I slide my hand down my leg, and reach for the knife that's strapped to my thigh. I tug it free and throw it at the man closest to my omega.

It embeds in his neck with a wet sound.

I expect her to scream, instead she goes completely still. His body crumples to the ground. Simultaneously, she plants her fist in the man closest to her. She grabs his shoulders and pulls up her knee, so she hits him in the groin. She shoves him aside and sprints toward me.

Another man blocks her way. He grabs her and flings her to the ground.

The sound of her body hitting the hard earth sends another ripple of anger racing down my spine. "Pick on someone your own size," I roar.

"We've delayed long enough." Harald glances at the man who holds down my omega. "Release her."

The alpha grabs her hair and raises her face. "I want her. She smells so fucking sweet." He licks her cheek.

And something inside me snaps.

Gritting my teeth, I flex my shoulder muscles and shove them apart. Pain burns down my wounded flesh and I ignore it. My chains snap, and I race for her. I am halfway to her when I am tackled from behind at the same time that another man slams into me from the side. I fling him off. A third comes at me from the front. I twist my torso so he arcs through the air and over me, hitting the ground to the side.

Another three spring on me. One of them holds my legs from behind, but I keep moving.

"Touch her, and you die."

I keep moving, dragging more than my body weight in men along with me.

"Release the omega," Harald's tone is hard.

"But…" the soldier whines.

"Now!" His voice booms out.

The soldier releases Lucy who rolls over, then springs up to her feet.

"Run," I growl.

She doesn't reply. She narrows the distance between us and tackles the man who is holding me down. He tumbles back and hits the ground.

She squeezes his neck between her thighs, grabs his head, and twists his neck.

The crunch of his spine cracking rends the space. She springs up to her feet and turns to me. Her chest heaves, her eyes glitter, and her hair sticks to her forehead. She is glorious. My warrior omega.

A warmth fills my chest. Whoa, hold on there? Now I am proud of her? Where are all these emotions coming from? I shake my head to clear it, then snap my gaze on her. "Woman." I roar, "Why can't you listen to me, just this once?" A bitter taste fills my mouth. It's fear… for her. The band around my chest tightens. I need to get her to safety.

"The same reason you refuse to recognize that I can take care of myself, Alpha." She blows me a kiss. Turning, she sweeps the legs out from under the second man who's come at her from behind.

Adrenaline spikes my blood. I hit out at the third guy blindly, take him down. I aim for the fourth when a gunshot explodes in the air.

I freeze; so do the other men. Everyone except Lucy, who dives toward me. She slams into my chest, and her weight feels sweet, right. I catch her and tuck her behind me.

"Who'd have thought"—Harald sneers—"that an alpha as powerful as you, as focused on revenge, would find a mate."

"Shut the fuck up." I thrust out my chest.

Harald raises his arm.

And I know it's a signal. I don't need to look around me to know that every single alpha in the vicinity is ready for the hunt. They are going to come after us, but they'll have to face me first. No way am I going to let them get to her.

I grab her arm and tug her so quickly she stumbles before righting herself. I sprint for the edge of the clearing pulling her along. "You remember how fast you ran when I tried to catch you the first time?" I pant.

"Y…yeah." She shoots me a glance over her shoulder.

"You'll have to run faster this time around."

72

Lucy

He yanks me along and I am half dragged in his wake. I'd always wanted to fight shoulder to shoulder with him, but had never thought it would turn out to be the two of us taking on the Viking contingent. The most brutal warriors in all the new world. Men who kill without mercy, who raped—no, I'll die before I let them get to me. I'll kill myself, I'll— Zeus increases his speed, and his powerful legs seem to eat up the distance.

I have to focus all my instincts on the path ahead to avoid tripping and slowing down.

His grip on my hand is bruising. My breath comes in pants, and my hair sticks to my forehead, but there's no time to push it away. The sound of a shout behind me sends a shiver of fear running down my spine.

Zeus swears and speeds up.

The muscles of his massive thighs undulate and the planes of his back flex. His powerful shoulders slice the air as he leans forward on his feet. The poetry is evident in every line of his body.

This monster is the most beautiful male I have ever laid eyes on. He makes me hate him, makes me lust after him, reduces my insides to a gooey mess, only to inflame me to anger the next. A ball of emotion clogs my throat.

"Fuck." It's my turn to swear.

"You're learning fast, Squirrel." He tosses over his shoulder. "At this rate, I am going to corrupt you completely."

"Not that you haven't already, Alpha." My voice trembles. "If anything were to happen to you…" I can't complete the sentence.

"I'm not going to let anything happen to you...or me." He doesn't look back, doesn't look around, just keeps his gaze focused forward.

The sounds of footsteps reaches us.

We hit a fork in the path, and Zeus comes to a halt so suddenly I slam into his back.

The scent of burned pinewood, of warmth and pheromones, all of it crowds in on my senses.

My belly trembles, and tears prick my eyes. "Why did it have to be this way?" I slam my fist into his chest.

I am not the kind to throw tantrums, but when I am with him, when everything I've ever wanted is right in front of me and I know I am going to lose it...well, something inside me snaps. The feminine part of me insists on coming to the fore and wants to cling to him. "I can't let you go, Alpha, I can't."

"Listen to me." He grasps my shoulders and hauls me to my toes. He
peers into my eyes. "I..."

"I—"

We speak at the same time. I gulp. His eyes, those beautiful blue eyes blaze at me.

There's fear, heat, and some other emotion that I dare not name.

He swears, under his breath. Tilting his head, he closes his lips over mine.

The taste of him sinks into my blood.

He thrusts his tongue inside my mouth and his teeth dig into my lips. The coppery taste of blood bursts on my tongue. Mine? His? He ravages my mouth and drinks from me, sucking out the very essence of me. He's storing up my taste, my scent, committing me to memory. My instincts scream a warning and I know he's going to put himself at risk. I tear my lips from his. "Don't you dare do it."

His lips curve up in a smile that reaches his eyes, and those blue eyes glow darker, indigo flames leaping up inside. "I fucking love you, you obstinate, stubborn omega."

I stare, "Now, you tell me."

"You need to hide." A pulse tics at his jaw, "Once I lead them away, you must escape."

"I'm not leaving you." I grab his collar and throw myself at him. But he holds me at arm's length.

"We cannot both die. *You* cannot die."

"I can't live without you." My throat closes.

"You can." He sets his jaw.

"No."

"You will." His features harden.

"No, no, no—" I dig my nails into his arm.

"For the child you are carrying."

I go completely still.

That's it—that's what is different about me. Why I have been so hormonal and my emotions so erratic that I am getting whiplash trying to keep up with my own feelings.

"How do you know?" Not that it matters, but I need to ask.

"Your scent." He swallows. "It's different."

Another shout reaches us, this one so close that I jump.

He grabs me close, and shoves me into the undergrowth, right there in the fork of the path. "Go."

"But—"

"For our child."

The fear in his voice, the devotion...all of it leaps out at me. I know I can't let him go without saying it. "I love you," I burst out.

He smiles. The resignation in his eyes clutches my heart. I've never known my alpha to seem so beaten. The band around my chest tightens. My hands and feet tremble, and I bite down on my lip to stop myself from screaming. He hauls branches over me, covering me completely.

His footsteps pound away.

Silence descends.

Sweat runs down my back, my chest, and the branches scratch at me.

The dust stings my nostrils along with the receding scent of burned pinewood. My alpha. I squeeze my eyes shut to stop myself from bawling. The tears leak past my closed eyelids, but I don't stop them. There are more shouts, footsteps racing toward me.

My heart hammers.

They come to a stop right in front of the bushes where I am hidden. I hold my breath.

They talk to each other, deciding which way to go.

There's an explosion in the distance. Him. It's him. Zeus did it to get their attention away from me.

Every instinct inside me wants me to throw myself at these men and tell them to stop, but I don't. No, I cannot destroy Zeus' effort. I need to get out, find the rest of his men and bring them here.

The men take off in pursuit. As soon as their footsteps fade, the breath rushes out of me. My lungs burn.

There's the sound of swords clashing, bullets firing, a man screaming... Zeus. Is he hurt? A scream wells up. I press my knuckles into my mouth and bite down on it.

They couldn't have caught him. Not my alpha.

My heartbeat thunders in my ears. Adrenaline spikes my blood. I slip out and run the opposite way.

Zeus is alive. He has to be. I race down the path. My pulse thuds at my temples, my breath screams down my lungs, and my eardrums ache like they're going to pop at any moment. I race past the tree line into a clearing and keep going until I hit the docks. I come to a standstill, panting. There, facing me is Ethan with Mirela next to him.

She looks at me and takes a step forward, but Ethan yanks her back. Something tugs at the back of my mind. My instincts scream at me to stop, that something is wrong, and I push it away.

I reach Ethan and grip his sleeve. "I don't know how you got here, but you have to help me. Zeus...they're hunting him."

He doesn't say a word.

Mirela begins to cry. "You traitor." She tries to hit him.

He grabs her arm and wrenches it behind her. She snarls in pain.

"What are you doing?" I stop, but I already know.

I'd suspected it all along. When you share a bond for any length of time with another person, you learn their secrets, what they are thinking about, their innermost emotions, and Zeus never trusted Ethan. Never.

"He was right." The words tremble from my lips.

"I am sorry, Omega." He raises his head, and those blue eyes of his are serious. "It's not what I wanted, but it had to be this way."

Footsteps sound behind me. A group of Vikings burst onto the shore. Two of them drag the body of an unconscious Zeus between them.

"No!" My pulse thunders at my temples and adrenaline spikes my blood. I will avenge my alpha. I will kill whoever has hurt Zeus. Is this what he felt when he decided to avenge his mother's death? I raise my fist and slam it into Ethan's side.

He doesn't duck. "You'll pay for that." He wheezes.

I raise my fist again, but a soldier steps up behind me, grabs my arms, and twists them behind my back. I don't resist.

Harald saunters into the clearing. "Get them to our temporary warehouse." He walks past me onto the pier. "We'll amuse ourselves with them tonight. I plan to take their bodies back to London as trophies."

73

Zeus

Consciousness creeps in at the edge of my mind, and I become aware of a low, soothing hum. Gentle fingers trail over my chest, and something cold touches it. A trail of fire burns down my front.

I groan, not quite understanding what's happening.

Something cold grazes over the inflamed skin, and the sensation subsides. A bandage is pressed over my chest. Water bathes my temples, and I sigh.

"You're hurt; you need to rest."

Her voice.

She makes to move away, and I snake out my arm. I grab her wrist and pull her to me.

She falls against my chest, and another flash of pain jolts me. I groan but don't let go.

"You are going to reopen your wounds."

Her voice is low, and I detect the edge of tension in it. I bring her close and bury my nose in her hair, breathing in that cool-rain-on-dawn-air scent of hers. It settles something inside of me. When I am with her the noise in my head subsides.

A tang of cinnamon and pepper teases my nostrils and my groin tightens.

She's pregnant, with my child. My eyelids fly open. "You're okay."

Eyes of shattered green blaze down at me. There are dark bruises under her eyes. Her hair is astray and all over her shoulders. I reach up, and touch her cheek, "You didn't answer me, Omega. Did they hurt you?"

"No." She shakes her head.

Her gaze flickers to the right, and I follow it to find there are bars enclosing us. My gaze rakes over the row of iron, and I cradle her closer.

Realization sinks in. "They imprisoned us?"

"Not only."

Lights blaze over us. I blink, blinded for a second.

"I see you are awake," Harald's voice booms out, slapping over my skin.

Her shoulders shake. I sit up and bring her close to me, wanting to hide her behind my back. A growl rumbles up my throat. It's meant to soothe, and a moan bleeds out of her.

Her entire body trembles; fear leaks from her.

I hold her close, not caring about the wound on my chest that throbs. Not caring that every part of my body hurts, my shoulder screams, my calves tense. I heave myself up to a sitting position and drag her up with me.

She climbs into my lap.

Her arms brush my chest, and her hips press down on my shaft. My *naked* shaft.

A door creaks open somewhere, and the wind sweeps in, bringing with it the scent of the sea.

Goosebumps rise on my skin.

That's when I realize that we are *both* naked. Our clothes are gone, and we are trapped in this cage.

A shiver of apprehension runs down my spine.

In my arms, she trembles again.

Fear rolls off of her in waves along with that cooler scent of her omega essence, and mixed with it is the sugary scent of her slickness. My shaft instantly hardens. Another purr grumbles up from me.

She burrows closer, all but climbing inside my skin. I wrap my arms around her, trying to make as much of her body come into contact with mine as I can. She folds her legs and brings them up so she's completely huddled into my lap.

I hunch over her. I want to shield her from prying eyes.

A wave of tenderness sweeps over me.

I had vowed to protect her... I had failed. I had faced Harald's men, killed at least five of the bastards. Another ten had ambushed me, coming at me from all sides. I'd fought them off, had even thought I was winning, but one of them had managed to ambush me from behind.

My last sensation was that of the blade slicing into my flesh. It had bitten into me like a son of a bitch, and I had blacked out.

"They won't hurt you, I promise."

She folds her head under my chin and moans. "They're going to kill us."

"Not yet." Harald's boots thud on the hardwood floor as he walks over to stand on the other side of the cage. "How the two of you comfort each other." He rocks forward on the soles of his feet and licks one of the bars. "A sight that should rekindle hope and melt the most cynical of hearts." His pupils roll back showing the whites of his eyes. Fucker is insane.

"Shut the fuck up." I should stay quiet. Now is not the time for bravado, to incite the berserker. I need to think, to find a way out of here. And yet that something inside me insists that she survived and never bowed her head to anyone so far. She is resilient my omega, and I will make sure she gets through this, unscathed.

I surge to my feet and bring her up with me.

"What do you want?" I set my jaw.

"To see the two of you engage in what you do so well. Fuck."

In my arms she freezes, and every muscle in her body tightens, echoing the same tension that grips me mine.

Another purr rumbles up my throat and I cradle her closer.

Her shoulders hunch. Her body melts into me.

I can do this much for her. I can keep her calm, help her to stay grounded, perhaps allow her to subsume her conscious mind in my ability to cocoon her, while I try to figure out a way out of this cage.

"Never."

"Have it your way." He thrusts his face through the gap between the bars. "Any of my men would gladly rut your omega." Without taking his gaze off of my face, he raises his arm. I follow the direction of it, and all of my muscles go solid. The fine hairs on the nape of my neck rise.

Gathered about the cage are Harald's berserkers.

I count at least twenty…no…there are fifty of them assembled past the bars that close us in, and that's not the worst. Where alphas never stay quiet, definitely not in the presence of an omega, these alphas are all standing at attention.

They are silent. Their gazes are all trained on me… No, not on me, on the woman cowering in my arms. I tighten my grip around her, my purring grows more agitated, and I force myself to lower its intensity.

I don't want these men to hear me purr for her, not what is a nuance meant only for my omega. Not when Harald means to strip us bare, to tear every shred of dignity from us, and exploit the purity of what is between me and my omega for their entertainment.

A chill grips my chest and expands out until every part of me feels like it's carved from ice. I will not let them hurt her. I'll do anything to protect her. Anything.

I wipe all expression from my face.

Harald narrows his gaze, "I see the seriousness of my intent is finally sinking in," he drawls. "You must admit this is a coup. I have the General of London and his omega at my mercy. Nothing like watching the alpha of alphas rut his mate to get my men in the mood. Besides," he leans forward on the balls of his feet, "they've been promised they'll all get a chance at your omega's cunt...after."

"You'll die for this, I promise you that."

"You're an optimistic man, Zeus. But you must know one more thing. It's thanks to your second that I find myself in this happy situation."

"Ethan?" Every instinct in my body goes on alert. No, it can't be. I form the words in my head, yet everything inside me screams that it's true.

Harald jerks his chin to his left.

I spot the traitor, and every muscle in my body coils. I only realize that I've taken a step forward, when she digs her nails into my chest.

"Don't, Alpha. Don't give in to your rage, not now." Her voice whispers over my skin.

My chest rises and falls, and my breath comes in pants. I need to stay calm, and find a way to shield her from the worst.

A low growl rumbles from me.

Next to Harald, Ethan strides to the bars. "I am sorry, it had to be this way."

"I am going to kill you." My voice is calm, my shoulders bunch.

"Sadly, that's not going to happen." Ethan widens his stance. "Accept it Zeus, you have lost this fight."

Harald jerks his chin. "It's time for you to begin your performance, General."

Everything inside of me screams a protest. My body tenses and there's a pounding in my ears. I'd always suspected Ethan's loyalty, had suspected he'd turn his back on me. I'd known it, and my ego had blinded me. I'd ignored it. I'd not trusted my own instincts, and my omega is going to pay the price.

74

Lucy

The look in their eyes…I am sure they are going to tear me apart. No, they want to tear into my body, rut me, punish me, and not for anything I've done wrong.

Simply because I am an omega.

Because they are alphas.

Because they can.

A soft purr rumbles up his chest, and the sound flows around me, soothing me, calling to me. I huddle closer to the heat of his body. Acutely aware that I am naked.

My hair falls over my shoulders, and I am happy that I have let it grow. When I had escaped from Russia I had contemplated cutting it short to disguise myself, but I hadn't. Small mercies. I hiccough. At least I have something with which to cover up my nakedness. That, and his arms, which he uses to shield as much of me as he can.

He's agitated. I can tell from the way his muscles clench, his shoulders flex, his chest rumbles as he purrs continuously.

The sound is comforting, alluring, yet it also unnerves me. The very fact he's trying to comfort me, soothe me, makes me aware that our situation is every bit as hopeless as it seems.

"You won't get away with this," his voice is harsh and a vein throbs at his temple.

Harald laughs, and the sound is so evil, so full of his intent to harm. No, more than that. He wants to see us suffer. He revels in our helplessness. And my alpha is not helpless. Neither am I. We are not going to die, not here. We can't. I must stay alive for my baby.

Our child.

His voice caresses my mind, and I shiver. Comfort bleeds down the mating bond and curls in my chest. His purring intensifies, as if he is trying to cocoon me with his tenor, trying to build a wall of sound between us and those…those animals.

How had I ever thought he was like them?

He had taken from me…and yet it had been different, because from the moment I'd seen him, I'd known he was it for me. It's complicated, of course, it is. He'd toyed with me, played with me, but he'd also protected me, tried to take care of me in his own overprotective way.

Zeus.

I can't stop myself from whispering his name in my mind, from reaching out to him through the mating cord.

His chest heaves.

"I am here, my love."

A shiver scrolls down my back. *"I can hear your voice in my mind,"* I pulse the thought back to him. *"You removed the barrier on the mating cord?"*

I'd heard of mated alpha-omega couples being able to communicate through the mating bond but experiencing it with Zeus…the intimacy of being able to share my innermost thoughts with another makes my breath catch. Goosebumps flare over my skin, all my nerve endings tingle.

Why'd you do it, Zeus?

I reach out to him again through our shared connection, trying to glean what he's not saying, trying to understand the moods of this complex man. What is he thinking? What is he going to do?

I had to Omega, he pulses back.

Why? I raise my head to meet his gaze. *Because we are going to die?*

We are not. He narrows his eyes.

Because you took pity on this omega and thought to share the real parts of yourself before I am thrown at the mercy of those berserkers, who are going to rip me apart. I jut out my chin.

Not as long as I am alive. One side of his lips curl up.

And after that?" I force myself to say the words.

"I am not going to die. He sets his jaw. *I cannot die, not as long as you are in danger.*

Didn't take you for such a dreamer, Zeus. I swallow.

I am not going to give up hope, and neither should you, Omega. He rubs his cheek over my head.

How do you know that? How can you be so confident?

He leans back and meets my gaze. *You need to trust in me. Can you?*

Can I? *I am not sure,* I pulse the thought truthfully at him.

We just need to survive the next few hours, Omega. His features set in hard lines.

I am not sure if I can. The band around my chest tightens.

All you have to do is follow my lead. His gaze softens.

It's so easy for you to say that. I press my palms to his chest. *Follow me, trust in me, be with me. Why should I?*

Because… I… He firms his shoulders. *I love you.*

My insides freeze. Did he just say that? Does he mean it?

Why…why should I believe you? I bite the inside of my cheek.

When a man faces danger like this, when he knows the only thing that makes his life worth living could be taken away from him, believe me, even an asshole like me will speak the truth.

Alpha-hole. I correct him.

One side of his mouth curls. *I'll take that as a compliment.*

Only you, Zeus, would stand here surrounded by these hungry alphas who are going to tear us apart, with the biggest monster of them all—yeah, more of a monster than you—watching us, and choose to have this conversation."

He grimaces. *We don't have much time, Lucia.*

A shiver of apprehension spills down my back.

What would you have me do, Alpha?

I hate what I am about to do. But despite all of my bravado and my posturing, despite my confidence, I didn't see this coming. I miscalculated, Omega, and now I have no choice but to ask this of you.

You're scaring me, Zeus.

Let me love you. He slides me down his body until my feet touch the floor.

Here? I whisper.

It's not how I'd have chosen it, but I have to work with the hand I've been dealt. It's wrong, so wrong of me to ask you this, and yet... He arranges my hair so it flows down my back to my hips, covering my back. *I know you are strong, Lucy. I know you are more resilient than anyone I have ever met. Just trust in me, allow me to take over, to block out everything else outside. Everything except us. Let me show you how it can be between us, Lucy.*

He folds his arm over my butt, and I realize he's covered most of my body from the gaze of those animals.

I know what he is asking of me and I don't want to...and yet...if this is the only way to have him, one last time... My belly tightens, and my thighs clench. I realize my body has already spoken for me.

I don't care if the entire world watches. They are not here, I am. In the arms of the man who was born for me, who is mine as I am his. I'll never be anyone else's, and if this is the way to show him how much he means to me, then I am going to do it.

I lean in, close enough for my lips to brush his ears. "Take me, Alpha. Knot me. Fuck me, Zeus."

75

Zeus

Her words shiver down my spine, and my groin tightens. My dick throbs. I shouldn't be so aroused, not like this, not in front of all those watching pairs of eyes. Gazes from the other alphas who want to be part of what I am going to do to her.

They want me to fuck her, to take her in front of them.

They want to experience the passion of a true alpha-omega bond through me. They want to partake of the pleasure that comes from a true couple bonding and fucking like they mean it. Like their life depends on it.

But what I feel for her is so much, for it's this need to take care of her, to protect her from them, and if that means having to claim her in front of everyone...

Taking her is no hardship, and yet I don't want to share what we have. I don't want to share the purity of my emotions for her. Purity?

A chuckle grinds up my throat.

I'd have never classified what I feel for her as that. But the lushness of her scent that sinks into my blood and twists my gut, that makes my muscles tense, my breath come in pants, all of it testifies to the fact that my response to her is very real. Real enough for me to have removed the barrier on the mating bond between us so she is aware of every nuance of my emotions.

Can perceive my intentions.

Know what I am thinking at the same time I am.

She can anticipate me. I let her in when I've never done that to anyone else before her. No one after her either. She has my complete trust—does she know that?

"Get on with it." Harald drags the blade of his sword across the bars. Sparks fly from the contact. The uneven sounds that the blade makes when it grates over each bar set my teeth on edge.

The hairs on my neck and arms rise.

She moans and cowers closer to me.

In that moment, I know I hate Harald even more than I ever loathed Golan.

"Forgive me, my love." I sweep her off her feet and lay her on the ground.

Her back comes in contact with the hard floor, and she shivers.

"When we get out of here, I'll ensure that you never lack for silks for your mattress."

"Cotton." Her voice trembles.

"Huh?" I plank over her. My shoulders bunch, and my biceps tremble as they support the weight of my arms.

"I prefer cotton sheets."

"You'll have it," I vow. "The softest of cottons that I can source for you."

"If you are in such an agreeable mood, perhaps I should ask you for more?" Her eyes gleam up through those long, dark eyelashes.

My heart stutters. I forget that we have an audience, that we are locked up in this cage, far from London, from any friends or allies, in the clutches of a monster who is going to kill us, or worse. All I know is that… "I am going to make this up to you."

Her chin wobbles. Color fades from her cheeks. She reaches up a hand and cups my cheek. "My alpha, my monster." Her voice is soft, so soft. Her gaze liquid, the curves of her body are perfect, made for my arms. Why hadn't I noticed that before? Why did I have to let things go so far before realizing what I want from her, from myself?

"Forgive me for what I have to do to you, to us. I reach down and brush my lips over her forehead. *If there had been any other way, I'd have taken it."*

Waves of helplessness roll off of her. "I am scared, Zeus." Her voice wavers, and fear bleeds down the bond.

Raw anger churns my guts, and my pulse thuds in my temples. My heart stutters as I drop down into that hidden part of me and draw up a harsh purr. I fucking hate that the alphas will hear this most intimate of sounds. I grit my teeth and push that thought from my head. I will do what it takes to comfort her and calm her, just for a little while longer. Just until I get her out of here. The growl resonates up my chest. I draw it out and spill it over her, looping it around her, cocooning her.

She shivers and thrusts up her breasts. Her spine arches, and her nipples pebble. I can feel their sharpness, how her flesh trembles against mine.

Blood rushes to my groin and my dick thickens against her thigh.

Her shoulders heave, and her legs part.

I draw out another purr, this one deeper, more sensuous.

I modulate my voice just right, just harsh enough that it will tug on her nerves and arouse her, while yet packed with my craving for her.

Her stomach trembles, her thighs clench, and a stream of slick gushes out of her.

Another purr, and her muscles relax. A hum creeps up her chest, her throat, and spills from between her parted lips. "Zeus…" she says my name on a sigh.

That's it, my love, let go of all your inhibition. Give in to me, flow with me… Trust me, my darling. I didn't know I had it in me to call her by those endearments.

A month ago, if you'd told me that I'd be so drawn to another, an omega at that, enough to take her as my mate, enough to profess my love, to soothe her, to call her by those intimate names that mates reserve for each other...well, I'd have said that you were insane.

Instead, it is I who lies here completely stripped of all ego, of all my bravado, those masks I had worn for the world.

All that posturing, the survival skills I'd picked up in the streets, the revenge I had nourished so carefully all these years...all of it is nothing compared to the overwhelming need to protect her from those animals, from the world, from myself even. My body stills, my muscles going solid at that realization.

She wriggles under me, parting her legs wider, bringing her arms up and over my shoulders. "Take me, Zeus." Her breath heaves.

I want to rise and angle my hips and thrust into her, and I can't, and isn't that a surprise?

My needs are no longer important; this is about her.

Her desires.

Her wants.

I want to make this pleasurable for her.

The fact that there are alphas watching and no doubt getting off on this display makes me want to cocoon her further.

I draw out another purr, and another, letting the sound waves build, letting the resonance engulf the space around our bodies.

I hold the purring steady, drawing each one out from the depths of my belly, my heart, my soul, layering each surge one on top of the other, fashioning an intricate wall of sound, a shield that weaves in over our bodies, holding us within its protection.

They can see us through the disturbance, catch glimpses of our bodies, but they can't hear us or scent us now. It's our very own fortress, a barricade to hold back the hunger that pours from our audience.

I rise onto my elbows, making sure to keep as much of her body shielded from their gaze as I possibly can.

Balancing myself on one arm, I slide the other under her hips. "I am going to make this so good for you, Princess." Lowering my head, I brush my lips over hers, nibbling my way up and over those closed eyelids which I kiss.

She trembles and raises those eyelids. She trains that green gaze, now drugged with need, on me. Those pupils are dilated enough to tell me she is at the edge and ready for me. *It was always you, Zeus*, she exhales. *Only you.*

Her words sink into me through the bond, warm my blood, and I know there is no turning back.

I pulse my need, my devotion, my hopes and dreams, my want to see her safe, to see us happy, for our child to be thriving, for so much of everything that I dare not put a name to it. I let all of it flow down the mating bond to her.

Sweat glistens on her forehead. *I love you, Zeus.*

I close my lips over her mouth, absorbing the words, then angle my hips. I nudge my shaft against her wet opening and slip inside of her.

76

Lucy

He slides into me, and his shaft fills up that empty space inside of me which aches with need.

This is what I missed: his hardness inside of me, throbbing against my channel walls, that feeling of utter fullness that takes ahold of me when my alpha's dick stuffs me to the brim. And it's different to how he's fucked me before.

He tilts his lips over mine, nibbling at my lower lip, licking the seam of my mouth, swirling his tongue over mine, drawing from me, yet pouring all of himself into that kiss.

He sucks on my tongue, then nips on my lower lip until I open my mouth completely.

His tongue thrusts inside, and desire radiates out, down my jaw to my chest.

My nipples tighten.

His fingers squeeze my flesh and my thighs quiver.

He scoops up my hips, and nudges his shaft farther inside, impossibly deep. His movements are sensuous, seductive, as if he's trying to please me. No, possess me, occupy every last untouched corner of my skin, my soul.

I try to understand what is happening to me, try to form the thoughts in my brain and find all I can do is pant and strain against his heavier weight. Heat from his body slams into me, rolls over me, and sweat drips down my spine and my skin, slipping onto the hard, stony floor. The still-thinking part of my brain pulses an alarm that there are people watching. My muscles tense.

He grips the curve of my waist, squeezing my flesh. Heat radiates out from his touch, and all of my attention zooms in on that space. All other thought flies from my head.

That purring of his increases in velocity, swirls over me, around me, hemming me in. The dense waves of sound push down on me, holding me in place.

I want to move and find I can't. A flutter of nervousness trickles over my spine.

I open my mouth to tell him, and he sweeps his tongue in farther, as if he's swallowing me whole, overcoming all of my senses.

A flood of heat strums the mating bond; there are so many layers to it. My head reels. I reach out to him through the bond, trying to decipher and make sense of the complex emotions that he's pulsing at me.

There's lust, a primal need, and laced with it is the white hot edge of fear, a desperation that holds me still. And it's all bound together with love, so much love… My eyes roll back.

My brain feels like it's melting, like all the cells are short-circuiting. He did tell me that he loves me, but those were just words…nothing compared to the sensations that barrel toward me now.

He lowered the barrier on the bond and opened himself to me, and I hadn't realized it, not until now. Not until he'd slowed his assault on my mouth, and his kisses had lightened; his mouth nibbles on mine. His hand sweeps up my back and slides under my hair to cushion my neck.

He raises his head and peers into my eyes.

Those brilliant blue eyes glow. Deep in them are flashes of silver—entrancing, overwhelming—and around them concentric circles of violet, indigo, and turquoise.

My heart lurches, and my breath catches.

I'll never get over that gaze. That heat. That possessiveness that rolls off of him. His chest heaves, and the low hum of his purr winds around me. Wrapping me up in an oscillation of sound.

He's been purring all along, holding me in the center of a storm of emotions. In the heart of the turmoil, he's built a nest of calm for me.

I swallow and want to say something, but find I can't.

Instead, I trail my fingers down his back to the taut muscles of his butt. Goosebumps rise on his flesh. He leans in close, impossibly close, until our noses almost bump, until our breaths mingle.

A small smile tugs at one end of his lips.

He smirks…but not quite. There's an edge of softness to it which hadn't been there before. *Mine.* He forms the words with his mouth, even as I hear his voice in my head, as if he's whispered it down the mating bond.

Yours, I pulse the thought back at him, and he slides forward, just another millimeter, just enough to fill me up completely.

His dick throbs, and his knot glides into place. *This* is where I belong, joined up to him. Connected to him, in body and in soul.

He closes the last remaining inch between us and brushes his lips over mine. A drop of moisture trickles down his cheek and plops on my face, and it's as if he's worshipping me with everything in him.

I knit my legs around his waist and take him in deeper.

The swollen head of his shaft sinks into that secret space inside of me. The climax swoops up the back of my thighs, over my hips, shudders up my spine and crashes over me.

I arch my back, push up my chest, and when I open my mouth to scream, he absorbs the sound, takes it all in.

Jets of warmth shoot into me, pulsing straight to my womb. My arms and legs tremble, my scalp tingles, every cell in my body seems to vibrate, and I shatter.

I hold on to him as I float in and out of that quiet space that exists within me.

I am aware of him holding me, cradling me to him, the deep hum of his purr all around me as if he's cushioning me and bringing me back to this plane, slowly, slowly.

There's so much sweetness in his touch, so much tenderness, almost as if it could be our last time together and he wants me to remember. Fear grips me, and my eyes fly open. "Zeus…"

"I'm here, Omega."

He's still inside of me and watches me with unblinking eyes.

"Why did you do that?" I force the words out through a throat so raw, that I am sure I have been screaming with pleasure all along.

"Why did I make love to you for the first time?" He tilts his head, and his lips twist. His gaze narrows.

"Tell me." I grip his shoulders so hard that my nails dig into his flesh.

"Whatever happens now, remember how it is between us, Omega."

"Wh…what do you mean?" My breath catches.

The mating bond screams in my chest, and my heart beats so fast I'm sure I am going to pass out.

"I love you, Lucia."

Above us there is a loud noise. The roof gives in.

77

Zeus

The bricks and stones pour down on us. They shower around us, hitting my shoulders, my legs. One of them slams into the back of my neck, and blackness threatens at the edge of my consciousness. Under me, she trembles and flings her arms around me.

"Zeus!" Her voice is high-pitched. Fear pours off of her in waves. "What's happening, Alpha?"

Even now, caught in a situation where she has no idea what's happening, she knows I am in control, that I must know the cause of this disruption.

The thought heats my blood and my groin hardens. She trusts me and that turns me on more than any physical act ever could. And it shouldn't be that way, it shouldn't... After all, isn't lust and the act of procreation the sole reason to knot an omega? This shows me otherwise, and for a second, I am humbled.

The realizations keep tumbling in, right as we are in the thick of a situation where our lives are at stake.

Or perhaps it's being at the edge of life, poised on the verge of death and being redeemed by the act of faultless lovemaking that's showing me a mirror of myself.

For the first time, pushed to the edge of my resources, put in a position where my entire life can change, I am finally finding out what I really am.

I stretch myself out as much as I can, trying to cover her body with mine, needing to shield every part of her from the debris that pours over us.

When it finally slows down, I raise my torso and shake my shoulders so the gravel slides off. "Wrap your legs around my waist, Omega."

She holds my gaze and locks her ankles into place behind my waist.

"Your arms now." I can't stop the soft smile that curves my lips.

I know I shouldn't be showing this depth of emotion for her, or perhaps it's myself I don't trust with sharing exactly what she means to me.

How much it would hurt me if something were to happen to her, how I couldn't live if I were to lose her...

The realization sweeps over me, and somehow I am not surprised. My instincts had known I was headed this way from the moment I'd first scented her. Something inside me had warned me that if I followed my instincts, I'd lose myself in her. Her breath, her touch, that maddening sweetness of her scent, that heat of her pussy, which clamps around my shaft, for I am still in her. Still knotted. And that's the way it should be. If I were to die now, I'd die happy, knowing I had done everything possible to keep her safe. Knowing this is where I belong. Inside of her.

"Alpha?" Her eyebrows draw down, and the green of her eyes grows deeper, a shimmering emerald.

There are questions in them, but no doubts.

She challenged me, fought me, but never once has she mistrusted me.

"I'll never let you down, Lucy." I cradle her close to me, holding her gaze with mine.

I know my voice sounds strained, and the seriousness in my tone takes me by surprise.

I've never had to explain myself to anyone else, but I want this slip of an omega to understand what I am, what I am trying to do, and I don't understand why.

"I know." She leans up and brushes her mouth over mine. "I may not always agree with your actions, but as long as I am with you, I know everything will be alright."

Moisture shimmers in her eyes. "Lucy, I—"

There's a shout from outside the cage. Heavy footsteps pound toward us. More blasts rend the air, and an entire wall on the far end of the stronghold caves in.

A breeze sweeps through, bringing with it the scent of seawater, the burning smell of explosives. More bullets whiz past us. There are more screams, this time closer to us, from the alphas who howl in pain as they try to move away from the stream of fire. Then, there's silence.

"Hold onto me." I tighten my grip on her, cradling her, until it feels like our skin is merging, then heave myself up to my knees.

"Ready?"

She nods. Her eyes gleam. Her breath comes in short puffs. She's not scared; far from it. She's looking forward to the confrontation, to taking these animals down and getting out of here.

I know now she is the one for me. There will never be another like her.

I slide one arm below her butt, securing her close to me. Bringing up one leg, I thrust my foot into the floor for leverage and rise.

She clings to me, and the walls of her channel cradle my knot which is locked inside of her.

I can't let her go, not now, not for a long time. I don't care that it's all wrong that I am still inside of her, connected to her, while around us the entire place lights up. Another sweep of explosions crackles through the space, the sound a staccato as it rips along the walls.

It fades away and there's silence for a beat.

A low groan, an inhuman sound, a rough creak echoes in the space, and one of the remaining walls of the stronghold on the far side crumbles. The lower part of the wall gives way, and the upper part collapses. And it's like a signal for the remaining walls to follow. The cracks ripple through the walls, and they topple. The noise overwhelms the entire space, mixing with the discord of the alphas growling at each other as they scramble to find the exit.

All through it, I stay there, holding the most precious thing in the world, the other half of me, connected to her in body and through the mating cord which pulses with adrenaline. My flanks tighten. Every part of me tenses. "You ready for this, Omega?"

"You bet." She snarls low in her throat.

The sound sends a pulse of desire shooting down the cord, straight to my groin. My dick throbs inside of her.

A low purr rolls out of me. It's filled with heat and anticipation, and the thrill of the chase.

I look to my right, to the dust swirling outside of the cage. There is a silhouette outside the broken wall and the familiar profile of Sol appears. He strides toward me.

The men in front of him...my men fire at the alphas on either side. The sparks from the stream of bullets burn through the dust that swirls in the place. Solomon stalks through. He raises his arms. Balanced on his shoulder is a cylindrical gun. He aims it at the bars.

I race aside, out of the way. A flame of fire shoots from it, and when he's done, the bars on the side melt, forming a doorway.

"Go," she urges me, and a chuckle rips out of me.

I should protest that I don't follow orders, not from anyone...well, not from anyone else. Just her. "I'll allow you to order me this one time," I murmur as I stride to the makeshift doorway.

I sense her chuckle. "Not that I'd ever try to tell you what to do when it comes to mating."

A part of me doubts that already, but I decide to let that one rest for now. I step out of the cage. Solomon nods to me.

I jerk my chin in thanks. One of Harald's alphas reels out of the smoke, lurching toward me. I hold up my arm and shove him aside.

"Zeus."

I look at her, and in my arms, she stiffens.

Ethan stalks toward me, stepping over the bodies of fallen men. He holds a sword in his hand.

"So all of the players are here then?" From my other side, Harald's voice mocks me. He swaggers forward to stop with his remaining arm resting on his hip.

The scent of burning flesh permeates the air. Mixed with it, is the scent of copper, the scent of the blood of his men.

Solomon stiffens. "I didn't think you'd betray us this way, Ethan."

Ethan purses his lips. "People always seem to underestimate me." He turns to me. "Not you, though, General." One side of his mouth twists in a smile.

"Finally, you reveal your true colors?"

78

Lucy

His shaft pulses inside of me as he speaks to his men. I should be conscious of the fact that we are not alone, that as he commands them, he's knotted inside of me.

My muscles coil, and the mating bond throbs in my chest.

A pulse of heat streams through me, calming, reassuring. My shoulders relax. The tension bleeds out of me.

All around me echo the sounds of groans, growls, and someone howls with pain. The scent of sweat and piss and fear taints the air. Clearly, Harald's men are hurt.

But here, in the cocoon of his arms, I know nothing can hurt me.

There's an itch between my shoulder blades, and I am sure it's the Viking leader's gaze sweeping over my back.

Zeus angles his body so I have a clearer view of what's unfolding.

Harald grins at us. Soot stains his face, his vest is torn, blood seeps from his one whole arm, but there's a look of triumph on his face. His features are flushed, and there's a glimmer of excitement in his eyes. His chest rises and falls. He stares across at Ethan.

Above me, Zeus' heart beats steadily.

A bead of sweat slides down his temple, and that's the only sign that he's tense and waiting for something to happen. Every muscle under his skin tautens. A pulse beats at the side of his neck. I follow his gaze to Ethan.

Sol takes a step forward, anger radiating off of him.

Zeus jerks his chin, and Sol pauses. He, too, looks at Ethan who holds the sword in his hand.

Ethan raises the weapon, pointing it at Zeus.

Harald chuckles. "Isn't it wonderful when friends kill one another in the pursuit of what matters?"

"And what is that?" Zeus doesn't take his gaze off of Ethan.

"Power, of course." He widens his stance. His chin firms. "You, more than anyone, would know that. After all, you killed your father to claim his title."

"The fucker deserved to die." Zeus' lips thin. He tilts his head.

Ethan's jaw tightens. It's as if the two are engaged in some kind of silent dialogue, one I cannot follow. Nor can anyone else, for that matter.

"No argument there." Harald bounces his fingers on his thigh.

"And I thought he was your friend?" Zeus' gaze narrows.

"Just like Ethan is yours?" Harald giggles.

The hairs on my forearms stand on end.

That thin, feminine sound from someone as massive as the Viking is downright creepy. And honestly, I know what it must look like, me with my legs around Zeus' waist, his dick in me, his arms holding me close, one forearm across the length of my hair that falls to my waist.

In the thick of what has to be the biggest fight of his life, for his power, for everything he's held important, he's making sure that my back is covered, that my hair hides most of my skin, while the width of his arm conceals the rest.

My heart stutters. The mating cord trembles, and I can't stop the pulse of heat that spools off of me, bleeding toward him.

His shoulders flex; the cords of his throat bunch. "Except he isn't." He firms his lips. "Ethan is my half brother."

Ethan stays quiet; he doesn't deny it.

Harald stills his fingers.

Sol freezes where he is.

No one moves. Around us, the groans of the others die down, as if everyone senses the importance of whatever is unfolding between the two men.

"Is he now?" Harald's voice is casual but there is an edge of uncertainty to his tone. His gaze swerves to Ethan's face. "Well, that's better. What are brother's and father's lives in front of true power? You can have it all, Ethan. You can finally take over the title of General."

"I don't want it, I've never sought it, not as much as Zeus. It's what makes me the perfect second." Ethan's lips widen, and it's the first genuine smile I've seen on his face. It reaches his eyes. Those gray pupils spark with a silver fire, so like Zeus'. He doesn't resemble Zeus in any other way, not like Kayden.

If Zeus hadn't revealed Ethan's connection to him, I'd never have guessed.

"It's not only that, is it?" Harald strokes his beard. He surveys Ethan from head to toe. "You've had me fooled this far, but clearly you are no alpha. You are a beta; it's why you've backed Zeus every step of the way."

Ethan squares his shoulders, drawing himself to his full height. He's almost as tall as Zeus, but not. Almost as filled out as Zeus, but he isn't. His build is much leaner, wiry. His features thinner. The skin stretches across his cheeks. "Apparently, even a blockhead like you sees the truth when it's rubbed in your face. Except—" He tilts his head.

"Except?" Harald drops his hand to his side, reaching for the gun.

"It's too late." Ethan flings the sword at Zeus who raises his arm, catches it, and in a smooth move, thrusts it at Harald.

The blade slams into his chest.

His gaze widens. He chuckles, and blood dribbles from his mouth. He glances down at the sword, at the hilt that juts out from his chest. "He who lives by the sword must die by it." His voice is strangely calm. "That goes for any weapon."

He raises his head, aims the gun at us, and shoots.

A scream boils up. A slight breeze flutters over my skin and Zeus shifts his position. His big body shakes.

The scent of burning flesh deepens and all of his muscles go solid.

White pain screams down the mating bond.

"No." I raise my eyes to his.

There's a look on his face I've never seen before.

It's unguarded. All the masks are gone. There are no more barriers between us.

So much love floods down the bond, pure, unadulterated love, unselfish love, and tenderness, the kind that clouds my chest, filling it, overflowing it until I can't breathe. "Zeus…" I try to say his name, but my voice is too dry.

He smiles.

His knot loosens inside me, and he lowers me down to the floor. His shaft pulses once. He pulls out and his cock slides free with a wet, sucking sound. His cum, my slick, the combined heat of our fluids gushes down my legs. "No." I shake my head and cling to his shoulders.

"So fucking beautiful, My Mate." One side of his lips lifts up in a smirk.

His big body sways, and I scream. "I am not letting you die on me, you hear me, Alpha?"

Those brilliant blue eyes spark at me, then the light fades out.

"Zeus, no." I try to hold him up, but he's too heavy for me.

His shoulders convulse.

He tilts his body, and I realize it's to hold his weight off of me so he doesn't crush me when he falls. His big body slumps and he slides to the ground.

"I love you, you hear me?" I snarl.

79

Zeus

"I love you…" I see her lips form the words and I open my mouth to reply, to tell her that I love her, too, but no sound emerges.

The mating bond screeches in my chest. A pulse of fear floods the connection, and laced with it is this heat, this incredible will to survive.

It's her will.

I've always knowns she was much more resilient than she looked, with so much fire, so much vitality that shines off of her.

It's why our child will live, not only because I want it to, but because his mother's one hell of a fighter. Like me. I want to hold on to life, to everything that it has to offer. My hopes my dreams…for my omega and my child, for both of them.

I close my fingers around her shoulders, and I know I am dragging her down with me, but I can't help it.

My back hits the floor. Pain rips down my spine and overflows my cells. My entire body spasms. I sense liquid pool under my skin, scent the coppery smell of blood. My life is oozing out of me, and all I can do is watch her face, trace her features with my gaze.

Ethan's face fills my vision.

"Take her." I grasp her hand, and she tries to yank it from me. I tighten my grip so much I know it must hurt, but it's the only way to make sure that she obeys. "Promise me you'll get her to safety."

"I promise." He takes off his vest and hands it to her.

She doesn't notice. "Don't you fucking talk like that." She tightens her jaw. "I am not going anywhere without you."

I jerk my chin at Ethan, and he slips the vest over her shoulders. A part of me hates that he gets to touch her. My guts lurch. I don't want her to wear clothes that belong to anyone else. So what if he's a beta? No one else's scent gets to be that close to her skin. A growl rumbles up my chest, and the pain fades away for an instant.

Ethan glances at me. "Only until we get back to the stronghold. I want to make sure she is covered, so she's shielded from the other alphas."

Solomon comes racing up to us. He drops to his knees. "We're getting you out of here, General." He slides an arm under my shoulders.

Ethan takes my other side, and together they heave me to my feet.

"I am not letting you go." She leans close to me, goes up on tiptoe and brushes her lips over mine.

Solomon freezes next to me. His gaze falls on her, and his nostrils flare as he scents the slickness that trails down her legs.

"Don't you dare look at her." My voice is harsh.

He draws himself up to his full height. "Well, then you need to beat what the bastard did to you, now don't you?"

I freeze, all of my instincts going on alert.

Anger twists my guts, and my muscles respond to it. My vision clears, and the pain recedes. I yank myself away from Sol, and he steps back. So does Ethan.

"No one gets to come near her, you hear me? Not one of those losers in my Council. Not any of my men, and not the two of you. Not that I don't trust you…"

"You don't." One side of his lips slides up as Ethan smiles.

"Yeah." I grimace. "That's right, I trust none of you fuckers, none except her." I train my gaze on my omega.

She stands there, green eyes blazing. "Can we get the fuck out of here already, before you bleed to death?" She plants her hands on her hips.

I draw my lips back. "There's just one more thing to do." My heart races, my pulse pounds, and the pain in my back where the bullet smashed into me ratchets up as if indicating my time is up.

She steps forward, and I hold up a hand.

She pauses and fists her fingers at her sides. But mercifully, she stays quiet.

"If anything happens to me —"

"What the fuck —" she swears.

"Listen to me, Omega." My voice echoes over the bodies scattered around us.

Someone coughs, then all noise dies down.

I take in a breath. "If anything happens to me, Lucy will take over the title of General."

Ethan freezes. The tendons of his neck bunch, and a pulse beats at his temple.

Solomon gulps. "You…you sure, Zeus?"

She swallows and her gaze locks, with mine. She opens her mouth as if to say something, then purses her lips tighter and nods.

Thank fuck.

I turn to Ethan. "Nothing to say, Second?"

He angles his head, and his lips purse. "As you wish, First."

Pain engulfs me, and I grit my teeth. A chill grips my chest and grows, spreading through me. I can't feel my feet, my legs, my heart…my heart.

Everything goes white.

80

Lucy

The mating bond pulses, once, and goes silent again.

"No," I scream and want to move toward him, but Ethan is already there.

He grabs Zeus' shoulder, and Solomon takes the other side. They half carry, half drag him between them. I try to move and find my feet are too weak.

I take a step forward and stagger. Liam reaches out a hand to steady me.

"No." My stomach twists at the thought of anyone else touching me. The scent of Liam's alpha presence taints my skin. My guts heave, and leaning over to the side, I am sick.

He waits until I right myself and wipe my lips. I square my shoulders and follow them out. Liam brings up the rear. I clamber into the massive SUV, and they place Zeus' body in the back. I cradle his head and hold him closely.

He's so pale, so silent. My heart lurches, my head spins. "Don't you die on me." Tears stream down my cheeks and slap onto his face.

"You're mine, Alpha." I kiss his forehead and push back the heavy black hair, matted with blood and sweat. I kiss his eyelids, brush my cheek against the rough whiskers on his jaw. *Mine*, I pulse the thought at him and it echoes through the mating cord.

"Stay with me, Alpha." I reach out to him again through the mating bond, but there's nothing. Silence. An emptiness that scares me more than anything else. My palms go cold, and my feet seem to be fixed to the floor of the vehicle that's speeding along. Sol's driving with Ethan next to him. Liam stayed behind to clear up some of the mess.

Harald is dead. My clan is safe. I've completed what I set out to do. So why is there a burning emptiness in my chest?

My throat hurts and a pressure pushes down behind my eyes.

The only thing that matters to me is here, right here in my arms, only he is slipping away, and I don't know what to do about it.

His skin is so cold. The color seems to have leached from his face. The rough dressing that Ethan had wrapped around his chest is already saturated with blood. His life is fading away in front of me. "Drive faster, Sol, faster."

The vehicle speeds up, the countryside blurs past, and all I can do is fix my gaze on his face, try to anchor him to me.

"I can't let him die, I can't." Tears trickle down my cheeks.

He doesn't stir. A ripple of fear trembles down my back.

"There's one thing you can do." Ethan turns to me. "If you want to save him." He hesitates.

"What does it look like?" I snarl. My chest hurts. The blood thuds at my temples.

His gaze falls to Zeus' face then rises back to me.

"Tell me." A sob catches in my throat.

"You can reach out to him through the mating bond and share your life force with him. Except…" His jaw firms. His gaze narrows, and he drums his fingers on the back of his seat.

"Now is not the time to keep anything back." I wipe my cheek on my shoulder and try to focus on his face.

My head spins with the effort, but I don't blink, don't look away.

"Tell me." I infuse as much authority in my voice as I can muster. I am not alpha, never will be. I don't want to be, not when I have a prime specimen of alpha male in my arms. He's alpha enough, macho enough for the two of us. But when he's down, damn if I am going to let him slip away without at least trying. He thought I was strong enough to fill in for him when he's not there. Well, I am going to do everything in my power to ensure that's never a reality. "Now." My voice echoes inside the vehicle.

His lips tighten. "If you do so it isn't without risks."

"Risks?" I frown.

"It means the bond will be irreversible. If something happens to him, you die, too, and trust me, he will not be happy when he finds out."

"Can't wait." I bare my teeth. The thought of Zeus awake and angry and raging at me…there would be no sweeter sight. My breath hitches in my chest.

"Just don't tell him I gave you the idea." He holds up his hands. But his gaze is serious, his features pinched.

"You want Zeus to live?" I frown.

"Very much." He holds my gaze

"You love him…like a brother." I sniff back my remaining tears.

"Now that may be stretching the truth a tad too much…" His gaze falls to Zeus. His jaw firms. "But yeah, the Bastard of the East End is the best leader we've got, and trust me, I don't want to lose him. For a beta…like me, he's the only way that I can partake of the leadership and not expose myself."

"You have a selfish reason in telling me all of this." I quirk my eyebrow.

"Completely selfish." His lips twist. "Don't delay, Lucy." All emotion fades from his features.

I square my shoulders, and straighten my back. I place one palm over Zeus' heart, and leaning in close, I kiss my alpha. I touch my forehead to his and tune in to him. I draw on all of my instincts, my past, all of my experiences, everything I've learned so far, and I open myself up to him completely.

I think back on how we met: his scent, his touch, how he first claimed me, how I'd bitten him, how he'd fucked me, knotted me again and again. He'd sunk his teeth into my throat, and later on the other side. The wounds swell up with blood, the skin around them bunches, pain flutters down my spine and I don't stop.

I drop all of me into the bond and push it at him.

There's nothing, then the cord bursts into fire.

It blazes a trail from me to him, flooding through him, pulling with it every last bit of my breath, my heart, my soul. All of it pours through.

I sense his shoulders heave, his breath rasping through his lungs.

I tighten my grip around his shoulders.

Heat slams into me, and I am sure every part of me is on fire, then there's only smoke.

81

Zeus

A day later

"How dare she put herself at risk for me? She's hurt, my unborn child is at risk, and it's all because of you." I stalk across the floor to the edge of the room to where Ethan stands, and smash my fist into the wall by his head.

My fist goes through the surface. There's a creaking sound from above as a crack spiders up to the ceiling, to where the light that hangs from the ceiling creaks. Bits of plaster fall down to flow over us like snow.

Fucker doesn't blink. "I trust venting your frustrations in a show of temper helped?" He tilts his head.

The man sounds so calm; there is no scent of fear around him.

"You should have been born an alpha, Second." I grunt.

His features tighten, his lips thin. "You sure know how to rub it in, Zeus."

"I meant that as a fucking compliment." Now I am softening my words. Bloody fucking hell.

I cannot recognize myself anymore.

Maybe it's time I stopped trying to hide my reactions for her, for Ethan, for those among my team who had put their lives at risk to get us out of there.

And to be honest, perhaps…I'd trust them with my life. But I cannot, will not, let any of them get close to her.

No matter that I had been out for hours as they'd driven us here, and had regained consciousness just as they had drawn up into the stronghold.

I had found my omega sprawled unconscious over me.

Her pulse had been weak, her breath shallow, and the mating cord between us had thinned to a thread of light. She'd seemed so cold, so silent, my heart had seized. I'd insisted on carrying her to the infirmary, no matter that my legs had wobbled under me, my muscles bunching, my chest heaving like I had run for miles. No one, no one gets close to my omega, no one takes care of her but me...and yeah the doc, and only because he's beta and he's the best in the city.

Yeah, so I had my men hunt him down and bring him here with his team. They huddle over her now, blocking my omega from my sight.

Fuck! If something were to happen to her...no, she is going to survive this. My Squirrel is strong and obstinate, she will get through this. She must. I clench my jaw.

"If this is your way of showing appreciation that I saved your hide..." Ethan clicks his tongue.

Right. I jerk my chin. "Thank you."

"The Bastard of the East End swallowing his pride and thanking me? This has to be a first." His lips curl.

"Better not get used to it." I tuck my arms at my side.

"Nah." He scratches his jaw, "I am going to be too busy watching you meet your your downfall, at the feet of a sassy omega, no less."

I frown, and he raises his palms face up. "Truce?"

I rub the back of my neck. "Yeah." I hold out my fist.

His gaze narrows then he nods. "Okay." He bumps my fist.

I step around him toward the transparent partition that separates the waiting room from the examination room, where the doc and his team are checking her out.

I can't get over how I'd woken in the SUV, with her slumped over me. I'd sat up, and her body had almost slipped to the floor, as if the life force had been sucked out of her.

And it had been. I'd done that.

She'd fed me her life breath down the mating bond, and I'd grasped on to it, had pulled it all into myself, used it to rejuvenate every part of me. When the doc had examined me, he'd glanced at me strangely, then confirmed what I already knew. My wounds were almost completely healed... thanks to her.

"Stop beating yourself up General." Ethan steps up to stand next to me.

I clench my fingers at my sides. A pulse tics at my jaw. In the spirit of trying to get along with him, I suppose I should hear him out, this once. "Spit it out, Second."

"She chose to do it; she chose to share her life force with you." Ethan steps up next to me and peers through the transparent wall.

And that, right there, is what's annoying me. "She endangered her life. Put our child at risk." Fear tightens my chest. I press my fingertips against the transparent barrier that separates me from my omega.

"She couldn't have known the impact it would have on her." Ethan places his hand on my shoulder and I don't shake it off. Fucking hell. I am actually accepting the comfort he offers, and damn if that doesn't feel right.

"She's a fighter." His voice softens, "You forget that she brawls as fiercely as you."

My lips twist. "You have no idea."

Truth is, I am not quite sure how to sort my conflicting emotions right now. Fear, disgust at myself that I couldn't protect her, that while she's close to death I am alive and waiting…waiting. "Fuck."

"You do know that you can speed up her recovery right?" Ethan mutters.

He doesn't elaborate. He doesn't need to.

I know what I must do. What I want to do. Every second since I met her has been leading up to this. This is the time to show that I am a true alpha, that I protect what's mine, even if it means baring my true self.

I press my fingertips against the transparent barrier that separates me from my omega,

I can't see her, but I sense her presence.

I'm aware of how close she is to me, even now. I hadn't allowed myself to think of the possibility of how I could help her…maybe because it's the last barrier that stands between us. Maybe because to reach out to her through the mating bond will mean acknowledging everything inside of me that's real and decent, that is alive.

And who am I kidding?

I'd begun to change from the moment she'd come into my life. Her presence, her essence inside of me, her scent…everything had dragged me from the dark place I'd been, showing up a mirror to myself.

I confess I'd seen myself for what I was. An alpha torn apart with hate, needing revenge. Someone for whom lives meant nothing, not even my own. Except hers did.

She and my unborn child, I need them to live.

I drop into myself, seizing the bond that nestles in my chest, and reach out to her. Images of those green eyes, her cries as I'd taken her, her trembling as I'd marked her. Her moans as I'd knotted her, the exact moment I'd sunk my teeth into her and claimed her over and over again…I bleed all those feelings into the bond.

I press my forehead to the glass wall and open myself to her.

My eyes flutter down.

I sense her presence: a vibrant green that swoops toward me, the golden thread of the mating cord that binds us and…twin violet lights that spark down the bond racing to get to me. They are a combination of us, of my essence and hers, of everything I'd hoped for but could never put into words, could never acknowledge. I swallow and my throat closes. I see them—my family, my flesh and blood. My world. Mine.

The doors of the infirmary swoosh open, footsteps walk up to me, and there's a touch on my shoulder. I raise my head and turn to meet the eyes of the doctor.

82

Lucy

The presence of my mate envelops me. I am surrounded by his touch, his heat, that burned pinewood scent of his teases my nostrils, and I moan.

Every part of me feels like it's been broken apart and put back together. My eyes flutter open, and I search for him, his gaze, his warmth. I need it. I crave it. A hand grips mine. Wide palm, fingers that are calloused and rough. His thumb rubs circles over my wrist, and I shiver.

"Alpha." I train my gaze on his hand.

I follow the honey-colored forearm over those muscled biceps where the tattoos ebb and flow as if they have a life of their own, up that tanned, beautiful column of his neck to his incredible lips.

"Lucia." His lips form my name.

Hope blooms in my chest.

His voice is rough, the tone so raw that I flinch. I raise my gaze to his face. Wetness glints on his cheeks.

"You're crying?" I breathe out in shock.

"Only for you." He leans in close and presses his lips to my forehead.

The touch is so tender, so filled with that longing, a yearning that I'd have never associated with him. He needs me, as much as I need him, and this is as close as he's going to get to admitting it. I take in the skin stretched over his cheeks, the pulse that beats at his temples, the bristles that cover his sculpted jaw. I swear he's lost weight since I last set eyes on him. "Your wounds." I try to sit up, and he presses me back.

"I am fine." His forehead furrows, and the skin around his eyes stretches. "Thanks to you."

"Oh." I sink back against the pillow, then swing my gaze around the room. "This looks like an—"

"Infirmary," he fills in for me. "I woke up to find you slumped over me. Your body was so cold, your color so low, I thought you were—"

"Dead?" I train my gaze on him.

He swallows, and a pulse flickers to life at the base of his neck.

"How long have I been out?" I croak.

"Two days. The doc says you are out of danger. You fucking scared me, Omega."

"No more than you did me, when the bullet hit you. You put yourself between me and that…that monster."

"It was my right." He sets his jaw. "I am alpha, I protect. I take care of what is mine." His gaze falls to my stomach.

I lower my palm to cup my belly. "The baby." Fear twists my chest. I reach for him, and he grips my arms.

"They are fine."

"They?" I frown.

His eyes gleam and his lips draw up in a smile that lights up his features. "Twins."

I blink. "And you know that, how?"

His brows draw down, "Trust me on this."

"Um." I gnaw on my lower lip, "Isn't it a little early in the pregnancy to confirm this?"

His shoulders stiffen. Is he hiding something from me?

"The potency of my sperm, Squirrel, it had to happen." A smirk curves his luscious lips. My throat goes dry. Heat snakes down my spine and all thoughts slip from my mind.

"No doubt." I cough.

He tucks his shoulders back. Pride radiates off of him. Okay, so the sarcasm is lost on him. I bite the inside of my cheek to stop the chuckle from trembling off of my lips.

He leans over me. This is when he thrusts his face into mine until our noses touch, until his breath sears my cheek and...he pulls back. Eh? Not what I expected.

"Doesn't change the fact that you put yourself at risk, despite my instructions to the contrary." His voice is gruff.

"I did what was necessary." I set my jaw.

"Obstinate omega." He reaches out to touch me, then seems to change his mind and tucks his hand into his side. What the--? The alpha is showing restraint?

"When will you learn that you cannot do what you want, at any time you want?"

"Never." I raise my chin.

His lips tighten. Finally a reaction I recognize.

"You have our children to think of."

My shoulders tense and my gaze skitters away. He knows just how to manipulate me with his words "You're right." I swallow.

A breath rushes out of him. "Look at me Lucy." This is when he grips my chin so I have no choice but to look at him. I can imagine the scrape of his knuckles as he feathers them over my jawline, but nope. Nothing.

I turn to look at him, and he's stays by the side of the bed, maintaining his distance.

"From now on you stay inside, rest, take care of yourself. I'll make sure you have enough to keep your mind engaged. Your priority is to ensure that you and the child are safe and content."

He presses a kiss to my forehead and gets up from his chair.

Hang on a moment, he kissed my forehead? Zeus gave me a chaste kiss? He's never done that before. Whatever happened to fitting his lips over mine and thrusting his tongue into my mouth and ravishing me? Even weakened from my ordeal, that is what I still want.

I snake out my arm and grab his wrist, then for good measure dig my fingernails into his skin.

He turns and his features form into an expression of polite concern.

Huh? My heart begins to race. "What are you doing?" I frown at him.

"Leaving you to recover."

"I don't want to be alone," I pout, Yeah I am acting childish, but gimme a break. I just found out I am carrying twins and that my alpha, the one who'd bonded me without my consent and who I have since realized is my soulmate, has decided that now is the time to go all well-mannered on me. "You're acting weird." I frown.

He drops his gaze to where I am still clinging to his arm and I let go.

He steps back, "Explain yourself."

"I am used to you taking what you want, fucking me until I can't move, rutting me until your cum drools out of my every hole, but this..." I swallow and squeeze my thighs together. Holy hell, just talking about how he'd taken me is arousing me, or maybe it's just my hormones, which seem to go into overdrive whenever this alpha is around, which is responsible for my shooting my mouth off.

"This?" A vein throbs at his temples.

"This." I firm my lips. "Your being all well-mannered is confusing me."

He grimaces. "I am doing what's right for you in this condition."

"I am pregnant not dying." I curl my fingers into fists.

"You need time apart to nest and let your body prepare for what is to come." He sets his jaw.

"If my emotional state is important to you—"

"It is and you won't be alone." He angles his body away. Can he not tolerate the sight of me anymore?

"Mirela will stay with you day and night and attend to your needs."

"But…" I swallow. What did I miss? Why is he acting so aloof? Keeping this distance between us?

I reach out to the mating bond and find the thread leading to him. I sense the shadow of his presence.

Gone is that fiery, all-powerful essence of his that pounded at the bond and overflowed my chest. It feels like he's hiding behind a screen. I see the shadow of his presence, feel him, but as if from a distance.

"Don't go." Panic coils in my chest.

I try to sit up, but my body is too weak to hold me up. My head hurts, my limbs tremble, even my toenails protest. Sleep tugs at the edge of my consciousness.

He turns around and stalks to the door then pauses. "You have nothing to worry about." He shoots me a glance over his shoulder. "No one will hurt you…especially not me." He turns and leaves.

I squeeze my eyes shut, "That's what I am afraid of."

83

Zeus

I pace the floor in the war room, looking out of the window. A cold wind blows in from the open panes, and I let it flow over my skin, taking away some of the heat that seems to burn through my veins. Well, I only had myself to blame. I've been avoiding her. It's been weeks since I last saw her. Twenty-one days, eight hours and six minutes since I last saw her, but who's counting? Me, the pussy-whipped motherfucker who's hiding from her, is who.

I can't face her after what I've put her through.

This should be the time that I spend every second with her, protecting her, cherishing her. Fact is, even now I am tuned in to her thanks to the mating cord.

The barrier between us is still in place, but that doesn't mean I can't keep an eye on her. I twist my lips. Okay so I am stalking her. I am all but physically in the same space as her, and alert for any signs that she may be in discomfort; otherwise I am leaving her alone. I have to.

I was the reason she'd almost died a second time. This time, it's not just her but the fate of our children at risk. Children... I roll the word over my tongue.

Father? Am I ready to become one? I'll be a better one than the loser, Golan, ever was, of course. I set my jaw. I'd mated her hoping for precisely this, and now, faced with the reality of what is to come, a warmth fills my chest. My throat closes and my pulse begins to race.

Ethan ambles up to stand next to me. "Interesting view?"

"Huh?"

"Whatever you are looking at."

"The fuck, Second?" I growl and rub the back of my neck. There's no reason to snap at the man. He's doing his duty, or whatever it is that seconds-in-command are meant to do.

Not that I would know.

I never could be second in anything. "It must be agonizing to live as a beta when everything inside you insists that you are an alpha."

Ethan's muscles coil with tension; he reels away from me as if I've struck him a physical blow. "Fuck, Zeus, do you need to continuously throw that in my face?"

"Hold on there." I turn on him, hands raised in front of me in an appeasing gesture. I'll never get used to this either… Me? Actually being conciliatory toward him? "I just meant to empathize, that it must be tough for you to be constantly at war with yourself?"

"Do me a favor Zeus?" He growls low in his throat.

I frown.

"Next time, don't try to make polite conversation. It has just the opposite effect." He swings around, then raises his fist and slams it into the wall next to the window.

A crack blooms up the wall, traveling up to where the light fixtures are. One of them shakes loose then crashes to the table below.

"Did I interrupt something?" Solomon stands at the entrance to the room. He looks from the light that's collapsed on the table, to me.

"Nope." I swivel away from the window and stalk to the front of the table. "Ethan here is just having a bit of a meltdown."

"Ethan?" His gaze widens. He rubs the back of his neck. "You sure it wasn't you, sir?"

I peel back my lips. The calm and collected second who never misses a chance to tell the rest of us off? Who could put a monk to shame with the kind of serenity he normally sheds. "Yeah." I jerk my chin toward the table. "Sit your ass down, Sol."

He moves around the table, seems to debate where to sit, then pulls up a chair in the middle. Wise man. "You're a diplomat, Sol."

"Just being prudent, sir." He grins at me.

"Fucker's gloating because all of the omegas in the harem have been vying to lay with him, given you are no longer in circulation, Alpha," Ethan bares his teeth.

"The fuck does that mean?" I roll my shoulders.

He stalks to the chair at the foot of the table and drops into it. "Word is that you are mated, your omega is pregnant, and you are giving her a wide berth, due to some misplaced sense of celibacy." His eyes gleam.

"Celibacy?" I go to pull out a chair, then change my mind and grab it and tip it forward, preferring to stand instead.

Anything to keep an edge over my men.

It's sad that I have to resort to cheap tactics to maintain the power balance with my men. What-fucking-ever. I am a little—okay, a lot—out of sorts, and Ethan is flipping the situation to his own advantage.

He tips back his chair to balance it on its hind legs. "Am I not right?" He twists his lips. "Sir?"

Fucker is always saying things as if he has a direct connection to my thinking process.

He has no idea what a surprise he is in for.

"Don't you men have anything else to do, like field exercises for yourself and your men to stay fighting fit, instead of gossiping like omegas?"

Sol glances at me, his expression pained. "That's low even for you, sir!"

"Just for that, all the soldiers, every fucking alpha in the Council, will put in an extra hour of fieldwork every day for the next week."

"No way." Sol's lips turn down.

"An additional hour in the morning, too."

Ethan sets his chair down with a thump. "Zeus, really—"

"Two weeks." I grin and rub the part of my vest over my heart.

Both their gazes drop there.

"Something on your mind?" I growl.

There's silence.

Solomon leans forward and places his elbows on the table. "She needs you."

I huff out a breath. "It's better this way. If I am not in her way, I can't put her in harm. I don't aggravate her, she doesn't challenge me, then I don't have to punish her and—" Fuck if my dick doesn't throb right now. The thought of all the ways I could punish her fills my mind in graphic detail.

The mating cord twinges.

I've retreated right back from it, yet, I am always conscious of her presence on the other side of the bond, and somehow, she always seems to know when I am thinking of her and she doesn't make it easy for me. Not at all. It's like she's stalking me, too, waiting for me to make a move. Like she's calling out to me, cajoling me, all without saying anything, and damn if my imagination is not being overactive.

I release the chair so it falls back with a thump.

Both of their gazes are fixed on me.

"So why did the two of you come here anyway?" I fold my arms over my chest.

Silence.

Solomon's lips quirk, and he looks to Ethan.

My second jerks his chin at me. "You called us here, General."

"I did?" I rub the back of my neck. Bloody hell, now I am forgetting what commands I have issued?

"We assumed you wanted an update on the aftermath of the encounter with Harald?" Sol scratches his chin.

"Fucker's dead. So are most of his men." I step back and pace. "Those who survived are imprisoned and being tortured so we get to know their plans."

Ethan drums his fingers on the table. "Well, that's what we want to talk to you about."

"Well, speak up then, man." The mating cord twinges. The scent of sweet honey spikes the air. I must be delirious, mistaken. Yeah, that's what it is.

I turn and widen my stance.

"Harald's son is planning to cross the seas and come over with a bigger army." Ethan stills his movements and leans back in his chair. "Apparently, he sent his father just as a tester to check the waters. If you thought Harald was a maniac, his son is much worse."

"Well, bring him on." I crack my knuckles. "A fight is exactly what I need."

"Maybe you need to stay with your omega until she's given birth." Ethan's forehead furrows.

"She's in my suite, she's comfortable, there are omegas attending her around the clock—"

"You mean Mirela." Ethan's features go solid, all emotions wiped from his face.

"What-fucking-ever her name is," I roll my shoulders. "Can you spare your omega to help Lucy until she has given birth?"

He notches up his chin. "Not my omega." Color flushes his face.

Well, isn't this interesting? "So you're hard for her. Not exactly a secret how you all but eat her up with your eyes."

Ethan growls.

I swallow down the chuckle, "Just trying to help, Second."

"Don't fucking try." Ethan springs up so fast his chair crashes to the floor. He raises his fists in front of him.

Solomon's gaze bounces between us. "If I hadn't learned that you two were half-brothers, I'd have guessed it by now."

"Shut the fuck up, Sol," I say at the same time as Ethan.

Sol firms his lips.

Ryker flings the door open and swaggers in. "Sir, you need to see this."

"We're having a discussion —" Ethan turns on him.

"Which is over." I walk over to Ryker in relief. Anything to get out of here and do something before I go crazy. "What is it?" I thrust out my chin.

He shifts his weight from foot to foot. "There's a delivery for you at the warehouse."

A prickle of apprehension slides down my back. The last time a delivery had arrived, Kayden had been responsible for it, and I'd unwrapped the package to reveal my luscious omega, speaking of which, "How's Kayden doing?" I shoot Ethan a glance over my shoulder.

"I'll check on him, make sure he's in the safehouse."

84

Lucy

I wait, rolled up inside the rug.

This is stupid, very stupid of me.

Why had I thought up another half-assed plan to get to him? He's not going to be happy when he finds out I sprang this surprise on him. Likely he'll throw me out. Not that I care. I snort under my breath. Since I'd shared my life force with him and revived him…and, well, so I did risk my life in the process, but the important thing is that nothing happened, right? Besides I don't remember much of what went down during the time I was unconscious, and since then…? I've been trying to make sense of why Zeus has been aloof. And that's stating it mildly.

I'd woken up in the infirmary, and he'd held me close and comforted me. I'd seen that haunted look in his eyes and known that I'd broken through all boundaries. That finally he'd revealed his true self to me. I'd thought this time around he'd accept me as his mate, after everything we've been through…Well, I did save his life, too, didn't I? But it had all backfired on me.

It's as if the closer I get to him, the more the alpha runs from me.

What is he afraid of?

Sweat trickles down my back, and my hair sticks to the inside of the tight cloth I've wrapped around my head. I'd tried to replicate the way we'd first met, right down to my clothes.

Except I hadn't been pregnant then.

The morning sickness had kicked in with a vengeance a week ago. I am sure Mirela has been reporting it back to Zeus. Not that it seems to have made any difference.

He'd given his suite over to me, and I haven't seen him since that day at the infirmary.

I'd heard from Mirela that he was spending his nights in the barracks with his men.

Apparently, he is comfortable there, too. It's similar to the quarters he left behind in the East End before he took over as General... All of it is supposition, just word-of-mouth gossip I've heard from Mirela.

I shouldn't lay weight by it, but what choice do I have? I've been starved for news about him.

I haven't seen him for weeks; in fact, I've been all but a prisoner in his suite. Okay, not exactly, I've been allowed to take walks on the grounds as long as I've been accompanied by Mirela.

He seems to trust her.

I should be jealous, but for the fact that on many occasions Ethan has picked her up and accompanied her to her quarters. It has been clear that there is serious chemistry between them.

"Why do you and Ethan not get together?" My voice echoes in the tube of fabric.

I'm sure she hasn't heard me, or if she has, she's ignoring me.

I pop my head outside and tug at the seam of her pants. "Don't pretend you didn't hear me."

"What's the question?" Mirela looks down at me from where she is standing.

I am wearing a shift borrowed from her. It's different from the jumpsuit I'd worn the first time I'd snuck into the stronghold wrapped up in a rug. Yeah, desperate measures. Not my normal attire, but figured I'd go all the way with this seduction routine.

Mirela has exchanged her feminine attire for, dark pants and a full-sleeved shirt. Still, there's no mistaking her curves or the stream of thick black hair that slides down her back.

She's 100% omega, a woman born to be knotted and bred, and she'd agreed to be part of my plan.

Perhaps, she has as much need to challenge the stereotype of omegas that all of these alphas subscribe to.

Little do they know.

I chuckle, and she frowns.

"There's nothing funny about what you are going to do," she huffs. "I must be insane for agreeing to help you."

"Nah, you're just avoiding the question—"

"I didn't hear one." She taps her foot on the floor.

"Ethan." I grin up at her.

She stiffens her back and raises her head. "What about him?"

"You two seem to have a love-hate thing going on."

"It's pure hate from my end." She huffs.

"I've seen the way he watches you when you are not aware, and my guess is that he feels something powerful for you."

"He's made it clear he doesn't want me, that he will not break my heat cycle. He's happy for any other alpha to have me...so..."

My forehead furrows. "Ethan said that?" I try to reconcile the hurtful words with the principled, steely man I know.

"Better believe it." She sets her jaw.

"And are you going to do that? Get another alpha to break your heat cycle?" I peer up at her.

"It's not like I have a shortage of alphas." She tosses her hair. "Every time I turn a corner, there is one of Zeus' men loitering around trying to petition me for an omega."

"Do they approach you to lay with you, too?"

"They wouldn't dare." She angles her head and grins down at me. There's something feral about that look.

"You're a tough one, Omega."

"Yeah." She shakes back the hair over her shoulders. "I've survived on my own and faced up to alphas far more vicious than Ethan, so he can take his dick and stick it in any other omega pussy and knot them, and you know what, I wouldn't care." She digs her heels into the floor and huffs out a breath.

A thought crosses my mind then; of course, she hadn't been there when Ethan had shared the reality of what he is.

She doesn't know he's not an alpha. I open my mouth to tell her, then purse my lips. It's not going to help if I reveal that now. Besides, it's Ethan's secret to share.

It's a testament to the bond that has formed between Zeus and his men who had been there at the scene. When the relationship between Ethan and Zeus and the true status of Ethan's standing had been revealed, no gossip had circulated in its aftermath. And I'm not going to tell either.

There's a knock at the doors to the warehouse. I stiffen and look at her.

"It's time." She squats down and grips my shoulder. "Good luck, Lucy." Straightening, she walks to the door with that smooth, gliding gait of hers.

Panic skitters down my spine, and I almost call her back.

But that's stupid. I need to see this through on my own.

She's already put her own life at risk by helping me set all of this up, including convincing Ethan and Sol and the men closest to Zeus to fall in with the plan.

Ethan had flouted Zeus' rules by coming to see me in the suite, and surprise…it had actually been to convince me to go through with it. He'd felt it was for the best, that Zeus just needed to see me, and he'd accept me and my unborn children, he'd said.

I brush away the tear that trickles from the corner of my eye. Not that I have a choice.

He's been avoiding me completely, has refused all requests for a meeting with him.

None of his team, not even Ethan, have any idea what is going on in Zeus' head or why he's been so adamant about avoiding me.

Definitely some kind of misplaced need to protect me.

Snatches of conversation from when I'd woken up in the infirmary cling to the edges of my memory. I'd known already that he was going to do something stupid. I'd thought he'd likely just send me away along with my clan.

Instead, he'd sheltered my people in London, accepted the omegas who'd come with me, including my sister Chloe, into the harem. He'd also given the betas among them roles within his stronghold.

He'd done everything right. Well, everything except his duty as an alpha, which is to fuck me and… I miss him. There, I admit it.

I miss his presence, his scent, his touch, the chafe of his hair roughened jaw over the soft skin of my inner thigh, his big body pressing mine into the bed, pinning me down and holding me in place for his ministrations. A shiver of yearning ripples down my spine.

My belly quivers and I place a palm over my womb.

He hasn't returned to check on the progress of how my pregnancy is developing, and that is unusual for an alpha.

As much as an omega gets possessive about her children, an alpha is as much protective about the omega, and especially a pregnant omega and his unborn children.

The mating bond pulses. I stiffen. I've felt his presence often shadow me through the bond, especially at night, but this is the first time that there has been any sign of life in it. Almost as if it senses his nearness. I know without a doubt that he's close.

He must be headed toward the entrance of the warehouse.

My pulse ratchets up, and my throat goes dry. My stomach heaves. I can't be sick, not now. I burrow back down into the rug, wrap the scarf over my nose and mouth, and take a deep breath to steady myself.

I hear the sound of the door being wrenched open, the hinges creaking, and the hair on my nape stands on end.

I am in for it now.

There's no way out but to go through with this plan. Excitement strums my nerves. I am going to see him. Finally, I am going to be close to my alpha. Heavy footsteps close in on me.

85

Zeus

I stalk toward the rolled-up fabric at the end of the warehouse. The colors glimmer blue and green in the light from the harsh fluorescent lamps in the ceiling.

My gut tightens.

I don't need to open it to know what's inside of there. The scent of her hits me as I approach the fabric. The scent of dawn air mixed with the sweet spoor of omega slick. She's inside there, balled up in it.

What is she getting at?

Is she toying with me?

Did she defy my command to stay within the suite and take care of herself? The thoughts race around my head. I want to be angry that she disobeyed me.

Want to feel something, anything other than this anticipation that fills my chest, a warmth that percolates from the mating cord. It fills my cells and overflows, until every part of me is taut with anticipation. I shouldn't be so pleased to see her.

Shouldn't feel the need build with every step that I take toward her.

My footsteps echo within the hollow space.

My pulse thuds at my temples. My heart hammers, mirroring the hope that bubbles up in my gut.

Bloody hell. When was the last time I was so filled with expectation? This. This elation that coats every cell in my body and urges me to thrust out my chest and roar my anticipation to the world—when had I last wanted to do that?

When I'd last been with her. That's when.

The fact is that I've missed her, and I don't want to admit it. I come to a stop in front of the rolled-up carpet.

It seems innocuous enough, exactly like the last time a rug was delivered to me.

Except this time, I know what's waiting inside for me. And something in me wants to draw out the suspense.

How does she feel wrapped up inside there, waiting for me to unpeel that cloth and expose her? What will she be wearing? Will she be naked?

Heat flushes my skin.

My breath stutters. My fingers tingle.

I squat next to the rolled-up material and trail my fingers over the fabric, over the hint of the curves that shape the cloth. Down the arc of what must surely be her hip and over her thighs, to her legs. I pause at her feet.

"You coming out of there, Squirrel?"

Silence greets me. There's no movement from inside, nothing. I can't fucking hear her breathe. Fear twists my heart. She's fine inside there, right? She has to be. She's pregnant, too, and is this right, what she's doing now? Wrapping herself up, smothering herself in this piece of cloth, and luring me here, and for what?

So she can talk to me?

Because I've turned away every opportunity to see her. I've refused her repeated attempts to meet me. I've made her go to these lengths. Replicate the way we first met. And a part of me wants to chuckle and puff up with pride. My omega is fucking clever, too damned clever for her own good. At this rate, she's going to end up hurting herself and the children all over again and… It's only when I feel the material under my fingers, I realize I've already reached for the seam of the carpet.

I grip the cloth and yank it with just enough force for the fabric to unravel. The colors stream out as the material unrolls.

Her body tumbles out, and I sweep her up and into my arms, "How dare you put your children at risk?"

"*Our* children." Those eyes of shattered green blaze up at me.

I cradle her close, taking in the shift she's wearing and the long sleeves that flow to her wrists. Hmm. "Isn't it time you put such foolishness behind you and give thought to recovering from your last encounter?"

"It's been three weeks, Zeus." She juts out her lower lip. "An. Entire. Twenty-one. Days."

"I can count, Omega." My voice is rough.

"Well, bully for you, *Alpha*." She hisses at me.

Her scent crowds my nostrils. Her skin is soft against mine. She is so tiny. So vibrant.

A splash of color in a life which had otherwise lacked purpose. Strange how quickly I'd gone from wanting to tear down everything about my past to wanting to build it up for her, as a legacy for our children. I hadn't been aware when it had happened. But standing here, holding my omega in my arms, seeing the expressions flit across her face, reading the yearning in her gaze, I know I have changed.

I am not sure how to react.

"So much planning, and just to see me?" I walk toward the exit, carrying her in my arms.

There's a blur of movement and she flips out the knife hidden in her sleeve. The one I'd noticed earlier, and hadn't wanted to call her out on. Where is she going with this?

"I'm not done talking." She raises the blade and presses it against my neck.

I chuckle. "You think you're going to scare me with that toy."

She pushes the tip of the knife into my throat—not enough to break the skin, just enough to send a shudder of heat from the point of the wound all the way down to the tip of my dick. Fuck. It's perverted, this reaction I have toward her. That her need to hurt me only seems to turn me on further.

"Stop, Zeus."

"Or what?"

"I won't hesitate to draw blood."

"You wouldn't dare." I infuse every bit of confidence into my voice. She wouldn't cross the line and actually carry out her threat, would she?

A part of me wants to goad her on, to see how far she'll go.

Just an excuse. I just need an excuse to get even, to take her and claim her all over again.

To push aside all of my arguments, all of those promises I've made to myself not to take her. That my being near her will only harm her. Just one little glimmer of—

Pain streaks down my throat. I glance down to see that she's drawn the tip of the knife down my neck. A trickle of blood streaks my skin. "You fucking stabbed me?"

86

Lucy

His muscles are wound tight, and the hard planes of his chest flex as he growls. My insides quiver in response.

How much can I push him before he gives in to the need that crawls under his skin?

He squeezes me closer and the knife edge opens more of his skin. Blood drips from his throat and the scent of copper rends the air.

Heat from his body pours over me, and I gasp.

Sweat breaks out on my brow. I've missed this. Missed his overwhelming maleness. That thrum of danger that coils just under the surface of his skin, ready to strike. I want to unleash it now and face the brunt of his anger...his feelings, well, anything except that quiet front that he's maintained with me over the past few weeks.

All along he's been at the other end of the mating bond, yet I couldn't see him or touch him.

Now he's in front of me, and my hands are numb with the need to draw him closer. To bury myself inside of him, to crawl into his skin and lose myself in him. My fingers shudder around the knife's handle, and the blade slides from my hand.

He leans over so it hits the floor and then kicks it away.

"You always did like to play with things that were more dangerous than you thought them to be." His chest brushes my breasts.

My nipples tighten.

A breath shudders out of him

"I like being burned." I lean up and lick the blood that drips down his neck.

A pulse flares to life at his temples. He's not as composed as he appears either.

He's so close to breaking. All he needs is a little push, one more tiny shove over the edge and —

"I know what you're doing, Omega, and it won't work."

"Oh?" I flick out my tongue and wipe my lips clean of all traces of his blood.

His gaze follows the move, his eyes hooded. The cords of his throat ripple.

"You think you can make me lose my control, and rut you like the beast I am?" His voice shivers over my skin. "You thought right."

A hoarse growl rumbles up his chest and pours out over me, tugging my nerves, heating my blood. All the pores of my skin seem to open to absorb every bit of that sound. To roll around in it and revel in it.

"What...what are you trying to say?" I try to form the thoughts in my mind into words, and come up empty.

I've been reduced to this mass of sensations, coming to life at the points where my skin meets his.

Where that rough sound of his purring throbs through me, heading straight to my belly.

My thighs tremble, and a burst of slick slides out from between them. The scent of my arousal grows heavy, and I don't want to hide it from him. If anything, I revel in how tuned in to him I am. How my body reacts to every nuance of his tone. I reach for the mating cord nestled under my breastbone and pulse heat through it — my thoughts, my needs, what I want him to do to me, all of it I shove at him, hoping, praying that it will infiltrate whatever barrier he's placed between us.

An answering surge of want spills down the bond and hits me square in the chest. I gasp and look up at him.

He's already striding to the door, his jaw clenched. Those blue eyes focused on the task ahead.

"Alpha..." The word spills from my lips, and I am not sure what I want to say next.

"Quiet." His voice has an edge that I have never heard before. Rough, threatening, as if something inside of him has snapped.

Anticipation stretches my nerves.

He steps into the space outside of the warehouse. The cool air rushes over my skin, and I shiver.

It's been more than a month since I came here to London, since I tried to kill him, and the weather has turned.

Overnight, the chill had crept in, rain falling steadily throughout the night and day. It's only a matter of days before the snow arrives. With climate change, the once temperate weather of this place has been pushed to an extreme summer and winter, merging into each other and yet distinct. Like me and him. Same and yet apart. Alike and so different. And now...our fates are wound together — our children have made sure of that. My skin puckers.

Another purr growls up his throat.

"How do you do that?"

"What?"

"Modulate the sound of your purr so it seems to break out of your vocal cords, then snake around me in a hail of protection, and then you wrap me up in the notes and pull me close and soothe me and turn me on all at once."

His steps slow, and he looks down at me.

His blue eyes are lit from inside as if there's an inner fire that's burst to life. "That was almost poetic, Squirrel."

One side of his lips curls in that smirk that I have missed and wanted to see so much. I reach up a finger and trace the outline of that luscious, beautiful lower lip.

He angles his head, and my fingers miss his mouth to slip down over his chin.

My chest squeezes.

Apparently, he doesn't like me touching him—yet. And he doesn't want to answer my question, not that he needs to. He seems to know exactly what I want, what my body needs. He's always known what to do on a physical level. Emotionally…well, we have an unseen cord that binds us, and the children in my womb who will soon be the evidence of what we share, a passion, a chemistry that is more than just the need to rut that takes over between an alpha and an omega in heat.

It isn't much, but perhaps it's enough to build something, a semblance of a relationship between us. If that's all I can get, well, then so be it. I am not going to shy away from it. I am going to use his physical need for me as a starting point.

I pull back and flatten my fingers over his chest.

He presses me closer, then picks up the pace.

The lush gardens, the pool with the fountain in the center, all of it rushes by. He sweeps past the guards, into the stronghold, and crosses the courtyard where his men are practicing.

I notice the sounds of fighting, of swords clashing, and swearing. All of it dies down.

He's done it on purpose, carrying me away in front of everyone, so that there is no doubt as to who is my owner. I should protest, should be angry, but there's only this weariness dragging me down. My legs grow heavy, and there's a band around my chest.

I am his property. His possession. Only his.

There is no turning away from the reality of my situation.

He's the alpha, I am the omega, and our roles will always come down to this, him taking me, possessing me, rutting me.

So what if he'd told Ethan that if anything happened to him, he wanted me to take over? He is confident enough of my ability to lead his men in his absence. But when we are together like this, we are just a male and a female. One takes, the other gives. It's what nature intended, right?

So why is there a lump of emotion in my throat?

Why do tears prick the backs of my eyes? Why do I squeeze them shut as he takes the steps two at a time, reaches the landing on the top floor, then stalks down to where his suite—my temporary prison—is?

He shoulders open the double doors and steps inside the room.

They slam shut behind us, and it feels…why does it feel like I've come home?

I know what is to come.

I know he will take me all over again, and this time I want it, and more. I want so much more.

I want him to tell me again that he loves me, that he sees me as his partner, his mate. I want his trust, his devotion, his everything, and you know what? I won't stop, not until I have it all.

The world tilts. I bounce on the mattress.

The bed dips under his weight and he follows me down.
He shoves his heavily muscled thigh between mine and wrenches my legs apart.

87

Zeus

I lean in over her and her shoulders shudder.

She seems so tiny, so perfect lying under me. It's hard to remember sometimes how fragile she is. When she's angry at me and challenging me, her aura is larger than life, and it always seems that she is taller than her height. I rake my gaze down her breasts, over her stomach that... will soon not be concave anymore, and a primitive need to protect grips me.

The anger beating at my temples dissolves.

In its place is a curious need to possess, and so much tenderness. I swallow and try to move but can't.

"You can touch me, you know." Her voice is soft.

My gaze narrows and my fingers tingle to close the distance and cradle the swell of her stomach.

It's only a matter of time before she swells with my children. I try to breathe and find my lungs hurt. *My children.* Will I be able to do right by them, more than what my father did for me?

My breath catches.

Why does the thought of bringing two vulnerable lives into this world scare me so? Me, the alpha who's brought down fierce enemies, I have never hesitated to rise to a challenge; but the thought of being responsible for another: an innocent child born of our union, my own flesh and blood... a surge of heat coils in my chest. My throat closes. What if I am not good enough? What if I can't protect these little lives, can't guide them or provide them with everything they deserve? What then? My throat closes, and a nerve jerks to life at my jaw.

Her forehead furrows. She reaches for my palm and tugs it over her stomach.

My fingers seem to develop a life of their own and I cup her belly. "Mine."

The sound of my own voice is a shock.

Low, guttural, like nothing I've ever heard before. It sounds different, like a man possessed. I am possessed by her...by the possibility of the life we have given form to, by what the future holds for us.

A dull ache knocks at the backs of my eyes.

There's a ball of emotion in my chest that grows and throbs. The mating cord tugs at me, pulls me down. I flip up her dress, then lower my head and touch my lips to her belly.

She trembles. "I've missed you, Zeus."

Her words hit me with the force of a storm. Warmth pools in my chest. My throat closes.

This, being here with her, in my space, in my bed. This is right. This is where she belongs. *This* is what I've been fighting all along. Everything I have ever wanted is here in front of me. I see it now. I swallow down the lump of emotion in my throat and trail kisses up over the cloth covering her breasts to balance my weight over her. "I am sorry I ignored you, Squirrel."

The breath shudders out of her. "Why?" She squeezes her eyes shut. "No, forget I asked, it doesn't matter. Except—"

"It does." I can't help the smile that curls my lips.

"Yeah." She cracks her eyelids open. "Sometimes I wondered if you did it on purpose."

"What?" It's my turn to frown.

"Shut me up in this suite which is filled with your presence."

I tilt my head, knowing what she's going to say, but wait for her to spell it out.

"Your scent in this bed, in the mattress, in the air. It's like every part of you is enmeshed within the bricks in the walls. In the very floorboards, in the clothes you left behind in the closet." Her gaze moves around the room before alighting back on my face.

"Now that you mention it, perhaps I did, I wasn't aware of it though. I don't overanalyze things, but maybe...subconsciously..." I frown. I am at a loss for words, and that doesn't happen often, I promise. "I guess I wanted you to ache for me as much as I did for you?"

"Well, it worked. You starved me of your presence, and now I need you, Zeus. I want you."

She rises and flings her arms around me.

I pause, my shoulders going rock-hard. "The children."

"Are safe in my womb." She drags her tongue over the outer rim of my ear.

Desire sweeps through me. My dick leaps in response.

"Perhaps we should wait?" I hesitate.

"Who are you, and what have you done to Zeus?"

"He's fucked, that's what he is." I half chuckle then lean back to peer into her eyes. "I haven't come to terms with my reactions to you."

"Which are...?" She tilts her head.

"Half the time I want to keep you safe, hide you away from everyone." I set my jaw.

Hearing myself, I realize I sound half out of my head with possessiveness.

Exactly how an alpha would behave. Yet, that's not enough. She deserves more, much more than being treated like just another omega.

"And the other half?" Her lips part, showing off those white teeth between them.

Teeth that have nipped and bitten me. My shaft hardens. I want to feel them on me again.

"The other half of the time…" I lean in close, so our noses bump. "I want to tie you up and fuck you so hard that my knot locks inside of you, with no room to move, and you remember the sensation for days."

Spots of color highlight her cheeks. A bead of sweat slides down to pool at the hollow at the base of her throat.

"I lie actually."

"What do you mean?" Her brows draw down.

"I want to do that to you *every* time I see you." My heart stutters. My thighs go solid.

She flicks out her tongue to touch her lips, and my gaze darts to her mouth. "Wha—" Her voice breaks and she clears her throat. "What else do you want to do to me?"

Our toes collide; my thighs press into hers. "I want to kiss you senseless, right before I take you, knot you, become one with you, until it's no longer possible to differentiate where I begin and where you end."

Her pupils dilate. The scent of her arousal deepens. "And?"

I lock my gaze with hers. "I won't stop, not until my skin fuses with yours and our breaths mingle."

Her chin trembles, and her head falls back, exposing that delicate neck. Even after the way I've ravaged her, how can she seem so pure? So untouched. That primal, possessive part of me wants to roar forward and mess her up again.

Her chest heaves. "Is that all?"

My vision narrows on her, and a snarl simmers up my throat. "I'll drink in your every last groan, every last scream that I wring out of you. I'll take everything from you and come back for more."

88

Lucy

His words shudder over my skin. His chest planes rumble as the purr roars out of him. Not soft or modulated, it's a primal call to mate.

And my body reacts. My womb spasms, the mating cord in my chest throbs in tandem, and slick flows out from between my legs.

His nostrils flare. A dense cloud of heat spools off him and slams into my chest. I can't breathe. Can't think.

His gaze locks with mine and those blue eyes darken.

I am completely enraptured by those concentric orbs of blue that draw me in, by the flares so silver, that burn in the depths of his eyes.

Something unspoken passes between us.

Without taking his eyes from mine, he pulls away and steps off the bed.

Grabbing the bottom of his vest he tears it off of himself. All that glorious muscle and hard planes and angles, covered in skin that is rough enough to chafe over my tender flesh. To bring me to the heights of passion which I suspect I still haven't fully experienced.

He kicks off his pants and his cock springs free—large, throbbing, its head an angry red. A bead of precum glistens at the slit. He's never seemed more animalistic as he stands over me looking down on me from his superior height. His nostrils flare, and a deep resonant purr rolls from his lips.

My pussy clenches. Slick pools between my thighs. I draw in a breath and my chest heaves.

His gaze drops to my breasts and color flushes his cheeks. Another growl tears out of him, then he swoops down on me.

He fastens his hands around the sleeve of my clothing and yanks with enough force for the fabric to rip in half.

I gasp.

He peels back his lips and glares at me.

It's almost reassuring to have this feral side of Zeus back. It's as much a part of him as the possessiveness that lurks inside.

As inherent to him as the glimpses of the caring man he's shown me. He's complex, my alpha and…I wouldn't have it any other way.

He drops his head and fastens his lips around the nipple of one breast. When he bites down on the nub, heat travels all the way down to my core. He brushes the whiskers of his beard down the side of my breast, and goosebumps rise on my skin.

"You are so fucking responsive." He growls.

The sound shivers over my skin, and I wriggle under him.

That emptiness inside me throbs and grows and I moan.

"So impatient."

A harsh purr flows out of him, and more slick slides out from between my legs. He trails kisses down my waist and licks my bellybutton. His touch is so tender that I shiver. He grips my hip, and I tremble. It's like every part of me is focused on his touch, his breath on my skin as he kisses his way down to the throbbing flesh at the apex of my thighs.

"You didn't wear underwear." He blows on my pussy.

I groan. "Didn't …" My breath hitches. "Didn't see the point."

"You did it to torture me, so the scent of your arousal would be thick in the air, and so I wouldn't refuse what you wanted." He peers up at me.

"Did it work?" I gasp.

His lips curl. "What do you think? You teased me, pushed me over the edge, little Squirrel." His shoulders go solid. The skin around his eyes tightens and his gaze narrows with intent.

"Wha...what are you going to do?" My stomach flip-flops yet anticipation tugs at my nerve endings. This is it, this is what I wanted. To unlock the monster inside of him. I'd poked at the beast, shoved at it until it had reared back at me, until it was crazed with lust and beyond rational thought. I gulp.

He cants his head, the movement so animalistic, and I know he's sensed my fear.

He settles down between my legs, his head pillowed on one thigh, "I am going to take pleasure in giving you exactly what you asked for." He draws a finger over my belly, making lazy circles all around my pussy.

My body trembles and I clench the mattress with my fingers.

He has me where he wants me.

In his bed, surrounded by him, under him...on the verge of submitting to him. Somehow I can't get over the suspicion that he played me all along. He'd waited for me to come to him, and now he wants me to beg?

He wants me to take that final step, to ask him to take me and put me out of my misery, to show that I have accepted him as my master, and something inside me refuses to give him that satisfaction. Yet.

A snarl rips from him then he thrusts a finger inside my wet cunt. The shock of it whips over my skin, all the way to my toes.

I squeeze my eyes shut and refuse to meet his gaze.

To do so will be to show him exactly the effect he has on me.

He lowers his lips close to my clit and purrs. The heat of his breath sinks into my tender flesh. The vibrations of his tone shudder over my skin, my womb contracts, and a fresh burst of slick gushes out of me.

He positions his face at the opening of my channel, then proceeds to lick up all my cum, every drop of it, before rising over me and kissing me.

He thrusts his tongue inside my mouth, and I can taste myself on him. It's so fucking hot.

He buries his fingers in my hair and tugs my head back so I have no choice but to open my eyes and meet that hot, burning gaze. It's everything I expected. The way he eats me up with his eyes.

My belly clenches, my sex quivers, and a whine dribbles from my lips.

His nostrils flare and he answers my unspoken plea with a growl.

I sense the pulse of desire that runs down his body. His shoulders flex, and his chest muscles ripple as if there is an unseen force inside that's eating away at him. "You will give in to me completely." The hushed edge to his tone sinks into my blood. The mating cord in my chest thrums. The command in his voice grates over my skin, propels through my veins until it seems to infiltrate every cell in my body. My breath catches in my chest.

His biceps bulge, a vein throbs at his temple and every muscle in his body seems to coil with tension.

Anger and lust and a brutal singlemindedness vibrates off of him. I shiver, and delicious need coils low in my belly. Heat plumes off of him and slams into my chest. Sweat breaks out on my brow. The weight of his dominance pins me down, the fine hair on my body rises and I can't move. Can't breathe. All I can do is wait for his next move. Wait. He is going to possess me and I can't stop it. I don't *want* to stop it. Tears prick at the back of my eyes.

He peels back his lips as if acknowledging the effect he has on me. Demanding it, taking it as his due.

He lunges down my body then fastens his mouth over the bud of my clit. "Zeus." A scream tears out of me.

He thrusts his tongue inside of my soaking wet channel and my body bucks.

He rubs the heel of his hand against my cunt, and sparks of pleasure shoot up my spine.

I bury my fingers in his thick hair. I cradle him close as he proceeds to lick and suck me, while his clever hand keeps up the friction on my clit. The climax sweeps up from my womb.

Waves of pleasure rip through me. I arch my back and raise my spine off of the bed. Red and white sparks flare behind my eyelids. My muscles quiver. It feels like my body has been stretched to its limit. All the fight oozes out of me. My limbs spasm and a trembling grips me.

All I can do is lay there as he pushes off the bed. He rises to his feet and towers over me.

"All that sass and fire; all of it is just a front. This is what you want—just sheer pleasure so you can forget to fight, forget everything except the need to open yourself up to me, to obey me so I can give you what you crave." I hear his words and know he is right.

"You want more, don't you, Squirrel?"

I blink my acceptance, unable to speak anymore.

"Do as I say, and you'll get it all, everything." He grabs the base of his heavy, swollen dick. "Even this."

89

Zeus

I want to be gentle with her, but one look at her, and all I can think is how I want to teach her a lesson for disobeying my orders. One scent of her, and I need to own her, possess her, destroy her. I want to be buried balls deep inside of her, until I forget everything except her.

She looks at my dick, and her lips part. Her pink tongue comes out to lick her mouth.

I feel it all the way to the tip of my shaft.

A growl rips out of me. The purr rolls over the space between us.

A visible shudder ripples over her body. Her thighs squeeze together, and more moisture streams from her pussy.

That sweet, sugary scent of her arousal is everywhere. It sinks into my blood, goes straight to my head. My dick throbs, and I grip the base harder.

"Get up," I rasp.

She raises her heavy eyelids, and when she peers up at me, her pupils have dilated. The black has bled out into the green, and she looks drunk with desire. Almost as gone with lust as me. It's that which tips me over the edge. I need to have her, but first she must understand the consequences of disobeying me. She put herself in danger again, and I cannot permit that. Ever.

"Up." I jerk my chin.

She winces, and her chest heaves. Her biceps twitch as she pushes herself to sitting position.

"On your feet."

Her gaze widens, but she doesn't protest. She pulls up her legs then sidles up to her feet, on the bed. Her eyes are at chest level with me. She's at the perfect height for what I have in mind. "Turn around."

She opens her mouth—

I shake my head. "You don't get to speak. You don't get to say anything. You defied my orders, and now you must pay the price."

She pouts and one side of my lips curves up in a smirk. I trail my fingers over my chest, down to where I grip my shaft with my other hand.

Her gaze follows my every move.

"You want this, don't you, Squirrel?"

Her breath rasps out. She nods.

"Do what I tell you. Take your punishment like the warrior you are, and you will be rewarded, I promise."

As I say it aloud, I know I am using words to cover for myself, for my emotions, for how raw I feel right now. Yet I can't stop.

"Do it." I growl again, and the sound rends the air and surrounds her.

A shiver ripples down her back. She turns on her heels.

"Open your legs."

She parts her thighs.

"Farther, Squirrel."

Her leg muscles tense, then she shuffles her legs wider.

The scent of her slickness deepens, and I harden further. I slide my hand up my dick to the tip and back. Blood rushes to my groin. "Now bend over and grab your ankles."

The planes of her back go solid. She doesn't move.

"You disobeyed me over and over again. You went toe to toe with me, knowing exactly what you were doing. Now do as I say, and we'll call it even." As the words leave my mouth, I know I have said the right thing.

I am treating her as my equal, not just in a fight but also in bed. I am appealing to that fighter in her, to play as rough as me. I am challenging her to take her punishment as she's challenged me all this time.

"Go on, Squirrel, you can do it." My voice is soft. The realization that I am dealing with someone who is every bit as strong, as willful as me, has changed the dynamics between us.

Is she aware of it?

I'd set out to make her submit to me but what I want is more. I want her to accept me. Need her to trust me enough to give herself up to me completely. Body and soul.

The muscles on her back bunch. The backs of her calves flex.

Waves of desire roll off of her.

She wants me. Wants to give in to me fully, and yet there's something inside of her that cannot, not until I say, "Please?"

No sooner is the word out of my mouth than her shoulders hunch, her head drops forward. She nods. Then, bending over, she grips her ankles.

Her perfect, heart-shaped ass rises. I see the succulent flesh of her pussy quiver between her legs.

I groan. "You should see yourself, Little Squirrel. So pink, so enticing, so bared for me."

She wiggles her butt; the muscles of her thighs ripple under her skin.

I shift closer to the edge of the bed, near enough for the warmth of my body to brush over her skin.

She shifts her weight from foot to foot.

I drag a finger over her ankle, up the back of her leg, trailing it over the inside of her thigh and to the swollen lips of her pussy. I pinch her clit and a moan spills from her.

She gnaws on her lower lip and a pulse of heat slithers down my spine. Leaning up, I blow softly on that wet center. Her entire body goes stiff. Her core tightens. She snarls low in her throat.

An answering growl rumbles up from me, and with it the need to see her come again.

To see her shatter until all the resistance in her dissolves and she lays herself bare and open for me, only for me. I cup the curve of her butt and massage it.

She shudders and moves her head. Her glorious hair streams down, covering her face.

"It strikes me, Squirrel, I should complete what I started before I left you the last time."

90

Lucy

Every part of me goes tight with anticipation.

My face warms, and I clench my butt cheeks. A shiver ripples down my back.

He won't, will he?

I almost voice the word aloud, then bite my lips. I am often spontaneous, aka stupid enough to be fearless, but if I push him this time, I may not be able to deal with the repercussions. He's skillful all right, my alpha.

He knows that the only way to make me comply of my own volition is to challenge me. It's that part in me that can never say no. Not to a fight. Not to this...duel, either. And not to him. I can't refuse him. I want to please him with every fiber of my being.

At some point, the tone of our mating changed.

It's gone from him wanting to make me submit, to *me* wanting him to make me submit... and it feels right. Huh?

I wait, watch, wondering what he'll do next. How far will he go?

The last time he'd said those very same words, he'd not gone through with it. This time I know he will not stop. And it's not about him teaching me my place. I pushed him to lose control and now he's asking the same of me. To give in and trust him.

I want to say something but I can't. So I stand there, bent over, waiting for him...waiting.

There's silence behind me. I sense his warmth, smell his presence, but he doesn't make any other move.

The moments stretch, and my scalp prickles, my fingers tingle with need. The blood rushes to my head, and I sway.

I'd have fallen except he grips my hips and kisses the curve of my ass. "I am going to take you every way." He nibbles on my butt and heat bursts over my skin. I gasp.

"That's right Squirrel, you are going to take it all and you are going to enjoy it as I pleasure you. " He kisses the sweep of my ass and I tremble. "Fill you up." He licks the dip between my ass cheeks. "Fuck you." He sinks his teeth into the flesh of my butt and I howl.

I want him to take me there, I do, but a part of me is scared of it, too.

Not just the pain that is sure to come, but the pleasure.

I am sure I will like it all too much, and that's worse. It holds up a mirror to what I am, ultimately. An omega who craves her alpha, wants him in every way possible. If he takes me there, too, he will own me completely. There will be nothing left of me. There will only be Zeus and his omega.

Will that be so bad?

The bed dips as he leans his full weight on it.

He comes close enough for his chest to brush the backs of my legs. He slides his arms up and around my back, holding me, covering me completely with his warmth. The heat from his big body surrounds me, and strangely, I find myself relaxing. Something inside me melts.

I open my mouth to speak, then hesitate. He'd told me not to say anything, but he'd forgotten there's more than one way of communicating between us now.

A smile curves my lips.

I reach out through the mating bond and pulse my thought at him. *"You can take me that way, too, on one condition: you never again put up this barrier between us on the mating bond."*

Every muscle in his body coils, and tension radiates off of him, and anger… There is complete silence. Then he chuckles. The rough sound glides over my back, and I shiver. A flood of heat comes down the bond and fills my chest. It overflows my cells and engulfs every part of me, until my muscles relax completely.

He purrs low in his throat, the sound deep, rough, and 100% prime alpha male. The vibrations sink into my blood, and coil in my womb. I can't stop the stream of slick that slides down from between my legs.

"So we have a deal?" He kisses the curve of my butt again, the touch tender, so tender.

My insides clench, and my pussy trembles. Does he want me to beg? I thrust my hips back at him, and he growls again. The sound seeps into my blood, and I tremble. My skin twitches with anticipation and sweat beads my upper lip. I dig my fingers into my ankles, waiting, waiting.

He dips his head and licks my slit all the way up to the space between my butt cheeks to my back hole.

The sensations stretch through me, radiating out from my core, tightening my insides.

I can't stop the mewl that escapes me. And it seems to urge him on further.

He darts his tongue into my hole. I wriggle my waist, not sure if I want him to stop or to continue.

He curls his tongue and thrusts it in even deeper.

The sensations pin and needle down the backs of my thighs, down my legs, and I shudder. I dig my toes into the mattress.

He plunges a finger into my pussy, pushes it into my wet, dripping channel, then slides another digit inside of me.

My entire body tenses, waiting, waiting for more. More. A groan draws out of me.

"Soon… I just need you to be ready for me." His voice is rough, and that sends me over the edge.

"Take me, Alpha. Do it," I pulse the thought at him.

His big body stills.

"Now." I growl the word aloud, not caring that I have broken his rules, that he may punish me for it.

He drags his fingers out of me, taking the slickness with it and smearing it up and over my back hole preparing my body to take him in.

My toes curl and a shudder runs down my spine.

Straightening, he pushes my ass cheeks aside with his hands and brushes the head of his shaft over my puckered hole.

My head reels with the strangeness of the sensations that course through me. Fear, need, lust, and above all, a primal instinct to show him I can match him step for step. I lean back and into him, so the backs of my thighs curve over his legs. My butt slots into his concave waist.

"I can't hold out anymore, Squirrel." He nudges the tip of his shaft inside of me.

91

Zeus

The throbbing head of my cock slides inside her puckered hole, and her walls clamp down on me. My balls harden.

"So fucking tight," I growl, "you're driving me out of my mind with need."

She shudders, and the scent of her arousal deepens. That sugary smell rocks through me, and my dick pulses inside of her.

I grit my teeth and hold on to her hips, wanting, needing to go slowly. "I don't want to hurt you, Squirrel." I pant.

"You won't." She rocks her hips back, and I growl.

"I didn't give you permission to speak."

"So punish me, Alpha—"

I nudge my shaft in just another millimeter and she gasps.

Sweat beads my forehead and I try to slow down further. Not yet, not yet. The deep purr builds up from my center, rolling up and flowing over her.

Her shoulders draw down, a moan dribbles from her lips. She relaxes her butt cheeks and I slip in all the way.

Her tight walls close in on me, sucking me in.

Heat flushes my skin, and the sheer pleasure of being so deep inside of her sweeps over me. The climax builds, tugging at my groin, and I know I need to slow down.

I want her to enjoy this.

Pulling her hips back, I bend over her, covering her back with my chest. Then slide my hand around her to play with the wet folds of her pussy. "You are dripping with need, so ready for me, my love."

A-n-d, the endearments pour out. Is that me? That overcome with emotions man who's found his mate, his world?

It's not in me to share my sentiments so openly.

But with my dick balls deep inside of her ass, as I thrust my fingers into her weeping cunt, as the shock of it sweeps over her and she raises her arm to loop it around my neck, holding on to me as she moans, I know I'll never meet anyone else like her.

She is it for me.

Why did it take me so long to realize that?

This omega who came to kill me...who is killing me all over again, only it's with her touch, her scent, her sweet core that pulses slick over my palm, while her back hole expands and I slip in, all the way in. So deep that the touch of her warmth jolts me to my center.

The sensation is so intense, the need to hold her closer grips me.

I raise my head, run my tongue over the nape of her neck.

She shivers. Goosebumps pop over her skin. I sink my teeth into her shoulder, holding on.

My balls draw up but I can't come, not yet.

I shove another finger into her pussy, and a third, hooking it inside her wet channel, hitting that bundle of nerves inside which I know will drive her crazy.

She presses her shoulders back, pushes up her breasts, and screams. The climax sweeps over her and her body bucks.

I pull out of her, then straighten.

I hold her arms and raise them before swiveling her around to face me. I grasp her waist and swing her up.

Her arms twist around my neck. Her head lolls on her neck. Pulses of the aftershock of her climax rock her shoulders.

"Look at me, Lucy."

She cracks those heavy eyelids open.

The black of her pupils has completely bled out into the green. She looks like she's been sucker punched, like she's high on me. It's exactly how I want her to be. I aim to keep her addicted to me, by my side, where she has no choice but to keep coming back for more. A hit of me, a taste of me. I'll keep feeding it to her, until she is so attached to me, that she'll never want to leave.

I raise her, then lower her onto my shaft. Her gaze widens, and color surges to her cheeks.

"Zeus..." Her voice is slurred.

"That's me, Squirrel, your mate. The only alpha who'll ever knot you and breed you. Only." I slam into her pussy, all the way to the hilt. "Me."

Her entire body shakes. She holds my gaze, and the black in her eyes swirls; she's feeling everything I am doing to her, and I can see its effect on her. It's like nothing I have experienced before. This complete abandonment with which I want to take her. No one else has seen me stripped this bare. And I know then, I cannot deny her that last part of me.

I open my heart, my soul, my very essence, and let all of it pulse down the mating bond to her.

She gasps, the skin around her eyes tightening. "I love you."

I lower my forehead to hers. "I can't live without you Lucy."

And isn't that a fact?

This need that courses through my veins, the emotion that blocks my throat, the way my chest tightens, my ribs ache, all of it points to only one thing—how much this omega has won me over. The thought of it is so freeing, a weight rolls off of my shoulders.

Blood rushes to my groin. My shaft swells further, and my knot locks into place behind her pelvic bone. It feels so right, so fucking good, that I can't hold back anymore. My butt clenches, my balls ache. The climax crashes over me. Streams of hot cum shoot out of me.

I am dimly aware of her digging her heels into my back and yanking me closer.

Then my legs weaken, and I lower her to the bed.

92

Lucy

He covers my body with his, pinning me down with his weight. I groan.

His muscles bunch. "Am I hurting you?"

"Yes."

He makes to raise his shoulders from mine, but I tighten my legs about his waist. "But in a good way."

A growl rumbles up his chest. "You're a tease, my love."

My chest constricts. "And you're...mine." A wave of possessiveness heats my blood. I tilt my head, and my cheek grazes the curve of his shoulder. I bury my nose in his neck. That sheer masculine alpha scent of his goes straight to my head. "I should put my arms around you and hold you closer, but I don't think I have the energy." I yawn.

He chuckles. "I have enough stamina for the both of us." Satisfaction drips from his every word, and really, I should protest. But then he scoops me up and flips positions so I am curled up on his chest. His warmth surrounds me. A hum of satisfaction drools from my lips.

And he's still inside of me.

The man knows how to manipulate my body to give him, *and me*, maximum pleasure. My toes curl. "When you do that, I feel small and vulnerable."

He trails his fingers down the curve of my spine. "Which you are."

"Yeah." I blow out a breath. It ripples over his skin, and the hair between his pecs trembles. "Unlike you. No part of you is weak." I place my palm over his chest.

"There is, actually." He folds his hand over mine and presses my fingers into the skin over his heart. Strong, steady, it beats with resolve.

"Oh?" I rest my chin on his rib cage.

"You…you make me weak."

"You resent it." I know he does, so why am I spelling it out? How is that going to help?

"I did." He lowers his head and gazes at me down that hooked nose.

"And now?"

"Now I realize you are the best part of me. You make me human, remind me that despite everything that happened to me, there is hope for the future. There has to be." He cups the curve of my waist, and his thumb slides over my belly.

"For them." I swallow. The intimacy of the moment as I hold his gaze makes my throat close. I hadn't thought it could be like this, that I could feel so close to a person who I don't know that well.

But maybe that's what the future is about, discovering everything I don't know about him.

"For our progeny." His shaft pulses inside of me. He frames my face with his other hand. "For you. I have to believe that the world will be a better place for all of you."

"*You'll* make it a better place." I set my jaw. As I say the words, a shudder of heat runs down my spine. The hair on my nape stands on end. I believe in him. I truly do. In his strength, his sense of fairness, that man who dwells inside of him, who is often seduced by the need for power, but who ultimately will always do what is right.

"So sure, Omega?" He drags his thumb over my lower lip and pulls it down.

I nod. "More than I've ever been sure of anything else."

"That intuition of yours?"

"Don't make fun of my foresight." I can't resist pulsing the thought at him.

His gaze widens, and his dick throbs inside of me. "It's so fucking hot when you do that, you know?"

"What? Talk to you through the bond?" I flutter my eyelids at him. "Or this perhaps?" I squeeze my inner muscles around his shaft.

He smiles, just a slight curl of his lips.

My belly flutters. "That smirk." I gulp. "It makes me hot, all the way down to my core."

"Does it now?" His grin widens. Those blue eyes gleam.

It's the only warning I get before he slides his hand that was already between us down to rub my clit.

I shudder and can't stop myself from closing my eyes.

"You like that, too?"

"Yeah." I breathe out.

"And this?" He drags out a purr, all the way up from his belly.

The vibrations roll up his chest, over my breasts that are flattened against his pecs, curling it around my sensitive nipples, dragging it up his throat until it spills from his mouth and flows over me.

My entire being quakes.

A pulse of heat floods the mating bond, down from his end, sinking into me, wrapping me up in warmth until it feels like I am floating.

Moisture gushes from my womb to bathe his shaft, and his knot grows bigger, impossibly big until it seems to fill me up more completely than it ever has before.

"Now you are showing off," I slur the words out.

He tips his head down and closes his mouth over mine and kisses me. It's like he's bleeding all of his essence into me, through me, while his knot throbs inside of me and the sweetness that floods the mating bond fills my chest. It flows down to envelop my womb.

He's opened himself to me, no more barriers between us.

I can feel his essence, the rawness of his spirit. He's gorgeous, my alpha. At heart he is that boy who fought for his mother, who wanted to protect her just as he'll protect me. Always.

A burst of love sweeps through me for him, for the ones I carry. It raises me with it, up and farther up, over the clouds, until I see the stars shining and the sun on the horizon. It crashes, and I drift down. My hair streams behind me as I cup my palms over my navel.

I crack open my eyes to find he's watching me.

His lips are turned up in a slight smile. Color flushes his cheeks, and those blue eyes glow at me as if there is a fire inside, as if he's enjoying a secret joke. "How did you do that?" I know I sound awestruck, but I can't help it.

"You like it, hmm?" He smiles, and it's almost sweet and definitely smug.

"That was the singular most beautiful experience of my life," I say, not wanting to hide the truth from him.

"The benefit of being mated, it seems."

"Can we do it again?" I reach up to kiss him, when there is a banging at the door of the suite.

93

Zeus

The sound of the knock jars through my head. My muscles tense, and anger floods my spine. I pull her close to me, cradling her to my chest. No one gets to my omega, especially not now when she's carrying my children.

She wriggles in my hold, and I rest my chin on her head. "I am not letting you out of this bed, not until I know who is at the door."

"Who do you think it would be anyway? Either Ethan or Sol."

I growl at the thought of any other man laying eyes on her.

"It's not like they are going to even glance at me, considering how possessive you are." She yawns. "I am sure you've warned them off of me many times already."

"They helped you set up this whole thing in the warehouse." I set my jaw. "They put you at risk."

"I didn't give them a choice." The dazed look in her eyes begins to clear.

Damn if I don't want to just send away whoever intruded and love her all over again. Keep her wrapped up in my passion, and high on my essence. The primal need to have her skin fused with mine sweeps over me.

I growl again.

She swats my chin. "Don't punish your men for what they did."

"Is that an order, Omega?"

She tugs at my hold, and I let her go.

She sits up with her legs locked around my waist. Her thick hair streams around her shoulders, strands falling over her breasts. I reach around and push it aside, making sure it doesn't cover her nipples.

Nothing comes between me and her.

"Like I'd dare order you around?" She peers at me from under those hooded eyelids.

"Yeah." I huff out a breath. "You *would*, and that's what I am afraid of."

"Afraid? Why?" She props her arms on her waist, and her breasts thrust out. She looks magnificent, my Lucy.

I link my fingers behind my neck. "Because, I won't be able to refuse you."

She bites down on her lower lip, "For a macho alpha, you sure can be charismatic."

"I know." I smirk down at her.

"I walked into that one didn't I?" She huffs out a breath.

There's another knock on the door, then, Ethan's voice filters in. "Sorry, General, I seem to be making a habit of interrupting you…but…"

I set my jaw, "That man seriously knows when he is not needed."

She runs a finger in the space between my eyebrows. "Don't frown, it will only add to those lines that you already carry on your forehead. Not that it doesn't make you look distinguished, but still…"

"I don't have lines on my forehead." I glower.

She snickers.

"Getting too cheeky for your own good, Omega." I wrap a hand around her nape, haul her close, and kiss her.

"General, you need to hear this in person." Ethan's voice is insistent.

"He sounds desperate enough to pound down the door." She flicks her tongue over my lips, and I growl against that beautiful mouth.

"He wouldn't dare."

"No, he wouldn't, not when you are being so moody and grouchy like this. But if you don't go, you'll miss the news, and it must be important to bring him to the door, when he knows we are…ah…" Her cheeks go pink.

"Fucking?" I supply helpfully.

She squeezes her eyes shut. "Thanks for clarifying that. He probably heard you too, and now I am just making it all worse." Her cheeks flush a bright red.

I stare. "Are you actually blushing after everything I've done to you?" Warmth suffuses my chest.

She makes an exasperated noise in her throat. "You have no…no shame, Zeus."

I chuckle, "And you have no need to be shy about us." I circle my thumb over the soft curve of her hips. "I will ensure that my team understands what you mean to me. I am going to introduce you to the Council as my mate and have them swear a blood fealty to you."

She opens her eyes and stares at me. "You'd do that?"

I stiffen. "Did you have any doubt about my intentions for you?"

"You know what a blood fealty means, right?" Her gaze narrows.

"Don't question my intelligence, Omega." I growl.

"It means none of them can rut me, not even when I am in heat and I need an alpha to break it."

"I am all you need." I squeeze her flesh harder.

"They won't dare look at me, let alone think of laying with me." She frowns up at me.

"Exactly." I can't stop my lips from curving.

The tendons of her throat move, and she tilts her head. "It means I am joined by blood to them, they regard me as their own flesh, the closest thing to a sister. It means they have to protect me when I have any needs."

"It won't come to that. I'll make sure I always stand between you and any threat." I raise my chin and wait for her to defy me on this, to ask questions. "It means they swear to protect our children."

She folds her palms over her belly. "I accept then."

"Good." I bring her down for another hard kiss, then grip her hips and lift her up. I slide out of her, and the sensation of my arousal dragging against her wet channel sends spirals of pleasure radiating from my core.

Rolling off of the bed, I hold out a hand and help her to her feet.

"Well, go on, Ethan, what is it?" I angle my head toward the door.

"It's Kayden." Ethan's voice sounds through the door. "He's escaped."

94

Lucy

"And so it begins." Zeus lowers his head and nuzzles my forehead.

Heat skitters down my spine. This alpha...I'll never get enough of him. I force myself to string the words in my head into a coherent sentence.

"You don't seem surprised that Kayden is absconding."

He straightens and stares at me.

"So his breaking out—"

He clicks his tongue.

"You anticipated it?" I stare.

"You don't think I'd have left Kayden with minimal guards if I hadn't wanted him to escape?" His lips curl and my gaze drops to that mouth of his.

That thin upper lip, the full bottom lip that I want to—I force my gaze back to his eyes.

"You want to give him a chance to redeem himself?"

"Something like that; apparently, when it comes to family, I have a heart." He cups my cheek, "I blame you for my attack of conscience, Omega."

"Me?" I blink.

"Since you flounced into my life, I can't recognize myself. You seem to ferret out every last bit of humanity in me. Every whorl of emotion that I have hidden away, you dig it out. You seem to bring out the parts of me that are—"

"The weakest?"

"Unexpected." He growls.

"It's your strength, Alpha." I place my palm over his. "You let your instincts guide you and that makes you the kind of leader that your enemies will fear, and your men will lay down their lives for."

"And I'd throw it all aside for just one more second with you."

"Wow!" I peer up into his eyes, "You are a romantic; you know that?"

His eyebrows draw down, "Is that praise?"

"Like you need any to inflate your already swollen ego." I can't stop the smile that tugs at my lips.

I have never met another man so in tune with his instincts, one who tries his best to hold back his emotions; and yet, they are there bubbling under the surface. Intense, passionate, just waiting to explode. And the person at the receiving end of all that goodness? Me.

He stares, those blue eyes sparkling with a possessiveness that makes my nerve endings tingle.

"What?" I squirm and try to pull away.

He slides his palm to the back of my neck and grabs my nape. 'You're going to deny me the pleasure of staring my fill of my mate?" His deep voice rolls over me.

Heat curls low in my belly and I squeeze my thighs together. "For a dominant alpha you sure know how to say the right things." My voice hitches.

"Not only, Omega." He moves in, closing that little half-millimeter of distance between us as if he can't bear to be away from me, as if he'll always be there wanting me, needing me, eating me up with his gaze, looking out for me, protecting me.

Tears prick the backs of my eyes and I sniff.

He frowns, "You're sad?"

I shake my head.

"You *are* sad." He growls. "Is it something I said?"

No. "Yes." Now why did I blurt the first thing that came into my head? Why do I want to bait this big hunk of an alpha, needing to see how he reacts to my distress?

A slightly panicked look flares in his eyes, his shoulders bunch, his lips twist. "Fuck. I screwed up, didn't I?" He swears, then without taking his gaze from my face, he half turns his head to the still closed door, "You are my Second, you handle this, Ethan."

There's silence, then Ethan's footsteps recede as he walks away.

I stare, "You should go, this is important for you, your half brother, your city —"

"My mate."

"Huh?" My throat closes. He can't mean it. He can't be looking at me like I am the only thing that matters, like I am his sun, his moon and his stars, his blood, his everything.

"You come first."

I swallow. "You're confusing me again."

I'd wanted to be the focus of his attention but no one warned me that it would be so overwhelming.

When my alpha gazes at me like he is going to put me ahead of everything else, including his own life, that I am the cynosure of all his intent, that he is going to possess me... love me...then...then, my hands tremble, my thighs quiver and my knees all but knock together.

"Good." He bares his lips and his smile... his smile is like that of a man who has found his passion, his calling, who's found everything. It's smug and hungry and lascivious. Holy hell! I gulp.

"I... I don't trust that look."

"Excellent, Squirrel, you are getting to know who I am." He bends his knees then lowers his head until his nose bumps mine.

"But I trust you." I angle my head and my lips brush his.

Every muscle in his body goes rigid. "Do you know what it does to me when you say that?" His lips twist.

"N...no." I stutter.

His eyes burn into me and his features resolve into an inscrutable mask. "It makes me want to take you all over again in every way possible, to imprint my touch into your skin, into your pores, your cells, until you are subsumed in me and I... in...you." His chest rises and falls.

My throat closes. My heartbeat ratchets up. Why does the thought of submitting to him again completely turn me on so? My skin puckers. My head spins.

"You ready for that little omega?" His voice is hushed, yet there is an urgency in it that touches something basic inside me.

My thighs squeeze together and I nod.

Color streaks across his cheeks. "Good girl."

Heat flushes my chest. Why does his approval make me feel like I've just been given the biggest gift of all. Him.

"But first you must recover from your exertions, I don't want to tire you out." The tendons of that beautiful throat flex and a vein throbs at his temple.

I reach up to touch it and he snags my hand. "Don't." His voice is harsh.

I gnaw on my lower lip and his gaze drops to my mouth. "Don't do that either." He groans.

O-k-a-y! So I'll do as he commands, doesn't mean I can't initiate some moves of my own, right?

I rise up to my tiptoes and sink my teeth into his lower lip.

A growl rumbles up his chest, heat jolts the mating bond, the planes of his massive chest harden, and his shoulders bunch.

The taste of blood fills my mouth and I lick his lip to soothe away the wound. I try to step back and he applies just enough pressure on my nape to hold me in place.

"Such a wildling and yet, so soft, so small."

My pulse thuds, my heartbeat ratchets up.

His gaze snaps on mine, "Why do I want to throw you down and rut you all over again when everything inside me insists I go slow with you and take care of my children that you carry within you?"

Say something, anything. I open my mouth and a moan wheezes out. Slick pools between my thighs, and that sweet scent of my arousal bleeds into the air.

His nostrils flare, and the blue of his iris' lightens until it's almost colorless and I can see myself reflected in his eyes.

"That essence of yours is going to drive me crazy. Every time I want to behave, want to be civilized, I just have to smell you and—" he brings my arm down and behind my back then slants the fingers of his other hand up to bury them in my hair. He tugs on the strands so my head falls back.

He buries his nose in the hollow of my neck and draws in a breath.

I shudder.

A hum drawls out of him. "So fucking sweet...one whiff and I am a goner."

Another moan whines out of me. There is a fluttering sensation in my chest and my toes curl.

He raises his head and his gaze meets mine. "Your features are burned into my head. I close my eyes and all I see is you. When I am away from you I miss you. When I am with you I want to be in you. Hell, I want to be buried balls deep inside of you when I am not with you." He hauls me close so my breasts press into his chest. "You are turning me into a wreck, Squirrel."

I chuckle and the sound comes out broken. "All the more reason for you to leave and take care of—"

"You. You come first. I must take care of you and—" He drops to his knees and kisses my belly, "them." He whispers, "I wasn't completely honest with you earlier."

"Oh?" I stiffen.

"I know you are carrying twins because—" he peers up at me from under hooded eyes. "Because I sensed them when I reached out to you through the mating bond when you were unconscious and the docs were attending to you."

The sight of this big dominant man, who never bends to anyone...the sight of him kneeling before me, gazing at me with that look of serious intent, with lust and adoration, with the need to share something he's never told anyone before...my heart squeezes in my chest. My pulse flutters. I cup his cheek "I guessed."

"How?"

"Even when I was out of it I knew you were with me. I knew you wouldn't let anything happen to me. Besides the bond between an alpha and an omega can manifest in many different ways. Like being able to communicate via the mating bond and on occasion even—"

"Sensing the presence of our unborn children?" He tips up his chin and brushes his lips over my belly.

Nature has brought us closer to our animal selves and that includes being more in touch with our instincts, more open to possibilities that the physical eye cannot always comprehend.

"I wanted you to know. No more secrets, Squirrel." He drags his whiskered jaw over my waist.

Heat flushes my skin, my stomach muscles quiver.

"Obviously the strength of my dominance had something to do with how powerful the mating bond is between us too." His lips curve against my skin.

"Obviously—" I chuckle, then squeak when his hands come around to cup my butt.

He scoops me close so his face, his lips, the outline of his features are imprinted on my skin. I bury my fingers into his hair but he doesn't stop there.

He drags his hand down the curve of my butt then lifts my thigh and hooks it over his shoulder. His breath sears the soft folds of my pussy and I groan.

He inhales again and my thighs quiver.

His flicks his tongue over my folds and a scream trembles from my lips.

I groan and clutch at his hair, raking my fingernails over his scalp as I pant. "I, I am too sore to take you inside me again."

He licks my clit, then plunges his tongue inside my channel, eating me out, sucking on me, and I shatter. Ripples of pleasure shoot up my legs and crash into my womb. My shoulders tremble, my leg gives way, and I slide against him.

He stands and lifts me up, maneuvering my body with ease. I tease him, "Didn't mean you had to stop what you were doing." Greedy, I am greedy when it comes to my alpha. I want more. I want all of him, I want every second of his time, don't want him to give his attention to anyone else. And I thought he was possessive?

I've gone from that haughty once-princess, wannabe-assassin to a woman who wants to be the object of her alpha's fixation, the nub of his desire, his only devotion. Hell. I cuddle closer to his chest.

He lowers me to the bed and the cool sheets of the mattress brush my back. "You need to sleep and recuperate." He kisses my eyelids shut, then brushes his lips over mine. There's a whisper of a touch on my belly, and I swear he nuzzles my pussy again. A sheet covers me, then his footsteps recede.

Goosebumps flare on my skin and all the heat seems to leave me, sucked away by him in his wake. I crack my eyes open. "Wait."

His face fills my vision, "Should I send Mirela to watch over you while I am gone?" His eyebrows furrow, and he looks so concerned, warmth fills my chest.

"You don't know much about pregnant omegas, do you?"

He frowns, then rubs his hand over the nape of his neck. "I haven't had much experience, but if you tell me what you want, I promise to get it for you."

I rake my gaze over his naked shoulders, that gorgeous sculpted chest, the concave stomach, and lower to that swollen shaft that hardens under my gaze.

"You did say that you were too sore... but if you've changed your mind." His gruff voice pierces the sexual haze that drags at the corners of my mind.

"You should go, your men need you."

He shifts his weight from foot to foot. "You need me more." He angles his body back toward me.

"I'll be waiting here for you here, in your bed." I rub my cheek against the pillow.

"I'll be more than happy to wait here with you." He takes a step toward me.

"Go Alpha, before I give in to my weakness, though there's one thing you can do before you go." I jerk my chin toward the vest he'd discarded. He tilts his head, then his forehead clears.

Reaching down, he grabs his vest, then walking over to the bed, he bundles it up and slips it under my head. The scent of him pours over me. My skin prickles, my scalp tightens, that part of me bunched up deep inside relaxes.

I snuggle into the bed and yawn, my eyes already closing.

He drops down to his knees, then dips his head and peers into my face. "I did wonder earlier..."

"You mean the nesting instinct?"

"I had heard about the need to nest for omegas, but you never exhibited any signs of it. Of course I've never mated before and none of the other omegas—"

"Don't talk about them." I pout.

He rubs his thumb over my lower lip. I suck on his digit, then release it so it slides out with a plop. "The nesting instinct takes ahold of different omegas at different times." I yawn again. "Guess I didn't felt the need before, but then, I wasn't pregnant earlier."

"You are now, very much so," he smirks.

That smile of his, it's so sexy. My heart flutters. "I am."

A low purr flows from his chest, cocooning me, pulling me into his heart.

His gaze widens. "And you feel safe and content enough to build a nest for our children."

"Mine." I smile and my eyes flutter down.

TURN THE PAGE TO READ KAYDEN AND CHLOE'S STORY...

PART IV

CAPTIVE

95

Kayden

In a heat cycle, an omega will do almost anything to feel an alpha cock between her legs. My pulse quickens, blood rushes to my groin. The hell? Have I been starved of pussy for so long that the thought of taking an omega is arousing me to this extent?

I stalk toward the omega harem in the stronghold of Zeus, the General of London. I'd saved his life from the Vikings and how does he reward me? He'd taken over my country and then he'd imprisoned me.

He hadn't tortured me though—*mistake asshole. You should have killed me when you had the chance.* My lips curl. Now I've broken out and you're never getting ahold of me again.

I may be the bastard son of a British general, but it was the leader of Scotland, who had brought me up. Yep, we are half-siblings, Zeus and I, and, no, there's no love lost there before you ask.

Golan, our blood father, had been barbaric in his sexual proclivities, shall we say? I snicker.

No wonder omegas looking for a safe haven had headed for Scotland. Like Lucy, the current General's omega.

I'd sent her to infiltrate Zeus' stronghold, and Zeus had mated her. The bastard found his soulmate thanks to me. Bet he's happily playing house with his little omega right now. My steps quicken. Enjoy yourself dear half-bro, for not only have I broken out of your safe house—surprise— I am going to penetrate your omega harem, literally. My lips curl.

The blood thrums at my temples and my shoulders tense. Clearly being in this space drenched with omega essence is also going to my head.

A scent of lilies laced with the deeper scent of honey...and a touch of something spicy tugs at my nostrils.

My dick twitches. Desire slides down my spine, slow, insidious.

Not any omega...it's the scent of this particular female that's making my head spin.

Only when I step into the whitewashed building do I realize that I have followed her spoor all the way in. I look around. Everything is quiet. There are no guards to stop me? Huh. Is this a trap? Nah! Not even Zeus could have foreseen my breaking out and heading here. I prowl to the staircase and take the steps two at a time.

When I reach the top floor, I walk up the corridor.

The heady cocktail of pheromones sinks into my skin and heats my blood. My skin tightens. Sweat breaks over my forehead, and I speed up my pace. I am running by the time I reach the single door at the top of the corridor. Yes! I gulp in the air, her scent is concentrated here.

My nerve endings spark. My gut churns.

I push the door open, and stepping through, I come to a stop. Shades of green unfold in front of me. I blink, and the rooftop garden resolves into its components. Creepers bearing bunches of grapes line one side of the path. There are bougainvilleas, palm trees, sunflowers on high stalks, bluebells, and there in the middle of the space is a glimmer of water.

I stalk up the path. Stems of roses scratch at my skin and I push them aside. When I reach the sunken pool of water in the center, I pause.

The rim of the pool is level with the ground. There is no one here.

The scent of lilies, spiked with the unmistakable tang of omega slick teases my nostrils. My heart beat quickens.

She rises from the shallow end of the pool on the far side and throws her dark-blonde hair over her shoulder.

The water streams from the wet strands, flows over her shoulders, and plops to the surface of the pool.

She cups more water and pours it over her shoulders.

Her back slopes down to a perfect, heart-shaped ass. Every curve is lovingly traced by her tunic. The cloth sticks to her skin, molding to every contour of her body before it dips into that crevice between her ass cheeks.

Saliva pools in my mouth. My fingers twitch to reach out and squeeze that flesh. To bury my teeth in those lush curves and mark her as mine. *Mine.*

She raises her head to the sun rays. Her eyes are closed; thick eyelashes sweep down to meet high cheekbones. My throat goes dry.

I am in some kind of glass house. The trapped warmth weighs down on my shoulders.

My shirt is already sticking to my back. Sweat beads my chest, but moisture of a different kind leaks from my cock.

She raises her arms over her head and trails the fingers of one hand over the other forearm.

The little tease. Bet she's aware that I am here, watching her. This omega is making sure that I am enticed enough to want to take her right here. The scent of her arousal fills the air, and I can't resist anymore.

I step into the sunken pool and the water drags at my pants. I wade into the tiny waves that lap around my waist.

She hums, a soft melodious tune that ebbs and flows.

A harsh purr rumbles up from me as I match my tone to hers.

Lust beads my skin, sliding to my groin.

My dick throbs with need, and I come to a halt behind her.

Whoever she is, I need to have her now. I reach out to touch her shoulder, when she turns and fixes her gaze on me.

96

Chloe

Amber eyes burn into me. They are golden and brown with flames that seem to rise from the very depths of his soul.

His gaze lowers to my mouth, then continues down to my chest to where my nipples are puckered and outlined against the fabric of my tunic.

He raises his eyes, and I gasp.

Everything I'd seen earlier, that heat, that life, that thrum of need is gone—replaced with a cold brown.

I shiver.

Who is he?

Why is he here?

He drops his hand to his side and curls his fingers into a fist. Does he want to touch me? *He is going to touch me...* Of that, I have no doubt. I need to leave before he does.

I try to move, but my feet are too heavy.

The sun's rays beat over my shoulders and seem to pin me in place with their intensity. Sweat beads my upper lip. A tremor snakes down my spine.

I can't be hot and cold at the same time, can I?

Not unless...unless I am on the verge of a heat cycle? Fear twists my guts.

Yet I hold his gaze. I will not glance away.

This stranger is massive. His shoulders block out the sight of the greenhouse behind him. I don't need to look around to know that I am alone.

My breasts are so heavy, they seem to be full and throbbing and...waiting. Waiting for his touch?

What am I thinking?

I don't know him. So how can I need him with such intensity?

My belly trembles.

A harsh purr emanates from him.

The sound envelops me—seductive, soothing—and is filled with so much promise.

I want to ask him who he is. He must sense my intention, for he shakes his head.

I open my mouth to tell him to leave when he raises a finger and picks up a drop of water that's slithering down my neck.

Pin pricks of heat radiate from his touch. My head spins. I pull back with a start and my calves hit the wall that surrounds the pool.

I stumble and he snakes out an arm and hauls me close.

My breasts collide with that solid chest, and my waist cradles his crotch. He's hard and throbbing. His turgid flesh tents his pants, leaving me in no doubt of what he wants. Me. He wants me.

I jerk back, straining in his hold, but that only pushes the lower part of my body into his.

The alpha peels back his lips, and a deep purr growls from him.

The vibrations radiate out from his center, up the sculpted pecs and the strong cords of his throat to pour out of him. Glorious subvocal notes that weave around me, curl around my shoulders, bleeding over my waist to nestle in my core.

My womb contracts, and slick gushes from between my legs.

Color burns his cheeks, and those brown eyes deepen in color. There's an edge of cruelty to his gaze, a need to punish. It's more than an intention to possess me. He wants to break me, to ruin me and…I… I want him to take me.

I need him to throw me down and slam his shaft into me. I want this alpha to fuck me. My stomach churns. The hell am I thinking? Adrenaline laces my blood. I need to get out of here.

I open my mouth to scream, but he clamps his big palm over my lips.

Only when his taste fills my mouth do I realize that I've flicked out my tongue and licked the palm of his hand—the salty essence of his skin, mixed with a deeper, more complex edge of chocolate. How could someone who looks so dangerous… taste that good?

Liquid lust drenches my core.

His nostrils flare, and the tendons of his throat slide over each other. That's the only warning I get before he lowers me onto the short wall.

The water sloshes over me, slapping me between my legs. My core clenches. My belly flip-flops with nervousness. But underneath it all is this crazy need to submit… no, to run.

I must break the hold he has on me. I angle my body and yank up a leg to try to slide it over the side. He steps into the gap between my legs.

I widen them to accommodate his massive body. His hardness pushes into the apex of my thighs.

A groan dribbles out of me, muffled against the palm he holds over my mouth.

The tendons of his throat bunch, then he slides his hand down and under my dress.

No. I try to shake my head.

Try to tell him not to do this, not to…oh! He slides his finger into my pussy.

A shock of pleasure shoots up my spine.

My nipples pucker, my back bends, and the breath rushes out of me. My entire body seems to tense and wait, wait… His gaze narrows, and he rams another finger, then a third into my dripping channel. He twists his fingers, dragging them along my weeping inner walls.

Red sparks flare behind my eyes. My body jerks forward, and my breasts thrust into his chest. My nipples tighten to pinpoints of pleasure.

He drags his fingers back, all the way out to the opening, then inside me again, this time hitting a spot inside I didn't know existed.

White-hot pleasure envelops me. My head falls back, and I moan. I hear the sound and only then realize he's removed his hand from my mouth.

I raise my eyelids to find him undoing the buttons on the front of his pants. His erection springs free. Thick, broad, and with precum leaking from the tip.

My belly contracts, and another burst of slick slides out of me.

I want to reach out and touch his beautiful cock. Want it throbbing inside of me and…no, what am I thinking?

I raise my gaze to his. I need to open my mouth and tell him no. *No, I don't want this. Not like this.* Instead, all that comes out is a moan. I am not encouraging him, I am not. I shake my head, then raise my hand to his shoulder and grip it so hard that my nails dig into the wet cloth.

Something of my terror must show on my face, for his features tighten.

He places his hand over my palm, then slides it over the V of his collar so my fingers are flat against his chest.

A dense plume of heat swirls off of him, and I gasp.

He draws my hand down his concave belly to cup his crotch.

I curl my fingers around his shaft and find my fingertips don't quite meet over his girth.

I gulp and touch my tongue to my lips.

He leans in close enough for me to see the lines that fan out from his eyes. Golden sparks leap in his irises. A deep purr rolls up his chest.

The subvocal vibrations sink into my skin and warm my blood. My pulse races. Whatever he is doing, whoever he is, I can't move, can't protest. I want him. I need him. He must take me. Now.

I bite the inside of my cheek. Is my first time going to be with a stranger? It's only primal lust, a need, a mingling of two different sides of a spectrum. The alpha and the omega, male and female, two extremes ready to be joined. A moan tumbles from my lips.

His shoulders flex.

He drags my fingers down the width of his shaft, then all the way up to the tip, then yanks my hand to the side. He pulls his fingers out of me, only to push aside my tunic.

Then he grips my waist, angles my hips up, and plunges into me.

97

Kayden

So tight, so wet. Her pussy clamps around my thickening shaft, and I brush up against a barrier. "You're a virgin?" My shoulders tense.

She swallows and tries to wriggle away, but I hold her in place.

"Answer me." I growl. "Is this your first time?"

Her eyelids flutter. "Yes." Her voice is soft and melodic, and it bleeds right into my skin.

My shaft thickens at the thought that I am her first. *Her only.* The fuck? Where did that thought come from? Why do I feel that once I take her I'll never have enough of her?

Why is she so familiar?

My heart stutters.

I should pull out of her and leave. Now. I shake my head to clear it. What am I thinking? This is the perfect way to take revenge on Zeus.

What better way to make my half-brother lose face than to take an omega from under his protection and rut her?

She peers up at me and her pupils dilate. Her shoulders pull back.

The sugary scent of her slick teases my nostrils.

My groin tightens, my balls ache. Will I knot an omega who is under Zeus' protection, under Zeus' roof? Abso-fucking-lutely.

Will I take her against her will? Without hesitation. I could make excuses and say I didn't have a choice, that I was too overcome by lust, but that's not me. I don't hide behind words. I will not hesitate to claim what is mine.

Zeus had taken Scotland. He had occupied my territory and it's only fair that I take what belongs to him: this omega with silken skin, and a scent that sinks into my blood, making my cock hurt.

I pull back and stay poised at the opening of her channel. "Look at me."

I pinch her chin and her eyelids flutter fully open.

Light-green eyes stare at me.

They are so pale that they seem to reflect the color of the water around us, picking up hints of green from the surrounding garden. The color deepens, hinting at her turmoil. I could lose myself in their depths.

Why does it feel like I have been searching for her? It's precisely that which makes me hold her gaze, as I kick my hips forward and pound into her. My shaft breaches her sensitive barrier.

She screams, and her entire body heaves.

My throat closes. Warmth pools in my chest.

It's her first time, she deserves better—tenderness, touches, kisses…none of which I can give her. But I can make this good for her. A deep purr rumbles up my throat. I twirl the notes over her, pulling her close.

I rest my chin on her head, knitting my fingers through her hair.

I gather her close and cradle her. I slide my hand down her waist, over her thighs and urge her to wrap her legs around me.

Her shoulders shake, and she begins to cry.

The band around my chest tightens.

Why does this feel wrong?

It's the wont of an omega to be rutted when in heat. And an alpha's right to take her.

Yet, that sense of rightness that my adoptive father had instilled in me, the one that said I should always treat omegas with respect, protect them, and make sure never to abuse my rights as an alpha, all of it crowds in on me.

But the circumstances are different here.

The only way to get back at Zeus is by hurting his ego. Which means hurting her.

I angle my hips, and she raises her tear-stained face to me.

"Don't do this." Her chin wobbles. "Please."

Seated on the rim of the pool, she barely reaches my chest.

Her heart-shaped face is perfectly formed. Wide forehead, big eyes, pink lips that frame a mouth that is slightly parted. Desire spikes my blood, and something else, a fierce need to protect. Not a surprise, for I am an alpha, after all. The need to safeguard is built into me. For a second I hesitate and I am not sure why.

Perhaps because I don't want to hurt her? But she shouldn't mean anything to me. She's an asset I own…temporarily.

My muscles tense, and color bleeds from her face.

She squeezes her eyes shut, and anger thrums at my temples.

"Open your eyes."

She swallows, but her eyes stay closed.

"Now."

Her eyelids crack open. She stares at me, her lips trembling.

I nudge my dick farther inside of her. Every bump and ribbed surface of my cock throbs. So hot. So soft. So fucking beautiful.

I angle her hips to further ease my penetration. "I will take you and knot you, any time I want to."

"No." The sound bleeds out of her.

"You will do as I say."

She shakes her head, and her pupils dilate.

"Accept what's going to happen to you, and maybe you'll enjoy it."

Her gaze widens, and she shakes her head. "No." The pulse beats wildly at her throat.

"Yes." I bring my palm down to the space between us, then rub the heel of my hand over her clit.

Her entire body jerks. Her breasts thrust up into the air. The nipples are dark shadows against the almost translucent material. Bending down, I close my lips around one and pull.

She cries out, and more of her slick flows out to cover my shaft.

My dick thickens, my thigh muscles harden. I raise my face to hers, then fix my fingers around her nape.

Her eyes flutter open, pupils blown; color sears her cheeks. So fucking gorgeous.

I glare at her and she gulps.

Her soft pussy contracts around my cock and the blood rushes to my groin. A pulse flares to life at my temples, my throat, even in my fucking balls.

"Come for me, Omega," I rasp.

Our breaths mingle. I draw in that honeyed, sugary scent of her slick. My dick lenthens, and my knot stretches the entrance of her channel. A tremor sweeps through her, and she shatters.

Her features tighten. Her nipples pebble. Every part of her seems to flare to life. Only then do I come, shooting hot streams of cum inside of her.

Her climax fades away; her muscles relax.

My knot loosens and I slip out of her.

Her body slumps and I squeeze her hip to keep her upright.

Sliding down to my knees, I cup some of the water to pour it over the triangle between her legs. When I see the traces of my cum on her inner thigh, a surge of possessiveness grips me.

My belly hardens and my dick thickens. I need to be inside of her again.

I turn my palm over so the water drops away, then scoop up the blend of my cum and her slick, rubbing it into her pussy. I sweep up some of the liquid and drag it up her waist, over her breasts. Reaching her mouth, I swipe the mixture over her lips, and she licks it up.

"Alpha?" Her chin trembles.

"Yes, I am your alpha now."

She blinks.

"But, not only." I bare my lips, and the color fades from her cheeks.

"I am your worst nightmare. I am the man your mother warned you about. I am what happens when you find yourself at the wrong place at the wrong time. You are mine now, Omega, and I will use you to get back what is most important to me."

I shove my thigh between her legs and position my shaft at the entrance to her wet channel.

98

Chloe

He kicks his hips forward and slams into me and I gasp aloud. Too much. Too hard. Every throbbing ridge of his massive dick seems to be etched into the walls of my channel.

My pussy contracts. Pinpricks of pleasure radiate from my core.

Bad enough that he knotted me once, why is he penetrating me again? Why had he made sure that I climaxed the first time. I should hate what he did, so why does my body say otherwise?

The pulse thuds at my throat. My arms and legs tingle, and a chill racks my body. Clearly the testosterone-filled presence of this alpha is driving me faster toward the impending heat cycle. I shove at his shoulders, and he raises his head. Amber eyes glare at me.

His chest swells; his biceps bulge. Every part of him seems to enlarge right in front of eyes.

"Let me in."

He growls, and the harsh sound ripples down my spine.

My thighs clench.

A whine spills from my lips. This can't be happening. Why does everything in me lean toward him? Why do I want him to drag his rough fingers down my skin, over my curves?

I wriggle, and his grasp on my waist tightens.

As if on cue my belly convulses. More slick rushes out to bathe his dick. A deep purr rumbles up his throat. Color flares on his cheeks. He tilts his hips and slides his dick further inside of me again. His balls slap against the sensitive skin of my inner thigh. His knot hardens inside of me.

His dick lengthens, pulses, and he locks it behind my pelvic bone. The heat of his body throbs around me, the very air saturated with his testosterone, his dominance a living, breathing, palpable thing that drenches the air in grotesque play.

I raise my arm, and he shoulders it away.

His hands grasp my waist, and he forces me back until my spine is plastered to the ground. My wet hair falls away from my shoulders.

He leans over me, his big body blotting out the sight of the green leaves above, the gray-blue sky between the patches of trees all gone.

All that is left is the sight of his beautiful face, fierce eyes, those gorgeous lips now stretched in a snarl.

He clasps a palm around my neck and squeezes.

"I should kill you for tempting me so. I can't get enough of your cunt, your scent, your sweet essence." A vein throbs to life at his temple. "What are you doing to me Omega?"

The breath thins in my lungs, the pressure beginning to cut off my air flow. Darkness crowds in at the edges of my mind.

A tremor runs over my skin.

I dig my fingernails into his muscled forearm and try to pull him away.

The movement only hardens his dick, filling me up as he shoves deeper into my channel.

A coldness fills my chest; my arms and legs quiver.

He places his other palm on my chest, pinning me down, then curves it around my breast.

He pinches my nipple, and pain explodes across my nerve endings. He lowers his head to the other breast and bites down on the turgid flesh.

A scream bubbles up, only to be caught in my throat. Goosebumps pop on my skin.

He lets go of my nipple then shoves his hand down between us. He pinches my clit, drags his fingers over my folds, and rubs the heel of his hand into my throbbing flesh.

White-hot pleasure sweeps up my spine, and I arch off of the flat surface.

He thrusts his face close to mine. His eyes hold every single strand of my attention.

"Come. Now."

His command sinks into my blood, down to my womb, and a flash-fire explodes out, vibrating over my cells, setting them twanging, sweeping up to crash behind my eyeballs.

No, not again.

My eyes roll back, my entire body goes rigid, then the storm slams into me and I come apart.

Slick gushes out to cover his dick, which grows harder. His knot locks into place behind my pelvic bone.

The sinews of his throat tense. A groan rumbles up that broad chest as he shoots hots jets of cum inside me.

My breasts swell, and aftershocks wreck my body. Darkness grabs at the edges of my mind, pulling me down.

"Stay with me."

He loosens his hold on my throat. I gasp, taking in a deep breath. Oxygen rushes in, blazing a searing path down to my lungs.

I crack my eyes open, and those golden orbs of his fill my vision. Flames flare and roll, and silver spots dart among them. So much turmoil. So much angst. Anger. Rage. This alpha is drenched with the need for revenge. It rolls off of him in visceral waves, crashing over me, tugging me to him. I am entranced. And I shouldn't be. The bastard took me against my will. I will not allow myself to be attracted to him.

I struggle in earnest, pushing, shoving, swiping out with my fist. He weaves, avoiding the hit, a graceful, sensuous move that makes my breath snag. My limbs flail.

He leans down, grabbing my wrists and wrenches them above my head.

"Let go of me, you...you heathen."

Heathen? Can't I think of a better insult? Blame it on my love for historical romance novels. It's those stories that have filled my head with dreams of a lover who would sweep into my life and surprise me. Which is literally what is happening —A sob catches in my throat—just not in the way I'd imagined.

"You will not fight me."

The hushed demand in his voice engulfs me.

A deep purr rolls up from him and twirls around me, lassoing me, and I pant. My mouth goes dry; my pussy clenches.

He leans more of his bodyweight over mine. His cock throbs inside my wet channel. Tendrils of pleasure shoot out from my pussy. "That's it, milk me, Omega, take my cock, for you want it."

No.

No.

I shake my head, and his jaw tightens. He twists his hips, then releases my arms, only to loop both of his hands under my knees. He raises my legs up and over his shoulders, then pins me with those burning eyes, and I swallow.

"Yes." The force of his dominance saturates the air, pressing down on me. I gasp aloud. My head spins.

His gaze narrows and the fine hair on my nape rises. I

sense his intent a second before he leans down. I lean away from him, try to pull away, but his body follows mine.

The hard planes of his chest flatten my breasts. His entire body envelops me.

Too late. It's too late. The words ricochet in my mind, as he buries his teeth in the skin between my neck and shoulder.

Red sparks flash behind my eyes.

A scream rips out of me. The burn travels down my side, filling my chest, coiling there, digging its claws into my rib cage, swirling there, radiating out. *Let me go.* I want to say that aloud and open my mouth, but all that emerges is a groan. Tears run down my cheeks.

He releases my shoulder only to move his face directly over mine. His gaze narrows, a frown between his eyebrows. Then he licks my tears, swirling his tongue over his lips. Tasting me. Absorbing me. He swallows, and a strange look comes into his eyes. A hint of confusion.

Surely I imagined that?

His arm moves between us. And my gaze darts down to find he's grasped the base of his dick, squeezing it. Another stream of cum flows inside, then his knot loosens. His grip loosens. I pull my wrists free then swing my fist at him.

99

Kayden

I see the flash of her fist a second before it grazes the side of my face. So there's still fight left in her, eh? My chest swells.

My dick slides out of her squelching wet entrance.

She swings again, and I tilt my torso.

She pulls back her legs, then rolls to the side.

I move forward, and my knees graze against the walls of the pool.

I grab the side, swing myself up, but she's already running toward the wall on the far side.

Adrenaline laces my blood.

Pausing long enough to tuck my dick back inside my pants, I speed up, my long legs eating up the space between us.

Her white sheath clings to the curves of her back, those rounded butt cheeks flexing under the fabric, and my dick twitches. The fuck? Anger hums over my skin; my heartbeat ratchets up.

I am going to catch her and then I am going to whip her so hard she'll never be able to move again. Not have the strength to crawl away from me. *Why the fuck am I so possessive about her?*

I put on a burst of speed and lunge for her. This time I wrap my fingers around her ankle, and she goes down.

I slide forward, twisting my body so she lands on top of me. Can't have her hurting herself now. Only I have that pleasure. Her curves cling to my hard planes. She's my perfect complement.

Huh? No, I didn't mean to think about her that way. All I meant was that she's light. Barely a handful. Just right to tuck into my side and take her out of here.

I spring up to my feet, holding her captive. She screams out, digs her fingers into my arms, her back chafing over my chest, her hips smashing my semi-erect dick. My thighs spasm; my groin hardens.

"Stop struggling." I growl.

She stills for a second, then writhes in my grasp. I tighten my arms around her, squeezing her against me.

A tremor shakes her body, her legs kick out once, then she stops. "I hate you."

"That's the idea." My lips curve up. "Best you hold on to that sentiment, for by the time I am done with you, that will be the most charitable of your emotions."

Her entire body goes still. Her shoulders tense and fear leaks from her pores. I want to turn her around, peer into her eyes and reassure her that it's going to be okay. *But it's not.* That I am making empty threats, but fuck if that's not true either. The least I can do is not lie to her. I owe her the clarity of my intent.

I swing her up over my shoulder, and she struggles anew. I bring up a hand and slap her butt. She screams. I spank her other butt cheek and she howls. The sound shoots straight to my groin. My dick throbs with the need to slam into her again. What the hell? This is not only about an alpha rutting an omega, there's something more here.

Her beauty calls to me. Her innocence seduces me. Her very essence proclaims that it is my prerogative to take her. Ruin her for anyone else. Make her mine. My breathing quickens. My vision tunnels. Adrenaline laces my blood. Take her, get her out of here away from prying eyes. Hide her away where no one else can see her, smell her, taste her. No one but me. A pulse beats to life at my temples. My heart aches. My balls throb. *The fuck is she doing to me?* I have never been so attracted to an omega before. I shake my head to clear it.

Lust.

A primal need to fuck. Yeah, that I understand. That's all this is: base chemistry between an alpha and an omega. Albeit a very desirable, sexy, curvy omega who's fidgeting over my shoulder, even as I proceed to slap her butt again and again in rapid succession.

I pause, breath heaving. Sweat trickles down my temples, to join the pool water streaming from my clothes.

A quiver shakes her body.

Her thighs squeeze together, and the sugary scent of her arousal rends the air.

The fuck? "You enjoyed that, hmm?"

"No." I sense her shake her head.

"Add dishonesty to your other faults then. One more thing I intend to punish you for."

"What?" She screeches out.

My ears ring and I wince. "Behave and I may let you come when I spank you the next time. That's after I tie you up and stuff your mouth with my cock."

"You sick pervert."

Yeah, that's me.

"I changed my mind. I am going to gag you and make you beg for my dick, and even then, I will not give it to you, not until you show me you are worthy of every single orgasm I can wrench from your body."

"You took my virginity, asshole."

And that had been a surprise. Not that I had taken her innocence, but that she had been untouched.

Perhaps it was why I had decided not to leave her behind? Oh, and to avenge what Zeus did to me, remember?

"Don't expect me to be grateful for that, by the way." I sneer. "Your being a virgin is overrated."

Her body goes still, then she beats at my back with her little fists. "Unhand me you...you fiend."

Fiend? Who uses such words?

"Not until I get what I want."

Not even then, but I am not going to reveal that.

There's time enough for her to find out that her future is mine.

All of her belongs to me. Every single twisted desire in my head is going to come to life, and she is going to be the recipient of all of them, willingly or not.

I need to use her to negotiate my terms with Zeus. Doesn't mean I can't use her body until then. That's all it is. A transaction...which is all one way. The winner is me. Of course, I'll ensure she enjoys her time, too...most of it, at least.

"What do you want?" Her breath hitches.

"For you to play your role."

"What do you mean?"

"Kayden." A roar fills the air.

I growl; a fierce surge of satisfaction tightens my chest. "That, sugar. *That* is what I was waiting for."

I turn around to face the alpha striding across the terrace. On his heels are two of his men. Ethan, his second, on his right, and on his other, a younger alpha, slimmer in build and almost as tall.

"Motherfucker." Zeus snarls.

"Hello to you, too, half-bro." I crack my neck.

Zeus' face reddens.

"It seems you don't have a sense of humor either." I cluck my tongue.

Zeus takes a step forward. His hair snaps around his face, his fists clenched on either side of his body. His vest is on askew, and his fatigues are not zipped up.

"Did I interrupt you?"

Zeus prowls across to the pool and comes to a halt. "You don't want to do this." He folds his arms over his chest.

"You seem afraid." I crack my knuckles, "But then you are a pussywhipped motherfucker, so I didn't expect anything else."

He makes a warning sound in his throat, and I grin. "That the best you can do now, empty threats?"

I take a step back, and another until I hit the wall of the terrace. Behind me, I hear the gushing of the Thames river far below.

Perhaps the omega senses my intention, for she strains over my shoulder. "Save me," she yells out.

Zeus' jaw clenches. His nostrils flare. "You dare steal from my harem?"

"You dare take my city?"

Oh, hey, good retort.

A vein throbs at my dear half-brother's temple. Short fuse and all that.

The tendons of his throat flex, "I did what was needed to put an end to the fight between our two regions."

"Not interested in your reasoning." I feign a yawn.

"Let her go, and we can discuss this like—"

"—Siblings?" I snicker. "I think we're doing a bloody fine job of that. A fight unto the death between brothers. Couldn't get more poetic. Except you have much more to lose now, Z. You're mated and all that, or have you forgotten?"

"Don't bring my mate into this." He snarls.

"Ah, but she's already making you weak, half-bro."

The woman over my shoulder wriggles her tight body. My cock twitches.

"Unhand me." She snarls and fuck if that isn't the sexiest sound ever.

I tighten my hold over her thighs, "We need to work on that outdated vocabulary sweetheart. Makes you sound ancient and I can assure you that from where I am—" I tap the curve of her hip, "—the view is anything but."

The tiny omega kicks out, and her foot catches me in the groin. I wheeze, and not in hurt. My balls go rock solid, that's how much her struggling to get away turns me on. She has spunk, this omega and fuck if I don't find that arousing.

I want her to fight me, hit out at me, scratch me up while she's at it. Gives me the perfect excuse to mess her up. To tame her and show her who is her master. It's going to make the inevitable fucking so much the hell sweeter. "Don't interrupt when the grown-ups are talking, little girl."

I spank her butt and her muscles tense.

"Little girl?" She elbows me in the back and fuck if I don't come right then.

"You called me little girl?" She yells and strains in my hold.

"Saying it as I see it, darlin'." I tighten my arms around her. Not letting this one go in a hurry. Too much free entertainment. I snicker.

"You seem to have your hands full." Zeus' eyes gleam. "You sure you didn't get the wrong omega?"

Fucking sure, not that I am going to tell him that.

"One omega, the other...doesn't fucking matter." I massage the rounded flesh of her ass, and she trembles. "She'll serve her purpose, and I'll dispose of her. I'll chop her into such tiny pieces that you'll never find her—"

Her body goes still. Her muscles tense; fear rolls off of her. Good.

"Unless?" Zeus slaps his palms on his hips.

"You know what I want. Come to Scotland, apologize for what you did to my citizens, then hand my city back over to me."

"Never." He scowls.

"Don't be so hasty. Think it over." I half angle my body away.

"You're the one being hasty. Don't throw ultimatums you won't be able to stick to." Zeus drops his arms by his sides again, his gait casual.

Fucker's sure changed his stance. Why does he seem so laid-back all of a sudden?

I ignore his words. "A week—that's all the time you have." Turning, I jump onto the wall.

"No, Kayden, don't do that." Zeus' voice rises in alarm.

For me? Nah. Not possible.

"Else she dies."

I throw the words over my shoulder, then I jump.

100

Chloe

The wind whistles past my ears, the sound so loud it fills my head with a howl. There's a screeching noise; someone is screaming. It's me. I cling to him, the only solace in a world gone wrong. No…he's not my solace; he's the bastard who got me into this situation. The alpha jumped…he…jumped?

We hit the river, and the impact consumes me. Then the water closes over me; the dank gray Thames pulls me under.

I sink down, dragged by the currents into a dark Hellscape.

Am I dying? I can't see anything, can't sense anything. Except the coldness that swirls around me, sinking into my blood, my cells. My lungs burn and I can't hold my breath anymore, I can't. My throat hurts, and there is a pressure squeezing down on the back of my eyeballs. The water eddies around me. I crack open my eyelids and spot a dark shape headed my way. It's coming at me. Straight at me. No… I swivel away from it. Which way is up? Which way is down? I have never been this disoriented…definitely going to die. Guess it was good I managed to lose my virginity huh? And to the most gorgeous alpha I have ever met, with the thickest, fattest cock. How about that?

Something hooks around my waist.

I open my mouth to scream, and instantly the water rushes in, burning down my throat, filling my lungs, pulling me under…under… Light pours over me, and I draw in a breath, and it hurts. It hurts. My lungs can't breathe any longer on their own. My throat is so raw. I gasp, and water spurts out. More pressure is applied to my back, ow! Is the entire weight of the Thames sitting on me? Pushing, prodding, not letting me sleep. I want to close my eyes and surrender to the darkness…blackness…the water, I am in the water drowning. My eyes pop open, and I see brown…

mud…leaves. There's more pounding on my back, more water spurts out of my mouth…ugh…I am going to be sick.

I cough, and all of the contents of my stomach flush out. I groan. Then hands grasp my shoulder and turn me over.

The world swings around me. I make out the face of a man…him…the alpha who'd knotted me.

"Kayden?" I pant.

"You're alive."

His lips firm.

He's not pleased I made it? Well, not that I am on his list of favorite people or anything. Something heavy in my chest claws from the inside, stabbing at me… struggling, twitching. "Why did you kidnap me?" My chest heaves.

"Well, you must be feeling okay if you are back to being your bitchy self again." He leans back on his haunches.

"You haven't known me long enough to find out if I am bitchy…" I gasp, then spit out more water. "Or not."

The light haloes his massive shoulders and throws his face in relief. The dark crevasses under his cheekbones draws attention to his harsh features. So beautiful. So lethal.. A shiver racks down my spine, and it's not because I am cold. In the deepening dusk, he seems like a monster, a man mountain not of this world. My very own personal nightmare. The alpha who claimed me. He claimed me? Oh my goodness, he *claimed* me. Panic bubbles in my chest and I gasp aloud.

His forehead furrows, "Don't lose it now Omega." He peers into my eyes, "I am not the kind who'd soothe you while you have a panic attack."

My stomach churns. Bile burns my throat and I scrunch up my face.

"And if you are sick, I'll throw you back into the river."

I glare at him and the sickness subsides.

"Asshole."

"Alpha-hole to you sweet one."

"Scoundrel."

"Need to wash out that mouth of yours...and it's not going to be with water."

I blink. What the blazes? What did he say?

My gaze slides down to the bulge between his thighs. Big, hard, throbbing. My mouth waters.

"So you're not averse to what I implied eh?"

My gaze swivels up to meet his. My cheeks flush and one side of his mouth quirks.

He rises to his feet, his movements lithe.

For a man who is at least six-feet-seven-inches tall, he has a feline feel about him.

Bet he's spent a lot of time learning how to blend into the darkness, learning how to take people by surprise, learning how to creep up on unwitting omegas and kidnap them.

"I abhor you."

His left eyelid twitches, "Up." He jerks his chin.

Didn't he hear what I said?

Guess he doesn't care what I think of him.

I am an omega he took. So what if I was a virgin? So what if I had saved myself for…who…? For him? For this unfeeling brute who is Zeus' half-brother. The man who had promised to protect me and my omega sisters but would have handed us over to the Vikings to ensure the safety of his city.

He turns and strides away as I lie there gasping. I try to push myself up and collapse back.

"I don't have all fucking day, princess."

"Yeah, I am a princess," I snarl.

"Right, and I am the Chief of Scotland." He looks at me from under hooded eyebrows, then snaps his fingers. "Oh! Wait, I am." He smirks. In that moment, I truly hate this man.

A low growl catches in my throat. Huh! I am not a fighter, or a warrior. No, I left all that up to Lucy.

When we had escaped the Vikings who had attacked my native Russia, my sister Lucy and I had made our way to Scotland with some of the other omegas.

It had been rumored that Kayden's father was one of the few alphas who respected omegas' rights and never forced alphas on them. By the time we'd reached Scotland he was dead, and Kayden—this monster—had taken over.

Lucy had been the one to appeal to Kayden, and I had never seen his face. But then, she was always the leader, the warrior. Not me.

I am an honest-to-goodness breeder omega, one of the few of royal blood. I had saved myself for my alpha, my soul mate, had only wanted to have babies, to marry the prince of my dreams, for hey, I am…*was* the second princess of the Russian royal family, until the Berserkers attacked and everything went to hell.

Kayden sent Lucy to assassinate Zeus, but she failed.

Lucy had mated Zeus instead.

Zeus had overthrown Kayden and imprisoned him.

And it should have ended there, except Kayden had escaped, and things have come full circle.

I have landed back in the hands of this man who will trade me in, given a chance, who will kill me without compunction. Unless I am smart. Strategic. Maybe some of the lessons I learned at my father's court will come in useful. Already some of the fighting skills he'd drilled into me had allowed me to escape after the alpha had mated me.

Tears knock at the backs of my eyes.

I will not give in to the fear, to the tiredness that drags at my limbs.

He doesn't know who I am, and I am going to keep it that way. In this situation, the more I can keep from him, the more I have to work to my advantage.

I raise my head. "You sure don't look like a leader." I rake my gaze over his massive shoulders, the torn and muddied shirt that clings to those sculpted planes of his chest, to the concave stomach and don't look down. Don't. My gaze slides further to where his pants tent. I gulp. Is the bulge bigger than before?

A cloud of heat spools off him and slams into me. The musky scent of his arousal fills the air and I gasp. How would it feel to taste him? Feel him pulsing inside me and filling me again? My pussy throbs and saliva pools in my mouth. The hell am I thinking?

He took me without asking for my consent remember?

I definitely don't want to taste him. I don't.

Had he purposefully planted that thought in my head?

I raise my gaze to his face, and catch him staring. My cheeks redden.

"You can't lie to save your life." The alpha-hole smirks. Then his lips smash together in a straight line. "Get the fuck up." He snaps his fingers. "I won't ask again."

The hushed dominance in his voice sweeps over my spine and tugs me up.

I look down to find I am standing. Oh, hell. He is so macho, so full of himself, so commanding... everything in me insists that I follow him.

That I throw myself on the ground, part my thighs, and ask him to mount me again and again. I don't want to submit to my base nature. And not to the man who has no respect for me.

He glowers at me. I shiver.

He jerks his chin, and I straighten my spine.

Perhaps it'll get easier if I play the role he demands of me? What if I pretend to be an omega who has given in to her needs? What if I take what he is offering? Can I use him to find my release?

I hold his gaze and walk over to him.

My knees tremble, but I keep moving. Put a little twitch into my hips, thrust my breasts out, and make it to him. I place my fingers on his crotch, and his pulsing length fills my palm.

His hips thrust forward, and I curve my fingers around his rigid shaft. Hot. Throbbing. So full of life. My throat closes. My breathing quickens.

His eyebrows slash down, and I almost keen with anticipation.

A growl rips out of him, and I can't stop the whine that bleeds out of me in response.

If I don't hold on to that secret part of me, I will have submitted to him before the night is over. And while that may be inevitable, I plan to hold on to some shred of my dignity every step of the way.

Which means I will do this...but on my terms.

I place my hand on his massive dick, and one side of his lips curls. "So, you've finally come to your senses?"

He folds his palm over mine and squeezes my fingers around his shaft. The shape of him is full and hard. The length of him is so enticing. Moisture pools between my thighs.

His chest swells; the cords of his throat move.

"Take it out."

"What? Here?"

I look around at the water of the Thames behind us, the banks beyond, and the building that marks the complex from which we escaped.

"Don't make me wait."

His free arm snakes out and grabs the nape of my neck. He firms his grip, and I part his already undone fly. His dick springs out. My gaze drops to his cock. Long, angry. The head is already purple and looking up at me. Moisture beads the slit.

"Touch it."

I fold my fingers around his dick and his thigh muscles flex. I scoop up the mixture that beads the head of his dick, then bring the moisture to my lips and lick it.

A low snarl rends the air.

"Fuck this."

He presses down with his fingers. I sink to my knees in the muddy sludge until I am at eye level with that monster cock.

Up close I can see the vein that runs up the back of the shaft.

I fold my fingers around his dick, and they barely meet around the girth.

It's bigger, more imposing than I had thought...and that...that thing has been inside of me. I swallow. No wonder it had hurt. He had filled me up and fucked me senseless.

A trembling sets off in my belly.

His dick lengthens further in my grasp. "How is it possible you are aroused after that near-death fall?" I jut out my chin. "Or maybe it's *because* of the experience that you are turned on? Does jumping into a river with a helpless woman in your arms make you feel all macho? Or maybe it's because you fucked me against my will? Bet that was a notch in your already-long list of accomplishments?"

His jaw hardens. "Less talking, more putting that mouth to use."

If he puts his dick in my mouth, I am going to —

"Don't think of it." He scowls. "If you bite me, I'll make you suffer so much you'll regret the moment you set eyes on it."

"I regret it already. I —"

He grabs my hair and tugs. My head falls back, my mouth opens, and he shoves his cock in.

Hot. Pulsing. So full again. My pussy clenches even as I cough.

My senses are full of him, tangy, salty, the skin so soft, and underneath it steel, throbbing life.

His cock slides over my tongue, bumping against my teeth, and he groans.

I peer up at him from under my eyelashes to find the skin pulled over his cheek-bones. His chest rises and falls, his gaze locked on my face.

I pull back then flick out my tongue and curl it around his flesh, and his shoulders twitch.

I close my lips around his dick and suck, and a growl rocks his chest.

I have never given head before but heard it described by the other omegas. That, and something insane inside of me directs me to squeeze my fingers around his cock and swallow.

He draws in a breath. "Fuck." His other arm drops, and he cups the back of my head. "Take me in."

He yanks me forward so his dick slides in and stabs at the back of my throat. I gag, tears spring up and run down my cheeks. He lets go of my hair long enough to scoop up a drop and bring it to his lips. He sucks on it. A strange glow comes into his eyes, then fades away. The planes of his face harden, and a shutter seems to close his features. His hand descends to the top of my head.

He lets go of my hair only to grab my nape. He pulls me forward, and again. With each move his dick slides down my throat. He goes at it, using my mouth to pleasure himself.

I am another omega who can give him what he needs. How many others has he fucked before me?

My belly clenches and a slow burn starts in my chest. Why should I feel jealous? No way. Not after how he took me.

The man's forcing me to give him a blow job, and all I can think is I can't bear to have anyone else near his dick. I swallow, taking him in farther down my throat. My gag reflex kicks in, and I choke.

A low purr ripples up his chest.

He squeezes my nape and I peer up at him from under my eyelashes. A muscle tics at his jawline. Color reddens his cheeks.

I must be doing something right for he's enjoying it.

I raise my other hand and grab his hip. My touch seems to fire him up. He yanks and tugs and shoves me back and forth, back and forth, until his dick lengthens, his breathing goes harsher.

Spit dribbles from my mouth, flows down my chin. Fresh tears leak from my eyes, but he doesn't stop.

His chest heaves; his hips jerk. He bites down on his lower lip, and the sight of his white teeth digging into that full, plump flesh sends a fresh burst of slick flowing out from between my legs. The scent of my arousal sugary, sweet, envelops us.

His nostrils flare, then his dick pulses, and hot cum shoots down my throat. It fills my mouth and overflows, and still he keeps coming. It's too much. I gasp, choke, and he doesn't let go. My body sways, and I grab his hip for purchase.

He holds me right there, daring me with his gaze to move away. Bastard. I fucking hate the hold he has on me.

There's a sound behind us, footsteps pounding up the riverbank. My shoulders jump, but he doesn't stop.

He restrains me, until I swallow down the last drops. Only then does he release me.

I open my mouth, and his dick slips out, still partially erect. What the hell, is he still aroused? Are all alphas this way? How long can he keep going?

I sit back on my haunches, and my butt lands in the mud with a wet plop

The taste of his cum...tangy, with an underlying hint of something else...a dark edge that is quintessentially him. The scent of him fills my senses. I flick out my tongue and lick my lips, and his gaze narrows.

More footsteps sound, closer, and I look over my shoulder, peering into the darkness. Zeus' men are no doubt right behind us, and he fished me out of the river, then couldn't wait for me to give him a blow job. Here. Either he's insane or he gets off on danger. Probably both. Sick fuck.

He snaps his fingers, and I swivel my head back to him. I hate it when he does that.

He grabs my wrist and breaks into a run.

101

Kayden

I plow into the undergrowth, not looking back.

I had been harsh to her so she'd stop feeling worry for herself. And no it wasn't empathy; I needed her to keep fighting, it was no fun if she didn't.

That blow job threat? It had been to provoke her. Hell, she was a virgin, I'd expected to intimidate her into doing what I wanted. Instead she had stared at my dick like she wanted to eat it. Then she'd grabbed my cock and fuck... all thought had spilt from my head. Yeah I had come close to spilling myself right there in my pants. It's why I had pushed her to the ground and then the way she had sucked and swallowed and taken me all the way in it had made me want to throw her down and slam into her all over again.

Her green eyes shining up at me, her mouth wrapped around my cock, her tongue sliding around the tip...She had to have practice in doing it. My shoulders tense.

Who had she done it with? How dare she have touched any other alpha except me? My chest hurts. A hot need coils low in my belly. Why do I feel this possessive about her? She's only the means to an end, remember? I pick up the pace and pull ahead.

Not caring that she can't keep up...no, not true. I want her with me, and surely it's only because I am all too happy to have my very own personal slave.

My omega, who I intend to use and abuse. I can't wait to be inside of her again.

Can't wait to slide my palm over her soft skin, slap her butt, mark that white creamy flesh, close my mouth around her nipples and tug and bite and lick and suck. I want to fuck her again, knot her over and over until every hole of hers has been taken and filled with me. I'd been her first.

Maybe that's why I'd claimed her?

My instinct had insisted and I had followed it. It doesn't mean anything, does it? I will not be tied down by a mate. Not now. Not when I owe it to my people to free their city from Zeus.

A jolt of fire digs behind my rib cage, and I rub my hand over my chest.

I increase my speed, and she stumbles, then rights herself.

"You're slowing me down, woman." I shoot her a glance over my shoulder.

Her forehead furrows, and her gaze skitters to the side, then back to me.

"If you try to escape, I'll hunt you down, and then what I did to you earlier will seem like I had been easy on you." I turn to go, stop again. Fuck it. I let go of her arm, then haul her up and over my shoulder.

"Let me down, you Neanderthal."

Neanderthal? Really? One side of my lips twitches and I swallow down my chuckle.

"I can walk on my own," She beats her fists on my back.

The patter of those small knuckles sends pinpricks of pleasure down my spine. She'll make for an interesting diversion on the journey to Scotland, where I'll recon with my team who have escaped Zeus, then wait for my half brother to find us.

I keep running, thrashing through the bushes, between the trees. Her body bounces against my shoulder. The hard planes must dig into her ribs and hurt her, but I don't stop. I don't care, I don't. So why do I speed up further?

Only because no way am I giving her up.

I can't let the other alphas catch up with us. When had this become about protecting her, taking her, keeping her, and less about winning back everything that is mine? I shake my head to clear it. The scent of her pussy wraps around me. The sweetness of her arousal seems to cling to my every pore. The skin of my hips where she had grabbed me burns, needing her fingers on my bare skin. Willingly.

The fuck? I don't need her to do anything for me.

I don't care if she's willing.

She is mine to use as I want.

Mine to take as I need.

My pussy. My cunt. That is all. My breath heaves; my lungs burn. I need to rut her and get her out of my system.

I burst out of the forest and onto the road leading away. And on the side is a parked SUV. Next to it a man taking a piss, his back to us. I keep going. He hears my footsteps, turns, his fingers still around his dick. I bend my neck, charge, head butt him in the chest. He crashes to the ground then starts to rise again and I bring my foot down on his head, smashing him back. He groans. The omega screams and thrashes in my hold. I tighten my grip on her, and moving to the SUV, grab the door on the driver's side and yank it open.

Fucker left it unlocked. Figures. Zeus' alphas are well-trained, but they are susceptible to bodily needs…like me. Yeah, she weakens me. It's why once I am done with her, I will walk away from her. Fucking her and knotting her is a way of pissing off Zeus. So he knows that I can mess with what belongs to him. It's a way of getting back at him.

Yeah, that's all this is.

I shove her inside, pushing her until she has no choice but to move over to the other seat. Then I follow her in.

Tearing the shirt from my chest, I grab her wrists and loop the fabric around them, then thread it to the door handle and secure it. She wriggles around in the seat, and frowns at me. How adorable. If looks could kill, I'd be bleeding on the ground. Still I don't put it past her to try to escape, not that she can, but hey, not taking any chances. I grab the sheath she's wearing and tug. The material is wet. I yank it once more, and it gives with a ripping sound.

She screams, then glances at her naked self.

My gaze rakes over her breasts, down to where her pussy glistens. The scent of her deepens in the air, and my cock twitches. Fuck. Need to get the hell out of here and to a place where no one else can see her, no one but me. I drop my head, and she screams and tries to sidle away.

"I am not going to hurt you."

"You already did."

Yeah, but if she knew what I really wanted to do to her...It would only scare her further, and I'm considerate like that. Better show than tell and use the element of surprise. No preconceived notions that way, get me? And she'll only be more open to enjoying the many ways I plan to take her. Tear up her pussy, take her ass, wrap my fingers around that glorious hair, and shove my dick inside her mouth again. Right before I drag her across my lap and palm her butt, the backs of her thighs, and come all over her. Mark her with the imprints of my fingers, streaks of my cum. Drag my tongue into every nook and crevasse of her body. My head pounds. I start the vehicle, and it leaps forward.

"You don't need to tie me up. I have already shown you that I will come willingly."

I shoot her a glance sideways. Right. I don't say anything, but I am sure my look communicates my level of incredulity. She sets her jaw. Is she going to argue the point? Her shoulders hunch, and a shiver ripples over her skin. She pulls up her legs and huddles into herself.

"You're cold."

"Your powers of deduction are incredible."

I glare at her. "Enough."

She shivers again, then firms her lips.

Bet it turns her on when I command her to do my bidding. Bet if I leaned across and fingered her pussy I'd find her soaking wet. Bet if I keep up this line of thought I'd come in my pants. I tighten my grip on the steering wheel. *Can't you go a few seconds without thinking of burying your dick in that soft pussy of hers?* I force my attention back on the road.

"We'll find a place soon where you can get a fresh set of clothes."

Headlights brighten the interior of the car. The fuck?

I glare at the rearview mirror, then swear under my breath. She'd distracted me, slowed me down enough that I'd let them catch up with us. Never again. Taking my hands off of the steering wheel, I lean around, grab the seat belt, and snap it into place around her.

"What the—?"

I tune her out, grab the steering wheel again, and press down on the accelerator. The SUV leaps forward, and she screams.

I keep going, but the car follows.

Another few minutes, and he seems to be getting closer.

I increase the speed, and the following vehicle accelerates further.

The tires screech, but hold.

I focus on the road ahead, stay on track, pick up the pace, up the next rise, then slow down to nudge the other vehicle aside and brake to a stop.

The SUV careens, then stops so suddenly that sparks trail the wake of my car.

The other vehicle pulls ahead. I step on the accelerator, then swerve to the left, nudging the fender of the car ahead. It crashes off the road and plunges into the undergrowth.

I stay on course and keep going.

Silence descends on the car, except for her breathing. I glance at her face. Sweat shines on her brow, and her knuckles are white where she's holding the door handle. She looks straight ahead, the skin stretched over her cheekbones. Her legs still curled in on the seat, showing the front of her legs. White, creamy skin that is soft to touch. I turn and focus on the road.

"I'll find us a place and get you some clothes."

She doesn't reply. Her teeth chatter, the sound harsh and I set my jaw. She's clearly going into shock. A pulse tics at my jaw. *Yeah, well, you did take her against her will, then dove off the building into the river, made her give you a blow job…* That's the kind of man I am. The man who'd adopted me was someone who'd respected women, who'd drilled into me the need to be different from the other alphas, who'd wanted to usher in a new way of living where omegas were given the same positions as alphas. "Equal rights," he called it.

He'd said that's how the world had been once.

I had believed him, too… I had wanted to be like him, idolized him. The same need to play by the rules, to be the kind of human he was, had caused his death. Killed by one of his own alphas. His closest friend and advisor.

When I'd seen Ethan, he'd reminded me of that double-timing bastard. I'd killed my father's assassin. Had sworn I'd never let another get close enough to kill me. My belief had only been borne out by Zeus. He'd taken my city. I'd taken an omega from his harem…quid pro quo…not.

This was turning out to be far more complicated than expected. But it didn't need to be, not if I simply stuck to my plan. Used her body to assuage my needs, then negotiated a barter with Zeus. Luckily, my half-brother has many faults. Ego is one of them. I can count on that for him to follow me to Scotland, to find a way to get her back. I simply have to regroup with my team before that.

She groans low in her throat.

I look to her and find her shivering. She leans her forehead on her knees, and her muscles quiver. Sweat beads her shoulders. The scent of slick saturates the air.

A growl rips from my chest. "You are going into heat?"

"Good guess." Her teeth chatter, making a sound that tears at my gut.

My belly clenches. My vision narrows. I can't let anyone near her when she's like this. One whiff of the potent omega slick is enough to send any alpha into rut. My dick strains, warning me I am not far from losing control myself. Oh, wait, I did lose it, not once, but twice with her already.

I press down on the accelerator, and the SUV picks up speed.

I need to put distance between us and Zeus. The farther away we are, the safer.

She moans again.

I shoot her a glance to find she has lowered her feet to the ground.

She wriggles her hips, her shoulders snap back and those full succulent breasts thrust out.

"The fuck you doing?"

102

Chloe

His gaze rakes down my exposed breasts, to my core. My feet are flat on the floor, and I rub my thighs together, again and again. I need to fill that aching space between my legs.

"Stop that."

His voice whiplashes over me. Dominant. Demanding. My thighs quiver, and I pause, heaving.

The gnawing sensation in my core only worsens. I curve my spine, and my head falls back. "I need..." I gasp, sliding my tongue out to lick my cracked lips. "Need..."

"You're going into heat?"

"It was a few days away." I choke out the words. "I'd felt the onset, but the stress of the forced..." I swallow. "The forced knotting, then the stress of the escape, it—"

"Sent you over the edge."

I raise my head and shoot him a glance.

His profile is regal. Hooked nose, square jaw, that beautiful neck and below that his cut torso of is bathed in water, sweat and mud streaks. I take in his concave stomach and gulp. One, two, three...eight. He has an eight pack. Who has an eight pack? I've never seen an alpha with an eight pack.

My gaze lowers and oh, wow! His half-undone pants ride low on his lean hips. That 'V' of his torso, is so defined. So this is what the other omegas refer to as a 'man chest' eh? I swallow and right on cue the fabric over his crotch tents, I swear his cock hardens, stretching his pants as I watch. Does my staring at it turn him on?

It must.

My lungs burn and I draw in a breath. The rush of oxygen goes to my head. The world tilts and I dig my feet into the ground for purchase.

"Don't faint on me."

"What?"

"If you do I'll have to fuck you back to consciousness and I don't like to knot inert bodies. Much prefer my omegas conscious and fighting."

I snap my head up to stare at him.

"That got your attention huh?" One side of his lips twists. "Bet you don't feel light headed either eh? And I was just kidding sweet thing. I wouldn't do that to you now." He shoots me a sideways glance. "Or maybe I would?"

Is he as mean as he makes himself out to be? Or is it all an act? I mean no one can be this...this arrogant. This full of himself. This much of an unfeeling brute, right?

A low growl rumbles in his chest. The sound coils around me, tugging on my nerves.

Heat fizzes down my spine, slapping into my womb. On its heels, a streak of cold coils in my chest. My entire body jerks and I moan. Darn it, it hurts. The estrus is creeping up on me.

I squeeze my thighs together, dragging the edge of my elbow down, trying to reach between my legs. "K...Kayden."

His gaze shoots to me. "Alpha." He glowers. "You call me Alpha. That's all I am to you."

"O...okay." Guess he is every bit as unfeeling as his façade. I swallow down crushing disappointment that coils in my chest.

"What do you need?"

The vehicle seems to speed up further.

Good thing there are no other cars on the road. Good thing I am near him. Near all that testosterone. That force of will which thrums against my veins, drawing me in, tugging at me, pulling at me. Urging me to go closer, closer.

I strain against the bindings. "Please." That hated word again.

He betrayed my sister. Stole me from my sanctuary, and I... I can't get enough of him. His cock...that's all this is about.

I drop my gaze to where his pants tent.

The hard column of his shaft strains the fabric. Precum stains the cloth and I lick my lips. I want to hold him, pet him. Take him in my mouth, feel that rigid muscle inside of me, tearing up my cunt, filling me...loving me. What? No. The thought shoves aside the sexual haze in my head. I straighten, breath coming in gasps, and shake my head.

"Changed your mind about asking me to rut you?"

Yes.

Yes.

"No."

Another moan wells up, and I bite the inside of my cheek.

"It's only going to get worse. Think about how easily I could put you out of your misery, when you're trying to give in to your instincts and find every part of yourself shuddering, and wanting to tear out your hair, your skin, your nails." He swivels around to look ahead.

A breath hitches in my throat.

He's trying to scare me. I've only heard about omegas going insane with heat, without medication to ease them through it, or alphas to break their cycle. He's using it as a subtle form of coercion, no doubt to force me into begging him. I won't. I will not.

Tremors flood my skin, pooling in my chest, between my thighs. I want him. I need him. I will not ask him. I will not.

Ask him.

Ask. Ask. Ask.

I drop my head and moan. "Drat you to Hell."

"That's, ah!" His mouth twitches, "drat you to Hell, Alpha."

"Fucking alpha."

"You only have to ask."

"Never." I squeeze my eyes shut. Straighten my shoulders. I have my pride...sort of.

"Or maybe you don't want to be given a choice. Maybe you want me to simply throw you down and rut into you and put you out of your misery, you little liar."

"Not. A. Liar." I hiccup.

The cold digs in its claws into my guts. Am I going to die from this need tearing me up from inside?

Why hadn't anyone told me this? Why hadn't they warned me that going into heat with a potent, muscle mass of sheer alpha male at hands-length is like sweet death? Like every single wet dream rolled into one double-fisted punch that will take every single thought, breath, coherent intent away from you?

I dig my nails into the palms of my hands.

He clucks his tongue, and I flinch.

"There you go again. You have two options. You ask me, and I rut you."

"The second?"

"You don't ask and I still...rut you."

The arrogance of this man. I draw in a trembling breath. "But... I... I thought you said you'd give me a choice?"

"I haven't decided yet. You have a choice until you don't. Maybe I'll lose my patience and take you anyway. Use you, then hand you over to my men to finish off the rest of the cycle, how's that?"

"You...you wouldn't." I stare at him in horror.

"Don't tell me what I can and can't do. It's up to you how this plays out. Satisfy me, be a good little hostage, and perhaps I may go easy." He shoots me a sideways glance under hooded eyes.

Is he lying? I can't tell if he is. He's wiped all expression from his face. Given how he's acted with me so far, chances are he'll carry out his threat.

"Bastard." My teeth chatter. My jaw aches. My very cells seem to be tearing apart. Anything, anything to be put out of this misery. Anything.

"Tell me something I don't know." His tone is flat, and something in it, a twist of hurt maybe, brings my head up.

I look at him, and his chest heaves. His biceps are rigid. Color stains his cheekbones and a bead of sweat trickles down his temple. Eh? "You want me?" I blink.

"I am attracted to you, but don't go making too much of that."

Ego much? You...brute?

He bends to peer through the windshield. Rain patters down, and the wipers flick on. "You, an omega in heat. Me, an alpha who can help you break it." He rolls his shoulders, "You do the math."

"Why did you claim me?"

His fingers clench around the steering wheel, "You don't get to ask the questions."

"You saw me and wanted me. That's when you came up with this insane plan to kidnap me, right?"

"Wrong. Even before I saw you, I scented you. That sugary, spicy, luscious slick of yours drenched the air and pulled me to that terrace. I wanted the source of that abundance of pheromones. Then I saw you and knew I wouldn't stop until I had learned your every secret. Until I had taken you over and over again and ruined you for anyone else."

103

The fuck? Did I say that? Hadn't meant for the words to come pouring out. It doesn't mean anything, of course. *Words.* What my adopted father lived by.

It's what I'm good at too. My gift for talking has allowed me to charm the omegas, to strategize the end of the alphas who stand up to me. It's how I had seized the leadership after my father's death. Twisted lies. Words that can be bent out of shape, made to mean anything. That's what I am good at. The truth…? I have never owned up to myself, until now. Until she'd asked and I'd wanted to lie…but this once the truth will work better.

I have nothing to hide from her.

She's already seen me at my worst. Yet I have never taken another omega against her will, before her. So why don't I feel more regretful about my actions?

I had scented her, had seen her and been instantly attracted to her. There was no way I would have left the Omega harem without her.

After all, we Alphas take. We rut. We demolish. Our base natures demand that. But we also protect what's ours. And she's mine. Mine. *Temporarily.* For a few days; until Zeus tracks us down.

The lights of a house glow in the distance, and I swerve off of the road.

"Where…are we going?"

"You don't get to ask me questions."

She shudders, then clutches at the door handle. No other sound emerges from her mouth. I don't need to look at her to know she is in agony.

I can't claim to understand what it is to be an omega, but my half sister, Reena, had mentioned to me the pure torture it is to face estrus without an alpha rutting her.

She'd managed it thanks to the suppressants that I'd procured for her. The drugs are not easy to come by. Which begs the question, how did this omega manage to survive so far?

I shoot her a glance. Her skin is pale, and sweat stains her upper lip. The strands of her hair stick to her forehead. Her shoulders twist; her fingers are locked together. She chafes her thighs and lifts her legs so her knees are pulled close to her chest again. Under her thighs, the seat glistens. Slick...heavenly slick. My mouth waters. It's only when her scent deepens that I realize that I have leaned in close.

I want to lick up that moisture from under her, right before I thrust my tongue into her wet cunt and tear into her. Fuck. The SUV tilts as the car grinds up the slight incline. The tires catch each rut and dip and jostle us side to side.

Her head hits the window.

The sound sweeps aside all other thoughts in my mind. I need to get her to the house before she hurts herself more. Another bounce, and her head falls back against the seat. She pants and gasps. Then mumbles under her breath. Sweat beads her forehead. Clearly she is in discomfort. Why should that matter to me? So I knotted her, and now she is my hostage. She is my best bargaining chip with Zeus, and that's one reason to make sure she survives this trip, right?

Besides, I'd have done the same for any other omega in need. Yep. That's all it is. I toss my head, then press down on the accelerator. I speed up until we hit the driveway.

The gates are open; one of them hangs off of the hinges. I veer around the winding road, then pull up in front of the house. A light comes on inside.

Leaning over, I untie her from the door handle. She doesn't react. Her eyes are closed. The tendons of her throat move as she swallows.

When I pull back, she moves towards me.

"Stay."

She angles her body and falls across the console between the seats. I catch her, and she moans low in her throat. She rubs her cheek against my hand. No words. Not needed. The need clings to her skin and saturates the air.

"Fuck this."

I drag her up and over to my side, then pull her out and haul her into my arms.

She promptly burrows into my chest, her shoulders, her hair, her cheek, the side of her thighs. She fucking plasters every available part of herself to every surface of my skin she can reach. She moans again and my heart thuds in my rib cage. I need to put her out of her agony. Something primal inside me insists I take care of her.

I stalk around the SUV and race up the steps. As I reach the doorway, it opens.

A man stands there, clad in pants and a long-sleeved shirt. His hair is gray and combed back. His face weathered.

"Marcus." I nod.

"Kayden?"

His gaze moves from my face to the woman in my arms. I tighten my hold on her. The skin around his eyes creases. He's noticed her bindings.

His forehead furrows. "The last I heard, Zeus had you under house arrest."

"I broke out."

Zeus isn't exactly the well-respected leader he is striving to be. He's made mistakes, and many of the old guard aren't happy with how he killed his father and took over.

At least, so I have heard.

Marcus nods and my shoulders relax.

"We need food, shelter."

"She needs more than that; she's bleeding."

I drop my gaze to her and find a trail of blood trickling down her forehead. She'd hurt it at some point. When she banged her head against the window? Is she that fragile? She's tiny, weighs hardly anything in my arms.

Yet, she'd held her own without the kind of aggression I associate with males.

It's a quiet strength, a fortitude that I had seen only in my mother. How she'd confronted everything life threw at her—the way Golan had raped her...the way I had taken this omega. No, not the same thing. My shoulders tense.

This is different. This for the sake of my clan, my people. Who'll never be happy under Zeus.

I don't trust my half-brother to do the right thing. I don't trust him to not kill my people, loot the city, take what is not his...no. My circumstances condone my actions. But do they? Do they really?

"I owe your father, Kayden. You can trust me." He swivels around to walk up a winding staircase to the first floor.

I follow him to the door at the far end, then shoulder it open and stride inside to the massive bed in the center.

There's a skylight overhead that lets in the moonlight.

Marcus follows me, then switches on a floor lamp.

I place her on the bed, and she moans.

"Shh." I touch her cheek.

She moves her head toward me, nuzzling my hand, and my gaze constricts. I straighten to find the man watching us at the entrance.

I tilt my head. "Why are you helping us, and it's not because of my father, is it?"

He drums his fingers on his chest, "I'm not a fan of Zeus, as you well know." A smile ghosts his lips, "Besides, your omega reminds me of my wife. If that had been her wounded and hurting, I'd not have wanted her to suffer."

"Your wife...she's..."

"Not here." His jaw tics. "I'll get the medical supplies."

He walks out of the door, which swings shut.

Her shoulders jerk, and I sink down to my haunches. "Shh. You're safe now."

She turns her face toward me. Her green eyes are glazed with agony. Or is it fear? She lowers her chin and stares at me. Burning sparks flare in her eyes. Her lips part, and she flicks out her tongue to wet her mouth. She pivots the upper half of her body, wriggling closer until her face grazes my palm, then licks the inside skin of my wrist.

Goosebumps flare over my skin. Fuck. I pull my hand back and surge up to my feet. No one is allowed to have that kind of impact on me.

No one gets under my skin. Definitely not her. So why am I hesitating? Why am I moving back and staring down at the woman who writhes on the sheets?

Perhaps she senses my perusal, for she pauses. Bending her knees, she brings her bound wrists down to her pussy and begins to play with it.

104

Chloe

Need him. I need him. Why is he standing there looking at me, when it's clear that he wants me? I stab a finger into my pussy, and he jerks. His shoulders flex; his nostrils flare. His gaze is entranced by the motions of my wrist. I add another finger then drag my fingers in-out-in to my dripping channel.

The wet squelching sound fills the air.

The scent of slick creeps over my skin. Sugary and sweet. I lick my lips.

I rake my gaze over his beautiful mouth, down that glorious chest to the thick bulge that strains his pants. The patch of wetness at his crotch has grown...he's definitely hurting, if not as much as me, enough for me to know that he's exercising a level of self-restraint I don't associate with alphas. Why? Why doesn't he fuck me and put us both out of our misery? Isn't that his job? A snarl drips from my mouth, and I start.

Is that me?

This ferocious, wanting creature who will do anything to get this alpha to put his cock inside of her?

He's more than a foot away, yet the warmth of his body embraces me. That wall of muscle that is his chest calls to me. A bead of sweat slides down between his pecs, trailing a line in the dirt that sticks to his skin, and I gulp. Why does he have to be this sexy? This delicious? This overpoweringly male? All the time I had dreamed of my alpha mating me, knotting me, impregnating me...his face had no features. A faceless, nameless, virile man who'd not stop until I was his. Who'd overpower me, fuck me, protect me. Save me. He'd done all of that. Not exactly in that order either. He'd also kidnapped me.

But he'd saved my life.

Only to satisfy his own ends.

His gaze flicks to the door, then back to me. He swoops down and I gasp and pull back.

He heaves me up in his arms, marches to the bathroom, and places me inside the tub.

"Stay."

Right, where can I go anyway?

Another tendril of heat sweeps up my spine, and I pant loudly. Darn it, I can't help myself. My belly clenches, and I hunch in on myself.

His jaw firms. Swiveling on his feet, he marches out shutting the door behind him. I hear the sound of low voices. A chill rattles my body, and I groan, clench my fists, curl my toes, curl in on myself. It hurts. Damn, but everything hurts.

My body doesn't feel like my own anymore and I am not fully into estrus yet. Every nerve in my body is sensitized. My skin stretches. The blood surges in my veins. Each cell in my body is attuned to him. Every sensation is magnified. Why does everything feel so... so intense? It has to be his nearness that's triggering this cascade.

Another shudder propels icicles through my veins, and a low scream spills from my lips. The chill seems to radiate out to my extremities until my fingers grow numb, my toes...until I can't feel myself. My body...cripes.

I bang my head against the side of the tub, and again. Need something more... more. More of him. Where is he, the jerk of an alpha? Where is he when I need him? I raise my head, and when I slam it back, it hits something soft. His palm cradles my head.

I wheeze, "Alpha."

He straightens, then flicks on the water, which streams over me. Heat. Warmth. The breath whooshes out of me. I lie back to find him shrugging out of his pants. He steps in behind me and slides down so I am held in the 'V' between his legs.

My back rests against his chest. The warmth is instantaneous. It leaps off of his body, cocoons around me. A low purr wrenches from his throat, bleeds into my skin, and I sigh. This...is what I want. This is what I've been missing.

Tremors rattle my body, and I hunch back, trying to paste myself to him. I need more warmth. More of that pine-filled scent of him. More of that cool, wind-touched essence that is uniquely him. More of his arms coming around me, a band of steel across my chest, restraining me. More. More. A sob catches in my throat.

He pushes me to sitting position, and I whine.

"Shh. Just taking these off."

He bends past me and unties the restraints around my wrists. He flings them over the edge of the bathtub.

I sigh aloud. My shoulders relax. I turn over and all but burrow into him. His skin. His scent. The essence of his protection. His dominance is what I need. This alpha is what I crave.

I rub my nose into the hard wall of his chest. Flinging my arms around his neck, licking, sucking biting whatever part of him I can get to. He doesn't protest, simply lets me breathe in my fill of him.

He pulls the hand shower, and flicking the lever, holds it over my hair. His fingers smooth over the strands, washing out the dirt, down my back. His hands trail over my skin, the curve of my hip, the flare of my butt, down to the sensitive underside of my thighs. His hardness digs into my waist, and I shudder.

He purrs again, and the vibrations roll up his chest, curving around me, entrancing me. He points the shower spout over his head, over his face and chest. The dirt leaches away, baring that caramel skin.

I dip down and lick the raised nub of his nipple, and he growls. The hand shower switches off, and he flings it aside. He straightens in one smooth move, bringing me up with him. Then he steps out of the tub and swings me over, his movements abrupt. His dick slaps against my thigh, and I look down at the hard, solid length and gulp. Angry, throbbing, it seems bigger. Saliva pools in my mouth.

I reach for his cock and he makes a warning sound in the back of his throat.

I blink.

What am I doing?

I shouldn't want this man, not after what he did to me. But my body has developed an agenda of its own.

It wants his cock inside of me, soothing my burning channel with his cum.

A jolt of awareness ripples down my spine, followed by a chill so intense that my shoulders tense.

Another day and I will be completely in thrall of the heat cycle.

If I escaped from him, I'd have to face it on my own. I'd also attract the attention of every single alpha in the square mile who'd sniff the pheromones and make a beeline for me.

And if I stay? I'll give in to the estrus. I won't be able to resist him then.

I'll throw myself at his feet, begging him to rut me. Goosebumps flare on my skin. If I do that, I have no doubt he'll take pleasure in enjoying my body in ways I hadn't known existed. My pussy squeezes; moisture wets my cunt.

Another wave of sensation spikes up my belly.

I am pulled up to the tips of my toes as if by an invisible thread. I stumble and he cradles me against his chest. He grabs a towel, then rubs it over my hair, down my shivering shoulders, over my hips. Dropping the towel on the floor, he scoops me up again and walks out of the door toward the bed. He drops me there.

I lie panting as he stalks over to where a tray of food sits by the entrance of the room. He stops in front of the double doors, then slams the bolt shut.

105

Kayden

The sound of the double doors slamming shut fills room. A gasp sounds behind me. I turn around to see her swing her legs over the side of the bed. She paces back and forth, muttering to herself.

"What's wrong?"

"Nothing...everything." She chews on her lower lip, then drops to her knees, sniffs the bedspread, and scrunches up her nose. "That...that's what's wrong."

I tilt my head.

"That..." She stabs her finger at the bed. "Can't you see?"

'It's a bed." I raise my shoulders and let them fall.

"That's what I mean... It doesn't smell right."

"Ah." My lips curl.

I bend and pick up the tray of food. It also has some medical supplies, antiseptic, bandages, even a rope and a pair of scissors. Efficient, Marcus.

I walk to the table in the corner of the room, place the tray on it, then jerk my chin toward it.

She frowns at me and rubs the skin over her chest.

"Does it hurt?"

"No."

"Liar."

She hangs her head and squeezes her thighs together. My groin throbs. *Bet the sweet flesh between your legs aches as much as my cock.*

I drop into the chair and tap my lap.

A shudder of breath leaves her chest. Then she raises her chin and walks toward me, her gait unsteady, her arms wrapped around her waist. Her shoulders hunch, and by the time she's reached me, she's trembling all over. She sinks onto my lap. I catch her, turning her so she's seated sideways.

Her gaze drops to the tray, and her eyes widen. "What?" She swallows, then points at the rope. "What is that for?"

"Guess?" I allow my mouth to twitch.

She juts out her lower lip.

Fucking cute. *Cute? Did I think cute?* I draw myself up to my full height.

"You intend to tie me up again?"

"Maybe…" I lean close enough for my breath to lift the hair on her forehead. "Maybe I'll whip you with it instead."

The color slides off of her cheeks. Her breathing goes ragged.

"Mark you across the backs of those creamy thighs, over the curve of your luscious ass."

Her eyes widen; the pupils dilate.

"Maybe you'd enjoy that too much, hmm?" I feather my knuckle over her cheek, then lift her chin until her gaze meets mine. "Perhaps once we reach Scotland I should throw you into the cellar and let you suffer on your own."

She flicks out a tongue to lick her lips. I press my thumb down on her lower lip, opening her mouth. I'd been inside that hot, wet cavity of pleasure. My dick throbs. I want her to wrap her lips around my balls and suck on them, right before she takes me down her throat.

Her shoulders bunch. The scent of roses and pepper teases my nostrils. Only then do I realize I've buried my nose in the crook of where her shoulder meets her neck.

"P...Perverted asshole."

"You weren't saying that when I shoved my dick inside of you earlier."

She flinches, and I lick the still bleeding wound.

The taste of her blood fills my mouth. Sweet, with a bite. My dick lengthens. I graze my teeth over the torn flesh, and her hands jerk in her lap.

"Does it hurt?"

She turns to me. "What do you think?"

Her green eyes bore into me. The emerald sparks ebb and flow, pulling me in. I want to lose myself in their depths. Want to sink into her and watch how that affects the change in their color. The fuck is that about? They are eyes belonging to my slave.

So what if they are beautiful, shining, with a stormy vortex boiling at the edges?

Why do I want to lean into them, close enough for the fire inside of her to burn me, to burn away all of the thoughts that crowd in on my mind, the past that weighs me down, the future that presses in on my rib cage, shoving at me, strangling me?

Since when have I begun to feel trapped by the promise made to my adoptive father?

My groin thrums; a vague discomfort tugs at my chest.

"I don't care one way or the other." Picking up a slice of cheese, I offer it to her. "Open."

Her lips clamp together. Her muscles stiffen. She folds her arms around her waist.

"You need your strength to fight me."

She doesn't react.

I wrap my arm around her and pull her close.

A low hum rumbles up my chest, twining around her, sinking into her blood. Her muscles relax. Her face twists.

"I hate—"

I pop a slice of cheese into her mouth. She presses her lips together; her jaw stays static.

"Don't make me force you to chew it."

I hold her gaze. Black pupils shining, dilating, and my dick hardens on cue. Huh?

The angrier she is, the more my body seems to relish it. Maybe it's because I've never been challenged by an omega before? Most of them are more than ready to lie back and spread, then are pathetically grateful when I rut them. Unlike her. She doesn't want to be here, and that makes her an irresistible challenge. How far can I push her before I break her?

How long before she surrenders to her needs and begs me to take her?

How long before I lose patience and knot her again?

"What's it to be then?"

She purses her lips.

"You going to eat this on your own or should I—?" I drop my mouth toward her breast and blow on the nipple. The bud pebbles. Goosebumps flare on her skin and I peer up at her.

She purses her lips, then her jaw moves.

I straighten. "Good girl."

I hold up another slice of cheese, and she opens her mouth and chews, then swallows. I feed her more cheese, some grapes, a strawberry, a small piece of bread.

"Enough."

She licks her mouth and looks at the food longingly.

"Behave and you may get more."

I grab a hunk of bread, place some cheese on it, and eat it up.

I offer her a few more bites, and she chews and swallows. She watches my mouth with hungry eyes, her gaze moving with my every bite, her lips glistening. By the time I am finished, my dick is throbbing, the pulse echoed by the blood pounding in my ears.

"Why do you care if I eat or not?" Her breath hitches.

"I need you to get your strength back to—"

"So I can fight you?"

"To resist me when I try to fuck you." I chew, then swallow the last mouthful.

Her breathing goes shallow.

I reach for the cotton, swab the cut on her forehead, then bandage the wound.

"You didn't have to do that; it wasn't life-threatening."

"You are my asset; I need to make sure you are in top shape when I return you to Zeus."

Her muscles go still; her fingers clench. "But you took the most important thing I had." A shiver convulses her shoulders, yet her body burns to the touch. The heat radiates off of her skin, tinged with pheromones and that sweet scent of slick.

I drag my fingers over her belly button to the flesh between her legs. Wet. So damned wet. Her arousal coats my fingers and I snarl, "You want me inside of you?"

"No."

"You want me to fuck you?"

"Never."

"You want me to throw you down on the bed…and knot you, take all choice from you, and put you out of your misery."

"No. No. No." She digs her fingernails into her palms. Her body quakes, her hair curling as it dries around the pale white of her face.

"You need to only ask, Omega."

"I will not." She hiccups.

"Fine."

I rise to my feet cradling her in my arms. "Time for you to sleep." I prowl toward the bed.

"Wait." She wriggles in my grasp.

I continue walking.

"I told you the sheets smell all wrong." She snarls.

Not surprising, neither that mattress nor those sheets belong to me.

I pause near the bed, then lower her to her feet. Her legs give way, and she falls against me.

I grasp her shoulders, then press down. Her knees hit the floor.

I grab my cock and slide my fingers up the length, squeezing out a bead of precum. She pants, and her gaze fastens on my dick. The skin stretches across her cheekbones.

"You want this?"

Her little tongue flicks out to lick her lips.

"You're not getting it, not until you ask for it."

I continue to slide my hold up and down the length of my shaft.

A moan wheezes out of her.

She raises her chin, her tongue caught between her teeth. Her eyes glaze. Her breathing roughens. Then she reaches a hand for my groin, and I growl.

She drops her palms to her lap then clasps her fingers together.

I increase the speed as I continue to wank off, up, down, up again, faster, harder.

Her breathing quickens in tandem.

Her chin wobbles, and a shiver runs down her spine; goosebumps flare on her skin.

I keep going.

I don't take my gaze off of her face, off of the way her entire body trembles. The scent of slick deepens in the air, and my muscles stiffen.

Fuck, I am going to come.

She whines and parts her lips. My thigh muscles spasm, my groin hardens. Then the cum spurts out. I step around her to jerk off onto the bed.

Squeezing out every last drop onto the mattress, I stop, my dick still semi-rigid, my breathing ragged. She tilts her chin up, her pupils blown.

On her knees, she stares up at me, her lips parted. Mouth glistening. The wound at the base of where her neck meets her shoulder cleaves the creamy flesh of her skin. The puncture wounds I left when I bit her is visible.

So beautiful. So fucking primal. I can't wait to mark every inch of that gorgeous body.

I peel back my lips. Her chest rises and falls.

I flex my fingers and her pupils dilate.

She locks her pleading gaze with mine, and something coils in my chest.

I jerk my chin toward the bed.

She springs up to her feet, pivots around, and throws herself onto the mattress.

The curve of her spine, the dimples over the flare of her hips flash, then she rolls around, streaking my cum all over her newly washed skin.

Over her hair.

She scoops up some and rubs it over her breasts, down her stomach, across the flesh between her legs. I can't stop looking. Can't stop myself from grabbing my dick.

"Part your legs."

She bends her knees, then slides her thighs wide.

"Play with yourself."

She drags her fingers between the folds of her pussy, rubbing my cum into the soft flesh.

"Deeper."

I grip my cock harder, the pulse thrumming at my temples, at my wrists, even in my balls. I don't stop. I tug and wank myself.

"Add another finger."

She slides another into her cunt.

"One more."

She adds a third, and that sweet little hole of hers expands to take it in, all right up to her knuckles.

"Faster."

She pulls out and shoves her fingers in, and again. The squelching noises sink into my blood. A shudder rolls up from my feet and my cock lengthens. The pinpricks snowball, racing up my thighs, contracting my groin.

"Come."

A moan bursts from her lips, her spine arches off the bed, her eyes roll back, as the hot bursts of cum spill from my cock.

I angle it over her, and the thick ropy strands coat her chest, her hips, over her pussy, her thighs. My breathing hitches, waves of tiredness engulf me, and I sway. My knees hit the bed, and I fall across it. She moans, and her breathing deepens.

I drag her body up next to me.

I position us, with our heads on the pillows, and pull the covers over us. I haul her close, then spoon her.

I've helped to ease her pain temporarily.

Wrapped her in my cum, in the tone of my purrs, in my heat, so she knows I am here, close. Enough to soothe for a few hours. My dick protests wanting more. Have I fucking lost it?

It's a glimmer of weakness. Something I will not allow myself again.

I need to get my ass in gear and fuck her out of my system.

Tear up her pussy, use her as therapy. She's so fucking gorgeous I want to fuck my entire childhood out on her.

My dick hardens.

I groan and lower my hands to where her ass cheeks thrust against my dick. All I have to do is bury the aching, weeping head of my cock inside her hole.

I bury my nose in her hair and her scent fills my senses. My breath deepens, my muscles grow heavy. I let my eyelids flutter down.

"Kayden."

Ma calls after me as I race up the hillside. My breath comes in pants. My pulse thuds in my ears. I pump my legs and speed up. Faster, faster. The wind slams into me, pushing me back. My heart begins to race. I have been here many times before. Have relived this scene too many times in the past. I am dreaming. But I can't pull myself out of it.

I brace my body against the breeze, keep going, don't stop. Maybe if I run fast enough I can outrun this nightmare? I put on a burst of speed and race over the last few feet. Reaching the peak I bend over panting.

"Kayden."

I turn back to see the woman walking up the slope. Her golden hair shines in the rising sun. Her dark pink scarf blows behind her. Her long legs eat up the distance between us.

No, don't come closer Mama, if you do you are going to die. Don't. I try to scream out to her, and tell her to stop, but no word emerges from my throat.

"You are getting too fast for me, Kai."

She smiles and her face lights up.

Footsteps sound behind me. She looks past me and her gaze widens. She hastens her pace, breaking into a run. "Stop, mama, stop."

"Kai." She races in my direction.

"No, you need to leave before he kills you." I moan aloud. Sweat pools in the hollows of my armpits.

"Kayden." She reaches for me and blood drips from her fingers.

"Kayden, wake up."

My eyelids snap open.

Green eyes blaze at me. Blonde hair streams around her shoulders. "Kayden," Her lips purse, "You were dreaming?"

There's a knock on the door. Every instinct in me goes on alert. I throw my arms around her and roll over so my body shields hers, "Who the fuck is it?"

"It's Marcus. Zeus' soldiers are scanning the grounds. You need to get out of here."

106

Chloe

He releases me, then rolls out of bed.

For a second I'd been sure he meant to protect me. The way he'd wrapped his arms around me, and planted himself between me and the entrance had been...unexpected.

Why did he do that?

He stalks to the door and cracks it half open.

Marcus hands over some clothes. "I have a new car with a full tank, enough to take you all the way to Scotland."

"I appreciate it."

"Your father was the one man who never let me down. He was there when I needed him most. This is the least I can do. Save his legacy, Kayden."

Kayden's shoulders go solid. He accepts the clothes and shuts the door. Then prowls back to me. Dawn lights up the window, caressing his body. The hard planes of his chest, the tapering waist. The thick, beautiful cock that hangs semi-erect between those muscled thighs.

He drops some of the clothes on the bed, then stalks toward me and hands over the rest. I accept them and he turns away.

"Alpha."

He pauses.

"Thanks."

"Don't thank me, thank Marcus. Left to myself I'd have preferred to keep you naked."

Does he have to twist everything I say to suit his needs? Why is he trying so hard to come across as unfeeling?

"But since I am feeling particularly generous and because Marcus has a kind heart, we may as well indulge the old man eh?" He jerks his chin toward the clothes. "Don't go reading anything into the gesture."

Don't worry I won't be making that mistake anytime soon.

"Get dressed." The hushed command in his voice sears my nerves. The hair on my nape rises.

Only when I turn my back to him do I realize that I have rushed to do his bidding. Damn it. He can make me obey him with a few words.

"Still modest, eh?"

I stiffen. Is he mocking me? I shoot a glance over my shoulder and find that he's staring at me, his forehead is furrowed.

I search his features for any trace that he's having fun at my expense, but all I see is curiosity.

I hunch my shoulders, "I am not used to... to... dressing in front of someone else."

Yeah, after everything he did to me, after the way he'd taken me, I still feel obliged to seek some modicum of privacy to getting dressed. *Such a prude.*

All this while, I still feel his dick throbbing inside of me; the taste of him is fresh in my mouth.

Once we get to Scotland he's going to knot me and fuck me senseless.

He won't stop until he's squeezed every last drop of pleasure from my body. Then what? Will he give me away once he grows bored with me?

I gnaw on my lower lip and his gaze drops to my mouth.

"Get used to it." He rakes his gaze over my breasts. "Your body is no longer yours Omega. It belongs to me. You'll obey me, fulfill me, you'll do everything in your power to make me happy. There is only one reason for your existence, to do as I ask."

"I'd have never guessed that."

The skin around his eyes creases. "Still haven't lost your sass hmm?" He smirks and the cruel line of his thin upper lip draws my attention. "You have more spine than I'd expected." His gorgeous lips part and he flashes me a smile...no not a smile, that's being too charitable. It's a declaration of intent. A smirk of a predator who's simply biding his time.

He cracks his knuckles and I blink. "There'll be enough time to whip that out of you...if you ask me nicely."

"You wouldn't." I gulp and wrap my arms around my waist.

"Don't mock it until you try it. You may even enjoy it, Omega. You may ask for a whole lot more before I am done with you."

"Never."

He clucks his tongue. "Where are your manners?"

I lost them the moment I set eyes on you, you cad!

He rolls his shoulders, looking so damned pleased with himself. "I have so much to teach you."

I curl my fingers at my side. What stops me from reaching across and scratching that smug expression off of his face?

He holds up a warning finger, "I wouldn't."

Hell, can he sense my every action? Am I that easy to read? I scowl at him.

His eyes gleam, one side of his lips twitches. He's trying to hold in a smile. Huh? So beneath that alpha-hole façade lives a man with a sense of humor. Who'd have thought? I almost wish I hadn't seen that. It humanizes him. Makes him regard him as something more than my kidnapper and I don't want that.

I stare at his face and he turns away.

Wow, he didn't take it into his twisted head to punish me for standing up to him...yet. In fact, he seems to have enjoyed the little altercation. I dig my fingers in my hair and tug on it.

Why am I surprised?

I may not have experience with men, but I have met enough dominant alphas in my father's team. They think that they want someone who submits to their every need. How wrong they are. They can't resist an omega who challenge them, one they can chase and try to break. The thrill of the hunt is as potent as the need to mate. The need to mark and take.

I wish I were strong enough to defy him, but every part of my omega core yearns to obey him.

I may put up a token resistance, perhaps manage to be bratty with him on occasion, but I'll never be able to deny him.

How am I going to keep him from abandoning me?

Or worse, from dominating me completely, until my very personality merges with his. The hair on the back of my neck rises. I can't let that happen. Enough subservient omegas have warned me about how it is to give in completely to the alpha. They'd lose interest in you and hand you over to another...and I...can't let that happen.

My only hope is to make my captor care for me, enough that he doesn't destroy me completely. But how?

He snaps his fingers and I raise my gaze to his face. "Wear your clothes."

Without waiting for my response he steps into a fresh pair of pants, then shrugs on a T-shirt and a jacket.

There's something strangely intimate about watching him dress. Yet with every layer of clothing that he pulls on, Kayden disappears. In his place the alpha who'd kidnapped me knits back together.

If the alpha senses my perusal he doesn't show it.

Sitting on the bed he slides one foot, then the other, into his boots, and begins to lace them up.

His movements are brisk.

Every twist of his wrist, every curl of his fingertips aimed and focused at the task at hand. Exactly how he'd claimed me. With ruthless efficiency. He'd done it without a second thought. As if he'd been sure of it. As if it had meant nothing to him.

Or perhaps his instincts had guided him and he had followed?

He had marked me as his. That had to count for something, right? Only he'd never mentioned it, not once. Does he regret that? Maybe it didn't mean anything to him?

I reach for my clothes and pull on the jeans, the shirt, the hoodie.

The bedclothes?" I nod toward the sheets.

"Marcus will wash them."

He glides up to his feet.

Every movement of his is lithe, nuanced. For a cruel he's almost beautiful. It's all a front for the dark heart he hides inside.

He swivels his head to glare at me. "What are you waiting for? Need some motivation maybe?" He flexes his fingers and my breathing quickens. My toes curl. The hell? I shouldn't find that arousing, I shouldn't.

I avert my gaze. Slipping on my sneakers, I tie the shoelaces.

The silence stretches. A beat. Another.

"Everything fits."

"They belonged to Marcus' daughter."

"You knew her?" I straighten.

His jaw hardens. "I did." His forehead furrows and the skin around his eyes creases. "She ran away when she turned eighteen." The chords of his throat move as he swallows and for a second he looks vulnerable.

"You haven't seen her since?"

"No." He rubs the nape of his neck. "Marcus and I searched for her but there was not a trace of what had happened to her. Of course when I asked my father to help he refused. It was more important for him to keep his team focused on the betterment of his city. His fucking city." He scowls.

"It's also your city."

"Is it?" His lips twist, his features harden

"Isn't it?

He glares at me and my throat goes dry. My thighs clench. This man, he can scare me and arouse me at the same time. That commanding look on his face, the arrogance that bleeds from his every pore... every angle of his body screams prime alpha male and the feminine core of me instantly responds to him. And I hate that I am so aware of him. So ready to do his every bidding. When every part of me wants to resist him, challenge him so he doesn't take me as being compliant to his every demand.

"Maybe she was kidnapped?"

His face whitens. His left eyelid twitches.

Don't say it. Don't. "Like you took me?"

He rises to his feet to tower over me. "Think very carefully about what you say next Omega."

A thrill runs down my spine. All my nerve endings tingle. Holy hell, why do I feel so alive when I go toe to toe with him?

"Or maybe she doesn't want to be found?"

A low growl rumbles up his massive chest and I wince. I want to pull back and cower. But I will not. I grind my heels into the ground and stay where I am.

"Maybe you drove her away?"

He takes a step forward. Anger leaps off him in waves, the sheer dominance of his personality seems to amplify in that space and I almost cry out. All the pores of my skin pop. My belly quivers, slick pools in my core and his nostrils flare. Damn him for instantly picking up when i am turned on. And I am, and I don't understand why. I should run away from him, hide under the bed or something. Instead I raise my chin, "Maybe she is happy where she is?"

"As will you?" He peels back his lips and his teeth sparkle against his tanned skin. He lowers his head, closer, closer, until his eyelids tangle with mine. Holy hell, is he going to kiss me? Do I want him to kiss me?

I flick out my tongue to lick my lips.

His gaze drops to my mouth.

His shoulders flex, those massive biceps bulge. He is going to wrap those powerful arms around me and yank me close. My eyelids flutter down.

"I never kiss my prey." He pats me on the head. "It's more fun to play with them."

Cool air glides over my skin.

I snap my eyelids open to see him saunter towards the door.

Jerk. My throat closes. Tears prick at my eyeballs. Clearly, he felt something for Marcus' daughter. Was he in love with her? Did he care for her? The band around my chest tightens. Why am I trying to engage him in conversation? Trying to reconcile the cruel alpha with the empathetic man I'd glimpsed when he'd taken care of me in the bathtub? That had been so he could take care of his property, as he'd mentioned.

To think I had actually thought he had a kernel of empathy somewhere inside. I was so wrong. He knows how to manipulate, how to use my feelings against me. I should hold back, rein in this crazy attraction I feel for him. I raise my chin and head to the exit, "I find you repulsive."

He glances at me over his shoulder, "I'll remind you of that when you are screaming to have my cock inside of you again." His amber eyes gleam, "And I won't stop until you are begging for your release over and over again and even then I won't let you come. Not until I have fucked your every hole and every pore in your body is leaking my cum."

My breath stutters.

The picture he paints. Those horrible, filthy words.

My thighs clench, my scalp tingles.

Why do they turn me on so?

He crooks a finger at me. "Come."

My belly flip-flops, my pulse thuds and my mouth goes dry.

He cants his head and the force of his dominance reaches out to me.

The very air seems to be saturated with testosterone. This man...his sheer will is a living, breathing thing that clings to my skin, sinking into my blood, making me want to accept my base nature and ask him to take me, to put me out of my misery.

Exactly what he wants.

His lip curls.

Fuck him but he knows exactly how his words affect me.

He saunters to the door and shoulders it open, "After you."

I keep my head straight, brush past him and to the staircase. Reaching the bottom of the stairs, I quicken my steps toward the front door.

"This way." Marcus beckons to me from the opposite side of the room. "The back door. Best to go the other way."

"Right." I cross the floor toward him and jam my hands into the pocket of my hoodie. "Th...thanks for the clothes." I shuffle my feet.

"You're welcome." Marcus' features soften.

I shiver, and he frowns.

"You okay--?"

No.

Of course not.

I nod, not trusting myself to speak.

"Take care of yourself, little one."

I swallow, then stand up on tiptoes and hug him on impulse. Marcus pats my shoulders.

There's a growl behind me, and I stiffen.

Marcus ruffles my hair then steps back. "Your mate is possessive of you."

I raise my head. "Not my mate." I frown up at him.

His lips curve. "Don't lose that spirit." He bends down and peers into my eyes. "Never give up on what you hold most precious."

I frown. What does he mean? What's the most precious thing to me? My parents? Myself... Kayden?

My thoughts whirl. I walk around him toward the back door.

When my next estrus takes ahold of me, nothing can stop the cycle. No drugs. Not the dominant commands of an alpha. I have Kayden to rut me...unless...unless he asks one of his men to do that.

Nope...he's too possessive for that.

I am counting on the fact that he won't trust anyone else to do what is needed. He won't risk his merchandise, his bargaining chip, as he calls me. I am what he needs. Only he doesn't know it yet.

I am going to crack that alpha-hole façade of his, and he won't realize what hit him. I am a breeder. I am conforming to my nature.

We are geared to be attracted to the alphas with the strongest genes, the ones who'll give our progeny the best chance at survival.

Who better than the Chief of Scotland to father my children? I am only sticking to the plan nature laid out for me. Survival of the fittest, the fastest, the canniest. The pure bloodlines of my Russian royal family, and Kayden's pedigree, yeah, can't get better than that.

He took my virginity, and I am going to make him give me the whole lot in return. Children, the position of an omega who belongs to one of the most powerful alphas in this region.

Insane. Insane plan.

This is the only future for me. For him to accept me. I can't go back to Zeus. There's nothing there for me, other than Lucy, but she's my sister and an omega. She'll understand what it means to want to find an alpha and a home of my own. I can't go back to Russia; the Berserkers have taken over that country. No, this is the only course of action. To stand up to the alpha, to make sure he sees me as a challenge, enough to come after me, rut me...impregnate me...? The breath rushes out of me.

Maybe once I am with child he'll change?

Surely, he'll not want to let go of me then?

Kayden prowls past me, out the door, then glares at me over his shoulder. "Get in the car."

Assuming I manage to survive long enough with him.

107

Kayden

An alpha's thirst for power is only surpassed by his hunger for omega pussy. *Fact.*

It has to be the explanation for how I lose control around her.

I look over at the sleeping woman curled up against the car door. Her lips are parted. Her skin is flushed.

Her eyelashes lie in a sooty fan against her soft cheeks. She'd walked to the car and seated herself without waiting for me. By the time I'd said goodbye to Marcus and started the vehicle, she'd shut her eyes.

There had been a moment earlier when I'd wanted to kiss her. I bet she'd taste sweet. Bet the mere feel of her lips against mine would turn me on more than having those lips around my cock. And isn't that a surprise?

A hint of her and I'd be a goner.

I'd never be able to tear myself away from her.

I'd keep going back for more. Until I'd sampled every inch of her body, until I'd sucked on those nipples, kissed my way down to the folds between her legs. Until I'd bitten her right there and thrummed her clit and slid my tongue into her hot sweet pussy.

I'd have sucked her juices, drunk my fill of her slick, until her cum had smeared my mouth, dripped from my chin, coated my skin and bled out of my pores. The way I'd wanted mine to drip from hers.

My fingers tighten on the steering wheel.

I'd eaten her out until she'd whimper and her breathing would get harder. Until she'd wrap those sleek thighs around my head, holding me in place; then I'd have thrust my finger into her back hole and her entire body would stiffen. She'd scream and come all over my face; and I'd lick up every drop of her cum, right before I'd tear my face from her core and bury my dick inside her.

I've wanted to fuck omegas. But making love to them? Pleasure them? It's the first time I've wanted that.

I want her to be aroused and throbbing for me until she is a dripping mess.

Then I'd mark her all over, rub my seed into her skin until she smelled of me...until my breath fused with hers, my skin melded with hers. Warmth heats my chest, my dick throbs, my balls harden and I have to part my legs to accommodate myself, the fuck? I grit my teeth so hard that pain tears up my jaw.

The woman's right next to me and I am arousing myself.

I'm jizzing myself thinking of taking her again.

She is dangerous. I need to get her out of my head. I need to find a way to break her hold on me. I thought I had kidnapped her? It's she who has taken me ransom.

Good thing I'd procured a rope from Marcus and tied her to the door handle. Not that it makes her less of a threat. I snort under my breath. Being in the same space as her makes my dick twitch. My chest hurts and what the fuck is up with that?

She mutters under her breath then sighs. My vision narrows, my biceps twitch. I glance at her from the corner of my eyes. I could reach for her, loosen her restraints enough to pull her across my lap. Massage that tempting backside, hold her down until her pussy makes contact with my aching dick. Only when the vehicle swerves do I realize that I have snaked out my arm toward her. Bloody hell. She's messing with my control. I return my hand to the wheel and right the vehicle..

Why am I so tuned into her?

Why do I want to own her?

This need to possess her and ruin here? It's different. This is not what I want. I can't afford this distraction. Best to get back to my clan in Scotland and then? I'd hand her off.

I'll turn my back on her and make sure never to see her again.

I need to rut another omega as soon as I get there. A cold feeling coils in my chest. I don't want anyone else. It's her innocence I seek. It's the melting cradle of her pussy that I need. The warmth of her mouth around my cock is what I crave. Those little moans as she comes, that's what I want to hear. And those archaic insults she insists on flinging at me? I'd miss them.

The smile fades from my lips. Why am I chuckling to myself? Why am I still thinking about her? She's softening me up, messing with my head. And it makes me uneasy. I rub my finger around the collar of my T-shirt.

Enough messing around.

I need to get back to my clan, at the earliest. Get on with the original plan of trading her in with Zeus. I step on the accelerator and the vehicle leaps forward. For the next few hours I focus on driving. The countryside flashes by and dawn lights the skies. Not far now, we are almost at the border to Scotland. Silence fills the car.

I turn to glance at her. She's so still, hasn't moved at all since we left. My shoulders bunch. Is she breathing? I lean across and hold a finger under her nose.

Her warm breath flutters over my skin, and my muscles relax.

Ridiculous. I straighten and rub the back of my neck. When had I worried about another before her?

I'd loved my mother and Reena; had cared for Marcus' daughter like she was my own sibling. When Adelina went missing I'd helped him search for her, but we hadn't been able to find her. I'd been a child when my mother had been murdered. In front of me. Golan had taken me...had whipped me for days. Then he'd turned me over to his alphas to make me a man. I'd been too soft he'd said. Too spoilt. I was a bastard and I had to be treated as such.

Those alphas had not been easy on me. They'd beaten me and buggered me.

I'd have died if my adoptive father had not rescued me. Another reason I owe him. I must stay true to his legacy.

I step on the accelerator, and the SUV speeds around a curve. A screech from the tires slices th the thoughts in my head. I slow down, glance at my omega's sleeping profile.

The regal curve of her neck, the parted lips, the sooty fan of her eyelashes against the flushed skin of her cheek... I blink. The way she wears Adelina's clothes, they could be cut from the finest fabrics. There's a sophistication to her, an almost royal bearing. I frown. The sheath she'd been wearing when I had first spotted her... it was made of fine spun linen.

And she'd been a virgin.

I turn back to the road.

A virgin omega is something unheard of. Most omegas come into their heat cycles when they reach puberty; many whore themselves out to survive. Those who hold out lurch from one cycle to the next, growing slightly more desperate with each one—no access to suppressants, which have been outlawed, their supplies all but vanishing from black markets, too.

Very few omegas reach adulthood without giving in to being rutted by an alpha.

You have to be a princess or belong to royal blood or have extremely rich parents who can source suppressants for you. Unless—nah! I shoot her a sideways glance.

That rich silk of her hair, the softness of her skin, the delicate features, that regal bearing when she walks, hell, when she'd dropped to her knees and given me a blow job—even then there had been a delicacy to the way she had eaten my cock. Clearly she is used to a privileged lifestyle? I drum my fingers on the wheel.

I'd called her a princess, and she'd turned up her pert nose and said she was before she'd retracted it.

Hang on a second.

I slam on the brakes right there in the center of a deserted road.

I take in a breath, and that pheromone-laced essence of her teases my nostrils. The one thing I can count on is my instincts.

It is that which had prompted me to send Lucy to Zeus. And Lucy didn't have a sister, did she? The omegas who had appealed to me for shelter...well, I hadn't seen all their faces. I hadn't bothered with them, really. Lucy had been the one who'd been of use to me. So...who is this omega?

First chance I get, I need to find out. If she's been withholding information from me...I'll teach her a lesson she won't forget easily. A growl rumbles up my chest. She moans, then shifts restlessly and rubs her thighs together. The sugary sweet scent of her deepens in the car.

My mouth waters. I want to reach over and rub the heel of my hand on the triangle of her pussy.

Scoop up the cream that pools in the hollow of her core, lick it, suck it, thrust my tongue into that moist channel and eat up that succulent flesh until she comes all over my mouth.

I lick my lips, and fuck if I can't imagine the taste of her. She moans and turns to me, her eyelashes fluttering as if she's responding to my thoughts.

Heat coils behind my rib cage. No. Keep away from her. Touch her now and you'll not be able to stop yourself from knotting her, claiming her again...and that would only consolidate the mating bond. And I don't want that. I don't.

I roll my shoulders.

The faster I get her to Scotland, the sooner I can hand her over to my clansmen and then I can refocus on my plans to spring a trap for Zeus when he comes for her.

I speed up the car and drive through the night. By the time dawn is on the horizon, we are approaching the border of Scotland.

My eyelids are heavy with tiredness, and I shake my head to dispel the sleep.

The headlights pick up the bumps in the unkempt road.

It's one of the first things I intend to do as soon as I take over Zeus' city—raid his treasury and use it to restore Scotland to its former glory, something that will finally bring peace to my father's spirit.

The outline of two parked motorbikes looms up, and I slam on the brakes.

108

Chloe

The sound of yelling fills my ears. Something heavy crashes onto the road and the SUV seems to shake.

I crack open my eyelids, and the move sends pinpricks of agony drumming at the back of my head.

Another shout, metal crashing, and my heart hammers. I fling out a hand, grasp the cushion of the seat, and straighten my back. Shake my head to clear it, then open my eyes. It's dark outside. I peer through the windscreen. The shape of moving figures greets me.

What…who are these people? A man taller than his opponent…broad shoulders, and the way he moves it has to be Kayden—he raises his fist and brings it down on his opponent. The shorter, stockier man reels back, then recovers and rushes at Kayden. Head down, he winds his arms around Kayden's waist, and both figures go crashing to the ground. They struggle. Sounds of scuffling. They roll across to the side of the road and over the edge. I am still tied to the door handle. I yank at my restraint, but it doesn't give. I shove open the door and tumble out. Clutching the car for support, I peer around it.

Where did they go?

What are they up to?

Is he okay? Why am I worried about him?

Footsteps approach me from behind, and I swing around. A man comes into view. He's tall, his shoulders almost as broad as Kayden's, but he's leaner. Muscular. Streamlined. He resembles a column of pure, lethal power. His features are harsh. There's something familiar about him. Have I seen him before?

His black vest clings to his chest, outlining every hard plane. He takes a step forward, and I scuttle back against the car door.

"Who...who are you?"

He moves closer, and the light from the car interior illuminates his body, making him seem larger.

"Why...why are you here?" My pulse rate ratchets up. My heart hammers, my breath catches in my throat. I am alone. Kayden is nowhere to be seen. Not that he is a savior, either. He, too, is a predator, but right now I'll take a known devil over an unknown enemy.

I open my mouth to scream and he raises his hands face up, "I won't hurt you Chloe."

That's what they always say.

I stare at his palms, scars mark the skin.

He's been hurt in a fight recently? For some reason that calms me. I blink.

"You saw me on the terrace of the Omega harem,

princess. I was with Zeus." He angles his head.

Right, I remember now.

"Nod if you understand Chloe."

I jerk my chin.

His shoulders relax. He drops his hand, then steps back.

"What...what do you want?" I square my shoulders.

"Zeus sent me." He bends his knees, drops his head, and peers into my eyes. "I am Ethan."

"Who?"

"I am Zeus' Second." He lowers his voice a notch, " I have a message from him."

I frown. "What do you want?"

"Not me, Zeus." His shoulders move as he raises them, "He needs you to play the role Kayden wants."

"What?" I blink.

"Zeus wants you to distract Kayden the best you can, until he has a chance of getting his team together and coming for you."

"Distract Kayden?" I press my lips together, "You mean let him fuck me?"

His features twitch. He's not as comfortable having this conversation with me as he thinks. Too bad. This is my life we are talking about.

"So the esteemed mate of my very own sister wants me to wear myself out. He wants me to give in to every depraved need of that...that..."

I jerk my chin toward where the two men had tumbled over the side.

And they haven't appeared yet.

My gaze flicks over to the dent in the bushes marking the spot. Dammit, Kayden should have managed to beat the other man and come back, and why should I care about that? He is my captor. He means nothing to me. He deserves every single hit he is getting. His body deserves to be beaten, bruised...worshipped, licked all over, sucked on, especially his cock. His big, beautiful cock.

"Not too easily."

Ethan's voice breaks through the clutter of my thoughts, and I swivel around to face him. The world tilts. I grab at the door to right myself. "What do you mean?"

"If you submit too quickly, he'll lose interest. Zeus wants you to resist."

"I don't understand." My gaze widens. My senses tingle a warning.

"Zeus thinks you need to ah...keep him engaged, give him enough but not submit so completely that he loses interest."

"So the General of London wants to dictate my sex life?" I stare, trying to get my head around what he's saying.

"Not yours." Ethan tilts his head in the direction of the edge of the road. "His."

"Ah! Zeus wants to use me to play his half-brother?"

Ethan nods.

"Zeus wants to use me to further his own interests?"

Ethan's features tighten. Maybe he doesn't agree with Zeus, but he's here, isn't he? And he's conveying the message.

"So it's not enough that I have this...this monster trying to rape me, and impose his will on me at every turn. Now my own sister's mate wants to use me in this whatever...sick one-upsmanship is going on between him and his half-brother?"

He drags his fingers around the collar of his vest, and ink peeps out for a second before he drops his arm to his side. "I am only the messenger."

"That's what they all say." I jut out my chin.

I thought, perhaps because I was his mate's sister, Zeus might want to come out to save me... I was wrong. I am alone. I am really on my own. "Lucy." I raise my chin and fix him with a glare. "Did she agree to this?"

"She was the one who suggested it."

"I don't believe you." My lips turn down. My stomach lurches. How could that be? My very own sister had agreed to this plan to humiliate me?

But then, Lucy had always been far ahead when it came to strategizing and plotting things out. She had been an avid learner at my father's lessons.

She had made sure to train herself in swordplay, in fighting, in matters of politics. It's why she had been the self-appointed leader of our little ragtag band of escapees from Russia. Going to Kayden in the first place had been her idea. And when she'd had to assassinate Zeus...she'd turned that entire series of events to her advantage.

"Damn it." A flash of sensation ripples down my spine, and a burst of chill follows on its heels.

Ethan's nostrils flare. His gaze widens. "You are close to estrus?"

My teeth chatter; my head spins.

"No...no kidding." My knees wobble, and I fall against the door.

Ethan leans forward on the balls of his feet then stops. "I can't...touch you... If I do, he'll scent me—."

"—And, of course, we can't have that now, right? After all, I am just a possession." *His possession.*

Everyone and everything in this world is hell-bent on making sure I belong to him...eventually. How did it come to this? How have I found myself so alone, with nothing and no one on my side? Except for the alpha who wants to make sure I obey his every command and fulfill his needs.

Ethan fists his fingers at his sides. "Do you have any message for Lucy?"

"Yeah, tell my sister to go fuck herself."

He winces, then straightens.

"Why won't you rescue me now?"

"Because Zeus..." he hesitates, "and Lucy need you to do this for them."

"And if I refuse?"

His forehead furrows. "Are you refusing to help Zeus the General of London and his mate Lucy?"

I swallow, then drop my gaze. Damn him for reminding me of exactly how insignificant I am in the scheme of things.

"Remember this is your only chance, Omega. You need to heed Zeus' commands; you need to hold back, keep him engaged. You need to do what it takes to keep him distracted."

"How...how long does he want me to keep up the charade?"

"Until the time is right."

I jut out my chin, "that's not very helpful now is it?"

"Trust us to come and get you when the time is right."

"You mean when I am well and truly fucked right?"

His shoulders stiffen. He pulls himself up to his full height. "I will be tracking you from a distance and keeping Zeus informed of the...the developments."

My stomach rolls. This entire scheme is a joke. "What if I do as he says and keep Kayden engaged? What if he enjoys it too much? What if he never lets me go?"

"You are a princess. You can play him, without letting him get too close."

"He's putting too much trust in me."

"Both Zeus and Lucy have full confidence in you."

If only they knew how close I am to giving in to him completely.

He turns to leave.

"Wait."

Ethan pauses and faces me.

"What if...?" I lick my lips. "What if...what if Zeus decides not to come for me?"

"He'll come for you." He touches his hand to the place above his heart. "I'll come for you. I won't let you down." His gaze swerves over my shoulder, and his muscles tighten. "I must go now. Take care of yourself."

He slips into the darkness. Drat them all to hell. I duck inside the car.

By the time Kayden stalks toward the front of the SUV and slides in, I am curled up against the door with my eyes shut.

He slams the door shut, and I sense his gaze sweep over my features. He leans in close. The scent of testosterone, that edge of darkness laced with cinnamon, grows deeper, and moisture squeezes between my thighs. *Don't move. Don't breathe.*

There's a light touch on my hair.

"I know you're awake."

I stay where I am.

"Your seat belt is not fastened."

Drat it. I open my eyelids, turn to face him, and gasp.

There are bruises on his cheek. The skin around his left eye is darkening, and his lip is cut, blood dripping down his chin.

"You're hurt."

He brushes the back of his hand across his split lip. Then flicks out his tongue and wets the wound. His full, pouty lower lip glistens. It's the only part of him that is soft, and somehow, it's obscene how much of a misnomer it is. It hints that there is something redeemable in him, that despite all evidence to the contrary, there is some part of him that still wants to do what is right. What is right? What he wants? What Zeus and Lucy want from me? What do I want?

Him. I want him.

Not him, only his body, his cock that I want him to thrust into me and use it to put me out of my misery. And it's all wrong. So damned wrong.

"What happened?" A low thrum coils in my stomach, and I fold my fists against my lower abdomen.

His gaze drops there, but he doesn't comment. "We were ambushed."

The leather of his seat creaks. He moves away, puts the SUV in gear, and we drive on.

"You defeated them."

He doesn't glance at me. Right. I am not the one asking questions, or in charge here. Blood drips from a cut at his temple. It slides down to his jaw, stands there stationary, then the droplet falls to his T-shirt...torn and dirtied already.

"If you untie me, I can take care of that wound."

He keeps driving.

"You'll bleed out."

One side of his lips twitches. "Hardly."

"You want to make sure you are fighting fit if they attack you again?"

"They wouldn't dare." But his shoulders flex. Maybe he's considering it?

"Just one arm. You can still keep the other tied up."

He slows down, then turns to glare at me.

I gulp.

"I don't want your ministrations." He snarls. "Or your sympathy, none of it. I am your captor. You are my slave. You do as I tell you, when I tell you. Do you understand?"

I swallow. The dominance rolls off of him and shoves at me, threatening me. I want to shrink against the door, throw my arms over my head and cower. And if I do that, I'll have no defense left.

Nothing to stop him from completely taking over and breaking me. My spirit. My intent. The force of my will, that's all I have. And it's not because of what Zeus and Lucy want of me...it's for my own self-preservation that I will not give in. I thrust my chin out at him. "And if I refuse?"

109

Kayden

After everything that's happened, after I'd already knotted her, made her suck my dick, warned her not to go against me, she still defies me? Why can't she be like the other omegas who'd have given in by now? Who'd be only too happy to spread their legs and allow me to rut them. Who'd fall in line and submit...why do I want to make her do all of that? Why do I want to break her will? See her fall apart, watch as I knot my dick inside of her and make her come all over my shaft? When I had seen the motorbikes stop our progress and known that it was possibly Zeus' men who had waylaid us, fear had clawed at my insides. And it wasn't for me. It had been for her. That she had been vulnerable and tied up. That Zeus' alphas could hurt her —worse, take her away, and I was nowhere near done with her.

She stares at me with wide eyes. Her throat moves; her chest rises and falls. A bead of sweat slides down her throat to the valley between her breasts. She isn't as unafraid as she pretends to be. I glare at her. Her cheeks flush, then she glances away.

"Do you want to find out what happens if you don't listen to me?"

She purses her mouth.

"Haven't we discussed this already? Did you think I was joking earlier when I laid out exactly what your options are?"

She shudders.

"Answer me."

"N...no."

"No what?"

"No, I know you are not joking."

"So what's the problem here, Omega?"

"N...nothing."

"Liar." My voice lowers a tone. Soft, silky. Hushed in the space between us.

She clenches her fists tightly, then squeezes her eyes shut.

"You're trying to push me over the edge, challenging me, waiting to see when I lose control."

She shakes her head. "You're wrong... I was trying to help." Her voice trembles; her chin wobbles. Fear rolls off of her in palpable waves.

"You expect me to believe that?"

She opens her eyes and turns away. "I don't care what you believe. I have basic decency left in me. You were hurting, and I wanted to help."

I slow the car and pull over to the side of the road, shifting into park. When I reach across she flinches, but I don't stop. I loosen the ropes. "Slide your arm out."

She edges her right arm back.

I tighten the restrain, then pull out the bandanna I had grabbed on my way out earlier. Her gaze widens.

"Wha...?"

I tie it around her mouth, gagging her. "Only to keep you quiet." I allow my lips to twitch, "you understand right?"

Sparks ebb and flow in those dark-green eyes.

Oh, yeah, there's plenty of fight left in her. My cock twitches. The thought of all the sass, all that resistance. It's going to make the inevitable surrender from her so much sweeter. And she is going to give in to me, make no mistake.

I lean back in my seat.

She doesn't move.

"There's a first-aid kit in the dash."

She stays where she is.

I glare at her, and her breath hitches. Her gaze lowers, then she opens the dash and pulls out the kit. I shift the car into gear and ease the vehicle back onto the road.

She leans over and dabs the antiseptic on my cut lip.

I can't stop the hiss that escapes me. The scent of her deepens and all my nerve endings seem to fire at once. My cock thickens. My thighs go solid. The fuck is happening to me? How can I find the task of her tending to me such an erotic experience? I press down on the accelerator. Her body jerks toward me, and I put out an arm to steady her. Don't want her hurting her creamy flesh now do we? Only I have that privilege.

"Put on your seat belt."

She mumbles something, the words muffled against the gag. Good thing I had the foresight to shut her up. I jerk my chin. "Get back."

Her jaw stiffens, then she retreats. She shoves the remainder of the bandages into the kit, and pushes it onto the dash, shutting it. She brings her free arm up and winds it around her waist.

"Get some rest. Once we reach our destination, I can't guarantee that you'll get any sleep for a while."

She straightens her spine, closes her eyes, and for the rest of the journey stays that way. At some point, her breathing evens out. I shoot her a sideways glance and find her forehead furrowed. Her face, or what I can make of it around the gag, is pale. There are dark shadows under her eyes. Her body is twisted in a position that surely can't be too comfortable for her.

My heart lurches.

Why should her comfort matter to me? I slow the car and bring it to a stop. Then, unfastening my seat belt, I lean over and loosen the gag. She moves in her sleep but doesn't awaken. I slide off the gag and shove it in my pocket. I ease her head back until her body rests in a comfortable position.

This is to make sure she survives the journey in one piece, that's all it is. It's what anyone would do to their possessions, making sure they are cared for.

Her eyelids flutter, and I pull back, start the car, and set off. She mumbles, then settles down.

I drive up the winding roads. The darkness crowds in, and I have to peer through the windshield to make out where I am headed. Lowering the speed, I navigate the circuitous slope. The headlights pick up the steep grassy incline on one side. We are far above Loch Ness. Heading toward Inverness. Where's the turnoff? I keep going, eyes straining, then find the small, almost hidden road.

I swing onto it, and the SUV bumps along the unpaved surface. I keep going until I hit a wall of foliage, then stay there idling. I flash the lights off and on, then switch them off. The silence is almost absolute. Except for the breathing of the woman at my side.

Within a few seconds, the foliage is pushed aside. I drive the car through, down the lane, until I reach a clearing. There are five bungalows set around the space. A motorbike, an SUV that has seen better days, and another car I don't recognize are parked there. Bringing the SUV to a halt, I jump out. Footsteps crunch on the gravel, then a man appears at my side.

"Kayden." He props his arms on his waist.

"Dominic." I raise my chin.

"Didn't think you were going to make it."

"Or was that what you'd hoped?" I bare my lips at my second.

"Knew you'd survive whatever Zeus had in store for you, especially after that hairbrained plan you came up with which led to…" He waves his hand around the place.

Anger thrums down my spine. "Perhaps my plan worked better than expected. Zeus is distracted, isn't he? He's found a mate; he has much more to lose. It makes him vulnerable."

"You made us vulnerable." He rolls his shoulders. "Look around you. We lost the city, lost the omegas, set ourselves up to be targets of the Vikings, who will not stop until they've gained back what you promised them—one way or the other."

He's fucking right. Not a moment has gone by when I haven't berated myself for losing the one thing I had promised my father. The one thing that I would protect with my life. But I intend to make sure I get it all back and Zeus pays the price for what he did to me.

"You forget one thing." I crack my neck.

He tilts his head.

I slam my fist forward and smash it into his face. His head snaps back. Blood spurts from his nose, over his lips, highlighting his white teeth. He snarls, then lunges at me.

I sidestep him, stick my foot out.

He goes sprawling on his front, and I leap on him, slam his head into the ground, then twist his hands behind his back.

"I am still the Head of the Clan, still the Chief of Scotland. What I say goes. If I ask you to jump, you do. If I ask you to throw yourself off the highest peak of the Highlands, you fucking do that. You don't question what I say."

He turns his head and spits out blood.

I lean my weight down and I bury an elbow into the small of his back. He pants and tries to draw in a breath. I lean in farther, pinning him to the ground.

"Do you fucking understand?"

He nods. I loosen my grip enough for him to take in a breath, and another.

The sound of the door of the SUV opening reaches me a second before the scent of honey and slick deepens.

"Alpha?"

I look up.

Dom angles his head toward the SUV. "So this is the reason for your foul mood?"

110

Chloe

"Get back in the fucking vehicle," he roars.

The sound grates over my sensitized nerve endings, and I jolt. His anger is a palpable force that slams into my chest. I slap the palm of my free arm over my ear and lurch back. I collide with the edge of the car and fall in.

"Who've you got here?" The man on the ground peers up at me. His nostrils flare; his gaze rakes over my body.

I know what he must see—a helpless omega who is ready for the taking.

"None of your fucking business." Kayden grits his teeth. His jaw tics. He rises to his feet in that fluid gesture that is so characteristic of him. He prowls toward me, anger fairly leaping off of his body.

A moan threatens to bleed from my lips, and I swallow it back. I can't show him how scared I am right now. He takes another step forward, his gaze holding mine. Those amber eyes flare. Golden depths roll with suppressed emotions. Anger? Something else. The need to mark me as his. The need to hurt. My breathing goes shallow. His hand snakes out, and I wince and squeeze my eyes shut. The next second, the bindings holding me to the car drop away. He grabs my shoulders, and fear spikes my veins. Anger explodes at my temples.

I fight him in earnest. "Let me go. Don't hurt me."

He yanks me close against the wall of his chest. Heat. Hardness. The kind of infallible warmth that only comes from direct contact with another human being. He is my captor, I want to be scared of him, I am afraid of what he can do to me, but he holds me tightHis arms restrain me and reassure me simultaneously.

"Shh," he whispers.

His breath is hot, his heart thundering against my ear. His chest planes heave. I try to free my arms, and his grip tightens, and somehow…somehow instead of it feeling threatening that he's got me locked and immovable, it feels almost freeing. Like he's giving me the permission to break down again, to let go of whatever I am trying to hold back, to give in to the fears that crawl at my gut, that grow in my chest, tendrils snaking out, winding around my thoughts, radiating out to my fingers, my toes.

My shoulders heave. I draw in gulps of air. A headache pounds at my temples, a combination of the estrus that surges in my blood and my restless sleep. I sag against him. My eyes burn; my chest hurts. He holds me until my knees buckle under me. Then, taking a step back, he grips my chin and lifts my head so I am forced to meet his gaze.

"I am going to take you inside."

I stare. The beginning of shadows stain the hollows under his eyes. The skin stretches across his cruel face. His lips purse. "Nod if you understand."

His voice chafes over my sensitized nerve endings. I jerk my head.

He bends, then winds his arms around my lower thighs and hauls me up over his shoulder in a fireman's carry. My head lolls, hair hanging down as the blood rushes to my face.

He turns, then walks away from the car.

Footsteps sound behind us. I guess the other man, Dominic, is following us.

"You going to tell us who she is?"

"A prisoner."

"That much is evident. What do you intend to do with her?"

"Trade her in with Zeus, when he comes looking for her."

Dominic swears. "You think Zeus values her enough to walk in here? If he hasn't tailed you already, motherfucker. You are putting the lives of our closest clansmen at his mercy."

"My clan. My decision," Kayden snaps back, his voice whirling around me, the tension from his body slapping my skin, my face.

My stomach lurches. I moan and wriggle against the hard bones of his shoulder. He rubs a hand over my back, patting my ass. His gestures seem absentminded. The warmth of his touch sinks in through the seat of my pants, reassuring me. Isn't that strange? He's made it clear I am a pawn in this, whatever power play is on between him and Zeus (and Lucy…yeah, I am not sure how much I can trust my sister now). Yet, something inside me insists that he cares for me despite everything. I groan, and his steps hurry.

"A decision that affects all of the rest of us," Dominic says.

"If you don't agree then you can leave."

"I am not here for you."

"You are treading on shaky ground, Second."

"I promised your father I'd stay with you."

Kayden's body stiffens. The tension crackles off of him, mixed with anger and a tinge of something else. Regret maybe? Nah, he may want to make sure I am not in danger and purely for his own selfish needs, but regret, now that's an emotion I don't associate with him at all.

"And that includes backing you in whatever insane decision you decide to take. Doesn't mean I won't fight you over it."

Kayden tosses his head. "You are too fucking rational, too logical."

"You and Zeus are so similar, it's no wonder the two of you don't see eye to eye."

Kayden swings around, my body lurching against his. "No more talk of that motherfucker."

"You'd think the two of you felt more for each other than being enemies. Maybe someone needs to lock both of you in a room, until you fight out whatever it is that claws at your guts."

"Maybe I need to thrash it out with you first?" Kayden rasps.

"We are evenly matched."

"I brought you down earlier; you are growing soft here without anyone to keep you on your toes…" Kayden's shoulders flex; the hard lines of his back dig into my chest.

"Whoever she is, this is wrong."

Now, I stiffen. So Dominic has a conscience. He and Kayden also seem to have a less-than-cordial relationship. Is it something I can use to my advantage? Not sure, but it's worth a try. I only need to wait for the right opportunity.

Kayden swivels around and continues walking.

"You are contradicting everything your father stood for. First, sending Lucy to kill Zeus."

"Which worked in our favor," Kayden's pace quickens.

"Now, kidnapping and holding this omega against her choice."

"Which is going to lure Zeus here, and when he comes, we'll be waiting." Kayden half angles his body, and the other man pauses.

"I have your back, Kayden." Dom sounds resigned.

"You could have had me fooled."

Dom huffs out a breath, "Have it your own way. But don't say I didn't warn you when we are caught between the Vikings and Zeus."

"You've had your say, now do your duty. Shut the fuck up."

111

Kayden

Dom's jaw tightens. He has my best interests as he insists, and I don't doubt that. Fact is, a lot of what he said is true.

It was wrong to kidnap her and hold her against her will.

It was wrong to have brought her here and endangered all of them.

The Vikings will pursue us until I make good the loss of omegas to them.

There is a chance that when Zeus comes, he won't be willing to negotiate.

Which leaves me where? Facing a possible rebellion among my team. They've been loyal to me. I have a chance at getting them to see my point of view. It is the only way out. I have to use all of the skills at my disposal to get them to back me up. Dom will come around. He always does. The man is older than me, in his late thirties; he's already seen a lot. No wonder he tends to be cautious in his approach. He prefers to take the more cautious way out. That's why he is my second. My adviser. I take the lead; he often acts as my buffer, to smooth things out in my wake. He needs to get with the program and do exactly that now.

I raise my chin and meet his eyes. "You're right."

"Huh?" He frowns, then folds his arms over his chest. Creases fan out from around his eyes.

"I shouldn't have endangered all of you this way. It was wrong to come here. But it's done." I toss my head. "I am here now, and I want to call a meeting of the entire team so we can decide on what we want to do next."

"You are actually going to consult the entire team and work out what's best for all of us." Dom rubs the back of his neck.

"Didn't I say that?" I narrow my gaze at him.

He stiffens but doesn't look away. "Now?"

"You gotta problem?" I tense, and the omegas muscles bunch. Is she so tuned into me that she senses my anger? She wriggles in my hold and I pat the curve of her ass. She draws in a breath, then her muscles relax. I continue stroking her body, from ass to thigh and back. The curves of her body under the fabric of her pants are soft, yet firm. I turn my head to nuzzle the side of her butt and Dom's eyebrows shoot up.

I drop my arm to my side. The fuck did I do? Do I want her so much that I can't keep my hands to myself in front of an audience. I draw myself up to my full height, "Besides, I am awake." I crack my neck, "No reason the rest of the team needs to sleep in."

I stalk toward the cabin at the end of the line. It's bigger than the rest and set apart a little. "Fifteen minutes," I tell him over my shoulder.

"Just to be clear no one missed you while you were gone."

"Ten."

He swears. Then marches to the door of the cabin on the opposite side.

I reach mine and shoulder open the door. I walk past the large room with chairs scattered around. It's the only space in this entire compound that accommodates all of us and which we use for meetings. I walk right through, past the small kitchenette to the bedroom.

I drop her on the bed. Her body bounces once then stills. She doesn't move. Her eyes are open but her gaze is fixed on a point past my shoulders.

"How are you feeling?"

She doesn't reply.

"Are you hurting anywhere?"

"What do you think?" She twists her lips, but still refuses to meet my gaze. Adamant omega. A pulse tics at my jaw.

Why do I care how she feels?

After today I'll never see her again. Not until I hand her over to Zeus and then things will go back to the way they were. I'd have lived up to the promise made to my adoptive father, my citizens will be happy. My clan will be able to go home. Everyone will have what they want. Including me. A heavy feeling rolls in my stomach. The blood pounds at my temples and I ignore it. I am doing the right thing. This is the only way to get over her. To forget I had ever buried myself inside her, licked her skin and claimed her.

She bears your mark asshole. And once I turn away from her, I'll forget about her. Forget the vulnerability in her that draws me to her. Forget how her innocence seduces me, makes me want to lose myself in her. Makes me want to protect her. Take care of her. And I can't afford that distraction. I can't allow myself to be emotionally attached to her.

It's why I must do this. It's the only way out.

I scoop her up in my arms and she doesn't protest. Her muscles are slack as if she's mentally checked out. It's a coping mechanism and it angers me.

How dare she allow her attention to drift away when she is in my arms. With me? How can she think of anything else but me? I snarl low in my throat, but she doesn't wince as I expect her to. My biceps flex, the blood thrums at my temples. Fuck this omega and her histrionics. It's all a bid for my attention, that's all this is. Well you got it little one, you asked for it.

Striding inside the bathroom, I lower her to the floor. She sways and I right her with a hand on her shoulder.

Her hair flows around her shoulders and I tuck a strand behind her ear. She blinks, her gaze widens. I tense. Why did I do that? Why do I constantly want to touch her, caress her, hold her... soothe her. *Soothe her?* I've never wanted to comfort any other omega I had fucked before. *She's screwing with your head and just by being in your presence.* I let go of her and fold my arms over my chest.

"Use the facilities."

Her gaze flicks across to the porcelain commode in the corner.

She takes a step toward it, and her knees buckle. I swear under my breath, and she flinches. That only makes me angrier. At myself, for allowing her to get so weak. I square my shoulders then scoop her up and deposit her near the commode.

I press down on her shoulders, and she raises her gaze.

"Some privacy, please."

"Nothing I haven't seen before." I glare at her.

She hesitates, then color flushes her cheeks. "Please." She squeezes her eyes shut. "Don't deny me this." Her features twist. A teardrop trails down her cheek.

Damn it, that look on her face. The pulse that thuds at her throat. All of it screams at me to show her mercy. Mercy.

My heart constricts. The hell does it feel like I am shattering a little inside.

I turn my back on her.

There is silence behind me. A beat. Two.

"You have two minutes."

A breath whistles from her. Then comes the rustle of fabric as she pulls down her jeans, then her panties. The tinkle of liquid hits the ceramic. She finishes, there's a whisper of cloth against skin, then she flushes. Footsteps sound toward the sink in the center. I pivot to find her washing her hands.

Her spine bows, and her thick hair fans around her shoulders, covering her expression. The scent of her is heavy in the space. That whiff of honey, the tang of pepper, and beneath it all that sugary scent of her slick which sinks into my blood.

Her shoulders convulse

Only when I am standing behind her do I realize I have moved. She stiffens. Then shuts off the tap, and looks around. I grab the towel and hand it to her. She dries her fingers. I watch her movements—slow, precise. Another ripple flows down her spine. She grips the edge of the sink, and her gaze meets mine over her shoulder. Green eyes dilated, the darkness of her pupils bleeding out until only a circle remains around the edges.

The pulse beating at the base of her neck accelerates. Thudding against her skin. I push the hair back from the curve of her shoulder, and she trembles.

The skin there is torn, beginning to scar. Beautiful. My groin tightens. I lean down and lick the scabbed skin, and she flinches. Another shudder grips her body; the scent of slick deepens. I place a palm at the small of her back and push. She bends over the sink, her spine straight, her butt jutting out.

I palm the curve of her ass, then shove my thigh between her jean-clad legs. She whimpers, my cock jumps, wanting to stab through my pants. I cup her pussy through the fabric of her pants. Moisture dampens the material that covers her crotch.

"You're soaked," a purr rumbles up my chest.

She closes her eyes and sways. A sweet hum floods out of her lips in answer, and my cock strains, begging to be let out of the confines of my pants.

"I could fuck you now."

I slide my hand in front to pinch her clit through the fabric, and she moans. Her head falls forward; her hair flows down either side of her face, the long strands grazing the sink. I squeeze her hips and fit my swollen cock into the groove between her ass cheeks.

A spasm whips over her back, and her spine curves. I plunge my hips forward, locking her between my thighs and the sink. Reaching down, I grab handfuls of her thick hair, winding it around my palms. I tug, and her face comes up, her gaze meeting mine in the mirror. Her pupils are blown, her lips fall open, and color flushes her cheeks.

"Ask me."

She opens her mouth, then closes it. The cords of her throat move.

I lean forward until my chest is flush with her back. The width of her shoulders is half that of mine. My torso crowds her, my chest surrounds her, overwhelming her. She swallows, and her mouth moves.

"I can't hear you."

"Please," she gasps. "Don't do this."

"Don't do what?" I turn her head around so her face is angled to me. "You mean this?" I drop my head and lick behind her ears, and she shivers. "Or maybe this?" I seize the hoodie and pull it back, along with her shirt, then nibble my way down her throat, to the strip of skin bared by the move. I sink my teeth into the soft skin, and she groans.

Another growl vibrates up my chest, undulating in the air around us, folding her to me, pinning her to my chest. My dick pulses against her core, and the scent of slick deepens. Soft. Sweet. Mine. A purr of satisfaction coils in my gut. The fuck? I let go of her so quickly that she stumbles. I

take a step back, and she raises her head and meets my gaze in the mirror.

Dazed eyes, twisted lips, heaving breasts, so easy to corrupt. So innocent. So ready to be taken. I shake my head to clear it, then swivel around to the door. I pause and throw her a glance over my shoulder.

"Time to get this over with."

112

Chloe

He strides out of the bathroom, and the breath whistles out of me. What was that about? For a second he'd seemed on the verge of losing control.

I was so sure that he was going to throw me down and take me right then.

Since we left Marcus' place, the tension in him has been building. I am sure it's all a ruse, this...act of not fucking me again until I ask. And I will not ask. Not only because of that message from Zeus and Lucy, which had only reinforced my decision to not give in. If anything, the very fact that they thought it necessary to tell me to resist makes me want to...throw myself at him and ask him to take me.

I bring my hand to my hair and scrape back the strands. My face is flushed, my lips swollen, even though he hasn't kissed...he's not kissed me so far. He wants to try to relegate me to the position of an omega. A nameless, faceless creature who he can rut to scratch an itch. I straighten. But I am not as weak as he thinks me to be. I am not as defenseless as he wishes I were. I am, was, a princess, albeit one without a place to call her own. But I have the most important thing—my genes, my bloodline, my dignity. I will not allow him to strip me of that.

"Don't keep me waiting."

His growl filters past the open door, and my nerve endings spark. My thighs squeeze. Why does his roughness only turn me on? I must be sick in the head. That hidden core of me responds to his dominance. Wants to be the cynosure of his harshness. It hints at a confidence, a brutality that will burn to the core. When he finally lets go, it won't be gentle. He won't stop. He won't care what I want. He'll simply take, and I... What will I do? Will I fight him, resist him? He'd knotted me and marked me just because he could. To show that he had the kind of strength that could overpower, bend me to his will.

The air in the space vibrates with unsaid emotions. The beast is getting restless. I square my shoulders then, tugging my hoodie and shirt back into place, I swivel around and walk to the door. My stomach twists and I double over, panting. The estrus is growing intense, the spasms coming faster, harder. Has it been this agonizing before? I can't remember.

It's his nearness.

All those pheromones, adrenaline—the proximity of a hot-blooded alpha male calls to the omega in me. It demands I submit. It's only a matter of time, but until then I am going to play my part. I am going to hold on to every last shred of my resistance.

I straighten, then walk out of the door of the bathroom. Crossing the bedroom and the kitchen, I enter the living room and come to a halt.

Faces turn around to stare at me.

One, two, three…there are seven alphas, not counting Kayden, who stands at the far end next to a small table. My heart thuds. I lick my dry lips then swing my gaze to his face.

All expression is wiped from his countenance. All signs of the out-of-control male who'd almost rutted me is gone. He stands head and shoulders above the others, his chest wide, his shoulders bunched.

He jerks his chin.

I take a step forward, and without exception, every man in the room leans forward to track my every move.

The one closest to me scowls, "This is her?"

My gaze flicks to him, and I swallow the sound of fright that bubbles up.

His hair streams in dark-blond clouds, his massive chest clad in a shirt that clings to powerful muscles. His nostrils flare, and his lips twist.

"What are you playing at, Kayden? She's in heat, and you bring her here among alphas who haven't had female company in months?"

Kayden's fingers clench into fists.

A ripple of discontent flows around the space. A low growl rolls out from the man next to him.

Across the room, another alpha digs his fingers into his knees and leans forward. The very air reeks of testosterone and male aggression. A whine floods my chest, and I bite down on my lower lip.

Kayden crooks a finger, his other arm hidden behind his back.

I hesitate, and he glares at me.

A ripple of apprehension shivers up my spine. Only when my knees wobble do I realize I have taken a step forward. I walk past one alpha, then another, all the while my eyes are on Kayden's, holding on to the strength of his gaze, pleading with him. He doesn't blink. Nothing reveals his awareness of the state of my confusion. *Don't do this.* I beseech him without speaking aloud.

His muscles stay solid.

What does he have in mind? What does he want of me? I reach him and stop. I am so much smaller that I barely reach his chest. I don't look up, don't dare meet his gaze.

He brings his other arm around, and a flash of silver catches my attention. He raises the knife clasped in his fingers, and my heart slams into my rib cage. Blood pounds in my ears. The muscles of my thighs tighten. I half-angle away from him, everything in me insisting that I get out of here. Get out of here. Now. He makes a warning sound in his throat.

I swallow and clench my fists at my sides.

I won't leave. I will obey him, and he knows that. How could he have trained me to do his bidding in such little time? The force of his influence creeps around me, tugging at me, holding me to him with chains of delight.

"Undress."

His voice whips over my sensitized skin.

"What?" I stare at him.

His face is a mask I don't recognize. His gaze is determined. All expression is shorn from his features. I don't recognize him.

Kayden holds my gaze. "Should I ask them to help?" He jerks his chin toward the men behind me. "Or will you do the honors…princess?"

I swallow, and the blood drains from my face.

"You…you know?" I wheeze. How had he guessed? What is he going to do next?

His lips curl. "Enough talk."

He lowers his arms. I flinch.

He flicks his wrists and I squeeze my eyes shut. He rips down the zipper on my hoodie then shoves the sleeves over my shoulders before wrenching it off. He grabs the front of my shirt and rips it apart. Buttons pop and fall to the floor. He yanks it off.

There's a whistling sound, and air flows over my bared skin.

He reaches for the buttons of my jeans.

"Wait."

I sputter, and he pauses.

"I'll do it." I bite my lower lip.

I will not give him the satisfaction of stripping me completely. It's a small gesture of defiance, but that's all I have left. I hold his gaze, then wriggle the jeans down my hips and kick them to the side. The cold air flows around me; my teeth chatter. I want to wrap my arms around my waist, but instead, I stay still and clench my hands into fists at my sides.

"Take off your bra."

I shake my head, a low moan of fear surges half-way up my throat. I will not scream, will not. How can he do this to me? What does he want of me? Why couldn't he have just left me back at the harem? Why did he bring me with him?

"Keep going." His amber gaze fills my vision. Fires banked, they are hard brown now. He's locked away a part of himself somewhere deep inside. He's distancing himself from what is happening here.

Is that the only way he can withstand this?

"You don't leave me a choice." He reaches for the knife on the table next to him.

My knees wobble.

He holds it up, and I gasp.

He sets his jaw, then slides the blade between the strap of my bra and my skin and flicks up. Another flash of steel, and he's cut the thin straps that hold up my panties. A sliver of pain tears at the skin over my hipbone, droplets of blood, and the material snaps. He slams the knife down, and the blade embeds in the wooden floor, the vibrations traveling up to me, swiping up over my calves. My fingers convulse and I dig my nails into the palms of my hand.

The bra inches down my shoulders to catch on my nipples. It stays there, poised.

There's an indrawn breath behind me, then the bra slithers to the floor.

His gaze holds mine all through. "Part your legs."

His voice is low, harsh.

"I'll make you do it; you know that."

Blood thrums at my temples. He'd do it, too. Bastard. I fucking hate him. He leans forward, and a small scream leaves my lips.

"Do it."

His voice is hushed. Dominant. My insides clench. Only when my panties slide down my thighs do I realize I have done as he commanded.

I am naked. Exposed. Vulnerable.

An inhalation rips the air behind me.

"What the fuck are you doing, Kayden?"

I recognize the voice as belonging to the same alpha who'd been talking to Kayden earlier. Dominic, that's what Kayden had called him.

"This is wrong, you shouldn't —"

Kayden raises his hand, and the voice cuts off.

One of the alphas shuffles, another snarls low in his throat, and the hair on my nape stands on end. I want to cross my arms in front and shield myself but I won't.

He thinks this is the way to humiliate me, and he is right. But I won't give him the satisfaction of knowing that.

Fear thrums at my nerves, crawls up my spine. It eats away at my chest, throbbing, pulsing. A primal need to scream fills my head, bile churns my stomach, and I swallow away that bitter, acrid scent of my worst nightmare come true. Trapped in a room full of alphas with no one to help me.

Kayden jerks his chin toward the table. The skin over his cheeks stretches white. I swallow, then turn and take a step forward. My head spins, my stomach heaves, and my legs threaten to give out from under me. The next instant, Kayden lifts me in his arms. Crossing to the table, he lays me across it on my back. I fold my arm across my breasts and place the palm of the other between my thighs. He grabs my hand and wrenches it to the side. The other he wraps it around the edge of the table.

"The fuck is this?" Dom stands so fast his chair spills over.

"A test."

"For her or for us?" He narrows his gaze.

"You thought I was wrong in bringing her here? Let's see what happens when a room full of alphas are exposed to an omega in heat."

"What do you plan to achieve?" his lips thin.

"You think you are more superior, Dom? We'll see how you are able to restrain yourself."

Another of the alphas springs up, his nostrils flaring. He slams his hands on the table and leans close. My heart jumps; sweat beads my brow. A whine squeaks past my lips. He reaches out a hand, and I scoot away only to brush up against another hand. I swivel around and scream.

A third alpha watches me from the side. His arms are crossed at the edge of the table, and he lowers his face to rest his chin onto his forearm. "Such a pretty little thing." He licks his lips; his gaze narrows. He sweeps his gaze over my stomach and to my exposed pussy.

I shake my head, and he blinks. His gaze darts to the foot of the table where Kayden stands.

"What are you waiting for?" His voice is cold.

The alpha turns back to me, and his features twist. He gets up and walks around to the foot of the table. Grabbing my ankles, he pulls me down, and a scream bubbles up. *I will not cry out.* I will not let these men see how afraid I am. The hum of growls pulses around the enclosed space. Is this what it feels like to be surrounded by feral creatures who have not one iota of sympathy for me? Except Kayden isn't like that. He isn't. Beneath all of that need to hurt is a man who will not let anything happen to me. This is a test; my instincts scream that's all it is. But tell that to my body, which yearns to cave in on itself.

I bite the inside of my cheek.

A touch on my shoulder makes my head swing around. The third alpha leans across the table. He trails his fingers down my shoulder, over my breast, and my skin crawls. A spark throbs in my chest, and I gulp. Pain fills my rib cage, radiating out, pushing out, reaching toward something, a distant space where all that exists is a golden nothingness. It calls to me, seductive, asking me to come. Telling me to trust. To jump. Where? My head spins; the room wavers around me.

There is a shift in the air, and the hairs on my forearms prickle. I turn the other way to find Kayden standing there. My gaze latches on to his. I can't look away. I hold on to his eyes, lose myself in the depths of the burning amber. *Help me.* I pulse the thought at him. The band around my chest tightens. The pulse at my throat thrums.

His jaw hardens. A nerve throbs at his temple.

He shifts his gaze and nods to the man standing at the base of the table.

Fingers circle my ankle, and then my body is yanked down until my legs dangle over the side. I scream and struggle in earnest.

Someone restrains my flailing arm. Another grabs my thigh. Fingers bite into my flesh as my legs are pried apart. I hold Kayden's gaze, let him see my pain, my fear. *Please. Please.* I reach out to him and beg him in my head. *Don't let this happen. You won't let this happen. Don't let them take me.* I swallow. Tears drip down my cheek and pool on the table.

Hard flesh bumps the inside of my thigh, and everything in me goes silent. My muscles coil, my belly clenches, and something inside of me snaps. The sparks in my chest blaze out, reaching for that amber of his on the psychic plane.

I hold his eyes, raise a hand to him. "I am your mate."

113

Kayden

Her lips move; the words scream across my nerves. "I am your mate."

My mate.

Mine.

She's mine to protect.

Mine to take.

Mine to break.

Only mine.

A fire bursts to life in my chest, and I gasp. It burns through all of the thoughts, all of my apprehension, every single barrier that I had put down between us. Everything in my life has been leading up to this moment. All that I want is right here in front of me and I hadn't recognized it. My instincts had known. Right from the time I had caught the first whiff of her scent, I had recognized her. I had claimed her for myself. But had refused to accept her. No more. A scream churns my guts.

I pound my fist into my chest, throw my head back and howl. "Get the fuck away from her."

Grange, the alpha holding her leg captive, swivels to look at me. He bares his teeth. "You said this was a test."

"You failed."

I lunge across the distance between us, then swing my fist under his chin. His back arches, and he crashes down onto the seated Lester who folds to the floor.

Grange springs to his feet. I lean forward, grab his neck, and haul up all six-feet-two-inches of him to his toes. My tendons stretch to breaking point, my muscles shudder, and my thighs groan under the weight of holding up the weight of both of us.

"Back. The. Fuck. Off."

Grange's gaze widens, he chokes, and his fingers clutch at my forearms. I shove him, and he loses his balance and stumbles over the other fallen alpha, then hits the wall. I turn to find Dom snatching up her torn shirt and placing it over her chest. He picks up her hoodie and hands it to her. I race around to the other side of the table and scoop her up.

"Get away," I bare my teeth.

Dom steps back and raises his hands.

"Leave." I glance around the room, fixing my gaze on each of the faces of the assembled alphas. My team. I fucked around with them. I screwed up. I'll deal with them later. "Go."

Another alpha lurches up to his feet, Shane. A young pup, that one. His nostrils flare; color suffuses his face. His gaze is fixed on the cowering woman in my arms. He moves forward, only to be yanked back by Dom.

"Get away, you heard the chief."

"But, she... I..." He rubs the back of his neck. "The fuck happened?"

"She's in heat. No alpha is impervious."

She moans in my arms, and Dom's face comes up. His face contorts. Sweat beads his brow. "Not even me." He snarls.

She burrows farther into my chest, and hides her face.

"Leave. Now." I narrow my gaze on Dom. "All of you."

Swiveling on my feet, I race out and to the bedroom. Then slam the door behind us and lock it.

The sound of the bolt hitting home seems to awaken her from her stupor. "Wh... what are you doing?"

I don't answer. I can't. I don't trust myself to speak right now. The fuck is wrong with me? What have I done? I had claimed her, then thrown her at the mercy of my own men. I had told them it was a test...but really, I had been testing myself. I had failed spectacularly.

I march to the bed in the center, drop her on the mattress, then pull her up toward the headboard. I look around for something to use. Letting go of her, I wrench my T-shirt over my neck. Bending I twist it around her wrists, then tie her to the headboard.

"Let go of me." She scrambles back as far as her restraints will allow her.

"No." I straighten and look down at her half-naked figure. I yank the shirt and hoodie away from her body and fling them aside.

Another scream leaves her mouth, and the sound sinks into my blood, lodging in my gut. I don't want to see her in pain, I don't want to see her unhappy, and yet the sounds she makes when she is afraid only add to this burning, throbbing need in my chest. I rub the skin above my heart, and her gaze drops there.

Her eyebrows furrow, and she raises her eyes to mine. "You don't want to do this."

One side of my mouth twitches. "You don't want to tell me what I can't do." I unbutton the waistband of my pants and she gulps. "Please..."

"You remember what you said out there?"

Her gaze widens as she stares at my crotch.

"Do you?" I growl, and her shoulders convulse.

"Y...yes."

"Did you mean it?"

Her breath hitches.

I glare at her, and she cowers, kicking up her legs, trying to scoot away. Blood thuds at my temples. My cock twitches. I massage my dick, and her gaze drops there. A low purr tumbles out of my lips, and her breathing grows ragged.

"I was only stating a fact."

"Oh?" I tilt my head. My vision tunnels in on her. "And what's that?"

"You claimed me against my will. You imposed your choice on me. You made me your mate…" Her voice fades.

Another purr rumbles up from me, and she flinches.

"Complete your statement." My voice lowers to a hush. I wipe all expression from my countenance.

Her gaze flicks to meet mine then skitters away.

"Say it, Omega. You've stood up to me so far. Don't disappoint me now."

"You won't appreciate it." She gulps.

"Has that ever stopped you?"

"I am afraid of what you'll do to me."

"Punishment is part of the process."

"What process?"

"Us getting to know each other."

"Is that what you call this?" She swivels her head to glare at me.

"Doesn't matter what it is. I am not one for giving names to things. Or classifying relationships. I left that to my father, and look where that got him…dead." Anger thrums my nerves.

He'd accepted my mother after what had happened to her, but the relationship between them had changed forever. He'd adopted me, tried to foster his goodness in me, almost as if he'd wanted to burn away the blood pounding in my veins. But my genes had manifested themselves after all.

I am just similar to my blood father.

Not very different from my half-brother.

I am a fucking alpha. This is what I do. I take what is mine.

She squares her shoulders. "Doesn't mean I accept it."

I swoop down on the bed, and she screams and kicks out. I grab her legs, fold them and shove up her knees so they are near her ears. The pink throbbing lips of her pussy stare up at me. Beautiful. The source of all of my pleasure. My pain. So fucking hot and moist. Saliva pools in my mouth.

"Why are you doing this?" Her voice wavers.

"I have to. Since I scented you, I knew you belonged to me."

"You allowed them to touch me." A sob spills from her lips.

I raise my gaze to hers. "I am sorry, I should not have let that happen."

She sniffles, "If you are truly sorry then you'll let me go."

"I can't." I drag my gaze down to the wound at her neck, across her heaving breasts, back to the focus of my fascination. Her beautiful, gorgeous, melting core. "But I can make it up to you."

I lower my head and lick her clit.

114

Chloe

Heat. Too much heat. The rough texture of his tongue grates over my pussy and my thigh muscles stiffen.

He swipes his tongue from my clit to my back hole then back to the top of my cunt. Ripples of heat flash out from my core. He hooks his tongue around the bud of my clit and my breath falters.

I open my mouth to scream, and all that spills out is a pant. "Don't."

He looks up at me from under hooded eyelids. "You know better than to challenge me."

He leans in, forcing me to part my legs farther. Then slurps his way up my melting, throbbing pussy, again and again. His tongue dips inside my channel, and I groan.

He blows over my clit, and I shiver.

A low purr vibrates his chest, curling around my waist, sinking into my belly. My nerves thrum. My hips rise off the bed. All of the blood rushes to my engorged pussy. Another growl vibrates from his throat, and my belly spasms. Moistures gushes from my core.

"Good girl." He drops his head and laps it up.

Warmth flushes my cheeks.

Why is my body obeying him? Why does everything in me want to open up, give in to his needs? Allow him to take?

"Untie me…please."

"I can't do that."

"You said you'd wait for me to ask before you took me again. Did you forget?"

"By the time I am done, I promise you'll be begging for me to rut you." Another purr rumbles up his chest, "and so much more."

He draws out the sub-vocals, swirling the notes around me, coating my skin with the intensity of his rich, deep sounds. The vibrations build, holding me down, pinning me to the mattress as surely as his tongue which cleaves my pussy, drawing out the moisture between my thighs, forcing my womb to contract again. A gush of builds at my core and clambers up my spine. It rises up to meet the burning in my chest, and I pant. The breath squeezes out of me; my rib cage tightens. A chill skitters in its wake, coating my blood with ice.

"No. Not now." I cry out.

I've been on the precipice of estrus for nearly forty-eight hours. On its own, it might have taken a day, maybe more to go into full heat, but that pine-and-cinnamon scent of his, the bite of testosterone crowding in on me, the rough thrust of his tongue in that most vulnerable part of me, it all shoves me over the edge.

My eyes roll back, and I groan. "Please."

I sense him glance up. "Look at me."

I focus my gaze on his features. His broad shoulders are poised between my thighs. His lips glisten with my slick; a flush sears his cheeks. He looks feral, animalistic, and so strong. So vital.

"See what you do to me?" His jaw tics. "You reduce me to the most basic part of myself. Force me to acknowledge I am nothing but a rutting, depraved animal at heart. The one I'd tried to discipline and failed. You make me aware of my vulnerabilities. That I am just a breath away from the beast inside me." His eyebrows knit.

"You…you hate me?"

He peels back his lips, "Hate is too mild a word for what I feel about you." He stares at my face. "I want to consume you alive. I want to lick up every part of you, mark every inch of your body. Shove you face down into these sheets and lick your pussy for hours until you come again and again. Until you lose every thought in that pretty little head. Until all you want is me. Ask for me, beg me to take you, and when you do…if you convince me that you really want it, only then"—his eyes burn with a cold heat—"will I rip into your cunt and knot you. I'll fuck your body through this mattress, fuck you for hours, only letting you up for air for seconds, right before I claim you all over again so you'll never forget who you belong to."

His words send a primitive surge of fear…and lust…I admit it; his possessive, filthy words shake me to my core. A primal need to be with him rears up from deep inside. He's strong. Virile. He's right for me. He's the kind of alpha I would have chosen…if I'd had a choice. But he hadn't given me that. He'd simply taken.

And I can't forgive that.

But I also want him.

"It's not you I hate, I hate myself." I swallow, "I loathe myself for being so attracted to you."

My belly clenches, my sex squeezes, and more slick flows down between my pussy lips. No. I don't want this. Once he starts, I won't be able to resist.

I'll submit to him; it's a foregone conclusion.

He'll take my body, make me experience the kind of highs I never thought existed. Drug me with endorphins, coat me in his cum, and spoil me for anything else. He'll have seduced my body, sated my appetites, but my mind is my own.

I'd been wrong to think he doesn't feel. There's an anger eating away at him. One he tries to mask, and mostly succeeds. But this fire that boils inside is the kind that, once drawn, cannot be pulled back. Not until it destroys everything in its path. Me.

"I'll never accept you." I spit out the words. "Never."

Those glacial eyes burn.

A harsh purr rips from his mouth, the sound so animalistic that I cry out.

His biceps bulge.

The fine hair on my forearms raises in alarm.

His shoulders expand as he draws in a breath. "Allow me to change your mind."

He dives down between my legs and nips on my pussy, and I scream. He licks me, sucks on my clit, shoves his rough tongue inside of my soaking channel. He lets go of one of my knees only to knock them together and restrain them with a massive arm. He shoves a thick finger into my cunt and bites down on my clit. The orgasm screams up my spine to smash behind my eyeballs. Flashes of red and white fill my vision. My spine arches, my head snaps back, and I howl.

"I hate you." The words tear out of me

"You don't mean it."

He adds a second finger, then a third inside my channel, pulls them out and shoves them back in, again and again. The squelching sounds fill the air. Obscene. Primitive. My entire body tingles in the aftershocks of the orgasm.

"I...hate—" He swipes his tongue between my aching folds and all my nerve endings seem to fire at once.

"Hate—"

He twists his tongue inside my channel, then dips a finger inside my back hole and I stutter. All thought spills from my mind leaving only intense sensations in its wake. He fucks me with his tongue, in-out-in, and hooks his finger inside my puckered hole. Sparks of fire ripple down my spine. A trembling starts up from my toes.

No, no, no. I can't orgasm. Not again.

Adrenaline laces my blood, and I fight him in earnest. I yank at the restraint around my wrists, strain against the solid barrier of his arm. He simply leans more of his weight on me, holding me immobile. Tears wet my cheeks; sweat trickles down the side of my chest and over my shoulder. A spasm ladders up my calves, up my thighs and every cell in my body tenses. Waves of heat, then chills slither over my skin.

My body seems to develop a mind of its own as I twist and buck, reaching for something. Something. Burning need claws at my chest.

A moan whines out of me, and my limbs quiver.

He releases my knees, which part on either side, baring me completely, only for him to wind one of my legs around his neck.

He continues to lave my pussy again, swiping his tongue up my melting folds and around the aching bud of my clit. He rubs the heel of his palm across my cunt at the same time that he thrusts three fingers into my pussy. All the while he's playing with my back hole.

I thrash my head from side to side, my hips arch off the mattress, and he still doesn't stop.

He sucks, he nibbles, he bites on my clit, all the time his fingers thrust in and out of me. More slick gushes out, and he releases my swollen bud long enough to lap it up, always returning to the throbbing, aching, swollen part of my pussy. The waves recede, and chills wreck my muscles.

My teeth chatter; my bones ache. I open my eyes and look down to find him staring up at me with that penetrating gaze.

"I will not…cannot…give in to you." I whisper.

"Then take from me, Cara, take everything I have to offer, and that which I can't. Fucking rip me apart to make up for what I did to you earlier."

115

Kayden

Her muscles tense, and her forehead furrows. Her gaze holds mine as if she dare not let go.

"What do you need?"

Her belly trembles, her breasts heave. "More..." She pants.

Before the word has left her mouth, I drag my fingers from her clit, and slick gushes out. I scoop up the liquid and smear it down the cleavage between her ass cheeks. Her hips convulse. I rub my fingers against her back hole, and color flushes her cheeks.

"Let me give you what you ache for."

I shove my tongue inside her wet channel, and she pants.

Her muscles loosen, and I glide my finger into her back hole. Her shoulders lift off of the mattress, and her head falls back, exposing the curve of her neck.

"Tell me you want me to pleasure you."

After what I put her through earlier, it's the least I can do. There's a strange satisfaction in seeing her fall apart around me. In making her come. In watching the color sweep up her shoulders, over her throat. In hearing her pant and moan as she chews on her lower lip, her entire body shaking, while she digs her hips into the mattress and tries to wriggle away from me. At the same time, her legs wind around my neck, urging me closer, nearer, faster. More, I need to taste more of her.

I rub my chin over her swollen pussy, around her clit, and she howls. "Ouch...that hurts." I blow on the throbbing flesh and she whines..

I slide my other hand up her torso to her quivering breast and pinch the distended nipple. She howls and thrashes around. Slick gushes out from between her legs, her head snaps back, and she screams as she comes. Her entire body tenses, then her muscles relax.

The aftershocks ripple across her skin.

Shivers ladder up her legs; goosebumps flare over her thighs. I unhook her legs from around my shoulders. Then

crawl up her body and plank over her. "Open your eyes."

Her eyeballs move behind her closed eyelids, her lips part, and she mumbles under her breath.

"Look at me."

She cracks her eyes open, and her gaze latches on to mine. Pupils blown, the dark black bleeds out, leaving only a green circle around the circumference. The heat in my chest flares; my groin hardens. My shaft brushes against her melting core, and she whines. I clasp her waist and slide my palm over her hips to squeeze her butt.

She licks her lips. My gaze falls there. I angle my head and slurp on her mouth. Sweet. Hot. The honey of her essence teases my senses. A purr curls up my chest, and I weave the sub-vocals around her shoulders, her chest, binding her to me as efficiently as the rope. I drag my arm up her luscious curves, over her arm, to twine my fingers around her hands. So tiny, both her palms fit into one of mine.

"I have to take you."

Her gaze widens. Her breasts heave. She opens her mouth, and I swipe my tongue over the seams of her lips, drag it over her teeth, filling her up, drinking from her.

A growl rumbles up my chest. The taste of her fills my senses. Sugar. A bite of pepper that tugs at my nerves, overwhelms all other thought. I tilt my hips and glide my shaft into her weeping pussy. Her muscles coil and flex, her curves move, adjust, and her inner muscles protest, then stretch to accommodate all of me.

I drag my hand down to support the back of her head. I balance my other arm next to her, trying to keep my weight off of her. Her body shudders, and I wait. Her pussy clamps down on my shaft, her wet channel clinging to the shape of my dick. I stay there and wait until the trembling recedes. Then tilt my hips and thrust into her. My dick slips all the way home, bumping against her cervix.

Too much.

Not enough.

The sensations crowd in on my mind. Blood pulses in my ears. My heart rate ratchets up. I tear my mouth from hers and peer into her eyes. "Take me in, Cara, all of me. Take what you need."

I reach up and over her and undo the ropes. Her arms come around my shoulders. Her nails dig into my flesh. Pain shudders down my spine to twine with the lust that expands in my belly.

Fresh ripples of heat flicker out, vibrating up to slam into the burning sensation in my chest.

Everything inside of me comes alive. All of my senses pop. My vision narrows in on her face. Those beautiful eyes. The flush of her cheeks. The swollen mouth. I loop my arms under her knees then yank them up again, "Hold on."

"Wh…what?" She blinks.

"I am going to fuck you now."

116

Chloe

"What the—?" I stare at him. Another wave of heat flushes over my skin, and I pant. "Wh...what do you mean?"

His lips twist; a nerve tics at his jaw. "Where you are concerned, I have no self-control." He kicks his hips forward, and his dick slams right inside, glancing off of my pelvic bone.

"Ow."

Pain sparks at my nerve endings. He crams every millimeter of my channel. The rough ridges of his shaft scrape over my sensitive walls, and I frown.

He braces himself on his elbows, the muscles of his biceps bulging and trembling as they hold up his weight. He's keeping most of his bulk off of me, but the position of his hips on mine, his dick throbbing inside of me is enough to restrain me.

The strength of his dominance pins me down. The scent of him, the thrumming purrs that reverberate up his chest, the overabundance of testosterone in the air crowds in and sends me over the edge.

I clutch his shoulders, and his muscles flex against my fingers.

I throw back my head, and he leans down to nip the exposed skin of my throat.

The breath slides out of me, my heart hammers, and my pulse pounds, a beat picked up by the sensitized flesh between my legs.

"Fuck..." his big body twitches.

Sweat coats his beautiful shoulders, and I have this insane desire to lean up and lick it. No. I don't want to do that. I will not participate in this brutal fucking of my body...so why do I enjoy it so much?

I squeeze my eyes shut to block out the sight of those gorgeous golden eyes. That stern countenance, those cruel lips. He is my nemesis. My master. The conductor of the orchestra that is the finely tuned nerves of my body, all of which flare, pop, and open for him. Liquid lust spikes my blood. My toes curl.

Then he begins to move. He pumps his hips, kicks forward, shoving his dick inside my poor channel, again and again. Each time he pounds against the sensitive inner muscles, sending out ever-widening whorls of heat, lust...pure sensation. This is what it must be like to be completely alive. To be taken and used like I am the last omega on Earth. And he is the only alpha who can do this. The other half of me. My captor who completes me.

It's thrilling and horrible at the same time.

My tendons of my throat move, and he sweeps his gaze down my flushed countenance. He watches me, studies my every reaction, searching my features. Every cry I stifle, every moan that slips out, every broken hitch of my breath is taken and stored away in a corner of his mind. I have no doubt he will use it against me. Even as he kicks his hips forward, he plunges his dick to the farthest extent inside of me. His knot blooms at the base of my channel, locking into place. His face hardens; his eyes glare at me. Is he still angry with me? What is he waiting for? What does he want from me?

His dick throbs inside, pushing, shoving, yearning for more, more than I can give him. More than what I want from him. Who is taking from whom? It doesn't matter anymore. He thrusts his hips again, and his dick locks behind my pelvic bone. And still he doesn't come. He waits and watches and studies my face. Then, balancing his weight on one elbow, he brings his other hand down, slips it between our sweating bodies, and thrums my clit. Goosebumps pop on my skin, my chest heaves, and white heat radiates out from where we are connected, swooping up to writhe in my chest. Swirling, twining, it shoots out, up my shoulders, behind my eyelids to my crown.

"Come."

His growl whips over me, and all of my brain cells fire at once. My womb contracts, slick gushes out to bathe his dick, and I explode. I throw my head back and open my mouth, and he closes his over mine, absorbing my screams as I hear his hoarse shout. His body shudders, his flanks flex, and then he shoots hot streams of cum inside of me.

My breath wheezes in and out and a chill sweeps down my body. All of my bones seem to rattle at once, and my teeth chatter. His dick throbs, and I realize he's still inside of me. Without disengaging, he flips positions so I lie on his chest. He brings my palms down to slide them between our bodies. The warmth of him...it's better than a furnace. It's living, breathing heat, different from the sauna cloying inside of me. It sinks into my blood, heats my skin. He rubs his palms over mine, cupping them in his. He closes his thighs around my feet—yeah, that's how much shorter than him I am.

I melt into his chest, my skin fusing with his. His deep purrs encircle my shoulders. He locks his arms around me, then tucks my head under his chin.

"Sleep," he commands, and I don't resist.

There's a touch against my forehead. Did he kiss me? Nah. The tenderness in that touch, that affection, all of it is an illusion. A ploy to get me to trust him, and that I will not.

The blackness tugs at the edge of my subconscious, when something niggling at the back of my mind comes to the fore. "Wait." I mumble. My eyelids close, "You called me Cara. What does that mean?"

117

Kayden

"Cara." I whisper. "It means beloved."

An alpha's instinct cannot be tamed, least of all by rational thought. It's why I had used the endearment without conscious thought. It's also what my father used to call my mother, before she was taken.

When had my feelings toward this tiny omega begun to change? When had she become more than a hostage? She's no longer only a pawn in this transaction between me and Zeus?

Her breathing deepens, and I clasp her over my chest. She snuggles in. Her softness curves into my hard planes; her hips fit into the hard angles of my waist. Her fingers are curled against my breastbone. I slide a finger through them, and she clutches at it.

A low hum of contentment rolls in her throat.

An answering purr rumbles from mine. Her skin glows with my ministrations. She's content, flushed with sex, and replete with my cum. Her body is spent from the orgasms I wrung from her. The high of endorphins from the knotting will ensure that she sleeps for a while longer.

I play my fingers down the ridges of her spine. Small. Delicate. So trusting. So fucking gorgeous.

I'd seen her and known she was my mate.

It's why I had claimed her on the terrace of the Omega harem.

It's why I had been trying to deny it ever since.

I was wrong in exposing her to my alphas, in allowing them to touch her, to fill their gazes with her curves, her scent infusing the space and driving them to want her.

I made a mistake and I intend to make it up to her. I intend to give her so much pleasure that she'll forget the pain I've inflicted on her so far—the emotional pain, that is. On the physical level...my demands go beyond a normal alpha-omega coupling. This was an initiation, meant to ease her into the heat cycle. Until she comes out of it, I will stay with her. Feed her and bathe her. Fuck her and rut her until her estrus breaks.

I will make sure she wants for nothing during this time.

And if it means I intend to use pain to push her over the edge of pleasure, I can be forgiven, right? The gratification from the experience will more than compensate for any gaps in my ministrations.

She mutters under her breath, and I increase the pace of my purring. Rolling out the vocals, the subtle tones, the hums, the lows of the vibes, twirling it around her and cocooning her in a space where she can float, content. Uninterrupted.

When her breathing deepens, I move her to my side. My knot loosens, and I slide out my dick. Moisture gushes out from her sweet channel. Scooping up a mixture of our combined cum, I rub it in over her pussy, her hips, across the curves of her stomach, her breasts, covering as much of her as I can get to, pausing only to smear some over her lips. I pull up an arm and tie her wrist to the headboard. I make sure the tether is long enough for her to sleep and move around the bed if needed, without restriction. Then, rolling off of the bed, I shrug into my discarded fatigues. Not bothering with a shirt or socks, I unbolt the door, closing and locking it behind me. I cross the kitchen floor, closing the door behind me there, too. Can't have any of my team coming too close.

Dom looks up from the chair in the corner. He marks his space in the book he's reading and snaps it shut.

"This place is going to be off-limits for a while, I take it?"

He waits as I cross the room and drop into the chair next to him. "I need food, clothes for her." Not that I am going to let her wear clothes, of course, but it never hurts to be prepared.

"The kitchen's stocked. I took the precaution to get these." Dom bends and picks up the bag I hadn't noticed. "I had Lisa pack some clothes for her."

"How's she doing?" I take the bag.

"She's turning eighteen in a few months." His jaw flexes. Lisa's his daughter, and one of the reasons he's perhaps overly-protective about omegas, in general. Doesn't help being the father to a breeder, and finding that overnight, she has blossomed into the kind of woman that every alpha in the square mile around her wants to rut.

"We need to find a way out of here and back into the city. If she goes into heat here in the wild, with nothing but me as protection between her and the rest..." His big palm clenches around the book.

My gaze drops down, and his clasp loosens. He smooths out the cover then sets it aside.

"It was my fault that the others turned on her." I jut my chin toward the kitchen door and the woman who is in my bedroom.

"Does your omega have a name?"

I peer at him. "Huh?"

"A name? She has one, right?"

I dig my fingers into my hair. "I...ah." I crack my neck. "You trying to tell me something, Second?"

"Only that you haven't the first idea how to treat omegas. Don't let what happened between your father and mother blind you to the possibilities of how it could be with a mate."

"And how do you know that? How do you really know what transpired between them? Other than her being raped and him taking her back, and then the two of them never getting over the incident. It would have been better if they'd lived separately than do what they did to each other. They destroyed each other slowly with words over many years. Better if he had broken off the mating bond. At least I wouldn't have had to watch each of them die slowly." My lips twist. By the time Golan came for her she'd been ready to give up her life. Is that why she'd sacrificed herself? To save me? Only her death had been in vain for Golan hadn't stopped there. The things he'd done to me afterwards...perhaps it was a relief that she'd been gone by then.

Dom doesn't know about it.

No one does.

"They stayed together for you." Dom places his elbows on his thighs and steeples his fingers.

"I would have been better off if they had stopped pretending and tried to be truthful about the fact that whatever had been between them was over the day Golan raped my mother."

"The way you are pretending now?"

"The fuck does that mean?" Springing up to my feet, I pace. "If it's about her —"

"The omega who you kidnapped and who's name you haven't even bothered to find out?"

"I didn't —" I clamp my jaw shut. I did take her. I did knot her. And, yeah, it was against her will. Oh, she enjoyed it, too...but I hadn't exactly given her a choice to back away, had I? I wouldn't have listened if she had said 'No' either. I am an alpha male, I take. That's what I do, right?

"What if one day someone does that to my daughter? I'd...I'd..." His voice breaks.

I swivel around to look at him. "I won't let that happen. I can't pretend to understand what it means to have someone depend on me. But I took an oath to protect my city and its constituents, and that includes my clan."

"And yet you agreed to barter the omegas who came to this country to seek protection from the Vikings."

"I had my reasons." I clench my fists at my sides.

He frowns; his gaze narrows.

Why do I owe an explanation to him? Why do I owe him anything? The man annoys me with his holier-than-thou attitude. He is cautious, more seasoned...everything I am not. It's why I need him. I may be arrogant enough to strategize. I can pull off the most audacious plans. I am cocky enough to try to bring Zeus to his knees. Assured enough to do everything in my power to take my city back from him...but I am also egotistical enough to not want to lose everything with one mistake. I am not my father. It's why I keep Dom around. Much as he drives me up the wall and frustrates me, I need Dom as a natural speed breaker. Someone who forces me to think things through...that's when I allow him enough knowledge of what I am up to.

"I didn't share the entire plan with you."

His chest rises and falls. He squints, but he stays silent.

"I had promised the omegas to the Vikings only because I was buying time."

"You had no intention of handing them over?"

"No." I drum my fingers on my chest. "I used it to play Ethan against Zeus, but that plan backfired."

"Something I'd have told you in advance if you had thought to confide in me."

"I wasn't sure who among my council I could trust."

"Hence the test earlier?"

He nods toward the table in the center of the room. The one where I had asked her to climb on naked. Had exposed her to the eyes of my fellow clan members. Had tempted them to get a reaction from them. I had tested them, yes, but I hadn't realized that it had been a test of my intentions. One way of finding out what I felt for her. I had claimed her, but refused to acknowledge it...until that moment when another man had had his hands all over her.

"I made a mistake."

My voice comes out gravelly, my tone unsteady. The fuck? It's the first I have admitted aloud to him that I was wrong, about anything.

He leans back in his chair. "You hurt her. She may never forgive you for what you did."

I clench my fists. A dull thud beats behind my eyeballs. He's right. Fuck the man, but he is. I can try to make it up to her, but doesn't change what I did to her.

I swivel around to face him. A flicker of of something... an understanding? — laces his features.

"I don't need your empathy." I growl.

"Not getting any from me, Kayden." One side of his lips quirks. "I've been there, you know."

"Huh?"

"I had Lisa when I turned eighteen. The physical attraction between me and her omega mother was the most overwhelming thing I had ever experienced. I carried Daria home, locked her up and knotted her." He swallows. "When I found out she was pregnant, I claimed her. It seemed the right thing to do...except...she was all wrong for me."

I fold my arms over my chest. "Is there a point to this, old man?" I toss my head. "Hearing about your personal life is all well and good, not that it's not interesting... not, actually." I pretend to yawn. "But if you came here hoping to come around to the fact that I am doing something wrong here in your usual convoluted Dom way, I can tell you for free that it's all wrong."

His gaze sparks, and he leans forward. The overhead light glances off his bald head, "First, I am only ten years older than you."

He rises to his feet and slams his palms on his waist. The muscles strain against the sleeves of his T-shirt.

"So you are in good shape for someone...your age." I smirk.

Color floods his cheeks. "I can outrun you, take you down in a fight anytime, fuck an omega for days at a time—"

"When was the last time you bedded a woman?"

His jaw tics.

"That's what I thought." I tilt my head. "All that celibacy shit is screwing with your mind. It makes you horny and brings you in here to live life vicariously."

"Fuck you." He closes the distance between us, his fist raised.

"Go ahead." I glare at him, voice soft.

He's a few millimeters shorter than me; his shoulders are broad. The tendons of his neck flex. His chest heaves. I stay silent, arms by my sides.

He may be an alpha male. Stronger than most men in my clan. But where I am concerned, he is my second.

We stare at each other, unblinking. Tension rolls off of his shoulders. The hair on my nape hardens. Then he lowers his arm, blinks, and looks away.

A breath whooshes from his chest. "I don't want to fight you, Kayden. We've had our differences in the past —"

"Something I respect you for."

His gaze flicks back to my face; his forehead furrows. "A second compliment in the space of less than ten minutes. You're losing your touch at being a dickhead."

"Yeah." I crack my neck. "You came here to impart some goddamned wisdom, no doubt." My jaw firms. "Have your say, before I lose my patience."

"Do right by her." He jerks his thumb toward the kitchen door.

"If not?"

He bares his teeth. "You will. You may have given in to your base instincts where she is concerned, and not that I blame you for it…it's reassuring actually, shows you are in touch with your emotions. Don't get me wrong, I am not condoning you for what you did either, but it shows that you are human, something a leader needs to be to stay connected with his people. You'll do what is best for both of you. Trust yourself, Kayden." He stabs a finger at me. "Stop fighting your true nature. It's okay to make mistakes. That's how we all learn."

He swivels on his feet and stalks toward the door.

"That's it?" I frown. "No long-winded lecture on doing my duty, staying true to the heritage of my father…?"

He stops at the door, then shoots me a glance over his shoulder. "Nah, you were right. I was beginning to sound past my prime. Fuck that." His features crinkle, and he tosses his head. "You have your faults…many of them. Doesn't make you a monster."

"Fuck, thanks." I roll my shoulders. I am not out to win the people's vote, I don't need to. I follow my instincts, differentiate right from wrong…largely. I play in shades of gray…but have enough confidence in my abilities."

He nods then turns to leave.

"Dom."

He pauses with his hand on the door.

"I was out of line earlier. You are doing an incredible job with Lisa. I can't understand why you thought turning celibate was important enough for that, but hey, I am the last one to judge your choices."

The skin across his knuckles tightens, then he jerks his head. He shoves open the door. "Me and Xander will take turns staying on guard."

He singles out the only other alpha in the room who had restrained himself when faced with Cara's pheromone-saturated presence.

Yeah, I can trust Dom with my life…and hers if it comes to it. Not that I am going to tell him that anytime soon.

A noise reaches me from the closed door of the kitchen. Turning, I race toward my omega.

118

Chloe

I lurch away from the bed, and the rope digs into my wrist. Bastard had made me orgasm over and over again, and I hate myself for it. I hadn't been able to resist him. My body had bowed to his will. I had been helpless in front of his intent. He'd licked every part of my body, fucked my pussy, sucked on my cunt until I had climaxed, and then he had knotted me. Again.

My stomach clenches.

I hadn't been able to stop myself from responding to him. My body shudders, then I straighten.

I need to get out of here before he comes and starts his assault on my senses. I won't be able to resist giving in to him. Another burst of tension slinks up my spine, and my vertebrae snaps back. My breathing quickens; sweat laces my palms. I wipe my hands down my thighs, and my hand comes away sticky. The hell—? I raise my fingers and smell them. Sweet, tangy, the scent of cinnamon mixed with that sugary essence that is mine. He coated me in our cum? I run my fingers down my stomach, to my swollen pussy and wince. I touch my thighs, my waist, my breasts….drag my fingers up to my cheek.

Every part of me is coated with the gooey mess.

My head spins. I am covered in the evidence of his arousal and mine. Even when he is not here, I can't get away from him. I race to the door. Halfway across the floor, the rope tightens and yanks me back. I cry out in frustration.

Footsteps approach the door. He's coming back. Another shudder ripples over my skin, and I pant. My belly spasms. My sex clenches. I squeeze my thighs hard as a gush of slick slides down between my legs. A moan rips out of me. Not good. This is not good. I am in full-blown heat. Hunger claws at my insides, gutting me, tugging at my nerves. My toes curl, my fingers tingle, and I drag them over my aching scalp.

I need him.

Need the alpha to come back and rut me. To shove his cock inside of me and push away that empty hurt that coils within.

My chest heaves, my spine curves, and my head jerks back. The door opens, and I turn away; my gaze roams around the place. Spotting the half-open door to the bathroom, I race toward it. I reach it and fall inside the doorway as the main door slams shut. I leap across the threshold and shove at it but…it won't close.

The rope is in the way.

I shove my weight against it, panting, shoulders rolling, tears flowing down my cheeks. I don't want to see him. I don't. Another spasm licks up my spine. My stomach contracts; my pussy quivers. I turn around, my back pushed against the door to hold it in place. I fold my legs against my chest then lower my burning forehead to my knees.

A knock sounds on the door, and I scream, then stuff my knuckles into my mouth. Sobs bubble up, and I bite down on my hand, trying to stop the noises from spilling out.

"Open up, Cara."

No. I won't.

"You don't want to make me angry."

Right. As if it makes a difference if he's upset or not.

Any excuse to throw me down and rut me. My pussy trembles. I clench my thighs. Isn't that what I want?

For this alpha to spear his cock inside of me and obliterate the seething emptiness that rattles around my insides, threatening to claw out of me? I throw my head back and it careens against the door.

Pain erupts behind my eyes, and I cry out.

"Get away from the door."

"No." The guttural cry emerges from my throat, and I blink. I sound like I am in pain. In agony. An omega in heat. Not for the first time, I wish I could control this primal urge inside of me. To pull myself back from embracing my destiny as a breeder. A woman. A mother. That's what I was born for, to be impregnated. But don't I have a say in who takes me? In who my mate is? I had dreamed of the day when I would go mate the alpha of my dreams. He'd soothe me, take my virginity, take me to the edge of the pleasure that a mating would bring on. He'd knot me and fill me with his child. And that's going to happen, all right. Just not in the sequence of events I had wanted or with the man I love. "I hate you."

There's silence, then he says, "I don't doubt that. But right now, you need me."

"No."

"You want me to come in and rut you, put you out of your misery." He lowers his voice to a coaxing tone, "You want me, Cara."

"Don't call me that." Why am I engaging in conversation with him? That will only encourage him. And I don't want that. I want him to leave me the fuck alone.

"Then what should I call you?"

"Huh?" I blink. He's never asked me that before.

"What does it matter?" I huff out a breath, then wipe my cheeks.

"It does. I should have asked you for it earlier. Shouldn't have treated you the way I did."

"A second apology, Alpha? You are losing your touch." I chuckle then choke as another wave of agony twists my insides. This is bad. The estrus won't allow me to stay in here. Will force me to go to him. I lower my head to my knees. I need a way out. But what?

"Come out and let me take care of you."

"You mean fuck me?"

"If that's what's needed."

"Why are you being so solicitous?"

"Why are you being so stubborn when everything you need is right here on the other side of this door? All you have to do is reach out and take it. What are you afraid of, Cara?"

Nothing. Everything. You. The words scroll across my mind, but I don't say them aloud. I grit my teeth, bury my nails in my palms, and ride out the chill that racks my bones. My teeth chatter, my toes curl, and my thighs spasm. A groan bleeds out of me, and the doorframe trembles at my back.

"Open. The. Fucking. Door," his voice booms out. "Now."

The dominance in his tone slams into my back. My spine curves. I push away from the door and it flies open.

I turn around to see him looming in the doorway.

119

Kayden

She lies there panting, curled into herself, on the cold, tile bathroom floor. Her shoulders tremble, her chest heaves, and slick pools under her on the floor. She's in pain, and yet the stubborn woman will not give in to me.

I cross the floor to stand over her, and she shudders. A moan leaves her lips. The ball of heat in my chest clenches. I scoop her up in my arms, then turn and walk over to the bed. Her skin is so cold to the touch.

She bangs her head against my chest. "Please," she whispers. Her throat moves; her chin wobbles.

I cradle her closer, and she whimpers.

"You will let me help you." I growl.

She nods. A tear slides down her cheek, and I lower my head and lick it up. Maybe the heat cycle has completely taken over her senses and that's making her compliant. Perhaps her body has given in to the hormones; the needs that course through her have made her a slave to her urges. Or she simply can't take the hurt that cleaves her body. Either way, I don't wait.

I lay her down on the bed and tear off my clothes. Her body bucks, and I lower myself over her. Keeping most of my weight off of her, I lean enough of my weight on her to push her into the mattress.

A sigh of relief gusts from her lips.

She raises her chin, and her forehead brushes my neck. Her arms come around my shoulders, and she parts her thighs. My dick chafes over her trembling core, and we both shiver. I lean my weight on my elbows then nuzzle her hair. A tenderness sweeps over me. I want to fuck her, but I also want her to feel how different it's going to be this time. My head hurts, a pressure builds behind my eyeballs. I may have taken her to hold her hostage, but it's me who is being held prisoner to her. Her scent. Her body. Her.

I rub my cheek against hers, and she whines. Her breasts strain against my chest. Her pelvis rocks forward. Leaning back, I peer into her face.

Her eyes are closed, the color of her cheeks flushed. Her lips are moist and trembling and waiting...waiting for me to kiss her. I lean down and lick her mouth. She parts her lips, and I slide my tongue in. Gently, slowly. I swipe the seam of her lips, swirl my tongue over the roof of her mouth, ease in and suck from her. I take and I share. I tease and nibble until she responds. Her mouth opens wide; her lips cling to mine. Her tongue slides over mine. I tear my mouth from hers so suddenly that a string of spittle stretches from her mouth to mine. I lick it up. The combined tastes of our essences, sweet and tangy, fills my palate. "Look at me."

She cracks her eyelids open. Her pupils are dilated, the black completely overtaking the green.

"I want you."

She holds my gaze.

"I am going to knot you, Cara."

She licks her lips, and her gaze drops to my mouth. She drags her hand around my neck, to the front and down my chest, heading lower. I lower my body to trap her restless arm between us.

"I am going to fuck you, do you understand?"

She jerks her chin.

"But first, tell me your name."

She frowns, then squints at me. A circle of green bleeds around the edges of her irises, and she sets her jaw.

"Say it."

She shakes her head.

I had held off finding out her name, worried it would only elevate my designs on her. But now, when she decides to hold it back from me, I can't stop myself. How dare she deny me this? My chest constricts. "What's your name?" I grit my teeth.

She firms her mouth, and that little act of defiance shoots a trail of fire down my spine. I am going to break her. And when I am done, she will deny me nothing. Not ever.

I shift my pelvis forward, and the head of my dick brushes her cunt. Her breasts heave, and she digs her teeth into her lower lip.

"Your name, Cara."

She swallows, and her features crumple. She squeezes her eyes shut, and her body goes rigid.

I run a hand down her side to squeeze her thigh and pry it to the side. "Don't make me wait."

She shivers; goosebumps flare on her skin. "Don't do this." The words tremble from her lips.

A whiff of fear leaches from her skin, and that only makes me harder. It shouldn't, but seeing her defy me, seeing her fight her instincts which command her to give in, seeing her stand up to me, makes my balls ache with longing. I want that spirit of hers. I am going to revel in that sweet, pungent essence of hers. I am going to possess her thoroughly, and when I am done, she will be mine. Only mine.

I growl, and she pales.

I cup my palm around her butt, and her shoulders draw back. She moves her head to the side; her body pushes back into the bed. I lower my chin and drag my whiskers up the exposed column of her throat. Her fingernails dig into my shoulders; more slick drips from her pussy.

"You belong to me." I infuse enough dominance in my voice, and she raises her head to meet my gaze.

There is a furrow between her eyebrows, and I want to smoothen it out. I want to give her so much pleasure that she forgets everything except how I make her feel.

Is that unusual? Maybe. I don't question why. Her body is already mine. But it's her spirit, her soul, her emotions that I hanker for. Her submission, her compliance. Her admission that I am her master.

"The more I share of myself with you, the closer I tie you to me."

I crack my neck, and she groans.

"The more time we spend together, the deeper I pull you to me."

Her head snaps back. Her breasts heave, and she pants.

"The longer you resist, the stronger the connection that binds us. The less reason for you to escape me."

Her entire body bucks.

"Your very instincts urge you to give in to me." I nod toward the stream of slick that pools under her. "The cells of your body thirst for me." I raise my head and sniff the air. "The essence of your desire coats the space, insisting that you need me. You can deny it all you want, but the evidence is to the contrary."

She pants. "You can twist anything to suit your needs."

"Including you."

"No." She shakes her head.

"You will not resist." My gaze holds her. "You'll do as I ask." My body pins her down. I tease my cock into the entrance of her pussy, waiting...waiting to breach her channel.

"You will. Tell me your name. Now." The hushed command in my voice pulses in the space between us.

Her pupils dilate. Her lips move, and I angle my head to catch the syllables.

"Ch-l-oe," she whispers.

"Do you want me Chloe?" I glare at her, and she swallows.

She stares, an agonized expression scrunching her features.

I slide my hand over the curve of her thigh to her melting core, then rub the heel of my hand against her clit. Her body writhes. Her shoulders push back; her pelvis kicks forward.

Her body wants me, but I want to hear it from her.

"Say it, and you'll get what you want."

"Rut me, Alpha."

120

Chloe

"Thank fuck."

His gaze bores into me, penetrating my soul, pinning me down as surely as his cock will pierce my body. And I want all of it. The stinging edge of his desire, the callused length of his dick, the rough scratch of his chin abrading my skin, the…heat of his chest enveloping me, his dominance overpowering me, the suffocating blanket of his self that holds me captive. I thought he was going to be tender, that he would pay attention to my needs, my choice… But I was wrong.

This balance between us of an alpha and an omega will never change. He is the marauder, and I am his prey. He is my master, and I am…I am his.

"No." I shake my head, and his frown deepens. "You may have asked me to divulge my name, but that doesn't mean anything." I gulp.

His lips pull back, and it's not a smile. It's a sign of intent. A sign that he is enjoying my discomfort, my helplessness. He tilts his hips and breaches my channel, and my pussy clenches. Pinpricks of pleasure radiate out from where he's joined to me. My hips jerk, and that hated smile widens.

"Keep saying that and perhaps you may convince yourself."

His finger pinches on my clit, and I shudder.

My body is not my own where he is concerned. And my will…he's broken me to obey him. His dominance insists that he won't be happy until he's owned every part of me. My body, my soul, my thoughts.

His scent swirls around me; his chest rumbles; a deep, resonant purr flows over me.

The sound pounds at my chest, shoves at my temples, and my vision narrows.

My breath comes in pants. More slick floods my channel, and the sweet, sugary scent of my arousal is unmistakable.

"So wet and hot." His nostrils flare, and his chest expands. Every muscle in his body seems to bulge and harden further. He could take me, and I would do nothing about it.

"Don't do this. I don't want you."

Another finger joins the first, a third, then he nudges his dick farther into my pussy, and the combined feel of his fingers curving inside of me while his shaft stretches my soft entrance sends tendrils of pleasure coursing up my spine. My chest hurts; my head swims.

"I don't," I gasp out. "Don't."

He peels back his lips. Color flushes his cheeks, then he kicks his hips forward and slides all the way inside of me. A low, keening cry spills from my lips. Too much. Too full. His fingers thrust in tandem with the hard column of his cock. He finds that spot deep inside of me, and I shatter. My pussy clamps down on the alpha's intrusion, and a growl rips from his chest.

"Good girl," he urges me on.

He shoves forward again and again, his fingers keeping pace. Pushing me toward that sliver of light so far on the horizon.

I pant and loop my legs around his waist, tilt my hips up to take in every throbbing centimeter of that source of pleasure.

Don't. The word echoes in my head. *Don't.* My eyelids flutter, and he nips on my chin. The pain fills my head, shoving aside all thought. My eyes narrow in on his face.

"Stay with me." Another purr wells up his throat.

My back bows, my belly trembles, "No." I shake my head to clear it.

"Yes." He frowns.

"I can't do this." I shove against the massive body holding me down.

"You can and you will."

I rake my nails down his shoulders, lower my legs, and try to knee him, but he leans more of his weight on my torso, flattening my breasts, then he lunges forward. His knot widens at the entrance to my channel. *No. No.* The words flicker in the corners of my mind.

Waves of pleasure stretch my veins. My womb spasms, and my channel squeezes on the alpha's shaft, sucking on it, begging him to take what is his. His cock locks in behind my pelvic bone.

"Come." The primal call in his voice rips me apart.

The climax slaps over me, and I howl.

A harsh purr rips from him, then he shoots hot streams of cum inside of me.

I float in that space for a while. Mind blank. Body pulsing in the aftermath. I hate... I hate myself. But I can't deny him. Every part of me needs him.

There's nothing I can do but comply as long as I am here, in this space with him.

Another aftershock of the climax jolts my skin.

He raises his head and licks the sweat that trickles down my temple. The rough sensation sets my nerve endings tingling, and my shoulders quake. A purr pours from his throat, and another. He builds the sounds around me, holding me in that space with him, demanding that my insides clench.

He pulls his fingers out, and the sensation pulses more heat to my core. He drags his digits over my pussy up my chest and rubs the cum into my lips. I lick it up, and those amber eyes glow. Gold sparks in their depths. He brings the fingers to his mouth and sucks on them. The sight of his tongue swirling around his fingertips sends my pulse racing. My heart thuds. Adrenaline laces my blood. His knot loosens enough, and he pulls out of me. Sliding to his feet, he looms over me.

"So fucking beautiful."

Blood flushes my cheeks.

His praise doesn't mean anything; it doesn't.

He scoops me up in his arms and walks to the bath. He moves to the shower stall and flips on the shower. The warm water gushes over me, and I gasp.

He lowers me to my feet, and I sway.

His arm comes around me, and he proceeds to wash my body, my hair, spending particular attention on my breasts, the apex between my thighs. When he's done with me, he lowers me to sit on the floor, and I huddle against the wall.

I look up to find his powerful body towering over me. The water from the shower pours off of his shoulders. He cleans himself with firm strokes, brushing his big palms down his concave stomach, to the jutting thrust of his shaft. My mouth waters; liquid lust coils low in my belly. He continues to wash his groin, sliding his hands over that throbbing muscle which elongates as he squeezes his cock from root to swollen head.

A drop of precum coats the slit, and I rise to my knees, my face now level with the object of my fixation.

I am revealing exactly how much I am turned on by him. How much my body craves him, and I can't stop myself. The scent of his testosterone saturates the air, and the tangy spoor of his arousal spools around me, thick, inviting. A moan bleeds from my lips.

His fingers brush my hair, then he coils the strands around his palm and tugs my head back. I raise my gaze to meet his and blink. His features are solid; the skin stretches across his cheeks. A nerve flicks at his jaw. He squeezes his dick and thrusts its head into my mouth. I curl my tongue around the swollen flesh, and he groans. The harsh sound skitters down my spine. My nerve endings fire. Then he moves.

121

Kayden

Heat, softness… I shove my dick down her throat, and she gags.

The sucking pressure swoops straight up my spine, and bursts of red and white spark at the backs of my eyes. My knees tremble…they fucking tremble. She has the power to knock my legs out from under me and she isn't aware of it. And I don't mean to tell her either. No one should have this kind of control over another. I need to put her in her place, use her for my pleasure. And once she is with child, tie her to my side. No one gets to come near her, no one gets to own her but me. She will not carry anyone else's seed but mine.

I pull at her hair, and her head falls back.

She drags her mouth to the head of my cock. I push her forward so my dick slides down the hot grasp of her throat. Goosebumps rise on my skin. I slap a hand against the wall of the shower with the water beating on my back. What am I doing to her?

What am I doing to myself?

It doesn't matter anymore.

My entire world is narrowed to the feel of her greedy mouth, the soft give of her tongue as I proceed to fuck her face.

I pull at her head, again and again, until my balls draw up, my groin tightens. A growl rips up my throat. The climax bursts over me, and another groan boils up my throat. Then I hold on to the wall for purchase as my spine arcs and I shoot hot streams of cum inside of her mouth. I keep coming and coming. I am never going to stop. I am never going to have enough of her. Her tongue, her lips, her breasts, her beautiful cunt. Her. She is my undoing. I look down to find her peering up at me.

Pupils blown, mouth coiled around my cock, tears streaming down her cheeks.

My cum drips from the edges of her lips. No one has the right to look this beautiful, this ruined, this possessed. She belongs to me, only me.

A harsh purr rumbles up my chest, and her gaze widens. I tug at her head, and my dick slips out. Then, swooping down, I grasp her under her armpits and haul her up. So tiny, so light, perfect for me to manipulate her body. I back her up against the wall. Gripping her thighs I lift her up and she wraps her legs around my waist.

I drag my lips over her mouth, and she pants.

"So fucking responsive." I growl, "Why do I want to bury myself in you and stay that way forever?"

Her eyelashes flutter. She raises a hand and cups my cheek. Something's in her gaze. Pity? Understanding? I am not sure. "I don't need your empathy, little omega." I snarl.

"You think you can fuck me to get over your demons?"

I frown.

"Nothing is going to help, nothing except going back and facing the past that you are running from." Her chin wobbles; her lips tighten.

"You don't understand anything about me." I glare at her gorgeous face.

"You don't share anything with me." She pouts, her full, lush lips glistening with the traces of my cum. Fuck me, but I want to be buried balls deep inside of that sweet pussy of hers again.

"You don't have the right to find out more about me." I roll my shoulders. "You don't need to understand me."

"No." Her mouth twists. "You only want to knot me and fuck me out of your system."

"That's right." I toss my head. When had I let her crawl under my skin? When had I allowed myself to want more from her? When she is only a means to an end? My gaze narrows.

"You are nothing but my hostage, remember that."

"You had me fooled there." She tilts up her head. "You claimed me, and there's no getting away from that. You took me against my will…"

"Didn't find you complaining once I started fucking you in earnest."

Her throat moves as she swallows. "Doesn't mean I want it."

"Your body needs it; not much you can do about it." I peel back my lips, and she blinks.

"So all you do is take, not caring how much it hurts me?"

"I'll make sure it's good for you." What the hell is wrong with this woman?

I have her naked and flush against the wall with the water pouring down on us, and yet she's trying to make me see reason. Doesn't she understand that where she is concerned, I have no modicum of sense left, none? I kick my hips and thrust into her.

Her spine straightens, she throws her neck back, and I place my hand behind her head to shield her. Can't have her hurting herself; only I have that prerogative.

She pants, her chest rises and falls, a pulse flickers at her throat, and the beat of it is echoed in my balls, in my dick that's buried inside of her.

She looks at me from under hooded eyelids. "Is that your answer to any question, Alpha? To fuck?"

I bare my teeth, and it's not a smile. Just a declaration of my intention. "Finally, you get me."

I pull back, then thrust forward.

Her entire body jolts. I wrap my other arm around her to protect her spine from scraping against the wall. Then I proceed to fuck her tantalizing cunt, watching her watch me.

Her gaze holds mine, her shoulders heave, the water grows cold at my back, and I still don't stop. I thrust into her again and again. Her body twitches and jerks with each thrust, but I don't care.

"I am going to make you come again." I grit my teeth. "And again."

I pound into her wet channel, and she moans, her breath coming in pants. Her hair is stuck to her forehead, framing those wide eyes. Eyes that look right into me, that pity me. How dare she look down on me? I am the alpha here. I am the stronger one. I am the one who can break her in half, who can pierce her with my dick so hard that it destroys every last secret place inside of her.

She blinks, her eyelashes spiky with water from the shower. With tears? Not that I care if she is upset. Why does it matter if I am hurting her?

"And when you can't orgasm anymore, I am going to suck on your sweet cunt. I am going to draw forth your slick, feed on that gorgeous essence of yours until you pass out from exhaustion. And when you wake up, I'll do it all over again." I punctuate my words by kicking my hips forward to bury myself inside of her to the hilt. My balls slap against her tender flesh.

Her chest heaves, her breath hitches, but she doesn't scream. Doesn't protest. She takes everything I impose on her, and fuck me, but why does that make me angrier? A tremor courses over my skin; my blood thuds at my temples. And yet she doesn't break my gaze.

The skin of her forehead furrows. There's a pleading look in her eyes. What? What does she want from me? Understanding? A happy ending? Me to tell her that I am her mate, that I want her, will take care of her and her children? Give her everything an omega needs to be happy? "When we finish fucking, you will build your nest."

The color drains from her face. "I will not."

I glare at her. "You will do as I say."

"No." She sets her jaw, and I smile.

This...this is her weakness. One that I am going to exploit to get what I want. But what is it that I want from her? What do I want for myself? I push the thought away and grimace. "Say that word one more time, and you will regret the day I walked onto that terrace and ever set eyes on you."

Her shoulders hunch, then she firms her lips. "I will not build a nest. I am not going to allow any child of mine to be born into this...hell."

122

Chloe

Mistake. I made a mistake. I shouldn't have declared my intentions aloud.

Why did I have to provoke him? Why did I have to blurt out what I was thinking? But a child…? That's what I have always wanted. The one thing I was born for; it's the only thing that's kept me going…that I could become pregnant and have someone just for me, but to have him or her with this alpha for a father?

He'd make a good protector, wouldn't he?

But that's not enough. I want more. When had my thoughts changed? I'd thought being pregnant was the solution to everything, but it's not. I want him to acknowledge me as his mate. I want the father of my child to be more, one who's proven himself in so many ways. As a human being who'd do the right thing, unlike this alpha who has failed me.

"Let me go." I struggle against him.

A growl pours from him; the anger in that single intonation is so loud that it slams into my chest, and I gasp. He thrusts his hips forward, and my body bucks.

His hand is cupped around my neck. The other is at the small of my back, protecting my spine from slamming into the glass wall.

Why would he do that?

Why would he want to protect me from physical harm even as he crams his cock inside of me? Slick gushes forth, and I clamp down on my inner walls to hold it in.

He groans; his chest heaves. All my attempts at escaping, at holding him back only seem to be arousing him more.

His cock lengthens, chafing against my inner walls. Liquid desire flushes my veins. "I will never give in to you." My voice shakes, yet I refuse to look away. Refuse to allow his personality to overpower me completely. He's taken my body, broken my will, and the only thing remaining is that kernel of resistance inside, the one that says I don't belong to him.

A vein throbs at his temple. His jaw goes solid, and a flush of red streaks his cheeks.

"I've been patient with you so far, Omega—"

Surely he's joking?

"—but no more." He thrusts into me and I whine.

I wriggle, then try to pull away but he grinds his chest into mine, flattening my breasts, and pining me in place..

"Don't do this," I pant. "You don't want me like this."

"I'll have you my way, any time, any place, and you'll take it. Your body is mine now." His knot hardens, and he thrusts again. "Mine." His dick locks into place behind my pelvic bone.

So much. So full. A moan whispers from my lips. His gaze drops to my mouth. He leans down to kiss me, but I turn away. He pinches my chin and angles my head so I have no choice but to glance at him.

His breath ghosts over my cheek, and I clamp my lips shut.

He presses a thumb to my lower lip, and my mouth falls open. He sweeps in. Sucking on my lips, shoving his tongue inside, swiping over my gums. I bite down hard, and his muscles twitch. But he doesn't react. He keeps kissing me, curling his insidious tongue over the roof of my mouth, over my teeth. The taste of blood fills my palate, and I swallow it down.

He tears his mouth from mine, and crimson drips down his chin. I am not a violent person, have never been in a fight, never wanted to resort to physical acts to prove my point... but this alpha brings out the worst in me.

"When you fight, you fucking turn me on," His lips curl, his eyes narrow, and in that moment, I am sure I've never hated anyone else more than him.

His fingers curve around my throat, and my breath stutters.

"What other surprises do you have left? How much more can you take?" he mumbles almost to himself.

His hold tightens, and a flicker of fear laces my mind.

His knot throbs inside of me. The weight of his chest punishes my tender flesh. I stay there panting, not daring to move, not wanting to give in to the thoughts that chatter through my head. He's going to squeeze every last breath out of me, and there's nothing I can do but take it.

He angles his hips and thrusts into me then tightens his fingers around my throat.

Darkness seeps in through the cracks on the edges. His big body trembles, a harsh purr rolls up his chest, and sinks into my blood, my pussy clamps down on his shaft, my womb spasms, and the orgasm sweeps through me at the same time as he shoots hot spurts of cum inside of me. The blackness envelops me, and I give in to it.

When I come to, I am on the bed, flat on my back, and he's between my legs.

His shoulders shove my thighs apart, and his mouth is on my cunt. He thrusts his tongue inside my channel, and I quiver. My limbs shake. All strength seems to drain from me. He hooks his hands under my knees and, raising my legs, he loops them around his neck. Then he goes at it, sucking on my pussy, licking, swirling that tongue of his between my folds.

I arch my spine unable to push him away, unable to accept the waves of pleasure that roll up my core. My eyes roll back in my head, and I pant.

He doesn't stop, not until he brings me to climax, and then he knots me again. And again. I lose track of the number of times he takes me, ruts me.

He buries himself inside of me and comes inside of me, filling me to the brim with his cum.

At one point he straightens over my inert body, then jerks himself off with a roar, coating me with the essence of his arousal. His desire, his need for revenge. He seems driven to whip my body into a state of heightened awareness. He doesn't allow a single millimeter of my skin to escape unscathed. He sucks on my toes, runs his tongue over the delicate skin of my heels, arousing me to fever pitch. Who'd have thought my feet were such an erogenous zone?

He nibbles on my nipples, sucks on the pulse at the base of my throat, then when I am sure I can't take a single touch more of his, he buries his teeth at the base of where my neck meets my shoulder, and rips open the half-healed flesh where he'd last claimed me.

I scream in pain, waves of pleasure spike my blood. Shrapnel's of red and white lodge in my chest as his knot locks into place and he comes inside of me. Then there is only blackness.

123

Kayden

An alpha in love...?—no...not possible—An alpha in *rut* is fixated on his woman.

That's all this is.

She went into heat and now I can't get my fill of her.

I stand over the sleeping omega. "Chloe." I whisper. The morning light creeps in from between the cracks in the shutters over the window. For three days and nights I had rutted her.

I had not paused, except for the brief snatches when I had lapsed into a semi-comatose state and napped with her on my chest.

I had needed her small body folded into me, making sure she was close to me. I needed her within reach so I could run my fingers over the curve of her hips, down to her sleek thighs. Every beautiful inch of her flushed with my cum, her slick, mixed with the blood that she had drawn. Not only had she bitten down on my tongue, she had clawed me, dug her fingernails into my shoulders, and raked scratches across my back. She had cried on me, sobbed her climax, screamed through her arousal.

I had reduced her to the very essence of the omega she is.

I had marked her again.

Drawn her blood, allowed it to flow down her shoulder and mix with our essence. It was only fitting that this union of ours was christened with something as violent.

The need to rut had filled my brain, flushed my blood, and hardened my groin until I had lost sight of everything else but her.

I had tried to pleasure her as much as I could.

I lick my lips and taste the lingering sweetness of her cunt...her pussy, the source of my obsession. I am fucking fixated on that triangle between her legs. I dig my fingers in my hair, and the wet strands coil around my palm. I had taken her with an intensity bordering on violence…couldn't stop myself.

The fact that she'd tried to resist me until the end had filled me with a strange pride. It had made me want to break her, show her that I could keep going for as long as was needed, to break her heat cycle. Now she lies spent. Her body is stretched out, one arm flung out, the other curved over her chest. Her long waist tapers down to the curve of her hips. And my gaze once more latches on to the strip of hair between her thighs. Her parted lower lips glisten, pink, throbbing…engorged.

Scratches mark the creamy flesh of her inner thighs, and I clench my fists. I hurt her. I had wanted to get all of my frustrations out on her. Wanted to let her experience the force of my desire, my needs. At some point I had lost sight of the fact that she was vulnerable.

I had been angry enough to try to prove her right—to fuck her out of my system.

My breathing quickens. I had claimed her again…I had wanted to do it.

If she doesn't belong me, she belongs to no one else. I made sure of that. I may have started this entire sojourn to use her as a means of getting to Zeus…but she's going to be my downfall.

Her chest is so still, her body so motionless… I lean over her and hold my finger under her nose. There's a slight rustle of air against my skin, and my shoulders relax. The fuck is wrong with me?

She has me all wound up, and the woman doesn't realize it. She's completely exhausted, thanks to the cruel ways in which I had taken her.

I sink to my knees next to the bed.

Her features are tense in sleep. There's a furrow between her eyebrows. She's unhappy, and what had I done? I'd redoubled my efforts to keep her tied to me. The emotions crowd in my head. What do I feel for her? Anger? A possessiveness? A need to protect? The flare of heat in my chest bursts into a flame. I need to make sure she doesn't escape from me. Not until I find out if she's pregnant.

She has to be.

I'd knotted her repeatedly over the last few days. There's no way she couldn't be…and if she isn't? Then I'll keep her here…I'll find a way to inject her with a heat-accelerating drug, keep her in a perpetual state of needing me. Keep her high on sex and on endorphins so her body is sated. As for her will? She'll never accept me, not after what I've done to her.

But once she is pregnant, she won't leave.

She has to start nesting; that is the only way to bind her to me.

When Zeus comes for her…I'll find a way to keep both her and get my city back from him.

And if she doesn't stay willingly? Too bad. I'll wear her down.

Besides, once she bears a child, she won't leave. Motherhood will shove all thoughts of escape from her mind.

She makes a keening sound in her throat, and her fingers clutch at the sheets.

I lean over her and purr. I draw out the most melodious sounds from deep inside of me, everything I am not able to tell her—my confusion, the grief of my past, the hope for something to call my own—all of it, I infuse into the notes.

I swirl them around her body, let them sink into her blood. I keep purring, building a cocoon of sound around her. Her forehead smooths out, her shoulders uncoil, and her fingers on the sheet relax. She turns her face toward me, and her lips tilt up in a slight smile. I still don't stop. I let the tone of my voice soothe her.

There's a soft knock at the door, and I frown.

"Kayden?" Dom inches the door open, and I glance toward the exit.

He peers in without entering. "I held off the rest of the team, but you need to come and see this."

124

Chloe

Awareness creeps up my toes. I turn over on my back, and the muscles in my thighs protest. My biceps burn; my throat feels raw. My eyes flicker open. Silence surrounds me.

It's warm in the room.

I crack my jaws open in a yawn, and a fiery ache tears down the side of my neck. I raise my right hand and cry out. The agony ratchets up in intensity. My hand falls back against the bed, and the blanket slips from my breasts.

I bring up the fingers of my uninjured arm to the side of my neck. The touch sets off a drumming behind my eyes, and I groan.

"You're awake?"

The voice echoes through my head. Sweat beads my forehead, and I turn toward the source. A woman leans forward in the chair placed at the far end of the room. She walks toward me, and I narrow my gaze.

"Who're you?"

"Lisa."

"Who?" I frown.

"I'm Dom's daughter."

"Dom?"

I hear her moving around, then the sound of water being poured into a glass. "Here."

I manage to open my eyelids, and the water appears in my line of sight.

She holds out a pill.

"I dare not come closer, else my scent might get onto the bedclothes, and, you know..."

I swallow.

Yeah, most omegas coming out of estrus would hate for a stranger to be so close to the nest, and after the marathon rutting session that I'd been subjected to, it would make sense that I would feel the same way.

But this isn't a nest.

And I am not an omega who had been willingly mated.

Her scent wafts over me, so different from the alpha's musky aroma that my stomach lurches. Bile rushes up my throat, and I stuff the knuckles of my uninjured hand into my mouth.

I bite the inside of my cheek until the sickness passes. When I open my eyes, she's moved away to stand by the chair.

She wrings her fingers in front of her. "I...I'd help you, but right now you're better off if I don't get too near."

"Whatever." I take a deep breath and try to calm my stupid stomach. When I feel better, I look at her.

She gestures to the side table. "I left the painkiller there for you. The chief was adamant that you take it."

"What's in it, poison?" I lick my dry lips. "Though that would be too merciful of him. Is it to prolong my heat cycle so he can keep me helpless?"

"Kayden is not as bad as you make him out to be." Her mouth firms.

"Oh, yeah?" I jerk my chin toward the throbbing mess of my shoulder. "What do you say to that?"

"He's a passionate man."

"A monster."

"An alpha who cares for his people."

"Enough to take a woman against her will and mate her, then arrange to exchange her back for them?"

She pales. "He...wouldn't do that."

I chuckle, and my throat aches. "Obviously you don't understand him as well as I do."

"He...must have his reasons for what he did."

"Nothing excuses what he did to me."

"You...you must have done something to provoke him." She bites her lips.

"Right...that's the oldest story in the book—one I did not think I'd hear from another woman, by the way."

Her glance skitters away, and I stare.

"But then you're in love with him, so I guess he can commit no wrong in your eyes."

She wrings her fingers, "Don't presume to understand me, Omega."

Obviously my guess was correct and now I've managed to piss her off, too. Which is not the thing to do.

I could do with all the friends I can make right now, given the alpha is set to ruin every last one of my stupid dreams. A romantic that I had been. A mate who loved me. A home. A family of my own...none of it is in the cards for me, at least not in the way I want.

"You're right." I swallow then squeeze my eyes shut. "I shouldn't have said that. And I didn't mean to be disrespectful to you...but...I am tired, and it's not been an easy few days..."

She huffs out a breath, then sinks into the chair. "You aren't far from the truth either. Apparently, you're insightful as well as beautiful. No wonder he wanted you for himself." She twists her fingers in front of her.

"He didn't want me...he wanted what I represented."

She looks up at me. "And what's that?"

"A way to get back at Zeus. A willing pawn. An omega who couldn't fight him, who knows only one thing. To be a breeder, hence..." A ball of emotion clogs in my throat, and tears prick the backs of my eyes. I will not cry, will not.

"You need to believe he's better than that. The Kayden I know...he's been nothing but good to me."

"Perhaps it's because I am not one of his people."

"You are his mate."

"That doesn't mean anything."

"How can you say that? Don't you realize what it means to carry the claim of a man such as him?"

"He doesn't want me."

"That's not what the evidence suggests." Her gaze roams over the bed, and I know what she's seeing. Soiled sheets, the scent of cum in the air, the evidence of our coupling rubbed into every inch of my body.

I lurch up to sitting, and my head spins. "I need to take a shower."

"Take the painkiller first."

I shoot her a glance.

"It is a painkiller, and it's made of herbs. No chemicals. He wanted to make sure that whatever you take does not harm..." She flushes. "You know."

A cold feeling coils in my chest. "He thinks I could be pregnant."

"He hopes you are."

"That's what he wants...a child?"

"He didn't tell me that..." Her voice tapers off.

"But you heard him talk about it?"

She firms her lips.

"Who was he speaking to?" I angle my head, "Does he go around sharing with his friends, assuming he has any?"

"He was talking to my father, his second, and he does have many followers."

"But not many whom he trusts?" The thoughts whirl around in my head.

"Oh, he trusts me." She raises her chin and her chest heaves.

She is lying. She isn't over him.

"You envy me?"

"Don't flatter yourself." Her gaze narrows.

Something in the angle of her head, the glint in her eyes makes the hair on my nape rise. It's as if the innocent girl who'd come in is gone, and in her place is a woman shrewd and calculating, one who'll not stop at anything to get what she wants.

"Be nice to me because I have something else that you may prefer." She dips her hand into the pocket of her dress and pulls out another pill that she holds out in her palm.

I hesitate, my glance bouncing from her face to the innocuous tablet in her hand.

"What's that?" My brows furrow.

"An abortion pill."

"Abortion — ?" I stare.

What in the blazes is she talking about?

"This one is concentrated enough to work for up to a week after copulation." She takes a step forward, and I scramble up the bed to put more distance between us.

"I am not following." I straighten my shoulders, and the sheets slip farther to pool around my waist.

Her glance rakes over my exposed breasts, and her nostrils flare. A harsh look comes into her eyes. Disgust? Hate? Perhaps, all of the above.

"You are too weak for him." She taps her boot-clad foot on the floor.

"I am?" I mean, I know I am, but something about how she says it makes me want to refute her words. I don't want her to see me helpless, and at her mercy. My gaze skitters around the room and alights on the door.

"I'd be more than happy to allow you to escape."

"What?" My gaze snaps to her face.

All expression is wiped from her features. "You don't want his child. I don't want you to have his child. Hence…" She jerks her chin toward the pill.

"You'd risk his anger to allow me out of here?" I don't understand what the relationship or lack of one is between this woman and Kayden. But I've seen enough of Kayden's dominance, the confidence with which he had handled my body, how he'd commandeered respect among his people to know that he won't let this go lightly. "He kidnapped me for a reason."

"Yeah, to negotiate a way to get back his land from Zeus." Her lips curl. "Zeus will never agree to that. An entire city for an omega?" She snorts. "What was Kayden thinking?"

"And you know that, how?" I tilt my head, looking, really looking at her for the first time.

The light from the windows haloes her features, making her skin seem almost translucent. She seems delicate, tinier than me in height. Her curves are lush and draped in a thick woolen skirt and a long-sleeved shirt that's tucked in. All in all, the outfit hugs her curves without attempting to be overt.

It enhances the image of the good little girl that she wants Kayden to see. No doubt he swallows the act whole. Alphas. I snort to myself. They think with their dicks…me, being the primary example of that.

She shakes back her long dark hair that curls in large whorls over her shoulders and around her face. Her skin glows, her gaze is wide. She's younger than she seems. Hmm. "You're a virgin?"

She pales. "Wha...what's that got to do with anything?"

I raise my shoulders and let them fall. I am missing something there, but what? Something about this woman doesn't add up. "Why should I trust you?"

She grins then, a baring of her teeth that gives her a sly look. So not that innocent after all. She's calculating, strong, she goes after what she wants.

"You want to hurt Kayden?"

She throws her head back and laughs. "In a matter of speaking."

"Revenge then?"

She straightens and stares at me, all expression wiped off of her face. Those eyes of hers are dark pools of resolution. How had I thought that I could trust her?

"What did he do to you?"

Why does it matter to me?

I had wanted to get away from him, and she is giving me a way out. I should take it and go…except something holds me back. I need to get to the bottom of what she has planned.

I am done being a pawn in this political game of hate and revenge that these alphas, and apparently also omegas in this clan take part in. If I am going to be used, I want to know what it is for, and oh, at the end of it, I am going to make sure that I get something out of it, too.

"Nothing." She folds her arms around her waist.

"So it's what he didn't do then?"

She glares at me. Her fingers close around the pill, and I am sure she is going to throw it on the floor and stamp on it. Instead, she squeezes her eyes shut and takes a deep breath. "Am I that easy to read?" When she looks at me again, the features of her face compose into a mask. "No matter, soon you will be gone, and he will forget you."

"What do you mean?" My heart thuds.

"Kayden has always thought I was a young, impressionable virgin." Color flushes her cheeks. "The last may be true, and I may be young, but I am far from naïve."

"You have thought this through, haven't you?"

"I have had my entire life so far to plot how to get his attention. Only, for some reason, he fixated on you first."

I sweep my gaze over her face. She twists her lips, and her throat bobs as she swallows.

"So not love, you are obsessed by the idea of him?"

"Shut up." She fists her hand with the pill inside it at her side.

"Guess you want to be mated to the chief. Power…is that what turns you on?"

She raises her fist, and I smile.

She draws in a breath and lowers her arm. The emotions fade away from her face, leaving those smooth, unlined features in place. I blink at the transformation. This girl is a darn convincing actress.

I yank up the sheet and tuck it under my armpits. Not that I am shy, but no way am I going to have this conversation with her half-naked. Not that covering myself up is going to help much, not when I am clearly at her mercy, but if she thought Kayden underestimated her, well, he doesn't see me as a threat either. Clearly, the alpha is used to omegas fainting around him and doing his bidding. But not me. I may have submitted to him so far…but face it, it was only because I'd wanted to. Because I'd wanted to see exactly what kind of twisted, depraved things he could do to my body, how he could bring me to climax. My virginity was something I had been proud of; he had rid me of that…so, well, I'd had nothing to lose.

"You have no idea what I am thinking." Her voice is low, and she rolls her shoulders as if preparing for a fight. And isn't that what this is? A battle of wills? Each of us trying to further our agendas? The girl is focused, and so confident. Hell, I could do with a smidgen of that kind of self-assurance.

I draw myself up and mirror the rigidity of her pose. "Don't I?" I take in her stance. "You've loved him from afar, maybe esaved yourself for him. Made sure not to give in to the agony of the estrus. Hell, I bet you turned down other alphas purely because you were so sure you could lure him in. Maybe seduce him into claiming you." Her jaw hardens, and I know I've found my mark. "Then he disappears and comes back with me."

"You don't matter in the grand scheme of things."

"He's half out of his head with lust, it's clear that he has claimed me." I motion to the mark on my shoulder.

She takes a step forward; her nostrils flare. Her shoulders stiffen, and she snarls, "It's a fledgling bond; he'll break it, and it would be as if you never existed."

"You forget I claimed him, too."

"No." She gasps, and all color leaches from her face. "And so what if he did...if you leave now...if you get out of here, you can put distance between the two of you and...and..." Her voice fades, and she curls a fist against her stomach.

"Relax, Lisa." I pretend to rub my nails on the sheet covering me then survey them. "I was kidding you." I peek up at her from under hooded eyelids.

A breath whistles out from between her lips. She closes the distance between us, and thrusts out her fist.

I duck.

She misses me and stumbles before righting herself. Then she places the second pill on the side table. It's blue in color. The painkiller is white. That is, if I believe her. *Which I don't by the way.* Everyone here is a conniving heel.

"Take the pill...or not." She raises her shoulders and lets them drop. "If I were you, I'd shower and eat to keep my strength up for the trip ahead." She tosses the hair back from her face. "I'll check everything is ready and come to get you in ten minutes."

She heads for the door.

"Wait, what do you mean?"

She pauses on the threshold. "You want to get out of here or not?" she flings over her shoulder.

I nod.

"Then do as you are told, no questions." She leaves.

For a second I stay where I am, and she pops her head back in. "Ten minutes, or you can forget this."

Right. I jump out of bed, head to the bathroom, shower off the gunk from my body. I am out in three minutes, wrapped in a towel, and find a fresh change of clothes on the chair. I snatch up the fatigues, T-shirt, the heavy hoodie, and pull them on. No underwear, but that's fine. Sitting on the bed, I shove my feet into the socks and the boots. They fit—are they hers? Probably. My stomach grumbles, and I reach for the tray and eat the fruits, cheese, and bacon.

I glance at the two pills. Nope, not taking either. If I am pregnant...? I cup my belly. No way am I going to destroy a child in my womb.

I reach for the glass of water and drain it. A faint metallic taste lingers in my mouth, and I try to swallow it away.

By the time I am done, warmth creeps up my body, my hands and legs tingle, and my head feels fuzzy. Maybe I am more tired than I thought. I lay back on the bed. The ceiling swims around me. I haven't taken any of the pills, so why am I so woozy? My heart begins to thud. Had Lisa used the pills to distract me? What had she laced? The food...no, the water. It had tasted funny. Had she drugged it? With what...? My eyes shut, and darkness steals over me.

I am aware of voices, my body being lifted.

I try to protest, but can't speak, then all consciousness leaves me.

When I come to, I see the gray skies crowding in on me. I am out in the open. The wind blows, and I shiver.

Snowflakes flutter down, tickling my cheeks, on my lips. I lick my mouth, and the flake melts. A low growl has me turning to see eyes glowing at me from the tree line.

Amber eyes that remind me of his. The beast moves forward, its shaggy head regal, nostrils flared. Its breath steams up the night air. It stalks closer...closer...and I watch, entranced. Why does this tiger remind me of Kayden? The fierceness of its pose, the dominant way it prowls toward me... Tiger? Hell!

I jerk upright, and my head swirls. The predator hunches low, its muscles tense. Holy hell. I spring up and run the other way. I am sure the animal is on my tail... I don't have a tail, the beast does...not the time for semantics...need to keep going, to get away. I should never have trusted that bitch, Lisa. Bet she conveniently arranged for the tiger to be here. I race past the trees and toward the sound of falling water. I reach the edge of the clearing when hooves sound up the path.

I look up to find a man on a massive horse bearing down on me.

Behind him, another rider turns the corner and pulls up, then another, and another.

The leader yanks on the reins on his horse. The animal rears its massive hooves up in the air then brings them crashing down on the ground. Reverberations from the impact echo around the space. Birds fly up in the distance. The man tosses back the blond mane rippling around his shoulders.

His chest is massive, his beard a darker shade of blonde. Piercing blue eyes fix on me. His shoulders block out the sight of the other men behind him. If I hadn't caught sight of them earlier, I'd have no idea they were there. He throws up his hand, and a sliver of light glints off his palm. He makes a rotating motion with his wrist, and a lasso twirls toward me.

I scream and turn to run, but the tiger crouches not four feet away.

My heart beats so fast that I am sure it's going to break out of my rib cage, and my throat closes; my pulse pounds. Who are these men? There is a whistling in the air, then the lasso settles around my arms, tightening instantly. The sound of thundering hooves echoes off the trees, then he sweeps me up and throws me over the horse in front of him.

He races ahead and past the tiger.

"Come, Bruno," the man's deep voice rings out.

The tiger swivels around and falls in line. The hell? This savage has a tiger for a pet?

Panic tightens my chest, and I begin to struggle in earnest. A heavy weight descends on my back.

"Stay still or I'll have to do this the hard way."

The gruff voice is cultured, so different to what I'd expected. The hair on the back of my neck rises. I peer up at him. "Who are you?"

He smiles. No, that would be too charitable a way to describe it. His lips pull apart. White, perfectly formed teeth flash at me, terrifying in their uniformity. His entire face lights up, and I blink. He's some kind of Nordic god, this man. He tilts his head, and a cold feeling coils in my chest. The Scots and the English hate each other... They both hate another race more.

"Vikings."

I try to scramble away, but he shoots out his arm and grips my shoulder. His features go blank, all expression wiped from his countenance. My throat closes.

"Who...who are you?"

"I am Talon, the leader of the Berserkers. And I am here to avenge my father's death."

125

Kayden

A bonded Alpha cannot be reined in. The fuck am I thinking? Is that what this is? This...this white-hot pain that pierces my chest?

I wince, and Dom stares at me. "What's wrong?"

I hear his words as if from far away.

Another wave of pain rolls in my chest, and this time a gasp leaves my mouth. I bring my palm up and rub at the skin over my heart.

"You've gone pale." Dom lowers his gaze to my chest then back to my face. "You're sweating."

"Thanks for pointing out the obvious."

I lurch up to my feet. I had been huddled with my team in the open a few miles away from the settlement where one of our trackers had claimed he'd spotted the Berserkers. "It's not possible that the Vikings could have tracked us this far up the highlands. They've never been seen in Scotland before."

It's one of the things about which I had been confident . That the Berserkers would never make it this far. They had always restricted their movements to the ports, their sights set on the grand prize: London. I had counted on Zeus to keep them occupied for long enough that I could regroup with my team, come up with an alternate plan to take him down. Hell, bringing her here had been the opening in my plan... Okay, so the part of mating her had been spontaneous...something I didn't have control over. But everything else had been thought through. All those weeks I had been stewing in Zeus' prison, I had come up with enough creative ways to get the better of him, but this, finding traces of the Vikings this far inland is very strange.

Another streak of pain spikes my chest, then trips down my spine. It's as if a red-hot sword has been skewered right into me and pulled down, tearing my guts apart.

My heart races, my spine curves, my chest pulls forward, and only when my feet hit the ground do I realize that I have already turned away and am racing back toward the settlement.

Dom falls into place behind me. "What is it?"

I increase my speed, but he keeps pace.

"It's her, isn't it?"

I don't answer, I don't owe an answer to anyone, definitely not to my second.

Besides, I am not sure why I feel compelled to head back to her. It's her. She's in danger, I am sure of it. Don't ask me how. Perhaps it's my instincts which scream at me to go faster, keep moving. Don't stop. Another wave of fear clutches at my chest. My shoulders bunch and A blinding fury fills my head. She's afraid. Someone is threatening her. How am I so sure of that? I've never felt this…this connection to another. So why her? Why?

"You mated her?"

My body twitches, and I stumble, but Dom seizes my shoulder and hauls me up.

"Please tell me that you knew you would be able to sense her when you claimed her? That the mating bond goes both ways. It changes both the alpha and the omega?"

Of course, I knew that. I did. Didn't I?

I shake off his grasp, then keep moving. "It's a fledgling bond," I bite out the words. "I can break it anytime."

"You sure about that?" A thread of amusement laces Dom's voice.

"The fuck you implying?" I keep my gaze trained on the path ahead.

"Nothing." He holds up his hands and motions forward with his chin. "Just that not all bonds are created equal. Sometimes a fledgling bond has as much depth to it as a finalized main bond…not often, but it's been known to happen."

"Not this time. I mated her as a means of getting back at Zeus. The fledging bond means nothing." My stomach cramps; a ball of emotion clogs my throat. "Nothing."

My chest hurts and my knees knock together. My very body, my instincts, every cell in my body seems to rejects my words. I huff out a breath. No fucking way. I am not going to be drawn into the trap of a mate.

The bond will tie her to me *temporarily*.

It serves the purpose of keeping her close and from trying to escape. Escape. Has she escaped? Is that what this is about? Is that why my heart races? I lengthen my strides and my breath comes in pants.

Dense waves of fears tug at me and sweat beads my forehead. My spine curves again, and my chest thrusts forward as if an invisible thread hooks me to her.

I break into a run.

Halfway to the settlement, I swerve right, heading toward the forest.

"You're going the wrong way," Dom calls out.

Sweat pours down my face, and I toss my head to shake it out of my eyes.

"Is she somewhere in that direction? Is that why you are headed there?" His voice follows me.

I quicken my steps, but Dom keeps pace. The fucker is right on my heels, right fucking there, not giving up.

I grit my teeth and focus on moving forward.

My knees knock together again. The fuck is wrong with me? I straighten my spine and focus on putting one step in front of the other.

The closer I get to the source of whatever has my chest twitching, throbbing, hurting like a motherfucker, the more I know it's all wrong. My feet grow heavy, my legs feel weighted down, yet I push on. I stumble again, and Dom grabs my arm, and this time I don't shove him away. I let him right me.

He drops his grip but stays close. Almost there…almost. I reach the clearing and burst through the trees. The men turn around to look at me.

The one closest steps in front of me. I twist my leg around his and trip him. He goes crashing to the ground, and a flash of gold tied around his biceps gets my attention.

"Vikings," Dom snarls from somewhere behind me.

I stare toward the center of the clearing, just as she raises her face and her gaze meets mine.

Terror twists her features. A rush of fear comes down the mating bond, and my vision tunnels. Her hair is disheveled, her clothes streaked with mud, and her shoulder is in his grasp. The man standing next to her has his fucking hands all over what's mine. Mine. She is mine. My property. My omega. Anger screeches up my spine; blood thuds at my temples.

"Let go of her, motherfucker."

The man draws back his lips, and his nostrils flare. He shakes back his long blond hair. "Or what?"

I snarl and move forward, but Dom grabs my arm. "We are outnumbered. It's best we retreat."

"No fucking way. He has her. I cannot abandon her."

"If you go in, there's no way he'll let you live. Then what use are you to her?"

"I cannot leave her." I roll my shoulders.

"I cannot let you kill yourself."

"Get out of here, Dom." I want to raise my fists and leap forward and tear the arm off of the man who's holding her. But that would be bloody stupid.

If I can keep their attention off of her, force them to watch me instead, maybe that will buy me enough time. Who am I kidding? Me alone, surrounded by so many of these Vikings, I don't stand a chance. But I haven't come this far without taking risks. I hadn't realized how much I had come to regard her as mine, not until this moment, not until I saw another man's hands all over her.

The Viking turns her around, then yanks her close. She stumbles, and her back hits his chest. Her skin grows pale, her eyes widen, and fear comes off of her in waves. She bites her lips, and the sense of futility, of utter helpless that bleeds off of her is my undoing. My chest stutters; my belly flip-flops. I square my shoulders.

"Go, Dom, get help," I snarl without turning my head. "I'll keep them occupied."

"You don't stand a chance on your own."

"Go." I raise my chin. "That's. An. Order."

He hesitates, then begins to retreat.

One of the men closest to me lunges forward to stop Dom. I step between them, hook my leg around the stranger's, and tug. The man crashes to the ground.

A ripple of emotion trips through those assembled. With a roar, five of the alphas leap on me.

126

Chloe

"No!" I run toward Kayden, only to be pulled back.

I shove at the grip restraining me, and Talon wraps those massive arms around my waist and yanks at me again. I dig my heels into the ground and resist.

I bury my nails into those muscles of his forearms, but I may well be trying to scratch a brick wall. I barely make a dent in those tough muscles. The hard wall of his chest at my back sends panic racing down my spine.

"Kayden," I yell out, trying to break Talon's grip. I kick back and catch him in the shin.

But the Viking doesn't move.

I rear back and smash into his chest. Pain lances down my neck. But the alpha gives no sign that he felt it. His breathing doesn't change. The alpha is almost as big as Kayden...as mean...only there's nothing remotely human about him.

Where there had been anger coiling around Kayden, and revenge...emotions that were extreme, at least I had sensed something. I had sensed the hurt in him. The primal need inside of him that had reached out to me and had urged me to try to share myself with him, to soothe him...somewhere we had been not only matched, but linked. Is that why I had responded to him?

Is that why, despite the fact that he had kidnapped me, I had only put up a token resistance when he had mated me?

Oh, at that time I thought I was trying to fight him off, but now I realize all of that was fake.

I had wanted Kayden from the moment my eyes had lit on him. I had yearned for his touch, his harsh caresses. His instinct to take from me had triggered the primal part of me inside that was designed to give, to embrace, to bear his children...his...I was his from the moment he had reached for me and I hadn't known it.

It had taken coming in contact with another alpha, breathing in the reeking, masculine scent of another male which was all wrong. There is only one man for me—him.

"Kayden." My voice cuts through the space, echoing over the writhing bodies of the men who are shoving punches, kicks, blows on my alpha. They crowd around him shutting him from sight.

"Let me go." I dig my elbow into the man behind me.

The next second, his big paw grabs my neck, and he lifts me up. His hand squeezes my nape as if I am a helpless kitten. I kick out with my legs suspended above the ground. Grab at the fingers wrapped around my neck. Try to take in a breath and find I can't. My throat hurts, my lungs burn. I gasp for air and come up empty. Darkness nudges the corners of my mind. My arms flail, then fall to the sides. Gurgling noises...oh, that's me. I am going to die, hung to death by the grip of an alpha...but maybe that is better. If he takes me, I'll not survive whatever other bodily harm he'll do to me. If he rapes me... I'll kill myself. I don't want anyone else, no one but Kayden. When had my kidnapper become the only man I wanted, who meant more to me than life itself? My throat closes. Oh, Kayden, what did I do?

I hear a roar as if from far away. "Chloe."

I crack my eyelids open. It's the first time my alpha has called me by my name.

Kayden, I try to whisper, but the words stick in my throat.

The scene sways in front of me. I spot the hazy outline of his beautiful form. Behind him are the bodies of the fallen men. Kayden flings his head back and howls. The sound echoes around the space. Talon's fingers close around my neck. The trickle of air to my lungs cuts out. I gasp, and my body twitches. His figure blinks in and out of focus. *Kayden. Kayden.* I shouldn't have tried to escape.

Shouldn't have let Lisa goad me on. I put not just my own, but also his life at risk. The thoughts race around in my head.

"Stop right there or I will twist her neck. I'll cast her aside without another thought."

Talon's voice echoes in my ears.

He doesn't mean it. He doesn't.

He's doing it only to provoke Kayden. To lure him in and make him trip. *Don't come closer,* I try to whisper, but all that comes out is a sob.

Kayden's body jerks. Did he hear me? His features twist. I force myself to meet his gaze, try to signal to him to stop. *Stop. Don't let the Viking hurt you. If something were to happen to you, I'd never forgive myself. Please. Please.* The words keep repeating in my head.

Then Talon raises me higher by the hold on my nape. My neck hurts; pain shoots down my spine. My belly trembles. My thighs spasm. Another growl fills the air and a ripple of fear screams down the mating bond. It fills my chest, my throat, my mouth. It bubbles up thick and strong and forces me to raise my chin and snap my gaze on Kayden.

His big body is bent low; his wide shoulders shove aside one man. He swings out at another, who falls to the ground. Another two step in front, and he kicks one of them away, a third, a fourth. He uses his fists again, flexes his muscles, the tendons of his throat bulge, and he keeps coming. More men pour into the clearing. They surround him, holding on to him. One of them jumps on his back, and he shakes the stranger off. I hold his gaze. That burning amber of his eyes floods me, filling my throat, my chest, connecting with a part of me that I didn't know existed. Deep inside. I know then, I'll never forget this sight as long as I live: Kayden inching toward me. He moves closer…closer… When he is less than a foot away, I stretch out my arm. He flings aside another man then reaches out, and his fingers graze mine.

"Mine," he whispers, then his eyes widen. His shoulders shudder. He looks down at himself, and the color fades from his cheeks.

I follow his gaze and see the tip of the sword that protrudes from his chest.

"No!" I open my mouth to scream, but no words escape. They stabbed him from behind.

He glance up and holds my gaze. A trickle of blood drips from the corner of his mouth.

"Kayden."

"Cara." He wheezes on a breath.

His arm falls to his side, his big body sways, then he crashes down, taking more men with him.

I struggle in earnest. Kick out with my legs. Tear at the fingers that squeeze my throat.

The pressure increases, my lungs burn as I try to breathe. Fail.

Darkness pulls me under.

Turn the page to keep reading…

PART V

SURRENDER

127

Kayden

"I need you."

Her scent teases my nostrils. Lilies and honey; underlying that is the tang of cloves...the same, yet not. Why does she smell different?

I raise my head and survey her flushed features. High cheekbones, skin flushed pink. Her beautiful bow-shaped lips part. I drop my head and lick her mouth. She shudders. I angle my head then sink my teeth into her chin. Her muscles jump.

A whine bleeds out from her. Those tiny sounds of need, of want—she's so greedy for me. My groin tightens, the blood pounds at my temples.

An alpha in rut is at his most vulnerable.

Damn her and the effect she has on me.

Tearing my mouth from hers, I roll away, then swing my legs over to stand next to the bed.

Her eyelids fly open. "Wh...what's wrong?" she stutters.

"You." I rake my gaze over her heaving chest, her puckered nipples pink and begging for my ministrations. "Me." I grab my dick through my pants and squeeze it. "All of this...is wrong."

She pushes up to a sitting position. "I...I don't understand."

I do. I want to taste you, to break you. I will not give in to this need that tears at my guts.

I move around to the foot of the bed and she doesn't take her eyes off of me.

Her fingers clutch at the bedspread. She flicks out her tongue to wet her lower lip and I almost come in my pants.

I am going to ruin her. To rip into her and satisfy my every depraved desire.

"What do you need?" I widen my stance.

She gnaws on her lower lip. Her fingers dig into the sheets.

I grab my crotch. "Tell me." I stroke my cock through my pants. Up-down-up. My dick extends, the musk of my arousal deepens.

Her nostrils quiver.

She lowers her fingers down between her legs —

"Stop."

She flinches.

"Did I give you permission to do that?"

She raises her heavy-lidded eyes to meet mine.

I glare at her. "Answer me."

Her shoulders hunch. "No."

"Yet you pleasure yourself."

She sets her jaw. Hmm. How much longer can she stand up to me? "You're making me wait, Omega."

Color fades from her cheeks.

"Did you or did you not touch yourself?"

She brings her hands down then grasps them behind her back.

A chuckle bubbles up and I bite the inside of my cheek to suppress it. "Lying, Cara?" I lower my chin and she gulps, but she doesn't deny it.

"What are you willing to do for this?" I grasp my dick and squeeze.

"What do you want?" She pants.

"You sure you want to find out? For once I ask, you can't deny me."

She blinks and looks away.

Disappointment squeezes my chest. I straighten my shoulders and turn, when she breathes, "Okay."

My balls harden and I swear if I don't bury myself inside of her I am going to come right now. I squeeze the base of my dick to hold myself in.

"I didn't hear you."

A snarl rolls from her lips and I almost fucking smile then.

She tosses her head, "Asshole."

"Insult me one more time and all bets are off...and oh, that's Alphahole to you, little Omega."

"I have a name."

"So I hear."

"Why don't you use it?"

"So much attitude, hmm?" I lean forward on the balls of my feet and her shoulders hunch. But she doesn't move back. She doesn't wince. Not even when I let go of my dick to snap my fingers at her.

"I am going to teach you a lesson in servitude. I am going to stuff my cock in your mouth, then your asshole. I am going to show you what happens to omegas who think they can take on the big bad alpha. You made the ultimate mistake."

She brings up her knees, then squeezes her thighs together. Her cheeks flush, her breathing hitches and my balls harden in response.

Fuck me. "Does nothing I say frighten you?"

She glances away then lowers her head. "Y...yes it does."

"But it also arouses you?"

Color flushes her cheeks and she nods.

"Let's see how far this can go before you lose your nerve. On your knees."

She snaps her head up.

"Now." I glare at her.

Before the word leaves my mouth, she is on her knees. On the bed.

I click my tongue then jerk my chin to the floor in front of me.

She gnaws on her lower lip as if considering my request. I press my lips together and she gulps. Then moves forward to drop to all fours. She crawls toward me, and seeing her lithe body inch closer, closer, her blonde hair in a cloud about her shoulders, her breasts swinging as she peeks up at me from under hooded eyelids, I swear it takes everything in me to not turn her around and slap her ass right then. Why does she invoke the predator in me?

The beast that wants to regress to the most basic of states.

An alpha male who wants to claim his female until her every last desire has been fulfilled.

She reaches the edge of the bed and hesitates.

Oh no, she's not going to lose her nerve.

Not now, not after coming this far. All she needs is someone she can trust to lead her, who'll take care of her and protect her. *Which can't be me.* For while I'll never hurt her, while I'll give my life to protect her, where Cara is concerned, my intentions are fueled by greed; by lust for her body, for the taste of her skin. The scent of her essence that drives me crazy. I clench my fists at my side.

"Down."

The edge of my tone curves into a purr. A harsh resonance that swells up from my throat and vibrates around the space. A moan wheezes from her throat. Then she swings her legs over and drops to the floor on her knees.

Seeing her there, on the ground, ready to do my bidding, I swear it's the most erotic sight ever. My groin hardens, and fuck me if I don't want to come right then and cover her in my cum. The fuck? Why does she have this effect on me?

I grab my shaft through my pants and squeeze the base to hold myself back.

She's an omega and I have had my fill of them. Women who are ready to do my bidding. To spread their legs, open their mouths to receive me; but nothing...nothing has prepared me for the pleasure that comes with the absolute submission of the only woman that matters: her.

"Take it out."

She hesitates.

"Now."

Her shoulders wriggle then she reaches for my zipper and pulls it down. She cups her fingers around my shaft and my groin tenses. She runs her fingers up my length and the hair on the nape of my neck rises.

She leans forward and curves her lips around the head of my dick. "Ah, hell." My thighs spasm, my knees wobble, I swear my legs almost give way from under me. *Sur-fucking-prise, asshole. You underestimated how much power she has over you.*

How can I be so weak?

So overcome by the pleasure of having her hot breath sear the ribbed skin of my dick.

I grab the back of her head, dig my fingers into her glossy strands and tug.

She raises her eyes and peers up at me, her mouth still embracing my shaft. The sight is so erotic that my cock thickens further. No, I am not going to allow myself to react to her. I will not show how much her touch affects me. How much I want her to take all of me down her mouth and suck me off.

I tug and want to pull her away; instead, I apply pressure, moving her head forward. My dick slips in further and grazes the back of her throat. Her cheeks are flushed, spit drips from her mouth. She swallows and the suction coils around my shaft.

My groin aches.

A pulse flares to life on my eyelids, at the nape of my neck, even in my fucking balls.

I lower my other hand and grip her shoulder then proceed to fuck her mouth. In-out-in, I pull her face back and forth, wanting her, hating her...how can so many emotions exist in the space of a second?

She grips my thighs, sucks, and swallows. My belly tightens, my balls draw up. Her green gaze holds mine. Unwavering, pupils blown. I can see myself in her eyes. See my intentions reflected in the sheen of sweat on her forehead, in the way the column of her throat moves as she gulps, how her narrow shoulders twitch. More. I want more.

I pull her head and move back.

My dick slips out and she pants. Ropes of saliva dribble from her mouth. Her gorgeous lips are swollen. This woman, this omega is dangerous. If I let her, she could crawl under my skin, into my heart. She could change me. She'd force me to explore the emotions I've never acknowledged I have. I slide my hand down to grip her nape. I tug and she rises to her feet. "Alpha?" She frowns.

"I will not allow you to weaken me."

Why do I want to hurt her so? Why do I want to ruin her and watch her cry? Why do I yearn to bury myself in her pussy until the numbness inside of me dissolves? "I am going to break you, Cara."

The skin over her cheekbones stretches, "What—?"

I turn her around and shove her onto the bed. She stumbles down on her front.

"Up." I hate the hardness in my tone. Hate the need that grips my veins. Pain stabs my chest. I wince.

She turns to look at me over her shoulder and I click my tongue. "Did I give you permission to look?"

Her lips firm. Her head straightens. Yeah, she hates it when I do that. It's the reason why I resort to it. I am a bastard that way. It's why I am going to order her around as if she doesn't mean anything. And she doesn't. *She doesn't.*

I glare at her and she swallows. Then turns around to face forward, on her arms and knees. Her plump delicious butt poised in the air. For me, for my touch. I trail my fingers over her ass cheek and her entire body shudders. "So fucking responsive."

My balls throb in tandem, mirroring her desire. We are too damned evenly matched. Beat for beat. Alpha to omega. She is the other half of my soul...it's why I am going to destroy her. I grab her waist and she moans.

I squeeze the soft skin and she trembles.

I pull her toward me until she is poised on the very edge of the bed and slick drools from between her legs. Her swollen cunt calls to me.

"Fuck you." I kick my hips forward and slam my dick into her pussy and her entire body moves forward. She pants, her shoulders tense.

This is when she cries and begins to struggle.

This is when she tries to escape.

When she tells me she hates me and can't wait to get away from me. This is when I force her to give in to me.

Her muscles tense, her ass cheeks quiver, then she squeezes her inner muscles around my dick. She thrusts her butt toward me and her wet pussy takes me all the way in. My balls slap against her tender flesh.

A whine spills from her lips.

Her back arches, she throws her head back, and that's when I lose it.

"I am going to knot you to me." I pound into her so hard her entire body moves forward. "Gonna own your essence. Your will. Your soul." I pull out of her until the swollen crown of my dick chafes the opening of her channel. "You are mine."

I slam into her again and she groans. "My property. My Omega. You are going to do what I ask of you." I thrust into her and her shoulders quiver. "I'll never let you go. Never let you escape."

She snarls low in her throat.

"There you are." A fierce satisfaction fills my chest. Underneath that coy omega exterior is a woman who stands up for herself. For what she wants. Why is that important to me?

Why do I want her to fight me?

I thought I'd wanted someone who would allow me to stuff my cock in them and then come on command. The kind who'd submit to my pleasure...and don't be mistaken, for I want that too... I want that from her. I *will* have that from her, just not without a struggle. I want her to challenge me. I lean over her until my chest is flush with her back. "Fight me."

She tenses but doesn't look back.

"Resist me." I squeeze my fingers over her waist and her shoulders curve. "Give me the satisfaction of breaking you, Cara." I lower my head and clamp my teeth around her ear lobe. She shivers. Her arms tremble and she groans.

I bring one hand around to play with her clit and her body shudders. "Please." She mewls.

"What do you want?"

She squeezes her inner muscles and I growl. The sound rumbles up my chest, over her back. Her spine curves, her entire body stiffens. She's close, so very close. I drag my chin across the sensitive skin of her nape and goosebumps rise on her flesh.

I pinch the folds of her pussy and she howls; that sends me over the edge.

I squeeze her hips, then pull out of her. The head of my dick stabs the folds of her wet entrance. My vision tunnels. "Tell me what you want. Now."

"You. All of you, Alpha. Your cock inside of me. Your cum covering me."

I drag my weeping shaft over her pussy and into the valley between her ass cheeks.

"What else?"

"Your skin grazing my flesh. Your fingers inside my mouth as I suck on them." Her voice breaks.

I tease my dick over her puckered asshole and she mewls.

"That all you got, Cara?"

She groans.

"What else?"

Her butt trembles.

"Answer me."

"Your thighs squeezing mine. Your body pinning me down—"

I lick the claiming mark on the curve of her shoulder and her spine bends, but it's not enough.

"More. Tell me more." I pinch her chin and tug so she's forced to look up.

"Tell me every depraved thing that you want me to do to you."

She swallows, "I want your dick hooked into me, knotting me, taking me. I yearn for every part of me tuned into you. My spirit reaching out to you. My will submitting to you. My heart...my heart is yours, Alpha. My body. My soul. My every thought belongs to you."

My chest hurts.

A ball of emotion clogs my throat.

Not what I expected. This is not what I wanted. Not this. Not her baring herself...so completely, utterly. Revealing her innocence, her vulnerability. Fuck me, what have I done?

"I am yours," her chin trembles. "Only yours—"

I allow my dick to slide down until the head grazes her melting slit again.

The pulse flutters at her throat. And suddenly I want it all. I want every last drop of her trust, her openness, that absolute willingness to merge with me. Fuse into my skin until there are not two beings. Just one.

"Say it."

She shakes her head.

I drag my teeth over the still healing wound where I had bitten her earlier. The scent of her blood teases my nostrils, and my heart flutters.

"It's now or never, Omega."

She swallows, her shoulders hunch.

I begin to pull out of her when she mumbles, "Claim me again."

My lips curve. Warmth coils in my chest. "I didn't hear you."

She freezes.

"Changed your mind?" I allow a smirk to tug at my lips.

Glancing over her shoulder, she fixes those beautiful green eyes on me. "Jerk."

"That's me."

"Alphahole."

"You got that right, sugar."

I flatten my palm over her waist, then insert my thumb into her asshole. "I have you at my mercy, Cara. Your every hole straining for me. You want me; admit it."

Color blooms on her face. So fucking adorable. So entrancing. Every part of her is screaming for me. Her body has always been drawn to what was right for her. But I need her to acknowledge it. "You will concede. You will give me what I want." I glare at her. "Now."

"I want you to claim me again and again and again." The words tumble from her lips. "Alpha." Her pupils dilate until every last whisper of green is swallowed up by the black. "I am yours."

I pound into her and she howls. Sweat glistens on her shoulders and I lick it up.

She raises her hips to meet my every thrust.

Every groan of hers drives me on.

Every broken hitch of hers fills my mind. Red fills my vision. My knot hardens, plugging the entrance of her channel. My dick hooks behind her pelvic bone. "Come." I bury my teeth in her neck.

"Kayden."

The taste of copper explodes in my mouth. The essence of her drugs my mind. My balls draw up, my groin contracts.

"Open your fucking eyes, Chief."

I snap my eyelids open and Dom's bald face fills my vision. "The hell?" Pain stabs at my chest and I wince.

"You okay?" He frowns.

"Where did she go?" I glance around the space. Nothing. "What did you do to her?" I spring up, then groan when pain tears through my chest. "The fuck?" I glance down to see the dressing that covers most of the upper half of my body.

"You were wounded."

"The Vikings knifed me from behind." My lips curl. "The cowards." My muscles go solid. "They took her." I rip the sheet off.

I swing my legs over and lurch to my feet. My knees tremble...they fucking tremble. "The bastards took my mate." The world spins.

Dom grips my shoulder to steady me and I shrug his hand away. "Back the fuck off."

He raises his hands, "You want to go after her. It's understandable. But there's a reason they left you behind."

"They thought I was dead."

"The Vikings are never careless." He leans forward on the balls of his feet, "Unless it's for a reason. Don't underestimate Talon."

The sweat breaks out on my forehead. "Zeus killed his father. He wants revenge."

My thigh muscles spasm and I reel. The next second I sink back onto the bed. I grit my teeth and ride through the pain.

"After what the Vikings did to Zeus and his mate you should have expected them to come after her." Dom's voice is grim.

"I screwed up. I should have tied her up and not allowed anyone near her."

"For a tough alpha you have no idea how to manage an omega."

"And you do?" I huff out a breath.

"Better than you."

"All of this is moot now. They have her and I am going after her." And when I find her, I am going to...to...whip her ass.

Tie her to my side and keep her captive.

That way she'll never be able to deny me.

I want her to be feisty. I want her to fight, but in the intimacy of my bedroom. I want her naked and writhing, and that fucking dream—my balls harden. It was all a dream. The way I had claimed her all over again and sealed the mating bond. The stabbing agony in my chest shoots up in intensity and I gasp.

"You feel her presence?"

"What does it matter to you?" Waves of fear pour down the bond. They crowd my chest, overflow my mind. I must be imagining it. No way can the bond have consolidated that soon. Could it? I had fucked her hard enough. What had I expected?

Darkness crawls at the edge of my subconscious and I shake my head to clear it. "How long have I been out?"

"Two days."

"Forty-fucking-eight hours?" A ball of emotion blocks my throat. They'd had her all that time? If they hurt her in any way...I'll, "I'll kill all of them." I push myself to a standing position. My thigh muscles cramp, my chest hurts, my side screams in pain.

"I'd expect no less..." Dom squares his shoulders.

"But —?" Sweat breaks out on my brow.

"But you need to rest and get your strength back."

Fuck that. "I need to go to her, is what I must do."

"It's a wonder you are standing." He rubs the back of his neck. "You must be in serious agony —"

As long as she's in one piece, that's all that matters, and I am going to do everything in my power to ensure that. I lurch forward a step and my ribcage screams in protest. "Fuck." I need to get rid of this lingering weakness. I must. As long as I am breathing I can leave here and get to her. I must.

"Stubborn motherfucker." Dom frowns. "Your willpower is something else, Chief."

A chuckle rips from me. "Keep going Second, I could get used to you singing my praises."

"You are the leader who is going to take on Zeus. You will find a way to get our city back." Dom shuffles his feet, "I trust you to do that Kayden..."

"I hear another fucking 'but' coming on."

Dom stays quiet. A beat. Another. Fucker is the too calm, and do I hate that? It's also why I keep him around. When things go to pieces, someone needs to think rationally, and normally, that's Dom. It's why I pause, then straighten my body, when every cell in my body screams that I should find my way to her.

"Well?" I dig my heels into the floor for purchase, "Can't read your fucking mind, Second."

"But when it comes to winning over your mate —"

I glare at him. "That's where you are wrong. I wasn't trying to win her over."

"That was the first mistake." He folds his arms over his chest and his features resolve into that mask which normally means he doesn't approve of what I've done. He has the audacity to question my actions, and I let him get away with it, occasionally.

A fine rage crowds my mind, my nostrils flare. "I am hurt, but not dead." I crack my neck. "Tread carefully, Dom. Think before whatever the hell it is that you are going to say next."

A small smile tugs at his lips.

"The fuck you smiling about, asshole?"

"You, my esteemed leader, you." His lips twitch.

I clench my fists at my side. I'd have stumbled to my feet and taken a swing at him, but I need to save my strength. Need to regroup the fuck fast and find a way to get to her.

"Now you are pissing me off."

"Yeah." He drums his fingers on his chest. "It's too easy to rile you, Chief."

I glare at him and he takes a step back.

"Only where she is concerned." He adds too quickly for my liking, but whatever. "He left you for dead, then kidnapped her. It's a..."

"Trap?" My left eyelid twitches. "Why didn't I see it?"

"You weren't thinking coherently when you rushed in to save her."

I bare my teeth.

He raises his hands. "No offense, Kayden, but you were lost in the mating lust."

"She's not my mate." The band around my chest tightens. The sliver of awareness in my chest thrums as if in warning. As if by saying it aloud I can ignore the presence that stabs at my ribcage. I'd heard that the mating bond went both ways, but I hadn't paid any attention to it. Hell, I hadn't cared if it did. When I had claimed her, I had done it with one emotion in mind. Revenge. Against Zeus. To take back my city from him. "I need to find a way out of this mess." Focus. I must focus on the task at hand. "And to answer your earlier question, I sense her."

The bond writhes. A piercing fear grips my chest, coils around my rib cage. When my feet slap on the cold floor, I realize that I have moved forward.

"What's wrong?" Dom drawls from somewhere behind.

"It's her." A coldness fills my chest. "She is scared and in pain. If they hurt her...I'll..." Another dense cloud of fear crawls across my mind. Dark, overpowering. "She's fucking helpless, wherever she is. She is afraid..." My palms grow cold.

My fingers tremble and I curl them into fists. Abject terror. Is this what she's feeling? Is that why my insides twist? My belly flip-flops. Bile rushes up and I taste the metallic tang of panic.

A touch on my shoulder and I whirl around, fists raised. Blood blooms on Dom's lower lip. He staggers back.

"Fuck." I drag my fingers through my hair. "Didn't mean to do that."

"How's the patient?"

I swivel around to face the newcomer. "Xander." I jerk my chin.

Dom walks to the table at the far end and grabs a towel. "Think you can talk any sense into him?" He presses the fabric to his lower lip and winces.

Xander scratches his chin. "Not when he's got his stubborn mind set on something."

"Why are we wasting time?" I take another step forward and my legs hold. Almost. The fire in my chest intensifies. My throat closes. Another step, then another. My shoulders hunch, but I stay upright. That's got to count for something, right?

I reach the exit, "Out of the way soldier."

Xander folds his arms over his chest. I glare at him and he swallows. Fucker's nervous, even when I am in this half-dead state. More wounded than alive. It's a miracle I made it this far. I dig my heels into the ground and straighten my spine. "What are you waiting for?"

I swing and he ducks. My fist jabs at thin air. The momentum takes me forward. He steps aside. "Oh, *now* you decide to give way?" I mumble. Darkness crawls at the edge of my mind. How strange.

And why is the floor rising to meet me?

128

Chloe

Kayden's big chest covers my back. His hands grab my hips. He raises me up until I am balanced on my hands and knees. His hot breath sears my neck a second before he digs his teeth into the soft skin of my shoulder.

"Ow." I try to scramble away, but he leans his weight on me. My biceps tremble. Darn, but he's heavy.

My shoulders bow, my spine dips under his weight, but does he move away? Of course, not. The brute kicks his hips forward.

He stuffs his dick into my pussy with such force that my entire body jolts. His turgid length extends inside of me. Every ribbed edge of that rugged surface scrapes over my melting channel. His fingers dig into my hip, the hairy, rough skin of his thighs scrapes over mine, and the walls of my cunt clamp down on his shaft.

A dense wave of heat plumes off of him. Sweat beads my skin. A pressure builds inside of me, tugging at me, pushing me to reach for something...something so close I swear I should be able to reach out and touch it. Something out of sight. Almost there. Almost. I groan and bite my lower lip.

If he doesn't let me come in the next few seconds, I am going to... I gulp.

He releases the bruised flesh at the curve of my shoulder, "You are going to...?" He licks the sensitized skin and I whimper.

"Cry." The sob hitches in my throat.

He kisses the skin behind my ear and I shiver. So tender, so caring. His dick fills me to bursting. "You're too big for me." I gulp. "If you get any harder, I am sure you're going to penetrate right through me.

His cock jumps. "Fuck, I love it when you talk dirty to me."

"It's you." I toss my head. "You overwhelm me. I speak my thoughts when I get frazzled."

"Is that the sole reason?"

His dick twitches inside of me and I whine.

"Answer me." His tone takes on that hushed edge. And I hate...I hate it. When he goes all alpha, I can't resist him. Can't hold back. Have to give him what he wants. I shake my head.

"Resistance is futile."

You don't say? I swallow. So why am I fighting him?

"Tell me how you feel." He purrs and I sigh. The velvety smooth sub-vocals curl around me, anchoring me. My thigh muscles quiver. My sex squeezes around the hard muscle of his shaft.

"Ah!" His groan of satisfaction washes over me. "Your body gives you away."

My cheeks flush.

"It's hot and so endearing."

I blink, then glance at him over my shoulder. "Endearing? Did you say endearing?"

His mouth curves. That thin upper lip stiffens, that plump bottom lip juts out. Moisture pools between my legs. "When you get that glint in your eyes—" I swallow. "I...I'd do anything for you."

"Anything?" His lips curl.

I squeeze my eyes shut. "Darn it," I mumble, "Why can't I stop myself from speaking what is on my mind?"

"It's why I can't stop wanting you." His voice is hoarse.

"Huh?" I crack one eyelid open. "I can't get used to this side of you."

"You mean this?" He rolls his hips and his cock grows bigger, heavier, straining the walls of my channel.

My pussy clenches and he groans. "Keep that up and I won't be able to stop." He rises to his knees, bringing me up with him.

My head falls back on his chest.

The heat of his body curls around me, his essence sinks into me. He rubs his whiskered chin over my unhurt shoulder and I shiver.

"You like that?"

Yes.

Yes.

I try to reply and all that comes out is a groan. His hand comes around to cup my breast. He squeezes it. Hard. The pain curves down to meet the burn crawling behind my rib cage. He thrusts into me and my entire body shakes. He lets go of my breast to wrap his massive arm around my waist. He yanks me close and his cock impales me further. "Oh." I writhe in his arms...or try to. He has me flush against the hard wall of his chest. He's overpowering me. Consuming me.

"Please... Alpha." All thoughts leave my mind.

He slams into me again and again. His fingers slide down to cup the flesh between my thighs.

"Mine."

His knot expands at the opening of my channel, melding me to him.

"Only mine." He pounds up and into me. His cock locks into place behind my pelvic bone. "Come."

The demand in his tone rings out over me.

A trembling starts from my toes and flows up my calves, my knees. My thigh muscles coil, my pussy quivers, a flood of slick gushes out to bathe his shaft.

"I am never letting you go."

His voice echoes in my ears and my eyes fly open. I look down to find my fingers are between the folds of my pussy. A dream? Had I been dreaming? It had been so realistic. The hard planes of his body are imprinted into the curves of my flesh. My scalp tingles. My toes twitch. I move my fingers in and out of my channel. The slap of my skin against my folds is heavy in the silence. Not the same. It doesn't feel the same.

I had been so full. Stretched in a way that was painful and pleasurable.

My sex clenches. My chest aches, a headache drums at my temples.

I arch my spine and my back scrapes over the muddy floor.

Where am I?

I glance up at the ceiling, then toward the window set high up on one wall. I'm in a cell of some kind.

I draw in a breath, and freeze. The scent of my slick is heavy in the air and something else, the smell of testosterone laced with bitter almonds.

"Who's there?"

I peer through the gloom.

A large shape moves toward me.

The hair on the nape of my neck stiffens and I swerve aside as a big body crashes down onto the floor. I scream and scramble away.

The alpha springs back and shakes his head.

Dirty matted locks fly around his shoulders. The howl that spews from between those stained teeth is feral.

He charges forward.

I scramble up to my feet. "Help!" My voice echoes off of the walls.

"There's no one here to help you." His footsteps thump closer.

My gut twists. I lurch to the side, but I am not fast enough. His fingers brush my ankles and hold. I tumble to the floor face down.

"No!" My nails dig into the dirt. Pebbles scratch at the inside of my palm and one fingernail breaks loose. Pain wrenches up my arm, tears blind my sight.

I am hauled back toward that vile presence. What the blazes is happening? Where am I?

"Omegas crave one thing." His voice is so close. "Let me give it to you."

I try to scream, but all that comes out is a wheeze.

"I'll show you how it is to be taken by a real alpha."

My skin crawls. My stomach twists.

"Get away from me."

I kick out with my free leg and connect with something fleshy...his thigh? Ugh! A groan tears out of the creature, and his grip loosens. Enough for me to shove away from him.

I rise up to my feet and run toward the sliver of light at the far end. I hit the door. It doesn't open. "Let me out." I hammer on it.

"It's locked, you whore. There's no one else here. No one to rescue you. What's your hurry? You escaped your master, and came here. Your ass is mine, Omega."

"Never." I snarl.

The sound bounces off of the walls.

The panting grows closer; that heavy, fetid presence looms behind me. Turning, I drop to the floor and roll, slamming into the gigantic tree-trunk-like legs. He stumbles over me and falls, crushing me.

His sweating, rancid body covers me. Crushing me. The scent of unwashed skin is thick in my nostrils, in my lungs. Bile rushes up my throat and I gag. I try to draw in a breath and can't. Tears pour down my cheek and I cry in earnest.

"Help me. Kayden. Alpha, where are you?"

Big gusts of words dribble from my mouth.

I strain and try to move my arms, my legs... nothing. I am imprisoned under the gigantic weight of whoever, whatever has me in his clutches.

He lumbers to his feet, and I cough. My lungs inflate. My head spins. I should move, get away. *Get away from him.*

My arms and legs are paralyzed.

I can't move.

Did he break all of my bones?

He looms over me. The white of his eyes gleams. He smacks his lips.

If I simply retreat into a corner of my mind, can I pretend this is not happening? That it's not me whose neck he grabs. It's not my body which he swings up. Not my feet which don't touch the floor anymore. Not my breasts he squeezes with such ferocity that a moan spills from my lips. He throws me down on the ground on my back. My head cracks against the floor. I tremble.

Not me.

Not me.

Not happening to me.

He reaches down and his fingers grab at my hip bone. I squeeze my eyes shut. *Not me.* I am not here. Darkness swirls around me.

He leans over me, and that putrid breath fills the space around me. I let my body slump, let every muscle go slack. He grabs my thigh and pulls it aside; his weight settles between my legs with horrible finality. *Kayden. Help. Me.* The next second, his weight is lifted off of me.

There is a crash. I don't open my eyes.

Sounds of grappling and snarling, like two beasts locked in a duel. *Help me. Help me.* The words roll around in my head, my heart. There is a sickening crunch, then silence. A beat. Two. Three. Nothing moves. I wriggle my fingers, my toes. I crack my eyes open to find the door to the space open.

Light pours inside and I gasp.

The body of a massive man lies near the door, slumped in an unnatural position. Next to him stands another alpha. Bigger. As massive as Kayden. He steps forward and the light flows over his face, illuminating familiar features. "You are safe."

As if I believe him? I gulp and my throat hurts. "Have we met?"

He tilts his head, "I may take prisoners, but none of my men are allowed to hurt them."

I sit up, trying to understand what I am seeing. "You are the Viking who kidnapped me?"

He tilts his head. "Talon, at your service, Princess."

Princess? "You know who I am?"

He stares, but doesn't reply.

"Is that why you kidnapped me?"

"Among...other things." His gaze rakes over me, and it should feel filthy, but all I see is an almost-polite curiosity. He's not interested in me? Not in *that way* at least. I bite the inside of my cheek.

Why am I here?

I want to ask him, but no, to do that will reveal my vulnerability, and I can't have that. Maybe if I keep him talking, I can find out what his plans are for me?

"He..." I jerk my chin toward the fallen alpha. "He tried to..." I can't bring myself to form the words.

"He wasn't supposed to harm you."

Right! Screams fill my mind...of fallen clan members as Vikings—as his people had swooped down on Red Square, hacking away at those trying to flee. One of the marauders had attacked me and Lucy had come to my defense.

My sister had saved me, only to send me a command to give myself up to another alpha. To Kayden. I don't understand it. I'd give anything for Kayden to be here. Kayden. *Kayden,* where are you?

Faced with the prospect of being taken against my will...once again...my ex-abductor has become my savior.

Is that why Kayden had taken me from the omega harem? Is that why my sister had nudged me toward him, very cleverly of course? By telling me to not give in too easily?

The thoughts whirl around in my head and I frown.

"I am sorry for what he tried to do."

Huh? I frown up at him, "Are you for real? You kidnap me, then you apologize for it?"

"He was on guard to protect you."

Heard that one before. I snicker and he frowns.

Have a breakdown. Why not? Go for it. You're the prisoner of an alpha...again! This time it's worse. It's a Viking. The most ferocious, most savage of all the clans.

The giant takes a step forward and I scoot back.

"Don't...don't come closer."

His lips curve, "You have fight left in you...perhaps that's what appealed to Kayden...hmm?"

He drums his fingers on his chest and an inquisitive look comes into his eyes.

His nostrils flare.

Is he smelling my essence?

His features harden. He drops his arms to his sides and steps back.

Huh?

"Did you tell him?" Talon growls and the sound rolls around in my stomach. My belly wobbles, the bile rises to my throat. I am not going to be sick. Not going to be sick. Not in front of this monster.

"Answer me." His tone is impatient.

I wait for my body to respond, for my cells to react. For that omega essence inside of me to surge forward and demand that I give in to the presence of a dominant alpha, but nothing. Huh?

So it's Kayden's voice that incites that need to submit to him?

I thought most omegas couldn't stop themselves from following any alpha's orders. Guess I was wrong. It's Kayden. Only Kayden's tone, Kayden's scent, Kayden's presence that presses down on my chest, raises the hair on my nape and insists that I throw myself down in front of him and ask him to take me. Fuck me. Knot me. Kayden, where are you?

A whine rolls up my throat and I clamp my lips shut.

I can't give any outward sign of what thinking of Kayden does to me. I am over the heat cycle; yet all I have to do is imagine Kayden's fingers touching me, caressing me, his tongue licking my folds, his cock inside of my pussy and the slick streams from between my legs..."No, no, no." I slap my hands to my ears and shake my head vigorously. "Don't think about it."

"What's wrong with you?" Talon's voice whips over me.

I hear his footsteps, then the heat of his body licks my skin. My pores cringe and seem to close up. I hunch my shoulders, try to draw into myself. "Go away, go away, go away." I chant aloud, not caring if he thinks I am crazy. If he did, maybe he'd release me? As if. He's going to barter me,

"If you don't stop that panic attack, I am going to open this door and allow the alphas circling around in the corridor to come in."

My heart begins to thud so hard I am sure it's going to jump out of my ribcage.

"Or maybe I'll hand you back to Kayden."

My eyes snap open.

Talon's face fills my line of vision. Closed features, broad shoulders that block out the rest of the space, and he's tall. As tall as Kayden.

But he's not Kayden.

"Kayden?" The sound of his name from my lips clears the rest of the thoughts from my head.

"Yeah, that's who we're talking about." Talon sets his jaw. "Does he know?"

"What?"

His gaze drops to my belly then back to my eyes, "Or maybe you were keeping it from him?" His lips firm.

"Wait... What?" My head spins.

My knees give way and I sink back onto the floor. I can't be what he's implying. No way. I mean sure, Kayden had knotted me...many times. Came inside me. Took me. But if I am pregnant, why haven't I sensed it?

Why hadn't he?

Is he not my true mate? Aren't mates supposed to be the first to sense the change brought on by pregnancy? Does Kayden not want me, after all?

Talon looms over me. "That's why my man couldn't restrain himself."

He takes a step forward; his chest muscles rise and fall. "There's something about an omega who's newly impregnated that sends every single alpha in the square mile around her into rut."

The skin around his eyes tightens and his biceps bulge.

Sweat breaks out on my forehead.

A newly pregnant omega is irresistible. My throat closes. The first few months is also when a pregnant omega's sex drive is unrelenting. When, despite the absence of estrus, they need to fuck. That's when omegas need their mates the most. It's when the urge to nest is the strongest and...when your body can't stop producing slick. My belly contracts. Just the thought sends my hormones into overdrive.

His head comes up and color burns his cheeks. A growl emanates from the Viking.

I open my mouth to tell him to stop, to not come closer, but the words stick in my throat. I shake my head and he fists his hands at his sides. He drops to his knees in front of me.

"I am sorry your mate was killed; my men give into bloodlust in a fight. They are also overeager to helping themselves to the spoils of a fight. Something I intend to fix. Meanwhile..." He thrusts his head forward until his nose is mere inches away from my skin. "Your scent...you need to be kept in isolation." He pushes away and to his feet so fast that I blink.

He swivels around to march to the door.

"Wait."

Only when my voice rings out do I realize that I had spoken. And I had commanded an alpha—the leader of the Vikings, to stop. I gulp. He's going to turn around and hurt me, but...but I don't care. I straighten and force myself to stand up.

He shoots me a glance over his shoulder. I hold his gaze. "Why did you kidnap me?"

"To hold you as ransom for Zeus."

Oh. I stare. Of course. I should have guessed it.

"Kayden...?" I force the word out. I don't want to know. It's best not to find out what happened...but I need to. I need to. "Is he really...?" My chin wobbles.

Talon jerks his chin. "My man stabbed him. He's dead."

"No!" The world spins.

It can't be true. I drop into myself, reach out for the mating bond coiled in my chest to find...nothing. Fog. Darkness, a screen that seems to have fallen between us. A hazy cloud, and beyond that, a nothingness so absolute. Why can't I sense him? Is it because I am pregnant? Expecting a baby often blinds an omega's senses. Makes her more dependent on her alpha. My heart begins to race. *Pregnant? I'm pregnant. I am carrying Kayden's child*. The band around my chest tightens.

I hear the sound of screaming.

The sound seems to go on and on. My head hurts, my ears ring. My vocal cords protest, but I can't stop.

"Calm down."

His voice whips through the space and I blink. I swallow down the scream bubbling up my throat. My stomach heaves. The acrid taste of bile laces my tongue.

"You are a monster. You killed him. Why did you have to tell me that I was pregnant? I was better not knowing. Not now, when Kayden is dead. How could you do this? I—"

"Stop it." I hear him as if from far away.

Tears slide down my face. Another shard of pain radiates down my throat to my chest. I can't feel my heart. My hands and feet are numb. Am I alive?

"It didn't work out the way I had planned."

His features fade in and out of sight. "Sorry about your mate. I'll take you to the omega quarters...you'll be safe there..."

White noise crashes over me.

When I wake up, I am alone, on a bed. I stare up at the ceiling. I don't want to live...don't want to...will not. I push up and slide my feet over the bed. Walking to the window, I shove up the pane. Then lean out and take a deep breath. Another. The view is so pretty, stretching out down the side of a hillside. Down to a steep drop to the river running below. I shove one leg over, then the other. The wind slaps the hair from my face. I open my eyes wide.

Then, I jump.

129

Kayden

The noise in my head fades away to be replaced by nothingness. My eyelids fly open.

I've been here for a week already. Every time I had regained consciousness, I'd tried to leave the room; had even made it half-way to the door before I'd collapsed.

This time around...I am going to get over the threshold and not look back. The doc had claimed it was a miracle I was already on my feet, but, whatever. My body has always healed fast from wounds—apparently the genes from my bastard of a blood-father were good for something. I snicker. The coldness in my chest snaps out, my spine bends. Something...an invisible force...the connection to her? Urges me to move. To leave. Get out of there. Now. I can't delay further.

My skin tingles. My arms and legs twitch. I lurch up from the bed and toward the exit. Sweat trickles down my back; the blood pounds at my temples.

Don't stop. Keep moving.

My feet slide a-n-d I crash down to the floor face down. The impact slams through my head, and the ringing in my ears slowly subsides. I slam my hands on the floor and push up. This time my legs hold up my weight. Thank fuck. Staggering to the door, I wrench it open. "Dominic."

He turns from the head of the corridor. "You bellowed?"

Next to him, Xander folds his arms over his chest.

"I can't feel her."

Since when do I speak out my thoughts to my men?

Her influence is seeping into me, making me more candid than I'd expected. Is this what Zeus experienced when he mated his omega. Why am I thinking of my bastard half-bro right now? My knees give way, and I grab the frame of the door to steady myself.

Dom leans forward on the balls of his feet, "What do you mean?"

I grit my teeth so hard that pain shoots up my jaw. "The Omega...Cara..." I rub my chest. Emptiness. Hollowness. Where was that irritating, stabbing pain that had curled behind my rib cage since I had claimed her...the second time? The fuck had I done that?

Why couldn't I have stopped myself?

Oh, wait, it's because I hadn't been able to resist that addictive taste of hers. Or the call of her skin, or her greedy pussy which had wrapped around my dick and made me want to wallow in her essence. Fuck! I drag my fingers through my hair. "She...she's in trouble." What had he done to her? "If he hurt her...if he...if..."

Panic grips my chest.

My stomach rolls. The fuck? I am not going to be sick, not now. Not when I need to get it together. My vision narrows. My shoulders hunch.

"I have to leave."

Turning, I stagger toward the closet at the far end. Thankfully, I had managed to reach my suite before collapsing again. For the third, or was that the fourth time? Whatever. It doesn't matter. Nothing matters except getting the hell to her. I should have done it earlier. I should have...could have...now I am crying over something I should have done.

Nice, real nice.

I wrench the closet open, then pull on fatigues, T-shirt. Sitting on the chair, I pull on socks and boots. I stand up and my head spins.

"Fuck. Fuck. Fuck."

I sink back onto the chair, my breath coming in pants. Fuck this shit. I need to focus, focus...ground myself.

"You know what sets us apart from animals?".

Huh? I glare at him.

"Hope." Dom's voice is sober.

"The fuck you going on about?" The pulse thuds in my throat, at my wrists, confirming I am alive. If I am, so is she. Isn't that how these mating bonds work? Not that I had bothered to find out about them or believe in them...because...because damn it, I'd never thought I'd find an omega I'd want more than life itself.

I'd seen her and felt it.

And I had denied it.

I am faced with the irrefutable evidence that my life has changed, that *I have changed*, because of her.

I can turn away from it. But I am not stupid. I can recognize the truth when it slaps me in the face. I lurch to my feet and sway again. Sweat beads my brow.

I should let her go, but I can't.

The lack of life in the mating bond tells me, she is...she is—I can't bring myself to say the words.

"Control your fears, Chief." Dom's voice is hard. "Don't give in to them. You have to believe that she is alive and waiting for you to rescue her."

I wheeze. "When did you become such a dreamer?"

"When did you become such a cynic?"

"Oh, let's see." I hold up a finger. "Was it when Golan raped my mother? Or when my father took pity on my mother and took her back in, but turned his back to her so she was a prisoner in her own house? Or perhaps it was when Golan killed her. Or when the omega who...who..."

"Stole your heart?" His lips curl.

"Fuck your sappy sentiments."

"Fuck your dominance that gets in the way of seeing what was in front of you all along."

Her. He means her. How I behave akin to an out of control asshole in her presence. "Enough."

I stagger to my feet.

Closing the distance between us, I grab his collar and raise Dom to his feet.

I am taller than him, and broader. I have defeated him in fights often enough. We are equally matched, but I have the upper edge in power...when I am in full health. My biceps flex, my chest hurts, my thighs struggle to keep me upright. Dom stares at me; his face wears that smug look, which I hate.

"Get the fuck out of my sight."

The skin around his lips tightens. "I am not the pigheaded one."

"No you are the pussy who's so in touch with his emotions that I should have put you in charge of the omega harem instead of being my next in command."

Dom's shoulders flex. "You are not thinking clearly, grief clouds your mind —"

"Making excuses so you don't have to fight?" There is a pressure knocking behind my eyeballs, but fuck if I am going to give in to it.

I glare at the man who's had my back since I was seven. The man who is quasi- guardian, friend, partner...who understands me too well. If I can challenge him to a fight...it might detract from the storm of emotions churning inside. "When I get my city back, I'll strip you of your post. In fact, you are too weak to be in charge of the harem. Why don't you become the Gardener, eh? You can tend to the flowers, surround yourself with the trees, whose company you prefer to that of other —"

His fist catches me in the side and I gasp. Pain explodes up my spine, framing the edges of my vision. "The fuck —?"

The words catch in my throat as I teeter on my heels.

His arms grab my shoulders, "Fuck, Kayden... I didn't mean to."

I bare my lips, then shake off his hold. "No. Fuck *you*, asshole." I snap my fist out and catch him in the face.

It's the same place I hit him the last time.

Crimson spurts from his mouth and a snarl bubbles up from within him. Then we are grappling and hitting each other. We tumble to the floor, go rolling toward the door. "Stop it...stop it."

I ignore the woman's voice.

"I know where she is."

I stiffen and Dom catches me in the jaw. White sparks flash behind my eyes.

"I can help you find Chloe."

I shove him away and spring up to my feet. "The fuck you talking about, Lisa?"

Dom rises up to his feet, "What did you do?" He frowns at his daughter.

"I...ah." She shifts her weight from foot to foot.

Dom prowls forward to halt next to me. "What are you up to?"

She swallows. Her gaze bounces between Dom's face and mine. "I am sorry."

Cold fingers grip my heart. I take a step forward and Dom steps between us. He turns to face me, his daughter hidden behind his bulk. "Let me handle this."

"You've done a fine job so far, keeping her in check..." I curl my fingers into fists.

"You couldn't control your omega either, so don't get me start—"

"Will you two listen to me?" Lisa swerves around to stand between us.

I glare at her.

"Kayden... I..." She looks away.

Dom props his hand on his hips, "If you've done anything to hurt her, I'll—" I hold up a hand and Dom falls silent.

"Tell me." I keep my voice shorn of all emotion and almost succeed. How can I sound so calm when everything inside of me is shattering into tiny pieces? She's dead...dead... I toss my head to clear it and she winces.

"Speak." I firm my lips.

Her shoulders tremble. "I laced her water so she lost consciousness and—"

"You what—?" Dom's voice thunders in the space between us.

I glance over her head and Dom's jaw hardens. His gaze meets mine, then he jerks his chin.

I bend my knees and peer into Lisa's eyes. "Who were you working with?"

The color leaches from her cheeks. "The Vikings." She swallows, then squares her shoulders. "I happened to run into one of them. He asked me to find a way to get her out of the stronghold."

"What did he promise you in return?"

She presses her lips together.

"You betrayed the leader of your clan. Do you have any idea what that means?"

Her chin wobbles, and fear rolls off of her in waves.

"Do you have any idea what you have done, Lisa?"

She raises her chin. "I had no other choice. You refused to notice me and I wanted to show you—"

"What?" I drum my fingers on my chest, "That I can count on you? That you were worthy of being by my side? That you were smarter than your own father, than everyone else in the clan?"

"Yes." She clenches her fists at her sides. "You don't listen to me because I am an omega." She turns sideways and jabs a finger in Dom's chest. "And you think I am too young. Too naive."

"Aren't you?"

Dom's expression is thunderous. His features contort. Considering I hit his face, that must hurt, but he doesn't show it...or if he does, he doesn't care.

"I. Am. Not." She stamps her foot.

Then draws herself up to her full height, which means she comes up to his chest.

She tosses her head. "You never listen to me. You are too busy being his second-in-command." She stabs a thumb over her shoulder, at me. "You and he...are forever in boring discussions. Or else you are off on some mission or other. You never spend any time with me. Never."

"You're a selfish brat," Dom's lips thin.

"Who's fault is that...Father?" She stamps her foot.

Dom growls deep in his throat, "Is this what I have brought you up to be? A self-centered girl who doesn't care about anyone else?"

"See?" she flings up her hands, "You treat me like I am of no consequence."

Dom grabs his hair and tugs. "You will fucking tell me what that Viking promised you in return."

"No."

"No?" His features darken.

It's fucking entertaining to watch my pompous Second losing his shit. Maybe I should get out of the way and let it play out?

But then he raises his hand and I have no doubt that he wants to slap her. Not that I care. Fuck if I want to interfere in their family drama shit, but if he does, Lisa will have a temper tantrum. She'd probably refuse to share Chloe's whereabouts, which I need to know. Now. "Stop it, the both of you."

Dom freezes. His features twist. I've never seen him this disturbed.

"Step back, Second."

His jaw tics. Then he lowers his hands to his sides. He takes a step back, and then another, putting distance between himself and his daughter.

"Look at me, Lisa."

Her shoulders slump as she swivels around to face me.

"Where is she?"

"At their temporary hideout."

"Where is that?"

"Not far...in Inverness."

"That's an hour away." Xander speaks up from his post at the entrance to the room.

"Who helped you to get her out?"

"I can't tell you." She clamps her jaw shut.

"I will find out who it is eventually, so how about if you spare us the trouble and tell us?"

She folds her arms around her waist.

"The hell did he promise you in return?"

She blinks, then swallows.

"Tell me, Lisa, or so help me, I'll—"

"You."

"What?" I frown.

"I wanted her out of the way so I stood a chance with you."

The fuck?" I glare at her. "All this so you could fulfill some romantic dream."

"Not a dream. I have always wanted you Kayden. You never noticed me."

"And now I never will." I prop my hands on my hips. "There's only one punishment for what you have done."

"Death." Dom crosses his arms over his chest. "She should meet the fate of any other traitor."

"Perhaps." I crack my neck. "For now, she will be confined to her room." I turn to Xander. "Take her away."

Lisa turns and walks to the door. "I can see myself out." She pauses, then turns to look at Dom. "You may be my father, but I can't forget that you would have me killed rather than support me."

The color drains from his face. His shoulders bunch, but he doesn't move.

Lisa brushes past Xander, who follows her out.

Walking to the safe in the corner, I flick it open, then pull out my guns and proceed to snap them on—one on my back, one in the waistband of my pants. My sword, I slip onto my back. My hunting knife, I snap onto the other side of my holster.

"I am coming with you."

I turn to Dom, "I need you here."

"I am not letting you go alone."

"Lisa needs her father."

His jaw tics.

"You promised my father to protect me. You have more than done your duty. Stay with your daughter. Talk to her."

He winces. "I've botched it up so far."

"You haven't." I straighten, then reach for a jacket and shrug it on, adding a whip that I hook to my side, another gun, two hand grenades, a rope. Hell, if I am going to take on Talon, I am leaving nothing to chance this time. "You brought her up to be smart, independent and to think for herself."

"She is an omega; she needs to behave like one."

"Reason it out with her. Find out who helped her from within the settlement. We need to flush out the traitor."

He straightens. "If you don't return in twenty-four hours..."

"I will."

"If you don't, I am going to Zeus."

"The fuck you will." I snarl.

"You need to bury your differences with him. Take his help to defeat the Vikings."

"I don't need his help. I'll find Talon on my own, and if he's done anything to her," My ribcage constricts. "I'll kill him."

"Twenty-four hours Kayden."

I jostle his shoulder on my way to the door," I'll find her before that."

130

Chloe

I glance around the clearing, a few miles from Talon's place. I had swung one leg over the window, half aware of what I had been doing. I'd had enough presence of mind to grab the ivy that clung to the walls and scramble to the ground before running here.

Okay, I admit, it had crossed my mind that I could jump. I had been ready to kill myself. Because...he...my alpha is dead. Why do I think of Kayden as mine?

He never was.

He'd never indicated that he wanted me for anything other than the omega he'd fucked to get out of his system.

Even his claiming—I touch the now healing mark on my neck—hadn't meant anything to him. If it had, wouldn't he have said something to me? A look, a touch...a glance to show that I meant more than a pussy to fuck? A womb to impregnate with his child? Is that what this was about?

Him wanting to use my pedigree to produce a child worthy of his lineage?

Not that he'd come outright and said it. But he'd realized that I was a princess; he'd revealed that much.

What more could it be? Darn it. I squeeze my arms around my sides and reach out to him through the mating bond. Nothing. The darkness rolls in my chest. He can't be dead. I refuse to believe it, despite Talon insisting that Kayden had been killed.

What is Talon's game? He'd insisted that he was doing this to draw Zeus out. Why would Zeus come to rescue me? Sure, I'm Lucy's sister but does that mean anything to him? No one is going to help me.

Talon wanted me to play my part. Be the omega in distress. Again. I fold my arms around my waist.

My tongue sticks to the roof of my mouth.

I hate these alphas for thinking they can ruin my life.

Manipulate me into being what they want.

A thumping reverberates toward the clearing. I look up to find the leaves of the trees in front of me shivering. The blazes is happening? I swallow. My heart begins to pound.

The crunch of heavy footsteps draws my attention to my right. There's something, no, someone moving toward me from my right.

A twig cracks and I snap my head to the left.

I take a step back. Another. I am surrounded. No, no, no. How did I let myself get into this situation? Why had I agreed to escape from Moscow with Lucy? But if I had stayed...I'd...I'd have landed in the same place. Being chased by Vikings. I snicker to myself. There was no way I could have avoided this situation. All that had happened in the intervening time was that...that I had met Kayden.

I slide back. My foot connects with something and I scream. Birds fly from the trees around me and my heart rate ratchets up. The hair on the back of my neck rises. I turn and my throat closes. A ball of fear squeezes my throat. No. No. A man steps into the clearing.

Larger than any I have ever seen. Massive legs like tree trunks. His shoulders so big, they seem almost deformed. Dark blonde, matted hair that flaps around his face as he moves. His biceps bulge and he has to hold his hands away from his side as he stalks forward.

Dark eyes gleaming. His nostrils flare. He's scented me. He picks up his gait and I stumble back.

My leg muscles tighten. My vision tunnels. Everything seems to slow down around me. The sound of footsteps reaches me. I swing my head to see another alpha enter the clearing.

Slimmer than the other one, but almost as tall. Dark hair cropped closed. A face that is so beautiful that it's almost hideous.

"There you are," he croons. "We've been looking all over for you." My throat closes. The fine hair on my forearms rises.

"Be a good little omega now and submit to us."

Never.

No way am I going to stay quiet while these monsters terrorize me. I am not going to give in without a fight. No. No. I swerve around just as footsteps sound from my other side. I turn and scream aloud.

Another alpha, this one less than a foot away. My heart rate ratchets up.

Get the hell away from them.

I scream aloud and the sound sends another wave of fear screeching down my spine. The closest alpha swoops toward me.

I duck. The breeze from his gesture sways the hair on my forehead. My pulse beats at my temples. I pump my legs and run, sweat pouring down my forehead, stinging my eyes. I race out of the clearing, taking the path through the trees. My hair snags on a branch and I wince. Don't stop. I keep going. Grunts sound behind me. Something crashes to the ground. Squirrels race past me in the undergrowth. A deer jumps across my path and I scream and stumble to the ground. The impact tears through my arms. My breasts hurt. My teeth chatter and I squeeze my lips together. Jumping up, I keep going.

"I saw her first."

"No, I did."

Don't turn. Don't. I sneak a peek over my shoulder and grimace. Two of the men are locked in fisticuffs. The third...the dark-haired one swerves around them, then grins at me.

He picks up his pace.

I turn around and leap forward. My feet slap on the ground. My joints ache, my chest screams, my throat is so dry. My vision narrows on the path. Everything else fades. Adrenaline laces my blood. I put on a burst of speed and pull ahead. I can do this, I can. I race out of the trees and cry out. I am at the edge of a steep cliff. Below me the river roars, the spray white where it hits the rocks and breaks.

"You can't escape."

I swerve around and hold up my fists. "Stop right there."

The alpha laughs. His steps slow and he prowls forward. "Don't die, little Omega. I promise it won't be all bad."

"That's what they all say." I grind my teeth. "I am not letting you hurt me."

"A quick grope." He wiggles his fingers and I wince. "A kiss, can I get a kiss at least?" He purses his lips and my stomach protests. Bile rushes up my throat. Gross.

"Stay...stay away from me."

"Of course." He bows low, "Your majesty." He leers at me and sweat beads my brow.

"We are here to obey your every wish..." he takes a step forward and terror claws at my insides. "Not." He spreads his arms wide and light shines off of metal.

A dagger is stuck in his belt.

I swallow. I will not be intimidated. My knees shake. Not.

He circles closer, closer. "That beautiful pussy of yours. That entrancing scent."

"Not for you. Never for you." Shut up, don't provoke him. Don't.

His nostrils flare, I can see the whites of his eyes. Darn it, but he is going into rut.

He lurches forward. Adrenaline laces my blood. I duck, and he totters at the edge. I snatch at the dagger as his body tumbles over the edge.

My fingers close around the handle of the dagger.

Got it!

I blink the sweat away from my eyes and turn, then scream.

The two other alphas face me.

"You haven't killed each other?" I try to smirk but my chin wobbles.

"Where would the fun be in that?" One of them scratches his crotch. Ugh.

"We decided we'd share you instead." The second grins.

"D...don't come closer." I slide back a step. The heels of my feet slip. I cry out and scramble forward.

The two men circle around me.

One of them holds out his hand, "Don't be scared, Omega. Talon promised that we could keep you when we found you."

"We'll take good care of you...and your...cunt." His gaze drops to my core. My chest squeezes. My skin crawls.

No. I shake my head. I am not going to let them touch me. I slide one foot back.

The wind picks up and slaps into my back and I sway. I half angle my head, not daring to look away from these two. But I can't look back.

If I do, I'll lose courage.

And I am not going to jump. Not this time. I don't want to be the victim anymore. I can't die, not when...I bring up a hand and touch my belly. Not when I have something to live for. "Don't come close."

A snarl spills from my lips and I blink.

I sound almost fierce.

How is that possible?

What has changed in such a short period of time? Is it the fact that I have someone else to live for? I hadn't been thinking straight when I had tried to jump out of the window. That terrible emptiness squeezes my chest...but there's something more. Love. So much love. Tenderness. Hope. For the life I carry inside.

I have to believe I can pull through.

I can live on my own terms. I can live for this new life. A surge of warmth coils in my chest. A calmness fills my mind. I widen my stance, place my feet firmly on the ground. "You are not going to touch me."

I can do this. I can. Father had insisted that I take part in fighting lessons with Lucy. I hadn't wanted to be part of it. But I remember them. I do. I tense my muscles. Train my attention on the face of the closest alpha.

"Oh, yeah?" The man angles his head. "You dare dictate to us?" He lumbers forward. A foot, half a foot closer.

The second one approaches me from the side. A bead of sweat trickles down my spine. I stay where I am.

Stay.

Stay.

The first one lunges and I drop low. I kick his legs out from under him. Then rush forward.

The second alpha swings, I duck, then kick him in the balls. He howls and grabs his crotch. I race forward. I did it. I did.

Adrenaline laces my blood.

I am going to get out of here, I am free. I—An arm loops around my waist. "Gotcha." I scream again.

I wriggle my shoulders, try to pull free.

The grip on my torso tightens. My heart begins to hammer.

No. No. This can't be happening. A pressure builds at the back of my eyes.

The second alpha stumbles around, his legs bowed, hands cupping his crotch. "The bitch needs to be taught a lesson. I am going to use her, then kill her."

He closes in from the front and I howl.

He raises his fist toward my face, but the next moment his body arcs through the air.

131

Kayden

"Hold on, Cara."

I fling the alpha away from her. He crashes onto the ground. I jump on his back and he screams. The sound of bones breaking has never been more satisfying. Springing off of him, I plant my knees on either side. Grabbing his big head, I twist it. His entire body twitches, his cry cut short. I drop him to the ground, his head at an unnatural angle.

"Kayden." Her cry has me back on my feet. I swing around and halt. My shoulders tense; my belly flip-flops.

The alpha holds her by her neck. Her legs dangle off the ground. She has her fingers squeezed around his forearms. Her face is white. She opens her mouth and a choking sound emerges.

"Don't." I take a step forward and the alpha swings her over to hold her over the edge.

He glances over my shoulder.

"How much will you give up for her?" A new voice rings out.

"Still getting others to do your dirty work, Talon?" I growl without turning around. Not taking my eyes off of the fucker who has my omega in his grasp. The man snarls. His shoulders go solid.

Cara gasps and her body twitches.

Anger coils in my chest. My belly is so fucking heavy. I will not let anything happen to her. I will not lose her. This time I will do right by her.

Footsteps sound behind me, then Talon draws level with me.

"Good of you to drop in, Kayden."

"The fuck you playing at, Talon?"

"Following your lead, my dear chap." So fucking polite. The hair on the nape of my neck hardens.

"The fuck you mean?"

"You started this game. Sending Lucy to Zeus. Then, going back on your word to my father."

"That's what this is about? Revenge?"

"Yes, but not the way you think it. I couldn't care less about the old man. But power... Yeah, that interests me. I want Zeus's city and yours. Call me greedy, but I believe in pressing my advantage when I have it. Can't have the two of you joining forces."

"No possibility there." I roll my shoulders.

"Not that I don't believe you. But power and pussy..." I sense him nod toward where the alpha dangles her over the edge, "have a way of complicating things."

No shit. My muscles bunch. Anger thrums my veins. "Let her go."

"As you wish." He snaps his fingers and the other alpha lowers his arm.

Cara's body dips. Her gaze never wavers from mine. Beseeching me. Pleading with me. I clench my fists at my side. My chest, my fucking chest hurts. Horror, pain...fear, white fear fills my mind.

"The fuck you up to, you bastard?"

"My mistake." He clicks his tongue. "That alpha is a little trigger happy, I'm afraid." He rolls his shoulders. "A small taste of what is possible here. One wrong move on my part and he may—" He lets my imagination complete the sentence. My muscles twitch. If only I could get near that man holding my mate...close enough to take him down. One wrong move and he wouldn't hesitate to let go of her. I dig my boots into the ground, don't take my eyes off her.

I hold her attention.

Stay strong, Cara. I pulse the thought at her and she blinks. *Don't give up. I am here. I am not going to let you go.* Can she sense what I am thinking? Can she understand what I am trying to convey to her? The mating bond writhes.

"You made your point, Talon." My fingers tremble. "What do you want?"

"Give yourself up to me willingly. Let me trade you and your omega with Zeus."

She shakes her head. "Don't..." she coughs, and her eyelids flutter down. "Don't do it." Her body slumps.

My guts twist. I need to get to her. I cannot let anyone hurt her. "Fine." I fist my fingers at my sides.

"I didn't hear you."

"I am here, aren't I?"

"Say the words..."

I turn, then lower my head, "Take me, asshole. Let her go."

He snaps his fingers at the other man, who turns and lowers her. When her feet touch the floor, he lets go. Her body crumples.

My heart stutters. I lunge forward and Talon clicks his tongue. "Don't be impulsive."

I pause, my shoulders going rigid. My attention is on her prone body. *Please don't die. Don't die. Not now.*

"On your knees, arms behind your neck."

I fold my hands behind my neck, then lower my knees to the ground. She's so still. *Wake up, Cara. Open your eyes.*

"I am sorry it came to this."

His words wash over me. He nods to the other alpha, who shrugs off his shirt. Then, turning to me, he uses it to tie my arms behind my back.

I dare not look away. Did her fingers twitch? No, that must be my imagination.

I flex the muscles of my wrists, hoping that when I relax them, I'll get some leeway to break out of my bonds. Her chest heaves. I flick my gaze to her face and her eyelids fly open. She swallows. Her lips purse.

I shake my head and she frowns.

Talon stalks around. He plants his bulk between us, cutting off the sight of her.

I growl in frustration. Fucking hell. Sweat coats my palm. The hell is she doing?

Did she feign being unconscious? Can't be. Well, if she did, she had me and Talon fooled. Should I be upset by that or...proud? My chest swells. What a strange reaction.

"Up." Talon jerks his chin.

I lurch up to standing, then plant my legs apart.

I hear the footfalls behind Talon a second before he stumbles forward.

"The fuck?" His forehead furrows. He brings his arm around to his side and that's when I notice it. A dagger sticks out from his side.

"She stabbed me?"

He yanks out the knife and throws it aside. Blood gushes out, drenching his side.

"I am going to need more than revenge after this." He swivels toward her and I lunge forward.

"Get out of the way, Cara."

She rolls to the side and I charge him.

132

Chloe

I stumble to the side as Kayden head-butts Talon. He stumbles back and Kayden slams his shoulder into Talon's chest.

Warmth floods my chest. Kayden is alive. So, why hadn't I sensed him earlier? It doesn't matter. I shove the thought from my head. He's here, and alive. And he came for me.

Another Alpha lunges for Kayden.

"Oh, no you don't!" I shove my foot out and the man stumbles, then rights himself. "You little bitch, I should have killed you...No, I should have fucked you when I had the chance."

He attacks me and I scream. Adrenaline spikes my blood. I lurch away from him, but he catches me and heaves me over his shoulder. "Kayden!"

The scream rips from me. My heart pumps, my head spins. No, that's the alpha swiveling around to stalk to the edge. He holds me up over the steep drop, "Say goodbye, asshole"

"No." Kayden's agonized yell fills the air.

I open my mouth but can't speak.

The breeze crashes over me, the emptiness swarms up to meet me. Then my arm is caught and almost wrenched out of my arm pit. I scream again in pain. "I've got you, Cara."

Kayden's voice fills my ears.

My legs dangle in free fall. Far below, the river gushes, the vicious rocks waiting, waiting... Had I really thought I could jump? How stupid I had been. I want to live...with him. I'm his.

"Look at me, sweetheart."

Sweetheart? I blink. Did he call me by that endearment?

His face fills my vision and I realize I obeyed his command. No, it wasn't a command, but I wanted to do what he said. I want to be with him. I need him. "Kayden." I hold onto that amber gaze. Burning fires in their depths. Why had I thought he was cold and cruel? All along, that fire had been banked. If I had glanced past the exterior I'd have realized that his need to hurt, was a kind of self-defense. Inside, he's a boy, trying to be a man, trying to show the world that he is fucking strong. Dominant.

"Give me your other hand."

I stare at him.

What am I thinking?

Why am I so drawn to him? Why am I making excuses for his behavior? Has he done anything to earn my forgiveness after what he did to me?

Taken me to use me as a pawn in his political maneuvers?

"I won't let you go."

His body slides forward and I dip. And scream. All the blood rushes to my feet and my head spins. My eyelids flutter. My lips tremble.

"Your arm. Raise your arm."

"I'm scared. I don't want to die." Tears spill down my cheeks.

"Do as I say, Chloe."

I raise my hand and he grabs it.

We stay suspended, his gaze locked with mine. His jaw tics. A drop of sweat slides down his temple and drops on my cheek.

The breeze blows and my body sways. A shoe slides off of my foot and I shiver.

"Hold on." His voice commands me. His will anchors me. His arms...his arms have me. His shoulders flex, biceps bulge. Then his body begins to slide toward me and a sob breaks free. "Let me go."

"No fucking way."

"I don't want you to die." I hiccup.

"Not gonna bullshit you... There may be a chance of that. But if you die, I die with you."

What?

I stare. For a second, the panic melts away. All thoughts filter out of my mind. What does he mean? Why is he saying that? "Don't lie." I stutter.

He frowns. "I am not. I love—"

His entire body lunges forward, caught in gravity, and I scream and squeeze my eyes shut. Only I am not falling. I am moving. In the opposite direction.

I crack my eyelids open as he crawls back, and with a heave, pulls me up.

We lay there panting. Sobs fill my chest. I take in great gulps of air.

He turns to lean over me. "You dare put your life at risk, for me?" His jaw tics, the skin around his eyes creases. He's angry?

Why is he angry?

I open my mouth to speak but all that emerges is a sob.

The skin around his eyes creases, "You fucking scared me." His voice shakes. Then his lips cover mine. His tongue shoves inside of my mouth and he sucks on me. And takes. And drinks of my essence. I want to raise my arms and fling them around him, but my body refuses to obey. A trembling sweeps up from my toes, up my stomach to my shoulders. Another sob hitches in my throat. I want to kiss him back but that seems like too much effort. So I open my mouth wider, and he obliges by sticking his tongue down my throat. He brings his palms up to cup my face, tilts his lips, and kisses me until darkness creeps up the sides of my vision.

I must have made a sound of protest...for he tears his mouth from mine. "The fuck?" He looks around. "They're gone? Talon called them off?" His jaw firms. "What's Talon planning?" He growls and the sound is so familiar. So right. So beautiful, so everything, that I begin to cry in earnest.

"Hey," He sits back on his haunches, then cradles me close. Gentle. Soft touch. Hard chest. Firm grip of his arms around me. Is this the Kayden who had...taken me against my will? Is this the same man? My head spins. I can't stop the sobs that wrench up from within me.

He rises to his feet and cradles me. "I've got you. I am never letting you go."

I don't believe him. I don't.

He breaks into a run; his arms squeeze me close to him. His testosterone-filled essence curls around me. I cuddle in, turn my head into the hard planes of his chest, and let my eyes flutter shut.

When I open my eyes next, I am alone.

133

Kayden

I slam my fist into the wall next to the window of the castle that has been in my family for centuries. The impact jars up my arm, setting off pinpricks of pain in its wake. I wince. I deserve this and more. I turn my knuckles and see the broken skin with droplets of red clinging to the jagged edges. Bringing it to my mouth I suck on it. The bitter taste of metal fills my mouth. So different from the sweetness of her flesh, her pussy..."Fuck this." My voice fills the space. "It's your fault she was taken. Your fault that she came so close to dying. Your." I raise my fist again. "Fucking." I punch it into the wall. "Fault." A crack opens up in the stone wall and debris from the ceiling plops down on the ground next to me.

"I thought I was the one who had this affliction of talking my thoughts aloud."

I stiffen, but don't turn.

Straightening, I glare out of the window at the view that stretches out in front of me. The rolling Highlands are dappled in shades of green. They stretch out far into the horizon. We are all the way up at the northernmost tip of Scotland. As far away from the rest of my clan as possible, and that suits me fine. They can all go fuck themselves for all I care.

Her footsteps sound across the floor and she comes to stand next to me.

The sugary scent of her essence crowds in on me. Sweet, sexy...with something else. A bite of pepper...something tangy I had picked up earlier. My mouth waters. Why am I so attracted to her?

From the moment I'd seen her, my life had turned upside down. Noth-ing...nothing has gone according to plan. And I have myself...my unceasing lust to be inside of her, to blame.

My cock stirs.

Yeah, especially that. It's my dick that got me into this predicament in the first place.

And the fucker doesn't care that she is recovering from a near-death experience. Her second one. Both times, thanks to me. Asshole that I am. I hate this, my trying to second guess my thoughts. Censoring myself. Trying to be fucking polite around her... me...polite?

Hey, okay, so I can be when I try.

My mother had drilled that much into me. Just haven't had much use for it recently. I've been too busy chasing after power...revenge. *Her. After her.* I had been blinded by my desire.

I had knotted her, claimed her...fuck this. I turn and stalk away.

"Run away, Alpha. Run and hide. You can't even look me in the eye. You can't take responsibility for your actions. You don't care what you've done to me. For how everything you do impacts so many around you. You are a coward, Kayden. A little boy who never grew up. Who's looking for acceptance from his father for what he's done. Who—"

I swivel around and she squeezes her lips shut.

"That's what I thought," I flex my fingers. "The little omega can grow a pair as long as my back is turned. Say those words to my face."

Her face pales.

I stalk toward her, "Say it."

She shakes her head.

I pause in front of her and she swallows.

"Open your mouth and repeat every single insult that you flung at me, Cara."

"I said." She tilts her head back to look at me. "Said—"

I glare at her and her shoulders quiver, "That you...you..."

"Me?" I lower my tone and she shivers.

"You are a..."

I drop my knees and peer into her face. "Don't disappoint me now, Omega." I allow my lips to curve. "Not after that flash of courage you showed earlier in stabbing that bastard Viking."

She blinks. "You...you are not angry."

"I am." I grind my teeth so hard that my jaw aches. I am angry, but *not at her,* and isn't that a surprise? "Everything you said earlier was true."

"No." She shakes her head and her gorgeous hair flows around her shoulders.

"It is." I straighten, then step aside and up to the window. I grip the frame. "I let what happened to my parents color my view of life. I let it influence me, mar my vision, my goals. I let it fucking rule everything. And now that I can see, I realize...if I take away my need for revenge, I have nothing."

"You do."

I toss my head. "Didn't take you for a liar, Chloe."

"Not lying... I—" she bites off the rest of the words.

"See...you may pretend otherwise but when it comes to detailing exactly what I have left in my life, you come up with the same answer as me..." I turn and hold up my thumb and forefinger. "A big fat zero."

"You have...have this castle." She waves her hand around her.

"Belonged to my father. Stones and crumbling ruins." I slap my hand on the weathered stone that runs around the window frame. "Not that I don't appreciate my legacy, but not exactly something I worked for either."

"Your clan."

"They owe loyalty to my father. They follow me because they think I can find a way to restore the city back to them. Besides, there's a traitor among them."

"Traitor?"

I turn to her. "How do you think Lisa snuck you away from the clan?"

"Oh." She gnaws on her lower lip.

Don't look at it.

Don't.

My gaze drops to her mouth. Pink, glistening, gorgeous flesh that I have tasted. That I want to bite into again. My belly hardens. I will not give in to this need to close the space between us. To drop my nose into the curve of her neck and sniff her. My nostrils flare. "Why do you smell different?"

"D...different?" She swallows.

I close the distance between us, then bury my nose next to her throat. The sweet scent of her arousal bleeds into the air, but underneath it is the unmistakable bite of something new.

Something fragile and about to burst into life. I draw back. "Something's changed and I can't put a finger to it."

"I am the same." She drags her fingers through her hair, then draws it over one shoulder.

She's hiding something from me.

My gut clenches. How dare she try to keep anything from me? I scan the other side of her neck.

"Why don't you sniff me there and tell me how I smell?"

I swoop down and bury my nose in the curve of her skin.

A moan wheezes from her.

The scent of her goes to my head and my knees weaken. My groin hardens and fuck me, but if I stand here another second, I'll have thrown her down and mounted her, and then all of the promises I made to myself to treat her differently from now on would have been broken. Bad idea, that. Whatever made me think that I could keep away from her?

I should have marched her back to Zeus; instead, I'd brought her here, to the place that holds happy memories for me, where my mother and I had spent so many summers. Why? I've never brought anyone else here. What was I thinking?

"Well?" Her shoulders tremble. "How do I smell?"

"Like someone I should avoid at all costs."

134

Chloe

"I... I don't understand."

I see something in his eyes, written into his features.

His jaw tics. A vein pops at his temple.

"Why...why are you upset?"

"*I'm* upset? What gives you that idea?" He begins to pace. Back-forth-back.

Huh?

He's always been controlled before. Okay, so he's been mean to me. Sadistic on occasion. He's taken pleasure in showing me how much I need him, that he is dominant enough that I have no choice but to obey him. But this...this uncertainty is new.

I almost open my mouth to point that out to him, then decide... Nah. Not the wisest course of action to do that. Sure, at some point the balance between us had shifted. I don't feel completely powerless when I am in the same space as him. And that's because...he admitted that I had saved his life.

That everything I had guessed about his childhood was right. Why had he done that? Revealing any vulnerability means giving me the upper hand. It's so confusing. I rub my forehead.

It was so much easier when I hated him.

So much more straightforward when the relationship between us had a name. Captor-captive. Coercer-coerced. Alpha-omega...that hadn't changed. His presence fills the room. The wide musculature of his shoulders flexes as he paces. The hard planes of his back seem unsurmountable, the tight flanks of his ass... He swivels around to catch me staring.

My face heats.

I force myself to stay where I am as he prowls closer, closer, then comes to a stop in front of me.

One side of his mouth twitches. *Jerk.* He's laughing at me. Taking great pleasure in my discomfort. Why had I thought anything had changed between us? Clearly, it was all my imagination.

My shoulders slump. "I am tired." I mumble. "It was a mistake to come here. I think...I'll...I'll go back to my room."

I swivel around and head for the door. Whew. My muscles relax and I release the breath I had been holding.

A heavy hand descends on my shoulder and I squeak.

"Nothing to worry about." There's a thread of laughter in his voice. "Just making sure you don't lose your way."

"I...I can find my way."

"Oh yeah?" He drops his arms, then folds them over his massive chest.

I look from him to the corridor stretching out in front, then back to him.

He jerks his chin forward. Asshole. Bet he's waiting for me to screw up. I am going to prove him wrong. I am. I stalk forward to the hallway at the far end of the corridor. There are three possible ways to go. Hmm. "Left...or right?" I chew on my lower lip. "Or should I go straight ahead?"

A draft blows up the hallway. I shiver. The wind whistles through the cracks in the wall and I jump. Keep going, pick a direction. I turn right, then walk past one door to the right, then the next...all locked.

I reach the door at the end, and grab the handle and shove. It doesn't open. It's locked. "Darn it."

I swivel and stalk back to the junction of where the four corridors meet. "Which way now?"

I glance around the hallway, take a step to the right. Stop. Turn the other way. My head spins. Dizziness assails me and I shove out a hand to grab at the closest wall.

I'm lost.

How is that possible? Hadn't I come from here? Hmm. Or perhaps it was the other side or— The lone torch in the corridor flickers and goes out; my shoulders stiffen.

In this post-tsunami world, skeletal electricity supply remains—and it's restricted to those in power— so this isn't uncommon.

But fold in an apex predator, aka an irate alpha, who lurks somewhere out of my line of sight, and well—you get the picture. The hair on the nape of my neck rises.

He's somewhere there, he's stalking me, I am sure of it.

The monster is playing with me and I should be scared. Instead, adrenaline laces my blood. My nipples pucker. Is being scared out of your wits supposed to have the same effect on your hormones as being turned on? Or is that me? *It's the effect the alpha has on you, admit it.* He's prowling nearby, waiting, waiting... Something moves in the shadows and I yelp.

I stumble, and brush against a hard barrier...which moves.

I scream, then slam my elbow back, to connect with an unmistakable bulge.

There's a low groan.

"Oh." I freeze.

Arms encircle my waist, "I'd prefer to keep my balls, sugar."

"K...Kayden?"

"Who else?" he growls.

Oh, hell. *Is he angry?*

He's angry.

But he's not the alphahole he was, right? I mean he's an alpha and an asshole but he's not an *alphahole* anymore, is he?

"If I let you go, do you promise not to elbow me in the nuts again? I am trying to be understanding but—"

Nope. Still an alphahole.

"Hold on a sec." I strain against his hold and he lets me go.

I whirl around and peer up in the general direction of his face through the darkness. "This is you being *nice*?"

"You are getting angry for no reason, Princess."

"Hate it when you call me that."

"Princess?"

"You're doing it again." I grit my teeth.

"I am calling you by the status of what you really are...*Princess.*"

"Aargh." I throw up my hands "I hate the darkness. I hate that I can't see your face. I hate—"

The torch lights up again. I blink.

The orange light casts shadows over the hard angles of his face. That square jaw, the thin upper lip, the hooked nose, and above that, amber eyes glare at me. A shiver runs down my spine.

"How did you do that?" I frown.

"What?"

I toss my head, "Get the light to come back on?"

He stares at me.

Right.

He's the alpha. The leader of Scotland. Controlling the lights in his stronghold was one of the tricks up his sleeve.

"Forget I asked."

"Hmm." He peruses my features and I shiver.

Damn him, but when he looks at me with that cruel intensity that is uniquely Kayden, I am sure he can read my thoughts.

"I can, you know." His voice curls around me.

"What?" I gulp.

"Read your mind. I know what you want, Cara." His eyes gleam, "I want to be patient with you, give you time to recover from almost dying...again."

"I was never in danger."

"Oh?" He tilts his head.

I bite the inside of my cheek. "I would have found a way to escape. I don't want to die, not when...when..."

He stiffens and the planes of his face go taut.

Say it, now is the time to tell him that I may be pregnant. But why can't he sense it?

If Kayden is my mate, he should have noticed the changes in my body. He should have recognized what it meant. So why hasn't he figured it out?

The light goes out and we are plunged into darkness again. The world tilts, and I squeak as he swings me up in his arms.

"What are you doing?"

"Taking you with me."

"Wh...where?"

"My intentions toward you are chaste, for now. You are safe with me. I am not going to touch you."

135

Kayden

A-n-d the lies simply don't stop coming.

I should have simply let her find her way back on her own. Hell, I had been ready to stand back and allow her to find her way back. I mean, she is an omega...but she's smart. And insightful, given how she'd look through me and figured out the demons that haunt my past...and she can defend herself in a fight. She is a princess, after all...something we hadn't discussed.

Discussed? I rub the back of my neck. Since, when did I want to trade words with a woman? They've been good for one thing so far...to fuck. So, call me a chauvinist. I am an alpha...the leader of my people. I am allowed to have my opinions. My father had thought otherwise.

He'd always maintained that omegas were nurturers, the seed of our race lay within them.

He'd given women their due respect.

The rest of the alphas believed it was their right to take. Like me. I'd thought I was my father's son. After all, I had sworn to avenge his memory by dedicating myself to the development of Scotland.

Somewhere inside, I hadn't believed in him.

He may have respected women, but when it came to his own household, he hadn't followed the rules. If he had, he wouldn't have ignored my mother after she'd been assaulted.

He'd adopted me...because he knew he was never going to touch my mother after that incident. For the remainder of her short life, he'd ignored her.

He'd made sure to turn a blind eye to her needs.

He'd tortured her, not with physical violence, but with something worse. By pretending that she had ceased to exist for him.

For all practical purposes, she had been dead to him...long before she'd breathed her last.

My arms tighten around her and she winces. "You're hurting me."

I ease my hold, then quicken my steps, making my way up the corridor and toward her room.

It's pitch dark but I can find my way around the place.

All the months I had spent playing in this very space with my mother and on occasion with Marcus' daughter, had made sure of that.

When I reach Cara's room, I walk across the floor, and reaching the bed, place her on it. I straighten and she grabs at the hem of the shirt that I had not bothered to tuck in. "Stay." Her lips quiver.

I hesitate. "I can't."

Her chin wobbles. "I...I need you, Alpha." A drop of moisture trickles from the corner of her eye, and fuck me, but my heart stutters.

It fucking wavers in my chest.

I can't leave her.

When had I become so in tune with another? I toss my head. Shove away the thought. It's normal, just something that comes with age. Clearly, I'm facing some kind of early mid-life crisis, or whatever. Maybe it's Dom's company rubbing off on me. What-fucking-ever.

"Fine." I crack my neck, then take a step back.

Her hand drops away.

Stalking over to the chair near the bed, I squeeze my frame into it.

She closes her eyes, then wriggles around. Her limbs twitch. Every cell in my body is aware of her.

I move around, trying to find a comfortable spot, then give up.

Fucking straight-backed chairs, they can barely accommodate my bulk. I shove my legs out in front, place my elbow on my knees. The fuck, am I doing here? Trying to control myself when she is not one foot away from me. If I slipped into bed and covered her body with mine, I have no doubt she'd part her legs. She'd wriggle her hips and allow me to nestle my dick between the soft folds of her pussy. I could push aside the tunic she's wearing, drag my fingers through that cunt, lap up the honeyed slickness, thrust my tongue inside her channel and bring her to climax over and over again.

My dick thickens, sweat beads my brow.

"If you keep doing that...there's no way I am going to be able to fall asleep."

She mewls, and something inside me snaps. Fuck this.

Then, reaching inside of myself, I pull on that part of me that I've never shared with anyone before.

I allow the purr to rumble up my rib cage, thrum over my vocal cords and pour from my throat. Deep, complex and layered notes curl around her. I project the sound, loop the gravelly tone over her, slithering over her throat, circling her breasts, sliding down her navel to the concave between her legs. Her cunt. Her core. Her fucking essence is what I want. I want to crawl over and settle between them. Lick her, suck her, pleasure her.

This time do it all for her.

Focus on her.

Her needs.

Her.

I open myself up, reach out through the mating bond and allow her a glimpse of what I am feeling. A strange tenderness...is that what this is?

This...vulnerability inside that I allow her to sense, as I soothe her with my thoughts. Calm her with my presence, then arouse her gently. All through, I keep purring. I allow the sound to build over her. Wave upon wave engulfing her with my presence.

My need. My thirst. My lust for her. I trickle it into the pores of her skin. Caressing her ankles, her calves, over the hollows behind her knees. She shudders.

I drag the vocal notes up her inner thigh and she squeezes her legs together.

I deepen the sound, lowering it until it's hushed. *Open up for me, Cara.*

I pulse my thoughts at her and she parts her thighs.

The scent of her slick deepens. I stare at the shadow at the center of her being. Her core. My life. Us. My groin hardens. A pulse beats behind my eyes, echoing the ache of my balls. Grabbing my dick I squeeze it. I draw out another purr and another. Never stopping. She writhes on the bed. Her fingers grab the bedspread and she moans.

I don't stop. I lean forward and loop another purr and another, slithering the notes in the gap between her thighs and the panties and then inside those gorgeous folds.

Her back curves and she throws back her head.

The white column of her neck gleams. I want to bend over and sink my teeth into the tender flesh between her legs. Bite her. Claim her right there. Fuck. I grab the rigid column of my dick through my pants and pump myself and squeeze. My cock thickens. My balls draw up.

"Come."

Her shoulders pull back. Her breasts thrust up. Her entire body tenses, then she shatters.

And I orgasm.

Right there in my pants.

Without touching her.

I pant and the sound of my purring cuts out. Silence. A beat. Another. I don't dare move. Can't take my glance off of the gorgeous omega who lays there on her bed, panting. One. Two. Three. Our heart beats in tandem.

"I am sure that will help you find relief." Springing up to my feet, I turn and march out of there.

136

Chloe

What the—?

Did he walk out of here without touching me? The exact opposite of the Kayden I had come to expect.

If I had met him in his earlier persona, I'd have never wanted to be acquainted with him. But this Kayden? He's trying to control himself. Show restraint. Hold back, stay in control...what? I blink and straighten my legs, then wince. My entire body aches. My limbs tremble, my pussy feels soft, melting...empty. I am empty because he didn't take me. Didn't shove any part of himself into me...huh? I miss him.

His touch, the scratch of his chin over my cheeks, the rough calluses of his fingers marking my flesh as he kneaded my hips, my thighs.

My belly quivers.

This side of him is intriguing. It also confuses me. It was easier to hate him when I could simply see him as all bad. Now...now I am not so sure.

The lights flicker and come on. I force my shoulders to relax.

I glance around, taking in my surroundings for the first time.

The space is comfortable but spartan. A worn carpet, a dresser in a corner. A closet on the other side. There's a door nearby, leading off into what must be an ensuite bathroom. So there are modern conveniences, at least. I blow out a sigh of relief.

Swinging my legs over the side of the bed, I walk across the floor and enter the other room. My bare feet slap the tile. Reaching the washstand, I lean across and flick open the tap. Cupping my palms, I splash some water onto my face and flinch.

The water is ice-cold. I glance up and catch sight of myself in the mirror. "Oh, hell." I grimace.

My face is streaked with dirt, except for where the water has washed away some of it. My eyelashes stand out, all spiky. My hair lies in matted strands around my shoulders. No wonder he hadn't wanted to touch me.

I huff out a laugh. Seriously, what is it with him?

He'd admitted that I had saved his life. He'd seemed grateful for it...in his own Kayden way, that is.

He hadn't seemed very happy that I had put myself at risk for him.

And that kiss...I bring my fingers to my lips. Holy hell, that kiss. It was...was... "Mind-blowing." My lips curl up. He had poured all of himself into that kiss. He had drunk from me...he'd never stop taking from me...but he had shared of himself. He had given for the first time...and now, when he'd made love to me with his voice? There was no other way of explaining what he'd done. He'd softened his purrs, crooned his emotions to me, modulated his tone to penetrate me. He had—there was no other way of explaining what had happened—he had fucked me with his purrs. I stare at myself in the mirror. Shining eyes, pupils blown from that orgasm he had wrenched from me, flushed cheeks, parted lips. I take in the almost healed bruise on the curve of my shoulder. He had behaved like a mate who was regretting what he had done...but he had no way of putting it into words. For someone who was dominant, and who could lead his people with a glance...who could control his alphas on command, he was being strangely reticent.

Why was that?

And why hadn't I sensed him coming to my rescue?

It's why I had believed Talon when he'd claimed that Kayden was dead. I reach out through the mating bond, and again, there's a dull silence. Static. As if there's a shield of some kind and he's on the other side of it.

I could have sworn that he'd reached out to me earlier. I hadn't heard him, but I had sensed his feelings.

I had understood what he'd wanted from me. To part my legs and allow him to caress me, seduce me. For the first time, he had coaxed me to give in to it. Not by force...but by the sheer intention of how much he wanted to pleasure me. I swallow. Kayden being persuasive is an entirely different beast.

His dominance, I expect.

His need to control?

Yeah, he's an alpha so it's in his nature. But him being charming—in his own way—him wanting me in that all-consuming way? Exposing his vulnerable side to me? No, not possible. My head spins and I clutch at the side of the basin with my fingers. My breasts heave. The nipples are large, distended. My stomach rumbles.... I need food. When was the last time I ate? I cup my belly, massaging the flatness. I don't feel pregnant. Is it too early to tell? I should be able to sense it if there is life flaring inside of me, right? Either way, I need to eat. As soon as I shower and clean myself up.

Twenty minutes later I walk into the bedroom, wrapped in the massive towel that I had found inside of the bathroom. I walk over to the closet, and opening it, survey the contents. There are long dresses, short dresses, skirts, dresses with long sleeves, cut off sleeves, cardigans...and more dresses. Oh wait, here are some frilly vests in different colors, all of which are small enough to fit me.

It's a woman's closet? I look around the room again, spotting the vase of dried-up flowers on a small table by the window. The curtains are made of lace...and had been cream colored not too long ago. This room belonged to a woman? Who? His lovers? The women he'd brought here when he'd wanted to hide away from his clan? He dared put me in a room that had belonged to them? Anger flushes my veins.

My skin tightens.

I don't want to wear the clothes, but the alternative is to wear the dirty, torn sheath I had on earlier. No. I am not going to wear that. I pull on a woolen skirt and the one vest in a natural shade...a pale pink, which to be honest, is not too bad. Soft cotton, slinky silks, luxurious wools. They were picked by someone who had taste and who loved colors.

A woman.

The same woman who had stayed in this room?

I pull out the drawer at the bottom and find rows of sandals, heels, stilettos. The blood surges at my temples. He dared put me in a room where he'd kept his lover?

I grind my teeth.

I slip my feet into sandals, then march for the door. I shouldn't be upset. I hadn't expected any more from him. But after that show of tenderness...after that kiss? That kiss had changed everything. It had promised me...what? Honesty? True passion? A future? Yeah. It had given me hope that things could work out. That he could be the tender man I had glimpsed behind that alpha who had hurt me so much. How wrong I was. No way am I going to stand for it. I am going to leave...right now. After all, I am no longer his captive, right? I stalk out of the door when the sound of a groan reaches me. I swivel in the direction of the sound. Up the dimly lit corridor to the other door that is ajar at the end of the hallway. The sound of something crashing to the floor slices through me. My heart begins to thud. Not again. Had the Vikings followed us here?

All the more reason to leave.

I turn to go, but a low cry reaches me. Kayden? My heart stutters. Another groan, this time cut off abruptly. He's hurting.

When my feet hit the floor, I realize that I am running toward him.

137

Kayden

My footsteps echo in the empty corridor. I run out of the courtyard, racing up the hillside. Adrenaline spikes my blood. I pump my legs and speed up. Faster, faster. The wind slams into me, pushing me back. I brace my body. *Keep going, don't stop.*

I laugh and the sound is high pitched and easy.

I am going to grow up to be a strong alpha like my father. But right now, I am a boy trying to hide in a place where it won't be easy to find me. *Keep going. Don't stop.* I put on a burst of speed and race over the last few feet. Reaching the peak, I bend over, panting. Sweat drips down my temples and the back of my neck, plastering my shirt to my back. Another gust of wind blows over me and goosebumps break out over my forearms.

"Kayden."

I turn back to see the woman walking up the slope. Her golden hair shines in the rising sun. Her dark pink scarf blows behind her. Her long legs eat up the distance between us.

"You are too fast for me."

She smiles and her face lights up.

I bounce on my heels. Another giggle bursts from my lips. "You can't catch me."

I turn and run up the path that runs around the side of the peak. Her footsteps sound behind me. "You are so naughty, Kai. And too old to be playing with me."

She huffs and I hear her speed up. "I love playing with you, Mama." I slow my footsteps so she can catch up.

"You should be playing with others your own age."

"I do, when I am back in the city." I turn around to face her, then jog backwards. " But it's more fun to spend time with you."

"Wait until you discover girls." She slows her pace and laughs. The sound is beautiful. Warmth fills my chest.

"I prefer you, Mama."

She smiles, and her face lights up. "I'll remind you of that when you meet an omega you want to mate."

"Is that how it was for you and Papa?"

Her eyes shine. "Oh, he was the most beautiful man I'd ever met. So proud and strong, and so kind." Her face closes. "But then he changed." She mumbles the words almost to herself and I have to strain my ears to hear her. I slow down, then come to a stop.

"It was my fault, Kai. All mine." Her gait slows. "I'll never forgive myself for what I did." She stops and wraps her arms around her waist. "I gave in to him."

"What do you mean, Ma?" I don't understand what she is talking about...no, I lie. I am eight, but my friend Dom who is almost sixteen has met the omega whom he intends to mate. He is older than me and I have to wait a while before I become a full grown alpha, but my instincts confirm that's what she is talking about.

"You didn't do anything wrong, Mama."

She sniffs, then wipes away her tears. "You are too young to understand, sweetheart. I was wrong. I should have resisted more. But when Golan pursued me, and I was in heat...and I knew it was wrong, but I wanted him. By the time I came to my senses and wanted to push him away, it was too late...he...he—"

The sound of heavy footsteps echoes through the hillside. She stiffens, then looks up and around me. Her face whitens. "What are you doing here?"

I swirl around and see him. A man taller than my father, broader. Black hair flows to his shoulders. He is wearing army pants, a vest that pulls across his immense chest. His heavy boots clank with each step. He is so heavy that the earth seems to shake as he moves.

"Golan," my mother whispers from behind me.

"Adele" He bares his teeth. "I have come for him."

"No." My mother steps in front of me, shielding me from the man. "You can't take him away."

"He's my blood."

"He's been adopted by the Leader of Scotland. He is the rightful heir."

He throws back his head and laughs. "Who'd have thought that in one stroke I'd have united England and Scotland by the seed of my loins?"

He pauses and slaps his hands on his hips. "Keep him...for now... When he comes of age, I will be back to stake my claim."

"No." I sense her muscles tense. Her hand slips to the small of her back. It's where she has her knife hidden. She's an omega, my mother, but she grew up in the Highlands. Had learned to hunt and fish by the time she was thirteen. She never left home without her hunting knife. She grabs the knife by the hilt, then slides it out.

"Yes." He snarls.

I step out from behind her, and shoving my body between them, I hold up my fists. "I will not let you harm her."

He frowns, then chuckles. "Look at you, little lion cub. You look like your half-brother."

"Brother?" I frown.

"His name is Zeus, and I can't wait for you to meet him. We'll be one big happy family, little cub."

"I have no brothers." I turn around to look at my mother. Why isn't she saying anything?

"Get out, Golan." She firms her lips.

He slaps his chest. "No goodbye kiss, Omega?"

She raises her head. "Leave." Her tone is hard, but her chin wobbles.

"Don't insult your master. Isn't that what I am? Your true love, Omega. He may have mated you, but admit it, your body responds to me. One rutting and I impregnated you. Something your mate could never do. Perhaps we should try it again, eh?" He closes the distance to us, until his body looms over me. He leans in, shoves me out of the way. I fall to the side, go tumbling down the steep mountain side. I hear the sounds of a scuffle, then a scream.

"Ma." I fling out a hand and grab hold of a shrub, then right myself. I leap forward, retracing my steps, to find her body prone on the ground. I reach her and cry out in fear. The hilt of her knife protrudes from her chest.

"No." I drop to my knees. "Mama."

"Kayden." She raises a hand, blood dripping from her fingers.

"Kayden, wake up."

My eyelids snap open. Green eyes blaze at me. Blond hair streams around her shoulders. Her lips tremble. "Kayden," she reaches out a hand. I grab it and tug. The next second she is on her back under me and I am planked over her. That sweet innocent essence of hers teases my nostrils. Her neck moves as she swallows. "You were dreaming."

"Not anymore." So pretty. So gorgeous.

So ready to be marked by my hand.

I drop my head and nuzzle her neck, she shivers.

"What was the nightmare about?" Her soft voice coils in my chest. My ribcage constricts.

Why does she not realize how dangerous I am to her? She should be struggling to get away from me. One word. One protest. That's all I need, and I'd let her leave.

"It doesn't matter."

I suck on her ear lobe and she moans.

She tries to pull her arms up from between us and I lean my weight on her, trapping her under my chest.

"It does. Talk to me, Kayden."

"Call me Kai."

Her eyes widen in surprise.

Yeah, that makes two of us. The fuck am I doing, trying to get her to call me by the name that my mother used?

"Say it," I growl, and she winces.

Good.

She should realize that my trying to keep away from her is an act. Me, trying to rein in the part of me that likes to torment, and failing. Miserably.

"Not easy, eh? Glimpsing the man behind the alpha? Very little separates me from the beasts that nature intended us to become."

"You're wrong... Kai."

My dick thickens. Fuck. Why had I invited her to show me the kind of intimacy

I had run from for all of my life? Why does it feel so fucking good to have her call me by my nickname?

"Again." I glare and she juts out her chin.

"It's all an act."

"What is?"

"Your acting like an alpha with a swollen head."

"That's not the only head that's swollen." I grab her thigh and pull it to the side, then settle my massive erection between her legs.

"You are being crude to get a reaction from me."

"No kidding." I grind my hardness into her core and she pants. "No need to ask if it's working either."

"Don't try to distract me, Kai."

My cock jumps. It fucking jumps in my pants. Hell, she has no idea how easy it is for her to control me. Say my name. Flutter those eyes. No...just be in my presence and let me sense her essence, and damn, if I wouldn't throw her down and lick her up all over. "Why do you screw with my head?"

She swallows, "Wh...what do you mean?"

"From the moment I scented you, nothing has gone according to plan. I was all set to get out of there, but then you stumbled into my path, and I can't stop myself from tracking you. From acting so out of character, from becoming another rutting alpha who can't get enough of omega pussy."

"Thanks for reducing what little trust you built up in the last few hours to this." She jerks her chin between us.

"Trust?" I laugh. "You shouldn't trust me, Cara. I take what I want, no apologies for it."

"At least, you don't cover up the alphahole you are."

"And that's good?"

She frowns up at me. "In a strange way, yes." She purses her lips. "And by the way, it was you who stumbled across my path, not the other way around."

"Yeah." I drag my hand over the curve of her thigh, and she trembles. "Perhaps Zeus allowed me to escape. Perhaps he made sure to have you there to entice me with your scent—" A coldness fills my chest. "Is that what this is? Are you working with him? I sent an omega to assassinate him and now he's paying back the favor? With no less that his own mate's sister. And it's definitely not a half-brother watching out for his sibling. Did you plan this all with him, Omega? Are you trying to trap me?"

138

Chloe

"No." I bite my lip. I shouldn't feel guilty. I mean, I'd had no idea who he was on that terrace until he'd told me, right?

"You lying to me?"

"Of course not."

He pinches my chin and I raise my eyes, look into his. Burning amber meets mine, and I flinch.

"You can't hide the truth to save your life, can you?" There is a note of wonder in his voice and I blink.

"I'm not..." I try to shake my head, but his grip firms.

I wince.

He is going to mark my skin, as he'd imprinted his touch on my body, my cells. How could he have made such a big impact on me in so little time? I swallow and his shoulders tense.

"Tell me." A growl rumbles up his chest.

The sound tears over my nerve endings, coils in my belly. My womb spasms and more slick flows out from between my legs.

His pupils darken, the dark centers deepening. The blackness in them grows, swirls. So deep that I could drown in them.

I want to hide my face in his neck, throw myself at his mercy and ask him to forgive me. For what? For doing what was needed to save myself? For falling in with Zeus and Lucy's plans? It had been Lucy's suggestion that I go up to the pool on the roof that day and cool myself off. I had agreed, had been so grateful to her that day. My sister, the General's mate, had extended the shadow of her protection to me. I had been sure then, that I was safe. Had allowed myself to indulge in dreams of a home, an alpha to call my own—for the first time since my escape from Russia. Had looked up and seen him then. Had thought my prayers had been answered—my alpha had come for me. I hadn't realized everything was but a game, for Lucy, for Zeus...for this man who looms over me. Whose gaze sweeps over my face, down to my breasts. Who pulls his fingers away from my face to cup my breast? "So heavy." His forehead furrows, "Your breasts are fuller than I remember."

He brushes his thumb over my nipple and I cry out.

"So fucking responsive."

His voice is matter-of-fact. Cold. As emotionless as it had been the first time he had laid eyes on me. But he's not the same alpha who had kidnapped me. He's not as heartless as he'd portrayed himself.

"K...Kayden."

He lowers his head to my other breast; his tongue pokes out to curl around my nipple. Soft, innocent...all a front. A trembling grips my limbs.

"K...Kai." I gulp.

He trails tiny kisses down to my belly button. My stomach flip flops. Not good. This is not good. The calm before the storm. He's being all soft in his touch, but the way he's ignoring me, the way his tongue darts out to trace the indentation of my bellybutton, how he drags his mouth down my waist to the valley between my legs sends another shiver tumbling down my spine.

"Don't do this." I can't stop the words that leak from my lips.

I am back to begging this alpha, wanting him, needing him, hoping he'll forgive me, and I haven't told him half of what had happened before he'd found me that day. Of how I had been maneuvered into this position, to defy him, push back. Yet I had been unable to hold back my reactions to him.

He'd noticed the changes to my body, but he hadn't questioned them. Small mercies. I can keep my secret from him for a little longer. I twist my lips. So why am I so disappointed that he hasn't figured out why my body is changing?

His fingers curve around my breast and he squeezes my nipple. The pain shoots down to meet the ache between my legs. Simultaneously he grips my thigh with his other hand and pulls it to the side. Cool air grazes my heated pussy a second before he drops his head and bites my clit.

"Kai!" I scream his name.

He thrusts his tongue inside my wet channel and licks, and again. He continues teasing my nipple, rubbing it, playing with it, until the flesh hardens into a painful aching point that I wish he would bite and suck and put me out of my misery.

He withdraws his hand and I whine.

He brings his hand around to cup my ass cheeks, then slides his fingers down into the valley between them to play with my asshole. "There is one virgin hole left where I haven't taken you, Omega."

Omega? Why is he calling me Omega? Why not Cara? Does he suspect something?

"How can you be sure?" I raise my chin.

He grips the curve of my hip, squeezing so hard that I moan.

He raises his head. "Do you know what I do to those who lie to me?"

And I'd enjoy his ministrations otherwise. I do. I do. And isn't that the most horrible thing of all. Even when he'd taken me against my will, my body had responded to him. I hate him. But I hate my need for him even more.

He watches me closely. There's no change in expression on his face. His features could be carved out of stone. His dark eyes are glacial. I shiver. Goosebumps rise on my skin. Is he angry? Upset? Does he want to take revenge? All of the above, I'm sure. But he's so remote that I can't tell. I reach for the mating bond and a dense cloud of chill stops me. No. No. He is aware that I was part of a setup. But, what choice did I have?

I had followed Lucy's directions; I had been doing what was right. I had no idea that Kayden would come on the terrace that day, or that he'd want me. Or that Ethan would approach me with Lucy's proposition that I defy Kayden, and if I told him all that now...? He'd never believe me. I thought things had changed between us? If it had, he would not be so quick to jump to conclusions about my intentions, right?

"Answer me." The hushed dominance of his tone sends a shiver of apprehension down my spine.

"N...no."

"No, what?"

"No...no don't do that."

"That's not what I asked." He thrusts his tongue between the wet folds of my pussy and my shoulders rise off of the ground.

"I don't know what you do to those who lie to you," I gulp, "but I have no doubt it's something that causes you much joy and much sorrow to those on the other end."

"Don't evade the question." He growls again and all of my nerve-endings seem to fire at once.

What is he doing to me?

I can't give in to him, I can't. If I do, all will be lost.

"Wh...what question?" I pant.

"You know exactly what I am asking." He slides his fingers down between my ass cheeks and I shudder. "You're a smart one, Omega. Excellent at evading, but this time I won't let you off that easily."

His fingertips probe my puckered back hole.

"You are at my mercy. Mine to do with as I want."

My stomach twists. He wouldn't, would he?

"You are hiding something from me and I am going to fuck it out of you."

He swipes his tongue up my slit and my sex clenches.

His fingertip slips into my backside and I freeze. My thigh muscles tremble.

He pushes another finger into my backhole and a fire flares in my belly. Why am I turned on by what he's doing to me? It's disgusting. No one has touched me this intimately before. Not before, not again. What is he going to do next?

"I am going to take you here. You can't stop me."

139

Kayden

Blood pounds through my veins. I had asked her a simple question. All she'd had to do was tell me that I was wrong. That she had been there on the terrace of the omega harem by chance. That I had come across her by accident and been entranced by her scent. I had claimed her and taken her, and yes, knotted her over and over again. I had almost allowed my men to have their way with her. My mistake.

I had been trying to prove to myself that I was wrong and that I didn't need her. Wrong again.

One whiff of her feminine slickness, one touch of her soft skin, the warmth of her kisses, her lips, her touch... Damn her to hell, but I can't live without her. The one omega I have wanted in my life. The one I had mated and had rescued; the only one who I had ever brought to my childhood home, and she had betrayed me.

I glare at her, "You deceived me."

Her chest heaves. Her lips draw down. *Open your mouth and deny it. Please tell me that you are innocent.*

She stays silent.

My guts twist. My chest grows heavy.

"Say it." I finger her asshole and she tries to pull away from me. I wrap my fingers around her thigh to hold her in place.

"Tell me that I am wrong. That you are not what I think you are."

A drop of moisture trickles down her cheek. "Kai, I am so sorry."

The band around my chest tightens.

"You don't mean it." My voice sounds desperate. What had I expected? That she'd throw her arms around me and tell me that she was my omega. Mine. My mate. And she is. Nothing changes that. Not the fact that this entire situation is twisted. That I had started out to get my country back from Zeus and had lost everything. And it hadn't mattered. Losing my birthright was not as painful...as...as this. This sense of being lied to. Of being betrayed by her. Of not having seen through her facade. And now...now it's too late.

An alpha betrayed will not stop until he's exacted his retribution.

I sit up and lean back on my heels. "You have one chance...to come clean."

She bites her lower lip. Her white teeth worry that plump flesh and I want to lean toward her and kiss her right then. Lick my tongue over that swollen mouth and suck from her. Drink from her. Fucking replenish that hopefulness that had bloomed somehow deep inside. Where, for a few hours, I had let myself dream...of a future. With her. A family of my own. All of it gone. I had been stupid. Fucking sentimental fool. How the mighty have fallen. I had taken her without giving her a choice and she had paid me back.

"You have one minute."

Her eyelids snap open. Her pupils dilate until the black of her irises bleeds out, a semicircle of green visible around the circumference. "I..." she swallows, then straightens her shoulders. "I was told to challenge you, to keep you interested enough to want to pursue me."

I tilt my head. "You were told to distract me?"

She nods.

"What else?"

She firms her lips. A bead of sweat trickles down her temples. Fear leaches from her skin and I want to hold her close and rock her and tell her it's going to be okay. When my breath raises the strands on her forehead, I realize that I have leaned up and planked over her. The fuck am I thinking?

Why am I so weak where she is concerned?

Is it because I did wrong by her? Because no matter what, I shouldn't have let the other alphas gawk at her? I let them touch her. I let another get close to her. And again, when Talon had taken her from me. Never again.

I'll never let her out of my sight. She'll be my prisoner. Mine to do with as I want.

"Speak."

I lower my head and nuzzle her forehead.

Her entire body tenses. She doesn't understand why I am being so gentle with her. *That makes two of us.* I should be raging right about now. Should throw her down and rut her, teach her a lesson, and I will, all right. Just not in the way she expects. I intend to keep her guessing. Play with her a little, and then overpower her with...not with force, no I did that already.

This time it's going to be different. I drag my lips to the edge of her mouth, and kiss her.

Her shoulders pull back. "That's all there is to it."

"It isn't though, is it?" I pause in my ministrations, then bend and bury my nose in the crook of her neck. "You knew when you were on that terrace that I would be coming your way. You were put there to get my attention."

"No." She shakes her head.

"Zeus planted you to tempt me. He'd hoped I'd leave with you."

Her pulse rate picks up.

I wrap my lips around where the pulse at the base of her neck throbs and suck on it.

She moans, and the sound is so helpless. So sexy. So fucking hot. My dick jumps in my pants.

I nibble little kisses to the valley between her breasts. The scent of her is concentrated here. Almost as complex as her cunt. I lower my weight onto her. My hardness thrusts into her soft core. "He wanted to throw me off track. And you helped him."

"No," she mumbles. Her legs part, allowing me entry. And I am so tempted to forget this entire conversation. To part her legs, and bury my length inside her wet channel. She'd wrap those gorgeous thighs around me, dig her heels into my back, and raise her hips to cradle me. Her pussy would clamp down on my dick and milk me, then I'd knot her and...the hell am I thinking? She deceived me and all I can think about is being inside of her. She has me at her mercy and I will not allow that. I need to stay in control, to show her who is in charge, that I own her body and soul and she can never get away from me. "Don't lie, Omega." I frown.

She juts out her chin. "I am not." Color burns high on her cheeks. She raises her fingers toward my face. I angle my head and her hand drops away. A wrinkle appears between her eyebrows.

"But you're not telling me the complete truth, are you?"

Her gaze skitters away.

"Admit it. You had an idea of what was happening."

Her lips turn down. She jerks her chin. "Lucy suggested to me to go up there and cool off. She told me..." Her voice trembles. "She said that if I followed her instructions...she'd help me find a suitable match. "

"And what were her instructions exactly?"

"To entice you. She said that you'd escaped, and if I managed to get your attention long enough, to keep you there, it would give Zeus and his team a chance to catch you."

"You're good at obeying instructions, hmm?" A coldness coils in my chest.

I'd been right all along, and she wasn't denying it. Guess I should be grateful the omega wasn't trying to lie to me, at least. I should be glad that she was coming clean, that I was finally making sense of this twisted tangled puzzle I had gotten caught up in. So why does my stomach twist? Why is my heart racing? A ball of emotion clogs my throat and I swallow it down.

"Then I read the intent in your eyes, realized that you were going to claim me, but by then it was too late."

Too late. It's too late. Her words echo around in my mind. I lower my mouth to lick her lips. Once. Twice. Sweet. So sweet. And it's all a fantasy. "You have been a very bad omega." I whisper the words and she shudders. "You leave me no choice but to punish you."

I push up to sit back on my heels then grab her under her arms and flip her over. Her entire body goes rigid. "Kayden." Her voice is muffled against the sheets.

"Alpha." I snarl. "You lost the right to call me by my name."

She turns to peer up at me, strands of blonde hair sticking to her face. "So easy for you to pass judgement on me." Her lips firm. "You don't understand what it's like to lose everything you own and have to beg for favors."

I angle my head, "Don't I?"

She blinks. "Zeus took your country. You had your followers with you. You are planning a way to get revenge. I was a refugee. The Vikings occupied my city."

"The Vikings took you from me." The words burst out of me. My heartbeat ratchets up as I remember the sheer terror when I saw Talon grab her.

"They almost killed you." Her gaze drops to my chest, to the dressing that covers the wound.

"I was ready to die for you. I put my life at stake again...to rescue you."

"And I'll never forget that...nor the kiss." Her features are pinched. She looks sad, miserable, and damn, if I don't want to kiss away her misery. I force myself to look away, to walk my fingers down the curve of her spine. "This fragility inherent in every curve of your body, it's a ruse to trap me."

"No."

I rub my knuckles over the rise of her butt and her back twitches. "Your gorgeous skin, your luscious pussy...all of it was made to seduce me." I grab her hips then pull her up so she is balanced on her knees with her shoulders pushing down into the mattress.

"Wh...what are you doing?"

I don't reply. Take my time as I grip her ass cheeks and part them.

"Kai"

My dick twitches.

My name from her lips is aphrodisiac. All the more reason why I need to shut her up. "Stay quiet. I have creative ways of shutting you up; don't force me to use them."

She purses her lips ,then turns to touch her forehead to the bed. She juts out her hips, and the heart-shaped backside of hers—I want to slap it, and mark it, see my touch bloom on her skin.

"This gets you off, doesn't it? This teasing me, taunting me, overpowering me and making me into your slave. Someone who can do your every bidding."

"You're wrong." I rise up on my knees so my crotch is level with her butt, then drag the head of my dick down the valley between her butt cheeks. "It's pleasuring you, driving you to madness, to the edge of your climax and then holding you there. Bringing you to the peak, again and again, until you flesh quivers, your pussy hurts, the slickness flowing from you in streams until you are covered in it and my cum, and yet not allowing you to come." She groans, and the sound is so needy, so full of unrequited passion that I can't stop the purr that rolls up my chest. "*That* is what gets me off."

She makes a choking sound, her ass cheeks clench. Her muscles tremble, then slick slides down from between her thighs. I scoop up the potent mixture, drag it to her asshole and coat the opening.

She shudders; her spine curves.

Then she turns to glance over her shoulder. "Wh...what are you doing?"

"Marking the different ways I want to take you."

She stiffens. Her gaze drops to where my flesh meets hers. "Will it...hurt?"

"What do you think?" My lip curls.

"I... I don't know what to think."

"Try again." I peel back my lips, and she swallows.

"I know...that it will hurt...but not for long."

Color streaks her cheeks. Her chin wobbles, but she doesn't flinch.

Warmth suffuses my chest. She is a fighter, this one. So much courage. Such instinct for survival. She'd never back down from a challenge. She hadn't turned away from me. It wouldn't have been easy to confess that she had been sent to set me up. No omega, however plucky, would have the strength of will to face up to an alpha, but she had. She hadn't tried to escape. She was here. With me, under me. My jaw clenches. She had been sent to take away everything I had fought for my entire life. She needed to be punished.

I lean down and swipe my tongue over the corner of her mouth. "Good answer." I position my shaft against the opening and her biceps wobble.

"Just for that, I'll ensure that the pleasure is more intense than anything that you have felt before."

I bring my hand around to play with the wet folds of her pussy and she groans. I slide one finger into her channel and a second, then curve them both and she pants.

Her spine curves, her thighs part, and I thrust my fingers in and out of her, and again.

A trembling sweeps up her thighs, up her back and she sways. I grab her hip and hold her firmly. Leaning over her I touch my lips to her ears, "Don't you dare come, Omega."

Her breasts tremble.

I add a third finger into her pussy and she cries out. Her body arches and she pants. "Please." She blubbers. Another wave of trembling grips her and she cries out, then thrusts her hips back.

"Let me in. Now." I kick my hips forward to slide my shaft into her puckered hole.

140

Chloe

It hurts. It hurts. Pain ladders up my spine and I moan. Too much. Too big. His dick stretches my backhole and I gulp.

"Relax," he purrs, and the hum builds up around me.

He draws out another growl and the sound loops over my shoulders. He presses the heel of his palm to my clit. All of my nerve endings seem to fire at once. My vision narrows, my throat closes.

What is he doing to me?

Every part of me is focused on this man. Every pore in my body tuned into him. The hum in my chest intensifies. Flashfires spark against my rib cage. He pushes aside the hair over the nape of my neck then kisses me there. The touch of his soft lips, the hardness of his dick that fills me up, the curve of his fingertips inside my channel—all of it seems to come together in one perfect hellish pinpoint that meets somewhere in my core. My toes curl. I dig my fingers into the sheets and groan.

"You will not come."

His hot breath licks the shell of my ear.

I turn toward him, pushing my cheek into the bed. Sweat beads form in the valley between my breasts.

The vibrations roll up from my feet, up my legs, and my thighs spasm.

"You will let me in.'

No.

No.

"Yes." He growls.

A moan wheezes from my lips.

Drat the man. I hate him. For a second there, I'd thought I felt something for him. That he had saved my life again. He'd faced up to Talon, fought off the alphas. He'd rescued me, brought me here...and then...I had myself to blame. I should have told him about Zeus and Lucy's plan the first chance I got, about how Ethan had approached me in the car. But I had been too preoccupied by the sensitive side of him. How he'd kissed me and held me and shown me that he was different. "All that alphaholeness is a front."

His muscles tense at my back.

"I know who you are."

"Oh, yeah?" He surveys me with unblinking eyes. "Pray enlighten me, Omega. Who am I?"

"Kai..." I swallow the dryness in my throat. "Kayden. Leader of the Scots. The man who cares for his people enough to take on his own half-brother. The boy who suffers from nightmares, who has been running from his past all his life. Who wants—"

"What?" All emotion is gone from his tone.

I try to peek at him, but my hair covers my vision. Damn it, I can't tell anymore what he's thinking. Not that I could tell otherwise either. But now, when I am laying myself bare...literally. Well, he's fucking my ass. A snicker catches in my throat. Doesn't get worse than this, right? I mean, when he had taken me against my will, I'd thought that was bad...but this...this...when he begins to move inside, when his dick throbs as he pulls back. He slides back in again, then stuffs three fingers all at once inside my channel. His other hand comes around to pinch my nipple and I am in hell.

In heaven.

Suspended somewhere in between, posted on that edge between pain and pleasure that he'd promised.

His shaft extends, thickens, stretching my back entrance, and pinpricks of hurt trail from his penetration. My pussy spasms, clenching around his fingers, and he groans. "Fuck Omega, you were made for me. You are dripping so much slick that I could cup my hand under you, collect the potent fluid, drink it up and it would go straight to my head. You drive me crazy."

Is that good?

Why is his voice so ragged?

Why is he panting so hard that the planes of his chest dig into my back?

The rough skin of his thighs chafes the soft skin on my underside. His dick extends, pushing in so deep that I swear he's going to split me in half.

His scent mingles with mine, teasing my senses. The ball of sensation in my chest grows and stretches my rib cage.

"I'm coming." I pant. "I can't stop."

"You can," he snarls, "you will."

He pulls his hands from my channel, drops his hand from my breast, and then he's gone. He yanks out his dick so fast that I am empty. Aching. Hurting. My arms and legs tremble and I collapse on my front.

The climax recedes, leaving behind...nothing.

I am nothing. No one without him. Hollowness fills my chest. I turn over on my back to see him stalk to the door.

"Wait." I surge up to my knees, and shove the hair out of my face. "What are you doing?" I scream. Not caring that I sound so horny, wanting, hurt. He's spoiled me for anything, for anyone else. The band around my chest tightens. The alpha made sure to hurt me until it had reached that threshold of pleasure that made me a junkie for him. I am going to keep coming back for more, no question. I hate him. I do.

He grips the door frame, "I told you I wasn't going to let you come."

"The hell?" I jump up on the bed then stamp my foot, "You asshole."

He shoots me a look over his shoulders, "Don't curse, Princess."

"Fuck you." I clench my fists at my sides.

"Not any time soon." Turning, he leaves.

"If you don't...take me, if you don't rut me...I'll—"

He swings around and his gaze burns into me. "Say it."

My mouth goes dry. There's no going back now. If I tell him what's on my mind, he'll...he'll never forgive me.

And since when has that stopped me?

He had taken me without my consent. But I had betrayed him first. I'd won this round...and it wasn't a fight. This was...is...my life. And he's my mate. And damn him, but I don't want anyone else. No one but him. Zeus and Lucy were right. I had to defy him. Challenge him. Keep him engaged. More so now, when the fragile trust between us has all but snapped. I hurt his pride and he's never going to forgive me anyway. So I have nothing to lose. Nothing but the alpha I want in my life. I firm my shoulders and jut out my chin. "If you don't rut me, I'll find someone else."

His jaw tightens. Color suffuses his cheeks.

Not good.

This is not good.

Anger spools off of him and slams into me. He takes a step forward and I scoot back on the bed. Lose my footing and fall back. I scramble to a sitting position, to find he's staring at me.

"I thought you were brave." He drums his fingers on his chest. The gesture should look casual, but coming from Kayden, it's...plain scary. My throat closes. My stomach twists in knots. Fear coils in my chest and the mating bond twangs. In sympathy? Empathy?

"You...you did?"

He takes another step forward, and I scoot back on the bed.

"My mistake." He widens his stance.

"Wh...what do you mean?"

"You are merely foolish."

"I...I am?"

He jerks his chin.

"Clearly, you don't value your life enough."

"I...I don't?" I sound like someone on the verge of a nervous breakdown. No...like someone who's lost all ability to think. I am repeating myself. I sound...like someone who is terrified. And I am. I gulp and his brow furrows. He cracks his neck and the joints pop.

My shoulders hunch, I draw myself into a ball and...he props his hands on his hips. His features twist into an expression of...satisfaction? Of looking down on me? He thinks I am pathetic. He does. I am not going to let him have the last word here.

I straighten my spine, sit cross legged. His gaze drops down to where the lips of my pussy must be visible. They are, for his nostrils flare. The brute must sense my arousal, for his mouth firms. "If you did, you wouldn't have said that."

"B...but" My heart flip flops, I fold my arms in my lap. "I...I did mean it. You are not the only alpha around. You were the first to hand me over to your team to gawk at me, to touch me, to—"

"My mistake." He holds up his hand, palm face up.

I blink. "You...you're apologizing?"

"I can accept when I am wrong." His lips turn up a little at the sides. "I should not have allowed my men near you."

He rolls his massive shoulders, his biceps flex, that hard chest rises and falls, and damn him, but he's so delicious, so beautiful. So big and gorgeous and 100% pure maleness that my leg muscles spasm, my stomach flutters and my heart...my heart flickers a beat, and another, and urges me to get off of the bed, to throw myself at him, for he'd catch me then...he'd always catch me.

He'd always take care of me.

I'd sensed it the moment I'd set eyes on his face. Oh, he'd take his pound of flesh, or my pussy, or yeah, maybe my ass first.

He'd be egotistical, and dominant, and demanding...but he could have been mine.

Mine.

I had screwed up. I don't stand a chance with him. Not when I had been set up, and by my own blood. It had to come to this. To him wanting me truly, saving my life over and over again, and yet, I can't give him the one thing he needs. A reason to trust me. Not yet, that is. Not until I try to put it right. Which is how?

By baiting him.

My throat closes.

By pushing him to lose control, by tearing at the walls he's built around his heart and forcing him to allow the Kai who lives inside to peek out. That vulnerable boy who had cried out in the middle of the nightmare and had brought me racing over to soothe him. To face the monster in his den. In his bedroom. He had let me into his bed and I am not going to leave here that easily. Nah, I've learned a thing or two from the heroines of my historical novels. They were no shrinking violets. Sure they may have fainted on occasion, but only when they needed to use their feminine wiles to get their own way. "Oh yeah?" I allow my lips to curl in a smile.

He glares. The dominance literally leaps off of him and slams into my chest and I gasp. A bead of sweat trickles down my spine. Everything inside of me wants to shove away, curl up into a ball near the headboard. I grip my hands together. "How do you plan to stop me?"

His features freeze. Then all expression leaches from his face, leaving behind a cold, hard mask. The face of the alpha who had walked onto the terrace and taken the most precious thing from me. Who had gone straight for the heart of me, my core, my feminine omega essence and possessed it. He becomes that alpha as he stalks forward to stand at the foot of the bed. He crooks a finger at me and I flinch. He tilts his head and I almost cry out in fear.

Don't be afraid.

Don't.

His jaw tics and he waits. Waits. When my feet touch the mattress I realize that I am walking on the bed toward him. And I have no recollection of having stood up. None whatsoever. That's the kind of hold this man has on me. And I had been trying to defy him? I must though.

I must, if I hope to come out of this encounter with any part of me alive.

My legs tremble and I force myself to put one foot in front of the other. I walk toward him and each step I take brings me closer, closer. When I reach him, I stop. This close, he blocks out the sight of the door, of the room, of everything but him. His entire body is a magnet. Heat. Lust. My thighs clench, my sex spasms. A dense cloud of anger spools off of him and folds over me. Intense. So intense. Why had I not realized that there was a churning writhing mass of need, anger—hatred?— pulsing under the surface, inside of this enigmatic alpha?

I had been too taken in by the hurt he'd inflicted on me, perhaps, to notice? I had been too focused on myself. My needs. How I wanted to get back at him. Now, when I have nothing to lose...everything is clear. All the distractions fall away and my vision narrows. I want to close the distance between us and touch him. Touch him. I raise a hand and he snarls, "You don't get to touch me, not until I give you permission, get me?"

I gulp.

He folds his arms over his chest. His biceps bulge, the cords of his beautiful throat flex. He looks remote and infallible, also vulnerable. Is that crazy? That act he puts on had fooled me thus far, but now I can see what he's all about. Hurt. Out for revenge. He'd let it rule his life, and then he'd found me, he'd been drawn to me. I made him vulnerable. It's why he'd taken me.

He'd recognized that I was his mate—but hadn't acknowledged it to himself. Oh, he had rescued me from Talon, but was that because his ego had been hurt that the Viking had taken what belonged to him. *Maybe.*

Maybe it was more. Maybe I'll never know. Not until I force him to tell me.

"Answer me." He growls.

"Fine. Got it. No touching." I hold up my hands, palms face up and he frowns.

"Don't sass me."

"Wouldn't dream of it." I bite the inside of my cheek.

As if I was going to obey him?

I am going to pretend, because I need to coerce him into trusting me, while I figure out my next steps. I peer up at him from under my eyelashes. "But I can let other alphas touch me—"

His fingers wrap around my neck. I gulp. How did he move so fast?

When had he leaned across the space between us and grabbed my nape? My throat closes. My heart hammers, my pulse pounds so hard at my temples that my vision wavers.

"If I see another man within ten feet of you, if I scent another male anywhere in your vicinity, I'll kill him. I'll tear open his chest, pull out his heart and crush it—" he flexes the thick fingers of his free hand and I stare. He raises those fingers to cup my pussy. "Who does your cunt belong to?"

The primal possessiveness in his voice washes over me. My toes curl. And I had thought he was that lost boy inside? Was I wrong? Had the experiences of his life scarred him beyond redemption? Is he every bit as harsh and emotionless as he portrays himself?

"Answer me."

When had he leaned down to peer into my eyes?

Swallowing up every bit of my attention. His nose bumps mine, his amber eyes glint, golden flecks of hellfire boiling deep inside. He is beyond angry. Dense clouds of feral rage plume off of him. Shards of coldness prick my blood.

How can he blow hot and cold at the same time?

I am riveted. I open my mouth to speak, but the words stick in my throat.

"Speechless, eh? What happened to all of that challenge inside of you, Omega?"

Gone. Swallowed. Disappeared. *When I am faced with the real you, that unfettered darkness that swirls around you, in you, when I see what you really are, I am scared, I am without defense.*

I am so turned on that if he pushes me down I'll spread my legs in invitation. I want him inside of me, taking me, possessing me, knotting me, wanting me...but on my terms.

Is that crazy?

Can a submissive breeder omega such as me tame him?

"I'll tell you." His fingers around the nape of my neck tighten. "Your pussy is mine. Your lips, your mouth, your breasts, your soul, your ass is mine to tap when I need."

He purrs and his massive chest rumbles.

"You will do as I command. Part your legs when I ask you. Orgasm when I allow you to. And if any man is foolish enough to glance at you, I'll..." A snarl bleeds from his lips. Wild. Animalistic.

In that moment I am sure that I'll never invoke the beast inside of him again.

The hair on my nape stiffens. My fingers tremble. All of nerve endings fire at once.

"I'll gouge out his eyes and eat them up. Then I'll chop him up into tiny pieces, make a bed of his sorry flesh, and fuck you on it."

He slaps his chest.

"I'll take you, and knot you, and bring you to the edge of climax and I won't let you come."

His nostrils flare, his biceps bulge, "I'll multiply the punishment I've meted out to you. I'll make you sorry that you were ever born."

His shoulders seem to broaden right in front of my eyes.

"I'll make you beg me, plead with me, cry in hurt, in pain, in arousal, in need, and even then, I won't let you orgasm." He peels back his lips, the tendons of his neck stretching. "I'll fucking cover you in my cum and bind you to me. I'll keep you hungry for my touch, my kiss, my cock, without allowing you to come. Do you get me?"

Kayden

The fuck am I saying?

These words filled with need and passion, with yearning and anger, with so much emotion that it fills my head and flushes my skin and pounds at my temples until the very fabric of my being seems to seep out of my pores...are they mine?

My vision narrows. Every cell in my body is on edge.

My hold tightens on her neck, my fingers curve up her pussy. She winces but doesn't take her eyes off of me. I should take my hands off of her, push her away.

I should walk out of here, set her free, and focus on what's most important. Defeating Zeus. Restoring my country back to my people.

Hiding behind the layers of revenge and anger that had been my salvation so far.

It had been so easy to barricade myself behind the walls of coldness that had shut me off from the world.

I look at her and everything is different. I scent her and my heart stutters.

Every fiber of my being insists that I take her, protect her, seal the mating bond and possess her, but I can't.

She betrayed me, remember?

All of this was a game...and is that so bad?

She worked with the cards that she'd been dealt. She made the most of the situation.

She did what was needed to survive...so why am I angry with her?

Why can't I forgive her? Why do I want more, so much more, from whatever this is between us? The stinging sensation in my chest digs into my rib cage and I gasp.

I let go of her so fast that she stumbles, then rights herself.

Her forehead creases. The skin around her eyes pinches. And the expression on her face...concern, mixed with the fear that I had placed there, leaps at me. I take a step back, then pace. Back-forth-back. I sense her watching me. Wary, uncertain. She doesn't skitter back, small mercies. So guess I didn't scare her off completely. My chest squeezes and I rub the skin over my heart. "My mother..." I clear my throat. "She was raped by Golan."

She blinks but doesn't respond.

"Zeus' father," I throw out without looking at her. "Who's also my blood father. I was brought up by my mother's mate. The Scottish leader, my adoptive father brought me up. And you'd think I'd be akin to him. Infused with his patriotism, his love for his country...turns out he wasn't perfect either. He couldn't accept my mother, not after she'd been tainted. My ma made the most of the situation. Every day she was alive, she loved me. Then Golan came for her again." I swivel around to see her.

She stands on the bed, not far from where I had released her.

Her arms are at her sides. Every muscle in that tiny, gorgeous, perfect body of hers is stretched with tension. Is she wondering why I am telling her all of this? *Yeah, me too.* Why am I sharing with her the one thing I've never told anyone? Why is it that I want her to see exactly what she's dealing with? *Doesn't matter.*

"She put herself between me and him. Told me to run."

"But you didn't." Her voice is soft, so gentle.

I wince. "I attacked him, tried to defend her. He struck me unconscious."

"You tried your best to save her."

Grief that I thought I had locked away deep inside surges forward. "I came awake to find him rutting her inert body. The handle of the knife stuck out from her chest. There was blood, so much everywhere."

The skin around her eyes wrinkles.

A pressure grows behind my eyes, the pulse thuds at my temples. "When he was done, he twisted the knife until her body stopped twitching."

She presses her knuckles into her mouth. Her throat moves as she swallows.

"Do you know the difference between a body that is alive and one that isn't?"

The color bleeds away from her face.

"Not much, yet *so much.*" My voice sounds as if it's coming from far away. A coldness radiates out from my chest. "A world, an ocean, a lifetime gone in a flicker of a second."

She inhales, but doesn't say anything.

Thank fuck. The first sign of empathy, and I'd have left.

She tucks her arms at her sides, her pose one of cautious waiting.

"Suffice to say, Golan and his alphas trained me well. By the time my adoptive father found me, I had been well-inducted into what it is to face monsters who'd taken away every shred of humanity from me. They buggered me well, those bastards."

Her shoulders tighten; she shifts her weight from foot to foot.

I wait. Wait for her to tell me how sorry she is. How much she regrets what happened to me. That this explains my behavior so far in treating her — As if anything can condone what I did to her? — But nothing.

Her green eyes grow stormy. So many emotions in them that I can't separate out the individual sentiments.

"Fuck me, for sharing this with you."

I dig my fingers into my scalp.

"Don't think it's to gain your empathy either. I don't care what you think of me. Your thoughts don't matter, Omega. All that matters is your body, your will. Your submission? It's what I crave. Owning you, possessing you, making you bend to my every depraved need, that's the only thing that gives me reprieve from the thoughts chasing around in my head."

"I understand."

"Excuse me?" I stare.

"I get it, Alpha."

"Oh?"

"We are not so different, you and I."

"Eh?" The fuck is this woman talking about?

She was unblemished, until I corrupted her. Tore into her, knotted her, penetrated her where no one had before. I marked her, and now I can't let her go. I can't have her either. I want to punish her for not living up to the expectations I placed on her. I am at a fucking impasse. Doesn't she realize that?

"I wanted you from the moment I saw you Kayden." She draws herself up to her full height.

Standing on the bed, she comes to the level of my shoulder. I peel back my lips, baring my teeth. There, that should scare her, right? But she doesn't flinch.

She doesn't blink. Huh?

"I hated you, for not giving me a choice when you took me." She juts out her chin. "You mated me. Sullied me. Bound me to you and spoiled me for anyone else. I loathe you." She shrugs. "But I can't live without you, either."

"You're not hearing me." I toss my head. "I want to make your life a living hell. For my dominance to consume you until there's nothing left of you. No free will. By the time I am done with you, the woman you were will be ground into dust. Broken by the force of my personality. Chained to me. Imprisoned to my destiny. You don't want that."

"Maybe not." She bites her lips. "But you give me very little credit. I've survived this far, haven't I?" She waves a hand in the air, then peeks up at me again from under those hooded eyelids. "Maybe I can hold my own. Maybe I would submerge myself in you, then find myself again?" Her chest rises and falls. "Maybe you will surprise yourself too?"

I throw back my head and laugh, and laugh.

Tears run down my cheeks and I wipe them away. "Think you can stand up to me?"

"Why not?" Her voice is fierce.

I look at her. "Right." I chuckle.

"You want this." She cups her pussy.

I stare at the succulent flesh.

"I want *you* to have this."

"So?"

"So, that's a start." Her lips curve in a smile. Her eyes sparkle.

So fucking vital. So alive, no wonder I had been drawn to her. I want to yank on that wellspring of anticipation and let it wash away everything that's tainted me. Something inside of me, some long dead spark of need, of wanting to thrive, of embracing everything fate had thrown at me and moving on, roars to life. My throat closes. My heart stutters.

"You won't let me orgasm, you won't let me find my release elsewhere, fine." She taps a finger to her cheek. "You forget I can pleasure myself."

I want to look away from her cunt, to read her face, understand what she's plotting, but I can't.

She widens her stance until her swollen clit peeks out from between her fingers. Then in exact imitation of what I had done to her, she shoves three fingers inside of herself, all the way up to her knuckles.

"The fuck you doing?"

My dick thickens. I have to shove my legs apart to accommodate my growing cock. I am mirroring her stance. *She's making me follow her moves?* The fuck I care?

All I can see is how she thrusts her fingers in and out of her wet channel. How the squelching sound fills the space. How slick drips down from her cunt, down her fingers to pool on the mattress. How her panting heats up the air. Her thighs tremble. The momentum of her fingers increases and so does mine. When my shaft leaps in my grasp I realize that I am wanking myself off.

I squeeze my dick and massage it from root to tip. I fucking grab at myself with such force that my groin protests, but it's not enough.

My movements grow more frantic. Faster. Deeper. I can't stop staring at her engorged clit. How the sound of her moans deepens, seeps into my blood, imprints on my fucking cells. I keep masturbating.

My cock lengthens.

My knot hardens.

Sweat pools under my armpits, but I don't stop.

A trembling grips my legs.

Her body jerks. Her hips wriggle. She brings her other hand to her clit and pinches it; and I explode.

I stumble forward, point my dick in her direction and let the cum gush out of me. Thick ropy strands mark her fingers, her pussy, her thighs. I keep coming, as the fucking orgasm rages up my chest to meet the mating bond, which flares out in a storm of rage, of heat, of lust...of love?

No, not that.

Never that.

I can't love. My past has made sure of that. But I can...possess, protect. I can hide her away where no one will ever find her. That much I can do. I will do. For she is mine. *Mine*. The orgasm fades away. I blink.

She dips her fingers into her pussy and scoops up our joined up cum. "This is us, Alpha." She holds her glistening digits out to me. "Our essence. What we are."

Us. I circle her delicate wrist with my fingers, bring them to my mouth and suck on them. The evidence of our mutual climax explodes on my palate.

My chest clenches, my pulse stutters. Bloody fucking hell. The hell have I done?

I release her hand, then stalk to the exit.

141

Chloe

He leaves the room and a coldness grips my chest. Goosebumps pop on my skin. My heartbeat slows. All the heat in the room seems to have been sucked out. Emptiness coils in my womb. My knees buckle and the back of my thighs hits the bed. I roll around, wrapping myself up in the covers, in the remnants of his cum. The gooey mess slithers over my skin, sinking into my pores, sticks to the insides of my thighs. I am empty, so empty. He's gone and I miss him already.

And I shouldn't.

Why is it that I crave him, his touch, his presence so much?

When he is with me, the vitality of his being, the sheer dominance of his being, grounds me. My head spins. Without him, I am nothing.

The evidence of how dependent I have become on him resonates inside. The mating bond simmers and splutters. Agreeing? Warning that I had pushed him. What had I been thinking?

Or rather I hadn't been? I had reacted from somewhere deep within. The feminine core of me had reacted on instinct. Getting my alpha to accept me was not going to be easy. It needed strategy. As much plotting as what my father had done with his team to shore up the defenses of our city against the Vikings. And where had that gotten him? Dead. Not me, though. I am here. I made it out.

I am here while countless numbers of my countrymen are gone.

I am alive despite everything that has happened over the last few days. I had gone toe to toe with a scary, forceful alpha, and I had survived. A chuckle rolls up my throat and I begin to laugh. I curl up in a ball and guffaw until my stomach aches.

Until tears run down my cheeks.

Until the sound of my mirth fills my ears and echoes through my head, until the blood pounds at my temples, and my cheeks hurt. I swallow down the last chuckle and hiccup. My entire body shakes. My shoulders quiver. Another hiccup jolts me, and another. Tears prick the backs of my eyes. And I let them flow down my cheeks. Cleansing. Refreshing. Another jolt punches my gut. My stomach heaves. Bile rushes up my throat. I clutch at my middle, my guts twist. I roll out of bed and stumble across the floor. My feet slip on the floor and I sway. Sweat beads my forehead. I stuff my knuckles into my mouth, lurch toward the bathroom and leap the distance to the ceramic commode. I bend over and the sickness gushes out. The contents of my stomach empty out. I heave and puke and manage to flush away the disgusting mess. Then lay back on the floor. I groan, then turning, press my cheek to the tiles. They feel cool and I sigh.

I bring my knees up to my chest, curl into a tight ball. A wave of tiredness washes over me, my limbs tremble and I clutch them closer. My chest hurts, there is a pounding behind my eyes. My skin tightens and I groan again. Something is not right. Something is missing. What? What?

My ribcage tightens, the ball of sensation in my chest screams. Go. Go. Where? What do I want? I crack my eyelids open and push myself up to my feet. At least my legs seem steadier. I walk out of the bathroom, cross the floor. The bed. The sheets. The scent of him. The taste of him is most concentrated there.

That is what I want. Him. All of him. On me. In me. Heat flushes my skin, then fades away. A chill slides down my spine. Insidious. Overwhelming. I shiver, then quicken my steps, and pulling up the covers, fall into bed.

The softness of the sheets, the overwhelming male essence that surrounds me, pours over me, in me...my heartbeat steadies. I pull the sheets up over my head, shutting out the light. Burrowing into the warmth, into the forbidden, familiar presence of him that lingers here. I wallow in it. I squeeze my eyes shut and can almost imagine that throaty purring of his. The vibrations of his chest that rock me, the largeness of his presence that overwhelms me and presses me down into the bed. Holding me down. Subduing me, caressing me, soothing me.

I should move.

Should fling off these covers, roll away, onto my feet. I should stand up to him and tell him he can't hold me here. I need to get away. No... I need to be here. Right here in his room, his bed, wrapped up in his juices. Ugh. What am I thinking? That's disgusting. Isn't it?

My throat closes. I try to lick my lips but my tongue feels swollen. My head hurts. Why does the back of my eyeballs feel so bruised?

Too hot.

I need to throw off the covers.

A chill coils in my chest. My belly heaves. No, I can't be sick. Not again.

I turn my head and my nose presses deeper into the pillow. I inhale, and my lungs fill with his essence.

If I pretend hard enough, I can almost convince myself that my alpha is in bed with me.

What am I thinking? Why do I miss him?

I shove off the cover, turn away. Cool air rushes over my face, shoving away all traces of him, and my stomach lurches again. No. No. I turn over on my front, press my nose into the pillow. Inhale his scent. Every muscle in my shoulders relaxes.

Hmm. Interesting. I turn my face slightly, his smell recedes. My stomach cramps. No! I push up on my knees, bury my head in the pillow and the world rights again. Him. I need more of him.

All of him.

Covering me.

Soothing me.

Where is the alpha when I need him?

I curl my arms and legs around his pillow. Clutching him to me. Smothering my face with the cover of the pillow. Making sure as much of me as possible can come in contact with him. The ball of heat in my chest flares out, reaching for him. Him. I need him. *Need you Alpha. Kai. Come to me.*

142

Kayden

An alpha never runs away. He turns and faces his monsters. And defeats them. *The day you let your nightmares get the better of you, the day an omega takes up too much of your waking time, you are in trouble.* Golan's voice echoes around in my head. *It means becoming vulnerable, letting your emotions rule you, and that is when you commit mistakes.* Bastard had done a number on me. Ingrained me with his filthy conditioning. Despite my not wanting to be influenced, clearly his philosophy had imprinted on my cells.

Pain grips my chest and I double over. Grip my knees and huff out a breath. The hell is that? Straightening, I shake my head to clear it, then jog up the slope of the hill.

I had avoided coming here for so long. Every time I retraced the path that my mother had taken on that last day when she had been alive, normally means a fresh burst of nightmares, so ideally, I should have kept away from here. But I'd walked out of that room aware that my life had changed. What had shifted between us in such a short time? I had been the hunter; she was the prey. The pawn in this entire fucking mess. But somehow the tables had turned.

No longer could I ignore my reaction to her.

Dismiss how I wanted to protect her. I am an alpha. It's natural that I want to protect my clan, that I hanker after omega pussy. It's my right, after all. And every other time that I'd been with an omega, I couldn't walk away fast enough.

But with her...I'd wanted to press on her shoulder until she was sprawled out on her back—legs wide apart, pussy lips bared to me—and taste more of our entwined essences. Bury myself in her and satisfy her. Bring her to climax, pleasure her. Take my time making love to her. *Love? Nah.*

I am not in love.

I *can't* be in love.

I haven't loved anyone since...my mother. Marcus' daughter, who had been the closest I'd had to a sibling, had never gotten this close to me.

I am incapable of emotions, remember? I know how to take, to wreak vengeance on the man who tore my life apart, except he is dead.

My blood father—the bastard—is long gone. Thanks to General-fucking-Zeus. He's the one responsible for this entire mockery of what my life has turned out to be.

Zeus killed Golan and deprived me of the chance for revenge.

He took over as the Leader of London—defeating me for it, but that's a minor detail. He had positioned Cara to seduce me and I had fallen for it. I had taken her from there and Zeus had let me. He'd known my life was going to get bloody screwed up. Bet he and his omega are laughing at me right now.

I quicken my pace, my legs pumping, feet pounding into the hillside as I race up the same steps that my mother had traversed. The only way to face your demons? Chase the monsters that scare you shitless.

Counterintuitive?

Maybe.

But it makes sense for I cannot face *her*. I can't. Sweat pools in my underarms. My legs ache. My shoulders tense, but I keep going. Keep pushing through the noise that crowds in my ears. Her screams as Golan had raped her again, as I lay there half-conscious.

Her voice calling for me, abruptly cut off.

Those choking noises issuing from her throat as he had suffocated her, until all that had remained was the pounding of my blood in my ears. I burst around the corner of the path and onto the peak, stumble over the uneven terrain, and sprawl on the ground.

I lay there, face pressed into the smooth marble, the frost bathing my skin. I turn my head, trace my fingers over the jagged lines. If I sit up and look at the design, it will form into the coat of arms that belongs to my father's clan. If I raise my eyes, I'll find the headstone. I've read the inscription so many times it's etched on my soul.

Adele Mcleod.
Beloved mother and wife.
She loved this hillside.

The one woman who had loved me. The first woman I had ever loved. The evidence was irrefutable. She was not the only one in my life anymore. Is that why I had come here? Why my subconscious had led me here?

Flipping myself over onto my back, I stare up at the skies. *You'd have loved her, Ma. Her spirit, the wildfire, the sunshine that she carries with her, trapped in those blonde locks.*

Her laughter... I'd never heard that. Her tears… I knew how they tasted. Her cunt… I knew how it pulsed. Her slickness, her arousal, how the skin tightened around the corner of her lips when she was tense. Her nervousness, the shy glance, the anger that tensed her arms as she curled her fingers when she was uncertain. Her sass, her ability to stand her ground even when she had to be terrified of the big bad alpha, of me. I had hurt her. I could spend my entire lifetime making it up to her. Yeah, she had been planted to be my downfall. But this one time, I couldn't fault my half-bro. Perhaps we knew each other too well?

We each had an inkling of exactly the kind of omega who would attract the other.

I'd sent Lucy to kill him.

He'd made sure I stumbled across Chloe.

I wanted her. But could I trust her?

I fling my arms out to my sides, squeeze my eyes shut. Count the beating of my heart. Thud-thud-thud. The noise fills my ears, my pulse speeds up, sweat slicks the underside of my palms. My left leg muscles spasm and I groan. Thud-thud-thud. My heartbeat gallops. The ball of sensation in my chest twangs. Tendrils of shrapnel dig into my rib cage and my eyelids fly open. I gasp. Something is wrong. What?

Thud-thud-thud.

My heart hammers. My guts twist. Her. It's her. Did someone get to her again? I left her unprotected. If something were to happen to her again, I'd never forgive myself.

I spring up and retrace my steps down the slope. Faster. Faster. My footsteps echo off of the hillside. The band around my chest tightens. Every step I take mirrors the beating of my heart. The pulse that pounds at my temples, behind my eyeballs, in my fingertips which tighten with fear. Go to her. Go to her. The words swirl around in my head. I pick up my pace. Stumble and slide down the last few feet as I hit the bottom of the hill, then begin to run in earnest. Arms tucked into my side, footsteps lengthening, almost not touching the ground. I reach the grounds of the stronghold, run through the half open gates, up the curving driveway. So vulnerable, easy to infiltrate. There were no guards, of course not. I hadn't told my clan members I was here. I had left to rescue her and then I had abandoned her when she needed me most. *She betrayed you, remember?*

Doesn't matter.

She is mine and I am not going to fail her, not this time.

Running up the steps of the entrance, I fling open the doors, pausing long enough to drop the deadbolts behind me. It wouldn't ward off anyone who was coming for long, but at least it would be a deterrent. Race up the winding staircase, down the corridor to the doorway at the end. I leap inside the room and come to a stop. The space is empty. I run to the bed, pull away the bedcovers, the sheets, the pillows, all of which have been scrunched up together into a ball, into a...nest? Huh?

I sniff the air and traces of her tease my nostrils.

She was here not too long ago. I angle my head. Something tugs at my subconscious mind. The slug of hurt in my chest yanks me to the right.

I head to the door on the far side of the room, shove it open and a sudden coldness hits my stomach. "Chloe!"

143

Chloe

That voice. Is it him calling my name? My alpha. *Mine*. I moan and try to move, but my arms and legs are bound. No. He didn't do this, did he? Did he tie me up again? But he'd left me and gone. He'd turned his back on me again. I had tried to sleep, tried to wallow in the scattered remnants of his presence, had tried to soothe myself, but it hadn't been enough.

"Omega, what's wrong?"

Nothing. Everything. How can I explain?

I open my mouth to speak, but the words stick in my throat. My mouth is so dry. I try to swallow, but my throat is too dry.

Footsteps thud on the floor, approaching me, and I lean toward him.

No, what am I doing?

He hurt me, over and over again. Yet I crave his touch. *His* presence.

This can't be right.

The heat fizzes down my spine and a coldness coils in my belly. The ball of emotions digs into my ribcage, and my spine curves. Not enough. Not enough. I need more.

More.

I flex my biceps, yank back my shoulders and my bindings strain. I turn my face and press my nose into the fabric. My senses fill with his presence. It's as if he's wrapped his arms around me, pulled me into him. I am melting into him, fusing with his skin. Burrowing into him. I tighten my hold around the soft fabric, pull it closer. Shove my nose deeper into the cloud of his scent. Draw it in. Fill my lungs with it. The tightness in my belly eases. There's a touch to my hair and I wince.

"Shh, I am here now." His voice is soothing.

I don't recognize it.

He'd been nice to me...briefly. Had pretended he cared for me...then...then I had told him the truth and he'd walked away. He hates me.

I try to pull away but his hold tightens.

"Stay with me Cara. Let me help you."

Cara, he called me Cara again.

I crack my eyelids and his features fill my line of sight.

The skin stretches across his cheeks. There's a streak of dirt on his temple. I want to reach up and touch it. I try to raise my arm but it's restrained. I look down at myself. What the—? I am on the floor, buried under mounds of clothes. *His* clothes. How did I get here? I frown.

"I found you." The tendons of his throat flex. "Will you let me help you?"

Huh?

Did he ask my permission?

Since when does Kayden do that? Doesn't he just take? Maneuver me until I am ready for him. Force his will upon me? This is a game. I hate it when he blows hot and cold. When he peels back the layers to reveal the tenderness that resides deep inside him, only to yank it all away. I shy away and he winces. "I won't hurt you, sweetheart."

I swallow. Sweetheart. He'd called me that once before, right before he'd kissed me. He'd tilted his lips over mine and slipped his tongue inside my mouth and shared himself. He'd taken and given, it had been a meeting of us, of the real us. My gaze drops to his mouth. That stern upper lip, that plump lower lip. My mouth waters and I lift my chin.

He leans in so close that his eyelashes twine with mine.

The hard planes of his features overwhelm me. His warmth sizzles around my shoulders. He's all around me. His big body dominates mine, and it's exactly what I seek. His hard chest flattens my breasts and my nipples pebble. His heart thuds against mine. The twined heartbeats fill my ears.

A purr rumbles from him, and another.

That sound curls around me, loops around my waist, fizzes down my spine. I shiver and he pulls me closer. The ground tilts and I try to clutch at him, but my arms are all entangled in his clothes. I wriggle in deeper and he cradles me. The purrs rumble up the planes of his chest, rolling around me, sinking in through the fabric that wraps around me. My skin tingles, my blood heats.

"I know what you want, Cara."

Do you?

Do you understand how it is to want another with every fiber of your being while your mind protests that it's all wrong?

As your heart aches with betrayal.

And your insides cringe at what you've done to him, to yourself. Even as your womb...your womb pulses with need. Wanting to be filled, needing to be bred. Yearning for a being that is mine. *All mine.* Who belongs to me, who I can hold in my arms, suckle on my breast?

I thrash my head from side to side, strain to get closer. Closer. I want my alpha's skin touching me. A whine bleeds from my lips and he hauls me to him.

His touch is fierce, yet gentle. His presence warm, yet demanding. Who is this man whose character changes so often? Who I want to trust...*trust?* He hurt me. I cringe and try to pull away. The next moment my back hits the bed. He moves away and I follow him up. My head spins. My chest tightens. I need him. Need him. It's wrong, but I don't care.

I want him.

I yearn for his touch, his kisses, his cock. I groan aloud. Saliva pools in my mouth. His big, fat, juicy cock. My eyelids snap open and a snarl leaches from my lips.

"I know," he murmurs.

The hell is he talking about? He has no idea how it is to have your body disobey your every thought. That inherent need from inside that rips out of you, that pushes you to strain up and slam your head against his chest. Feel the reverberations of his heart, the surge of the blood in his veins. A growl fills my ears. Him? Me? I don't care.

I am empty, aching, and this time I don't want him to stop, not until every part of me is crammed with him. Until he fills every writhing, wretched hole in my body. Until he ties me to him and fucks me until I can't think again. Anything...anything to get rid of this horrible yearning that pushes me to rear back and thrust my breasts into his chest, my pussy into the hardness that strains his crotch, my toes that curve against his legs.

I snap my head forward.

My forehead connects with his chin.

144

Kayden

My head snaps back. Pain cracks down my neck.

"Cara."

She shudders at the sound of my voice and bangs her head against my chest. She burrows in closer, trying to connect the maximum surface area of her body with mine. "Sweetheart, let me get these clothes off from around you."

She tilts her head. Her eyes are half open. She stares at my lips. Does she want to kiss me? I move in closer and she frowns. "What do you want, Darling?" A-n-d the endearments pour off my lips. But I mean it...kind of. Calling her Cara, my Omega, Chloe, none of it seems to fully convey the depths of my emotions. A confusing sensation that clogs my mind, digs into my heart, settles deep in my groin. So fuck that! I don't care how I sound. I need to...what? Strip off all barriers and share what I feel? Show her what she means to me. "What do you need?"

Her brow clears, a hum strums up her throat.

"That's it, little one. Don't fight your impulses."

She sighs and gnaws on her lower lip. Then her shoulders flex as she inches closer. "I have to get you naked Cara." I move away from her and she whines. "Yes darling, for a few seconds, that's all it will take."

I tug at the sleeves of my sweatshirt that is looped around her and she winces.

I'd walked into the closet and found her wrapped up in the contents of most of my wardrobe. Somehow, she'd crawled in and tugged the clothes off of the hangers, my underclothes off of the shelves, she'd emptied out the contents of the laundry basket, and she'd wrapped herself up in what I had worn next to my skin. In my essence. My scent. She'd tried to get as close as possible to me in my absence. "You didn't need to do that. I was coming back to you."

I was. I was.

I was, wasn't I?

I shove the thought from my head.

She groans and her head thrashes from side to side. She was going to hurt herself. My heart thuds. My throat hurts. Fuck this. I rise up to my knees and strip the rest of my clothes from her.

She surges up toward me and I restrain her easily.

So tiny. So beautiful. So filled with a raw need that oozes from her every pore. I want to lick every inch of her skin, mark her with my fluids until she's coated in my saliva, my cum. Yeah, gross, but what-fucking-ever. That's me, a primal, rutting, beast, who wants one thing: to mark my territory, my property, mine. My omega. My gorgeous mate who I was going to teach a lesson for what she'd done. "I am going to punish you, Cara."

She wriggles around, yanks at the restraint of my hold and strains to get closer. I throw the clothes away and she surges toward them.

I cover her body with mine, lower enough of my weight on her, so she can't move.

Her body strains in the direction of where I had tossed away the garments. She turns her head and whines.

"What?" I frown.

She raises her chin, then tosses her head.

"You want the clothes?"

She nods.

"You don't need them, not when I am here."

She glares at me and a chuckle catches in my throat. "So much fucking fire, little one, I can't wait for you to burn me. Singe me, while I lick every inch of you."

She stiffens, then her gaze narrows. The next second she struggles. She shoves at me, wriggles, tries to knee me, digs her fingernails into my shoulders. I scent blood in the air. The hell?

"Little wild cat."

I loosen my hold, move back to sit on my heels and she points at the clothes on the floor.

"You want them?"

She tosses her head.

"Well come get them, Omega."

She frowns.

"I am not stopping you."

She folds her arms around her waist, and those gorgeous mounds of her breasts push up. Nipples pink, puckered. My mouth waters. I lean over her and she slaps my face. "The fuck?" I jerk my head back.

She juts out her chin, then tilts her head toward the goddamn contents of half my wardrobe, which I had dumped on the floor.

"You want me to get them for you?"

Her forehead smooths out.

"Fine, so why don't you open your mouth and tell me that, hmmm?"

She shivers, goosebumps rising on her skin. She's fucking cold. I forget then, that I am angry with her, or that she'd demanded that I get the clothes for her, or that she slapped me. Yeah, me...the fucking alphahole, swing my legs off of the bed, scoop up the sweatshirt, the pants, the briefs, the used towel. I turn and begin to arrange it around her, but she snarls.

"What?"

She sits up and holds out her arms.

"You want them?"

She angles her head.

"You got them."

I dump the clothes on her. She grabs them, then begins to arrange them around her on the bed. Tugging at them, folding the pants, smoothing out the damp towel, balling up the briefs, twisting the sweatshirt. She sits cross-legged as she works, hums to herself. Mumbles under her breath. Her blonde hair flows around her shoulders, her breasts jiggle as she moves. She sways in tune to some harmony in her mind. I touch her on the shoulder and she shoots me a frown.

"Fine, okay." I shuffle away to sit on the chair. Watch as she weaves her nest. Nest? I freeze.

She's nesting?

Of course she would. She's my mate. I'd brought her to the place I felt safe. The space where I could be myself. I'd brought her home, and she'd picked up on my sentiments. I should have been here with her as the urge to build a safe haven for herself and her progeny had taken over. The primal instincts that nature had instilled in us to come forth when the timing was right. I should have watched over her, helped her, and I had turned away. No wonder she had tried to get to my clothes, to pick up the scraps that had remnants of me in my absence. My breathing quickens, my groin hardens. I dig my elbows into my knees, place my chin in my palm and watch her.

She bobs her head in tune to some internal music I can't hear. Fucking adorable. I swallow. Something hot fills my chest. An emotion I don't dare name. Not yet. Not now. *Don't complicate anything. Don't slot anything into a niche.* This...whatever this is that shines in the air, stretches between us, joins us, enfolds us in its embrace...this...this is right.

She glances at me. A furrow between her eyebrows.

"What do you need?" My voice cracks, but she doesn't notice.

She peruses my body, no not my body. She points at my sleeve. "You want it?"

She nods and I chuckle. Of course she'd want the clothes off my back. I rise to my feet, shrug off my shirt and hand it to her. She snatches it out of my hand, then nods toward the pants. I can't stop the laughter that wells up. The tables have well and truly turned. This woman can ask me to roll on the floor, to crawl on my hands and knees, and I'd fucking do it. Right before I threw her down and ripped into her cunt.

I step out of my jeans. She snatches them from me, then stares at my crotch. I step out of my briefs. She reaches for them and I pull back, "I am going to remind you of how you stripped me of my underwear when your estrus fades."

Estrus?

She'd completed a heat cycle already, so what was this? Did the nesting instinct overtake everything else? Had it been that long since... I pause. I had been out of it for nearly two weeks. It had taken me another five days to find her and then we'd spent another two days here...three weeks. A little short for another cycle to begin, but it was possible.

And this was the start. It would take her another day or two before the estrus took over completely. It could also be my nearness and the emotional turmoil of the last month that could have accelerated it. Not to mention bringing her to my source, my home, my bed...my true origins, which had clinched the deal.

She snarls and I blink.

She scoots forward on the bed and grabs my briefs then sniffs them.

My dick is instantly hard.

She sighs, then buries her face in the fabric. My balls harden.

No other omega has been this intimate with me. No one else will be again. I clench my fingers into fists.

She arranges my underwear, my pants, tweaks a protruding sleeve, then sighs. Turning around she sinks into the mess of clothes. A crooning sound warbles from her lips. Then she sits up, looks around—ignoring me completely—of course. She yanks up the futon cover over herself. Then frowns and throws it off. She looks around the room. Her gaze comes to rest on me. She sniffs the air, moving in my direction. "I want you."

145

Chloe

I hear my words and some subconscious part of my mind rejoices. I'd said it. I'd done it. I'd been truthful with him. My throat closes. My heart hurts.

I lower my hand to my side.

He glares at me. His dominance seems to intensify. His biceps bulge, his very shoulders seem to broaden.

He draws in a breath and the connection between us crackles.

Tendrils of awareness reach out from him, slide around me, slip down my spine. I should be afraid. I should cower. Hide under the bedclothes and pretend I didn't do that. But something stops me. My heart skips. My womb clenches. My sex hungers for him.

He rises to his feet and I tilt my head back. And further back. I crane my neck to see his face. He's so damn tall. His shoulders block out the sight of everything else.

He takes a step forward and my scalp tingles.

Another step and my toes curl.

So close. Nearer. Faster.

A moan leaches from my throat and he growls.

A purr rumbles up his chest, and another. The harsh, guttural cries wrap around me, skitter over my sensitized skin. All of my nerve endings flare. My thighs clench. Slickness drips from my channel. My core contracts. Thirsting. Needing. Wanting him. He stops next to the bed.

"I'll let you get away with your commands—" He swoops down and I cry out. "—this once." The next second he planks over me.

His massive arms cage me in. His biceps flex as they hold up the weight of all that gorgeous maleness. His gaze is fierce. Amber, gold, glitters of brown flare out from his eyes. I am entranced. Enraptured. He is a magician. A sorcerer...and I...I am all too happy, too entrapped. Ensnared. I drop the hold on my cover and it slips down. His gaze darts to my bared breasts. "You are confused. The impending heat cycle clouding your senses. No one can resist the mating call little one, not even me." He nuzzles my neck and I moan. His words fill my ears. Harsh. Rough. Just what I want.

He pulls back and I chase his presence.

"You thought when I knotted you last it was intense. It's nothing compared to how it's going to be now."

I peer up at him. I know that. I want to tell him. I sense it. I am not stupid. I am as tuned into you as you are to me. I can't stop myself. I want to cry out to him. I want to scream at him and demand that he take me now. But I can't. I scan his features. His thick corded neck. His sculpted pecs. The chiseled eight pack. The concave stomach...that...that monster cock that stares up at me. Precum drools from the head.

The essence of him fills my senses. He's so near, yet he's not. I open my mouth and he shakes his head. "No, you don't get to dictate further. You invited me in, Omega, do you understand?"

I frown. *Of course I did, stupid.* Why the hell can't I open my mouth and tell him that? I want to, but my throat is clogged with emotions, a need to not speak and break this...this connection. I reach for the mating bond and trace it to him. I pulse everything I am feeling and can't say aloud at him.

His throat moves as he swallows. "I sense it too. I don't understand what the fuck is going on, but I can't ignore it." He drops his head and licks my lips and I shiver.

"It's why this time will be different." He stares at my features as if memorizing my face.

"It's why I am giving you one last chance to back out. There's no turning back after this, Chloe."

I blink. Some of the haze clears from my head. Is it the shock of him calling me by my name to my face? Or because he's giving me a choice. Because he's acting so weird. So out of character. He's showing me that he cares in his own way. Now, as I open to him, when I am contemplating accepting the bond, he's...he's making sure I understand what I am doing. I shrink back and his shoulders slump. "I thought so." His gaze holds mine for a second more, then he begins to retreat.

He turns his head away and the warmth diminishes.

The ball of awareness in my chest screeches. "No." My voice rings out.

His entire body goes solid. He whips his head around. "No what?"

"No, I don't want you to go. Stay with me. I wasn't lying when I said I need you. I understand what I am doing. I am aware that once we...we—"

"Fuck?" His lips curl.

"Once you make love to me, once I claim you, I can't change it."

"Love." He rolls the word around in his mouth, tasting it, as if allowing the sensations to grip him. "I don't think I am capable of that." His shoulders rise and fall. "But sure if you want to call it that—"

I place my palms on either side of his face, and tug until his nose bumps mine. He stares into my eyes and I let him. I open myself up to him, allow him to read me. "I see you, Kayden."

He grimaces. "The hell do you see in me?"

"Hurt, need."

"That emo mumbo jumbo." He shakes his head.

"Lust, desire."

His lips curve, "That much, I confirm."

"An alphahole who ruts."

He purrs and the sound nearly breaks me.

"The meanest, baddest male I have ever met."

He smirks. "Keep talking, sweet thing."

"A beautiful soul."

Color smears his cheeks. "Enough."

Did he blush? No way. I open my mouth to ask.

Only he drops his head and thrusts his tongue between my open lips.

146

Kayden

For the second time in my life, I tilt my lips and swipe my tongue over her teeth and she moans. The way she mewls when she's aroused? —a sure sign that I am pleasuring her, lighting up her blood, arousing her. All of it goes to my head.

I plunge my tongue over hers and she strains toward me.

I wrap my arms around her and yank her closer, then proceed to plunder that heady taste of her. I nip on her lips, close my mouth over hers and suck on her. I open myself and pour myself into her. I kiss her until my head spins, until the blood rushes to my groin and my dick lengthens, my balls harden, and every part of me insists that I treat her body with as much reverence. Slow. Take it slow. No rush. Not this time. I tear my mouth from hers and she chases my mouth. "Open your eyes, darling."

She glances at me from between her eyelids. Blown pupils. Flushed cheeks. Hair mussed around her shoulders. "Don't look away." I hold her gaze and slide down her body. She doesn't flinch as I settle between her legs. I run my palms up the sides of her thighs and she swallows. The scent of her arousal deepens. "Hmm. The thought of what I am going to do to you is a turn on, eh?"

She licks her lips, and fuck me, if I don't come right then. I pillow my cheek on the buttery soft inside flesh of her thigh and her breathing quickens. I inch closer to that succulent core of hers. I blow over her pussy lips and her thighs jerk. I glance at her and her nipples distend further. Interesting.

She's so damned responsive.

So ready for me.

I swipe out my tongue over her cunt and her back arches off of the bed. The taste of her is fucking nectar and honey, every forbidden aphrodisiac rolled into one. No, better.

A growl rips out of me and she moans in response. Fuck this going slow shit. It's not me. I intend to pleasure her...take her along with me, just...it's going to be how I am best. Deep, intense and with no wasted actions. I straighten and my shoulders shove her legs apart. I grip the swollen curves of her ass and she pants. I drop my head and bury my nose in her core. She squeals and wriggles, and my balls fucking tighten. No getting away from it. I am the fucking hunter. She is my prey. I do best when I chase. When I catch and then...I demolish. I cup her butt cheeks so her core is arched up and ready and positioned just right.

"Hold on, Cara."

I drag my tongue from her asshole up to her cunt. She grips my hair and tugs so hard that pain flashes down my spine. My chest lurches. My groin throbs. Then I eat her up. I lick her up, again and again. I drag my tongue between those swollen pussy lips. I bite on her cunt and she howls and pulls at my hair so hard that I see stars. A snarl twists my mouth.

I close my lips over her pussy.

I suck and tug and bite, then drag my whiskered chin over her soft core again and again. She screams and loops her thighs around my head, pushing her pussy up into my face, even as she yanks at my hair trying to pull me off of her. Nah. I am just getting started.

I thrust my tongue into her wet channel, nudge my finger into her puckered back hole, and her body bucks.

Liquid slickness creams her core and I lick it up, swallow and go back for more. Seconds. Thirds. I drink up every last bit of moisture that splashes over my mouth. Then bring up my other hand to cup her breast. I squeeze her nipple so hard that she screams.

Words leave her lips, but I don't understand them.

She's lapsed into the language of her ancestors and the cadence of her tone is harsh and alluring at the same time. Fucking potent. When she swears like this, while lost in the pleasure of our mating, she destroys me.

My shaft aches. A vein pounds at my temples. A pulse flares to life at my throat, on my eyelids, at the backs of my knees.

My balls grow so hard that I can't wait.

No longer.

I crawl up her body and plank over her. "Look at me, Cara."

Her dilated gaze locks with mine. The hair sticks to her forehead. A bead of sweat rolls down my temples and splashes on her cheek, I lick it up. I position myself at her entrance, slip my finger further into her asshole. Her mouth falls open and I am there. I swipe my tongue between her lips at the same time that I thrust my dick into her.

She surges up to meet me. She wraps her legs around my waist, loops her arms around my neck and kicks her core forward, taking in every millimeter of my shaft. I slip so deep inside of her that my heart stops for a fraction of a second. The head of my dick nudges that secret core of her.

I tilt my pelvis, drag her hips up, and my cock lengthens, slipping in deeper than I have ever been inside of her.

My knot broadens, fills her entrance. Stretching her, readying her, and all along, I can't stop kissing her. I dance my tongue over hers, open myself to her. Let the pounding ache in my chest flare out until every centimeter of skin on my body tightens in anticipation. Until I am sure I am consuming both of us.

I curve my finger inside her back hole and lock my dick behind her pelvic bone.

147

Chloe

Drat him.

Drat him.

My belly clenches, my eyes roll back in my head. Waves of sensations wash up my legs, my thighs, crowding in on my womb, swirling there, thrusting up my spine to meet the aching, screaming ball of fire in my chest. The storm of sensations crashes around me and my body bucks. My shoulders lift off of the bed. I fling back my head and scream. He swallows up the sound, sucks up every last whine of need. His dick seems to thicken, stretching my channel. I want to come. I need to come. A scream wells up my throat. My body vibrates with the intense, horrible, aching stretching, yearning. I have to...got to orgasm...

You don't come until I let you.

I freeze.

My shoulders tense.

My thigh muscles tense.

I wait. Wait. For his command. For the alpha's permission. His body seems to grow heavier. A cloud of heat spools from him, hovering over me, holding me in place. For a beat. Another. We stay suspended. What is he waiting for? He's filling me up, yet I am so empty. A yawning, mass of something whirls inside of me, aching for him. Can't he understand that I have to come? A sob wells up, fills my throat. Please. Please. Then his big body trembles.

A purr jolts up his massive chest and coils in mine.

Are we on the same wavelength? Can he feel everything I am? Flashes of white and red blaze bright behind my closed eyelids, another vibration squeals up my spine. I stretch my body, dig my heels into his back. Press my palms into the unforgiving muscles of his shoulders. He's all around me, surrounding me, his weight pushing me down into the bed. His shaft pulses, his knot hardens even more. Too much. Too full. He kicks his hips forward and my entire body rocks up the bed. The weight of his body holds me in place. The penetration of his dick tethers me to this plane. He tears his mouth from mine. "Come for me."

I shatter.

Waves of lust scream over me. I open my mouth, but no sound emerges. I am too far gone. My entire body bucks, my neck snaps back. The sensations don't stop. Don't stop. My body gives in. My mind shuts down. My brain cells seem to fire all at once. Something snaps in my chest, my womb spasms. Slickness flows out from my core and every muscle in his body goes solid.

"Fuck, Cara."

He drops his head and digs his teeth into the side of my neck. On the other side from where he had bitten me last. Pain blasts down my spine, crashes down to meet the ball of hurt in my chest, and I squeal and try to wriggle away. But he holds me. The merciless brute shoves more of his weight on me until I can't move. My chest feels like it's going to burst, and yet, he doesn't let go. My pussy clamps down on his cock, and his big body shudders, and that's when he comes. He shoots hot bursts of cum into my womb. Too much. Too full. He growls and the sound rakes over my sensitized skin, "Open your eyes."

I raise my eyelids and fire, amber, flames...his burning gaze fills my vision.

"I wanted to trust you, to share my life with you, but your betrayal changed all of that. I tried to leave you... I did." His eyes narrow into slits and I try to focus. His face fades in and out of my line of sight.

What's he saying? It's important, whatever it is. I stare at his features, try to read his lips.

"But the mating bond connects us."

I blink up at him. He is my mate, so a bond between us is expected, right?

"We are stuck with each other."

His breath whispers over my cheek. A lover's touch. His sweat stains my skin. His presence holds me captive. And it would be so easy to simply give in. To waft along on this beautiful sensation that fulfills everything I want. And I want what it means. I want to roll in his essence and allow him to do as he pleases with me. He'd pleasure me. He'd hurt me, but even that would feel good. He'd use me and I'd let him. He'd breed me...and that...my womb trembles, reminding me of the biggest secret that I have yet to tell him.

"I'd wanted to give you your freedom, to make you my rightful partner, but clearly, I can't trust you, so why do I want you so much?"

He stares at me intently.

"Why do I want to protect you?"

A vein throbs at his temple.

"And punish you?"

He's not making any sense. I clear my throat to ask but he shakes his head. O-k-a-y. He doesn't want me to speak. Apparently, that alphahole part of him is back.

"You're fucking mine, Cara. Mine to rut when I need. Mine to love if I choose. Mine to breed. To hate. To knot..." His cock throbs. Every ridge of that turgid muscle seems to be imprinted into my channel. "I decide when you come. Your every single orgasm belongs to me."

He tilts his hips and a wave of awareness vibrates up from my toes.

He slides a second finger into my back hole and my butt clenches.

"Your every hole is mine to ravish." He leans down and licks my lips. "Your mouth is mine to plunder." He drags his hand up my body to cup my breast. "Your flesh is mine to mark." He rubs his thumb over my nipple and I want to pant. Want to moan. But my throat is dry. I stare, part my lips and his jaw firms. He lets go of my breast, smooths a tendril of hair from my forehead. His touch is light, the gesture so gentle, I could almost pretend that we were lovers. That he cares for me. And he does, in his own way...but it isn't enough. He tilts his hips and his crotch presses into my cunt. Pinpricks of awareness flare out, ladder up my back. "I can't return you to Zeus."

Eh?

"I am going to have to find another way to negotiate with him."

He doesn't want to let me go? Isn't that what I want?

He leans down and kisses me. Hard lips. Soft touch. He nibbles his way down to the hollow of my neck.

The sexual haze crowds in on my mind and I blink. Try to clear my mind. I need to think, think. Something is not right. He drags his lips up to my temple. He presses a kiss to the wrinkle between my brows and I shudder. I can almost believe that he can be gentle.

"I want to treat you right, take care of you, but how can I do that when every time I turn my back, I am convinced that you will pull a fast one over me?" His forehead furrows, then he firms his shoulders, "I am afraid you leave me no choice but to make you my captive again."

No. No. I shake my head and he pinches my chin, restraining me.

"Yes." His gaze is cold, emotionless. "I'll feed you and protect you and rut you when needed. Our child—children," the skin around his eye softens. "Will be my successors. They will have the best of everything.

Child. My child. Our children. I will never allow that. Never.

"You will do as I command."

No.

"Your choices belong to me."

Something inside of me snaps. I'd preferred to escape from my home country than to give up my freedom to the Vikings. I'd survived Talon. I want this alpha. Need him right now...but submit that completely? Give up the ability to decide my own future? I toss my head, "Never".

148

Kayden

"What did you say?"

My voice comes out harsh and I hate myself for it. Anger surges under my skin, and the band around my chest tightens.

She tosses her head. "You can control my body, Alpha, but not my mind."

"You will not deny me."

I thrust my face into hers and she doesn't blink. Doesn't wince. Huh?

The little thing has so much courage? She'd never back down from me. She's proven that to me over and over again. Is that why I am so addicted to her touch? Heat flushes my chest. She's a challenge I'll never grow tired of.

"You will agree to my every demand."

She shakes her head and my groin tightens. Every time she defies me, it's a fucking turn on. The more she pushes me away the more I want her. The more she goes toe to toe with me, the more I want to make her submit. The more she defies me...the more I fucking care for her. It's fucked up, this...this link that connects us. The chemistry that sizzles between us.

My knot loosens and I slip out from her; a stream of liquid gushes out from between her legs. I pull away and she follows me up. A smirk curls my lips.

I can't let her leave me, that much had been true. Fact is, I need her more than I am letting on. Her softness, her very presence calms me. Her soul soothes me. And our children— My heart stutters. Her growing big with my child, mine. I cannot let her out of my sight. If I do, she'll leave me and I cannot lose her. And that...that is the reason for my being an overbearing, overprotective, alphahole. Not that it's very different from what I am inside. What had she called me? Neanderthal. Yeah, that's what I am.

I am acting true to my real nature, so why is she so surprised? Why does she try to wriggle away from me?

She slides down toward the foot of the bed, then swings her legs over.

I click my tongue.

She stills, her spine snaps straight.

"Turn around."

Her hands curl into fists at her side. But she doesn't move away. Interesting. Can I have that much power over her? Can she actually not break this hold I exert on her? I flip myself on my back, fold my arms behind my head.

"Now." I infuse enough dominance into my tone and her shoulders hunch.

She's fighting the attraction. A flush crawls up her spine and she brings up her knees to her chest. Goosebumps dot her skin and she rocks herself from side to side. She's going to try to resist me. *As if she stands a chance?*

I draw out a purr from the pit of my stomach, up my chest. I draw it out, let the sound loop around her, and she stills.

I project my voice around her, swirling, merging my presence with hers. She shudders, then shoots me a glance over her shoulder.

Pupils blown, the dark irises so huge that they fill her eyes. A sliver of green peeks out from the edges.

My groin tightens.

That visible evidence of her arousal, it's a fucking turn on. A sign of how connected we are. Of how she can't resist me. Of course not.

I draw out another purr and she turns around on her hands and knees.

Another purr and she crawls toward me.

Her cheeks are flushed. Her blond hair tumbled about her shoulders.

I growl and she snarls. She bares her lips, shows me her little teeth, and fuck me, but I almost come right then. The blood rushes to my groin, my dick lengthens, and her gaze darts there.

She scuttles right into the 'V' between my legs, until her face hangs over my crotch. She licks her lips and my shaft distends further. The head swells, shining from the mixture of our essences. "You want me, Cara?"

Her breathing deepens. She doesn't look at me, doesn't glance away from my cock.

I click my tongue and she swivels her head. Her features twist in pain? In lust? Need. Sheer need. Agonizing. Craving. I am as much a drug to her as she is for me. My chest seizes. Why is that so beautiful? So...so everything I want. What I desire.

"You need to earn the right to suck my dick."

Her gaze narrows. Fuck me for toying with her. Why am I denying her, denying myself? Why am I being so mean? Why can't I show her what I truly feel? This emo shit? I suck at it. I am pussywhipped as it is...pussy...her cunt. A purr surges from my lips. I slap my chest, "Come 'ere."

Before the words have left my lips, she jumps...she leaps onto my chest and I catch her around her waist. She squeaks, her eyes widen. I haul her up and position her with her core over my face. "Hold on."

I lower her until her thighs are on either side of my face.

Her knees dig into the mess of clothes...her nest, on which we lie. I may own her, but she has exerted her control on me as well.

She's surrounded me with her claim, her nest that she had fashioned with her own hands.

I may have built a clan, but she had built the space inside which I wanted to claim her. My chest hurts. My temples throb. Everything in me pushes, tugs, fucking urges me to raise my chin and bring her down so she's riding my face.

I lick her cunt and she mewls. I drag my tongue up her swollen pussy folds and she squeals and mumbles in that exotic language that goes straight to my head.

I fuck her with my tongue, in-out-in from that melting, beautiful channel and she flails and wriggles her waist and tries to pull away and I've had it. I'm never letting her go, no matter what she thinks.

Her freedom, her choices, belong to me.

I lift her up, tearing her from my mouth, and she freezes.

Slick drips down in a long thread from between her legs and I lick it up. I flick my tongue over my lips. Are they as swollen as the flesh of her cunt?

"Not fair you have all the fun, sweetheart. It's my turn now."

149

Chloe

I hate him. Hate him. Savage. Beast. A brute who takes, who commands me, who denies me.

I peel back my lips and snarl, and he laughs.

He raises his chin, showing off the beautiful sculpted chords of his throat, and my belly clenches. Spectacular. How can someone so, so mean be so...so gorgeous? I am entranced. Can't look away from him. "You want me?" He trains that burning gaze on my face and my heart...my stupid heart skitters.

"Answer me."

I nod.

"Good girl."

I flush. My cheeks burn. Why does his approval mean so much? Why do I want to find a way out of this beautiful mess of my own creation?

He deposits me back on his chest. That massive wall of muscle that ebbs and flows under me. I scramble down, my legs slip off, and I grasp his waist on either side with my thighs.

"Show me how much you want me."

Huh?

He folds his arms back behind his neck. The impressive biceps bulge. I want to reach and touch them, drag my fingers over the mass of muscles and trace their sculpted firmness. I clutch my fingers at my side and one side of his lips lifts up. "Your expression tells me how much you desire me, so why don't you give in to it."

What? What in the blazes is he talking about? I frown at him and his grin widens. "Guess I have to tell you everything, hmm?" He jerks his chin towards his chest. "Touch me."

No.

He angles his head, "I can make you."

Yes he can, and all without trying.

He has to start that blasted, infernal, beautiful purring, that sound that is fast becoming the anthem of my life, the bane of my existence, and I'd do anything he wanted. I huff out a sigh and his features relax. Huh. Guess he hadn't been that sure of himself either? Hmm. I bring my palms up and place them on his chest. I flatten my palms over the vital planes of his flesh. Warmth, heat, pulsing energy sparks up my fingertips and I almost pull back.

"I won't melt."

I glance up at his face.

"Touch me like you mean it, Cara."

Maybe it's because he called me Cara, or perhaps because he asked me...almost politely. An underlying whiff of need streaks his words and a yearning flares to life between my legs.

I dig my fingernails into his planes and he groans. Huh? I drag my fingers up his chest and around his nipples. His muscles bunch.

"Bloody hell."

The harsh edge of his tone scratches over my skin. My thighs clench. I flick his distended male nipple and he growls. Warmth swells my chest. This is...different. I can make him respond to me. Why hadn't I thought of that before? The flesh between my legs throbs. I lean down and bite his nipple and he snarls. Waves of awareness swell around me and I gasp.

He's angry with me.

He's going to punish me.

I peer up at him from under my eyelashes and his features are flushed. A vein pops at his temple. "Don't. Stop."

O-k-a-y.

I let go of his nipple and move to lick his other one and he groans. I circle his other nipple with my fingers then nip my way down his chest. His muscles flex under my fingers, sweat beads his flesh and I lick it up.

"Fucking killing me." His voice rings out, an edge to it I recognize as desperation? Ah! I slide down his body and my butt hits a turgid hardness and I gulp. His dick teases the valley between my butt cheeks. A whine swells from my throat.

"Take me in your mouth."

I straighten and stare at his face. His eyes are squeezed shut. His throat moves as he swallows. I've never seen him this...this vulnerable. Is this the only way to communicate with him? Sex? He's an alpha with a massive appetite for me...of course, I am his weakness.

He wants me; he's never hidden that from me.

So why can't I use it to get what I want?

If I give him what he wants… If I pleasure him, play his body as he has done mine. If I submit to him completely...will he trust me again?

All of my cells resonate with the truth of what I am thinking.

Give in.

Pleasure him.

Show him how good it can be when you are willing...and then...then take what you need from him.

My muscles tense and he raises his eyelids. Fixes those burning amber eyes on me. "Do it."

I scramble down his body until my face is poised over his crotch. His cock is thick, swollen, and juts up toward his face. I lick the dark blue vein that runs up the underside and his hips jerk. "F-u-c-kkk," he gasps.

Oh, yeah. My chest contracts. A surge of satisfaction shoots up my veins. I nibble my way up to his cock, then close my mouth around the massive head. A tremor runs down his body and he stills, waiting. I tilt my head and take him further into my mouth. My teeth graze over his skin and he snarls. The taste of him fills my palate, my throat closes and I gag.

"Keep going." The thickness of his desire pushes down on my shoulders. And that...that needy edge to his tone warns me that he's close. So close to losing control. I grip the base of his shaft. He's so big that my fingers barely meet around the circumference.

He thrusts his hips and his shaft slips down my throat. Saliva drips down my chin, and I gag again. "Jerk me off, Cara, please."

Please?

He's never said that before.

Is that how much he's a slave to his base instincts?

I'd thought omegas in heat were helpless? Apparently, alphas in rut are as in thrall to their desires; and Kayden is in full blown rut, I am sure of that. No other reason he'd plead with me. Ask me to pleasure him. And he had rescued me from the Viking. He needs me as much.

My chest swells.

My pussy contracts.

I pull back and his dick slips out. The swelling head of his cock touches my lips and I close my mouth around him again. A purr swells from him, and another.

Sweat beads my brow. I take him down my throat, pull back, and take him in again. I suck his flesh, curl my tongue around the pulsing head.. His dick lengthens. His muscles tighten. Then I cup his balls and he comes.

150

Kayden

Fucking hell. Too fast, I am coming too soon.

My groin tightens, my cock elongates, my balls draw up and I shoot my cum down her throat. The orgasm tears through me, swells my chest, hardening my biceps and sweeping up my neck. It explodes behind my eyes, and fuck me, but I see stars.

When I open my eyes, she's staring at me.

Her chest heaves. Her shoulders pull back. My cum drips down her chin, over her throat. Her breasts tremble, the areolae around her nipples glistening from my earlier ministrations. Perfectly broken. Perfectly marked. Perfectly mine. Something snaps deep inside of me.

All thoughts drain from my head just as she had drained my balls earlier. A piercing need twists my guts. My cock thickens again, standing to attention. I swoop down and grip her waist. She shivers. I lift her up and position her over my erect dick and she gulps. Her pupils dilate further, all trace of green leached from them. She's so light, so small, how did I fit inside of her? I need to find out.

I lower her onto my shaft.

She wraps her fingers around my wrists, pushes down with her knees on either side of my waist. She slips down my turgid dick. Hot. Slick. Fucking beautiful. I drop my gaze to where her cunt snaps around me.

She takes me in just as she had sucked me down her throat earlier. This woman...? She won't stop until she's consumed me. And I'd gladly allow her.

My chest throbs.

I kick my hips and thrust up and she drops down further.

She locks into place, the missing piece of my puzzle. My knot wedges inside of her, thrumming, expanding. I can't stop the purr that throbs up my chest. She sways over me, her hips circling; a hum vibrates from her lips. We're locked in a dance, in a space of our own, one where no one else can intrude and it's...it's something I'd never thought I'd experience.

A pressure builds behind my eyeballs. The fuck is happening?

All of these emotions are messing with my head. An alpha who loses control is worth shit.

His men don't respect him.

His clan senses his weakness and dismisses him. And his omega...? She raises her chin and meets my gaze.

Her features light up. Her eyes shine. Her thick, glossy hair waves about her shoulders. She senses it. Loves it. She feels all of it, all of me, and it's so intimate. I thrust up into her. My dick locks into place behind her pelvic bone. I slide a hand up her curves to grip her nape. I hold her in place. Imprisoned. Riding my dick. I plunge into her like I want to break her in half. And I do. Except she's also broken me.

"Come."

She throws her head back. Her cries echo around the place. Her pussy milks my dick and I explode, shooting hot streams of cum into her. She slumps, her body twitches, and I lower her to my chest. My knot loosens and I slip out of her, but don't move. Her breathing deepens. Her heart beats steady. When the silken strands of her hair wrap around my palm I look down to find that I am running my fingers through the spun gold.

This once, I'll allow myself to touch her. I'll indulge the heavy sensation that weighs down my limbs. My shoulders jerk and sleep drags me down.

I come awake with a start.

It's dark in the room. Starlight pours in from outside. Warmth tickles my skin. I glance down to find Cara snuggled up on my chest.

She's curled up, legs drawn up, her cheek pillowed under her arm. I feather my knuckles over her chin. She mumbles, then quietens.

I wait another beat.

When she's completely still, I scoop her up carefully and deposit her next to me on the sodden nest of clothes. She doesn't move. The breath whooshes out of me. Right. Now I am worried about waking her up? I shake my head to clear it.

My shoulders ache. My balls throb. Cara's doing a number on me, and strangely, I don't mind it. I don't trust her, but hell if I don't want her with me, around me. I slide to the edge of the bed, swing my legs over the side and stand. My stomach rumbles. Food. We need food. I look around for my pants. Oh, wait, she'd stripped me of them.

My lip curls.

I'd asked her suck me off, and she had. Her mouth...her mouth was a potent weapon. And no, I'm never gonna tell her that. To do so will reveal how much control she has over me. I turn to glance at the sleeping woman.

I tug at the nest of clothes, cover her with it, then smooth the fabric under her chin. Now I am tucking her in? The fuck? Turning, I rise to my feet and stalk to the closet.

I pick up a pair of pants and step into them, then swivel around and to the door. My bare feet thump on the wooden steps as I walk down and to the kitchen. I am almost at the door when I hear it. The sound of cabinets being opened and closed, the rattle of crockery... I stiffen.

Who could it be?

Very few people are aware of the location of this place, for a reason. It's tucked away in a remote corner of the Highlands.

I grip my fists at my side, then step into the room. Someone's bent over and rummaging around on the lower shelves. I curl my fingers into fists and charge in. The person straightens, turns around, and drops the plate she is holding.

"Kayden?"

"Lisa?" I change the angle of my hit.

My fist grazes her shoulder.

She stumbles, the plate falls toward the ground. I swoop down and catch it, then straighten and place the plate on the island. "The hell are you doing here?"

She clasps her fingers together in front of her. "I...I..."

I frown and she gulps. "I came here to apologize."

I glare at her.

She swallows, "I am sorry for what I did."

My guts twist. "If not for the fact that you were Dom's daughter, I'd have killed you on the spot."

She shuffles her feet, "I came to thank you for your generosity."

"Don't thank me. I did it for Dom."

She stiffens, "My father doesn't care about me."

That's where she's wrong. Dom would lay down his life for his daughter. Not that it's my place to tell her that. This father-daughter impasse is something they have to figure out. "Speaking of which, why did he allow you out?"

She straightens her spine, "I escaped."

"You disobeyed my direct order?" The blood thuds at my temples. "You defied me, again?

"Kayden... I...I had to see you." She takes a step forward and her scent washes over me. Syrupy and sharp. It's all wrong. I lean back on my heels and she frowns. "Give me a chance to make it up to you."

"You put my omega at risk," I roll my shoulders. "You wanted to hurt me. Why should I forgive you?"

She shakes her head and grips her fingers together so tightly that her knuckles whiten. "I had no idea the Vikings would harm you. If I had, I'd never have trusted them." Her jaw firms.

"What did you expect?" I fold my arms over my chest. "They loathe us. They'd do anything to take over our cities and kill our people."

She squeezes her eyes shut. "I thought...I thought that I could use that hate to my advantage."

"You put her at risk, and endangered the lives of the clan. What did you think you'd get in return?"

"You." Her eyes snap open.

"The fuck you talking about?"

Her features twist, "For an alpha who leads one of the most powerful clans in the region, you've never seen what's right in front of your eyes."

"Enough." I plant my palms on my hips. "Say what's on your mind before I lose my temper completely."

She takes a step forward and this time I don't move. I wait. She pauses not a few inches away and lifts her chin. "I thought if I got her out of your sight you'd notice me."

I straighten.

"I want you, Kayden. I always have."

I shake my head.

"I wanted to be yours."

I rub my hand over my face. Bloody hell, I fucking hate this emo shit. "I've always thought about you as...as..." My mind comes up blank. Fact is, I had never noticed her. She had been Dom's daughter. Period. A girl who had grown up in front of my eyes. She had been out of bounds for me and I had never felt anything with her. Not the way it had been with Cara. That explosive chemistry, that insane need to throw her down and rip into her, to rut her, kiss her, make her orgasm...nope, there had been not a smidgen of that need with Lisa.

"It's not too late, Kayden, I don't care what you did or didn't think of me, just give me a chance." She sinks to her knees in front of me and I stare.

The fuck?

She reaches for my zipper and I don't react. Maybe I am too surprised by her boldness. Maybe the fact that she is Dom's daughter makes me hesitate from shoving her away? Perhaps Cara is already making me so weak that I want to find a way to let Lisa down gently.

Or perhaps...perhaps my base nature comes to the fore.

Do I want to find out how it would be with another woman, after being with Cara? Would I feel anything at all? Am I actually turning down the offer of free pussy?

After all, I am an alpha. I take. Nothing binds me down. I can do as I want, right?

Right.

Lisa lowers the zipper and takes out my shaft, then dips her head toward me.

151

Chloe

Kayden's broad back is naked. His legs are spread wide. There's a woman on her knees in between them.

I watch from the doorway, my line of sight unrestricted, as she raises herself up on her knees. Her face and hands are blocked by his body but the jerking movement of her torso leaves no doubt of what's happening between them.

She's blowing him. Not hours after I had made him come in my mouth, and all over me.

The hell?

I curl my fingers into fists and squeeze so hard that my nails dig into the flesh of my palms.

He had fucked me in his bed, on the nest I had woven.

He had claimed me again.

He had marked me and then he had left. He had walked down here to be...serviced by another omega? How could he?

Why wouldn't he?

I had betrayed him and he had clearly indicated to me that I had shattered any chances of our truly being together. He was going to keep me as his captive...though he hadn't bound me this time, nor locked the door. *Your mistake, asshole.*

He can't be that careless, can he?

Did he do it on purpose? Did he want me to come down and find another woman servicing him?

Is this how he was going to get back at me?

A ball of hurt coils in my chest, clogs my throat. I hear the murmur of his voice. Her body goes taut. She replies, but I'm too far away to discern the words.

She sits back on her heels and I catch sight of her face.

Lisa?

The omega who had drugged me and had me taken to Talon? The woman who wanted Kayden, and apparently he wasn't averse to her touch either.

She wipes the back of her palm over her mouth, then looks straight at me. Her mouth curves in a triumphant smile. My chest heaves. My eyeballs hurt. I am not going to cry. I am not. I look down at myself and realize I am dressed. I am not sure how, but I had paused long enough to pull on a dress.

I am barefoot, but that's too bad.

No way, am I going to stay here.

No way, am I going to allow him to hurt me again. I had given him my body because I wanted to. I am drawn to him...sick as that may be. *Who developed emotions for the man who'd once taken her without mercy?* But his dominance, his personality, his sheer will is my aphrodisiac. When I was with him, I knew what I wanted. I knew who he was. My other half. My opposite. He defined me, and how pathetic was that?

How could I let one man rule my entire life?

I had submitted to him completely from the moment I'd seen him. That omega essence of me had resonated with him. No other male could arouse me this way.

I was bonded to him.

Okay, so I hadn't actively accepted him — The ball of heat in my chest stabs into my ribcage and I wince. Apparently my body thinks otherwise.

I swivel on my heels and walk toward the exit. The bond flickers, fades in and out, yanks at me with such force that my shoulders pull back. My back curves. No, no. I will not give in to this pull toward him.

I will not allow him to insult me.

Surely, he'd arranged it all? He'd set up that little scene. He'd ensured that I would see him being...unfaithful?

What had I expected?

That despite his alphaholeness, the meanness, the way he'd treated me so far, he'd never stray from me?

Everything he'd done, the way he'd claimed me, had allowed me to feather my nest with the clothes he'd been wearing...he'd been tender in his own way. Caring. I hiccup, then thrust my knuckles into my mouth to contain the pathetic noises that emerge from my throat. How wrong I'd been. *How right.* Not that whatever was between us could ever last. Never. My chest grows heavy. My head begins to pound.

I quicken my footsteps to the main door, fling it open. I step into the fresh air and shiver. No time to stop. Don't look back. Don't turn. Keep going.

I stumble down the steps, then lurch around the drive. Out of the main gates. I need to get away before he discovers my absence. If he does, he'll come after me and I don't want that.

I can't let him get to me.

I will not let him cast that mesmerizing alpha net over me. One touch of his and I'll give in. The sound of his purring will seduce me, will draw me back into his sphere of influence. I have had enough. *Enough.* The heat courses through my veins and I pant. A chill chases it down and I gasp. Run. Chloe. Run. I race down the slope, gravity carrying me down. I sway wildly from side to side. My legs hurt. My thighs bunch. No, I will not stop, no. I pick up my pace. Keep running. Toward the tree line, then farther. As far as I can get away from him. The sweat pours down my forehead into my eyes and I blink.

I keep going, stumble over a rock, then tumble over the side of the path and toward the undergrowth.

When I come to, it's dark.

I try to sit up and my head spins.

"Stay still, you're hurt."

I peer through the gloom. The harsh features of a face peer down at me. *Kayden?* I reach out a hand. The man tilts his head and moonlight haloes his head.

Blonde hair, skin so pale that it glows, cruel lips. No. Not Kayden. I shrink back and he raises his hands.

"I won't harm you."

Right. I've heard that one before.

I twist my lips, and that little move sends pain vibrating through my head. I groan and sink back against the ground. Pebbles bite into my back and I wince.

"Sorry, I didn't want to move you, in case you were badly hurt." Talon squats down next to me.

"How long..." I swallow. "How long have I been out?"

"Half an hour, maybe a little more."

I blink. Little pinpricks of pain knock at my temples, "What are you doing here?"

He doesn't reply, just holds up a canteen filled with water. I reach for it and my biceps protest. A moan of pain swells up my throat.

"I'd help you, but..."

"But?" I take the canteen and raise it to my lips. The water soothes my parched mouth, the scratchy itch in my throat.

"Then he'd scent you on me, and we don't want that."

"We don't?"

He shakes his head.

I hand back the bottle and he corks it, then slings it over his back. "I have a proposition for you."

"And I should entertain you, why?" I cough and my entire body shakes.

He leans in closer and my hackles rise. My stomach twists.

He stares at me.

"Hear me out, and in return, I promise I will not touch you."

I frown at him. "You saved me from your alphas only to send others after me." I shake my head. "Why?"

"Bait."

Huh? I stiffen.

"Your mate was alive. I needed to find him. I had no doubt that he'd come for you. It was the most efficient route." His piercing blue eyes are placid. So cold. I shiver and pull my legs closer to my chest.

"Not my mate," I mutter.

He leans back on his heels. His features compose into a bored look. "Doesn't matter to me what he is to you. You are Zeus' mate's sister. Kayden has shown he will put his life in danger to save you."

If only he knew how wrong he is. I bite the inside of my cheek. What does he want? Why does he keep appearing out of nowhere? He has something in mind. A plan of some kind. "You hate them both because their actions killed your father?"

He pauses, as if considering my question. His face is impassive. The man has no emotions. No soul. I'd thought Kayden was mean...but I've always sensed the maelstrom of confusion that lurks under the surface. It makes him more vulnerable than I'd care to admit. But this Viking? He is unstoppable. Nothing will get to him.

"The world is a better place without that old bastard."

What the — ? I stare.

"What is it with you alpha males? All of you seem to have a hate-hate relationship with your old man."

The wind changes and he sniffs the air. His nostrils flare, his pupils dilate. "I don't desire you, Omega, but I can't resist your pheromone saturated scent."

I dig my fingers into the ground and push a few inches away from him. "What do you want from me?"

He inclines his head. "My father was wrong about almost everything. But he was right to go after Zeus and Kayden. I want their territories. Power, dear Omega. I am far more ambitious than my loser of a parent. He thought with his dick."

And you don't? I bite the inside of my cheek. Every alpha ultimately gives in to the lust inside of him. The need to rut and possess is a far more potent urge than he realizes. No alpha can resist the right omega. They are as beholden to their cocks as we omegas are to our estrus. A surge of warmth pools between my legs. My limbs tremble and I pant.

He leans in close. His chest heaves as he fills his lungs. This is when he shows his true colors. When he grabs me and threatens me, or worse, forces his way with me. His jaw firms. His shoulders grow solid, then he rises to his feet.

The hell? This alpha means what he said? He's actually going to walk away from me? No way can he exercise such restraint. Not unless...unless, "Do you have an omega of your own?"

He stiffens, "Why do you say that?"

"Because..." What should I say? How can I put into words what I am thinking without insulting his ego?

He may have greater restraint than other alphas, but the hard set of his frame, the way his shoulders bunch as he paces, his fingers clenched into fists at his sides; all of it indicates he's hanging onto his control with difficulty. But hell, I'd faced Kayden. I hadn't come this far to shy away. I raise my chin, "Because you stepped away."

He pauses, then swivels around to face me. "I need you to return in the same condition that I found you."

My lips twist. "With his scent imprinted into my skin?"

"Exactly." His lips flatten. "It's the only way for you to play the part I have in store for you."

"Which is?"

"You will engage with Kayden. You will keep him occupied."

I start to speak and he holds up a hand.

I flatten my lips.

"In fact, you will submit to him with such passion that he cannot think of anything else but you."

"You want him...distracted?"

"I want him prisoner." He widens his stance.

"You want to use him as leverage with Zeus?"

His lips draw up in a smile that doesn't meet his eyes. "My men were too quick to draw the last time." He shifts his weight from foot to foot. "This time, I won't leave anything to chance. I intend to plan carefully. You keep his attention diverted. Once my reinforcements arrive, I'll move in and take him by surprise."

I throw up my hands. "Why do all of you want me to fit in with your plans? Why is it that everywhere I turn, one of you asks me for help?"

"I am not asking you." He drums his fingers on his chest. "If you don't comply, I'll get my alphas to finish off what your mate started."

My stomach twists. Of course he would. So easy for these men to demonstrate their power over us. Just because they have cocks and wield them like weapons. Use them to spread their seed and bring errant omegas like me to heel. Except they haven't reckoned with me.

None of them have.

If he wants to use me, so be it. I can play him too. I can play all of them. I am not an omega who schemes. What you see is what you get with me. But these monsters...all of them...including Kayden and yes, his alphahole of a half-brother Zeus...all of them had manipulated me, had assumed that I'd do what they wanted. And I had. And now I am done. Now it's time for me to be smart. To be the kind of princess that Lucy has always been. Strong. Taking no shit from these men. Going after what I hunger for most.

"Fine."

I lurch up to my feet. My knees almost give way and I stumble, then right myself. It's agony to be upright, but no way am I letting another alphahole gain an advantage over me. If I am going to have this conversation, it will be standing up. The alpha hulks over me.

He's as big, as massive, as broad as Kayden. Except his face is all wrong. His features fade in and out in front of my eyes and I shake my head to clear it.

"I'll do what you want."

His shoulders relax. Huh? Honestly, he'd actually thought I wouldn't fall in line? Or does he want me to do as he asks so desperately?

"But you must first answer my questions."

He snarls. And the sound is rich, heavy, all wrong. Not like Kayden's voice. His laugh. His rasp, his growls. His groans as he'd come inside of me.

Goosebumps flare on my skin. Why am I thinking of him, again?

"Well?" I frown.

His features harden, "Let's get one thing straight. No-one, certainly no woman bargains with me—"

"Except you need me and so you'll listen to me."

He growls, the tendons of his neck flexing.

I've done it, he's going to kill me now.

His shoulders go solid, "Speak."

My muscles relax, the relief so strong that my knees weaken again. I press my feet into the ground and steady myself, "Why are you letting me go unscathed?" *Why do I need to know?* Isn't it enough that he isn't touching me? But my darn curiosity. When I see something I don't understand, I need to pursue it, need to find out why.

The skin creases at the corners of his eyes. "You're not the omega I seek."

"You have someone else in mind?"

He glares at me. Dominance leaps off of him in a dense cloud and I look away. Okay, don't push this one further. Don't.

This Talon? His control is greater than Kayden's, but when that breaks, the beast that emerges will be far more violent. God help the omega he has set his attentions on. And he has someone in mind. That much is clear. More heat flushes my skin. Sweat breaks out on my brow. A ball of fear bubbles up and I swallow to clear my throat.

"I'll do as you ask, but in return, you grant me my independence."

He frowns. "You can't survive without an alpha and you want —"

"Choice."

His biceps flex.

"I want to decide my own destiny." I lower my chin to my chest. "Is that too much to ask? All of you men take what you need. You give in to your impulses, indulge your passions. Why is an omega asking for the same such a surprise?"

"My sister would applaud your sentiment."

I raise my gaze to his face, "Sis — ?"

"Enough." He tosses his head. "You keep him distracted enough for me to capture him. The rest, I don't care about."

"So...deal?"

"It's your life..." His lips twist, "or lack of."

152

Kayden

"Where the fuck is she?"

I grab the pile of clothes from the bed and fling them on the floor. They smell of her, of us.

They remind me of how I'd taken her, wanted her...fucking lost myself in her. And now she isn't here. I growl, glance around and spot the iron stand next to the bed. I stalk toward it, grab it, then swing it at the wall. It hits the barrier; chunks of brick and plaster from the ceiling crash to the ground. I toss my head. Not enough. It's not nearly enough. I snatch up the chair near the bed and fling it toward the far end of the room. It hits the floor and shatters. More. I need more. I need her. But she left. I've searched the entire bloody place.

Gone from room to room calling out her name.

I had shared myself with her. No, I had held back. I had allowed my physical urges to come to the fore—that was easier than revealing my true sentiments. All that emo shit...I don't believe in it...but hell, what do I call this hurt that coils in my chest? This pain that snakes over my shoulders, around my neck, pulling tight, so tight that my lungs compress.

I had broken her, I'd thought... I was wrong. She had betrayed me and I had let her live. I had been thinking with my dick. I am *still* thinking with my cock. So what? I am an alpha. It was my prerogative to bury my cock in my...my mate. I had willed myself to not move as Lisa had taken out my cock. As she had reached for it, opened her mouth...and I'd realized that I couldn't let her go through with it.

Me!

I chuckle, and the vibrations hurt my throat.

Me, the alphahole who had never turned away an omega in his life. Who knew how to satisfy every single woman who I had taken to bed...my fucking cock had refused to rise in her grasp? I had stepped back and tucked myself into my pants, had ordered her to leave.

She'd wiped her mouth, looked ahead, and a smile had curved her lips. My heart had raced and I had swung around, my senses screaming, but there had been no one. My blood had pounded in my temples and I had raced up to the bedroom, but she had been gone. Had she seen us? Nah, I don't think so.

Hadn't stopped me from bustling Lisa out of there. I'd marched her to the door and commanded her to go to Dom. To stay with the Clan until I'd figured out what to do with her. I stiffen. Mistake. I should have locked her up in one of the rooms, and kept her prisoner until I'd been ready to leave. But the thought of any other woman in the same building as me and Cara had made my skin crawl. Nothing...no one was allowed to stay under this roof, except my mate. This space was...my child-hood home...it was sacred. Only my parents and Marcus' daughter, who had been the closest I'd had to a sibling, had been here. Until Chloe. A-n-d, I didn't want anyone in the vicinity when I fucked her again.

I blow out a breath.

Fucking sentiments hidden inside of me have a way of revealing themselves when I least expect it.

It has to be this connection with Cara that's making me weak. It's why the thought of what I'd allowed Lisa to do rankles in my mind.

I mean, I had turned Lisa away, right?

I had done nothing wrong.

So why is it that my muscles bunch, my shoulders grow tense at the memory of her fingers on my dick? I had let another omega touch me. I had entertained the fleeting thought of allowing Lisa to seduce me, to test myself. To see how far I could push it, if I could go back to being what I had been—a bastard alpha who never walked away from omega pussy...and that...that fucker is gone.

Replaced by this sorry pussy-whipped asshole. Fuck! I throw my head back and howl. The noise echoes back from the empty walls. Mocking me. Taunting me.

I let Chloe get away.

Why hadn't I locked the room, why?

I had trusted her. And she had broken my belief in her. Again.

I lurch forward, glare around the space. There. I walk to the mirror in the corner. Bloody antique. Hate it. Hate looking at myself in it. My fucking reflection that reminds me of my blood father. The asshole who I had hated more than anyone else... No, not true. I hate myself even more.

I grab the relic with both of my hands and heave it up and over my head. Biceps straining, shoulders aching, I bend my knees to accommodate the extra weight. Sweat pops on my brow and I growl. The tendons in my throat pop and I turn around and aim at the door. When she walks in.

The fuck?

She sidles in, head bent, eyes downcast. Huh? She shoots me a glance from under hooded eyelids, as if waiting for the other shoe to drop.

My legs scream with the extra weight I am carrying. I take a step forward, and another, straighten my arms and she flinches.

Fear leaches from her, her scent teasing my senses. Beautiful. Familiar. What I want.

"It's bad luck to break a mirror." Her voice cuts through the noise in my head.

"The fuck I care?"

She bites her lip. "It's dangerous to have glass shards all over the floor."

Right. I don't want her getting hurt. Don't want the sharp edges to dig into the soft skin of her feet and draw blood. Nah. Only I have that prerogative. Ha! I lower the heavy-ass frame. Don't miss how her shoulders relax.

A warmth fills my chest and I push it away.

Why does it matter that she is relieved?

I stalk to the corner and lower the mirror to the floor. I swing around. She's still there, thank fuck!

I drag my fingers through my hair.

My bloody hand is shaking. Must be from the strain of carrying that heavy furniture. Yeah, that's all it is.

I take a step forward and my thigh muscles lock. The fuck? I shake out my leg to loosen the stiffened tissues. Move forward. Cautious? Huh? Why am I tip-toeing around her? I didn't do anything wrong. Nothing.

I straighten my shoulders, then clomp toward her. When I am a foot in front of her, I pause. "Where did you go?"

Her gaze skitters away, and she swallows.

Somehow that movement angers me more, and I am not sure why. I want her to be scared of me. I want her cowering and subdued and... No. I want her to reveal that sass which she hides so well. I want her hellfire to burn me. Cleanse me of my past. I want her to want me... The fuck?

I toss my head.

What am I thinking?

She licks her lips and my groin hardens. My dick lengthens. So I was right, my body responds solely to her. My mind is fixated on her. I growl and she shivers. I draw out a purr. She clenches her thighs. Hmm. Nice.

Then she looks at me and my gut twists. A pulse tics at my jaw. Her chest rises-falls. I can see the outline of her breasts through her dress. She has no underwear on. *Good.* She wriggles her hips, and fuck me, but precum oozes from my cock. I am not impervious to her, either. "Why did you leave?" My tone is soft. Not the tone I intended. Not the words I had wanted to say either. But it was there between us. The hell is happening to me?

She lifts her chin, "I came back."

"You did." I lock my fingers around her nape. My fingers meet around the front of her neck. Her pulse races at the hollow of her throat. She's alive. She's here. So am I. So what the fuck is my problem?

"Please don't do that." She tilts her chin up. Sweat shines on her skin. Her color is pale. Her skin so translucent that I swear I can spot the blood running in her veins.

"Do what?"

"That." She touches my throat and pinpricks of awareness flare from the contact. That's when I realize that I am growling under my breath.

"Why?"

"Because...because it turns me on." Her gaze flicks to the mess of clothes on the floor. "And I am not sure I have the strength to...to..."

Fuck?

I almost say it aloud to see the effect it has on her. She knows my body more intimately than any other woman. Only she can please me. And I am going to show her just how good it can be with me. My dick throbs, my balls harden. I am going to take her again. Just not yet. I jerk my head toward the door.

"You hungry?"

153

Chloe

"Huh?"

He stalks past me and out the door.

The brute did not scream at me.

He did not hurt me.

He did not throw me down and rut me. He didn't punish me in any way. I glance around the room and gulp. The furniture had not escaped so easily.

Clothes dot the floor. The chair lies upturned and broken in a corner. The bed stand is smashed into the wall. It protrudes from the barrier and I blink. He must have thrown it with vehemence...took serious strength to do that. And he is strong. But for the metal to break through the stone wall?

I gulp.

Fear twists my belly; my pulse begins to thud. He had been more than angry. He had been worried... He'd thought I had left him. That I had escaped... Yeah, that's what it was. He was upset that I had gotten the better of him. That's all it was.

"Don't keep me waiting."

When I reach the door I realize that I have followed his command. *That* hasn't changed. Nor the confidence in his voice. My nerve endings spark. I had missed that. What in the blazes am I thinking?

I was barely gone an hour and everything in me aches for him. My footsteps slow. He hadn't come after me. He had given in to his frustration, and instead, taken his temper out on the furniture. I swallow. What did that mean? And why hadn't he shown me his displeasure? Why had he, instead, opted for words? And then he'd asked me if I was hungry. What next? Is he going to feed me? I laugh and the sound rolls around the space. It intensifies my nervousness. Heat skitters over my skin, chills snake down my spine. Damn the man for keeping me guessing. I walk down the steps, reach the kitchen, and halt.

He's standing in front of the cooking range. His broad back is to me. That massive wall of muscles, those planes that move as he reaches for something in the shelves above. The last time I'd seen this view, he hadn't been alone. Lisa had been there. Had he sent her off? Bet he got her to blow him quickly first. Anger rolls in my gut. The greasy taste of...bile...of jealousy fills my mouth. I hope he burns in hell. And that bitch omega? I hope she meets someone like Talon who'll teach her the most awful lesson ever. I snarl in my throat, and he glances at me over his shoulder.

"Sit."

He jerks his chin toward the chairs pulled up to the island.

I hesitate and he glares at me.

Right.

That...stupid male part of him which would never be restrained, no matter how much he might ever try. That's the part I respond to. That primeval female core of me aches for the hardness of him to take. To instruct. I am his pupil, his slave... Damn me to hell. I walk to the chair and slip onto it. He stalks to the island, then slides a plate over to me. Cold cuts, cheese, pickles. I blink. "What...What's this?"

He seats himself next to me, but at right angles to me. "You haven't seen food before?"

He picks up the meat and bites into it. I look up to find his jaws moving. He swallows and the tendons of his throat stretch and flex. My mouth waters and it's not from the food in front of me.

I snatch up a pickle and nibble on it. My stomach rumbles. He chuckles and my cheeks flush.

"Where did the food come from?"

He frowns, bites into a sausage, eats it all up, then looks at his plate. "I had one of my...clan members come by earlier."

Lisa. He means Lisa. I stare at my plate. Hunger tugs at my belly. I grip the table. I can't eat what that woman brought. I can't.

"What's wrong?" He growls.

Moisture pools in my core. His nearness is enough to get me needy and wanting. I shove the plate away.

"Food not up to your standards, Princess?"

I fold my arms over my chest. "Nothing wrong with the food; it's the man who served it who annoys me."

He tilts his head, "Oh?"

I am baiting him. That thick taste of jealousy is overpowering. It's the first time I've tasted it and I can't understand it. What do I care if he touches any other woman or sleeps with them? After all, in a few days Talon will return with his men and then Kayden will be history.

Right?

He deserves to be taken prisoner. To be punished for what he did to me. I need to be subservient to him until then. So why can't I stop challenging him? I pinch my fingers together in my lap, return his stare.

He reaches for the cheese on his plate, then holds it to my mouth. "Eat."

I shake my head and he swears under his breath. "You've been without food for too long. You need your energy."

"To fuck, you mean?"

His left eyelid twitches.

Anger leaps off of him, swirls over me, and I shiver. He's going to lose it any moment. Throw the plates...and me on the ground. He's going to rip my clothes apart and bury that hot, juicy, throbbing dick inside of me. I clench my thighs. Slickness drips from between my legs. His nostrils flare. "You are hurting, you need me, Princess. But you need to eat first."

"Since when do you care about my needs?"

The planes of his chest flex, "I have...always cared about you. From the moment I saw you I knew I couldn't walk away. It's not easy to put what I feel into words."

I stare at him; my mouth opens then closes. I open it again to speak and he slips the slice of cheese between my lips. The food touches my tongue and I chew on it. I am hungry and the cheese tastes so good. Besides I do need my sustenance for what is to come. For my freedom. My independence. Hang on a second — "You...you care for me?"

"Or something." He rolls his shoulders.

He does that when he's uncomfortable. Hmm.

"You were upset that I left?"

He stiffens. Then picks up the meat and offers it to me. "Eat"

I firm my lips.

"Eat, and I'll answer your question."

I frown at him.

"Please?"

154

Kayden

Her gaze widens. "Say that...say that again."

I glare at her. Yeah, I said 'please' and it was in normal conversation, so what's the big deal?

Why is she looking at me like I committed another crime?

I admit I am not the type to request... Hell, I've never asked anyone politely for anything. Perhaps my mother, but that was so long ago that I don't remember the details.

I lower my arm and she shoots out her hand to grasp my wrist. Pinpricks of awareness shoot over my skin. It's always been like this...this arousal that writhes between us, binding us in a cocoon of such excruciating connection that my chest throbs. My rib cage compresses. That ball of emotion in my chest grows bigger, louder, stretching out toward my extremities until every part of me is throbbing, yearning with the need to touch her.

My gaze drops to where her fingers are pressed into my skin and she drops her hand. She pushes back her chair and this time it's me who swoops down to grip her shoulder. "Stay."

She swallows, then glances away.

"I won't...do...anything you don't want me to."

A laugh bubbles up from her. She blinks and a tear rolls down her cheek. My chest constricts in what is getting to be a familiar sensation. My throat tightens. "Fuck, don't."

Her tears...her crying cuts a swathe through my insides. My guts churn.

"I...I am sorry for what I did to you."

She snorts. "Can't believe you said that."

"Yeah, fucking me too." I pull back my hand, then drag my fingers through my hair. Grab at tufts of it and yank. Pain slithers down my neck and I huff. Much better. Something I recognize. Something that belongs to the world I come from. Something that isn't soft and sexy and tastes of everything forbidden.

"What are you doing?" She looks up at me.

"Isn't it obvious?"

"No." She wipes her cheek on her sleeve, "Nothing is obvious with you, Kayden. When it comes to you, how I react to you, how you force me to act so out of character, it's all confusing."

Eh? I drop my arms at my side, "Explain."

She waves her hand between us, "You, me...this," she motions to the room, "it's unreal."

"Why?" I place my elbows on the table.

"Do you really have to ask?" She blows out a breath. "We met in less than ideal circumstances, and you were mean, so horrible to me. You still are." She wraps her arms around her middle. "But you aren't..."

"Aren't—?"

She hesitates, flicks me a glance, then looks away, "—aren't the same."

That's putting it mildly. That encounter with Lisa brought something home. It made me realize what Cara means to me. That despite what we had done to each other, I ache for her. There is no one else for me, but her. But how can I explain that to her, when I, myself, am trying to figure out what the hell I am going through right now?

I quirk my lips and watch her.

She wriggles in her seat, rubs her fingers together, a shiver rolls over her. "You're cold?"

She nods, rubs at her temple, "And hot." She begins to rock herself from side to side, and I recognize the signs. She's going into the next phase of her estrus, and this one will be more intense. After all, she's in the presence of her mate. Mate. I roll the word around in my head. It doesn't seem strange. It feels familiar. O-k-a-y. Gotta roll with the surprises. Clearly, there are more headed my way.

"You need to eat, sweetheart."

Yep, *like that*. Me using endearments? I rub the back of my neck.

"See," she stares at me, "that's what confuses me."

"What?"

"That," she stabs a finger at me. "You called me sweetheart once before."

"I did?" I frown.

"When you kissed me last."

"When I..." Ah! When I had hauled her up from the edge of that damned slope where Talon's alphas had pushed her over. "I was scared." I rub the back of my head.

"And now?"

I straighten, then stare down my nose at her. "I am furious now."

"You are?"

I nod.

"Wh...why?" she pouts.

So fucking cute. When she gets into this phase where she forgets to be prickly and scared, and I am not being an alphahole, the dynamics between us switch. If she were always in heat, it would make for a healthier relationship between us. Relationship? I am thinking emo shit now? I chuckle and her frown deepens. "You're laughing at me?"

"No, I'm concerned because you are not eating."

"Not hungry," she juts out her bottom lip.

"You must get your sustenance." I reach for another slice of cheese and offer it to her.

"I am not a stupid mouse that you keep feeding me cheese."

I jerk my chin. She opens her mouth and I pop the food in. She bites, swallows, then grimaces.

"You're not a mouse, but you are little." I smirk and she hunches her shoulders. "And I promise I'll get you a variety of your favorite foods when we get out of here."

"Hmph." she opens her mouth and I slide a piece of meat inside. She chews and swallows. "Cake?"

I frown.

"Can you get me cake?"

"I could." I hold up more food and she closes her mouth around my fingers. Her lips slide over my skin. Soft. Wet. My pulse begins to race. Feed her. Make sure she is replete. That's what you need to focus on, asshole.

"Not strawberry."

"Huh?" I frown at her.

"I hate strawberry cake."

"Right." I scoop up more food and she obediently bends forward and swirls her tongue around the morsel. The sight of her pink tongue swirling around my fingers...? Fucking turns me on. I widen my legs to accommodate my arousal.

"Chocolate."

"What?" I stare.

"Gotta be chocolate, Kai." She pouts, then reaching for her plate, yanks it close and begins to shovel the food into her mouth. I watch as she munches her way through everything on her plate, then looks up at me. "I am ready now."

"For what?"

She pushes back her chair, then comes around to stand next to me. "Can't you see?"

Okay, I have no idea what she's talking about.

She throws up her hands, "I am ready to be fucked."

This woman, when the estrus takes over, it strips back all of her layers. Reveals the wild, wanton omega at her core. Fucking seductive.

I turn my chair around so I am facing her, legs wide, "Come 'ere."

This is when I call her bluff. When she pulls away, or begs me to let her go. She gnaws on her lower lip, then draws herself up to her full height...which means she's eye level with me as I'm seated.

She steps into the 'V' between my legs. Her pupils are dilated. Color floods her cheeks and she mutters in that guttural language, that coming from her little mouth, makes me more horny. "You've got to tell me what you want, sweet thing."

She tosses her head. "Do I have to do all the work myself?"

Hmm. That sass, how I want to turn her over on my lap and beat it out of her. Bet it would turn her on too. Bet she'd never admit to enjoying it, either.

She reaches out and cups me through my pants.

"Fuck," I swear, and she grips me tighter.

"I want you to put your cock inside of me and fill up the emptiness. Break this cycle of heat and cold that is tearing at my skin."

She lets go, then bends and whips off her dress in one smooth move.

My heart stutters, my pulse rate shoots up, and heat coils in my chest. The ball of emotion there? It pumps out to my extremities and seems to explode. Every cell in my body seems to be on fire. I pant, chest heaving, and peruse her body. Luscious breasts, tiny waist, voluptuous hips, and that juicy flesh between her legs...lower lips plump and glistening. A trickle of liquid slips down her thighs. Reaching out a finger, I scoop it up and bring it to my lips.

I suck it in and she whines.

She shifts her weight from foot to foot, twists her fingers at her side.

"Shh, this time, I want it to be different for you."

155

Chloe

"I want to make it up to you for everything I put you through. Will you let me?"

His voice washes over me. Soothing, calming...my belly flutters. Delicious. I moan and reach out to touch his face but he grips my wrist. "Let me." He brings my hand to the side and pats it. I curl my fingers into the palm of my hand.

Why is he delaying? What is he talking about? What does he want to do? The emptiness inside writhes and I pant. "Please."

"I promise I am not keeping you waiting. Just making sure that you enjoy my ministrations."

He smooths his palm over my hip and I tremble. My knees sway and he tightens his grasp.

"So beautiful." He runs his fingers up the curve of my waist, then down over my belly. Closer. Closer to my aching core.

I chafe my thighs together and one side of his lips quirks. "We need to go slow."

No. No. What's he talking about? Is he toying with me?

He raises his head. "Not playing with you. I promise, Cara. I want it to be good for you." His forehead crinkles.

He means it. He's looking at me with such intensity. Those golden flecks in his eyes swirl, punctuating his words. A tendril of gold whips out to me and I gasp.

I dig my fingernails into the palm of my hand.

He jerks his chin. The sinews of his throat move as he swallows.

He perceives it too...this connection I had yearned for. He's not saying anything, but he doesn't need to. Our bodies, our souls are communicating in tandem. It's everything...and nothing like what I have ever felt before.

The thoughts whirl around in my head.

The ball of emotion in my chest digs into my ribcage. Heat, cold, the contradictory sensations whip over my skin. My fingers tingle, my toes curl. My head whirls with the intensity of the heat cycle drawing me in. I am losing myself, but the still-thinking part of my mind marvels at how he's changed. How he handles me with such care. How he leans in close and blows over my core, and when I shiver, he massages my skin, calming me, driving me toward that crack of light on the horizon. He swipes his tongue over my clit and I rise up to my toes. He licks me again and I moan.

He sucks on my pussy, his lips clinging to my throbbing flesh, and I want more. More.

I bring my palms up and grab his hair, holding his head in place, thrusting my pelvis closer, begging, mewling, and he obliges. He cups my asscheeks, brings me close, and eats me out. He slides his tongue into my wet channel again and again. He tilts my hips, angles me and twists his tongue inside of me, finding that aching hollow deep inside. He purrs and the vibrations curl over my throbbing clit, strum my pussy lips, delve into my melting channel. A low growl from him ladders up my skin, meeting the throbbing ache in my chest.

"Come."

I shatter. My thighs clench and a gush of slick flows out to meet his penetrating tongue. He laps it up and the sensations ebb and flow deep inside. My heart pounds in my chest. I cry out as I shatter.

"That's it, sweetheart, come all over my mouth. Give me all of you, Cara. Don't hold back."

His words cleave through the noise in my head. Push all other thoughts away. It's so hot. So intimate. The most beautiful thing I have ever experienced. My legs give way and I slump over him. The next second he stands, taking me up with him. "Hold on," he supports my butt as I wrap my legs around him. The world tilts again.

I hear the sound of crashes as if from a distance.

Then my back slips over the wooden surface of the table. He bends over me; his face fills my line of sight. "You're gorgeous, you know that?"

I blink. Not used to this side of him. Is this another of his games? Will he go all tender on me, only to turn back into that dominant alphahole—a side of him which I admit makes me wet to think of it. I swallow, and try to focus my mind. I mumble and he quirks his head. "You're speaking Russian, darlin'"

Am I? I frown at him.

"You do that when you are lost in your head."

Huh?

"That's how I know that your estrus is taking over. It's when you become all pliable. When your prickliness fades and the hidden fire inside of you comes to the surface."

He's right, but it's more than that. It's being near him, in the vicinity of the alpha who impregnated me that is causing my cycle to peak with such intensity. Is this what some omegas refer to as entrapment heat? This need to entice the father of my unborn child to fuck me again, then cover me with his body and hide me away from the world? He will protect me and my child. He can satisfy me. Only with him am I secure. *Him.* I make a sound deep in my throat.

His lips curve wider. "You have no idea what I am talking about, do you?"

I do.

I do.

And I want to tell you about the life growing inside of me. I want to share this with you, so much Kai. So tell him. Tell him. I open my mouth, but all that emerges is a groan.

A rush of heat sweeps up my skin, a chill grips my shoulders. I frown up at him. Why am I choosing this moment to have a conversation? When all I want is the taste of him, the touch of him deep inside of me, the rough calluses of his palms marking my flesh, the hair of his forearms brushing the underside of my breasts. I arch my back, wriggle my hips and he growls, "I can hear you think, Cara."

The creases around his eyes tighten.

"It fucking turns me on."

Me too.

The amber of his iris flares and I am lost. Gone. I reach up a hand and cup his cheek.

"Beautiful," I breathe.

"No that's you, all of you."

He turns his head and nuzzles my palm. Goosebumps flare over my skin. My sex clenches and I can't wait. I wriggle my hips and arch my back. He makes a sound deep in his throat. His chest planes flex. "I want you." He growls.

Subvocal purrs cascade from his throat.

He swirls the notes over me, on me, looping them around me. He's serenading me. Is that possible? Seducing me. I am addicted to his essence and it's not enough.

I raise my chin but he's already there.

Our lips meet.

He tilts his mouth, cups my face and it's the deepest of kisses. He gives, this time. He pours so much of himself into that touch that my head swirls. My mind goes blank.

I loop my arms around his neck, tighten my thighs around his waist. The hardness of his arousal teases my opening and I widen my legs. I dig my heels in his back, kick my hips forward, and the throbbing thickness of his cock slips inside of me.

Every single ridge of his hard shaft is imprinted on my channel, and still, he doesn't stop kissing me. He nibbles on my lips, sucks on my mouth, swipes that rough tongue of his over mine.

Too much.

Too intense.

The heat from his body crashes over me and I moan.

He drags his fingers up the underside of my arm. I shiver.

He twines his fingers with mine and tears prick the backs of my eyes. And he still kisses me.

He cups my breast with his other palm. Gentle. So tender. So real. My pussy clenches. More slick flows out to bathe his shaft and he groans.

His knot hardens, stretching the entrance to my channel.

My pussy clenches. I tilt my hips up, wanting to take in all of him, needing him inside of me, coming in me. Now.

He seems to understand, for he thrusts into me. His cock lengthens, extends, and I strain closer. His dick locks behind my pelvic bone. All of my nerve endings fire at once. The climax whips out from my core, extending out to my extremities.

My toes twitch, my fingers tingle, and I scream.

He swallows down the sound.

His muscles grow heavier, his body goes rigid. His shaft throbs inside, filling me up, pushing at my walls, and yet, he doesn't come. His knot stretches my entrance. Is he going to split me in two?

He tears his mouth from mine and gazes deeply into my eyes.

"You will forgive me." His growl slices through the sexual haze in my head and a chuckle bubbles up my throat. Can't let go of the alpha male side of his personality, can he? That hard tone of his tugs at my nerves. I tilt my head and take in his features.

Color flushes his cheeks. The tendons of his throat flex. He's looking at me with such intensity, such need. My stomach flutters. I'll never get used to the intensity of what there is between us.

He glares and I jerk my chin.

Damn him. I can't say 'No' to him. And here's the thing. I don't want to deny him. Even as my mind says not to do it. That I am stupid in giving in to him again. That every second in his presence binds me to his will. I am drunk on his strength. Floating in the high of his presence. Every cell in my body replete with how he'd made me come. As if sensing my thoughts, his dick thickens inside, his knot widens, and a moan wheezes out of me.

"Thank you," he rasps.

I blink.

The blazes was that for? Why does he confuse me so? He demands, he takes what I give him only to thank me for it? I frown.

He dips his head and brushes his lips over my forehead.

Mean lips. Soft lips that can arouse me to fever pitch. The world tilts and he straightens, holding me. He strides to the door with me in his arms.

"I am going to love you now."

156

Kayden

"Fuck Cara, you consume me."

My cock jerks, dragging over her soft walls, and we both groan.

Her thighs tighten around my waist. Supple muscles flex and twist as I pick up my stride.

Had I demanded that she forgive me?

Yes!

Did I command that she do as I ask?

You bet.

I had accepted her words.

A-n-d, I'd thanked her.

Fucking thanked her?

Don't forget I had apologized to her earlier, eh?

It's clear she's bemused, the way she'd stared up at me.

Don't blame you, sweetheart, I am too.

What happened to the Kayden who took, who schemed, plotted, demanded that his clan mates fall in line with his plans? *He's been seduced by a woman who's as gorgeous as she's fierce.*

Who had the courage to take me on. Who played me without my realizing it. Who swept in and crawled under my skin without my being aware of it.

I thought I was taking her by force, when all along, she'd been creeping into my heart. My chest tightens and I push away the thought. It's too close to what I am feeling. But I don't have the courage to face it.

I toss my head and she strains her head to look up at me.

I lower my head and kiss her. The taste of her slams into my gut and I almost stumble.

I cradle her closer, fold my arms round her so she's protected from any fall, from anyone else who'd dare harm her, then reach the top of the staircase and head up the corridor for my suite.

I enter my room, cross the floor and sink down onto the nest. The joined scent of our essences surrounds us, cocoons us in that intimacy which I'll never get anywhere else, but here. In this space I call my own, with the woman of my dreams. And I had dreamed about her, I admit that.

When she hadn't been with me, I'd been lost.

When she had been in danger, I'd been out of my mind with fear.

When I'd thought I'd lost her forever, I'd been wrecked, and when I found that I'd been betrayed by her, I'd come close to having a breakdown. Yeah, this woman, she is it for me.

I lean my weight on her, pressing her into the mess of clothes, and she sighs. Her pupils are blown, her color is high. She coils her arms about my neck. She pulls me to her and I go willingly. I allow her to kiss my mouth, my chin.

She rubs her nose with mine and I can't stop that stupid grin that tugs at my lips.

I balance my weight on my elbow, bring my other palm to cup her face. She turns and nuzzles me and a shiver runs down my spine. I bend and kiss her eyelids shut.

She sighs, her muscles relaxing.

I kiss her mouth and her lips part. I lick her chin and she giggles. The sound is so lilting, I bring my fingers to her waist and dig them into the curve of her belly. She wriggles and laughs and I can't stop the chuckle that rolls up my chest.

She pushes at my shoulders and I grab her wrist and bring it up over her head. She brings her other hand to my cheek, scratching at my whiskered jaw. I growl. "Harder."

She rubs her fingernails up my cheek, into my hair.

Digs her fingers into my scalp and pulls at the strands. Goosebumps flare over my skin. My dick leaps inside of her, turgid, swelling. "Enough or I won't be able to hold back."

Her eyelids close further. She tugs harder and my groin tightens.

"Stop Cara, or I won't be responsible for the consequences of your actions."

She smirks.

The woman curls her lips and I stare. That naughty set to her features, the shine in her eyes, fuck me, but this side of her turns me on further. Every time she reveals a side of her I hadn't seen before, she takes me by surprise.

I can't wait to understand her better.

To find out what other dimensions of her personality she's hidden from me so far. I want to rip through all of the barriers she's built between us, to taste her, hold her, kiss her, to consume her and be consumed. To discover everything about her. Share my life with her.

I stare, frozen.

My muscles go solid. My groin tightens further. That thought shouldn't be such a turn on. This...this wanting to tie myself to her is all wrong.

Would I willingly give up my freedom, possibly the goal that's driven me for so long?

Yes

Yes.

And there you have it. I am well and truly fucked. In over my head, no opportunity to escape. And it doesn't bother me. The warmth pools in my chest. My shoulders tense.

She slides her palm down and flattens it over my chest.

My heart hammers. Can she feel how fast it's beating? How my pulse thuds at my temples?

I let go of her hand, to slide mine under her head. I pull her close, until her breasts press into my chest, her legs wound around my waist. Until she loops her hands around my shoulders, and her pupils dilate. Then, I tilt my hips and slide further into her. Her pussy tightens, slickness flows out to bathe my shaft.

A harsh purr rolls up my throat and she shivers.

I angle my body. My knot throbs.

Another purr and she strains closer; her nipples pebble and I am sure they'll cut right through my skin. Draw blood. Reveal everything that I feel for her.

My shaft thickens, then my balls draw up.

"I love you, Cara."

157

Chloe

I come awake with a start. Light pours in through the open windows. I glance around the room, the walls, the ceilings. I am in Kayden's home. In his bed. I look down to find his massive arm wrapped around my waist. His forearm is so colossal, it covers the width from the skin above my pussy to the curve of my rib cage. Heat warms my back, the hard walls of his chest fold over me. The planes rise and fall. I move my head, peer at him from the corner of my eyes. Oh! He's tucked me into his side.

Fit my head under his chin.

His other arm pillows my neck. The biceps so sculpted, the muscles so hard. I turn my cheek into the defined shape. His skin is soft. The underside of his arm is inked and I suddenly want to see all of him.

Naked and uncovered and bared to my perusal.

He'd made love to me; there was no other way to describe how he'd handled my body.

Touched me, held me, knotted me with such delicacy, that it had felt like a dance.

A mating dance.

He had indulged himself with my body. Had touched every inch of my skin, kissed every curve, licked every dip and sucked on my nipples, my lips, my earlobes...my clit. He had paid a lot of attention to my pussy.

He had fondled my flesh, grazed his fingertips over that little triangle, barely touching, breathing heated puffs of air over the throbbing flesh, playing with my slit, my puckered back hole, drawing lazy circles over my back, my asscheeks, my calves...my toes. He'd sucked on my toes and I had come. He had blown over my pussy and I had gone wet. He had dragged his fingertips over my scalp and I had shattered. Who'd have thought I had so many erogenous zones in my body. He had paid attention to every part of me. Imprinted his touch onto me. And when I had begged, pleaded, screamed at him that I couldn't possibly orgasm again, he had smirked, then dropped his head to my squelching core. He had slipped his tongue over my folds, slid his fingers into my channel, and of course, I had orgasmed. So intensely that I had blacked out.

When I had awakened, he had fed me... Sneaky man had used my lack of consciousness to head to the kitchen for enough supplies to last us a few days. He had fed me, insisted I drink some of the wine. When I had refused, he had poured it over my chest and proceeded to lick it all up. He had placed slices of meat and cheese over my pussy and eaten it up...and me. I had begged him then to take me. That I was empty. That I needed him. Had threatened to leave if he didn't bury that thick pulsing dick inside.

Had he relented?

Nope.

He had slunk up my body and kissed me. He had drugged me with the taste of his mouth. The potency of his embrace. How had I thought he was rough? He had swiped his lips over mine, danced his tongue over mine, and I was gone.

Drugged on his touch.

His searing presence.

His bigness that owned me, dominated me, clawed at me. Still kissing me, he had positioned himself at my entrance, and slid in. By then I was so wet, so embarrassingly slick that he had slid all the way in. His dick had leaped forward and locked behind my pelvis bone. His knot had slotted into place at the entrance of my channel and he had groaned.

So had I.

And we had climaxed.

Together.

That had been...two...three days? Maybe.

After that he seemed to lose control completely.

He had fucked me from every angle. On my back, on my front, on my side. At one point he had simply held me up, maneuvering me first over his mouth so I was riding his face. He'd encouraged me...no, demanded, that I come all over his face. I had obliged. And he had grinned and licked up every last drop of my cum. Then he'd positioned me over his dick—that muscle never seemed to relax, I swear, not once in the last few days of our mating had he been without a hard on. I mean, is that anatomically possible? —and then he'd lowered me onto his shaft, crooning to me. He'd demanded that I not hold back and I had orgasmed, all over his dick.

I had come so hard that moisture had splattered over his crotch, his balls, and he had loved it. He had lowered me to his chest after that and—that's all I recall.

My pussy clenches, my muscles scream in protest. My hips hurt, my thighs ache. Even my eyelashes protest as I squint against the light. The pressure in my lower belly grows. I gotta pee. I push at his arm and, eh? —I manage to lift it long enough to slide out from under his hold. I scoot over to the edge of the bed and stand. My legs protest. The space between my thighs throbs. I roll my shoulders, and the muscles loosen, one by one.

I walk around to the foot of the bed, turn toward the bathroom. Can't look away. He's sprawled across the bed, over the pile of clothes that I had fashioned into the nest. He's so big... My fingers curl with the memory of the hair-roughened skin. The sculpted eight pack of his abs.

He turns over on his back and I freeze. His chest rises and falls. His hand is flung to the side. Big palm. Gigantic fingers that he had slipped inside of me. My cheeks flame at the memory.

When he's conscious, his presence is so powerful that I can barely allow myself to look at him. Now, sleeping soundly, all but knocked out cold—thanks to the pleasure he had drawn from me, and I had given him all of that willingly—he stays silent. I relax my shoulders.

Let my gaze roll down his chest to his crotch. His monster dick is hard. Of course, it is. The size of my forearm, the huge muscle points toward his chest. The head is swollen, a vein runs over the underside. He'd fucked me with it...and, he'd told me that he loved me. The blazes? *He loves me?*

I jerk upright.

Had he said those three words? Had I imagined it...? No, even in that intense sexual haze I'd heard him, and a part of me had responded. I had given myself over to him. I'd submitted completely. I bring a knuckle to my mouth and chew on it.

I hadn't expected that.

Had never thought Kayden would say that. More than his words...it's how he'd held me, how his touch had been delicate, his kisses fierce, his gaze intense as he'd taken me. His dick had throbbed and extended, and his knot had expanded my channel. It had been the same, yet not. This time, he had paid attention to my needs, to what I wanted. To how nibbling behind my ears had made me gasp. How sucking on my nipples had made me pant. How grazing his fingers in between my pussy lips had made me almost climax.

Not once had he stopped, never had he pulled back. There had been no hesitation, no second guessing. He'd set his mind and heart and soul to it and his body had obeyed. He'd worshipped me. Tears prick the back of my eyes. He'd given himself over to me and it had been incredible. Seamless.

He'd fused me to him. And I was going to tear myself away.

I had to.

I couldn't give in to whatever game he was playing this time. And that's all this was to him. A way of keeping me his slave...willingly. No way am I going to become anyone's possession again. I am tired of the games these alphas play as they thirst for power.

This is my time to break away. To live life on my terms. To become independent.

I bite the inside of my cheeks. It hadn't been what I'd wanted. I am not one to defy nature. I don't have the courage to stand up for the rights of an omega. I leave that up to Lucy. But I am not a coward. I don't like to be pushed around. And that's what had happened. And now I have to do what's right for me.

I run my gaze over his features. Those gorgeous high cheekbones, the eyelids closed and framed with dark sooty lashes. The hooked nose, the beautiful lips that had kissed me senseless. When my knees graze the foot of the bed, I realize that I have taken a step forward.

I curl my fingers into fists.

Leave, now. Before you do something that you'll regret.

I head out of the exit to the other room with the wardrobe of women's clothes. Pulling on a shirt, dress-pants—can't find any jeans, so they'll have to do. Better than a dress, at any rate. For the journey, I need to be adequately dressed. I pull on shoes. Straightening, I march out, down the staircase, out the front door and come to a halt. I walk down the steps to the muddy ground. The morning fog swirls around the shoulders of the man who is going to take away everything that could belong to me. Who is going to release me from everything that holds me back? Who will allow my child to be brought up as they should be? Free of any encumbrances. Free to be themselves.

When I reach the last step, Talon towers over me, "Where is he?"

Before I can reply footsteps sound behind me.

"Chloe, get away from him."

158

Kayden

She swings around and her gaze widens.

"Chloe."

I take a step toward her and she flinches. Behind her Talon tilts his head. He curls his fingers into a fist, and that's when I lose it. He is not going to harm her; nothing is ever going to get to her. Not when I am here and alive. Anger bubbles up my gut. Fear twists my chest. The ball of sensation behind my rib cage screeches and twists. My spine arches, a bitter taste fills my mouth. "Don't hurt her."

My voice is harsh. There is no mistaking the tone of helplessness that laces it. Me, the alphahole who would never give in, has been rendered a blubbering fool because of my love for a woman. Not any omega. Mine. She is mine. And I'll do anything to keep her safe. I square my shoulders and widen my stance. "Take on someone your own size, asshole."

"I intend to." Talon's features stay impassive, but a flare of something brightens his face for an instant. He turns to my omega, "If you are going to leave, then now would be the time."

Leave? What is he talking about? And why is he speaking to her like they have met before?

Because they had?

He had taken her...just as I had kidnapped her. But he hadn't touched her. If he had...if anyone else had, I'd have smelled it on her. Only I had knotted her, fucked her, made love to her. *Fucking love.* The sentiment that I had never believed in. Still don't...but this twisting, hurting, ache in my chest. This blackhole of fear that crawls in my gut and forces me to not take my eyes off of her for fear of losing her, it is that. I know.

It's why I had revealed my feelings to her. I couldn't have held back. The words had simply poured out of me and it had felt right. But I had to stop her now. "Chloe."

She stiffens. She straightens her spine, then skirts around him and walks down the path.

The fuck — ? I jump down the steps toward her, but Talon steps in front.

"Back the fuck away."

I should fight him; I need to teach this motherfucker a lesson. That he can't come onto my property and take away what belongs to me. Except he hasn't made a move toward her; and she is walking away from me.

"Stop," My voice rings out.

Her shoulders hunch. She stops, and a breath rushes out of me.

"Don't leave." Bloody fucking hell. Since when have I asked anything of an omega? I'd meant that to come out as a command, meant to demand that she stay and what? Put her at risk again. The Viking was here. Her life was in danger. Except he'd let her go and I couldn't. If I allowed her to leave, I'd never see her again. My heart twists. The mating bond groans. I raise my hand to find it's trembling. The fuck?

Ahead, she draws herself up to her full height, then turns to glance at me over her shoulder. "Did you think I'd accept you? That I'd let any child of mine be raised in your shadow?"

"Child?" I blink.

She smiles and it's a twist of her lips. Her eyes shine with tears. "You didn't realize I was pregnant."

Pregnant? She's pregnant? *Of course she is.*

It's why her estrus had come around with such intensity, and I hadn't thought to question it?

Oh, my subconscious had known.

In my dream, she had smelled different; a scent that had torn at my heart and I had not asked her what had changed.

"All this time..." The words catch in my throat.

She'd had my child growing inside of her, and I hadn't noticed. I had been intent on how it could be between us. I had been focused on my pleasure...on relieving my conscience. I had wanted to make her forget what I had done to her. To figure out a way to bind her to me willingly. I hadn't thought to tune into her, to ask her how she was, what she was feeling. Whether she wanted to be with me? Why her body had seemed more luscious, her breasts fuller. I had put it down to my nearness. Me. I had been thinking with my dick, had allowed my ego to overwhelm all other thoughts.

I had been selfish, again. I don't deserve her. I drop my hand to my side and she nods.

"What kind of alpha doesn't sense his mate's pregnancy?" Her features tighten. "And you say you love me?"

"I do." I grip my hair and tug on it. Needing the sharp pain that slices my scalp.

"You don't." Her eyes blaze. "The only person you love is yourself. You are obsessed by the need to avenge your past."

I shake my head. Not true. She's got me all wrong. Why can't I tell her that? Why can't I open my mouth and simply tell her to give me a chance. A bloody chance. The ball of emotion in my throat grows. A coldness coils in my chest. I take in the set of her back, the curves of her hips, the cloud of thick hair that swirls about her in the gust of wind. *Come back, Cara.* I pulse the thought at her.

Her gaze widens. Did she hear me? She must have.

Don't do this.

She gasps, then brings up a hand to rub her chest.

I can't live without you.

Her shoulders stiffen.

I love you, Chloe.

Color fades from her cheeks. She tucks her elbows into her sides, and presses her lips together.

"Goodbye, Kayden."

She swings around and breaks into a run and I know why. If she goes any slower, I'll coerce her into staying. If she slows her steps, I'll use my dominance to make her obey. Of course, I will.

I leap forward. I am going to snatch her up and take her back inside and—the next moment I am on my back on the steps. Motherfucker. I look up to find Talon raising his fist again. Fucker took me down? Only because I was distracted. He's the cause of all of this. Somehow, he'd gotten to her. He'd taken her away from me.

"I am going to kill you." I kick his legs out from under him.

Talon falls, then rolls down the steps. I spring and throw myself at him. He moves out of the way. I stumble. Before I can right myself, he's already on me. He grabs my arms, twists them behind me, then wraps his arm around my neck squeezing down, trying to block off my air supply. My lungs burn, my throat hurts. My mind zings with one thought. Kill him. Kill the bastard who took her away from me. I grab his arm, bend and heave him over. For a second I bear his entire weight and the man is as heavy as me. My knees bend, my thigh muscles scream, my shoulders give, then he goes flying over me. His body crashes into the ground. Above us, birds screech and fly off the trees. I look up, but she's gone. "Chloe." I leap over him, racing toward the tree line, then pause. The sound of heavy footsteps echoes through the space. Sweat drips down my forehead, and I blink it away.

A man clomps forward from between the trees, another, and another. The entire clearing is edged with Vikings. Anger claws at my chest. Rage crowds in on my mind. Chloe. I need to get to her. I shake my head, take a step forward.

"I wouldn't." Talon widens his stance.

I huff out a laugh. "Fuck off."

I move toward the men who stop; they take a step back. Huh? I angle my body, glance at Talon who stands with his arms at his side.

"Not getting your men to carry out your instructions?"

His gaze narrows. "Last time was a mistake. I never meant to kill you."

"You intended to take me hostage?" Something clicks in my head. "You want to use me to get to Zeus?"

"Your omega was smarter; she guessed my plan much before you."

"Don't you talk about her, motherfucker." I raise my fists and advance on him.

"An alpha in love is truly fucked. He loses all sense of perspective. All focus. An alpha in love is no good to his clan."

"You're wrong." I crack my neck. "An alpha in love is aware of what's at stake. An alpha in love will never give up what's his. Not his people...not his mate."

The skin around his eyes tightens.

"An alpha in love—" I bare my teeth and snarl, "—will lay down his life before he loses the only thing that matters to him. Her."

I charge at him.

He raises his hand. Sun glints off the metal. Sur-fucking-prise, asshole. Only this time the joke's on me.

I duck, but it's too late.

There's a flash of light, a loud bang, then something tears into my chest.

The mating bond screams, surges up to flare behind my eyes. Green, so green. Amber fire licks at my nerves, consumes my cells, overflows. I sink to my knees, look at the burning hole on the left side of my chest.

159

Chloe

The loud bang echoes off the trees. My heart stops, then starts again. No. No. No. Talon couldn't have shot Kayden. He'd said he was going to take Kai prisoner, use him to negotiate with Zeus. I had believed the word of a Viking? What's wrong with me?

I stop running so suddenly that I stumble and fall.

I throw out my hands at the last second and my palms slap onto the mud. Pebbles, thorns bite into the palms of my hand. A part of me registers the pain. But my heart...my heart is racing. Pulse pounding. Adrenaline fills my blood.

I spring up to my feet and begin to run back the way I had come. *Don't die. Don't die. I didn't mean to give you up. I didn't mean to walk away. It was... I wasn't thinking. I wanted to teach you a lesson.* Show you how it had been for me, when you had taken me that first time.

My gut clenches. *Liar. Even then, you had been attracted to him. One look at him and you'd wanted him. You'd recognized that he was it for you.*

It's why I had been disappointed when he had taken. He'd held me and rutted me and then...he'd loved me.

He loves me.

The world closes in; my vision wavers. He'd proclaimed his loyalty to me and I had...allowed my jealousy to get the better of me. I had watched him with Lisa...but what had I actually seen? Not her giving him a blow job. I hadn't actually observed that.

I had believed the worst of him.

I had preferred to hand him over to the enemy rather than talk to him. I had allowed the father of my child to walk into a certain death. Had never told him directly that he was going to be a father. And he'd have been good at it. A sob rolls up my chest. My throat closes.

The mating bond slams into my rib cage and I scream.

Flares of amber lick the edges of my vision.

He's in pain. He's hurting.

"Kai!"

I yell his name and race so fast that my feet don't seem to touch the ground. I reach the tree line, burst into the clearing, but there's no one there. I pause, panting. My side hurts, my leg muscles spasm. My entire body is one large ache, but my heart...my heart is silent. Emptiness in my chest. Cold, so cold. I take a step forward. Another. When I am a few feet from the steps that lead up to the house, I see the stain in the mud.

I drop to my knees, reach for the wetness.

When I raise my fingers, a sob wrenches out of me.

It's Kai's blood.

Talon shot him. Then took him. I stay there transfixed. The world swims around me, my vision tunnels.

"Chloe."

I don't react. Can't look up. It's not Kai's voice. I don't care who it is. I did this.

There's a touch on my shoulder and I glance to my side.

"You killed him?" Zeus frowns down at me.

"Let's not jump to conclusions." Another male voice interrupts, and Zeus glares at him.

I swing my head around to Dom's face.

"She didn't mean it." Dom's gaze meets mine, "I am sure it's all a mistake."

I shake my head. "It's my fault."

"What do you mean?" Dom's forehead wrinkles.

"I led Talon to him and now Kai..." I swallow. "He's gone. Talon shot him and I am to blame."

TURN THE PAGE TO KEEP READING...

PART VI

MATED

160

Kayden

"Stop Cara."

She races up the slope, her blonde hair streaming behind her. Her hips rise and fall with each step.

"You're making it worse for yourself. If I catch you, you'll regret it."

She tosses her hair, "Promise, promises." Her eyes gleam.

"Why you little thing." I lunge forward.

She squeals, then turns and leaps forward. So agile, so feisty.

I swipe out a hand and my fingers graze the material. She yells and pulls ahead. I grasp at the material and yank. There's a ripping sound, and the fabric comes away in my hand. She pulls away and I stumble, then hold up the material. "Keep running, sweet thing. Now I can see your ass."

She yelps, then pivots to face me. Her breasts heave; her face flushes. "Gimme that."

"This?" I twirl the piece of cloth. "Come and get it."

"No way." She blows the hair out of her face.

"I won't touch you, promise."

She glowers.

I thump my chest, "Don't you trust me?"

"Never."

"Aww come on, Cara." I allow my lips to turn down at the side. "I've always been true to my word."

"Right," she huffs out a breath, "and alphas fall in love, huh?"

"Now, now," I waggle my finger at her, "play nice."

"No."

"You've got to learn to use less of that word."

"Gah." She throws her hands up. A gust of wind ruffles her dress, which promptly slips down her shoulders. She squeaks, then tries to cover herself with what's left of the dress, fails. "Fine, keep it." She tosses her hair, "I don't want it."

"You sure?" I bring the scrap of cloth to my face and bury my nose in it. "It smells of your essence."

She scowls, "You're uncouth."

Huh? I lower my hand and glare at her. "What's wrong with my sniffing your scent? Why should I hide the fact that it arouses me, hmm?" I widen my stance, and her gaze drops to my crotch.

My dick throbs at her perusal; bet the fabric of my pants is pulled tight across that turgid muscle.

She reddens. Hm. I grab my dick, adjust it. She gulps; her tongue flicks out to lick her lips. Blood rushes to my groin.

I shove the fabric inside my shirt, then quirk a finger. "Come 'ere."

She chews on her lower lip.

I lower my voice and she stiffens. "I won't ask again." Our eyes lock. I jerk my chin. She stumbles forward and every muscle in my body hardens. So damn obedient.

She takes another step forward, then stops. An alpha is patient. He stalks his prey; allows her to think that she has a choice. *As if.*

I peel back my lips and she gulps. Her knees bend. Now is when she takes off running. *Do it, little one. Give me the chance to chase you. To capture you again.* Adrenaline laces my blood. My vision narrows. All of my senses home in on her. *Do it. Now.*

She blinks, then pulls herself up to her full height.

Huh?

She swallows, folds her fingers into fists at her sides. Then she puts one foot in front of another. She approaches me and I track her progress. I watch her come closer, closer. When she's in front of me, she stops.

Her breathing goes ragged. "Now what?"

I take in her pale face, the pulse fluttering at the base of her neck. Her chest rises and falls. Nipples outlined against the soft fabric. My fingers tingle.

All I have to do is close the distance between us, drop my head and bite down on that hardened flesh.

She gulps; her shoulders twitch.

Definitely not as impervious to me as she's trying to pretend.

I drop my gaze to the strip of ground between us, then up to her face.

Her lips firm. "No."

"Oh?" One side of my mouth twists, and I assure you, it's not a smile.

She chews on a fingernail, "I…I mean. Not yet."

Interesting. I stay quiet. Allow my perusal to dwell on her face. The strands of hair that cling to her forehead, the gentle slope of her pert nose, the full lush lips, so soft, so enticing. Her chin wobbles; a hint of fear creeps into the air. "I…I'll do what you want." She tucks her elbows into her sides. "On one condition."

My jaw drops open. *Oh, really?* She actually thinks she can negotiate with me? I can't stop the chuckle that vibrates up my throat.

She flattens her lips; the green in her eyes darkens. "You could at least pretend to listen to me, you jerk."

Oh, she's pissed.

Color flushes her cheeks, and she jams her hands on her hips.

I swallow down a laugh, "You think you can win this, hmm?"

Her stare deepens. She seems about ready to stamp her little foot. Cute. She snarls, showing her little teeth, and damn, if I don't want to feel their pointed tips on my skin. Dragging down my chest, over my stomach, while I wrap her long strands around my palm and tug. Her mouth would fall open and I'd stuff my cock inside—

"—Hey"

I blink.

"Get your head out of the gutter, dickhead."

Yeah, and said dick would very much like its head to be someplace else.

She snarls and I stab my tongue into my cheek. Not that I mean to consider her 'request' but hey, she'll never find out about that. Don't want to scare her too much and bring us to a total impasse. Not that I wouldn't enjoy bringing her down a peg or two, but best to give her something to save face, huh?

"Right." I raise my hands face up, "Okay. What's your request?"

"Tell me something you haven't told anyone else, and in return I'll—" Her cheeks tinge pink. So damn adorable. After everything I've done to her, she can't quite bring herself to spell it out.

"You'll?" I tilt my head.

"I'll... You know—"

"No, I don't."

She blows out a breath, "Give you a blow job."

"Give?" I raise an eyebrow and she swallows. "Fine, you can take a blow job from me." She waves her hand in the air, "Whatever."

"Hmm."

You have to admit the way she sprang that on me was clever, and sneaky. My Cara is full of surprises, and damn, if I don't like that.

"Well?" She hops from foot to foot.

I tap my finger to my temple. "I'm thinking about it." I lower my hands to my sides, "All done."

She frowns, "So?"

"After giving it careful consideration, I have arrived at the conclusion that—" I pause.

"That?"

"It's a hard no."

She freezes, then her features contort, "Fine, then you'll have to catch me first." She pivots, then darts forward.

"Don't you want to find out what I said 'No' to?"

She pauses so suddenly that she stumbles. I lunge forward as she rights herself. She pivots, and I retreat.

Don't want her to see how concerned I was, that I didn't want her to hurt herself. If anyone has the right to mark that pretty skin of hers, it's me.

She shuffles her feet, "What do you mean?"

"I said 'No,'" I link my fingers together, "to the blowjob."

"Meaning?"

"I'll tell you a secret, however, in return, you'll have to do more."

She twists her lips together, "You mean…you want to fuck me?"

I make a twirling motion with my fingers.

"You want more?"

I stare at her and she wriggles her shoulders, "Wh...what else is there?"

I allow my lips to curl.

Her breath hitches, "No."

"Yes."

"Not that."

"*Only* that."

"You want to tap my—"

"Ass."

"Why?" She wriggles her hips, "What's this fascination with that..." her cheeks turn fiery, "that part of me?"

"Isn't it obvious?"

She shakes her head.

"It's the only virgin hole left in you, Sweetheart. The one part on which I haven't imprinted myself."

"And is that so important?"

"Yes."

She frowns, "You won't settle for anything else?"

I shake my head.

"First you'll tell me a secret about yourself."

I hold up my hand, the other on my chest, "A promise is a promise."

She lowers her head so her hair covers her face, "Where have I heard that before?" she mumbles.

"What was that?"

"N... nothing." She peeks up at me from under those hooded eyelids.

"Want me to spank it out of you?"

She shakes her head.

"Do you know what happens to little brats who sass their masters?"

"Are you... are you?" Her pupils dilate.

"Your master?" I snake out my hand; she squeaks.

I wrap my fingers about her nape and her pupils dilate. "Any doubts in that regard?"

She shakes her head.

"There's one more thing."

She gulps, "Wh...what?"

"This time you initiate the fucking."

"Do you have to be so coarse?"

I smirk, "What do you mean?"

"You keep using that four-letter word."

"You mean you want me to use other four-letter words, preferably beginning with 'L'?"

She jerks her chin.

I exhale, "You can show me how much you lust after—"

"Not that four-letter word."

"Then, which?"

"You know."

"No."

She bares her teeth, "You want me to say it first?"

I raise my shoulders, "If you wish."

"You don't believe in it?"

"I already told you how I feel."

"That...didn't count."

"Why not?" I frown.

"That was in the heat of a life and death situation."

"And so is this." I lean in so close that our eyelashes kiss.

"H...how?" Her breath wheezes.

"You are my life; without you I'd die." I stare into her eyes. "Without the taste of you, I'd starve. Without your touch," I grip her hand and place it over my dick, "I'd never feel again."

"So poetic, and you said you didn't believe in emo shit?"

"I don't." The back of my neck heats, "You make it easy to forget what held me back previously."

"You still won't say the 'L' word?" She massages my hardness and I groan.

"When you have me by the balls, Sugar, do I have a choice?"

She squeezes and blood rushes to my groin. My dick thickens. "Wanna fuck, darlin'?"

"Let me think." She tilts her head, "That would be a hard...yes." Her lips curve, "But first, you promised." She strokes me.

My breath catches. "What?"

"One secret." She leans forward and her breasts graze my chest. "That's all that stands between my licking you, sucking you —"

"You're the first woman I've brought home to the stronghold."

A furrow appears between her eyebrows, "And the clothes you loaned me?"

"Belonged to Marcus' daughter."

She chews on her lower lip. "And Marcus?"

I rub the back of my neck. "He was in love with my mother."

"I guessed."

I lean forward on the balls of my feet, "He'd have given his life to rescue her, but she didn't want to leave her mate."

"She...loved your father?"

I nod. "And that's three," I cup her face, "secrets."

"Not fair."

"Neither is this." I pinch her nipple and she gasps.

I plunge my thumb into her mouth. She sucks on it and heat fills my chest. I place my other palm over hers, on my crotch. Grind the heel of her hand into the hardness.

"Kayden." Her breathing grows shallow.

"Kayden, wake up."

I snap my eyelids open. Light shines into my eyes and I blink.

"He's alive."

I blink; my eyes adjust to the semi-darkness.

"I've bandaged him... It should last, for now." An elderly man pushes his chair away. His hair is graying at the temples. He wears a faded shirt and pants that have seen better days. His eyebrows are grey and bushy. There's a calmness to his demeanor, a clinical thoroughness as he surveys me. A doctor of some kind?

"Just so long as he lasts for a couple of days." A voice speaks from my left.

I turn my head and pain explodes in my chest. "Fuck." Sweat pops on my brow. My vision wavers. Nausea wells up and I bite the inside of my cheek to swallow it down.

"Oh, he'll survive alright. He has a strong constitution." The older man gets up from the chair, then moves away.

I shake my head to clear it.

An arm appears in my field of vision. The same man holds out a glass of water. I raise my hand to take it—the hell? My arms are tied behind my back.

I strain against the bindings and my chair teeters forward.

"You don't want to open the stitches now." He raises the glass to my lips, "Drink it. You'll be needing your strength.

No kidding. Not sure what I'm more upset about... The fact that the bastard Talon shot me, that he has me tied up here, or because it was all a dream. At least it wasn't the nightmare about my mother and Golan. The same one that has come to me almost every night. One reason why I've managed to survive on a few hours of sleep each night. But after meeting her, hell, if my dreams haven't turned erotic.

You'd think I were a randy teenager, the way my mind keeps zooming in on one thing. Her smile, her lips, her cunt... Fuck. I toss my head and the glass jostles; water spills across my chest.

The older man doesn't react. His hand is unshakable as he cups the back of my head to hold me steady. When he touches the glass to my mouth, I drink from it. The liquid is cool as it slides down my parched throat. When I am done, he rises.

"You can leave, Alan."

The man places the glass on the floor, next to a pitcher. Grabbing his medical bag from the floor, he leaves.

I straighten, track the progress of the new arrival. He straddles a chair and surveys me. Blonde hair, eyes light blue. He tilts his head and the light from the single bulb above picks up the gold in his hair. Talon. His features seem familiar, and not only because I've run into him a few times. I blink. *No, what am I thinking?*

He watches me from under hooded eyelids. The silence stretches. Fuck, if I am going to break it. Not going to give him that advantage. My chest throbs and I wince. I flex my wrists and the ties don't give. The last thing I'd seen before I'd blacked out was her. "Chloe," I growl. "She led you to my stronghold."

"Took you long enough to put it together." He folds his arms over the top of the chair and regards me, emotionless.

A whiff of unease crosses my subconscious mind. His expression is so similar to someone else. But who?

"You coerced her into it."

"Did I?" He angles his head.

"There is no reason for her to have worked with you."

"Isn't there?" He swings his leg over the chair, rises to his feet. "Your ability for self-delusion is extraordinary." He walks toward me. "It's the first indication of an alpha in love."

Love? Why did he have to use the same four-letter word that she wanted me to confess to her in that bloody dream? My muscles tense.

He stops in front of me, props his hands on his hips, "Who'd have thought you would be next in line after your brother—"

"Half-brother."

"—to fall for an omega. Mate her, trust her enough to share your secrets with her. Except she betrayed you…a second time."

"She didn't." Anger thrums at my nerve endings; a cold sensation coils in my chest. *She did, you asshole.* As if the first time wasn't enough, she went behind my back, had a téte-a-téte with this Viking, kept me occupied. My heart stutters.

He nods. "Took you long enough to figure that out. It must be love."

"Shut the fuck up."

"And you're close to losing control. What would you do if I brought your omega here—"

I charge forward, my head connects with his abdomen. He huffs, staggers a little, only to straighten. He slams his fist into my face.

Sparks flash behind my eyelids. My chair teeters then falls to the side. Pain explodes in my chest, down my side. Sweat pools under my armpits. He grabs my chair, straightens it. The legs thump down on the ground; the vibrations jerk my insides. My belly shudders and bile rushes up my throat. I growl, shake my head and swallow down the acidic taste. No fucking way am I going to lose control. Not. "You don't have her here. If you did, you'd have produced her already."

"True." He flexes his fingers. "Maybe that jolt did you good, eh?" He shoots out his fist. I duck. He misses, stumbles a little, then brings his joined fists up. My jaw snaps shut; blood fills my mouth. Pain rolls down my neck. I spit out the blood, then glare at him. "Motherfucker, when I get my hands on you, I'm going to kill you."

He grins. "Can't wait to see the end of you and your brother."

"Half-fucking-brother."

"No love lost there then?"

I firm my lips. He's right, but the fuck, am I going to allow him to see that?

"Don't blame you though, considering it was your brother who set you up with the omega in the first place. That's after you did the same for him—not that he is complaining. He's busy playing house with his mate, and you?" He drums his fingers on his chest, "You, on the other hand, don't look so good." He peruses my throbbing countenance. "Not good at all. In fact, by the time I'm done with you, I wager none of them will recognize you."

Whatever.

He weaves his fingers together, then raises them above his head. Stretches from side to side.

"If this was meant to seem threatening—"

The door opens; a man bends, then ducks inside. His shoulders brush the width of the door. His head grazes the ceiling. He cracks his neck…and glowers.

Talon moves the chair to the side, then straddles it again.

"Getting someone else to do your dirty work?"

He props his elbow on the back of the chair, then rests his chin on his palm. "For once, you're right."

The big man walks up to me. He folds his fingers into a fist—it resembles a hammer. He raises his arm, blocks the light from above—No, make that a snowplow.

"Oh, by the way, Clod…?"

Talk about stereotypes. I was going to be pummeled to within an inch of my life by a giant named… Yeah, Clod.

"Don't kill him. Work him over, enough that he's compliant when I use the threat of him to blackmail Zeus."

My muscles tense and I force myself to relax.

"And spare his face."

Clod snarls, "I was hoping to rearrange those pretty features. Why can't I — ?"

Talon glares at him. Clod snaps his mouth shut.

"Not that it is any concern to you, but I need Zeus to be in no-doubt of the identity of his half-brother, you get me?"

Clod jerks his chin.

Talon pivots and leaves.

Clod advances one me. I tense. I survived Golan; I'll survive this too. The trick is to retreat to a corner of my mind... To where the scent of her, taste of her, coils behind my ribcage. My heart stutters; my limbs tremble. *Fuck, should have told her I loved her one more time, when I had the chance. So what if it was in the dream?* Clod's fist slams into my side.

161

Chloe

Pain shoots up my spine; my chest hurts. Why does it feel as if someone stuck a knife into my side?

I push myself up to a sitting position and my shoulder protests.

I scan the room—the simple furnishings, the closet in the corner, a table and two chairs by the window. I am in Kayden's room in his clan's hideout. I hadn't thought I'd see this place again, or at least, not without him. "Kai." My heart begins to thud. *What have I done?*

I'd heard the gunshot and run back, to find him gone... And the blood. The blood. Kai's blood was on the ground. I raise my fingers. They're scrubbed clean. Look down at myself. I'm wearing a different set of clothes.

Not mine, of course. I left everything behind in Moscow when I escaped. It should get easier surviving on what belongs to others, but it never does. Not my fault that I was brought up with the best of everything.

I hadn't realized how lucky I'd been.

I'd lived every little girls' dream. I'd been an honest to God, real-life princess. I'd found my prince... No, my king. He'd sought me out. He'd taken me for himself, had vowed to protect me, had confessed he loved me, and I... I had betrayed him. Twice. My hand falls to my side. I tug on the cover, bring it up and bury my nose in the soft fabric. Kayden's scent fills my head. Sinks into my blood. My pulse rate ratchets up.

Kai. I didn't mean to hurt you. It is right that I was brought to his room, in his clan's stronghold. Surrounded by his presence. The taste of him fresh in my mouth. The touch of him still sears my skin. I breathe in deeply, drawing in the perfume of our joining.

This is where he'd imprisoned me, tied me to the bed, taken me with a passion bordering on obsession.

He'd knotted me so many times. My sex clenches. I chafe my thighs together. Bend my legs then bury my head in my knees. I'd give anything to relive those moments when he dominated me. What does that say about me? A woman who fell in love with her kidnapper. I am conforming to every stereotype of a helpless female. Except I hadn't been.

I swallow down the lump of emotion that fills my throat.

I had walked out of Kayden's stronghold. I had stood up to Talon.

I had negotiated my freedom, and that of my child. I stiffen. My breath catches. I raise my head and cup my belly. Kayden's successor. I am carrying his son or daughter. And I sent my unborn child's father to his death.

Something hot stabs at my chest.

It's not my fault that Talon didn't keep his word. I delivered Kayden to him and Talon freed me. Why would he fulfill his promise on that and not when it came to Kai?

I chew on my lower lip. Of course, Talon hadn't indicated that he'd take Kayden alive. He hadn't said otherwise either. And why had he not taken me prisoner? Why let me go? My head spins.

I drop into myself, reach out to the ball of sensations in my chest. Nothing. I stiffen. Bring my awareness to the space within my ribcage. It's silent. I'd felt the anguish when he'd been shot. The mating bond had screamed in pain—that's when I had run to him. Now he's gone.

A pressure builds behind my eyes. I bite down on my lower lip. I will not cry. Will not.

The door swings open, and I glance up.

Broad shoulders fill the doorway. The shock of dark hair, the chiseled countenance, the menacing air that leaps off of him as he strides in. My heart stutters. "Kai?" I whisper.

The man pauses halfway into the room, "Not quite."

I blink and the image resolves. "Z…Zeus?"

"Not flattered to be mistaken for him, Princess."

The dominance ripples off of him in waves. It fills the space, weighs down on my shoulders.

The man is massive. Thick corded muscles wind about his forearms, a narrow waist, tapering down to meet corded thighs. He's a powerhouse. He's almost as beautiful as my alpha. *Alpha. Mine.*

I squeeze my eyes shut.

I won't allow myself to be sorry for what I did. *You took the choice out of my hands. It's your fault. You are responsible for your own demise.*

"I take it you're not happy to see me, hmm?" His voice sharpens.

Zeus isn't Kai; doesn't mean I can ignore him. He is the General of London. And technically, he is in control of Kayden's territory as well. The man is dangerous, as power-hungry as Kai had been, as filled with the thirst for revenge. The two are so similar, it's no wonder they're at loggerheads.

It's fitting that they are half-brothers; they were tainted by the same man.

I straighten my shoulders. "I won't deny I'd hoped it was someone else." I open my eyes.

His glare holds mine. I should cower, feel afraid, say something to reassure him…but nothing.

Why do I feel so numb inside?

Because what you did was wrong. You delivered Kai to his death.

"I failed you. I let Kayden escape." I raise my chin. "I am ready for any punishment you deem fit for me."

"Any punishment?"

He takes a step forward and the scent of him creeps into the room. Strong, male, all wrong. My stomach churns and bile rushes up my throat. I swallow. It has to be my condition that's making me so sensitive to another alpha's presence. Only my mate's scent, his touch, his essence would soothe me. Only his scent would calm me and I'll never have that again. A sharp pain pinches my chest and I huff.

Zeus frowns. The skin at the edges of his eyes creases. The shape of his countenance is so similar to Kai's and yet, not.

Where there's a cold menace to Kai's presence, Zeus is all raw power, unleashed energy. They are two sides of the same coin.

Both alphas. Both ready to pounce at the slightest sign of weakness.

I gulp, force myself to square my shoulders. "I will abide by whatever you decide."

"Your punishment is—"

There's a commotion; the door flies open.

A small figure rushes in, two alphas on her heels.

"Sorry, General, she insisted and ah, we couldn't stop her."

Zeus angles his body; his shoulders brace. *Huh?*

"How dare you?" The woman halts in front of him. Anger pours off of her. Her hair falls in perfect waves to her waist.

"Lucy." Zeus' voice holds a tinge of resignation, and something else… Is that, fear? Nah. The big bad alpha afraid of his omega? No way.

The tiny woman stomps up to him, "I told you not to speak to her without me."

"Uh—"

"You left me alone and slunk away when I wasn't paying attention."

"Lucy, I—"

"You should have waited."

"But you were—"

"No, don't give me any excuses. I told you I'd come with you, and you purposely sneaked off behind—"

"Enough, woman." The alpha roars.

His voice bounces off of the walls. I wince.

This is the first time that the two have openly traded such emotional dialogue in front of me.

Guess, both are trying to find a balance? After all, it is early in their relationship as a mated couple.

Lucy huffs out a breath. Her eyes gleam. She opens her mouth, when he lurches forward and raises his hand.

When my feet slap on the floor, I realize that I am halfway across the room to them.

Lucy gurgles. *What? What's he doing to her?*

His big body hides the sight of her, so I can't see what he's doing. Another sound of flesh hitting flesh. *No.* Is he hurting her? No way am I going to let that happen.

"Unhand her." I raise my fists, ready to what? Hit the General himself?

Yeah sure, and strike my death knell? I draw in a breath. Maybe being with Kayden had influenced me to an extent I hadn't been aware of. He'd pushed me so hard that I had been forced to hold my own. I'd learned that the way to handle a bully is to confront him. If you give in, they'll never respect you. And that... That was as important as love. "Let her go."

Zeus swings around. I blink.

Lucy is tucked into his side. His palm covers her mouth. Her eyes sparkle with...defiance? Her shoulders shake, and a tear rolls down her cheek. "Lucy, why are you crying?"

She shakes her head, waves her hands in the air, a sign that she's trying to communicate something. The words are lost against the broad palm of her mate.

She shoves at his thick forearm. He removes his palm, then enfolds her in his embrace. Her chest heaves.

"Lucy...you...you okay?"

She holds onto him, tries to speak but no words emerge. More tears run down her cheeks.

My heart begins to race, "What have you done to her?"

Zeus frowns. "What are you talking about?"

Her shaking grows more violent. She snorts, chokes. He releases her, then strokes her hair. "You all right, Sweetheart?"

His features soften.

No. Wait. "You were—"

"—play acting." Lucy huffs out the words. "He'd never hurt me, Sis.'

"You thought I'd harm her?" Zeus's voice hardens. "You think I'd lay a finger on my mate?" He pulls her closer and Lucy all but mewls in delight.

My cheeks redden. "Um... I..."

She clearly relishes being surrounded by his physical dominance. As I do with Kayden. And I walked away from it. Worse, I had made him vulnerable. I'd softened him up, so he'd lowered his barriers. I'd hurt him. How could I live with myself?

A sob catches in my chest. My head spins and I put out a hand to right myself.

"Chloe." Lucy rushes forward and grabs my arm. "You poor thing, you've experienced so much in the last few weeks." She pats my shoulder.

Zeus takes a step forward and Lucy shoots him a glance. "I need to be with my sister."

His gaze moves from my face to Lucy's. "I need to debrief her with my team."

"And you will." Her voice is firm.

"The information she has is vital." His voice is hard. He moves closer and I cringe.

"The sooner she tells us what she knows, the faster we can plan our next steps. Timing is everything—"

"My point exactly."

He huffs out a breath. "How am I supposed to stay away while you're in this condition?"

"Just this once." Her voice turns pleading.

He frowns.

She shakes her head. "I'll make up for this, I promise."

"I'll hold you to it, hmm?" His voice lowers to a purr.

Lucy shivers. "You can count on it."

"Five minutes."

"Twenty."

"Ten."

"Done."

"If anyone else would dare negotiate with me—" Zeus grumbles.

"I'm not anyone."

"You bet your sweet ass, Squirrel, which by the way, will never be the same again after I've tapped it this time."

"Zeus." She squeaks, then covers my ears.

How cute. What does she think I've been doing all these days with Kayden? Kai. Drat it, why does my every thought lead to him? My chest tightens, another sob swells up, and I squeeze my eyes shut.

"Alpha, please, my sister needs me."

"Woman, you try my patience." Another growl rumbles from him. Then he tosses his head. "I'll be outside." He moves away and the door snicks shut.

My shoulders slump. I hadn't been aware how much Zeus' presence had put me on edge. Not that I'd thought he'd hurt me. Well okay, earlier I had reacted from instinct, thinking he might hurt her. I know better now. What I had witnessed between them? The chemistry, the way she had played him. No, how Zeus had allowed himself to be played by his mate… Wow. It had been enlightening, to say the least.

He would do anything for her—protect her, cherish her, even listen to her…on occasion. He doesn't fool me.

He was simply aware that he was being manipulated and he let her. Is that how it could have been with Kayden? My chest tightens; a pressure builds behind my eyes.

Lucy turns to me; her gentle warmth surrounds me.

Her strength is so different from Kayden's. Feminine, vital. Since our Mom passed away, Lucy has been the one constant in my life. Our father had been too busy attending to matters of state, while fighting his own grief at the loss of his mate. Losing his wife had hit him hard, but he'd put his feelings aside.

He knew he had to be there for his daughters, for his country. Yet his strength had waned over the years. Most mated pairs often die within months of each other. The mating bond feeds both partners in the relationship, keeps them going.

My father had pushed on.

He'd relied on Lucy for emotional support in those early months. You see, I have our mother's coloring. Her dainty features. I reminded him too much of my mother. Her essence as an omega breeder is something I inherited.

I've known my purpose from the time I hit puberty. Known that one day I'd find an alpha, mate and have children—a family of my own. I'd stumbled upon my alpha, all right. Except he'd turned out to be nothing like the mate I'd envisioned for myself.

Tears flow down my cheeks.

I turn my face into Lucy's familiar shoulder. She's always been the stronger of the two of us, and fiercely protective of me. She'd made sure I'd had a roof above my head. Yet she'd maneuvered me into putting myself in Kayden's path. "Why?" I choke out the words, "Why did you do it?"

She tenses, then pulls me closer. Tucks me into her side, much as Zeus had done to her earlier.

"Why, Lucy?" I hiccup, "Why did you ask me to put myself in his path? I should have never met him. He was all wrong for me... " *And nothing had felt more right.*

My heart seems to crumple in on itself. I have reined in my emotions for so long. Hadn't let myself go, even when I'd found Kayden with that...that woman. Interesting, right? It wasn't Kayden kidnapping me, or my near-death experiences, that had affected me as much as

finding him with another woman. An omega with her hands gripping him, a female blowing him...and he had let her. A snarl catches in my throat.

I bet the alphahole would find a way to justify all that had happened. Except he couldn't. I'd made sure he wouldn't be able to.

A fresh burst of sobs wells up. Damn it, I shouldn't give in to my grief. I can't stop. Something pent up inside of me seems to have broken. My shoulders shake and I hiccough.

"Shh, honey. It's okay, let it all out."

She pats my hair, so motherly, so affectionate. "I miss her." I sob out.

She hugs me tighter. "Me too, doll."

"Why did she have to leave us?"

"She was selfish, Chloe."

Huh? I lean back in the circle of her arms, a headache pounds behind my eyes. "Wha...what do you mean?"

Her features harden.

"I know you loved her. I did too."

She urges me toward the bed. I sink down and she sits next to me. "But it's time you knew the entire story."

162

Kayden

Water slaps my face and fills my nostrils. It drives away the scent of her.

I crack my eyelids open.

That infernal light. Sparks flare in front of my eyes. I swear my eyeballs have caught fire. A headache thuds at my temples. Fuck—a groan wells up and I swallow it down. Not gonna be a pussy. *You can take the punishment. You've faced worse.*

There's a click; a flame ignites. The scent of burning tobacco seeps into the air. My mouth waters.

Cigarettes are rare to come by. Cigars even more so. The sticks are worth their weight in gold. Or omega pussy. What's his game in smoking one?

He straightens, then walks forward to stand in front of me. He places the thin cigarillo to my lips. I draw on it. He pulls away the stick. I drag in the smoke. It sears my throat, burns its way down into my lungs. I cough, then sigh as the nicotine sinks into my blood.

Don't inhale; you puff a cigar. My father's voice admonishes me. *Yeah, pater. Sure. Such a stickler for rules, eh? Except when it came to my mother. Where did all your rules go then, eh? You allowed her to stay under your roof, yet ignored her. You cheated on her, and you thought you were being so discreet, eh? She chanced upon you with another omega.*

And that had been the final straw.

She'd taken me away to the Scottish stronghold, had isolated herself there. A sitting target for when Golan had come for her. My father hadn't been able to protect his mate. Hadn't been able to keep it in his pants either. Like me.

Twenty years later, I am repeating the cycle. I had allowed Lisa to seduce me… So, I had stopped her at the critical juncture. Perhaps I'd needed that test to understand the strength of my feelings for Cara?

I stiffen. *Did she see me with Lisa? Is that why she ran away that first time? Had she met up with Talon and struck a deal then?* She'd returned to me, and by that time, I'd been too distraught to ask her where she'd gone.

Yeah, my dick had insisted that I claim her once more. Show her who was her master. I had allowed my needs to take precedence. A part of me had noticed that she'd been withdrawn, even shaken on her arrival, but all of that had been pushed aside. My need to be inside of her, to brand her pussy as my own, to ensure that she hadn't been with another in the short time she'd been away. I'd been jealous as a new groom. Hell, worse. I had been a coward all along. Unable to face up to my intentions for her. It's right that I pay the price.

"Hit me."

Talon stills. He holds the cigarillo to my lips. When I refuse, he raises it to his mouth, puffs on it.

"Strike me, you bastard."

"That's you, not me."

What-fucking-ever.

He takes another drag, blows out the smoke. Fucker doesn't inhale either. The scent of tobacco deepens —rich, complex. Sweetened at the edges. Like her. That inherent perfume that clings to her curves. Concentrates between her legs, at the nape of her throat. If I could see her one more time…I'd…what? Apologize to her? Beg her to forgive me for the callousness of my ways with her? My lips twist. Fucking fuck. I'd throw myself at her mercy. Beg her to accept me. And if she refuses?

I'd lock her up.

I frown. That'd upset her. Too bad. For the sake of her child…my child… I swallow.

Child. I'd missed that? She'd been right to betray me. What kind of a mate doesn't spot that his omega is pregnant? My subconscious had known though… I hunch my shoulders.

That change in her scent, in her more sensitive than usual breasts. In how she'd given herself completely to me that last time. Had opened herself up, allowed me to possess her with abandon. She'd been insatiable. So had I.

I'd lost myself in her. The voices in my head had stilled for the first time, but I hadn't questioned any of it. Had taken it as my due. And it had been… It is my prerogative to do what is right to ensure her safety. To protect my family. My family. I had had everything in the palm of my hand and I had lost it. I had squandered it. She'd been right. I am selfish. I had hurt her. Broken her. I don't regret marking her, ruining her... But betraying her? I had been doing that from the moment I'd laid eyes on her. *An alpha who fails to defend what is his deserves to be punished.*

"I…I need this." The words rip out of me, and I don't stop them. "Go on, you want to beat me up, so what's stopping you?"

He surveys the butt of his cigar, takes a last drag, then places it on the ground next to him, in an ashtray I hadn't noticed.

Straightening, he cracks his neck. "Absolution, huh?"

I bare my teeth. "What's it to you, mofo?"

"Let's agree to leave our mothers out of this, hmm?"

Interesting. Seems we have that much in common. A weakness for our omega mothers.

"Harald, he treated her well?"

His features darken.

"Guess not." I curl my lips. "Did he fuck her? Or no, that's not his style. Did he cheat on her? No, don't answer that." I smirk. "He buried his dick in as many omegas as he could find. Did he hurt her? Did he beat her up? Did you try to stand up to him?"

He growls. His shoulders tense. *Come on, come at me, you dickhead. Bury your fist in my face. Hurt me as much as I hurt her. No worse. Smash me up to within an inch of my life. Do it.*

"Mama's boy, huh? Unresolved daddy issues, no doubt. Did your father ignore you? Maybe he preferred the company of his soldiers to that of his son? Every time he saw you, did he fuck you up? Play mind games with you, perhaps?"

His chest heaves. He curls his fists at his sides. "I know what you are doing." He bares his teeth. "And it's not working."

"'Oh yeah?" I shift in the chair and my entire body protests. Fuck that. Fuck him. Fuck me and my entire warped perception of what I wanted from life. All wrong. Everything I'd thought I deserved—my bloated sense of entitlement was what had landed me in this mess. Oh, not being captured by Talon, but my turning my back on her. My becoming like my father when I had allowed another omega to get near me.

A part of me had hoped Cara would chance upon me. Maybe it was my subconscious, but the unspoken is so much more powerful, eh?

I am using exactly that to manipulate Talon.

At least I am using my ability to influence in the right way. Not to benefit me, but to cause me harm.

"What?" I pretend to yawn. "Lost your balls? As much of a pussy as your ma who couldn't stand up for herself?"

"Shut. Up." He lurches forward, his cheeks flushed.

"Oh, but I'm just getting started." I bare my teeth, "Bet he shared her with his alphas. Did she like that—?"

He buries his fist in my solar plexus.

Flashes of white and red flash behind my eyes. I wheeze, struggle to find my breath. My mouth opens, but no sound emerges. Finally, I gasp, "That's it, then? Didn't take you for a coward. Didn't your mama teach you to stand up for yourself? Oh, wait, I forgot, she was too busy being fucked—"

He swings at my side; my body bucks. He lands another in my gut; then sinks his fist in my chest. There's a cracking sound; white pain fills my ribcage. The emptiness there. The hurt. It hurts.

Good. This is how she must have felt, when she saw me the first time in that pool on the terrace of the Omega Harem. She'd spotted me and her gaze had widened. I'd seen my reflection in her green eyes. Dark pupils that had dilated. The blackness had extended out, until all the remained was concentric circles of green. Beautiful eyes that belonged to my angel. My omega. Mine. *Cara, wherever you are, forgive me.*

His joined-up fists fill my line of sight.

My entire body arches; the chair tilts. *Why is the light so white?*

163

Chloe

Cara.

I jerk my head toward the sound of his voice.

Here.

I run across Red Square. It's empty. Why is the entire place desolate? Where is everyone?

This way.

I still, then turn right. Pick up speed. The blood pumps at my temples. Where is he? *Kayden.*

There's no reply. Not good. Why is he not talking to me? Is he angry with me? *Alpha?* The sound of my labored breathing greets me. My heart begins to race. "Kai." I scream.

Kai, Kai, Kai.

The sound echoes around the space. The hair on my forearms stands on end. "Kai," I sob. "Don't die."

Die. Die.

The voices whisper.

"No," I gasp. My legs hurt. My lungs burn. Keep going. One step in front of the other.

The distant sound of galloping reaches me. I pivot and freeze. A lone rider on a horse comes into view. The pounding of the hooves on the paved stones grows louder. Louder. Heading to me. I can't see the face of the man. A big man, massive shoulders. He's dressed all in black. A devil. A dark angel? He heads closer.

I should turn, run. But my legs refuse to move. My knees wobble.

"Kai," I form his name on my lips.

The horseman looms large. I can't see his face. Why can't I see his face? It's all blurred out. The features are indecipherable. My stomach churns; bile sloshes up my throat.

He leans low in the saddle; he's readying to swoop me up. He's going to take me away from here, away from my family. I should turn, put distance from him, save myself.

Save me. I whisper but nothing comes out of my mouth. Fear laces my blood. Adrenaline spikes my veins. Run.

Run. Run. The words pound in my head, mirroring the beats of the hoofs. My pulse thuds. I angle my body. But it's too late. He's at me. He reaches out, grabs for me. I see him then. The blood that flows from his ears, his eyes, down his cheeks, pooling at his throat, running in rivulets down his shirt.

"Forgive me," his voice is harsh.

"Kai," I reach for him and clutch at air. He's gone. The horse thunders past me. "Kai," I shriek.

"Chloe." My eyelids snap open. Lucy's worried face fills my vision.

"Kayden," I whisper, "he's alive."

She frowns. "You were dreaming."

"No. I mean, yes." I sit up, and she fluffs a pillow behind me. "I may have been dreaming, but I am sure he's alive."

"The mating bond?" She sits on the bed. "Do you sense him?"

I press a palm to my chest. The thud of my heart greets me. So lonely. It's not right that I am alone. I can't be. He can't have left me. "I can't feel him." I swallow. "I haven't for a while, not since…"

"Not since you fell pregnant?"

I stare. "How did you know?"

"That you were pregnant or that you couldn't reach him?"

"Umm, both?" I lace my fingers together in front of me. Kai. He has to be alive. He must be. That dream. I shiver. She leans forward and grips my joined-up palms.

"The first I guessed… The second I knew."

"You…knew?"

"A pregnant omega loses the ability to sense her mate. Something to do with all of your attention needing to be focused on the child in the first trimester. Sometimes it lasts the entire pregnancy."

"It's why a mate becomes overprotective?" I swallow. "Guess that's why your sex drive goes up at the same time."

"Kind of to attract your mate to you during that time. So they want to literally knot themselves to you." She huffs out a breath. "Tell me about it."

"You… you know how it feels?"

Lucy stares at me, a look of expectation on her face. Expecting. She's expecting? "Lucy, you're—"

"Pregnant."

We say at the same time.

I blink, then hug her. "Oh, my God!"

She pulls me close, "Ma would have been thrilled."

"You never allowed me to feel the loss of a parent, Luce."

"You were so young when she died, Sprite." Her voice breaks, "Now I can't believe you are having a child of your own."

I swallow. Lucy's been more than a mother to me. With our father often engaged with matters of administration, she often filled in the role of both of our parents.

It's why I can never challenge her.

It's probably why Zeus agreed for her to question me, knowing she'd have better luck than his heavy-handed techniques.

Oh, and she called me by the name only she ever uses. I frown. She does it when she's trying to suck up to me. Hmm.

She squeezes my shoulder, "How do you feel about that?"

"What?"

"Both of us are going to give birth almost at the same time."

"And I thought you telling me that Ma being in love with her bodyguard, enough to leave us and run away with him, was the sole secret you were hiding from me?"

She peers into my eyes. "You missed her so much, I didn't want to tarnish the image you had of her. She returned after they broke up, but she was never the same. She died soon after."

I swallow. "And father never recovered from what she'd done to him."

Her jaw firms, "He loved her; she broke his heart." She cups my cheek, "I wanted to protect you from the truth of their relationship, which was far from perfect."

"I can withstand the truth." I push the hair from her face. "I'm not so little anymore."

"You were so little when she died, she made me promise that I'd take care of you."

"I appreciate everything you did for me; I do." I straighten my spine. "But I'm grown up now. I can decide my own future, Lucy." I jut out my jaw. "I am going in search of him."

"You can't do that." Her forehead furrows.

"Why not?" I release her, then scoot back until I am close to the headrest.

"You're not a fighter."

I set my jaw. I may be a breeder, but I'd stood up to Kayden, hadn't I? Hell, I'd even negotiated my freedom with Talon. I am stronger than I thought. I'd underestimated myself... Never again. I firm my shoulders, "And you are?"

"Yes." She juts out her chin. Her features mirror a familiar adamancy.

Well, I am not going to retreat either. I fold my arms over my chest. "He's my mate."

"I know."

"Wouldn't you do the same if Zeus were missing and you were sure that he was alive."

"No." She blinks.

"Bull-fucking-shit."

"Chloe." Her mouth falls open. "You've changed."

You have no idea.

"Things...happened, you know." I raise my shoulders and let them fall.

"It's my fault." She chews on her lower lip. "I never should have suggested to Zeus that you were the perfect candidate to entice Kayden."

"So, you admit it?" I stare.

"Well..." She wriggles around on the bed, "you know—"

"No, I don't." Anger crawls at my nerve endings. My own sister... I'd known that she wanted me to manipulate Kayden. That's what Ethan had implied to me as well. But to think she'd purposely put me in Kayden's path? Heat fills my chest. "You knew Kayden would escape?"

Her shoulders tense. "Zeus had set things up so Kayden could find his way out."

"You had an inkling that he'd head straight for the Omega harem?"

"There was a possibility of that." She shifts her weight from foot to foot. "I mean, there was a slim chance of it—"

"Don't lie to me Luce." I swallow, "I couldn't bear it if you didn't tell me what actually went down."

Her chest rises and falls, "Zeus didn't want to lose Kayden. He also wanted his brother to learn a lesson." The skin at the edges of her eyes creases, "Zeus wanted revenge for what he did."

"Because Kayden sent you to assassinate him?"

She nods. "When news of Kayden's escape reached us, I prompted you to go up on the roof. I thought," she swallows. "It was a chance for you to find an alpha of your own, you know? I was sure that he'd fall for you. I had no idea that he'd… he'd… kidnap you."

I peruse her features, so like mine. Her shoulders, the frame of her body, similar to mine, except she's leaner.

Me? I'm soft, curvy, smaller than her; the right size to melt against Kayden's chest. I squeeze my eyes shut. *Kai, oh Kai.* "You've always had my best interests at heart, Lucy.

The breath rushes from her.

"It's thanks to you that I found my mate." I crack my eyes open. "Not your fault he turned out to be uh, not quite what I expected, huh?"

Her forehead crinkles.

I continue. "We play with the cards we've been dealt, Luce. We do what we have to do to survive."

She grips the bed clothes.

"And it's not as if I am blind."

"What do you mean?"

I place my palm over hers, mirroring the earlier reassurance she'd tried to communicate to me. "What you and Zeus have is pretty incredible, and I can understand that you wanted to please him."

"Get to the point, Chloe." She pulls her hand away, her tone sharp.

"I'm so pleased it turned out right for you. Really, I am." I bite the inside of my cheek. "Besides, it's not as if we can say 'no' to our alphas, right?"

"Wrong."

I link my fingers together. "You wouldn't challenge Zeus." I incline my head, "Clearly, he wants you to talk to me, and get all the information from me, and you have to obey him."

"Hmph." She purses her lips.

"You're being a good omega," I waggle my head, "one who'd do whatever her alpha wants."

She gnashes her teeth. "Just because I am mated—"

"And knocked up."

She scowls, "—doesn't mean I'm helpless."

I flutter my eyelashes, "You'd never challenge Zeus. He's the General of this city."

"And I'm his mate."

"His mate doesn't hold any sway." I tilt my head, "Right?"

She slips off of the bed and pulls herself up to her full height. "Nice one, Chloe."

Oh, shit. "Wh…what do you mean?"

She waves her finger at me, "Well played, little Sis."

I hunch my shoulders, "I…I didn't do anything."

"Sure, you did." Her lips curve in a slight smile, "But you're right, I'd do the same if I were in your place."

Hope blooms in my chest, "Y…you would?"

She jerks her chin. "It was wrong of me to suggest that you manipulate Kayden."

"It's because of that, I fell in love with him."

Her features twist, "Oh, honey, I'll never forgive myself for playing you that way. I had no right to interfere with your life."

"You wanted me to be happy." I peer up at her from under my eyelashes. "You had my best interests at heart, Luce."

"So…" She blinks, "You… you're not angry with me?"

"Hmm."

Her features break into a broad grin.

"Doesn't mean that I forgive you."

"Aww… Chloe—"

I hold up a hand, "Maybe… On one condition." I fold my fingers. Turn them up and pretend to examine my nails.

Lucy shuffles her feet, "You want me to let you go so you can search for him?"

I nod my head.

"Okay."

"Okay?"

There's a gleam in her eyes which I don't trust. Not at all. Not one bit.

She tilts her head, "I have a condition of my own."

164

Chloe

This was not what I'd had in mind when I had agreed to her condition. Lucy, of course, hadn't told me what, exactly, her stipulation would be. She'd made me promise I'd go along with it, and I'd had no choice but to agree. She hadn't wanted me to go alone in search of my mate. So, she's concerned and that's fine. She's allowed. After all, she is my sister. But to insist that the woman accompanying me be this one? I mean… Honestly, how could she?

I walk forward, head held high. I refuse to talk to her, refuse to have anything to do with her. She draws abreast.

I increase my pace and she matches me.

"Stop following me." I grind out the words.

"I am not here of my own volition either," Lisa mutters.

"So why did you agree to Lucy's proposal?"

"You want to see him, so do I—"

I turn on her, "How dare you?"

She holds up her hands, palms face up. "Don't get your knickers in a twist. I want to apologize to him."

I glower at her. "It's me you should be apologizing to!"

Her lips quirk, "Not that he protested too much, by the way."

I step forward, "Take that back."

She tilts her head, "Or else?"

"Really? You want to get into this with me now?"

She stiffens, then jerks her chin. "You're right. We both want the same thing."

"Oh?"

She shuffles her feet, "We want to see Kayden safe."

A hot feeling stabs in my chest, turns out I am jealous, insanely. "Don't talk about him."

She frowns, "Whoa, girlfriend... possessive much?"

"You bet." I close the distance between us,

Bitch put her hands on him, she touched him, she tried to blow him off, and yeah, he went along with it, until he didn't. He'd been tempted all right, and damn, if I was going to let her close to my man again... *My* man. I blow out a breath. Hell, why can't I stop thinking of him? I curl my fingers into fists, "You are the last person I want to trust, but I have no choice."

I don't know where Talon's camp is situated, but Lisa does—or at least she claims to—and I have to get to Kayden before it is too late. He is alive; I am sure of that.

I can't sense him, but I am confident that he is at the other end of the mating chord. After all, when he'd been shot, I'd felt his pain as if it were my own... My heart stutters; my stomach twists. The taste of fear coats my mouth and I swallow it down. He's alive. He is. My instinct tells me I'll find him. It's all I have, and I am going to lean into it.

I take a step forward, and a wary look comes into her eyes.

I lower my chin. "One wrong move when we get there... If you try to take what's mine, I promise I'll kill you with my bare hands."

She stares, then her features brighten. "Hot damn." She chuckles, "Guess I misjudged you, huh?"

"Wouldn't be the first time."

"You have more courage than I gave you credit for."

I toss my head, "If that was meant to be a compliment—"

"It was. Honest." She shuffles her feet, "Listen, I really am sorry. Can we bury our differences, at least for the length of this trip?"

I purse my lips.

"Just until we get to Kayden, and find a way to rescue him."

I jut out my chin, "Why should I trust you, huh?"

She swallows, "I want to apologize to Kayden for what I did. I've known him since I was so little. Followed him everywhere. I had this massive crush on him, except he never noticed me." She inclines her head. "It's you he wants, Chloe. You don't need to be jealous of me."

Her features twist. Her eyes glitter with unshed tears. Damn it, I shouldn't feel sorry for her. I shouldn't. The band around my chest squeezes. But I bet it sucks to be in her shoes. Besides, she's right. Kayden had turned her away; he had chosen me.

My pulse begins to race.

"Fine." Me and my stupid soft heart, I snort, "You apologize, then you get the hell out of there, you hear me?"

Her forehead clears, "Deal." She holds out her hand.

I snort. "Let's not go that far." I turn, then march forward. There's silence, then I hear her following me.

I increase my pace, "How long, until we get there?"

"On foot, at least 3 days."

"What the hell?" I round on her.

She smirks, "On the other hand, by car it's a few hours." She walks past me, up the slight slope, and pushes past the tall shrubs. "Coming?" She disappears.

I follow her, step onto a road. Huh? Why hadn't I seen it? It had been hidden by the thick undergrowth. I turn to find her standing next to a jeep. A man steps out of the vehicle. I freeze, then watch as he walks toward her.

He hands over the key and she takes it from him. "Thanks, Xander."

Of course. He is the one alpha, other than Dominic, who hadn't touched me when Kayden had forced me to walk into the meeting with the other alphas in the room — when he had invited them to touch me, have their fill of me. I curl my fists at my sides. He'd apologized for that. In a way, it was that incident that had changed the dynamic between us…and now I had Kayden's child in my belly. I touch my stomach. *For you, I'm doing this for you, little one. We're going to rescue him, you and me. I grew up without a parent. Whatever happens, I am not going to let that happen to you.*

Xander hesitates. "You're putting yourself at risk, Lisa."

"Not out of choice." She tips up her head, "It's the fastest way to redeem myself."

"You don't need to do anything." He pushes away a strand of hair from her face. She doesn't respond.

He drops his face and she shuffles away. His features twist, then he composes himself. Ah, so the man is in love with her? He's an alpha, yet he doesn't force her. He'd restrained himself earlier with me, as well. A gentleman alpha? Huh. Imagine that.

I walk toward them, as he wrenches open the door to the driver's seat. She moves past him and seats herself.

He shuts the door, "You sure I can't come with you?"

"You would be missed. It would alert them to our having left."

"They'll realize that anyway."

I round the car, open the door on the passenger side and slide in. "Not if Lucy manages it correctly…and she will."

Xander peers inside the open window, "I don't want to leave you alone, Lisa."

"I think you should get used to the idea."

He draws in a breath, "Woman, you hit me where it hurts the most."

She stares ahead, her fingers gripping the steering wheel. "There's no future for us, Xane."

His jaw tics, "You've only ever had eyes for him."

"He was never mine." She starts the car.

"Then… Why do this?" He glances at me. "Why risk your life for her?"

"I…put Chloe in danger, tried to tempt him even after he'd made his choice." She swallows. "He hates me for that. This is the best way to show that I am sorry for what I did. I wanted my Dad to be proud of me." She tips her chin up. "You understand that, right?"

"No, I don't." His chest rises and falls. "But I know that once you decide to do something, nothing will sway you from your goal."

She chuckles, "You know me too well."

"Then, let me accompany you."

"I can't."

"Why not?"

"Because… " She firms her lips, "Because I…I don't want to lead you on."

His muscles tense; his shoulders bunch. "Fuck Lisa, you could give a man some hope, at least."

"The way I held on for Kayden?"

I clear my throat. What is it with these guys? Don't they realize I am listening? Or maybe they don't care?

He's certainly focused on her, and she...she's too busy feeling miserable. I touch her shoulder and she straightens. "I...I have to go Xander. Don't wait for me. Find someone else."

He swears, then slams his fist on the roof of the car. The vehicle shudders and we both yelp.

"Shit." He raises his palms, "Sorry, didn't mean for that to happen."

"No, *I'm* sorry." She snakes her arm out and grabs his hand, "If I felt something for you. If I could accept you... It's just, I don't want to settle—"

He winces.

"I don't mean it that way... Xane..."

He retreats, "You're right. Why should you settle for me when you're searching for that burning feeling that comes when you find your other half?" He rubs his chest, "And you let them go in the hope that they'll return to you."

"Not fair." She swallows. "You're saying it to make me feel awful."

"Maybe." He chuckles, the sound bitter. "I hope you find what you're searching for, Lisa." He firms his lips, "You can be sure of one thing..."

She tilts her head.

"If you don't return in 24 hours—"

She frowns, "3 days."

"24 hours." He sets his jaw.

"2 days."

He shakes his head, "Twenty-four hours, and then I'm going to Dominic and telling him everything."

"Hell," she mutters.

"You can say that again." I blow out a breath, "Speaking of which, we'd better get going. The clock's ticking."

She shifts into gear, steps on the accelerator, and the car leaps forward.

"Hey," I grab for the dash.

"Fasten your seatbelt." Her voice is hard, "It's about to get bumpy."

165

Kayden

Clod raises his massive fist. I stare at it from under swollen eyelids. I brought this beating upon myself and I don't regret it. The only thing I wish I hadn't done was treat her with such utter contempt. If I see her again, I'll make it up to her. First, I must pay the price for what I did to her. I raise my head, "Tired, motherfucker?"

Clod lands his hit into my side.

My entire body spasms. *Fuck*. Good thing I am numb. He must have broken something, probably my shoulder, the way it hangs down on my side. He's dislocated it… And that's not all that's off. My arms and legs are numb. Even the burning feeling in my chest has receded. A shiver rolls down my body. Why am I so cold? The scene in front of me wavers. I blink away the sweat that drips into my eyes. Or is that blood?

Clod pauses, chest heaving. Sweat glistens on his torso. His features twist as he scans my physique.

"That bad, huh?" I laugh. "Or maybe you've lost your nerve."

He rolls his shoulders.

"Tired already?" I smirk, or at least I try to, considering I can't feel much of anything, actually.

True to his word, Clod had spared my face. Small mercies. I huff.

The rest of me is one large blob of broken bones, sweat, and tears… The last? Yeah, I am not ashamed to admit that somewhere in the last hour I had broken down. Not from pain, or from the days of being beaten up. It was when I'd remembered her face. How her features had grown ashen when she'd stepped into that room filled with alphas, when I had invited them to have their fill of her.

I swallow, squeeze my eyes shut.

Fuck me. Fuck me for what I did to her. I don't deserve to be alive. I shake my head, crack my eyelids open. "That all you've got, you cunt?"

He growls, cracks his knuckles.

I bare my teeth, "I'm so scared."

He interlaces the fingers of his hands together. Fuck. When he puts the width of his body behind that punch, it more than hurts. He's gonna knock me out cold in the state that I am...exactly what I want. I angle my head. "This side."

He hesitates.

I glance at him and almost laugh out loud. The man has a confused expression on his face. *Don't blame you.* I am surprised by how much self-loathing I have in me. It's not just from how I treated my omega. Guess somewhere inside of me, I've held myself responsible for what happened to my mother — for not saving her from Golan, for not standing up for her with my father. *I should have forced him to take better care of you, Ma. I was too young, too messed up in my h I did the exact same thing my blood father did to you... ead with what was happening between the two of you.* I'd sworn never to let that happen to another woman in my life...and then, guess what? I had inflicted that, and more, on the one thing that was precious to me. Her.

"Hit me, bitch."

He snarls, steps forward...when there's a knock on the door. He freezes. I blink.

"Expecting someone?" I ask him, not that I expect an answer. Clod doesn't speak, I don't think, or maybe he's been instructed to stay silent. Either way, at some point I'd stopped caring, and decided to hold a monologue with him. Was it to simply voice my thoughts aloud?

To goad him on, to ensure that I push him until he, too, loses control, gives me his worst... A death wish? No. I won't die from the beating. Bet my body is bent all out of shape though. At some point I'd long gone past the point of pain, floating in that strange sub-space where you're outside your body and watching everything as if from far away. Clod opens the door and a woman walks in.

Huh? Am I hallucinating?

He stares and she brushes past him. She crosses the floor to stand in front of me. "So, this is the prisoner, eh?"

The fuck? I blink at her face, those familiar features. Green eyes blaze at me. Horror, fear, pity? Yeah, all of those emotions swirl in those big eyes.

"I'm dreaming."

When her face pales, I realize that I've said it aloud.

"You are a figment of my imagination."

She gnaws on her lower lip. "I've been sent by Talon to ensure that you're doing your job."

He peers in her direction, his mouth half open.

She angles her body, and his breathing deepens.

He leans forward. "Who're you?"

The man speaks? And he's addressing his questions to her, which means... I am not dreaming.

"The hell you doing here, Ca—?"

She swoops down, slaps her hand over my mouth. "What... did...you..." I mumble through the cloth she stuck in my mouth.

She fucking gagged me?

I yank at my restraints. The chair teeters forward, then slams back on all four legs.

She flinches, but doesn't turn. Her attention is focused on the asshole who peruses her face, her breasts. He fucking eats her alive with his scrutiny. And I... I'm here, helpless. Anger pulses at my temples, flares down my spine, and with it, pain. My leg muscles scream; my biceps bulge. I strain against the ropes that bind me.

He takes a step forward and she parts her legs. She drags her palm down her chest, and props it on her hip. "See something you want, big boy?"

He snarls, then lurches toward her.

She puts up a hand and he freezes. *Huh?*

She flutters her eyelashes, licks her lips, and my dick throbs. Blood rushes to my groin. Bloody hell. Apparently, *that* part of me functions with 100% efficiency. She's leading him on, trying to distract him. Why? I glance past the dumbstruck alpha to the door.

It opens and another woman steps in.

She scrutinizes the room, spots me, and color drains from her face.

Lisa? The fuck is she doing here? And are the two omegas working together?

I shake my head to clear it. Stare at the scene unfolding in front of me. Nope, they're both still there.

Lisa shuts the door, turns the key in the lock. The snick echoes across the space. Clod freezes. He angles his body. *No, don't look back, asshole.* I shove my heels into the floor, drag my chair forward, but Cara is faster.

She closes the distance to Clod, reaches up and places her palm on his chest. I bet that she's doing it to distract him, but fuck that. He's dangerous and dumb...but lethal with his blows. If he dares hurt her, I'll kill him. I'll —

"Guess why I am here?" She flicks back her hair. Her scent intensifies.

I stiffen; so does Clod.

His attention is focused on her; he seems to have not noticed Lisa, who moves toward him. What the hell is she doing? My muscles tense. I glance from her to my omega. If he lays one finger on her.

"You're so purty," his lips twist. He raises his hand and she sidles out of reach.

"I am your prize, Alpha."

"You are?" The fucker pants. He actually pants. When I get my hands on him, I am going to tear him from limb to limb, drain his blood, splatter it on the floor, then make love to her right there. A snarl rumbles up my throat.

Cara flinches. So, she hears me. Good. She's putting on an act to free me, but fuck that. Nothing is worth her putting herself at risk...this way. When we get out of here, I'll ensure that she understands that.

"Talon sent me to reward you for your efforts." She wriggles her hips, and his pupils dilate. He grabs his crotch and thrusts forward into his hand.

Fucker's masturbating to her presence. How dare he? No one disrespects her... no one else gets to cum looking at her, except me. I flex my biceps, firm my thigh muscles, take in a deep breath, and yank. My arms scream in protest. Sweat breaks out on my forehead and flashes of light go off behind my eyes.

The restraints around my shoulders snap.

His head jerks toward me; his face hardens. He shoves her aside. Anger pounds behind my eyes. All of my muscles tauten; the tendons of my throat strain. Pain explodes down my spine; my stomach churns. The taste of bile fills my mouth and I swallow it away.

I grit my teeth, yank forward, and the bond around my thighs loosens, enough for me to straighten to my feet, the chair still bound to me. I pounce forward, as he swipes out his fist. His gaze widens. He roars in pain, turns, and I see the knife sticking out from his back.

He hauls Lisa up by her neck, then flings her away.

"Move aside, Chloe."

She scrambles away. I bend forward from the waist, rush him. Head butt him below where the knife is stuck into him. I collide with him with such force that he shoots forward. The heels of his boots scrape across the stone floors, then he falls on his face.

I collapse on top of him, holding him down with my weight.

He snarls, tries to crawl away. I snap my head forward; my forehead connects with the back of his head. Sparks of white flash in front of my eyes. I swear my brain is on fire. I shake my head to clear it. The noise in my head ebbs away. I glance down to find he's unmoving. Motherfucker.

"Kayden." Chloe crawls toward me. She shoves aside her skirt, flashing me a long line of her leg. "Umm, Cara...I know you're eager to see me but—"

She reaches down, pulls out the knife stuck into the band around her thigh.

Ah. She saws at the rope that binds my arms; it falls away. I shake off the chair and spring to my feet. My shoulder screams in pain again. I ignore it. I use my still-working arm to reach for her at the same time she does.

"You've changed Cara."

166

Chloe

"You haven't, Alphahole."

Our fingers touch before he circles my wrist. I allow him to pull me to him, to lift me up in his embrace, tuck my head under his chin.

"I missed you." His breath ruffles my hair.

So did I. It's why I came for you. Except now that I am here, I 'm unsure what to say. I want to embrace you, bury my nose in your chest. Breathe you in, fill myself with your essence. Burrow into you. I can do all of that because I am in the circle of his arms, except... I don't. I stand silently as he rocks me, pulls me close until my breasts are pressed into his chest.

The 'V' of his pelvis cradles the softness of my pussy. The hard length of his shaft —no. I pull away; he lets me go. I turn away and he squeezes my arm. "What's wrong?"

Nothing.

Everything.

I don't understand why this awkwardness grips me. Why I can't meet his gaze. His scent surrounds me, the warmth from his body a potent force. Calling to me, urging me to wallow in his nearness. I twist my body and he releases me.

"Cara."

"We have to go." I march to where Lisa is beginning to stir. I hold out my arm. She hesitates, then grips it. I pull her to her feet. "Thanks…I think."

She sways "You saved my life."

I tighten my hold on her. "Least I could do under the circumstance."

Kayden stalks past me to the wall. His movements are jerky. He shoves his shoulder against the barrier.

"What are you—?"

He twists his torso, his shoulder strains, then, there's a popping sound.

I wince.

A groan leaves his lips and color fades from his face.

My stomach churns, my spine bends, and every instinct in me pushes me forward. *Go to him. Go.*

He straightens, "Snapped the sucker into place."

Right.

He pivots, then prowls toward me.

I anchor my feet into the floor, stare straight ahead.

He stops in front of me, fills my vision. He's too big, too large. His bulk surrounds me. Dominance pours off of him, pushes down on my shoulders. My chest. My throat dries. I can't look past him. Can't ignore him. *Damn you, Kayden.* The heat from his massive frame slams into me.

I gasp, drop my arms to my side. "We need to get out of here," and not only because we may be found soon. It's because…I am too attracted to him.

I want to fling myself at him, beg him to take me again. My thighs clench, slick pools between my legs. I shift my weight from foot to foot. Not yet.

This time I will hold my own.

I am pregnant with his child. My child. My fingers tingle; my belly quivers. Something warm coils in my chest. Physically, I want him. No denying that. He is my mate. My throat closes. Except, will he accept me on my terms?"

"You?" Kayden's voice sounds from somewhere above me. He clenches his fists, "What are you doing here?"

"I came to apologize." Lisa stutters. "I'm sorry for what I did, I—"

"Apology not accepted."

I pivot in time to see her face turn as chalky as the wall behind her. She sways and I step forward, grip her shoulders. "She's the reason I could find you. That you are now free."

"She's why you were taken in the first place, why I was shot." His voice hardens.

I wince, "No, that was me." I refuse to meet his gaze, "Don't go passing off the blame on her for that."

"Not here to negotiate, Omega." Anger radiates off of him, "She worked with an informer in my clan. She put your life at risk."

Sweat beads my palms. Do I have any hope of winning this argument? "And she's sorry for it. Besides, she made up for it by leading me to you."

"Doesn't negate what she did."

"And what will negate what you did to me?" I raise my gaze to his face, gasp, when I get my first good look at him.

Blood stains his temples, drips down his chin. Dark blotches blot his torso. There's a dressing above his heart. Imprints of fisticuffs mark his chest. Wounds, scratches, grooves mark that beautiful torso.

My heart stutters and my guts twist.

He pulls himself up to his full height. "Not discussing that with you here."

"Right." I curl my lips. "Never the time is it, for you to be accountable for your actions? I always have to fall in line with your plans. Well, I have news for you, Alpha," I close the distance between us and stab my finger into his chest, "You're not always right."

"So much sass." A low purr rumbles up his chest, and I'm instantly wet. *Oh, my God. Seriously? Why can't I control myself when I am with him, huh?*

I withdraw my hand; he swoops down and grabs my wrist. "I relish this version of you, Cara, all strong and brave and spitting fire." He widens his stance. "It's a fucking turn-on."

"I hate every version of you," I snarl, "Mean, domineering, and so full of yourself."

My sex clenches; my toes curl.

"Liar." A smirk tugs at those gorgeous lips.

My nerve-endings spark. Damn him, he's right. I toss my head, "It makes me want to put enough distance between us to never see your face again." I return his perusal. *Don't blink. Don't.*

"You don't mean it."

I huff, "You telling me what I should be thinking?"

"Damn right." His jaw tics, "And you'll listen to what I have to say."

"No." I raise my chin.

He glares at me. "Yes."

My scalp tingles. All of my synapses seem to fire at once. I gulp.

Lisa clears her throat, "Can we get out of here before we are found?"

Behind us, there's a groan from the fallen alpha.

I pivot at the same time as Kayden. He stalks up to the man, raises his foot—

"Kayden, no."

He brings it down on the man's face.

There's a sickening crunching sound. My stomach heaves. My knees buckle and Lisa grips my upper arm, "Stay strong," she hisses.

I swallow down the bile that threatens to rise. Square my shoulders.

Kayden turns toward me. The light from the bulb above casts his face in shadow. The rest of his battered, bruised body is in relief. Angles crevices, hollows, dips, planes…an expanse of pure male beauty, wild, untamed, savage.

He steps forward and his face comes into view.

I swallow. "You needn't have killed him."

His features harden, those dark eyes growing so black, they resemble pools of cold hate. "He touched you."

A shiver runs down my spine.

"He touched what was mine."

His voice whips across my skin; my pulse begins to race. My limbs tremble. A few seconds in his presence and I'm ready to do as he commands. I clench my fists at my sides. I must resist, I must hold my own…until I have established the rules of a level playing field. I can't give in.

His nostrils flare, his jaw tics, and he opens his mouth. "We need to get out of here."

I march toward the exit, unlock the door and shove it open. Talon's shoulders fill the frame. "We meet again."

167

Kayden

"Get away from the door." I leap forward so fast I am sure my feet don't touch the floor. My muscles scream; the tendons of my legs strain. "Cara!" I hear my voice echo in my ears, then I am there. I plant my body in front of her, slap my palms on my hips. "Don't touch her."

Talon's mouth curls, "You're hardly in a position to give me orders."

"Take me, let her go."

"I'm willing to consider your request." He jerks his chin, "Let's discuss this in a civilized manner."

"Don't believe him." Lisa bursts out from somewhere behind me.

Talon swings his face toward her.

His features harden. The veins on his forehead pop. He glares at her, "Who the fuck are you?"

Lisa shrinks closer to my omega.

"Answer me."

"I...I..."

"She's with me." I widen my stance, shielding both girls from him. Strange, huh? A few weeks ago, I was the one in his place. The marauder, the berserker, the one with the agenda to displace. To take. Now the boot is on the other foot, the tables turned... Fuck, these metaphors are fucking with my head. Clearly, I am not thinking straight. Thanks to fucking Clod. I'd felt each of the hits from his massive fists; I also have my faculties intact, mostly. Not complaining about that.

I can walk, can swing my fists.

I clench my fingers, hold them up in front. "Let them leave."

"No." He clicks his tongue. "Your mate is with you. This other one, though, I wonder if she's the reason for my losing two of my best guards?"

I smirk. "You really think a helpless omega could take on two of your men?"

There's a choking sound from Lisa. "Who are you calling helpless?" She steps forward.

I frown at her. *Idiot.*

She glowers back. "Honestly, Kayden," she stabs a finger at me. "After everything I did to reunite you with your omega, you'd think you'd be more grateful, you —oh." Her gaze veers to Talon and her breath hitches.

Her chest rises and falls.

"Do all of the omegas in your clan have such fighting spirits?" His eyes glitter.

She juts out her chin, "What do you think?"

He looks her up and down, "Seen better."

"Wha—?" She blinks.

He jerks his head, "Out of the way."

"Anyone tell you, you're impolite?"

I snort. Talon frowns. Cara steps closer to me. "Did she insult him?" she mutters under her breath.

"Didn't you hear me?" Talon clicks his tongue, "Step aside, Omega."

She leans forward on the balls of her feet, "Make me."

Talon steps in, shuts the door, locks it. He pockets the key. "Can't have you running off now, not until I conclude my business."

"Don't trust me to stay?" Lisa thumps her chest. "What a shocker."

His features take on a bored look. "I don't have time for feminine tantrums; however, since you insist." He moves so fast that he seems to blur. The next second he grabs her by her shoulders, lifts her and sets her aside.

Then jerks his head toward the chair, "Take your seat."

I hesitate.

"I won't ask again."

I growl deep in my throat. Fucker knows I am at a disadvantage. Not only am I hurt—fuck that, I don't care about myself— but no way am I going to endanger Cara's life. "Fine."

I turn to her, bend my knees and scoop her up.

She squeaks, "What are you doing?"

I stalk past the fallen Clod, to the overturned chair, and kick it upright. I drop into it and place her on my lap. She struggles and I tighten my hold, "Cooperate for once."

She huffs out a breath. "Why should I?" She whisper screams.

"If not you, think about the child you carry. You don't want to endanger his life."

"You're so sure it's a boy?"

"I know." I stare ahead.

"You've definitely not changed." She scowls up at me, "Still every bit an asshole."

You have no idea.

I track Talon's progress.

He takes in Clod's body, but there's no change in expression on his face. He picks up the other chair and places it across the fallen man's corpse. He straddles it. "Wish we could have met under better circumstances."

Cara stiffens in my arms, tension leaping off of her body in waves. Surely that can't be good for the child, eh? And to think she'd come all the way here, and teamed up with someone whom she must hate. Yeah, I have a lot to make up to her. Don't even blame her for being all standoffish with me, eh? A harsh purr rumbles up my chest. I haul her closer so she's tucked into my side.

Her soft curves melt into me.

Such a contrast. So fucking luscious. My dick is instantly hard, and yes, I'm turned on. After all, I have my mate in my arms. But so not the place. And it wasn't for that I'd pulled her into my lap. It's simply so I can protect her.

"What about me?" Lisa stalks up to stand next to Talon. She's tiny enough that she is at eye-level with him seated.

He ignores her, jerks his chin at Cara, "You shouldn't have come here, Chloe."

I frown, "Talk to me."

"But—" Cara protests, and I clap my hand over her mouth.

"Don't interfere."

She wriggles her little butt, which brushes the rising bulge in my pants. She freezes, I tilt my head. *Told ya. Stay put.* She bites down on the fleshy part of my palm and my dick twerks. Yeah, I used that word. No other way to describe the vibrations of pleasure that crowd in on my groin. My nostrils flare. Little hellion.

She brings her hand to my chest, digs her fingers into the bandage. Pain radiates out from the impact. Sweet justice. *I caused you so much grief, little one, this is nothing. I'll take anything you hurl at me and return for more.* I'm a sadist that way.

She drags her fingers down my chest, leaving a trail of fire in her wake. I don't flinch, watch as she huffs out a breath, then tucks her elbows into her sides.

"This is not right, Kayden," she mumbles, "Lisa's the one who convinced Lucy to let her go, for me to accompany her, so she could bring me here."

"You?" Talon glares at Lisa.

"Oops." She swipes her hair back from her face. "Sorry, not sorry."

He raises his chin, "Tell me more."

She pulls her shoulders back, "Nothing more to say, except..." She bounces on the balls of her feet, "Uh, I think I feel a nap coming on."

"What?" He stares at her.

"You know—" She pretends to yawn. "A siesta? Don't you want to snooze in the afternoon? I do...I—"

He quirks a finger and she shakes her head.

"Come 'ere."

She gulps, shoots me a sideways glance.

I raise my shoulders, let them drop. Nope, not getting involved. Firstly, I'm pissed that Lisa brought her here. Secondly, it's too entertaining how she seems to be crawling under Talon's skin.

I don't think I've heard the Viking so preoccupied, as when he's trying to simultaneously fend off Lisa and put her in her place.

When it comes to her, it seems that he has a weak spot—or is that a hard one? Interesting. Gotta see how this plays out.

I don't want to abandon Lisa, but my mate comes first; and if Lisa's presence serves to keep Talon off balance, then so be it.

Talon lowers his chin. "Don't make me repeat myself."

Lisa pales. She takes a step, another, until she's standing right next to him. He drops his gaze to the ground.

She frowns, "No way. If you think I'm obeying you, you're wrong."

"Oh?" He glares at her and she swallows.

"Down." He clicks his tongue and she firms her lips.

His glare intensifies. "Last chance," his voice lowers to a hush.

She gulps, sinks to her knees, peeks at the lifeless body strewn a few inches away. Her features twist. She opens her mouth, and he shakes his head. Her shoulders hunch; she folds her arms about her waist, stares at a point beyond him.

"Now, where were we?"

Talon turns to face me. He takes in my stance, the omega in my arms. "Seems I have not one hostage, but three."

"You don't need the two of them." Lisa mutters.

"Stay quiet." He grumbles.

She flinches, lowers her head further, mumbles, "It's true. I am the one to blame. You should release them."

"You have spirit." His eyes gleam. "You need to be punished."

She stiffens.

"And that pleases me, so I'll tell you. I can't release them. What kind of an example would that set, hmm?" He scratches his chin, "They killed my guards. They must pay for it."

Cara freezes in my arms. So, she is concerned about me? Of course, she is. That's why she came here. So why did she withdraw when I tried to touch her? Why had I been so distracted by her arrival? I should have scooped her up in my arms and run out of there. I hadn't. I'd dawdled here...and endangered her life.

She shudders and I pull her close, tuck her head under my chin. A subvocal hum rumbles up my chest. She presses her palm into the skin above my heart. The vibrations seep into her, travel up her arm. Her body relaxes again.

Lisa raises her head, "I killed the guards."

168

Chloe

"You?" Talon's attention snaps to Lisa, "You killed the guards at the door?"

Her shoulders hunch, but she doesn't shrink away. "All of this," she waves a hand in the air, "is my fault."

"It is, hmm?" He strokes his chin.

"That's why you must let them go."

"Oh?"

She bites on her lower lip and Talon's gaze drops to her mouth. "You should punish the real culprit... Me."

"Lisa... " I try to speak, but of course, Kayden slaps his palm over my mouth. I shove at his chest and he tightens his hold.

He angles his body, squeezes his palm across the lower half of my visage and my breath cuts off. I mumble, scratch at his wrists.

He loosens his hold enough so I can draw in a breath. "Stay quiet," he hisses. "Listen to me this fucking once."

I stiffen and he draws me close. "Please, Sugar," his breath sears my cheek.

I pause, something warm flaring in my chest. Damn it, one endearment from him and I'll lay down at his feet and beg him to take me. I force my muscles to relax and the breath whooshes out of him, lifting the hair on my head.

Ahead, Talon reaches out a hand and Lisa flinches. He tugs at a tendril of hair; her shoulders go rigid. Fear trembles off of her; her spine curves as if she wants to run the hell away from there. Don't blame her. If it wasn't for the big bad alpha who holds me in his arms—huh? —I shouldn't feel so safe with Kai—*Kayden, think of him as Kayden.* Why am I sure that he won't let Talon get to within an inch of me?

Except, I am not the one Talon wants. It's Lisa who bears the brunt of his scrutiny.

"Soft." He drawls out the word, and she winces. He leans forward so the chair tips to the side. Then drops his nose toward her. She sidles away. He clamps his palm around her nape.

Kayden's muscles tense, but he stays silent. Why isn't he doing something about this? Why is he allowing Talon to treat Lisa that way?

I dig my elbow into his chest, right into the wound there. He huffs out a breath, then turns to me.

I glower at him, then jerk my chin toward Lisa. *Do something.*

He glares back. Of course, he knows what I'm saying, but he doesn't respond. I look sideways, to where Talon pulls Lisa forward.

He buries his nose in her throat. "Mm," he inhales, his biceps bulge, and his chest seems to grow larger. He straightens, then urges her closer until her body is fitted against his thigh.

He coaxes her to lay her head down on his lap. Like a dog? He's treating her as if she's some kind of…animal, a slave. Someone he means to own? I sit up, or try to. Kayden's arms tighten. He shakes his head.

I jut out my chin, bite down on his fingers again. He doesn't even flinch. He glares at me and I sigh. Fine. Let's see how this plays out.

"A fight." Talon rumbles.

I freeze, jerk my head in the direction of where the other alpha runs his fingers over Lisa's hair. His massive body dwarfs hers. His strokes are long, hypnotic. Her eyes flutter closed.

Huh?

She is positioned on her knees; it's got to be uncomfortable. Except you wouldn't think so the way her muscles relax, her body curved to conform to the massive column of his thighs.

"What's at stake?" Kayden's voice is calm, but a pulse flares to life at the corner of his jaw.

"You win," he jerks his chin at me, "she goes free. If you lose—" he angles his head, and a small smile curves his lips. The unsaid words hang in the air… He doesn't have to complete the sentence. I am sure that, given the opportunity, he'd kill Kayden.

I gulp. This had been a bad idea. What had I been thinking, flouncing in here without a real plan?

Kayden glances at Lisa. "And her?"

Talon's fingers tighten in her hair, "None of your concern."

The hell?

I rear up, and Kayden slams me into his chest. His big arms squeeze my shoulders. He wraps his palm around my head, mirroring how Talon had subdued Lisa, and now he is doing the same to me.

He is shutting me down. He is going to let Talon have his way with Lisa. Exactly as he'd taken me without giving me a choice, and there was nothing I could do about it. Nothing.

I slam my body against his, push, shove, bite down again, try to bring my knees up. He simply tears his fingers from my face. I open my mouth and he kisses me. *Wha*—He thrusts his tongue between my lips.

I jerk away, and his fingers dig into my scalp.

He applies enough pressure that I can't move. Can't think, can't do anything but submit to him. He sucks from me, drinks from me, draws on my essence. He kisses me with the kind of passion I've always wanted him to demonstrate... That he'd shown me the last time I had been in his bed.

No, more. There's a desperation to his touch. His body hunches over me. Protective, hiding me from the other man's perusal. He teases me, seduces me, slurps from me, and gives in return. It's a submission from him too, a statement that he'll never let me go, a plea to trust him…and I do.

And that's the fucked-up thing about all of this. Despite everything he did to me, there was always an underlying emotion that connected us. The one that made me return to him again and again.

The sentiment that allows me to relax in his presence, open myself up to him. Bend my spine, thrust out my breasts, throw my arms about his shoulders and kiss him.

He tilts his head, swipes his tongue across the seam of my mouth. The pressure on the back of my head reduces. He drags his fingers down my spine, then grabs my ass and squeezes.

I groan; a deep purr rumbles from his chest. So hot. So sweet.

He plunges his tongue inside of my mouth again. My sex clenches. He continues kissing me, not coming up for air, not stopping, not until my eyelids flutter and my body slumps. My arms and legs grow leaden. Can't feel my toes.

Darkness swirls at my subconscious mind.

169

Kayden

Talon had left, taking Lisa with him, and I had watched silently. I'd felt a stab of guilt, but more than that, I'd been thankful that his focus had been distracted from Cara. He'd been riveted by the other omega and I had not interfered.

I hadn't encouraged him either.

I'd let the scene play out to its logical conclusion. I had protected my omega. That was my priority. That *is* my priority. This time I won't fail her. This time I'll make sure she is shielded from harm.

I watch her sleep.

Her dark eyelashes fan against her cheeks. Her cheekbones are so prominent. And her color seems too pale. I cup her face and she doesn't stir. My heart stutters. Is she okay? Was I too rough with her? I'd meant to quiet her before Talon changed his mind. Not that I wanted him to take Lisa, but if he'd touched Cara... Hell, I'd have lost it. As it is, I am barely keeping my temper under check and—my dick twitches—yeah, my cock in my pants. I am a prisoner and so is she. We are both in danger, and yet, I want to be buried balls-deep inside of her?

I drag my finger to the hollow at the front of her throat and her pulse thuds against my skin. My muscles unclench. She's fine, just tired. She came to save me. Me. The man who'd kidnapped her. She still hates me; that much is clear, from her prickly disposition. Still, she is here, isn't she?

She came for me.

Perhaps she feels the same connection I do. She must. It's why she is here, coiled up in my lap as she sleeps.

I smooth back the hair from her forehead. She mumbles, then burrows closer;

goosebumps dot her forearms. I undo the buttons of my torn shirt, and nestle her into my bare chest. Her skin warms. So soft, my beautiful mate.

I whisper my knuckles over the curve of her shoulder, up her throat to drag it across her jaw line. So prickly when she is awake. I prefer her like this. Compliant, quiet, melting into me.

Her breathing deepens; her chest rises and falls, the nipples peaked against the fabric of her shirt.

She's dressed in dark pants that match. The first time I've seen her in a masculine outfit. It suits this new her. The little fighter that she is turning out to be. Did I do that? I firm my jaw.

Am I responsible for this feminine omega transformed into a woman who doesn't hesitate to use her fists? My fingers still. I tip up her chin, survey her features.

When she's angry or pissed off at me, a little groove appears between her brows. Delicate arches that flow down to that nose, turned up slightly. She's always been spirited. She just didn't realize it. It was because I'd pushed her to the edge of her control that she'd held her own. That's good.

She needed to hold her own, had to learn to survive on her own.

Not that I won't be there to take care of her. I plan on being her shadow, stalking her to ensure that she never undertakes the kind of crazy risk she took by tracking me down. She put herself in danger. I haul her closer.

All that matters is her, the child she carries inside of her. I draw my fingers down to her stomach, cradle her belly.

My child. My guts churn. She carries my child and she put both of them at risk today.

Never again. I'll not allow you to endanger yourself or my child again, Cara. Not as long as I am alive. I plan to protect you, take care of both of you. I'll envelop you in the deepest of caresses, kisses, embraces. A low purr rumbles up my chest. It spills from my lips and I project it around her shoulders, waft the subvocal notes over her chest.

Mine, sweet Cara. All mine. To cherish. To shield. To ensure that you'll never want for anything in your life. I'll wrap you up in the finest of silks, give you all the comforts you once had. I'll treat you like a princess. My queen. The ruler of my heart. I bend down and press my lips to hers. So sweet.

I draw in her breath. Orange blossoms and honey, with an underlying trace of pepper. That was the change I had noticed earlier. I should have known then, that she was pregnant. I had been too embroiled in my need, my thirst for revenge. No more. I lean down and kiss her again. *It's all about you from now on, Sugar. Your life, your needs, our child.* I have everything I need right here. Everything else comes second.

She stirs; her eyebrows twitch.

"Shh." I draw out a purr, another, let the vibrations from my chest soothe her. I hold her close. Hum under my breath and she sighs.

Her brow clears. Her breathing evens out. "Sleep, Cara. When you awake, it will be the start of our life together."

I stretch my legs out as darkness drags at the edges of my subconscious mind. When I snap my eyes open, her green gaze locks with mine.

I hold her focus. Survey her features. Her cheeks are flushed. Good. Her color is normal. Tendrils of hair stick to her forehead. I reach out to swipe them from her face and she flinches.

My heart stutters, "Are you afraid of me?"

She bites her lower lip.

"Tell me."

"Will you hurt me if I don't?"

"Huh?" I frown. "What gives you that impression?"

She huffs. "Oh, please. Are you going to deny everything you did to me earlier?"

"You mean the fact that I kidnapped you and mated you?"

"You're going to stop at that?"

I stiffen, "How many times will you have me apologize for it?"

"Not enough."

I survey her features, how her eyes gleam. "It won't work anymore."

"What?"

"You're trying to make me angry enough to do something I'll regret."

She purses her lips, "You mean the alphahole who thought with his dick is changing?"

Hearing that from her mouth, my cock lengthens, stabs into her side.

Color burns her cheeks, "Thought not." She strains in my embrace.

I tighten my grip around her shoulders.

"Let me go." She hits my chest.

I wince, "No."

"Why not?"

"You came for me."

"I felt sorry for you."

"Oh?" I tilt my head. "Try again, Sweetheart. I don't believe what you're saying."

"I put your life at risk. I believe in correcting my wrongs." Her chin wobbles and her features twist.

"You're lying." I stare deeply into her eyes. "Tell me what you feel. Please, Cara, this once, come clean."

"You're right." She raises her chin. "I'll never forgive you for what you did to me."

170

Chloe

Something flickers in those dark eyes. Hurt? Regret?

A hot sensation stabs at my chest. I wince. I will not feel sorry for him.

I pull away and he loosens his grip. Cold air rushes in between us and I blink.

Why do I already miss his embrace? Why do I yearn for his affection? His fingers on my skin, on my cheek, in the valley between my breasts.

Why do I want his lips to tug on my nipples, to suck on the cleft between my legs? Slick oozes out from between my thighs. I press them together. His shoulders bunch. Of course, he noticed that tiny action. Nothing escapes him, after all. He doesn't comment. Huh?

He lifts me off of his lap and places me on the floor next to him. Goosebumps pop on my skin.

He shrugs off his shirt and hands it to me. "You're cold."

I take in his bare chest, the beautiful sculpted planes, the eight pack abs, now marred with fresh bruises. Concave stomach, and below that? His pants tent. Oh! My cheeks heat. Of course, he's aroused. I'd slept on his lap, and he'd held me, crooned to me. Yeah, I had been half awake then. I'd felt his erection pulse, but had given no sign that I had noticed it. No such luck now. The blood rushes to my cheeks.

A pulse flares to life at his temple, "I am not going to take you without your consent."

"Unlike the other times?"

"It was only that first time…" His brow knits, "Maybe."

"No maybes about it." I grab his shirt and shove my arms into it. "You took me without caring what I thought."

"Don't twist everything we had into that grey area."

"Is that what you're calling it now?" I draw up my legs. "How diplomatic of you. Must be nice to use words to justify your deeds."

"I don't regret what I did."

A coldness coils in the pit of my stomach. "No?"

"No." His jaw tics. "I wish I had tied you up that last time in my stronghold. If you hadn't escaped, I could have wooed you."

"Fucked me into submission."

"I would have courted you."

"Used sex to shove me into some kind of haze where I couldn't think clearly."

He frowns. "What's so wrong about that?"

"Can you hear yourself?" I straighten my spine. "You haven't changed... Not one bit."

"*You* have."

"So you keep saying." I dig my fingers into my hair. "Yeah, I am pregnant. Let's not go making a big deal of it—"

"You're carrying my child, Cara." A vein pops at his temple. "It's the biggest fucking deal ever." He moves so fast that I blink. He squats in front of me—big, imposing. His shoulders block out the light and I stutter. I scoot away until I am plastered to the wall.

He flinches, "I already told you I won't hurt you."

"Hmm."

He raises his palms face up, "I won't touch you until you give me permission."

I laugh, then clap my hand to my mouth. Oops. Hadn't meant to do that.

His eyebrows draw down. "You don't believe me?"

I cough. "What do you think?"

"I think," he massages his temple, "that I need to start building bridges with you."

"Keep trying." Another chuckle builds in my throat and I swallow it down.

He's trying to be nice to me. Bet he's trying to lull me into a sense of complacency, and when I least expect it, he'll jump on me. He'll use my lack of attention to his advantage. He'll take what he wants; he always does.

He rises to his feet, retreats a step, and another. He reaches the opposite end of the cell, then slides down to sit with his back close to the wall.

"See. I can put distance between us."

"But can you keep it?"

I frown, a shiver runs down my spine, and I yank the shirt even closer. His dark masculine scent surrounds me, tugs at my nostrils. *Drat him.* Did he hand over something he'd worn so close to his skin, to show me what I was missing?

He brings up his knees, thighs spread wide. The bulge between his legs thickens. I gulp, look away.

"You can stare at me." He spreads his legs wider. "I'm yours, Cara."

"No, you're not."

His eyes gleam. I shouldn't have responded to this strange mood he is in. A mix of playfulness and desperation? Nah. Neither characteristic fits the image of the man I carry in my head. Sure, I know his background and that he could be hurt…but all of that is in the past. When he was a child. It was those experiences that made him the ruthless man that he is.

An alpha who doesn't hesitate to snatch to fulfill his needs. So why is he toying with me? Why is he playing games? And it is a game. That is what it is. I squeeze my eyes shut. I will not be seduced by his rippling chest, the sweat that beads the ridges between his abs, the tightness of his pants across his massive thighs, the monster cock that—*no, no.* I squeeze my fingers together. *Don't go there, don't.* There's a beat of silence. Then a sharp rip. *What the—?* The unmistakable sound of a zipper being lowered. My shoulders tense. My sex clenches. He didn't do that.

"Look at me."

"No."

"Please."

No way. I grit my teeth, squeeze my eyes shut. Start counting back from 10, 9, 8...

"Sweetheart—"

"Don't call me that."

"Then open your eyes."

"And let you seduce me again?"

"So, you admit you allowed yourself to be seduced?"

"That was a mistake." I bite the inside of my cheek. This entire conversation is insane. Why am I not able to resist this alpha? My belly flutters. My sex clenches. Yeah, that's my answer. It has to be the fact that being pregnant is making me overly-sexed. I snicker. Nice excuses, huh?

The sound of a palm slapping against wet flesh fills the space. *Don't look, don't.* A groan bleeds into the air. My eyes pop open. *Oh!*

My gaze lands right there between his thighs. His fingers grip his thick shaft.

His palm is wide enough—I know because I've felt him cup my ass and I can vouch for the fact that his cock is every bit as massive as the girth of his hand promises...b-u-t that's not what is at debate here. So, what is...Huh? What am I thinking?

He squeezes the hard column at the base then drags his grip up to the tip. A drop of precum glows at the slit of its head.

My mouth waters.

My throat dries.

Heat swirls down my spine, pools between my lower lips. Hell, I want to taste him again.

A growl rumbles from his lips. "Come closer."

I shake my head.

"Don't deny yourself."

I huff. There are worse things than watching my alpha jerk off. It's the most erotic sight I have ever seen. My throat closes.

I squeeze my thighs together and his nostrils flare. "You are so wet that if I flicked your cunt you'd come right there on the spot."

No.

No.

I nod.

He draws in a breath. Massages his dick with such pressure that the skin across his knuckles whitens. "Fuck." He snarls.

Exactly. Only I am not going to ask him to do that. Never. My fingers clench.

"Will you do one thing for me?"

Why should I oblige him?

"Please." He lowers his voice.

No.

"Please, Cara." The tendons of his neck bunch. His biceps strain. He's holding himself back. It's a wonder he hasn't closed the space between us and grabbed my hand and... forced me to stab my finger inside of myself, find that throbbing aching center inside of me, and press down until I come.

"Do it for me?"

No. Something hot crawls inside of my chest. I nod. *What is wrong with me?*

"Touch yourself."

171

Kayden

Her fingers tremble, then she slides them inside her panties. No doubt they are poised at the entrance of her sweet pussy. "Let me see you, Sweetheart."

She hesitates.

I frown. *How dare she deny me?* Anger coats my blood, floods my veins. *Stop it. Would it kill you this once, to ask her politely?* Okay, so that's expecting too much. *Lower your voice. Draw in a breath, rein in your anger.*

"Push aside your panties."

My voice seems too loud in the enclosed space. I wince. Not good. *How the hell do I train myself to request what I want?*

My fingers tighten and pain coils up my dick.

Fuck, at this rate I am going to hurt myself...and that's definitely not part of the plan. I intend to use that particular appendage for a very long time.

"Please." I lower my voice. "Do it for me, Darling."

A soft moan spills from her lips. My groin throbs. My dick elongates further. *If she doesn't do as I ask, I —* She yanks her underwear aside.

I stare. Pink swollen flesh captures my attention — throbbing lips distended and wet, the bud of her swollen clit peeking out between them. A harsh sound fills the space. My throat hurts. My chest tightens. Fuck, it would have been better if she hadn't obeyed me. I wouldn't have seen what I've been missing then. Pain licks low in my belly, flares out.

I grab the base of my dick, squeeze hard to stop the climax from spewing out.

"Touch yourself."

She slips a finger inside her pussy, then another.

I groan.

She shoves a third finger, stretching the entrance, then pushes them in all the way until her knuckles.

So fucking hot. Sweat beads my forehead. "Keep. Going."

She pulls out her fingers, then slides them in, and again.

A pulse beats to life at my temples, at my wrists, even in my balls. I grit my teeth, "Don't stop."

She sets a pace, plunging her fingers in and out of herself. The strokes mirror my actions. I drag my fingers up to the head of my dick, then down again, and up.

Her chest rises and falls in tandem.

Her thigh muscles spasm.

"Come."

Her spine curves, her breasts point up. She throws her head back at the same time that slick gushes out of her.

I groan.

Could anything be hotter? My balls draw up and the orgasm screams up my dick; the cum geysers from my shaft, coats my chest in white strings of gumminess. I keep coming. Don't take my gaze off of her body. The sound of our breaths mingles.

She juts out her chin, cracks her eyes open. Her lips are parted, swollen as if I had kissed her. She scans my features, tracks her attention down to my chest. Her pupils dilate and she pants.

"You want me?" I glare at her.

She nods.

"You can have me."

She swallows. Her hands jerk.

"Come to me."

She rises to her feet, crosses the floor to stand in front of me. I tip my chin up to peruse her flushed features. Then slide both of my legs in between hers.

Her chest rises and falls.

My fingers grasp the base of my dick—which is, of course, completely erect again. Don't judge. That bout of masturbation had been hardly satisfying. Nothing comes close to being buried inside of her beautiful cunt. My shoulders go solid. My thigh muscles bunch. A moan spills from her lips. She lowers herself until her soft pussy is poised exactly above my aching shaft.

"I fucking hate you, Kayden." She impales herself onto my cock.

Her pussy clamps around my turgid shaft and a growl tears up my chest. I drag my hands to the side, curl my fingers into fists.

She lifts her chin, her hair flowing about her shoulders, the column of her throat bared to my scrutiny. I want to lean in and drag my nose down to the hollow of her neck. Wait. *Wait.* I want her to decide. I drag in a breath, hold the purr that tightens my chest.

Her hips twitch and she presses her knees into the floor on either side of my thighs. Another moan swells up, parts her lips, "I hate..." she raises her body until my dick slips out to be poised once more at her entrance, "... you." She impales herself on my dick again in one smooth move. A growl rips up my chest and she trembles, brings up her hand, and I grab it, flatten her palm on my chest. Thud-thud-thud, my heart beat ratchets up. "See what you do to me?"

Color flushes her cheeks. Her chin wobbles. "This doesn't change anything," she pants.

"Doesn't it?" I pump my hips and my dick leaps up her channel.

Her entire body shakes, and she sways toward me. I grasp her other shoulder to hold her steady. Peer into those blue eyes, reach out to her via the mating bond. "You're mine, Cara, and nothing you say or do will change that."

She swallows; her eyes shine. She bites on her lower lip and heat sears up my spine.

"Let me love you, this once."

She nods.

I swoop up, flip her over so she is on her back, my arm under her neck to protect her spine. I drag my other arm up her thigh, loop her ankle around my waist. "Hold on to me."

I propel my hips forward, enough to slip in another inch.

She groans, opens her mouth. I lower my head and lick her lips. Press little kisses up her face, close her eyes with my lips, flutter kisses across her temples, her hair, her forehead. I cover every inch of her beautiful visage with the tokens of my affection. Does she get me yet?

She swings her other leg around my waist, locks her heels at my back. "Still hate you," she pants, "but I can't stop you."

One side of my mouth curves. I lean back, "You ready for me?"

Her chin wobbles, "Wha—?"

I nibble on her lower lip and she trembles. I tilt my mouth and drink from her.

Her entire body goes pliant.

She mumbles deep in her throat and I smile. I raise my head and she stares, her eyes dazed. The black of her pupils expands to fill her irises.

I wind her arm about my neck, then the other.

"Hold on." I thrust into her and her entire body bucks.

Her chest heaves. Sweat beads her forehead, drips down her temple. I dip my head and lick it up. I cup her breast and she shivers, squeeze her nipple and she moans. Draw my fingers down to the curve of her hip, grip it, and she shudders. Damn, she's always been responsive to my ministrations. A musical instrument that I can fine tune. A woman who responds to my touch, who burns for me as I do for her. I cup her ass cheek and squeeze.

She whines. Her nipples pebble, their hard edges thrust into my chest. Goosebumps flare on my skin. My balls draw up. "Fuck, I'm close."

She whines, reaches up, and I cover her mouth with mine.

I dance my tongue over hers, slide my finger inside her asshole, and propel my hips forward. My dick extends, locking behind her pelvic bone. *Come for me, Cara.*

Her body bucks.

A groan wells up her throat and she shatters. Her pussy squeezes my dick; the walls of her channel tighten. Slick flows out to bathe my dick and... I can't hold back. My balls draw up, the tension inside of me snaps, and I empty myself inside of her. I drag my mouth from hers, tuck her head under my chin. Then flip positions so she is on top. I am still inside of her, her cheek plastered to my chest. I cradle her close. "Sleep now."

Her body slumps; her breathing relaxes. I slide my dick out, then swoop her up in my arms. I hold her as she sleeps.

When she stirs, morning light slants from between the window panes.

She stays still, but she doesn't fool me. She's putting off the inevitable confrontation that we seem to be so good at. Except this time, I won't let her get angry with me. Not again. I don't want to upset her. My dick begins to harden again. Not now. I shouldn't need her so soon again. But she's my mate. And my body reacts to her nearness. It's time. I sit up, then swing her off of my lap and place her next to me.

Her eyelids flutter and she turns her head to me,

"When we get out of here, you are free to leave."

172

Chloe

Chills creep up my spine. I huddle into myself, trying to seal in the warmth. The floor is hard against my back.

I open my eyes and find I am alone. I sit up, scrutinize the room and spot him. He pushes off from the floor on his arms and feet, then again. Umm...what's he doing? He's working out?

Yesterday, he'd seemed as if he'd been beaten half to death. Somehow, he'd flipped me over, fucked me senseless. Now here he is, exercising?

"Shouldn't you be resting your muscles... "

He pauses. His biceps strain, his thigh muscles tense, he lifts the weight of that massive body, balancing on his limbs. He gave me his shirt, so the entire expanse of that massive torso is exposed. I gulp, peruse the angles, the planes and indentations of that beautiful body that bears bruises, which are turning purple.

"I heal fast." He lowers himself until his chest almost touches the floor. Then winces.

"Right." I bite the inside of my cheek.

"No, really." He pushes up again. "My metabolism is such that I recover quickly from fights. I need to keep moving though. Else my muscles lock up."

I scrape the hair away from my face.

His shoulders bunch; the tendons of his throat strain. A bead of sweat trails down his temples and plops to the floor. Oh! The power writ in every last contour of his body? It's something. It's awesome and magnificent and... I am so much smaller than him. I pull my knees up and into my chest. Watch him as he continues his push-ups. 1-2-3...25.

"Doesn't your shoulder hurt?"

"I won't let it stop me." The corded columns of his thighs strain the pants he is wearing.

The veins of his forearms pop; his chest heaves. Sweat runs down his pecs, drops to the floor.

"You're in pain."

He grunts.

"You're too pigheaded to admit that your body needs more time to heal."

He pauses, his chest resting in close contact with the hard ground for a beat; he starts again.

I count…and count. When I cross 100, I lose count.

A groan rumbles up his chest, his biceps tremble, and his thighs spasm.

"Oh, for heaven's sake." I throw my hands up. "What are you trying to prove?"

"That I can protect you." He lowers himself, then pushes up, every muscle in his body curled with tension. Waves of pain and anger radiate off of him. "I need to keep alert, at my full senses, and fighting-fit for when the Viking returns for us."

"Oh."

He keeps going. Sweat beads his shoulders, the curve of his spine. He grunts on the next push up. His biceps tremble. He's tiring… He should be. I mean, the man's not a freakin' machine, though, to see him own those push-ups, you'd think he was.

I've felt his skin slide over mine, heard him cry out in the midst of a nightmare, seen him writhe in the grasp of the terrors that plague his mind. He is human and vulnerable. He has the same fears I do; he feels pain. Yet he hadn't hesitated to put himself at risk to save my life… So why can't I forgive him for how he'd taken me without giving me a choice?

I curl my fingers into fists.

There's no denying that I am attracted to him, that he can wring orgasms from me, bring me to climax, ensure that I'll be happy for the rest of my life, if I give him a chance. Except… He's never openly acknowledged that I am his, that he wants me by his side. He wants…the child I carry. There is no question of that. He's so macho, so alpha, that he'd take pride in being a father. He'd protect the child as he did me. He'd cherish the little one…and me? What does he feel for me? He'll ask my permission before he'll make love to me…*make love*, those were his exact words. He'd professed to love me earlier. Does he care for me enough to let go of me?

"Do you mean it?"

He pauses midway through the next pushup. The veins in his forearms bulge. Another bead of sweat sliding down his cheek to stay poised at the tip of his chin. I stare at it, fascinated. *Will it fall off? Will it?*

"What?"

Huh? I jerk my gaze to his.

He angles his head and I flush, drop my chin onto my knees, "You said earlier that you'd let me leave. Did you mean it?"

"Do you doubt it?" He pushes up to stand.

His chest heaves. He holds his arms slightly apart at his sides. In that full-frontal position, I can see every inch of his beautiful chest, the sculpted eight pack, the concave torso, the stretch of his pants across the bulge at his crotch. "No, I don't doubt it at all."

"We talking about the same thing here, Cara?" Humor laces his voice.

I flush, tilt my head up. "Most definitely." My voice comes out strangled. I clear my throat. "Did I imagine you saying earlier that I was free to leave?"

He scratches his chin and his biceps flex. *Stop staring at the man like you want to jump him. Stop eating him up with your eyes.*

"What if I said I did?"

"I'd say that I don't believe you."

He lowers his arm, "You calling me a liar?" His voice lowers an octave. "Are you?"

I shake my head.

"I never say anything I don't mean."

"But," I swallow, "you'd let me leave despite the fact that I am pregnant?"

"What do you think?"

He wipes his chest, mops his forehead. It's such a masculine gesture, so confident. The man's completely comfortable in his own skin. It's the one thing that I had noticed right from the beginning. His dominance is so ingrained in him, that you react to his presence without realizing what it is about him that sets you on edge. Grown men sense a predator, the challenge of an alpha, and women like me? We don't stand a chance.

I should have submitted to him long ago…but if I'd done that, he'd never have respected me. He'd never have allowed me to come into myself. If I'd let him, he'd have overpowered me until I had become a shadow of my former self, and that…I couldn't bear.

I had thought I was a breeder, first and foremost, and I am that…but I'm also more. My individuality and my identity are as important. Me… The Chloe who had survived this far…would not give in, not that easily.

"Cara?"

I jerk my chin up. "Kayden?"

His forehead furrows, "What are you scheming in that pretty little head of yours?"

"Scheming?" I flutter my eyelashes.

His throat moves as he swallows, his attention riveted on my face. So, I am not the only one affected by his presence. Guess we rub off on each other. I freeze.

There is so much about this man that I find irresistible, so why do I want to leave him?

Do I actually want to ignore the emotions he elicits in me?

Heat flares low in my belly, that little flip-flop that only Kayden can evoke. My throat closes.

Could I actually leave all that behind? I must. I have to. If he wants me…it will have to be on my terms.

"I know you, Omega. You're always thinking, planning, trying to figure out how to get to what you want next."

I stare. How strange. Kai's the first man to see beyond my soft feminine facade, to acknowledge that I am every bit as strategic as my background prepared me to be. That I had absorbed all of the lessons in manipulating emotions, that had been drilled into me by the tutors that my father had employed for me and Lucy. Not my father, not Lucy, not even my mother when she'd been alive, had known what I was capable of. No one except Kayden. And I am going to leave him?

I straighten my shoulders, "Glad you don't underestimate me."

"I wouldn't dare."

"So, you'll understand when I tell you that I want your word in writing."

"In writing?" He frowns.

"Preferably in blood," I jut out my chin, "that you'll let me go."

"Blood, hmm?" He widens his stance; his thigh muscles coil. *Don't stare at him. Don't admire his physique. Stop being aware of how virile he is, how damn gorgeous, how he seems to take up all of the oxygen in the space so you can barely breathe.* I swallow, retreat until my spine is pressed against the wall.

"You heard me, Kai," I bite my lip.

Why did I have to go and call him by his nickname, now of all the times? When he glares at me with those dark, piercing eyes, I am sure he can see right into my soul, and I am already regretting that I challenged him on his word. Should have quietly taken it as a fait accompli. Now, there is no way he is letting me go.

He stalks forward, one step, another. I freeze, watch his progress as he crosses the floor. He stops in front of me, squats down. I tilt my head back, scan his features —the high cheekbones, the hooked nose, the thin upper lip. I shiver. The heat from his body envelops me; his dominance surrounds me in a cocoon of protection. Damn it, this is not right.

A slow burn starts somewhere behind my breastbone, creeps out across my chest. My nipples pebble as sweat slicks my palms. He leans forward, stretches out his hand.

I squeak.

He reaches to the side, folds his thick fingers around a nail embedded in the wall. His shoulders bunch as he yanks. The nail comes free; bits of dust float to the ground. "You'd have hurt yourself."

"Oh."

"Can't have that now, can we?"

He holds out his forearm; my gaze drops to it. He drags the pointy end of the nail across his skin. Blood oozes out. "Kayden…what are you doing?"

"You want me to write it in blood, right?" He continues to scrawl. More blood pours out of the wound, spreads across the skin. I crane my head, try to decipher what he's writing.

He reaches the edge of his wrist, then pockets the nail. He drags his palm across the skin, clearing away the blood.

What do I care what he wrote? I chew on my lower lip. Still, I want to find out. "Show me."

He holds up his arm and I gasp.

173

Kayden

"You didn't have to do that." Color fades from her cheeks, her lips tremble.

I glance at my arm. *I promise.* That's what I'd written, in my own blood, on my flesh.

So that was a dramatic gesture. But Cara...she was testing me. She wants to be free. I can see the reasoning behind it. Hell, I understand what it means to be able to follow your own mind, to live life on your own terms. I've spent my entire life trying to live up to the reputation of my father. My promise to him to take care of our people, and ensure our family remains at the helm.

Strangely, she is playing her part in it and not even realizing it. I hadn't meant to get her pregnant...nor had I expected it to happen, though it is the logical conclusion to the number of times I had made love to her. Yeah, that's what I call it now, so call me pussy-whipped. Except, Cara doesn't seem to share the same sentiments. Isn't it enough that I love her? I've told her in so many words. But she wants something more, and I am not sure what that is. And there is only one way to find out. By obeying her wishes...or at least, pretending to. Yep, she's pregnant with my child. No way am I letting her out of my sight. No reason for her to be aware of it either.

Hell, if everything goes as planned, she won't even be aware that I am lurking not far away from her. Keeping an eye on her. She'll have her freedom all right... within the parameters I've set for her. Stalker much? Maybe. Her safety is paramount and no way am I compromising that.

"You asked for it, Cara."

"Do you always agree to everything I demand?"

I tilt my head. "When it suits me."

She throws up her hands, "You did not say that. Tell me you did not utter those words."

I lean back on my haunches, "What's wrong with what I said?"

"Seriously?" She lowers her arms, wraps them about her knees. "You have no idea how arrogant you sound, right?"

"So?" What is she upset about? I am an alphahole, dominance is my middle—no, make that my first name.

She knows that I must get my way. I have listened to her so far, right? I had indulged her, given her proof that I intended to be seen to comply with what she wants… So, why is she throwing a fit?

"You shouldn't be getting angry."

She snarls.

"It's bad for the baby."

"Shut up," she growls low in her throat.

"You know I am right."

Spots of color burn on her cheeks. She tosses her hair, the thick strands floating about her shoulders. She drops her arms, sits up on her knees. "So sure of yourself, Alpha?"

"Always, Omega."

"You didn't have to answer that."

"You asked."

"Oh!" She throws up her hands again, overbalances and falls into me. Her breasts graze my thighs.

I right her, keep my palms on her shoulders.

She winces.

I search her features. "What's wrong?"

"My breasts are tender." Color stains her cheeks.

So fucking adorable. This woman has me in the palm of her hand, and she seriously thought I'd let her walk away? Not happening. N-a-a-h. Never.

I massage her muscles and she groans. "You're too tense."

"And who's to blame for that?"

Her nipples harden. I know, because they thrust up and through the fabric of her shirt and stab into my bare chest. My dick twitches. *Down boy, not yet.* Her breathing heightens; her pupils dilate. Just gonna pretend it's because of my ministrations. I am taking care of her, that's all. "You've had a rough night."

"No shit."

"Why Cara, you sure swear much more than when I first met you."

"Your company must be rubbing off."

My lips quirk. "I prefer you like this."

She frowns. "When I am angry with you?"

"That too," I drag my palms down to her biceps, squeeze.

Her head falls back; her shoulders relax further.

"I prefer you going toe to toe with me...rather than submitting."

She angles her head, giving me more access to that creamy length of her throat. I draw my fingers up the contours of her shoulder, wrap my fingers around her neck; rub tiny circles over her nape.

Her entire body trembles, "Oh, that's good." She swallows, "Your massages are almost as good as—" she firms her lips.

"Almost as good as?" A smile threatens to curve my lips. I wipe it off, school my features into a mask, "As…?"

"Oh, you know." Her voice is thready.

"No." I lean in close enough for my breath to lift the hairs on her forehead, "Tell me."

"As your love-making," she mumbles, her eyelids closing as she sways toward me.

I allow her to lean into me, taking her full weight. Her body twitches. That's when I sit down, pull her into my lap. Tuck her head under my chin, and let her sleep.

It wasn't right to allow her to spend the night on the hard floor, I should have taken better care of her, but damn it, she'd made me angry.

Enough for me to spend the night apart…as I suspect I will be for a little more time.

Just as long as I am able to keep her in sight. That's all that counts. A harsh purr rumbles up my chest. I weave the vocals around her shoulders, watch her breathing deepen as her eyelids flutter down.

Her stomach grumbles and she blinks. "Wha…what happened?" She yawns.

"You fell asleep."

She sits up, scans her surroundings, "You mean, I dozed off?"

"Yeah."

"Wow, I must be more tired than I thought."

Her stomach grumbles once more, "And hungry."

I lift her up and place her on the floor, then stand up.

"Where are you going?"

"To get you something to eat."

I walk to the heavy iron door and bang on it. "We need some food in here."

No answer.

I ram my shoulder into the barrier. Pain ladders up my side. I ignore it. "Hey, open up."

The door swings open.

"You?"

Chloe

"Lisa?" I spring up to my feet.

Kayden stalks forward. "The hell you doing here?" He pauses in front of her, "How did you get in?"

She holds up a pair of keys. "Sneaked it off the alpha guarding my room."

I cross the floor and stand next to Kai.

"You expect me to believe that you overpowered him?" He huffs.

"With my charms." She thrusts a food hamper at him.

He makes no move to take it.

"He let you escape?" He cracks his neck, "It's a trap. And you came right here. If you put her in danger, so help me Lisa—"

She drops the carrier on the floor. "You bellowed for food? I'm bringing it to you."

He frowns, "Where did you get this?"

I interrupt, "Lisa, you okay?"

She juts out her chin, "Why wouldn't I be?"

Right. My cheeks heat. Granted, we are not the best of friends, but Talon deciding to keep her for himself? That is not okay.

I survey her features. The skin across her cheekbones stretches tight. There's a touch of blood at her temple. I close the distance between us, "What happened?" I reach out to touch her forehead and she winces.

"Nothing." She turns away. "We need to leave."

"After you answer my questions." Kayden glowers.

I twist my fingers together, "Why don't we get out of here first?"

Lisa clears her throat, "The faster you eat, the faster we can leave."

"She's right." He rolls his shoulders, "We should eat first, keep up our energy. Besides, you're hungry."

He squats on the ground, opens the carrier. The scent of food teases my nostrils; my stomach rumbles.

He tugs at my arm, and I sink down next to him.

"Eat."

He holds out a sandwich to me.

I frown. "I'd rather be hungry and safe, than sated and dead—"

He stuffs the sandwich in my mouth. I take a bite.

"Good." He smirks, "Chew now."

I scowl at him. *Jerk.* I move my jaws, swallow, open my mouth, and no, it's not because he asked me to. It's because I am very hungry. When I take the last bite of the sandwich, he reaches for the second one. I flatten my lips.

"You going to eat it or should I force feed you, Cara?"

I hear a snort and jerk my head up. "What?" I glower.

"Finish the food, *Cara.*" She bites the inside of her cheek.

"Don't be snarky." Kai's voice is mild.

She scrapes her hair back from her face, "That's what *he* said too."

"Who?" His eyebrows knit.

I reach for the sandwich again. He evades, holds it up. I sigh, take a bite, chew. "She means Talon."

He glowers, "How do you know?"

I blink, take in his features. His nostrils flare, a vein throbs at his temple. That's not a good sign, is it? I gnaw on my lower lip, "Who else could she mean?"

Color smears his cheeks.

"What's wrong?"

A snarl rumbles up his massive chest. "Don't say his name again."

Ah! "You're jealous?"

The tendons of his throat move as he swallows.

"You're jealous that I mentioned him?"

The muscles of his shoulders bunch. He leans in close enough for his lips to almost touch mine. His hot breath sears my cheek. "I'm jealous of the very air you breathe. I can't stand anything to be closer to you than me."

"Oh." My toes curl. That alpha male possessiveness of his. It should be cloying...

It should weight me down, hold me captive. Slick pools between my thighs. So why am I so turned on instead?

"You feel me, Cara?"

My throat closes. I can't even blink. Can't take my eyes off of that gorgeous countenance.

"Answer me."

All of my nerve-endings seem to fire at once, "Y... yes."

"Good." He raises the remainder of the sandwich to my mouth.

I nibble on it, then curl my fingers around his wrist. The muscles of his forearm jump. His nostrils flare. A deep purr rumbles up his chest. My belly flutters; sweat beads my palms. I swallow, "Your turn." I angle the food toward him, "You should eat."

He hesitates.

"You need your strength to protect us."

His jaw tics, then he nods. I let go of his hand, but he catches my palm, "We're not done."

The breath I'd not been aware of holding rushes out. I rise to my feet.

Kayden finishes off the remaining sandwich then jerks his chin at Lisa, "How long until they discover the missing food?"

"There's plenty more where it came from; they won't miss it."

"Hmm." He straightens, then pivots and walks to where his shirt is heaped on the floor. "And the guards outside?"

"There were none."

He freezes. "Too convenient," he mutters. "Something's not right." He straightens, shrugs into the shirt, his biceps rippling, those beautiful shoulders bunching and curving as he slides into the fabric. *Snap out of it.*

"Chloe."

I turn to Lisa, "Yeah, let's leave."

"Now." She jerks her chin toward the door,

I move toward the exit, but Kayden steps in front. He shoulders open the door, a crack. Glances both ways. "Let's go." He steps into the corridor.

I follow and Lisa brings up the rear. We head to the end of the corridor, up the stairs.

"It's quiet." I whisper, a chill running down my spine.

"Too fucking quiet," Kayden mumbles. "Something's not right." He picks up his pace and I break into a jog.

He shoots me a glance, "You okay, Cara?"

I nod.

"I'd have carried you but —"

"No way would I have allowed that. I can walk on my own, thank you very much. I'm pregnant, not unwell."

"You're pregnant?" Lisa exclaims.

"Shh!" I frown at her.

Her gaze flicks to the side, "Congratulations, I guess?"

"You could say it, like you mean it." I grumble.

"I do." She lowers her chin, "I was just surprised to hear it," she quirks her lips, "or maybe not —"

"What's that supposed to mean?" I glare at her.

"Nothing." She shuffles her feet.

"Lisa!" That entire dialogue about our burying our differences? Forget that.

"What?" She throws up her hands, "Now I can't even speak without you getting all hot under your collar."

"Keep your voices low," Kayden growls.

Lisa huffs out a breath. "Sorry Chloe... " she sneers, "being a bitch—"

"—is second nature for you." I toss my head.

"I've had a lot of practice." She looks down, links her fingers together in front of her, then peeks up through her lashes. "Congratulations, I am happy for you."

"Okay."

She pauses.

I stop, look at her.

She holds out a hand. I ignore it, step forward and pull her into a hug. "Thanks for bringing me here."

"Thanks for... ah, being so gracious." She pats my shoulder.

Kayden comes to a standstill. He pivots, then frowns. "Someone care to enlighten me on what just happened?"

I release Lisa, then sniffle. No reason to get all teary; must be the stupid hormones.

Kayden stabs a finger at Lisa, "You made her cry."

I frown up at him. "She didn't."

"What?" He looms above us, "Now you two are best friends?"

"No." I step away from Lisa.

"Nothing like that." Lisa sidles to the side.

"We were just agreeing to disagree... " My voice trails off, "I mean, she did bring me here."

Kayden turns away, "Nothing she does negates the fact that she put your life in danger."

I follow him, "And she's repaid the debt. She helped me find you, gave herself up to Talon, and broke out again to help us escape."

"Except," Lisa chews on her lower lip, "I think he's already found us."

"Who?" I still.

"Talon." Her lips firm, " I think he—"

"—is not far behind." Kayden completes her sentence.

"What…what?" I halt so fast that Lisa bumps into me, "Kai you are not making sense. He had us imprisoned, so why would he let Lisa escape to help us, then follow us, only to catch us again?" My head whirls. Why is the Viking toying with us?

Kai stops at the entrance to the building.

"No guards," he hisses.

I pause behind him. Next to me, Lisa stiffens.

"It's a fucking trap." Kayden tenses.

"What are we going to do?"

Footsteps sound behind us.

"Kayden."

"I hear it." He straightens, squeezes my arm.

I swallow. "We're going to have to make a run for it?"

"You ready?"

Before I can nod, he dashes out, dragging me along. Lisa follows at my heels.

We run across the clearing, past the undergrowth and up a winding path. The green of the trees envelops us.

There's a shout behind us, more footsteps.

"Stop."

174

Kayden

I brush past the girls to stand in front of them.

A man walks past the tree line—tall, broad-shouldered, features so similar to mine.

"Zeus?" I stiffen, "The fuck you doing here?"

"Good to see you too, bro." He stalks forward. "Why is it that every time I see you, you are running away from me?"

I thrust my neck forward, "Not running away, you asshole."

Another man steps up from behind him.

"Dad?" Lisa breaks into a run, then throws herself in his arms.

Dom lifts her straight off of the ground, "My little girl, you gave me a bloody scare."

"Sorry Dad." Her voice falters.

"I was worried about you." He lowers her to the ground. "If you'd told me what you intended to do, I'd have never refused you."

She scoffs, "You'd have stopped me from leaving."

"Do you blame me?" Dom surveys her features. "You're fine, not hurt or anything?"

She sidles away, "No…"

Ethan walks forward. "She will be, if we don't get out of here."

"Bloody hell." I plant my palms on my hips, "Did you bring the entire city with you?"

Ethan scowls, "You could be a little more grateful to see us?"

I glower at him.

More thrashing sounds emerge from outside the periphery of the clearing. A shout rings out in the distance; a returning voice answers.

Cara steps up from behind me and I thrust out a hand, "Don't move."

She juts out her chin, "Says who?"

"He's right." Dom jerks his chin to the side, "We're surrounded."

"The hell do you mean?" I lean forward on the balls of my feet.

"You're losing your touch if you can't keep her safe."

"Shut the fuck up." I curl my fingers into fists.

"Save the anger, First." His shoulders tense; he surveys the clearing, "You are going to need it for when the Vikings attack."

My gut churns. All of my senses go on alert. Next to me, Cara tenses, "What's he talking about?" She swallows. Fear bleeds off of her skin.

Fuck, this is my fault. I had been too intent on getting away from there. I'd known it was a trap. Hell, I'd seen Lisa enter the cell and I'd known there was no way she could have made it there, unless...he'd let her come to us.

Talon had been stalking us, watching our every move. He'd had us followed; I'd expected that.

I'd weighed the options and decided to go with it. If there had been even a chance of getting her away from him it would have been worth it...or so I'd thought. Now the thought of being recaptured by the asshole Viking... I set my jaw. Not gonna happen, not on my watch.

I push Cara behind me. "Stay out of sight."

She hesitates, then sidles closer. The heat of her body invades my skin. Good. I want her safe. Need her fucking out of sight of those animals.

"So, you're the rescue party, huh?" I draw myself up to my full height, roll my shoulders.

Zeus stalks forward. "I am here because Lucy was worried about her sister."

"Oh?" I angle my head.

"This has nothing to do with me feeling sorry for you. You deserve to be kept under lock and key. You are a fucking menace, Kayden, an out of control deviant who should be put away for life, except..." Zeus scratches his chin.

"Except?"

"My woman would have never forgiven me if I hadn't rescued her sister, and because you are mated to her."

"It doesn't mean anything." Chloe pops her head around me, "He was ready to let me go my own way."

Zeus lowers his chin, "Was he now?"

I snarl, "Don't talk to her." I shuffle sideways.

She moves with me. "In fact, that's the condition on which I agreed to go with him."

"Oh?" Zeus' mouth quirks. His eyebrows shoot down in an expression that indicates he clearly does not believe my intention.

"Hey, you direct your questions to me."

"He promised." Cara chews on a fingernail.

"You believed him?" Zeus' shoulders shake.

Fuck me. "Enough," I roar.

Ahead, Dom stiffens. He pivots and plants his bulk in front of his daughter.

"Nice Kayden, real nice." He pulls out the modified gun from his holster, "You're losing your touch."

He's fucking right. I did lose it there for a second, and gave away our precise location. Not that the Vikings wouldn't have found us, but I had hastened the process.

"Fuck." I bury my fingers in my hair and tug at the strands.

"You're not alone, bro. We'll get out of here, I promise."

"Since when do you care about my life?"

"I don't...but..." Zeus raises his shoulders and lets them fall, "Lucy seems to value it so..." Zeus holds out his hand.

I glance at it then at his face, "So.."

"You need our help.

No way. No fucking way am I going to join forces with him.

"Only way to keep her safe." He scowls past me to where Cara peeks out her head from behind my back.

He's right. If it were only me, I'd never bury my differences with my enemy. If I had been on my own, I'd have told him and Dom and Ethan to fuck off. It's because of her that I was captured by the Vikings. Because of her that I had insisted we eat first before we got the fuck out of there. Because of her that I had almost killed myself twice to save her. A-n-d, given a choice, I'd do it again.

I'll do anything to ensure the safety of my mate and my child. Anything. I bunch my shoulders.

A bullet whizzes past, the breeze raising the hair on my forehead. Cara shudders. Zeus pulls out his own gun and fires.

The bullet slams into the Viking. He crumples to the ground.

There's a howl, and five men rush in. One of them trips on the body of his fallen comrade and sprawls to the ground. The soldier behind him stomps on the fallen man's back, and jumps forward. He raises his gun, shoots.

Zeus swerves. Something hot explodes across my upper arm. I grunt. Pain slices up my spine. I swallow down the scream, then straighten.

"You're hurt."

Cara grabs my arm and I flinch, "I'm fine."

"You're not."

I scowl at her, "Stay back, Chloe." She shuffles her feet and I squeeze my eyebrows together, "Don't."

She sets her jaw.

"Please, Cara." White sparks radiate from the wound. I stumble, then straighten. I've been hurt worse; this is nothing. Doesn't mean that the pain is easier to bear, but damn if I am gonna give into it. "Stay behind me so I can protect you."

She scans my upper arm; blood drips from a wound. "Kayden." Tears fill her eyes. Something hot springs to life in my chest.

"If we weren't in the middle of a fight, I swear I'd kiss you right now, then lick you from top to bottom.

She gulps. "Oh."

"What?" I curl my lips, "No smart rejoinder?"

"Umm."

Another bullet whizzes past. "Dammit." I shove her behind me, then turn on Zeus, "We are sitting ducks here."

"You're telling me." Zeus fires off a series of rounds. Ahead, Dom and Ethan fire in tandem. Silence. The last remaining Viking falls to the ground.

Zeus rolls his shoulders, "Let's get the fuck out of here."

"With pleasure, but first," I hold out my hand. "I need a gun."

Zeus frowns, "Not the time to debate."

"My point exactly."

"Think I can trust you with a weapon, little brother?"

I thrust out my chin, "Can you?"

Cara bends, grabs the edge of her shirt. She rips out a strip, then steps up, to press the cloth to my wound.

Motherfucker, that hurts. I huff.

"Don't be a baby." She ties the fabric around my arm.

"Yeah, exactly." Zeus's voice sounds from somewhere behind me.

"Stop riling him." Cara frowns.

Zeus quirks an eyebrow, "Your woman has spirit, huh?"

"Stop calling me that." She concentrates to the task at hand, secures the dressing.

"The gun." I jerk my chin.

Zeus flips his gun and hands it to me. "Just do me a favor and don't shoot me in the back."

I scoop up the gun, aim it at Zeus, "Don't tempt me... But, I am not our father. If I wanted to kill you, I wouldn't need this." I lower the weapon.

Zeus scratches his jaw, "Not sure why, but I believe you."

"You guys done with the family reunion?" Dom stalks up, Lisa in tow, "Let's get a move on."

I grip Cara's hand, "You ready, Sweetheart?"

Lisa's gaze widens.

Yeah, so the endearment surprised me too. Clearly, being under pressure has addled my mind, or it must be the blood loss. What-fucking-ever. I stalk forward, taking the lead. Zeus falls in line next to Cara.

I snarl, pull her to my other side.

"What the —?" She raises her chin.

I shoot her a glare and she purses her lips, but stays quiet. *Thank fuck.*

We pull forward, and Cara increases her speed to keep pace. *Good girl.*

Dom and Lisa are right behind and Ethan brings up the rear.

"Where are we headed?" I scowl at Zeus.

"A safe house."

"The one halfway to London?"

Zeus's shoulders stiffen, "You know about that?"

"Of course," I chuckle.

"Hmm." Zeus frowns.

"Didn't expect that, eh?" I smirk. "I have my spies everywhere in your city."

"Had."

"Huh?"

"First thing I did after you escaped," Zeus scoffs, "I rounded up your men, and shoved them in prison."

What the hell! "If you've hurt them —"

"Relax bro, they're in safekeeping," Zeus' grin widens, "until you join them."

"And I'll come willingly, because —?"

Zeus scowls in the direction of Cara. Yeah, okay, he has me at a disadvantage. I'd do anything to keep her safe, but this?

Would I give up my freedom for her? *Gladly.* I stumble. Zeus grabs my shoulder, rights me.

"Kai?" She grips my forearm and I shake it off, "I'm fine."

Her features pinch and my heart stutters. Why does her every hurt seem like my own? The fuck is happening to me? Is this what it feels like to be mated, to sense another's every emotion as if it were your own? I rub the skin above my chest.

Zeus lowers his brows, "Growing up finally, little brother?"

"Oh, fuck off." I turn on him and stab my pistol into his chest. Cara draws in a breath. Dom and Ethan stop in their tracks.

Zeus doesn't react. Doesn't move a muscle. "You don't want to do this, bro." His voice lowers.

"Why do you think so?"

"I know it can be confusing, finding yourself vulnerable and exposed, a mate and your soon-to-be-born child in tow."

"Don't profess to understand me; we may share a bloodline on one side—"

"We *are* blood brothers."

"Pulling the family card, huh?" I chuckle, "Didn't think you'd stoop that low."

"You can deny the truth, Kayden. It doesn't change the fact that we have much in common."

"Oh?"

"The old man screwed us both over. Our mothers met with deaths they didn't deserve. We have both been given a second chance, with a soul mate, the chance to start our own families…carve out our own little slice of—"

"Shut the fuck up." I dig the gun into his chest and his shoulders bunch. Fucking finally. A bead of sweat runs down his temple.

The strange thing? I know what he's saying is true. My heart begins to thump. He's my half bro, technically the only blood family I have left. Until the child is born. And my soulmate? She goes beyond blood… She is a soul bond. A promise to cherish and protect.

My palms dampen. My gut churns.

This fucking emo shit, it never gets easier. Since I'd opened myself up to Cara, everything had changed. The damn has broken and now there is no going back. Everything I love in this world—and that includes Dom, and even that traitor of a girl Lisa—is right here. And fuck me, but Zeus? There is no denying the connection between us. He's right.

Our father left us both with a legacy that joins us… Question is, what am I going to do about it?

I step back, raise the gun, and pull the trigger.

175

Chloe

"Kayden... No."

He swings the gun over Zeus' shoulder and fires. There's a howl from somewhere ahead. Zeus swivels, drops to the ground. Dom shoves Lisa behind himself and fires.

Another Viking drops to the ground.

Ethan raises his gun and scans the surroundings. "All clear."

Silence. Kayden's shoulders rise and fall, his breathing harsh. He surveys the area, turns to me, "You okay?" His voice is hard, his features shuttered.

No. Not really. Not when you're hiding from me again. I swallow, nod.

He peruses my face, his inspection a physical touch that sears my eyes, my mouth... He scans every inch of my body, before jerking his chin. He pivots, offers his arm to Zeus, who takes it. Kai pulls the other alpha to his feet.

"Thought you had me there." Zeus' lips firm.

"Thought I had you too." Kayden draws himself up to his full height.

The two of them grip hands, don't let go for another second. Something passes between them. Something unspoken in the way men often communicate. Alpha to alpha, equal to equal. Then Zeus raises his free hand, pats Kayden on his shoulder, "Thanks."

"We are even."

"We'll see about that."

Kayden chuckles, "Stubborn bastard."

"Takes one to know the other."

Ethan snorts, "About time you two finally patched things up."

"Who said anything about patching things up?" Zeus drops Kayden's hand.

"The fuck you mean?" Kayden retorts at the same time.

Dom slaps Kai on the back then, grips Zeus' shoulder. A grin lights up his features. "Too fucking similar, the two of you. Arrogant, and way too lucky for your own good."

"Lucky?" Kai frowns. "What're you talking about?"

"You have each other, young families in the making. You have your futures in front of you. Don't mess it up."

"Too much philosophy for me." Kai mutters. He pivots, grips my elbow and strides forward, then slows his pace. *Huh?*

Did he do that so I can keep up with him? Not sure what to believe about him. This alpha is so confusing. So volatile. He seems to be working through something in his head...or is that his heart?

Zeus prowls ahead, and Kai doesn't compete. They seem to have come to an understanding of some kind. Dom and Lisa follow us. Ethan brings up the rear, gun drawn. He scans our surroundings, his features hard. All four of these men together? It's an awesome sight. But walking shoulder to shoulder with my alpha? It's an indescribable feeling, one I didn't think would ever happen for me. I link my fingers with his.

His wide palm engulfs mine and a shiver runs down my spine.

I lean in closer, brush my chin over his bicep. So hard, so unforgiving. Deep inside, is a man who truly cares...if he'd let go, and share all of himself with me. My heart feels too heavy. Tears crowd my eyes and I stumble.

The next second he scoops me up.

"Kayden," I squeak, "I can walk."

"Not when I can carry you."

"But—"

He frowns at me. "I can't let you exert yourself."

"Of course, the baby." I chew on my lower lip. "And here I was, thinking it was my well-being you were worried about."

"That."

"That?" I huff.

"I think about that...all the time."

"So, you'll keep your word?"

He stares ahead; his jaw tics. I raise my hand, place a finger against where the pulse throbs. He flinches, jerks his head aside. "You still want time alone, after all of this?"

"Especially after all of this. I need to figure out who I am, Kai, away from—"

"Me."

"Yeah." I toss my head. "Guess you're not a complete asshole."

"Alphahole."

"Whatever."

I slap his chest, and his mouth curls. "Careful, Princess, or I'll think that you want any excuse to touch me."

"Not."

He lowers his voice, "You have no idea what your touch does to me, do you?" He jerks his hips forward, and his hardness thrusts into my thigh.

My belly flutters; saliva pools in my mouth. "Drat you, Kayden." My cheeks heat.

"So fucking coy, after all this time, Cara?"

I scrutinize the area, notice the others avoiding us. *Either they can't hear us, or —*

"They don't care either way."

"Stop reading my thoughts."

"It's second nature. I am tuned into you, Sugar."

The ball of heat in my chest magnifies. I stutter. "How can I forget that?"

"So, change your mind."

"Hold on." I glare up at him, "You're trying to influence me?"

"Be thankful I am not forcing you to submit."

"Jeez, your ego," I huff.

He smirks. "You're welcome."

"Kai."

"Chloe."

"Ugh." I train my attention on the men ahead... Drat it, none of them are my Kai.

Stop thinking of him that way.

But he is mine, isn't he? So why am I fighting the inevitable? Because, if I give in without staking out my space... I'll never respect myself.

A low hum rolls up his chest... The subvocal notes envelop my skin, sink into my blood.

Heat fills my core, runs down my thighs. My bones seem to melt. "I know what you're doing," my voice sounds as if it's coming from far away.

"What?"

"You're trying to distract me."

"Is it working?"

His purrs intensify. They ripple up my spine, slither across my scalp. Tendrils of heat bind my legs, my arms. My eyes flutter shut.

When I awake, it's dark. I try to move, but a heavy weight pins my waist.

I turn my head and my nose brushes something hard. The masculine dark scent laces my nostrils. I draw it in and my lungs smile. I swear, they smile their appreciation. His warmth pins me in place. He turns on his back, and I cuddle closer.

A deep purr strokes up his chest, filters up my side, my back, slips between my legs, my toes. I draw in a breath, another. I am filled with his essence, his scent, his eloquence, the dark heart of seduction that is Kayden.

"Sleep, Cara."

I want to protest. I should protest. Try to open my mouth, but my body refuses to obey. The thick tones of his purr intensify, cocoon me. My limbs grow heavy, and drat him, I can't resist. The warm darkness covers my chest, my shoulders, and I let it overcome me.

A scream pierces the honeyed heat and my eyes snap open. My heart begins to race. "Kai."

"Shh."

He sits up, places me on the bed next to him. He slides down to the foot of the bed, then swings his legs over. He heads to the door, cracks it open. More shouts, another scream.

My throat closes. "Lisa," I scramble up to the edge of the bed.

He stalks toward me, holds out his hand. "Let's get out of here."

Kayden

Her gaze drops to my palm and she hesitates.

"Cara, I won't hurt you."

"I know."

"So, what are you afraid of?"

"You."

Huh?

"Myself."

Ah! I nod. "I promise not to seduce you."

She raises her chin. "Very sure of yourself?"

"Always." I allow my lips to curl. My heart thumps in my chest. *Come on, little one, trust me. I will not force you, not again. I can't let you stay here unprotected either. Come with me, Chloe.*

The ball of sensations in my chest throbs; I reach up with my other palm and massage the skin above my heart. She follows my actions, the skin at the edges of her eyes creasing. She nods, places her palm in mine.

I turn, head to the window; she follows me. I shove up the pane.

"What are you doing?" She whisper-screams.

A crash sounds from within the house, and the entire structure seems to shake. I frown at her, "Whoever is there is not going to let us pass."

"Who do you think it is?"

"One guess."

"Talon?" She breathes.

"Probably." I square my shoulders, "Either way, I am not waiting to find out."

I gesture to my back, "Hop on."

"What?" She pinches her fingers together in front of her, "No."

The sound of voices reaches us. It's muted, so I can't decipher the words. Another crash, a third. A feminine voice rises in pitch, then is abruptly cut off.

"Lisa." She gnaws on her lower lip, "I can't leave her."

"And I can't leave you."

"You'd abandon your own clan?"

"She abandoned you first."

"I can't win with you, can I?"

I cup her cheek, "I'd do anything for you, Cara, but I can't endanger your life. If it means I am seen as being cowardly, then so be it."

"It could have been me there, and Talon having come to take me back." She shakes her head, "Oh, wait, that did happen. *You* kidnapped me, and there was no one to help me."

"Now you're mine." I refuse to feel guilty for what I did. I'd followed my instinct and it had turned out so right. She is my future, and if she thinks I am knowingly going to thrust her into danger, she is wrong. "You carry my child."

"My child too." She cups her belly, "All the more reason that I lead by example, and it's why I can't leave her behind."

Pivoting, she races for the door.

"Chloe." I run after her. "Stop."

She reaches the door, wrenches it open. I follow. "Don't do this."

She runs across the landing, down the stairs. I am right after her. Too late. I am going to be too late. She careens down the steps, reaches the bottom, then comes to a standstill. I take the steps two at a time, reach her, brush past her, and plant myself in front of her.

Ahead, Lisa stands in the center of the room, facing her father. Talon is by the door, Zeus, Ethan and Dom on the other side. "Don't come closer." Lisa holds up her hand.

Dom snarls low in his throat, "Get out of the way."

Lisa shakes her head. "You've done enough for me, Father. This is something I need to face on my own.'

"But—"

She pivots to face Talon. "You came for revenge?"

"You escaped. Did you think I'd let you get away?"

She thrusts out a hip, "Maybe." She raises a hand. "Maybe not. Maybe I didn't think about you at all. I was busy running for my life, remember?"

Behind me, Cara exhales.

Talon's nostrils flare. "My men have surrounded the house." He widens his stance. "Didn't think I'd get lucky enough to trap the Alphas of the two biggest powers in the land, and their Seconds, all in one place."

Cara draws closer, her heat a welcome contrast to the chills that race down my spine. I prop my palms on my hips. This is why I'd wanted to escape through the window... So I wouldn't put her squarely in the eye of the storm. I'd expected Talon to find us. I'd hoped to be with my clansmen by then. Hadn't thought it would be Zeus who'd come in search of me. He'd left his pregnant omega behind to come here and put himself at risk. Why would he do that?

Talon takes a step forward.

Every muscle in my body coils, "Stop right there."

Talon stiffens. Dom and Ethan tense.

Zeus stays silent, his gaze fixed on the intruder.

"You can't win this." Talon glances from Zeus to me, "My men will attack in precisely five minutes."

"I'll take my chances." I bare my teeth.

"Against a hundred?"

I clench my fingers into fists. "If it means I go down fighting, so be it." *Not.* I have no intention of dying. Not when I am so close to realizing everything I want. My mate, my child. *Mine.* A growl rips from my chest, "Just give me a chance to take you down, bastard. Let's go one on one, you and me."

He angles his head, "Let me think about it." He shakes his head. "Nope. Much as my ego would love to take you down a notch or two, I'm afraid my better sense prevails. I'm not as hot-headed as you...or your half-brother. He gestures to Zeus, who glowers back.

Had he been expecting Talon? Is that why he'd suggested we come here? I scowl at him, then at Talon.

"Didn't figure you for a pussy."

"Didn't figure you for a talking kind of man." His lips curl, "Use your fists instead of your words."

Heavy footsteps sound outside the door, echo from outside the window. I draw myself up to my full height. Cara brushes past me and I growl, "Stay back."

She twists her lips, "I am the one who got us into this situation... I...I should be the one to pay."

"No, I should."

176

Chloe

"Lisa!" I jerk my head toward her.

"It's my fault." Her voice cracks, "All of it. The reason Chloe was kidnapped the first time, then Kayden and Chloe being imprisoned, and then I took his bait. I escaped knowing full well I'd be endangering all of us. But I...I couldn't stop myself. I had to try to claim my freedom." She bites her lip; a tear runs down her cheek.

"Don't blame yourself." My fingers tingle to grip her arm, "I'd have done the same in your place."

"Oh?" Lisa's mouth twists. "Would you have colluded with the enemy, betrayed your own clan?"

I swallow.

Kai steps up, enfolds me in his embrace. I allow him to draw me back, sink into his side, draw on that solid hardness. Damn it, I should protest, say something to show solidarity. I'd started out hating Lisa... but the conflict in her is palpable.

Her eyebrows scrunch. She wrings her fingers together in front of her, shuffles her feet.

I understand her situation. Am aware of what it is to be torn on so many different sides. My omega personality, my instincts as a breeder, clashing with my need to assert myself. Hell, it's similar to the dilemma I am caught in right now, only...the man I'd thought of as a monster has turned out to be so much more complex. Layers upon layers I am trying to uncover.

I may spend the rest of my life trying to solve the puzzle that is Kayden fucking McLeod.

"Lisa."

"Chloe." She raises her chin, "Stay happy."

"Wha—?"

Dom growls. "Lisa, the hell you talking about?"

"Don't interfere, Dad. You promised."

"Oh, for fuck's sake girl…"

"Don't swear, Father."

Dom's features twist, "I'll never forgive you for this, Daughter."

"Just as long as you don't forget me."

"The hell—?" My heart begins to beat fast, "Lisa, drat it woman, why are you talking in riddles? If you think you are going to do, what I think you are—"

Kai claps his hand over my mouth. I stare up at him and he shakes his head. His chest rumbles; a purr spills from his lips.

The beautiful subvocal notes ripple down my stomach and coil between my legs. My knees tremble.

He pulls me closer. I turn my head, watch as Lisa steps up to Talon. His big body dwarfs hers; his shoulders shut out the sight of the exit. His gaze narrows as he glares at her, stalks her as she moves toward him. Her shoulders tremble; she straightens her spine. "Let them go."

He blinks, then one side of his mouth curls. "What will you give me in exchange."

"What do you want?"

"What do you think?" His eyelids lower as he peruses her body.

She swallows, "Take me."

Dom snarls, his muscles tense. Ethan grips his shoulder.

Talon glances from Dom to Lisa. His eyes gleam. Was the alpha enjoying seeing the father hurt, while his daughter negotiated her life for ours?

Talon hums under his breath, "That's what you said the last time, then you failed the first test I set for you." He drums his fingers on his chest, "So why should I believe you this time?"

"This time." Lisa's knees seem to wobble, then she pulls herself up to her full height, closes the distance between them until there's less than half an inch between the two of them, "This time, I won't fight you."

"Lisa—" Dom's entire body goes rock-solid. Tension leaps off of him. Zeus's biceps bulge. Ethan draws in a deep breath.

What is she doing? Why would she voluntarily offer herself up to that Viking? Doesn't she know that they are meaner, more cruel, than either the Brits or the Scots? The race that everyone hates?

Talon reaches out a hand, trails a finger down her cheek. She shivers. Dom's features tense.

Talon's jaw tics, "You'll submit?"

"No," Dom snarls.

"Yes." She hangs her head.

Dom leaps forward. Ethan yanks him back, and Dom shrugs him off.

"Stop." Kayden's voice rings out.

Dom pauses, his shoulders heaving. "Lisa, why are you doing this?"

She turns her head, her face in profile, "You're the one who taught me that no one is bigger than the clan, certainly not me."

"You are my child." His chest rises and falls, "For me, you are all that matters."

"You don't to me." She twists her lips. "Not anymore."

Dom's face pales. "You don't mean it."

She lifts her chin, "Watch me, Dad. Hear me as I say it. You. Don't mean anything. To me." She turns her head to glance at Zeus, then swings her gaze back to Kayden, then me. "None of you do."

Her chin wobbles. She bites her lips.

"Come back, we'll fight together, Child," Dom's chest heaves, "or die together."

"I've made my choice."

Talon wraps his arm around Lisa. She shudders; her shoulders hunch.

He pulls her close, and she seems to shrink into herself. He drops his head to her neck, inhales, and a cry escapes her lips.

Dom howls, "Let her go." He jumps forward.

Zeus and Ethan grab either side of his shoulders. He puts up his arms, his biceps bulging. "How dare you touch her?"

"Oh, I'll be doing more than that." Talon grins. He cups her cheek. "Isn't that right, my pet?"

She swallows; her jaw firms.

"Answer me."

She nods. "Yes."

"Now tell them to retreat."

"Stay back, Father. You did your bit bringing me up. I am of age now and I have made my choice."

Dom snarls deep in his throat, "Lisa, don't do this."

"You heard the omega." Talon straightens. "She's mine now."

Kayden tosses his head, "On one condition."

Talon's head jerks toward Kayden.

"You leave, and never come back. You leave this continent, and relinquish all claims on our lands."

"Kayden." Dom's features twist. "How could you?"

"She betrayed us. Now she's redeeming herself. It's fair."

"Fair?" He spits.

"He's right." Zeus raises his chin. "One life in exchange of the futures of two clans."

Dom pales further. "Fuck you, Kai." He looks at Talon. "Let me say goodbye." He pulls forward and Ethan and Zeus release him.

Talon growls.

"Surely, you can allow me that much?"

"He's right." Kayden jerks his head.

Talon frowns. He glares at Kai, then drops his head and whispers in Lisa's ear.

The color burns high on her cheeks. Her eyes gleam. She whips her head up, but he's already stepping back. "You have one minute."

She shoots him a look filled with contempt, then schools her features into a mask. She straightens, then moves forward. Dom closes the distance, lifts her off of her feet. He kisses her forehead. "I love you, Daughter."

She sniffs. A tear rolls down her cheek. "I…I…"

"You don't need to say anything."

She nods as more tears roll down her face, "Dad, I—"

"Time to go." Talon glares at the tableau of the father daughter duo.

Dom curls his fingers into fists, "When you have a daughter and you're forced to see her leave, we'll see then how you feel. I promise I'll be there to witness it, asshole. I'll have the last laugh."

Talon grins, "I'm laughing now." He quirks an eyebrow at Dom, "Unlike the rest of you."

He holds out his hand to Lisa, "Come."

Dom curls his fists at his sides.

"Goodbye, Father." She turns, marches up to Talon, then past him. He angles his head, a glimmer of something—*Interest? Lust?*—laces his features. Then he follows her out.

The door bangs shut.

Silence, a beat. The sound of footsteps recedes.

Ethan prowls to the window, peers out, "They left. He kept his word." He pivots, angles a look at Dom, "At least in this."

Dom stalks to the door and slams his fist into it. The frame cracks. "I failed her." He pounds his forehead against the barrier, and the entire structure shakes. "What kind of a father am I?"

"A good one." Kayden squares his shoulders. "You did your best to protect her, but she chose her path."

Dom pivots and his nostrils flare. "Whose fault is that? Just because you took what was yours by force, doesn't mean—"

"Hey," Kai snarls, "Don't insult my woman."

My woman? Am I his? Do I want to stay his? I bite the inside of my cheek.

"Oh yeah? What're you gonna do about it?" Dom's eyes bulge. His biceps flex and anger rolls off of him in dense waves. Kai raises his fists, stalks forward.

A piercing whistle rends the air. "You alphas want to fight?" Zeus' voice drawls, "Let's take it outside, shall we?"

177

Kayden

I let the Viking take one of those under my protection. I did what was right, to protect the most important thing, my mate.

I bend my knees, take my stance in the courtyard outside the house.

Ahead, Dom waits at the edge of the makeshift arena. It's demarcated by the circle that Ethan drew in the dirt, not that it matters. The mood that Dom is in? No way is he going to stick to any rules.

I don't blame him.

If I had been in his position and it had been my daughter who'd chosen to barter herself for my freedom... Sweat beads my palms.

It nearly had been Cara, there in that prison, when we'd been locked up.

She'd come so close to being in danger, again. I had seized the first opportunity to get away, knowing it was a trap and that I'd have to pay a price for it. Except I hadn't expected Lisa to step in to save the situation.

"Our debts are square, Dom."

"Fuck you." He slaps his chest. "If you think I am going to let you live after what happened earlier—"

"You can and you will. You are well aware that Lisa chose that path because she wanted control of her own fate. There was no other way out."

Zeus scratches his chin. "You guys gonna fight or what?"

I glower at him.

Fucker came out of this smelling sweet, with nothing to taint him. Now he has the gall to seem bored? He shifts his weight from foot to foot.

Yeah, he wants to return to his omega, no doubt. Too fucking bad. He'll have to wait his turn for his shot at marital bliss, if I have any say in it.

"Stay out of this." I snarl.

He spreads his arms, "I am but a spectator."

"I wonder why?" I crack my knuckles. "Not your style, half-bro. You prefer to own the spotlight."

"Not always." His mouth curls. "You forget that I am the more prudent of the two of us. Sometimes I am happy to withdraw and give up the stage..." He gestures toward me.

I growl, "Why don't I trust a word of what you say?"

"Why do I think that you are getting cold feet?" He turns to Dom, "Seems, my ass wipe of a brother doesn't want to fight you. He's afraid he's going to lose."

Ethan swears from the sidelines. "Fuck off, Z."

"Happy to oblige." Zeus ambles away, drops down onto a tree stump, "This is me being very patient. And waiting to see who kills the other first. Less shit for me to deal with later, you get me?"

The hair on my nape prickles. Nope, not like him at all. All of this was some kind of crazy, elaborate plan hitched by my asshole of a sibling. *Why would he do that?* "Is this some elaborate plan to distract the Vikings? To get them off the shores of your city with minimum collateral damage, perhaps?"

Zeus smirks, "You give me too much credit."

Dom's face darkens, "The fuck you calling collateral damage?"

"Not me," Zeus stabs his finger at Kai, "him. He's the one who failed to protect Lisa; he agreed to Talon's terms and abandoned her."

Dom snarls; his biceps swell.

"Not to mention he's laying the blame for everything squarely at my feet, when he could have suggested another plan."

Dom holds up his fists. Sweat sheens his forehead. The big guy is more than angry. He is furious. Rage spools off of him in a dense cloud, so thick I can taste his need for vengeance.

"Stop it, Z." I snarl. "Don't play him."

"See." He flicks his thumb at me. "Talk about the pot calling the kettle black. All of this is his fault Dominic. Don't hold back. Whip his butt. Avenge your daughter."

Dom slaps his chest and howls.

The sound echoes off of the trees; a cloud of birds races away, their squawking filling the air.

My skin tightens. Dom's hurting. Understandable. He's helpless, filled with grief. If this is the way to help him, then so be it. I'll take him on, give him a chance to vent his frustrations.

I glower at Zeus. "I'll get even with you for this."

"You'll have to face me first, asshole."

He bares his teeth. The wind drops. All of my instincts go on alert. I brace myself. Wait. Wait.

Dominic lowers his chin, charges.

I stay where I am, dig my heels in, harden my ribcage, hold, hold. He slams into me with all the power of a battering ram. I could have stepped aside. I'd seen Dom coming at me, known he was charged with anger which made him sloppy, but no. That won't help him. The only way is to take the punishment he is hellbent on meting out, confront him head on, give him the outlet he desires. My entire body shakes. My bones rattle—they fucking rattle—the breath rushes out of me, and I stagger back. My heels dig into the hard soil, and my feet protest. My calves strain; my thighs flex. Dom comes at me again,, raises his head and snaps it forward. His forehead connects with my nose.

"Fuck me." Pain explodes behind my eyes. I hear the crunch of flesh and carti-lage. If he's broken my face, I'll—

"You're going down asshole," he bounces on the balls of his feet, "if it's the last thing I do." He circles me, moves in closer.

"You're not thinking clearly, Second." I shake my head to clear it. "I've gone easy on you so far, but—"

He hooks his leg around mine, tugs. The world tilts. The back of my head connects with the ground. Sparks flare behind my eyelids. I groan, "Fuck you, Dom."

He raises his massive foot. I roll aside.

I'd intended to be a punching bag for his hits, but damn, if I am going to kill myself.

He throws his head back and howls. Anguish pools in my chest and my throat closes. "Dom, I understand that you're grieving. Just give me a chance to help you."

His features contort. "You know nothing." The whites of his eyes gleam.

I've never seen him in such a state. Well, to be fair, he's never lost his daughter before…except, she isn't dead.

"Dom, Lisa's too smart to walk into a trap. She wouldn't have offered herself, if she didn't have a plan."

Color sears his cheeks. "Shut the fuck up. Don't talk about my daughter, asshole."

He raises his foot. I grab it, flip him.

The big man arcs through the air. He hits the ground with a thud that seems to shake the ground beneath me. I spring up, jump on him, land on my knees—fuck that hurt—on either side of his torso.

I grab his neck, "Listen to me, Dom."

"Fuck off."

"You have to trust her."

"What do you care?"

"I have a mate, brother, a child on the way. I understand how it feels to have the one thing you were responsible for torn away from you." I peer into his face, "Lisa knows what she's doing. She is not a child."

"She'll always be my daughter."

"Of course, but she chose her path. She's a bloody martyr. You should applaud her decision."

"Oh?" He bares his teeth, "And if your mate decided to leave you and offer herself up—"

Anger crowds my mind, "Not the same bloody thing."

"Isn't it? Mates, daughters… They are all the same." His features harden, "Women who love you and leave you. They break your heart, and leave you to fucking rot inside."

"I understand, brother."

"Stop saying that." He shoots out his arm, wraps his fingers around my neck.

I increase the pressure around his, and his chest hitches. His shoulders shudder.

I don't let go. The bad news? Neither does he. He tightens his grip. Black spots flicker at the edges of my vision.

Dom and I have sparred many times in the past. His strength is equal to mine, except right now, his anger gives him an edge. And my singular fixation on Cara means that, as I try to center my attention on the man who's trying to choke me, I find I can't. My senses focus on her, as she raises a hand, her cheeks losing color.

She races towards us, "No, Dom, don't kill him—" She leans over us, "Please let him go. It's my fault as much as Kai's. I shouldn't have let Lisa offer herself up l, I—"

Dom swipes out his fist; I duck from instinct. *No, wait!* I grab at his arm, but I am too late.

The breeze from his blow abrades my cheek.

His fist connects with her stomach and there's a cry above me.

"Cara." My heartbeat ratchets up.

I let go of Dom, twist my body and catch her as she falls.

178

Chloe

"Cara." Kayden's worried face fades in and out in front of me.

I crack open my eyelids, my stomach lurches, and I groan. "Wh...what happened?" A headache knocks at my temples. He shifts me closer and a lightning flash blazes between my eyes.

"Oh," I hiss out in pain, and he growls. "Please...don't do that," I try to whisper; at least, I think I do. Except I am not quite sure. My tongue feels too thick; my arms and legs seem to be entirely weighed down. "K...Kai," I whisper.

"I have you, Cara."

"Something's...not right."

"The bastard decked you."

"Wh...who?"

"I'm so sorry, Chloe." Dom's voice sounds from somewhere above me.

I wince. Pinpricks of pain flare across my skin. Something liquid gives between my legs. "K...Kai." My heat begins to race. Sweat beads my temples.

"What is it?"

"I'm hurt."

"I know, sweet thing." I sense him look up, "I am going to kill you, motherfucker."

"Later." Dom sinks down next to me. "She's bleeding."

"No shit."

The violence in his tone sears my nerve endings. I cringe. "Kayden...help me."

"Are you in pain?"

He sounds almost panicked. How strange.

"What do I do?" He swears aloud.

I've never known my alpha to sound so frazzled. A vein throbs at his temple; his face pales. Is he having a breakdown?

Pain coils deep inside, drips down from between my thighs. I moan.

"Kai…" I grip his forearm, "the baby."

"What's wrong with the baby?" His arms tremble; he pulls me close to his chest. His essence surrounds me, his scent teases me, and for a second, I inhale his familiar presence. Wallow in his nearness. My womb clenches, pain scours my insides, and I huff out a breath. "I'm bleeding, Kai."

"What the—" He glances down and pales.

"She's bleeding." His voice sounds dazed. "What should I do…? What—?"

"Take her inside." Dom's voice is brisk.

"What?"

"Inside Kayden, take her in where you can care for her."

"Oh."

The world moves, I moan. Damn it, I sound pathetic, even to myself. This shouldn't be happening. Isn't being pregnant supposed to be a happy space? Not for me, apparently. From the moment I'd found out I was carrying, nothing has gone right… *Don't think like that.* It will be fine, it will.

"Chloe."

His features are so pale. I lift my hand, touch his cheek, "So handsome." My voice seems to come from somewhere far away."

"Stay with me, Cara."

"I love you, Kai."

"The fuck you talking about, woman? Like these are your last words."

Kai.

"Stay with me, damn you." He's biting his lips. Moisture glistens on his cheeks. *Is he crying?* Nah, he can't be. Kayden fucking McLeod doesn't cry for anyone or anything. Unless, "Am I dying?"

"You're not." His tone is fierce, "I am not letting you leave me."

Something soft gives under me, my skin tightens, and I moan again. Pain blooms between my thighs, travels down my legs.

"Definitely…dying." Darkness clouds my subconscious mind.

"Cara, open your eyes."

I turn toward him. Cold chills rack down my spine, I shiver. My blood rushes to my fingers, my toes; every part of me aches. Pins and needles grip my extremities. *Where am I? What's happening?*

"Kayden?"

"I'm here, Chloe." Warmth envelops me. A soft purr vibrates up my back; my spine curves. I lean into the sound, the heat.

Another melodious hum twines about my waist. My toes curl. *Hmm. Much better.*

A gentle touch whispers across my forehead. Did he kiss me? *Nice.*

"Let her rest, Kayden." A second voice… *Is that Dom?*

"It's all your fault." Kai's tone is harsh.

"It is, I accept it." Ah, so it is Dom. But it's not his fault.

It was mine; I got in the way. I open my mouth to say that, but my throat hurts. A ball of emotion grows in my chest. My child. My baby. Wetness trickles down my cheek.

"Don't cry, Cara."

My baby. I don't need to glance down at myself to know there'll be blood between my thighs. The little thing growing inside of me is gone. Emptiness. So much nothingness. A hiccup clogs my chest. My lungs compress. I try to breathe, but there's no air. No oxygen. *Kai, help me.*

"Fuck, she's turning blue."

"Breathe into her mouth. Inflate her lungs."

My chin is jerked up; my entire body bucks. Friction fills my ears, tugs at my nerves. Something pops between my ears. Then I am falling.

My eyes snap open and I know instantly where I am. In a strange bed, with a man who's my mate. And my child? "I lost her."

I raise my fingers and someone grips them. *Kai? It's him.* His large palm caresses mine; his thick digits twine with mine.

"Shh, Cara."

A low hum convulses up his chest, his throat vibrates, and the subvocal notes consume me.

I turn to him, bury my nose in his chest, and draw on his familiar scent. I fill my lungs and wait for that familiar numbness to fill me. Wanting, craving, an escape from the nothingness that threatens to overwhelm me. My head throbs, my throat closes, I wait for the tears, wait... My lungs burn, my chest hurts, there's a heavy feeling in the pit of my stomach. *Drat it, why can't I cry?*

"Chloe."

"It's your fault." I curl my fingers into a fist, slap at him. "Your fault. You started it all. You took me from the life I was living for myself, thrust me into the unfamiliar, made me hope for something I could see, hope, feel... It was all within reach... then..." I choke, slap the broad wall of his chest again. "All your fault, asshole."

He doesn't correct me. For the first time, he lets it pass.

"I hate you." I snap my head forward, until it collides with the planes. Pain flickers at the edges of my mind. *Good. I deserve it.* I couldn't carry her to term. I'd not acknowledged to myself that I was pregnant, that I had life inside of me... I hadn't been far enough along to understand what it meant to carry another and give birth...but this horrible emptiness inside of me, it hints at the fact that it's over. *Over.* I launch myself at him. Hit him, shove at his shoulders, head butt him, again and again.

"Cara, stop." He tugs me close.

I scream, struggle... He doesn't release me.

"Let it all out, Sweetheart."

Oh, I want to. I yearn to cry, but something inside of me is too big, growing, so heavy. It binds me, holds me captive. "Damn you, Kayden. I'll never forgive you."

He winces. "Hate me, Cara, as much as you want."

"Hate?" I snarl. "I loathe you for what you've reduced me to. An empty shell of what I was before. There's no future for us after this, Kai, none."

179

Kayden

I stagger out of the bedroom in the safe house. The door snicks shut behind me, and I flinch. The noise seems too loud in the silence that has captured me. My arms and legs are weighed down, my chest too heavy. What happened? How did everything go to pieces in an instant? How did I go from being a dominant alphahole to a sniveling, scared, shadow of myself?

I hurt her. I broke her heart. I'd held her as she'd dry heaved, then purred for her, soothed her, until she had fallen into a restless sleep. I'd carried her to the bath, divested her of her bloodstained clothes, run a washcloth over her tired body, then put her to bed.

She hadn't stirred, her skin stretched over her cheekbones, damp strands of her hair clinging to her forehead. Her lashes fanned out against her cheeks, eyeballs moving restlessly behind her closed eyelids. I didn't want to leave her, but I couldn't bring myself to stay with her longer. It is my fault that she is a shadow of herself, a grieving mass of emotions with no outlet. I stumble down the steps into the living room…seeking what? Something, anything to numb the pain that coils in my chest. That clogs my throat and threatens to overwhelm me.

She lost our child.

And I am to blame.

"Here."

A glass appears in front of my eyes. I follow the hand holding it, up the arm, the neck, to Dom's face.

"Drink."

I take the glass, toss it back. The whiskey burns its way down my throat. I cough, blink away tears. "More."

He grips my shoulder, guides me to the chair at the dining table. I scan my surroundings. Apparently, I've reached the kitchen. Dom pours more of the amber liquid into my glass. I down it. Fire burns the pit of my stomach. My chest heats. Tears gather at the corners of my eyes, run down my cheeks. "Top me up."

He pours again; I sling it back.

"More."

He screws the cap on the bottle, sets it aside.

"Gimme that." I reach for the bottle and he shoves it out of reach. "Anymore and you'll keel over."

"Finally," I raise my eyes skyward, "he gets it." I lower my chin, glare at him, "Don't remember you being so slow."

"Don't remember you being so dumb."

"Hey." I scowl, swipe out my hand for the bottle again.

He slaps away my hand. "If not you, think of her."

"Don't speak about her. It's your fault she's in there."

He squeezes his eyes shut, "You're right." He grabs the bottle, tears off the cap and raises it to his lips, and drinks and drinks. Some of the liquor spills down his chin. He empties the bottle, then sets it down with a snap. His cheeks are flushed. "Fuck me, for what I did." He slaps at my shoulder and my body swings back.

"Watch it." A fine anger laces my vision. I strike out with my fist, he ducks, and I hit the bottle, which crashes to the floor.

"See what you did." He shakes his head. "Poor Kayden, always moaning about his misfortune. So, papa took you and buggered you, and left your mother for dead."

"The fuck —?" I snarl.

He springs to his feet, plants his palms flat on the table, and leans toward me. "So, you lost a child. Now you understand how it felt when I had to stand by and watch my daughter give herself up? And for what?" He leans across the table and stabs a finger in my chest. "To save your sorry ass, is what."

I lurch up to my feet; the world swings. Fucking liquor. I drank—not nearly enough. I scan the room. There. I march to the makeshift bar situated in the corner of the room, grab another bottle of whiskey and twist the cap off. I tilt it to my lips, chug down the liquid. The liquor goes down smoothly, but it's not enough.

I'm still standing. Still listening to him go on about my misfortunes. *Say one more thing, motherfucker, give me one more reason to deck you.* Anything to get into a fight, and feel something…anything other than this horrific guilt that's clawing at my insides. The ball of sensations in my chest whines, flares out.

I gasp, bend over with the bottle held in my hand. Liquor drips out onto the floor. The scent of alcohol deepens, overpowers me. Good.

"Running from facing the repercussions of your actions, Kai?"

Dom lumbers over. He grabs the bottle from my hand, drains it, then flings it aside. It crashes against the wall, the pieces shattering onto the floor.

He straightens; so do I.

He throws the first punch. I duck. His fist whizzes past my head. I move to the side, kick his leg out from under him. He falls, the back of his head connecting with the floor with a crack.

I jump on him, my knees on either side of his chest. I grab his neck and squeeze. "What did you say? Now, I understand how it feels when you lose a child? Well, how does it feel when your life is draining away from you, huh?"

He chokes; his eyes bulge. He scratches at the floor; his nails scour the floorboards.

"Die, motherfucker, for what you did to her."

It's not his fault. It was an accident.

No, he started the fight. It's because of him that she's out of her mind with grief. That she lost a part of the both of us that could have set everything right. Our hope, our future, a life together…all of it gone. I increase the pressure on his neck. His chest heaves and his shoulders hunch.

"Fuck you, Dom."

His body jerks.

"I am going to kill you."

Footsteps sound behind me, hands grab at my shoulders, and I shrug them off. Intensify my hold. Color fades from his face, his lips turn blue.

"Kayden, stop," Zeus' voice whips across the space.

"Not until he pays for what he did to her."

"She's gone."

"What?" I scowl at Zeus.

"Her room is empty."

I release Dom, and he heaves a breath, chokes, splutters.

"What do you mean?" My pulse begins to race.

"While the two of you were indulging in some very mature man-to-man talk," Zeus shakes his head, "she left."

180

Chloe

I stumble through the night. How long have I been walking? Hours? Probably minutes. I'm not sure. I woke up alone in the room, naked, of course. Even then, the alphahole couldn't let me be, eh? After everything we'd experienced together, he'd stripped me. Had he taken me again when I was unconscious?

Not even Kayden could be that heartless, surely?

I have a vague recollection of hitting him, trying to hurt him, then nothing. He hadn't even bothered to stay with me. I'd heard sounds of a scuffle from downstairs. I'd managed to find a skirt and blouse in the wardrobe, had pulled it on, along with shoes... Who did they belong to? No matter. They're not Kai's...Kayden's. *Call him Kayden. Bastard. Monster is better.*

I chuckle. He'd been all that once...and my beloved. No more. He's dead to me. As dead as the child I once carried. I press my hand to my flat belly. It feels the same, except for the faint ache between my legs, similar to how it felt when he fucked me. No, it had hurt more then, to have his cock pressed into my cunt. Now...I feel nothing. No pain. Not physically, at least. Damn it, why couldn't I have sensed something of the life I'd carried? A flutter, a jolt, a whisper of a touch deep inside.

I hadn't felt any of it.

A pressure builds behind my eyes. I stumble and almost fall, then right myself. I have to keep going, have to understand what happened ... Except, nothing makes sense anymore.

There is no logic, no reason for what happened.

Fate? Is that what it is?

That unseen force that had guided me to escape with my sister from Russia, to follow her and Zeus' directives, to bend to Kayden…to submit? And where had that gotten me? Alone. All alone. This time though, it is my choice.

I had walked down the stairs, seen him and Dom brawling. They'd been oblivious to me…not noticed as I'd slipped out, and I'd been glad of the reprieve. And angry. I'd wanted him to stop me, to be focused on me, not trying to bash out his own feelings in some stupid fight.

Clearly, he'd been selfish even then. He'd only thought of himself all this time. And now…it is time I watch out for myself. I don't need him, or Lucy, or Zeus… don't need anyone to survive. I have myself. I am alive…and what purpose does that even serve?

I push on past the undergrowth, shove aside the shrubs that scratch at my arms, my legs, keep going. Keep walking. As long as I am moving, I don't have to face up to what I left behind. My child—a part of me that never was. And him? He is alive. That doesn't mean anything. The ball of sensations in my chest stutters. *He* doesn't mean anything.

Heat, flushes my skin, a strange force tugs at me, my spine curves, and my breathing deepens.

Turn back. Turn back, Chloe.

I won't. There is nothing there for me. I pick up speed, focus on the path ahead.

A branch whips past me, scratching at my cheek. My hair snags on another, I tug, wince as it is pulled out of my scalp. Keep moving. One step in front of the other. My stomach churns and my knees tremble. Why do I feel so weak?

Come back, Chloe.

No.

Return to me.

I won't.

You must.

Why? Because you say so?

That's a start.

Not.

I huff out a breath. As if he can command me? *Yank my leash and expect me to come running?*

Yes, exactly.

Fuck you, Kai.

Language, Chloe.

You can't stop me from what I am going to do next.

I can and I will.

That's what you think.

I know.

How can you, when you've never bothered to ask me how I felt? You were too busy blaming yourself, Kai.

Because I was at fault.

See? I toss my head. *There you go, assuming you know everything about me, when you don't. You hadn't even realized I was pregnant, not until I'd told you.*

My mind was too full of you then. I didn't notice anything else. Don't you understand?

Ha! I increase my pace. *Excuses, so many of them. You're good at that, Kai. Finding a way to absolve yourself of the consequences of your actions.*

This was my mistake, Chloe, I accept it.

All of it?

Huh?

Everything you did wrong, Kayden, would you apologize for that? How you kidnapped me, took me for your own, never gave me a choice —

You wanted it too, Cara.

Don't call me that.

Why not?

Because I hate that name.

I love how it sounds, my Cara.

Don't distract me, Kai.

Am I now? A smirk laces his thoughts… Yeah, there's no other way to describe the flavor of that sentiment. Even during this strange internal monologue that I swear I am imagining now, for it is all in my head, of course, I don't doubt it, not at all, even now…the ego of that alphahole comes pouring through.

It's what had gotten me into this trouble in the first place.

The strange allure of his dominance. The one I've never been able to resist. Until now. For it's all a front. A sham. A way to get what he wants. He'd been so sure of himself, huh? What happened to all that self-assurance? *Where were you when I needed you, Kai?*

Right there with you…

And yet not. Your pride, your need for revenge, your unquenchable desire to get your own way, it's what led us to this place, where I stand poised at the edge of a decision.

I step out from the tree line into a clearing. The ground tilts up, and I walk up the slope. In the distance the sky begins to lighten. Grey and silver laced with pink hinting of the coming dawn. A new day; nothing has changed. Everything has gone back to when I was on my own. When my womb was empty. Empty. I flatten my fingers across my stomach. My child is gone. Something heavy knocks behind my eyes. My foot slides, and I freeze. A stone tumbles away. I peer down to where the waves crash against the rocks. The foam of their peaks sparkles, beckons. Closer, I need to get closer to that ethereal lightness.

The wind slams into me. I sway, catch myself.

What am I doing?

How did I get here? My subconscious led me here, perhaps. What do I intend to do?

Jump. Do it. Put it all out of your mind. Leave the pain, the loneliness behind. Join her… *where she is.* A whisper, a touch, a kiss. My heart begins to race as adrenaline spikes my blood. I curl my fingers into fists. One step, that's all it would take. One move to end it all.

I lean forward into the breeze.

181

Kayden

My heart rams into my ribcage and the jumble of emotions in my chest explodes out. I stumble, fall over, and hit the ground. Dead leaves and mud coat my mouth, the insides of my nose. Something cold coils in my stomach. I flatten my palms against the ground, shove myself up to a sitting position. *Where is she?*

Footsteps approach, then I am grabbed and hoisted up to my feet.

"Something's wrong." I stare into Dom's face.

"No shit." He jerks his chin toward the path. "You took off without warning."

"Chloe," my heart begins to race.

I pivot, race toward the source of my unease. She's there; she called to me. I swear I did not imagine that entire conversation in my head. I'd spoken to her, had sensed her fear. She'd been angry with me—that's fine, I can deal with it. She'd been afraid—understandable after everything she'd experienced.

But there was something else—a despair, a dense cloud of hopelessness, one that had sent fear shivering down my spine. That's when I had rushed out of the house.

"Hold on," Dom pants.

I bow my head, increase my pace.

He swears, "At least tell me you're going to her."

I run faster. Harder. Heart beating, pulse pounding. The burning sensation in my chest grows bigger, more urgent. My spine bends and I thrust out my chest, *gotta get to her.*

Dom keeps pace, his footsteps pounding right behind me.

I come to where the path forks in two. I turn right, pound through the undergrowth. Shove away the branch that slaps across my face, duck under the low hanging vines, tear away the foliage that stretches across the path.

"You sure she came this way?"

Am I sure? No. Am I going forward anyway? You bet. I lower my shoulders, pull my arms closer to my body, charge forward. My footsteps echo in my ears... Or is that the beating of my heart?

Sweat beads my forehead as a pressure builds between my temples. The intense need to move even faster overwhelms me. Adrenaline laces my blood, and I shoot forward.

The mist clears, as the first rays of the sun light up the horizon. My foot slips, I tilt forward, hurtle through the space, and am yanked back.

"The fuck you up to?" Dom holds onto my arm, almost yanking it from the socket. Pain explodes down my side, behind my eyes.

I gape down at the whites of the waves far below. "No!"

The cry is torn from my lips, ripped apart by the breeze. I hang there, suspended over the ledge, my body inching down, down, pulled by gravity.

Dom's voice calls to me from somewhere above. "Give me your other arm."

I search the rocks below. The waves crash over the surface; the sun's rays bend, illuminating every nook and crevice of the steep drop below the cliff. She couldn't have survived that.

I had turned away from her and she had left.

I had been selfish—again—thought only of myself, of taking out my grief, of finding an outlet to vent my frustrations.

That's why I had left the room. I'd drunk myself into a blind numbness while she… Cara had been racing away from me toward her death.

Dom grabs my other shoulder. I wrench it away, "Let me go."

"No, asshole, can you hear what you said?"

"If she's dead…I…"

"She's not."

"She went over the edge."

"How can you be sure?"

Because…because what? I sensed it? Felt it? All of that emo shit I'd disbelieved… All of it points to only one thing. She's gone. And I'm here. And I don't want to be. Not anymore. "Let me the fuck go." I jerk my body, and descend another inch…a centimeter? What does it matter? "I'm coming, Cara."

My head snaps back; I blink, look up as Dom slaps me again.

"The fuck—?"

"Yeah, there's more, asshole, if you don't give me your other arm."

"Arm?" I frown.

"Give. Me. Your. Arm. Or so help me, Kayden, I—"

I raise my free hand; Dom grabs my wrist.

My entire body sways, I sink another centimeter.

Dom grunts. "I fucking don't want to die, and I am not gonna let you pull me to an early death."

His fingers grip my forearms. The weight of my body is suspended from my arms. The pressure on my ribcage increases; the hollowness inside of me grows. My arms feel as if they have been torn out of their sockets. I can only imagine how Dom manages to hold onto me while somehow gripping the side of the cliff with his feet. He's carrying the weight of both of our bodies…and one wrong move... My throat closes.

I swing my leg and my toes brush the rocky surface. I wedge my feet in a crevice, taking some of the weight off of both of us.

Dom growls low in his throat, yanks me up an inch.

I swing my other leg up, find another toehold, hoist myself up another inch, another.

"I am going to kill you for this." With another grunt, his chest seems to expand and his biceps bulge.

I push away from the cliff's surface, and he yanks me up at the same time.

I swerve my leg up and over the edge, hold, then dig in with my knee and propel my body forward. I seem to fly over the last few inches, onto solid ground. I roll down the slope, then come to a halt.

Dom's breathing sounds from somewhere to my side.

Sweat pools under my armpits; I blink more out of my eyes. My breath comes in hard puffs; my chest heaves. The nothingness gnaws at my rib cage. I sit up and my entire body protests. My arms are numb. I swear I've torn them out of their sockets. My knees tremble—they fucking tremble—when I take a step forward. Another. I walk to the edge, peer down.

"I swear if you jump again, I am not coming after you."

I hold up my hand and he falls silent.

"Hear that?"

"What?"

I walk by the edge, follow my instinct. Yeah, seems I do believe in all that emo shit… Don't tell Cara… Better still, I'll tell her when I find her. She has to be alive, has to. No way am I letting her cheat me of the chance to punish her…when I finally track her down. I… "There!" I race to the far end of the cliff, then jump.

182

Chloe

Did I break my back?

No, I can move, so guess not. I turn my neck and pain erupts behind my eyes, flashes of red and white. I groan aloud. I hadn't meant to do that, honestly. I mean, the thought of taking my own life had crossed my mind. I'm not proud to admit that. Truly, I hadn't meant to go over the side.

By the time I'd realized that I was in momentum, it was too late.

And those last few seconds... I gulp... I'd thought of Kayden. Of us. Of the life we could have had together.

Of how much I want to slap him for what he put me through, fight him, and challenge him. Go toe to toe with him, kiss him.

Smell his masculine essence, revel in his nearness... I want all of that.

I'd been stupid to think I had nothing to live for. Maybe I was overreacting?

Maybe it took a brush with death for me to understand the gift I had been given. A mate. A *soul mate*. One who is mine, who seems to both love and hate me at the same time, who is so annoyingly full of himself that I often want to jump on him, tear his clothes off, and hit him at the same time. Such conflicting emotions... I mean, the man is 100%, grade-A, alphaholeness, but he is mine to hold and cherish.

Mine to ignore and punish.

If I had another life... What am I thinking? This life. I want it all in *this* life. *Now.* I crack open my eyes. His face comes into view.

"What the—"

"Cara?"

"Go away."

"Huh?" His eyebrows knit.

"I'm dreaming."

"Umm..."

Yeah, definitely dreaming. Kayden never hesitates. He never stops mid-sentence. Definitely doesn't have his hair all mussed, with dirt streaking his clothes, a slash of red across his face which doesn't take away from the beauty of his features, by the way. It only lends him a dangerous air, makes him even more appealing. Damn the man. I gnaw on my lower lip, and don't feel any pain. Well, how could I, given all of this is a dream, right?

"Chloe?" His biceps bulge as he balances the weight of his body on his massive forearms. He winces; his features twist. He seems both in pain and deathly afraid, at the same time. Of me? Nah...told ya, I'm dreaming.

"You're not really here, you're not." A rippling emotion coils in my chest. The pressure builds behind my eyes. A gust of wind crashes into him. He sways, then his body topples over.

"Oh, hell." I squeeze my eyes shut, wait for the impact, for my bones to be crushed. One...a beat...another.

"Open your eyes."

I blink, see his face suspended above mine. Those dark eyes, the emotions swirling in their depths. "The fuck did you do that?" He glares at me.

"At least in a dream, you could be polite?"

"Is that what you want, Cara?" He glares at me. "Fucking etiquette?"

"And why not?" I jut out my chin. "I am a princess, after all. Time you treated me as one."

"I always have." His jaw tics, "I mean, I could have... " He blinks and his gaze sidles away.

"Wow." I stare. "The great alphahole himself, speechless?"

"There's a first time for everything." His throat moves as he swallows. He straightens, peruses my features. "You're okay."

"Umm...yeah." I swallow.

"If I get up off of you, you won't try to...you know..."

"What?"

He jerks his chin towards the edge...gestures to the waves.

"Nope."

He pushes up to standing, holds out his hand. I grab it and he yanks me up.

"Let me help you." I peer up to see Dom. I hold out my hand and Kai makes a noise deep in his throat.

"What?"

"I'll do it." He swings me up in his arms, "Kai, what are you doing—?" I squeak as he jumps up the side of the cliff. His feet don't seem to touch the surface. "How did you do that?"

I look past him to where the ledge juts out, the whites of the waves breaking far below. "Oh." My head spins. I hadn't realized I'd been so close to falling over the edge. I grab at his shoulders. "Wow."

"Exactly." He huffs, "You see how careless you've been?"

"It was an accident."

"I don't believe you."

He stalks forward.

Dom follows. "Let the woman be."

Kai's jaw hardens. "You keep out of this."

"Fuck me," Dom mumbles. "You're as obstinate as ever. Why had I thought you'd have changed?"

"He hasn't." I lean up and pain grips my side. I whimper.

"You're hurt?"

That's putting it lightly. No way am I going to let on exactly how much pain I am in. If I do, he'll, no doubt, reprimand me, and right now, I can do without that. I relax, close my eyes, sense him perusing my features.

"You're in shock."

"No."

My limbs begin to tremble. *Drat him, but he's right.* Definitely not going to tell him that either.

A harsh purr flows up his chest. My blood heats and my pain subsides.

I focus on his voice, the subvocal notes that cocoon me, pull me close to him. Hold me, caress me. A sigh spills from my lips.

"You found her?"

A new voice interrupts my thoughts. I want to open my eyes but my eyelids seem to be weighed down.

Kai keeps walking.

"Perhaps this time you'll put her needs first?"

"Shut the fuck up." Kai's voice vibrates up his chest. The words are angry, but his tone is mild. I really should open my eyes and figure out what the hell is happening, but I'm too comfortable. Too warm. Strange, I'd have sworn I was cold a few seconds ago.

"How long do you intend to stay here?"

"Until she's strong enough to travel." Kai's voice rumbles.

"When will that be?"

"She needs to be checked out by a doctor."

Kai hesitates, "I'll wait for a day, at least."

"Don't think you need me anymore. I was thinking of returning with Zeus." Dom's voice draws closer, "Just as long as you don't do anything foolish."

"Look who's talking?"

I hear the smirk in Kai's voice.

Dom snarls. "What do you mean?"

"You don't fool me. I'll let you go on the condition that you agree to wait until I return to London."

There's silence. I tilt my head; I can almost hear Dom think. Clearly, he hadn't been planning to return. Bet, he wants to go after Lisa, and Kai doesn't want him to. Strange, I wouldn't have thought Kai cared for his friends so much. Not after how he'd tested his alphas the first time he'd brought me to his stronghold.

My belly clenches... That was one of the times he'd used me as a pawn in his game. Not the first time. What about now? Will he do the same? Is he planning something else? Is that why he wants me to himself for a few more days? I struggle in his embrace and his grasp tightens.

"Shh," he leans in close. "What's wrong, Cara?"

Let me go, is what I want to say. All that emerges is a whine.

"Get her inside," Zeus sounds preoccupied. His mind is already elsewhere. He intends to leave me here with Kayden, but I don't want to stay.

I'd much prefer to be in the company of Lucy. Ideally, I'd have all of them in the vicinity. There's safety in numbers, right? Though where this alphahole is concerned, I'm not sure if that holds true either.

I wriggle again, crack my eyelids open.

Kayden's' hard profile fills my vision. He lowers his chin, until his lips brush my ears, "I'm not letting you go that easily, Cara. Best you accept your fate."

No. I shake my head, at least I think I do.

His eyes glimmer and his jaw hardens. "You don't have a choice."

"We'll be heading off then." Zeus' voice recedes.

Dom hesitates. "You sure she's okay?"

No, I'm not. I turn my head in the direction of his voice, but Kai yanks me close. His arms tighten so my face is buried into his chest, and that's not all bad. That dark edginess of his scent fills my senses and my head spins. I'm fine, right? So why am I resisting? Why are all of my senses on high alert? I moan, try to pivot my head.

"Shh, I have you, Cara."

183

Kayden

There had been a second there, when I'd been sure I'd lost her. I'd leaned over the edge and seen the waves, and every part of me had gone numb. The truth had been laid out for me then. I am nothing without her, and that is a sobering thought. I hadn't felt as bereft when my mother had died in front of my eyes... Perhaps I'd even anticipated her death, known the time would come when my blood father would take her away from me. The event had shocked me, but also filled me with rage. Wrapped me up in the need for vengeance, which had driven me until I'd seen her.

My Cara.

The omega who turned my world upside-down, and now here she is, in my arms. Broken, grieving, and I am the cause of her sorrow. I tighten my arms about her, stalk up the path to the safe house.

I scrutinize her features, the planes of her cheeks, the dark circles under her eyes. She feels too thin, too fragile. I could snap her in half easily. I'd been the one who'd lost control and cracked, until I'd leaned over the edge and seen her. The hope that had filled my heart propels me forward.

I race up the stairs, to the room we'd occupied not too many hours ago. A lifetime ago. When things had been different...and yet, the same?

I lay her down on the bed and my arms tremble. I raise my palms and my fingers jerk. I curl them into fists, tuck my elbows into my sides. Leaning over her, I pull the covers up.

Her eyelids flutter open.

"Sleep now."

She tucks her palm under her cheek. Her gaze follows me as I prowl to the chair on the far end of the room.

She bites her lip, then opens her mouth and I shake my head.

She desists. Her forehead crinkles.

"I'll be here when you wake up."

Her shoulders hunch.

"Yeah," I rub the back of my neck, "not that I kept my promise the last time...but you taught me my lesson. No way, am I letting you out of my sight." I huff out a laugh, then sink into the chair.

She turns on her side and pillows her hands under her head.

"No, I don't mean that in a creepy, stalkerish way..." *Not quite. Except, that's exactly how I mean to be.* I'm going to shadow her every move, ensure that she's always safe, never allow another man to get close to her. Hell, I'll protect her from herself, if that's what it takes. But I don't say any of that aloud. Don't want to scare her more than I have already, hmm?

I fling my arms behind my head, spread, my legs wide.

"You going to stick to your promise?"

"Huh?" I raise my chin.

"I still want to spend some time apart."

"So fucking civilized." I bare my teeth.

"Don't change the topic."

I glare at her; she doesn't blink.

What the—? When had this entire relationship turned on its head? The balance of power is...evenly distributed between us, and strangely, it doesn't feel all wrong either. I scratch my jaw. "The faster you're back on your feet, the faster we can come to a decision."

"If you're playing with me, Kai—"

I hold up a hand, "I promise I'll consider it."

"You gave me your word." Her lips firm.

"And I won't break it—" *At least not yet.* I shift my bulk, trying to find a more comfortable position in the chair, "Get some rest, and we'll talk about it when you wake up."

"Kai, stop."

Ma's laughter floats across the valley.

My lips curve. Her laugh is beautiful. Ma is a true princess. Her glowing limbs, her long blonde hair that floats to her waist... All of it entrances me. There's no one else in all of Scotland who can rival her beauty, that's what my father's clan says.

I've heard them whisper this when they think I can't hear them. I snicker cause I can. I have sharp hearing. Ma claims I can hear the grass rustling from meters away. She may be right, but I haven't tested it. I am very attentive to my surroundings. At the same time, I find it very difficult to concentrate in class. Except for math. I love all of those figures, the addition and subtraction. And multiplication tables? Those are my favorite.

Ma says I am different from the other children in that, and not because I am heir to the clan of Scotland. Her face always grows sad when she says that, and I hate that. I never want to do anything that hurts her. She's my best friend. I love playing with her as much as with the boys from the stables. They're the ones who taught me to race through the fields and hide in the undergrowth.

"Kai, where are you?"

Ma's voice grows nearer. I giggle, then stuff my knuckles into my mouth. Father says boys don't laugh so openly. In fact, boys don't smile at all, and boys who are heirs to the Scottish clan, definitely not. I need to be more serious, pay attention to my fighting lessons with more in-ten-si-ty. Intensity. He uses that word a lot, and also other four-letter words that Ma always shushes him about. It's an insult to use them, she says. It's why I have stored them away in my head, to use when she's not around.

"Kai, stop hiding and show yourself."

Ma's voice rises in pitch. Oh, she's worried. I bite the inside of my cheek to stop myself from calling out to her. Just a little closer. I can hide myself until then, and spring out at the last minute. Ma will be happy to find out how clever I have become. She always tells me that I'm her little man. Her hero. I straighten my shoulders. I'll always be there for her.

When I grow up, I'll defend her from her enemies, including when Father gets angry with her. I won't allow anyone to hit her. I hate it when Father does that. I curl my fingers into fists. That's when I'll step between them, take the hits meant for her. No one hurts her on my watch. No one.

"Kayden... Kai—" Ma's voice cuts out. I stiffen. Peer around the bush. She's facing a man— Father? When did he arrive in the Highlands? He hates it here, says the place is too beautiful for warriors. He prefers the gri-ti-ness of cities. He's never come here before, has he?

He walks toward her and pauses. A bottle dangles from his left hand. His figure dwarfs Mom's tiny frame.

His face grows red; his nostrils flare. He raises his other palm and Ma winces. I jump up, rush out of my hiding place. "Stop."

Father glares at me. His face... He's not my father... He's someone else. His features distort. "Bastard child." He swigs from the bottle.

What does he mean? "Why is he calling me that?"

Ma's shoulders sag; she doesn't reply.

"Tell me, Mama."

Her spine hunches and she drops to her knees. "I am sorry, little man." She begins to sway, back and forth, back and forth. My head spins. Why am I so dizzy? She sobs, big gushing noises that pour out of her too-small body.

"She'll never admit this to you, but you are not mine."

I frown. "You're my papa."

"Adoptive father."

"Colin." She jumps up, "You promised you'd let me tell him the truth of his identity."

"You promised to be faithful to me, Adele." He bares his lips; his cheeks are so ruddy. The wind blows and the scent of something foreign...hits me. I cough, tears squeeze out of the edges of my eyes. "Don't hurt her."

"Fuck off, little bastard." He swigs from the bottle, then throws it aside. It crashes. The noise echoes around the hill side. I jump.

He stoops, picks up a piece of glass. The jagged edges glisten in the sunlight. "I should kill you for what you did to me, Adele."

"I...it wasn't my fault." She raises her head, her hair swirling about her shoulders. "I was in heat, and he was there... Where were you when I needed you, Colin? Away on another of your conquests?"

"Excuses, huh?" He tosses his head, "Typical of an omega. Can't control your instincts when you are in heat. Is that why you allowed him to impregnate you? Five years Adele. We'd been mated for five, bloody, long years, and you never got pregnant. He fucks you once and boom..." he smashes the glass to his forehead. Blood blooms at his temples, runs down his cheeks. I growl. Ma cries out. She jumps up, runs to him. "Colin you're hurting yourself."

"Not as much as you hurt me, bitch." He grabs her hair, tugs. Ma howls in pain. She clutches at his wrist, "Please...don't."

"I can... I will."

"Let her go." I rush forward, throw myself at him.

His big body shakes, "I hate the both of you." I sense him move, then pain explodes on my left shoulder. I scream.

Ma yells, "Don't hurt him, he's only a child."

There's a crash. I peer sideways. The shard of glass glistens in the grass. Its edges are red. *Blood? Is that my blood?*

Something trickles down my back, and my knees buckle. I slide down and Father stoops, grabs my shoulders, and I howl. White and red flashes behind my eyes, "Oh, dear Lord, Kai." He sinks down, cradles me, "What have I done?"

"Kai, my beautiful son." The sound of ripping jars my nerves. I turn to find Ma huddled next to me. She presses a cloth to my left side. Her beautiful dress is torn. She grabs my father's hand—which trembles. How strange. Father is not weak. He is a strong man, a warrior. But he threatened my mother and he hit me. Do soldiers abuse those they love? Oh, it's so confusing. Pain slices down my spine. I moan. Mother's face wavers. Her lips are bitten, tears streaming down her beautiful cheeks.

"Ma."

"Kai."

"Don't leave me, Mama."

"Kai, wake up."

I snap my eyes open.

Green eyes, red lips, beautiful blonde hair that swirls about her face. "Please don't leave me."

184

Chloe

"I won't."

The words dribble from my lips. The hollowness in his dark gaze grows deeper, more infinite. My heart twists. Pain...so much pain. The sounds he'd made in his sleep had woken me up. A groan, a low cry, an animal who was hurting so much. He was trapped in a nightmare from which there was no escape. Except there is. I am his salvation. As he is mine. Why have I found it so difficult to accept that?

"Kayden."

He doesn't respond. He studies my features, searching for something, lowers his gaze down to my chest, then back to my lips. Stays.

My throat dries.

"Kai."

"Did you mean it?" His voice is tentative.

I don't have to ask what he's referring to, though I am strongly tempted to ask. But that would be cheating, being cowardly, and that's the one thing I am not. Oh, I'd thought I was weak, a breeder made for just one thing, to procreate.

I know I am more.

I want an us. I want my independence, and I want another shot at everything that had been within reach, before it had slipped out from between my thighs. This emptiness inside of me crawls, begs for more.

I nod.

He swipes out his arm, I squeak, and the next second, I am sprawled across his lap. A lick of pain flares between my legs. I gasp.

Finally...something other than that churning nothingness that had crawled inside of me. I turn my face, scan his features. All expression is wiped from his face.

But his eyes... That dark gaze burns a trail up my spine, whispers across my cheek. He palms my butt, "Beautiful."

He drags his fingers down the valley between my butt cheeks. My skin tightens; my pussy clenches. More pain stabs between my legs. And hurt. And desire. All of it a potent combination. I'm not ready yet.. I can't be.

Not when I've been through something as traumatic as feeling the almost-life I'd carried slip out from between my thighs. And yet…I can't stop him.

I won't stop him.

This… What we have here is real. It's gritty. It stings. It's too soon after what happened, and it's exactly what I want. His fingers cup my pussy; I clench my thighs. A shudder of heat curls at my core.

"Kai."

"Shh." He draws his palm over the back of my thigh, down my calf muscles. Tendrils of sensation pop in the wake. He's arousing every millimeter of my body with his touch, his gentleness, a forewarning of the storm to come.

"Kayden, what do you want?"

"Huh?" He winds my hair around his other hand, and tugs. My scalp tingles. Pinpricks of awareness flare down my nape.

I hold his gaze. "Tell me." Something is different between us and I can't put a finger to it. I can't question it. Don't want to understand it. Sometimes it's better to follow the path where it leads.

He slips his palm under the hem of my skirt, drags the cloth up with his move. Cool air hits my heated flesh, goosebumps pop on my skin. "I want you." His voice is toneless, "I want to possess you."

"Why?" I peek up at him.

"When you cry out in response to my ministrations, it is an affirmation of life."

Oh.

"When you weep with pleasure, it turns me on."

I swallow.

"And when you come…" He lowers his head until his breath nuzzles my nape. "It's the sexiest thing in the world."

My breath catches; my throat closes. I want to tell him, no. Not now. Not when I am this vulnerable and open and exposed. Not when I lay here with my heart ripped open, the very essence of me fertile and trembling, ready to be taken… Now, if he makes me his again, I can never leave. Do I want to leave?

I nod and his lips curve. "My gorgeous Cara." He nibbles on my skin. "My luscious mate." He presses tiny kisses on the skin exposed by the collar of my blouse. "The beautiful mother of my as-yet unborn child."

"Kayden—"

He hooks his thumb in the collar and tugs. The material rips in half, falls to either side.

I huff, "Kai…"

"I told you what I want. Will you deny me?"

"Let me up." I strain against him and he leans his weight on me.

"No."

My heart begins to thud. "Please."

"I like it when you beg." His fingers slip in the gap between my panties and my lower lips, I shudder. "Love it when you swell under my touch."

He flips me, so I am facing him.

Then he scoops me up and stands. He cradles me against his chest and stalks toward the bath. "I should stop myself, Cara, it's too soon."

I reach up, trace the outline of his gorgeous lips with my fingers, "It's not."

"What if I hurt you?"

"I need this."

"What if you're too sore?

"I am." I swallow, "But I am so empty, Kai." I cup his cheek. "I want you to fuck me."

His nostrils flare; the skin at the edges of his lips tightens. He shoulders open the door of the bath, heads for the tub, and sets me down on the rim.

Leaning past me, he flicks on the tap. Water pours down and steam rises in the air. I swoop forward and kiss his cheek. He straightens, color burning his cheeks. *Huh?* A simple gesture of affection and my alphahole is reduced to a puddle. Imagine that.

"You were dreaming."

He grips the edge of my torn blouse and eases it down my shoulder, then the other side. My nipples pucker. His gaze drops to my chest, stays. He kneels down, and I spread my legs. He cups a breast, then the other, "I want to see them grow heavy as you fill with my child, again."

Me too. Tears prick my eyes. The words tremble on my lips, my chin wobbles, and just like that I am crying. The moisture gushes out of me; my shoulders heave. He pulls me to his chest. A deep purr rises from him, another. The tone soothing, almost sweet. The wavelengths envelop me, shiver down my spine. "I am sorry I couldn't carry her to term."

He tucks my head under his chin and his breathing deepens. "It was my fault."

I hiccup. "It was meant to be. The other omegas tell me when this happens, it means that the child was better off not born."

"Don't think about it."

"I want to." I pull back in the circle of his arms. "I didn't feel a thing, Kayden. All those weeks, it was too early, I didn't feel any different."

"And yet you are."

"You changed me." I blink. "You pushed me out of my comfort zone, forced me to find the woman I truly am inside. You broke me, then recreated me, Kai."

He grimaces, "Not sure if I appreciate the sound of that."

"I meant it as a compliment..." I huff, "Sort of."

He closes the distance between us, kisses me on the cheek, then slurps up the remaining moisture. "Yum."

I frown.

"You taste sweet."

"Thought that was a myth propagated by nosy older omegas."

"It's true." He scoops up a teardrop from the other cheek, brings it to my mouth. I close my lips around his finger, suck.

"I taste salty."

The blackness in his eyes deepens, "Not to me. You taste almost as sweet as..." He flips up my skirt, then dips his head between my legs.

185

Kayden

Lilies... She smells like lilies. The tang of pepper explodes on my palate. I groan as my dick lengthens. "Fuck, Cara, I need you."

I pull away, grab the collar of my shirt and yank it off.

Her breath hitches.

I throw the fabric aside, take in her luscious curves. The blood drums at my temples.

She peeks up at me from under half-closed eyelashes.

The heat in the enclosed space ratchets up.

She opens her mouth, then flicks out her tongue, to touch her lower lip.

My groin throbs.

I reach out, tuck a tendril of hair behind her ear. She raises her hand and I shake my head. "Not yet." I lower the zipper of my pants.

She exhales.

I step out of my shoes, kick off my trousers.

Her chest rises and falls. Color singes her cheeks. "Let me." She reaches for my briefs and I hesitate.

I've never allowed a woman to undress me. It's too intimate. Something hot sears my chest. The ball of emotions digs into my ribcage and I stutter. *Stay. Stay.* She slides her fingers over the bulge at my crotch. I groan. She squeezes my hardness and my legs tremble. She presses her face into the bulge, then bites down on the thick column.

A deep purr rips out of me, "Cara." I tug at the thick strands of her hair, "You're killing me."

Her lips curve. She shoves my boxers down my legs.

I kick them off, widen my stance. My dick swings free; my balls harden. She grips my cock, and massages my erection from base to head. A bead of precum appears. She drops her head, licks it off.

A growl rips out of me. "I wanted to pleasure you first, ensure that you were okay—" I huff as she closes her mouth around my cock.

She digs her fingers into my hip, slants her mouth. My grip tightens in her hair.

I jerk my hips and my dick slides down her throat. She moans deep in her throat and a snarl rips up my chest. She sucks on my thick column, hollows her cheeks. I yank down on her hair, and she peers up at me. The darkness of her pupils bleeds out until only a circle of green marks the circumference. So hot, so erotic. My heart squeezes; my rib cage tightens. "Suck me off."

She pulls back, until her lips are wrapped around the head of my shaft, then waits. Waits.

"Do it." I glare at her.

The skin at the edges of her eyes creases. She lowers her head, and takes me in, all the way in. She hums and my cock jerks. She hollows her cheeks again and the vibrations tug on my groin, travel all the way up my spine. "Fuck me." I can't hold back, but I must. I need to show I trust her. That I can allow her to set the pace... this once.

I grip her shoulder, tug at the thick strands of her hair.

She dives in, pulling me down the moist heat of her throat. And again. And again.

Stars explode behind my eyes. My balls draw up —the tension builds, coils, bursts out from my groin. I arch my spine, squeeze my eyes. Can't stop the growl that rumbles up my chest as I come. And come.

My shoulders shudder, my knees rock, and I glance down to find her staring at me.

Tears squeeze out of the corners of her eyes; strands of cum drip down her chin. I pull out, then drop to my knees, peer into her eyes. "I fucking love you."

An alpha who confesses the depth of his emotions after the most phenomenal blowjob in the world...speaks the truth. Yep, "I mean it, Cara."

I frame her face with my hands, my palms dwarfing her small visage.

"You could ask me this anytime of the day or night, and I'd swear to it."

I reach behind her, turn off the tap.

She straightens, stumbles, and I right her.

I lower my head, swipe my tongue over her mouth. The salty taste of my essence streaked with the honey of her lips. Pure heaven. I tilt my head, and kiss her. I absorb her sweetness, drink from her, fucking nourish every part of me with the vitality of her. I open myself up to her. Body and mind and soul. My chest tightens as the ball of sensations in my chest explodes. White streaks dance behind my closed eyelids. She shudders, winds her arms around my neck. Still kissing her, I lift her up in my arms. She relaxes in my embrace.

I step into the bath, lower both of us in.

When I finally break the meeting of our mouths, she turns to the side and blinks. Color fades from her cheeks. "That... What was that?"

"You enjoy the way I kiss?" I can't stop the smirk that curls my lips.

She blinks, nods. I love the slightly dazed look in her eyes. Love it even more when she grumbles, "Don't look so pleased with yourself."

"Why not?" I prop my arms on either side of the tub. Water sloshes over the edges.

"We're making a mess."

"You're changing the topic."

She groans.

I chuckle.

She balances herself on her knees, leans in close enough for our eyelashes to twine. "I fucking hate you."

I stiffen.

She continues, "And love you."

My shoulders unclench; the breath I'd been holding shudders out.

She rests her forehead against mine, "You're so damn beautiful, it should be illegal."

"Keep going." I bet I'm wearing a shit-eating grin right now, but what-fucking-ever. I'm not going to begrudge myself this moment when I have the woman of my dreams in my arms. So what if I have a whole world of fuckedupedness to deal with when we return to London?

She frames my face with her hands, in a mirror image of how I had touched her not too long ago. "I want to be your mate, build a life together, have children, but I also want my independence. Do you understand?"

186

Chloe

Shut up, what are you going on about?

The alphahole told you he loved you and he meant it. Yeah, so it was at the end of a phenomenal blowjob.

I'd promised myself a while ago that I was going to suck his soul through his dick, and I can bet my breeder omega nature that it was all that and more. But that was not the only reason he'd laid himself bare. I believe him. I do.

Which is why I can't stop myself from opening up to him, either. A furrow appears between his eyebrows.

"Hmm," He grabs a washcloth, dips it in water, then proceeds to wash my shoulders.

"Is that all you can say?"

He draws the soaking cloth down my breast, rubs my nipple, which pebbles instantly.

I frown. "Now who's changing the topic?"

"That is not changing the topic."

"It isn't?"

He throws the cloth aside, then grips my thighs below my asscheeks. The next second he raises me so my knees are balanced on his shoulders.

"What the—?" I glance down to find I am positioned strategically, with my pussy ripe for the taking, right in front of his mouth.

"You wouldn't," I squeak.

He flicks out that long, broad tongue, and swipes up my lower lips.

"Oh." I gulp.

One corner of his mouth curls, then he angles his chin and licks me again from my backhole all the way up to the nub of my clit.

My thighs tremble, I sway, and his grip tightens.

His nostrils flare, then he repeats the action; only this time when he reaches my clit, he swipes that wicked tongue across the swollen nub.

"Gah." My body bucks.

He chuckles, "Your range of expression is bloody limited, you know that?"

"Hmm." My head spins. "Stop talking." I blink, clap my palm over my mouth, "I mean—"

He retraces the direction to my back hole, then thrusts his tongue inside.

"—Please," I blubber. Heat sears up my spine; a moan whines out of me.

Yep, illegal, what he can do with that tongue of his… He slurps his way up my slit. He swipes his tongue inside my wet channel and my breath catches.

"Kayden... Stop."

His jaw tics, "Does it hurt?"

I shake my head.

"Then?" His brows draw down.

"I am sore... from the earlier... " Can't bring myself to say it. "From, you know... "

His features soften, "Let me ease your pain."

He drops his head, licks my pussy. Warmth vibrates out from his touch.

The lingering emptiness at my core recedes, to be replaced by a melting sensation.

"How?" My voice trails off.

"Just following instinct, babe." He blows on my core and a pleasant heaviness radiates out to my extremities. I dig my fingers into his hair, tug. A growl rumbles up his throat, the vibrations sinking into my sensitive core. My toes curl. "Oh, Kayden."

A purr rips from his lips. He yanks me even higher, holding me suspended right above him, then sucks on my pussy, licks my lower lips, slurps his way between my thighs, slides his tongue gently, so gently, inside my channel, filling that soul-shattering emptiness inside, cocooning me, caressing me, overwhelming me. *Ah!*

He's right. My repertoire of words is woefully limited right now. I want to say something else… What, what? My brain cells have all melded together. I crack my eyelids open as he thrusts his thumb inside my back hole.

Heat slashes up my spine, and I hunch my shoulders, squeeze my eyes shut.

He closes his mouth over my pussy, swipes his tongue once more inside my aching core, then tears his mouth off of my center. "Come."

His voice whips over my skin and all of my nerve endings fire, all at once. The climax rips up my legs, pours into my womb. I cry out. Slick rushes out from between my legs, gushes down my inner thighs; his warm tongue scrapes across my throbbing pussy. I sense him lick it up, gulp down my essence. A low purr vibrates up his chest, and my sex clenches.

"Look at me."

I crack my eyelids open. He lowers me onto his chest. I round my spine, touch my forehead to his. "That, Cara. That is how I change the topic." He quirks his eyebrow, a smirk tugs at his lips, and the hair on my nape rises. I gulp. *Okay.*

"What were you saying earlier?"

What? I blink. Try to focus my attention on the thick hair that curls on his forehead, that patrician nose, the cruel upper lip. I shiver. Trace that full bottom lip of his with my thumb.

"You want to be independent?"

Huh? I nod.

"You got it, babe."

187

Chloe

The alphahole has been true to this word.

One week. An entire seven days, he has kept his distance from me. Enough for me to have recovered from the... the incident.

I pace up and down the length of the decking. We'd reached London in record time.

Turned out Ethan had left him an SUV. He'd raced it, never taking his foot off of the accelerator. *Had he been in such a hurry to get rid of me?*

Of course, I had been the one to ask to be autonomous.

I huff out a breath.

Hadn't thought he'd be so quick to deliver on that, considering the last few times he'd promised me a measure of freedom, things hadn't worked out quite the way I'd wanted.

I had not expected for him to confess his feelings so openly for me, either.

I step up to the railing of the balcony. I am in a bungalow in one corner of Zeus' stronghold. And Kayden? He opted for his own space. In the building opposite the square from mine.

It's what I'd wanted right? To be away from him? My throat closes. So why am I so disappointed at the distance between us?

Set apart from the rest, we are in a small complex that affords an uninterrupted view of the Thames river that winds its way lazily below. The waters are thick, a dark green, and even from this height, I can't see through the depths.

In the distance, the Tower Bridge arches between the two sides of the river. It soars high above the surface of the water. I catch my breath. The majesty of the architecture... Oh, my God.

My throat closes.

It's a testament to how creative humans can be. The only sight more spectacular than this is the onion-shaped domes of the church on Red Square. I could see it from my bedroom in my father's home.

From being the daughter of a powerful man to the mate of another... *Mate.* My belly flutters. There's no getting away from the fact that I belong to him. Just as I had once been the prized possession of my father.

I grip the railing. In this world where omegas need an alpha to keep them safe, why is it that something inside of me insists on a measure of being able to strike out on my own? Apparently, I am more similar to Lucy in that respect than not. Who'd have thought?

The doorbell rings. I pivot, walk out of the room, down the staircase and to the front door, and fling it open.

"Hello, Sprite."

"Lucy."

My sister grins at me, her expression alight with mischief. "You've been hiding yourself away," she accuses.

"Me?" I school my features into what I hope is an expression of innocence.

"Don't give me that, sis." She brushes past me, onto the landing, and surveys the space. "What do you think?"

"Of what?" I shut the door, follow her in.

"The place, dummy." She waves her hand in the air.

"It's... nice." Drat it, I sound ungrateful, which I am not, truly. Just...my mind has been full of thoughts of the alphahole who's apparently imprinted his essence into every cell of my being, and hasn't come to see me.

"Hmm." She turns, surveys me up and down. "You look terrible."

"Thanks, sis." I can always rely on Lucy to tell me the brutal truth.

"You've been hiding yourself away in here."

"Not." I wrap my arms about my waist.

"I'm so sorry, Chloe." She closes the distance between us and hugs me. "It's so not right, what happened to you."

"Umm." A pressure builds behind my eyes. "I don't want to talk about it."

She releases me, steps away, "You sure?"

No. Not really. I chew on my lower lip, nod.

"It's not good to keep it all bottled inside."

"Oh, I am not." I drag my fingers through my hair. "I had my breakdown already; the alphahole saw to that."

"Speaking of," she peruses my features, "has he been here to visit you yet?"

I twist my shoulders, shuffle past her. "You want a cup of tea?"

"That bad, huh?"

I glance away. My sister's way too astute for her own good. If I stay in her presence longer, she's bound to figure out how on edge I am, and right now, I don't want that. "I'm not really in the mood for a heart-to-heart, Luce."

"Oh, pfft." She tosses her head. "Let me get the tea. You sit."

Gosh, I'd forgotten how bossy she could be. She flounces ahead of me to the kitchen, walks straight to the kettle on the stove, and flicks the burner. The flame flares up.

She reaches for the cups, pulls out two of them.

"Make yourself at home."

"I will."

"Aargh." I stomp to the chair by the island, drop myself in it. "Since when did you become so bossy."

"Ah—"

"No, don't answer that." I lean my elbows on the platform. "You've always known your mind Luce; I've admired that about you. But you've grown into yourself since you met Zeus."

She sets the kettle on the stove, "Is that good or bad?"

"It suits you." I cup my chin, "You're glowing."

"Oh." She blushes. "It's the weather, all the moisture in the air here—"

"Pregnancy suits you, Luce."

She smiles; her features soften. She seems so at peace. My heart thuds. I'm not jealous of her. No really… Just… I wish I could figure out how to come to some kind of understanding with my alpha.

"I wasn't sure whether to refer to it or not, you know." Her gaze drops down my body, then returns to my face. "I mean, I can only imagine what you've been through. If it had happened to me, I'd… " She rubs her belly, winces.

"You okay?"

"Yeah," she huffs out a breath. "I'm not even showing yet, but I swear the babies moved."

"Babies?" I blink.

Color flushes her cheeks. "Twins, Chloe." She beams at me. "I'm having twins."

"Wow." I jump up, walk toward her, "Can I feel?"

She clutches my hand, places it on her belly. We wait a beat, another.

The kettle whistles, and just then, there's a tremor as if the little lives deep inside of her heard the noise.

"I felt it," I swallow. "That was…" I try to form my emotions into words. "It was—"

"Yeah," She nods. "They react to noise. Especially when Zeus is close, they get restive. Z says it's because they recognize their father. I tell him, he's just too loud for his own good, and—" her features twist. "Jeez, I'm sorry Sprite. I didn't mean to go on and on."

I shake my head, "I want to hear about it, Luce. I am coming to terms with what happened, honest."

"Are you?" She raises her hand to my cheek, pushes at a strand of hair that clings to my temples.

She turns to the stove and switches off the burner, then pours out the water into the two cups. "Get some cakes."

"Cakes."

She frowns. "You do have some, right?"

Ah! My cheeks heat. I'm not sure. Truth is, I haven't spent any time in the kitchen. I've been eating, because… someone—Kayden?— has been stocking my fridge. Cooked meals have been appearing on the table, and I haven't questioned it.

I walk toward the cake box, open it, pull out some of the baked goods, and place them on a plate.

I pivot, cross the floor and join Lucy at the island. I take a sip of the tea, "Mm," and another. I drain the cup.

"I'd forgotten how you prefer to drink your tea boiling hot." She blows on her tea, sets down the cup.

We both burst out laughing. "We are so different..." she chuckles.

"Not that much," I mumble.

She angles her head.

I wave my hand in the air. "Why do you think I am here on my own?"

"Because Kayden decided to give you space?"

"I asked for it." I hunch my shoulders.

"Um, not following." She reaches for a piece of cake, bites into it.

"I told him I wanted to be with him, but also wanted to be independent."

She blinks, polishes off the cake, then reaches for another. "I see."

"No, you don't!" I jump up, "Now you're judging me." I begin to pace.

She eats her way through the pastry, then sits back with a sigh. "Don't be so hard on yourself, Sis."

"What's wrong with me? I've only ever wanted a mate, a child, a family of my own. Now, when all of that is so within reach...I...I—" I pivot and march toward her, cross her. Then turn and retrace my steps, "—want something else."

"An identity."

"Huh?" I glower at her. "I know who I am."

"Do you?"

"Stop talking in puzzles. I have enough of one alpha doing that."

"Sit."

"No." I grit my teeth.

"You're making me dizzy."

"Too bad." I pout, stalk past her, then retrace my steps.

"Oh," She clutches at her stomach.

I pale. "What's happening, Luce. What?"

Her eyes twinkle, "Now that I've gotten through to you."

"Not funny." I swallow, "Especially after the events of the last few weeks." My voice trails off and tears prick my eyes.

She grabs my hand. "Jeez, sorry Sprite, I wasn't thinking."

I angle my head, "It's okay." I swallow. "I mean, sometimes it all seems like a dream, because I didn't quite feel pregnant. Then I hear something, or see something, and my spirits plummet for no reason and it's because—"

"Muscle memory."

"Eh?" I plop down in the chair.

"Your body knows how it was to be pregnant, and your subconscious recognizes it." She winds her fingers with mine, "It will all turn out all right, I promise."

I twist my lips, "I'll let you know when your words come true, for now—"

"Focus on him."

I frown.

"Own him, embrace him, Chloe. Open yourself up completely to him. Let him see how vulnerable you are. Subsume yourself in him until you forget who you are, then find yourself again."

"Is that what you did?"

She tilts her head, looks off into the distance. "I hadn't thought about that, but yeah." She drags her fingers through her hair, "That *is* what I did. You look at me and Zeus today, and think that we have a wonderful relationship, except it wasn't always this way."

"I believe you." I place my other palm on top of hers, "Are you sure about this?"

She holds up her hand, "Give it a try."

There's another knock on the door. Lucy lets go of my hand and jumps up.

"Were you expecting someone?"

She bites her lip, "Umm... "

"What are you not telling me?"

She leans forward and straightens my collar. "I have your best interests at heart."

"You didn't." My pulse quickens; my heart begins to race.

"Trust me on this." Lucy pivots, walks to the door.

"Luce, I swear if this is who I think it is, you could have at least given me fair warning. I am going to get back at you for this, you—" She swings open the door.

188

Kayden

I glance over Lucy's shoulder. Cara's green gaze clashes with mine. She stands at the far end of the foyer. I peruse her features, down her chest, to her concave belly. I squeeze my fingers at my sides.

Not a day passes when I don't blame myself for what transpired. It's why I brought her here to London, on the turf of my mortal enemy, no less.

Zeus had been gracious in his welcome. In fact, it was he who had insisted I bring her here. It could be good for Cara to be close to her sister—her pregnant sister. I raise my gaze, "Are you well?"

Fucking polite conversation. Yeah, that's what I have been reduced to. Next, I'll be asking about the weather, but fuck that. If this is what it takes to win her over, then so be it. I'd wear a fucking bowtie if it was required to win her over. Okay, maybe not that. I snort under my breath.

Lucy quirks an eyebrow.

I nod. "Zeus is on his way."

"Not that he'd let me out of his sight for one minute," she smirks, swipes her hair away from her face. "He made me swear that I'd stay here until he comes to collect me, and I keep my promises, unlike the men in your family."

"We don't belong to the same family."

She tosses her head, "Oh please, the two of you are too similar for your own good."

I frown, "Not sure if I welcome the comparison."

"Oh, it's a compliment, dear brother-in-law."

I stare.

"You are mated to my sister, so that makes you my brother of sorts, huh?"

Hmm. I shift my weight from foot to foot, "Well, when you put it like that—"

Footsteps sound and Ethan walks up. "Weren't we going to have a meeting here?"

"Were we?"

"We are." Zeus announces as he steps onto the patio. He spots Lucy and his features seem to lighten.

She ducks under my shoulder, brushes past Ethan, and throws herself at my half-brother. Zeus swings her up and the two kiss.

I can't stop the growl that rumbles up my chest. I turn and glare at Cara, who's watching them. Her face flushes, she twists her fingers in front of her, then turning, walks into the kitchen. I close the distance between us and catch up with her, "Chloe."

She rounds the island, busies herself with putting on the kettle.

Is she avoiding me?

I stalk forward and come to a stop behind her. I touch her shoulder and she stiffens.

Heat sears my chest. "Didn't mean to scare you."

"You didn't." She sidles away, reaches up on tiptoe for the cups.

"Let me." I pull open the cabinet door, my forearm brushing hers. Goosebumps flare on her skin. She twists away. Her elbow sinks into my belly, and the cup slips from my hand. I swoop my other hand out, catch it.

The breath rushes out of me.

"Good save." She ducks under my arm, scuttles to the other corner of the kitchen, then bends to pull out more crockery.

"Cara." I place the cup on the island, then prowl toward her.

She straightens, hands me a bunch of plates, and I take them from her. She moves away, heads for the door.

The fuck? Is she evading me? I tighten my grip on the plates.

Can I simply throw them to the ground, then stomp all over them for good measure? A growl rips up my chest and she trembles. Then she steps out of the kitchen.

I slap the plates down on the island; the crash resounds across the room.

Dom walks into the kitchen, "You okay there?"

"No." I stomp toward the doorway, brush past him. He grabs my arm.

I jerk my head, "Back the fuck off."

"Whoa." He releases me. "Easy." He raises both his hands, palms face up. "Someone's wound up."

"Not."

"Hmm." He scratches his chin, "You two, fighting?"

I frown, "It would be easier if we were."

"Thought you would have been spending quality time together," his eyebrows knit.

"The fuck you getting at?" I turn on him, advance a step, "You trying to rub me up the wrong way? If a fight is what you're itching for..."

"Ah, I get it." He waggles his head. His lips twitch.

"The fuck you laughing at?"

"You, alpha." He looks me up and down. "Sucks huh? Caring about someone?"

Tell me about it, not that I'm about to admit that aloud, definitely not to him.

He surveys the kitchen, "Think there's alcohol here?"

I nod toward the shelf at the far end.

He heads in that direction, "Familiar with this space, huh?"

I tense. If he makes one more half-assed remark about my current situation, I'm going to throw him out bodily, and fuck the repercussions.

He pulls out a bottle of whiskey, grabs two of the cups, then sets them down on the island. He pours out the spirits.

"The fuck are you doing?"

He raises a cup, drains it, then slams it back on the table. "Zeus has good taste in whiskey, I'll give him that."

"You done?" I scrutinize the space.

Where is she? Did she go up the stairs? Why the hell is she avoiding me?

"Get a drink, Alpha."

Why not, huh? I close the distance, grab the other cup, drain it. The liquor burns a fire down my belly. I cough, wipe my face.

He pours more into our cups. "Now speak"

I glare at him. If he thinks I am going to air my feelings, he's got another think coming.

"If you keep it bottled inside, you'll blow a vein."

I draw in a breath, "Just because you saved my life…"

"Again." He tosses back the alcohol, pours some more, "You're welcome."

Fuck, if I don't hate my Second's guts, but he's the closest I'll get to having a friend, so…I shift my weight from foot to foot.

"Women." I gulp down the liquor.

It goes down smoother this time.

Heat scorches my chest; the tangle of sensations stabs into my rib cage. I huff, hold out my empty cup.

He pours some more. "I take it you two have been having differences."

"If only it were that simple." I throw back the liquor; the heat radiates to my extremities. "The woman doesn't give me the chance to speak."

"What, when you're sharing the same house?"

"We're not."

He chokes on his whiskey, "What do you mean?"

My face heats; I glare at him, "Just what I said."

"You mean," his shoulders shake, "You mean you don't live here?"

I shake my head.

"So where…?"

I jerk my thumb over my shoulder.

"The house next door?"

I frown. "Across the courtyard."

I grab the bottle, pour more into my cup, then chug it down.

The alcohol slides down my gullet. I can't feel my toes anymore. Good.

"The alphahole who wouldn't let his mate out of his sight, is practicing abstinence?" He raises his head skywards. "It's definitely not going to rain today."

I return the cup, taking great care not to thump it back on the table. "We are in London. Of course, it's going to rain."

He snorts.

I frown.

"Kayden, you've lost your sense of humor."

Along with my balls, obviously. I growl, "The woman wanted space. She made me promise to keep my distance. She wanted to be independent." I knead my temples, "This interpreting what she wants is fucking driving me up the wall."

"You're not the first." He turns the bottle upside down, pours the rest of the alcohol into my glass. "Not the last. You've made the classic mistake of—"

He takes a sip of his drink, "Of?" He angles his head, drums his chest.

Anger explodes in my gut. I swoop forward, grab his collar and tug, "Spit it out, asshole."

His lips curl, "Say, please."

"Fuck you."

"Pretty please?"

I raise my fist, and that wipes the grin off of his face.

"All I'm saying is that what a woman says she wants, and what she actually needs from you, are two different things."

I scowl "Meaning?"

"Release me first."

I make a noise deep in my throat, then loosen my grip.

He grins. "Say, please."

I set my jaw, "Fucker, start talking or else."

He rolls his shoulders; his eyes glint, "You ready?"

189

Chloe

I wake up with a start. Blue light streams through the windows. Is it morning already? I shrug off the covers and frown. I don't remember slipping into bed. I'd crawled onto the seat by the windows, watched the sluggish flow of the Thames. The lights twinkling in the distance had come on, and I'd switched on the lamp, picked up my favorite historical romance novel. I'd drifted off to sleep there, so how had I gotten into bed? Someone had carried me here. Kayden? Did he come in without my being aware of it? I glance at the chair and the cushion is indented. Did he watch me as I slept? I bite my lips. No, that's not creepy at all. Not that I could have stopped him if I'd been awake either, but at least I'd have some semblance of control. I swing my legs over, yawn. The scent of coffee creeps into the room. Huh? I walk to the bathroom, brush my teeth, then stare.

There's a second toothbrush laid out.

I take in the shower; droplets of water coat the walls. What the—? Did he shower here, in my bath? While I was asleep? He hadn't asked me permission. He hadn't informed me that he'd stay the night here either. I rinse out my mouth, return the toothbrush to the vanity.

If he thinks he can simply move in here without telling me... I blow out a breath. How typical. Can't take the dominance out of the alphahole, huh?

I scrape my hair together into a bun at the top of my head, then head out.

I flounce down the steps, walk into the kitchen, and blink. The plates are set out on the island with cutlery, and there's a rose. I blink. A rose? In a vase set between the tableware.

"You're awake?" Kayden ladles out scrambled eggs onto a plate. And that's not the only thing that he's cooked.

There are slices of toast, butter, marmalade, French toast, waffles, fruit.

"I wasn't sure what you'd prefer."

I frown, "What are you playing at?"

"You didn't eat last night." He gestures to the bar stool, "Take a seat."

I cross my arms over my chest.

"Come on, Cara, you must be hungry."

My stomach grumbles on cue, and he smirks, then schools his expression into one of solicitous caring. Yeah, doesn't fool me. Not one bit. He nods towards the spread, "Come on, you don't want my efforts to go to waste do you?"

I do, actually. I stomp forward, pile a plate, "Thanks." I pivot, flounce toward the exit.

Now is when he'll call my name, and glare at me; then scold me, turn me over his lap and…my sex clenches. *No, no, no, don't think of that. Keep walking.* I make it to the steps, up the staircase, to my room. In one piece. There's no sign of the alpha. My shoulders slump. I march to the loveseat by the window. Sitting down I help myself to a mouthful of scrambled eggs.

The taste bursts on my tongue.

"Good?"

He walks in carrying his own plate, then sinks down next to me.

His thigh nudges mine; I shrink away.

He doesn't say anything, just digs in. I finish off the scrambled eggs, and the French toast. Watch him as he devours everything on his plate that had been piled twice as high as mine.

He scowls at my plate.

I shrug. "I'm full."

He takes my plate, places it on his, and proceeds to wolf it down. The man practically inhales the food.

"Are you hungry?"

"Yeah." He smirks, "What are you offering?"

The blood rushes to my cheeks.

He chuckles. "Did you blush?"

"No." I jump up to my feet, stride to the other side of the room.

"I make you nervous?"

*Yeah, but not for the reasons you think. It's because I am no longer sure how I'll react to you. You confuse me, and I'm not sure what you want from me…*is what I want to say, but of course I don't. I stand in the corner of the room and watch him.

He places the plates on the side of the loveseat, rises to his feet. I shrink away, and he holds up his hands, palms up. "We should talk about this."

"Eh?" I tilt my head, "When was the last time you wanted to talk instead of commanding me to do what you wanted."

"I'm trying to turn over a new leaf."

I snort.

"You don't believe me?"

I shake my head.

"What would it take for you to see that I am serious?"

I sneak a peek at the door.

"Don't run from me, Cara." He rolls his shoulders, "I promise, I'll do what you want," he shuffles his feet, "when you want." He cracks his neck, "How you want."

I huff out a breath.

Should I believe him? Why does everything he says have a sexual connotation to it? Are we not capable of a single straightforward conversation about something inane?

"Chloe?"

"Y...yeah?" I straighten my spine.

His eyebrows knit; he looks like he's about to say something, then purses his lips. A low purr rumbles up his chest.

The heat from his body seems to reach out to me across the distance of the room. It sinks into me, slips in between my thighs. It isn't him. It's me. I have never been able to resist him. From the first time I saw him, I was his, so why am I resisting? What am I waiting for? What do I want from him? From me?

"Anything you want, Chloe." He lowers his chin; his biceps bulge. The skin across his knuckles stretches white. He's not as composed as he seems. Not as confident as he wants me to believe. Perhaps it's that which convinces me to lift my head. "Anything?"

His shoulders bunch, "Anything."

"You sure?"

His nostrils flare. "Sure."

"100%?"

A growl rips up his chest and he glares at me, "Chloe." The hushed tone of his voice shudders down my spine. I shiver.

"Don't test me, Sugar. I've indulged you so far. If I were you, I'd take this opportunity...before I lose control and decide to do things my way—"

Heat curls between my legs. Drat him. Why does the thought of giving up control resonate with something deep inside of me? Once a breeder, always a breeder, subservient, submissive...maybe. Doesn't mean I can't try to do things my way. If not months or weeks, just this once, I can strike out and claim a sliver of my independence, right? I press my lips together, "Fine."

He stiffens. His jaw tics and a vein throbs at his temple. He doesn't move a muscle.

He waits. Waits. Makes a noise low in his throat.

My toes curl. I jut out my chin, "Lie down on the bed."

190

Kayden

I glare at her and her chin wobbles. Good. She should be afraid. Very afraid of what I am going to do to her when this is over. She dares command me? The fuck? I clench my fingers at my sides, thrust my head forward.

"You…you promised."

So what?

"You never go back on your word."

There's always a first time.

"Kai." She wrings her hands in front of her, peeks at the bed then back at me, "Please let me do this my way."

No.

"This one time, darling."

I blink. Something hot curls in my chest. I am not one for softness. The only thing sweet in my life so far has been her. Her touch, her kisses, the honeyed scent of her essence. I draw in a breath, fill my lungs with the anticipation. Being with her, forever. Do I even dare hope for that? After everything I did to her? I owe her, though that's not the reason I'll comply with her wishes. I snap my eyes open, take a step forward.

Her legs tremble; she curls her fingers into fists.

I move closer. "You'll hurt yourself."

"What?"

I nod toward her hands, "You'll dig your nails into the softness of your palms and mark yourself, and we can't have that."

"We…can't?" she squeaks.

"No, only I get to do that, Sugar, or have you forgotten?"

"Have you forgotten," she firms her lips, "what you told me?"

I growl, take another step forward, another. Her little body quivers. She doesn't move away, though. Doesn't run from here screaming. Hmm. Interesting.

When was the last time a woman stood up to me in any form? I blink. Never. She is the first.

It's right that it is her. If I want to spend every night with her, wake up with her next to me, then it is important she hold onto her identity. I don't want her to feel overwhelmed... Okay, not completely. I smirk. She narrows her gaze. I don't want her to submit so fully that she loses that spunk which is the most attractive thing about my mate. *Mine.* I am never letting her escape; I have my entire life to show her exactly how I'll take my revenge for her daring to think she can boss me around... this once.

Can I let her take the lead? I huff out a breath. Stalk toward her. Her breath hitches. Closer. She stares, the color from her cheeks leaching out.

I close the distance between us, pause less than a foot away. She freezes, every cell in her body on alert. Good. This wasn't meant to be easy for either of us. I swerve to the bed, fling myself on my back. "There."

The breath rushes out of her, relief bleeding off of her skin and into the air, surrounding me, heating my blood. A low hum rises up my throat. "What now?"

She gulps, the sound hot and heavy, and my dick twitches. *Down boy. Don't rush this. Don't let her see how fucking turned on you are.* What does that say about me, hmm? There is a certain seductiveness in allowing my mate to have her way with me, apparently. I ball my fists at my sides, "Cara."

"Patience, Alpha."

Her tone is light, a smile lacing her words. She glides across to the foot of the bed, then pivots and walks toward the seat by the window. She grabs the plates, "Don't want anything to take away from this moment."

The fuck is she playing at?

She walks to the bed, her pace unhurried.

"Chloe," A snarl rips up my throat and she shivers. *Hmm. Two can play at this, Sweetheart.* purr rumbles up my chest and she freezes.

I project the sub-vocals, twining the notes over her chest, between her breasts, to the source of my anticipation. Her beautiful cunt. She moans.

"Come on, Sugar, don't make me wait."

She swallows, lurches to the door. There's a crash as she drops the plates outside the room, slams the door shut. Turning, she walks to the foot of the bed. "You have too many advantages."

"Too fucking bad." I fold my arms behind my neck; her gaze flicks to my biceps. I flex my muscles and she shivers. "I intend to use every last bit of advantage I have to good effect."

"No shit."

"What did you say?"

She squeaks, "I...I mean..."

I quirk an eyebrow and she wriggles her hips, "Ah, I think it's time to undress." She reaches behind her, unhooks the dress and the fabric pools at her feet.

My heart stutters. I stare at her. Can't take my eyes off of her perky tits, the pink nipples that pebble immediately, the concave of her stomach, the glistening lips of her pussy. "You shaved." My voice cracks and I clear my throat. She's fucking bare, as naked as the day she was born. "Come 'ere."

"Now, Alpha, behave."

I growl.

"Thought you kept your promises."

I clench my teeth so hard that pain rips up my jaw. I take a deep breath, another. Force my shoulders to unclench, my muscles to relax. When she's done with this stupid foreplay, I'll —

She reaches above her, pulls the pin from her hair, and the glossy strands cascade down her back. Fucking siren. The sunlight pours from behind her, bathing her skin, shadowing that hourglass figure. Those curves. Those hips that will swell further when she's heavy with my child. *Mine.* I swallow. A pressure builds in my chest. My cock lengthens and I spread my legs further to accommodate the hard length. She climbs up onto the bed, and into the 'V' created.

I tilt my chin up, peruse her beautiful body. A low purr winds its way up my throat. Her pupils dilate.

She hums under her breath, then kneels between my thighs. Her fingers brush my lower belly.

I stiffen. "Chloe."

"Hmm."

"The fuck you up to?"

Her lips curl.

Did she smirk at me? The little tease. I unlock my fingers from behind my neck, reach for her, when she drops her head.

191

Chloe

I unzip his pants and his turgid shaft swings free. I close my mouth around the head and he snarls. He drops his hands to his sides, tucks his elbows in. Whew!

If he'd touched me, I'd have lost what little focus I'd managed to gather so far.

I squeeze the base of his shaft and he thrusts his groin up. His dick slips in further and my eyes water. Damn alpha, dominance is imprinted into every cell of his body. He simply can't let go and allow me to do this my way, huh?

I cup his balls and a snarl rips from him.

I peer up from under my eyelashes and flinch.

Color burns his cheeks and those dark eyes glare at me. His massive chest rises and falls, the force of his will slamming into my shoulders, pinning me down. I gulp and his cock lengthens further. "Take me in."

I pull back and his length slips out. The vein on the underside pulses. I hold him poised with the head of his dick bumping my teeth.

"Chloe." The tendons of his throat flex; a vein beats to life at his temple. Sweat beads his forehead. Wow. He's reining it in, holding onto his control. The ball of sensations in my chest slams into my ribcage and I gulp.

A snarl rumbles up his chest, another.

"Do it."

His voice is thick, the dark scent of his arousal crowding my nostrils. I bob my head, take him down my throat, and gag. Saliva drips down my chin, my breasts hurt, and my sex clenches.

"You're killing me."

His raspy tone snakes over my skin. All of my nerve endings flare. I pull up, then lower my head, swipe my tongue up his hard length, squeeze his balls, and a growl rumbles up his chest. His thigh muscles clench. His gaze intensifies, the strength of his desire grips me. Slick gushes out from between my legs, and I pant. A trembling starts from my toes, sweeps up my thighs.

"Come."

His voice snaps something deep inside of me. The climax engulfs me. Sparks of white flare behind my eyes. More moisture gushes out from between my legs.

His cum swells my throat, pours into me. Seeps down the corners of my lips.

I lean back, and his shaft swings free. I scramble up, straddle him, then lower myself onto the hard flesh. A moan spills from my lips. So thick, so hard, he stretches my channel, fills me up, extends inside me. He thrusts his pelvis, drives his dick up and into me.

I gasp, raise my hand and he grabs my wrist.

He twines his fingers with mine, brings his other palm to my hip and holds me in place. "Ride me, sweetheart, take what you need."

With a twist of my hips I pull him in further. My pussy clamps around his dick, which surges. *Oh!* I drop my chin, open my eyes, and my gaze locks with his. The ball of heat in my chest detonates. Warmth snakes down my spine, grips my extremities. He drags his palm up my arm then grips my nape, pulls me down, then rises up, "You've done it your way, Cara, it's my turn now."

The next second I am under him. He's above me, inside me; his dominance engulfs me, pinning me in place. I blink.

He bares his teeth, a low purr swirls up his chest, my belly flip flops, and my channel weeps. He drags my leg up and around his waist, then the other. "Hold on."

"Wha—?"

He propels forward, and his cock plunges into me so deeply, I am sure he is touching my womb. My throat closes.

He locks his dick behind my pelvic bone, his knot snapping into place. I cry out. A rough purr rumbles up his throat. His chest seems to expand as he lowers his head and bites the curve where my neck meets my shoulder.

Pain lashes down my side.

He releases me, only to drag his mouth to mine. He kisses me, dances his tongue over mine, sucking from me.

A trembling starts somewhere at my toes, then whooshes up.

Every part of me tenses, tenses. He tears his mouth from my body, glares at my face. Blood coats his lips. My blood. A blistering feeling coils in my chest. I can't take my eyes off of him. Moisture drips down my cheek, slickness pours into my channel.

"Come for me, Baby."

My body bucks, my spine curves, and the climax grips me. A scream swells up and he covers my mouth with his.

When I open my eyes, I am curled on his chest. Tendrils of heat sizzle up my spine. My limbs twitch. I turn, peer up at him. "You promised."

"I kept my word."

"Hmm." I should protest some more, tell him he didn't allow me to make love to him the way I wanted. I open my mouth, but all that emerges is a sigh.

A smirk curls his lips. I reach up, brush my finger over his pouty lower lip. He sucks on my digit. He flings his arm behind his neck; a low purr rumbles up his chest. His heat envelops me and I sigh.

"I'm home."

"You bet your sweet tush, you are."

"You are mine," he turns his face into my palm. "Always."

"I belong to you."

His lips quirk, "Was there any doubt of that?"

The wound at the curve of my shoulder twinges. "You're a beast."

"Especially with you."

"A monster with a heart of gold."

He quirks his eyebrows, "A bit too emo for my liking, but I'll accept it."

"You'll let me seduce you?"

He firms his jaw, "Is that a trick question?"

"Me?" I flutter my eyelashes and his throat moves as he swallows.

Oh, I am loving this softer, mellower version of him.

"You are more relaxed."

He nods.

"Why?"

"Not sure, Cara." He pulls me up, licks the fresh claiming mark, "Seems we've arrived at some kind of understanding.

"You mean you fucked all the fight out of me."

"Same thing." Another purr, more intense, with deeper sub-vocals, cocoons me in its vibrations.

I yawn. Yeah, that's how comfortable I am too.

Something hard stabs into my waist. Maybe I spoke too fast. "Again?" I stutter.

He reaches for me. "And again."

192

Kayden

I slide the French toast onto the plate, drizzle more syrup on it, then top it with strawberries. I place it in front of her. A smile lights up her features. "You remembered?" She bounces on her seat.

"I remember," I bend my head, peer into her face, "everything."

She stills, her cheeks redden. So fucking cute.

"I'm hungry." She picks up her knife and fork.

"So am I."

She giggles, then cuts a piece of the food I cooked for her and places it in her mouth. She chews, her movements delicate. She swallows, then angles her head, her delicate eyebrows arching, "You're insatiable."

"Only for you."

Her smile widens, before she wipes it off of her face, schools her features into a look of stern admonishment. "Flattery will get you..." her mouth twitches at the corner, "... everywhere. Keep feeding me, and I'll do anything you want."

Hmm. I can demand anything of her and she'll give it to me, but I've found a better way. Food. Yeah. Turns out my little omega sucks at cooking.

After that day when I'd cooked breakfast, before she'd proceeded to seduce me and I had turned the tables on her, and fucked her completely, marked her all over again, and not let her out of that bed, until my stomach had grumbled rather loudly... She'd offered to cook a late brunch... Or was that an early dinner...? No matter, I'd accepted.

She'd whipped up a dish...or tried to.

The results had been less than palatable. I smirk. I'd eaten it, of course, without complaints. When she'd asked me how it was, I'd lied and said, not bad. A first.

I am learning how to rein in my instincts so I don't blurt out the first thing that comes to my mind. Don't want to upset her in any way. I shake my head... All that emo shit? I am living it; b-u-t...it has its perks.

More than anything, it has her willing, responsive, in my arms, in my bed, and of her own accord.

There is something enormously satisfying about having my mate submit to me... on her terms. With a giggle and a smile on her face...and a belly full of happiness, thanks to my cooking. Yep, I've taken over in the kitchen. I am more than happy to cook for the both of us, by the way—if that means I can spare my stomach the ordeal of eating another meal cooked by her. Don't tell her I said that.

She polishes off the food, smacks her lips. "What's next?"

Her mouth glistens. I reach out, rub at the corner.

"Oh."

I bring my thumb to my mouth, suck on it. "You had some sugar stuck there."

"Ah."

"Not that you need anything to sweeten your taste. You're more honeyed than anything that ever existed."

Her cheeks flame, "Drat you, Kai, you're so good with words."

"Only words?" I waggle my eyebrows.

She throws up her hands, "Anyone ever told you you've a one-track mind?"

"You're complaining?"

"Umm." She pretends to think, "Yes, but only when you're not touching me."

"We can rectify that." I swoop down on her, and she squeaks and springs away.

"Wanna play, Sweetheart?" I round the island and she screams.

I lunge forward. She ducks.

"What the—?" I reach for her and she yells.

I grab her collar, "Gotcha." I haul her close, and she giggles. The sound ripples across my skin. My dick twitches and my heart flutters... So fucking adorable. I tickle her and she laughs. Run my fingers over her waist and she screams, laughs again. I dig my fingers into her side, and she snorts, tries to pull away. "No, Kai, please, ah—"

There's a hammering on the door. "Go away."

"It must be Lucy."

"She can fuck off." I haul her in, kiss her again.

There's another loud knock, then another.

She tears her mouth from mine. "If I don't answer, she'll get Zeus to break it down."

And my half-bro would happily oblige. Talk about being under the thumb of his omega. Umm...okay, pot meet kettle, and all that.

I let go of her, push her into the chair, "Eat." I stab my finger at her, "You need your energy for later."

She tosses her head, smirks, then reaches for the stack on my plate and helps herself. I turn, stalk to the door, yank it open. Lucy brushes past, "Where is she?"

"She's—"

"Is she okay?" Lucy peeks into the living room.

"She—"

She pivots, glares at me, "If you did anything to hurt her, I'll—" She shakes a finger at me.

Huh? I raise my hands, palms up, "Why would I hurt—?"

"Chloe."

Lucy takes off across the foyer.

"Don't run, in your condition—" Zeus' voice tapers off.

She disappears into the kitchen.

I blink. What was that? How does she have so much energy? And what did she mean about me harming my own mate?

Zeus steps in, "Shut the door, and your mouth."

I snap my jaws shut, then slam the door.

"Is she always in such a hurry—"

His shoulder jostles mine. Asshole. He glowers at me, "What do you think?" He grips his hair and tugs; his forehead crinkles, "Has a mind of her own, that one."

"Tell me about it." I draw abreast with him.

"You too, eh?" He stares ahead, a dazed expression on his face, "How does it feel to be mated to an omega who runs you ragged?"

I smirk, "Sounds to me like you are pussy-whipped, is what."

"Kayden."

I whip my head toward the sound of her voice, break into a jog. Bursting into the kitchen, I race toward her, "You okay, Cara?" I drop to my knees next to her, pat her face, her shoulders. Not hurt or anything, whew. My shoulders sag.

"What were you saying earlier?" Zeus chortles from the doorway, "Pussy-whipped, huh?"

"Zeus!" Lucy makes a warning sound deep in her throat.

He drums his fingers on his chest, "Nothing Chloe hasn't heard before, considering," he jerks his chin toward me, "she's spent days locked up with him."

"Really, Z," Lucy huffs out a breath. "You could pretend to be polite, at least when we are with company."

"Polite?" Cara pats my cheek, "This one has not one iota of gentility in his bones, definitely not restraint... Not when it comes to me."

Lucy's mouth falls open, then she begins to laugh. "Oh my God, what have you done to my meek, shy sister?"

I fucked it out of her, is what. A smirk tugs at my lips and I straighten. "Guess you're all right then?" I cup her cheek.

She turns her face into my palm, kisses it, "More than."

Zeus clears his throat. "So, guess they are doing okay?" He prowls forward to stand behind Lucy. "It's time to break the news to him. Can't delay it any longer."

"What?" I slide behind Cara's chair.

"Not yet, Z." Lucy leans against him, "Can't we give them a little more time? They seem happy together."

"About time," Zeus snorts.

"What are you two talking about?" I growl.

"Your Second."

"Dominic?"

"He—"

Footsteps sound. Dom appears in the kitchen doorway, his shirt torn, blood oozing from his forehead.

"Guess we're too late." Lucy mutters.

"Best to let it play out, huh?" Zeus leans a hip against the counter, pulls Lucy into him. The two of them settle there, like they have center court seats to whatever is about to unfold. My heart begins to thud.

I turn around, place myself in front of Chloe.

I incline my head, "The fuck happened to you, Dom?"

"Got in a fight," He mumbles.

"Not the first time," Zeus snarls. "Asshole's been threatening to leave. Had to put him under house arrest, only he broke out."

"I can vouch for that." Ethan's voice sounds behind him. He shoves Dom aside, who turns on him.

Ethan, raises his chin, "Not everything can be resolved by your fists."

"It's not your daughter who decided to leave with the enemy."

"Thought we'd discussed this, Dom?" I firm my jaw. "You need to let her go."

"Oh yeah?" He stalks forward, "What if your mate decided to turn her back on you—"

I grit my teeth, "Not the same thing."

"Isn't it?" He rocks forward on the balls of his feet, thrusts his neck out, his eyes bulging. "I'll remind you the next time you go apeshit, when you are on your own." His nostrils flare and a vein pops at his temple. His hair is in disarray.

I frown. "What happened to you?"

The Dom I know has a cool head on his shoulders. I've rarely seen him lose his temper, and that was only when I messed up... as I had with her. But never again. Of course, he's worried about Lisa... but there's something else at work here.

I stare into his face, peruse his features.

He raises his fist; I block his hit. "Get a hold of yourself."

He blinks; his chest heaves, "I am here talking with you guys and drinking and eating, all cozy and safe." He grabs the short tufts of his hair and pulls, "While my daughter's somewhere out there alone, God knows in what state."

"She's a big girl, Dom." I curl my fingers into fists, "She made her choice."

"I can't stop wondering if I could have done anything differently. If I had found her earlier, if only I could have saved my daughter."

He drops his arms and his shoulders sag, "I am out of my mind with worry."

"Don't be."

A new voice sounds. A woman's voice.

"Lisa?" Dom swings around.

"Lisa?" Behind me Cara jumps up from her chair, tries to brush past me.

I haul her behind my bulk. "Stay back."

"What? Why?" She grabs my forearm, digs her fingernails into my skin, "She's returned to us—"

"No, she hasn't." Zeus prowls forward. He plants his body between Lucy and the rest of us.

Dom stops halfway to the door.

Ethan, who'd turned at Lisa's arrival, retreats, until he's abreast with Dom.

It only took the arrival of the Viking who towers over Lisa to unite Zeus and my team.

I scowl, "The fuck you doing here?"

Talon wraps his arm around Lisa. He yanks her close, and she winces.

Dom's features tighten, "Let go of her."

"I don't think so." Talon bares his teeth.

"What are you doing here?" I widen my stance, "Thought you'd have gotten off this island already."

"That was the plan, but turns out this Omega is a good negotiator."

I glance at Lisa's pale face then at him. "Explain yourself."

He drops his head, until his chin rests on her head, "You have something to tell them, Omega?"

Lisa swallows, "I wanted to come by to say that... " She hesitates, her gaze darts to Dom, then she lowers her eyes.

The muscles on Talon's forearm jump and a low purr rumbles from his chest.

She stiffens, raises her chin, "I am in good hands, Father."

Dom snarls low in his throat; he fists his fingers at his side, "Don't lie to me, girl."

Her jaw firms, "I am in a better place than I was in your clan."

"You don't mean it." Dom takes a step forward; Ethan grabs his shoulder and he pauses. "You don't have to pretend, not to me. Did he bring you here under duress? Is that what this is? A show and tell to throw us off your tracks?" He glares at Talon.

"See?" She stabs a finger at him, "You are not listening to me... again. You've never heard me, Father. I was your little girl, always. Well, I have news for you. I am grown up. I can make up my own mind."

"Oh, yeah?" Dom snorts. "So, you've chosen to tie your future to a monster?"

"No more than Lucy has."

Zeus makes a noise deep in his throat.

"—or Chloe."

"Stop right there." All of my muscles tense as my senses arrow in on her, the man behind her. Something is not right. *Why are they here? Why is he letting her speak?* Chloe's grip on my arm tightens; comfort bleeds in from her touch, the warmth of her tiny body seeping into mine. I draw in a breath, another. "Why are you really here, Lisa?"

She gnaws on her lower lip. "I came...because...because..." Her chin wobbles.

"Tell them," the Viking lowers his head until his cheek grazes hers. His voice lowers to a hush, "Or I will." .

She shivers, shifts her weight from foot to foot.

"Last chance."

Her shoulders hunch, then she raises her chin. "Don't try to follow us." She directs her words at Dom, "I know you, Father. You'll come after us, and that will only endanger your life. Talon," she swallows, "uh, he has promised not to hurt you. Just...don't follow us."

Dom's chest rises and falls. He fists his fingers at his side.

Lisa gulps, then juts out her chin, "Promise me you won't."

Dom flinches, "How can you ask this of me? My life has had only one goal, Lisa, to protect you, now—"

Lisa shakes her head sadly, "You don't need to protect me anymore."

Dom's entire body goes solid.

Chloe inhales a breath, then peeks out from behind me.

"As for the rest of you..." She surveys the room, "Stay away. This is my life."

"And if we don't?" I drum my fingers on my thigh.

"Then I'll kill her." Talon whispers his fingers across her throat, "I'll throttle her, or maybe—" He releases her, only to cup her breast. "I'll subject her to a fate worse than death."

Lisa pales.

"Don't hurt her—" Chloe leans forward.

The woman has no self-preservation. The last thing I want is for her to draw Talon's attention. I pull her into my side, so her face is hidden by my shirt.

"Let her go." Dom jumps forward. Ethan trips him. Dom stumbles to his knees and Lisa cries out, strains in Talon's grasp.

Talon swings her up and over his shoulder. He pulls out his gun, aims it at Dom.

"Leave." Anger thrums at my temples. I fucking hate this. How am I supposed to stand aside while he leaves with one of my own clan? But I have no choice.

This is the only way out. For now, I must let him leave. Just until we've figured out a plan.

Talon angles his head; he nuzzles her thigh, "You come after me and I'll make her life so miserable, she'll wish she were dead and even then, I won't kill her."

He retreats, carrying a limp Lisa. She doesn't struggle. If this was a ruse to convince us that she was going willingly with the Viking then—Dom races to the door—guess *he* wasn't buying it.

"Don't endanger your life." I call after him.

Dom pauses, then glares at me over his shoulder, "How can I stay here while my daughter is in danger?"

"What are you going to do?"

"I am going after them."

I lower my chin, "He told you explicitly not to follow them."

"The fuck I care?"

"If he gets wind that you are in pursuit—"

He curls his fingers into fists, "I have a plan."

WANT MORE FILTHY ALPHAHOLES WHO KNOT? READ MY FAE'S CLAIM SERIES. START WITH DANTE AND GIA'S STORY IN STOLEN BY THE FAE.

"★★★★★READING THIS BOOK IS LIKE BURNING IN FLAMES OF PASSION, LUST, AND DANGER. A TURBULENT RACE TO AN EXPLOSIVE CLIMAX." AMAZON TOP 250 BESTSELLING AUTHOR SKYE JONES

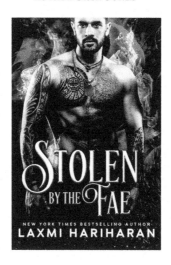

Gia

"Incoming heat missile." The bartender stares past me.

I turn, and he clicks his tongue. "Don't be that obvious."

Right. I bite the inside of my cheek, then straighten to peek in the mirror above him.

A group of men talking, two women conversing at the far end. Everything seems normal. Exactly why I'd chosen this watering hole at the edge of Red Square in Moscow.

Then, one of the women points to the entrance of the bar.

I follow her gaze.

The figure of a man fills the doorway. He's tall enough for his head to graze the top of the frame.

The hair on the nape of my neck rises.

Sunlight pours over him, and his features are in shadow. Yet there's no mistaking the sense of danger that radiates from him.

The bartender lowers his voice. "Good luck."

I grip the bottle of water, the skin over my knuckles stretching tight. "What do you mean?" I swig from the liquid, wishing it were something stronger. But I can't afford that, not when I have to return to duty with the Bureau of Shifters later today.

"Alpha-hole headed your way." He chuckles.

"Wait. What?" Every instinct in me snaps to attention.

He jerks his chin in the direction over my shoulder, then moves away.

Don't look, not now. I hold my breath. Then heat slams into my back. It's as if a furnace has been switched on behind me.

My mouth goes dry.

The scent of the first rain on parched earth teases my nostrils. My blood thumps.

I raise the bottle of water to my lips again, when arms cage me in on either side.

I peer out of the corner of my eye and see a corded forearm peppered with dark hair.

Muscles flex under the tanned skin and flow down to meet long, tapered fingers.

Hands that could trail over my skin, grasp my curves, squeeze my flesh, and massage them and... Heat flares in that secret place between my legs. I clench my thighs.

A flutter of lust licks my belly.

I lower the bottle. My fingers tremble, and my palms go slick with sweat.

I swivel around on the barstool and stare at the widest pair of shoulders I have ever seen. The man is massive; his big body blocks out the sight of the rest of the bar.

He doesn't move. Just stays, hunched over me. He's all around me.

His perfectly sculpted pecs are accentuated by a plain white T-shirt that clings lovingly to every single muscle. Dog tags nestle between those hard planes, and his nipples are outlined against the fabric.

My mouth goes dry.

I want to lean in and lick the valley between those chiseled planes, then drag my tongue over his skin, across to that nipple and bite it.

I swallow and raise my eyes.

The tendons of his beautiful throat flex as I move my gaze up to his square jaw. There's a shadow of a dent in the center of his chin. My fingers twitch. I want to reach up and trace the furrow.

One side of lips turns up in a smirk.

Bet he knew exactly what I was thinking just then.

A shiver runs down my spine and my nerve endings stretch with anticipation. He won't be gentle, this man. He'll take without regret, and... I want him to do just that. I want to nip on his pouty lower lip, then swipe my tongue over his cruel mouth... A mouth made for snarling, for sucking... for taking... Heat sweeps my skin.

I tilt my head back, and farther back, forcing my gaze to climb over that hooked nose to the furrow between those hooded eyebrows and... I gulp. Blue eyes blaze at me.

They are turquoise and sea blue with a hint of green, and there are amber flecks that ebb and flow in them. It's as if there's a fire that's lit inside, one which is reflected in those irises. Yet his pupils are so dark. Empty. Cold. So cold. A shiver ripples down my spine and... whoa! Is it possible for one pair of eyes to have so many conflicting emotions?

This man could rip me apart and not care. He would own me, possess me, make me scream with pain, he'd bring me so much pleasure. Damn!

My thighs clench. My fingers tremble, and the bottle of water slips from my grasp.

I keep waiting for the crash of the bottle hitting the floor, except this gorgeous, otherwordly, heat-inducing, moisture-drawing, perfectly beautiful hunk of a guy swoops down and catches it.

His muscles uncoil as he straightens. Every move of his seems to be etched in sheer poetry. I try to move, and it's as if my body is weighed down.

He raises the bottle and holds it right in front of my nose. "Yours?"

"Mine." I force the word out through a throat that feels it's lined with shredded glass. Does he realize that I am staking my claim on him already with that word? "Impressive catch." I jut out my chin.

"I know." His voice is low and husky and tugs at my nerve endings.

There's no mistaking the innuendo in his tone. He's so damn self-assured, so confident of the impact of his nearness on me. It should annoy me, but the truth is that his arrogance is a turn-on. Sheer charisma oozes from his every pore, threatening to overpower me with the dominance of his personality.

My belly flutters. Heat flushes my cheeks. I reach out and grab the bottle from him.

One side of his lips quirk.

A kind of know-it-all, I-know-the-effect-I-am-having-on-you kind of smirk. The kind of smile that does not quite reach his eyes. The kind that promises that lurking just under the surface is a male who will take without permission.

It's bad and oh so good.

Every part of my body seems to wake up and scream for attention. For *his* attention. His very careful ministrations on every inch of my skin, my body, my soul.

Someone opens the bar door at the front. A breeze sweeps in and flows over me, bringing with it more of that fresh rain scent. It's laced with a hint of something dark. Forbidden. Out of bounds. My heart stutters.

He tilts his head. His hair is cut close to his scalp. The strands rise, spiky in the front.

I have a sudden image of my thighs framing his face as he dips his head between my legs.

My belly tightens. My pussy is instantly wet.

"You are not human," I state the obvious.

He's too well built for us to belong to the same species.

He could be a shifter… except for the way he moves, it's too smooth, too fluid, not like their more deliberate gait.

"What are you?" A ripple of apprehension slithers down my spine. And yet I can't stop staring. Can't take my gaze off that perfect face.

"Wouldn't you like to find out?" he purrs.

Goosebumps flare on my skin. I gulp. I've never had such an intense reaction to a complete stranger, not like this.

"You okay?" He peels his lips back.

It's not a smile but a declaration of intent. A promise to take without mercy. Anticipation tightens my skin. My scalp tingles.

No. "Yeah, of course. Why wouldn't I be?" I tilt the bottle to my lips and take a sip before lowering it.

Perfect white teeth flash at me, setting off that honeyed tan of his skin. That, combined with the lines that stretch from the corners of his eyes, tells me he spends a lot of time outdoors.

The man reaches out with his finger and touches the corner of my lips. "You left some behind."

Heat flickers out from that whisper of a touch, down to my core, and I stiffen. Every muscle in my body tenses.

The man brings his finger to his lip and sucks on it.

The sight of those gorgeous lips closing around his digit sends a shiver of anticipation down my spine. My belly quivers. My heart stutters. More moisture slicks my core.

What the bloody hell?

Who is this man? And why am I reacting like he is the last male I'll ever see? Probably because it is true? Because I am about to embark on the most dangerous part of my mission, and I don't want to die a virgin? Because I want to know how it is to be taken, possessed… by him? No way am I letting that happen, not by a complete stranger.

I sidle off the barstool, still holding the bottle in my hand, then duck under his arm. He lets me go and my breath comes out in a rush.

Don't turn around. Don't look at him. I stumble up the corridor. When I reach the ladies' I lunge for the door and fling it open. I cross the floor of the restroom and lurch to a stop in front of the sink.

Close call. At least I escaped.

I plop the bottle on the counter and grip the edge of the sink.

So why does it feel like I am missing out? That I'll never know how it feels to trace those biceps with my fingers, to rub my face against the rough whiskers of his chin, to have him bend me over and slam into me, and… My belly twists, my pussy clenches, and the moisture flows from between my thighs.

Heat sweeps over my skin chased by chills. Sweat beads my forehead. I don't have a choice. Looking around to make sure the space is empty, I swoop under my skirt, push aside my panties, and thrust my finger into myself.

"Ah." My groan fills the space; the sugary sweet scent of my arousal spikes the air.

I plunge the finger in and out of my dripping channel, then add another. "It's not enough." I grit my teeth.

"Maybe I can help?"

My eyes fly open, and I see his blue eyes in the mirror.

Dante

It was my presence that aroused her, so it's up to me to help her, right?

Silver eyes meet mine in the mirror. She stares at me as if she can see into my soul. Maybe she can see who I really am and why I am here?

And now I am getting fanciful.

She's only a human I happened to spot while on this mission to Moscow. Except as I had passed this bar at the edge of Red Square, I had caught the scent of orange blossoms and pepper, a spoor so irresistible that I had stepped into the bar. One look at her, and I had to have her. Just the kind of man I am. I want something, I take it. Especially curvy sprites with soft skin, and an arousal that bleeds into the air, seducing me to get closer, closer.

"Starlight." I suck in a breath. My voice echoes in that enclosed space.

"Um… what?" The heat in the space turns up a notch. A bead of sweat trickles down her temple.

I grip the ends of the basin, blocking her in. "You have stars in your eyes, and yet when I touch you"—I place my cheek next to hers— "you flinch, wanting to draw into yourself; even as every part of you blooms for me, aches for me, wants me to scoop you up and lick you all over. Everywhere, in every secret nook of yours." My heart thuds. "I want to destroy your every hole. Fulfill your every fantasy. Fill you to the brim and make you come over and over again."

Her pupils dilate.

Her cheeks flush.

I am sure she is going to run out of here screaming, or perhaps turn and slap me, either of which will only add to the pleasure. For when I have her, she will forget everything, except me. My touch, my fingers, my lips as I make her scream with pleasure. As I break her.

The witch pulls her hand out from under her skirt. She straightens, then brings her fingers to her lips and sucks on them.

Desire roars in my blood. I feel the suction of that rosebud mouth as if it isn't her fingers but my cock that she sucks.

My pulse thuds.

My shaft goes rock hard.

Whaddya know? This one is feisty. One who'd dare to go toe to toe with me. She has no idea what's in store for her. No woman has tamed me yet. And it's certainly not going to be her.

The things I want to do to her, to bring her to her knees, literally; just the thought of fucking that mouth of hers makes my balls draw up.

Only when the touch of her skin filters into my blood do I realize that I have wrapped my fingers around her wrist.

I tug on her hand, and she doesn't resist. I bring her glistening fingers to my lips and ease her forefinger inside my mouth.

The taste of her infuses my veins.

I bite down on her finger lightly, and she shivers. She wriggles her hand in my grasp, and I tighten my grip.

Coercing her hand to the side, I slap her palm down on the sink in front of her.

Her breath hitches, but she stays where she is. Impressive.

Still holding her gaze, I reach for her other palm and place it flush on the surface as well.

She gulps but doesn't say anything, just holds on to the edge of the basin with her hands. The skin stretched over her knuckles is white.

I take a step back, hold my hands up to show her I am not forcing her. I tilt my head.

She raises her chin and her lower lip quivers.

I want to tell her that now is her chance to leave. If she doesn't want this, doesn't want the pleasure I can give her, then she should get out of here. But something warns me not to speak. If I do, it will break this strange trance that holds the two of us. This communication that we have established on the unspoken level.

So I jerk my chin toward the exit, all without breaking contact with her gaze in the mirror.

Her eyes follow the direction I've indicated. She frowns, her muscles go solid, then her eyes skitter back to hold mine in the mirror.

In a very deliberate gesture, she widens her stance. She pushes back from the sink, so her butt is poised in the air. Still, without breaking the connection, she circles her hips, and again.

Each move of hers is meant to seduce. Her skirt rides up just enough so I can make out the edge of her panties. White seams, simple cotton underwear. She hadn't come here to pick up a male. She hadn't intended to part her legs like this and invite someone to glide their fingers inside her and… What the hell is this? An attack of consciousness?

"Last chance." My voice comes out on a growl. "If you want to leave, then now is the time."

Yeah, okay, so I know it's a mistake to speak, but I can't help myself. I need to share what I have in mind; and in a fashion, that leaves no room for misinterpretation.

Blame my chivalry on pure greed.

I want her to remember me with unadulterated lust. I need her to understand that she yearns for this as much as me.

Her eyes sparkle. "Who said anything about leaving?" She darts out her tongue and runs it over her upper lip.

Heat flushes my skin and sweat breaks out on my forehead.

What is it about this woman that I have such a visceral reaction to her? I've never felt this turned on, this needy for a female before. And I won't again; not for anyone else. The thought sends a skitter of awareness prickling at my nerve endings. I hesitate.

She holds my gaze in the mirror. "I want you." Her gaze scrolls down my chest to my crotch where the evidence of my arousal must clearly strain against my pants.

Even before the words have left her mouth, I close the distance between us. I shove her skirt aside, seize her panties, and tear them off.

To find out what happens next read ***STOLEN BY THE FAE HERE***

❀ Created with Vellum

Made in the USA
Las Vegas, NV
20 June 2022

50484880R10420